ONE DARK SUMMER

Sarah Hornsley started her career in publishing in 2012 at Orion Books, followed by a short stint in script development before becoming a literary agent. She was selected for the Bookseller Rising Star list in 2019. She lives in Essex with her husband and their two daughters, and writes alongside working as an agent at Peters, Fraser + Dunlop Literary Agency. Her debut novel, *Bad Blood*, was published in 2025 and is set in Essex. *One Dark Summer* is her highly anticipated second book.

Also by Sarah Hornsley

Bad Blood

ONE DARK SUMMER

SARAH HORNSLEY

HODDER &
STOUGHTON

First published in Great Britain in 2026 by Hodder & Stoughton Limited
An Hachette UK company

The authorised representative in the EEA is Hachette Ireland, 8 Castlecourt Centre, Dublin 15, D15 XTP3, Ireland (email: info@hbgi.ie)

1

A CIP catalogue record for this title is available from the British Library

Hardback ISBN 978 1 399 72591 0
Trade Paperback ISBN 978 1 399 72592 7
ebook ISBN 978 1 399 72593 4

Typeset in Sabon MT by Hewer Text UK Ltd, Edinburgh
Printed and bound in Great Britain by Clays Ltd, Elcograf S.p.A.

Hodder & Stoughton policy is to use papers that are natural, renewable and recyclable products and made from wood grown in sustainable forests. The logging and manufacturing processes are expected to conform to the environmental regulations of the country of origin.

Hodder & Stoughton Limited
Carmelite House
50 Victoria Embankment
London EC4Y 0DZ

www.hodder.co.uk

For Luke, Hazel and Florrie x

I'm only four, or maybe five, my parents don't seem to know exactly, but there's one thing I've become sure of over the past few weeks: I'm not like other children.

I'm used to being hungry but it's already getting dark outside, and I still haven't had anything to eat. My stomach rumbles and I squeeze my eyes shut, praying to a God I'm pretty sure my parents don't believe in, that they didn't hear anything. I hold my breath and count to ten. When no one comes, I let it out slowly and quietly.

My back is hurting where my spine is curved and twisted. I'm outgrowing this cabinet. They'll have to find a new space for me soon. I must have had a recent growth spurt as my body feels even more curled over than usual. How much longer will they make me stay in here?

I can hear them watching the small box television upstairs. It's loud, far louder than it needs to be, but Dad likes it that way and what Dad wants, he gets. I can't wait until I'm a grown-up and I can get everything I want, too. I think he must be going deaf, but I'd never say it to him. I'm not stupid.

This isn't how parents are supposed to act. I'm starting to understand that now. The thought has been knocking on my mind since I started school. **Knock, knock, let me in.** *Mum doesn't always take me to school, and when she does, I don't have any friends. I'm not like them.*

Our teacher is called Miss Nightingale. To me, she sounds like honey, the way her voice is soft and how her words run together.

Less clipped and sharp than I'm used to. Mum and Dad are crunchy and dry, like cereal. Not long ago, Miss Nightingale read us a story by a woman named Charlotte Rice called My Dad and Me. *In it, the dad runs a bath before bedtime for his little girl. The picture showed steam rising up from the tub. I know that means the water must have been hot. I'd raised my hand, confused. Did everyone have hot baths? The other children laughed as if I was telling a joke, but I hadn't been trying to be funny.*

Miss Nightingale had looked at me strangely, but she'd carried on turning the pages, which showed even more ridiculous pictures. Dinner plates piled high with potatoes and sausages. Jelly and ice cream for dinner! At bedtime, the parents had kissed the little girl goodnight. Her dad even pretended to steal her bad dreams away, catching them in a tin he kept under his bed to keep her safe. I'd looked around and realised that it was only me who thought this story seemed wild and fantastical. That the other boys and girls sitting crossed-legged on the mat next to me also had someone at night to take their nightmares away for them.

As I sit here, my neck hot and sore, but too afraid to move in case my body bangs against the side of the cabinet and makes too much noise, I promise myself that one day I'll have my own family. A picture-perfect one. Just like in the story Miss Nightingale read to us.

Chapter One

Lily, now

His fingers are fat, his hands large; the perfect size for grasping my throat and not letting go. He could hold me under the water for as long as he wants, and I wouldn't be able to do anything about it. I watch those hands closely as my body skims past in the lane next to him. On high alert for any sign of movement. For danger.

The water rushes past as I tumble-turn, my feet pushing hard against the side. The jolt through my body always gives me a little thrill. Out of habit, almost subconsciously, I count how many people are left in the pool. The man with the fat hands is still here, but everyone else has gone. It is only us. His pasty legs shine through the water. I am aware that he'll likely be watching as I speed along. Men's egos are always fragile.

I turn, push and glide through the water. Logically, I know I am safe but still I can't stop myself from imagining the man with the large hands swimming towards me, staying out of sight until it's too late. I picture him holding my head underwater until I have no breath left. One hand squeezing my throat, the other on top of my head. My body sinks to the bottom of the pool, as lifeless as a ragdoll. I shake my head and tell myself there is no reason to be afraid and that, despite my mind protesting otherwise, I am perfectly safe. I refocus by counting each stroke.

One, two, three, breathe.

I don't remember a time when I didn't feel fuelled by fear – constantly imagining the worst is about to happen and catastrophising. Specifically, I am acutely aware of the power dynamic between me and most other men. How, if they really wanted to, the majority of men could overpower me. I don't know when that awareness started. Are girls born with the knowledge as an innate sense? Is it a survival instinct? Or do we learn it? Through the warnings we're told, 'don't walk home at night by yourself', to the stories we hear and for many of us . . . through the events we survive.

Perhaps I'm particularly attuned to it through my job as a therapist. You don't only have your own life experiences to process, but your clients' too. Their own traumas soak into your skin; they change the shape and weight of us through osmosis. I'm early on in my career and I wonder if it will always be like this. It is taking its toll, that's for sure. Without fail, my Apple watch aggressively alerts me to the fact my cortisol levels are always significantly higher at the end of a working day than at the start.

I'm not long into the job, only recently leaving the NHS after three years to start my own private practice. I like being completely in charge of my own day. I've sought to control every aspect of my life. I'm like Dad in that way. Often, I'll feel my jaw physically tighten when things don't go exactly how I'd planned them to. It is as though I take a sudden nose-dive into the feeling of the unknown, no matter how big or small the change in plan. And so, when Dad suggested he built a garden office for me so I could run my own business from home, I couldn't resist the opportunity to at least try it – what better way to stay in control than being my own boss.

My clients don't need to know I still live with my dad; there's a side entrance to our end-of-terrace and the office itself is gorgeously made at the bottom of our long narrow garden. Dad's a handyman and generally he's good at anything that involves building or fixing something. He always tells me his career may not sound fancy – not like my other friends' dads who are all lawyers, doctors or 'work in the city' – but he says he wouldn't change it. That his skill has allowed him the ability to do whatever he's wanted, whenever he's wanted to. That there is no better feeling than being free, living unrestrained by society's rules and regulations.

Dad's been like this for as long as I can remember. He is often out of the house, keeps himself busy and works hard. He has friends but he's never the one to host. I invariably get the feeling that, since Mum left, he's always seemed distinctly alone. Separate, somehow. While I may be like him in the sense of my need to control things, I certainly don't ooze his confidence or independence. It seems to me that Dad relishes his ability to control things and take the lead, whereas my desire for control comes from something else. Though what and where from exactly, I'm not sure.

I push off from the other side of the pool and as I feel the whoosh of water against my face, I think about how rigid my life has become. I have squeezed myself to fit into every box. No adventures, no dramatic love affair or betrayal. A good enough relationship with my father. No rebellious years. But the thought of it is no longer something that I'm proud of. Quite the opposite, in fact; I'm starting to detest it about myself. Because if all I am is the sum of 'fitting in' and 'doing well', of controlling my environment so far that I never push myself outside of it, then I can't help but wonder what's the point of me at all. I could be anyone. Faceless. A simple blend.

I can feel the burn worming its way through the tops of my arms each time I pull the water towards me; my trail of thought is making me drive forwards harder as the panic sets in, affecting my stroke. Sometimes I simply glide, taking my time, and other days I push my body to its limits. Today has been one of those days where I have barely stopped for a drink, allowing the repetitive stroke to take over. I can feel the heat in my cheeks even when they're submerged in the cold water.

On days like this, I find training meditative. Where the counting and the laps, up and down on repeat, help shut everything else out and I'm focused only on the few metres ahead of me. The goggles provide a kind of tunnel vision. Some think swimming laps is boring, but I find it relaxing knowing there is nothing unexpected about it, nothing I can't control. Just up and down.

One, two, three, breathe.

As I end my session, I roll my shoulders back and haul myself out of the pool. It's early still and I have a long day ahead of me at a conference for work. It would have been easier to have skipped today's swim, but I know that in the end it will do me good to have trained this morning. I never do that well in crowds. People are not my strong point.

I find small talk almost physically painful, which means I never manage to make it past the awkward formalities to find out whether I'd be any good at having real friends. My work as a therapist is different, I can step into a clear role where the rules are already set for us. There are social structures in place that mean I can be comfortable enough to get through, but socialising is a different matter entirely. I've never found it easy – or perhaps its other people who don't find me easy.

I've always thought trusting others feels like the most dangerous thing in the world. It's true that feeling of danger follows me everywhere, and even as I exit the leisure centre I notice a man on the corner of the street opposite, watching me, and feel as though I've seen him before. I look over my shoulder to see if he's following me.

Chapter Two

Penny, 1990

With her head resting against the train window, Penny watches the houses whizz by before the view opens out on to the countryside. She is headed to Essex to spend two weeks at her family's holiday house on Osea Island, leaving London far behind.

They haven't spent any time there in recent years – both her and Rosey having reached the age where they feel the need to spread their wings. Or at least, that's how Penny has been feeling lately. The need for space and to find out who she is without Rosey. Without being part of an already formed pair. But even more than that, it's been nice to have some space from their mum, Chrissy, and from the expectation of always putting everyone else's feelings before her own.

When her dad called inviting her to join them for a last-minute holiday back on Osea Island, she'd immediately wanted to say no. Nothing good could come from the four of them under the same roof; surely her parents knew that. Her and Rosey are better when they see each other infrequently. They love each other, of course they do – they are as much a part of each other as they are themselves – but too much time together only ever makes things complicated. Two weeks? There is no way they'll come out from that much time unscathed.

'Please, it's important. Your mother wants us all together,' her dad had said, and in the end, Penny didn't have it in her to decline. He'd played the mother card. He was always going to win with that.

In many ways, Chrissy is more like a child than a parent. Not because of how she acts particularly – at least, not in recent years – but because of how people treat her. She is kind and generous, fragile and small. The cancer had seen to that.

For as long as Penny can remember, even before the cancer diagnosis, people have always felt the need to protect Chrissy Taylor. As if she is a precious stone they might lose at any moment. Growing up it had felt almost impossible for the world to have revolved so heavily around her mum when all Penny needed was for it to envelop *her* instead. To cushion *her*.

She kicks her sandals off, rests her head against the window and closes her eyes. She is tired from training hard for an upcoming swimming competition. That's all her days consist of at the moment, swimming. Training and coaching. Laps, laps and more laps. She has never been into books or studying. It's one of the few things that distinguishes her from Rosey. Instead, swimming is her thing. She has always excelled at it and dreams of running her own club one day.

She can remember exactly when her fascination with water and swimming began. They were eight years old sitting at the table having Sunday lunch when her grandma had mentioned 'the accident' and the room had fallen silent.

'They still don't know what happened?' Grandma Rose asked, her eyebrows raised poignantly towards Chrissy. Judgement filling the small room.

'What don't we know?' Nothing ever got past Rosey, even back then.

'Who had an accident?' Penny chimed in, copying her sister as always, and their mum had put her knife and fork down with a clatter.

'They're still a bit young,' she'd replied, hesitantly.

'We're eight and three-quarters, actually.' Rosey was outspoken even at such a young age. Fiery and loud. Always so determined.

'I'm not sure, darling. In the end everyone was OK. I know it was terrifying, but maybe it's time?' Their dad had spoken softly, placing a hand over Chrissy's while the girls teamed up to start chanting *tell us, tell us,* banging their cutlery in time on the table. They'd been too young to read the room. Their emotional intelligence not yet fully formed.

'I think it's a bad idea,' Chrissy warned again in a small, resigned voice. 'But if your father says it's fine, then I'll try to explain.'

She'd paused, taking a big breath in, readying herself to begin, and Penny can remember excitedly thinking '*wow, what are they about to tell us?*' She had been blissfully unaware that her relationship with her mum and sister would be irrevocably changed from that moment onwards. That everything has consequences.

Chapter Three

Lily, now

The conference is held in a very fancy building in Bloomsbury Square, where the exposed sandy stone interior and overwhelming smell of eucalyptus feel more akin to a spa retreat than an office space. Still, I'm not surprised that the organisers have pulled out all the stops; the headline speaker, Dr Lisa Higham, is of A-list celebrity status in the therapy world. She's written countless bestselling books and while she has made that rare, almost impossible move, into mainstream media with a weekly column in *People* magazine, she's also part of a top academic research programme funded by Harvard. It is the work she's doing about whether trauma is inherited through the generations via our genetics which has drawn the crowds here today.

It's a fairly modern school of thought, and nothing has been entirely proven yet, but the question of why we respond to situations in seemingly preprogrammed ways is, essentially, at the core of any therapy business. What makes us tick? Why do we react the way we do? When faced with conflict – why do some run while others fight?

Dr Lisa Higham is mesmerising. Her voice is loud, clear and assured; I am quite in awe from where I sit at the back of the lecture theatre. Although I'm intent on listening to every word she utters, I keep finding myself imagining her in other settings. What's she like outside of her work life? What food does she like? Does she have a family? Children? I picture her at school drop-off, conjuring up an image of her in a long beige trench coat with her hair tied neatly in a perfect bun.

I know I'm projecting the absence of my own mother on to another woman I respect, but I can't stop. I take a sip of my too-hot coffee and force myself to concentrate. It's why I'm here – Dr Higham is the main event, the conference highlight, the draw for selling tickets.

'It's undisputed that trauma affects the next generation – whether that be the impact of the stress on a baby caused by the biological mother's own stress levels while pregnant, or the family dynamic between parent and child which is informed by the parent's own trauma. But, what we're here to debate today is the ability trauma may or may not have to impact on our epigenetics. Crucially, whether trauma can be inherited.'

I flip open my notebook and ready myself to take notes as the first slide appears on the presentation board. The words BIOLOGICAL MOTHER glare at me in big bold type at the top of the screen. It doesn't always hit me as hard as it does today, though increasingly I've felt Mum's absence affecting me more than it ever has before.

I wonder if it's because I'm no longer a child. At twenty-five I'm growing into the woman I'm meant to be. I run a business and look after my own clients. The way I computed Mum's absence worked for me back then, but now there are new questions and feelings which need addressing.

I don't know a lot about my mum. Penelope – Penny, to those she was closest to. I know she was beautiful – I've seen the photos hidden in boxes and locked away in drawers. Dad says I look like her, but I'm not convinced he isn't just being kind. Regardless, I definitely have his teeth. They cross over at the front.

I stare again at her presentation. Dr Higham is still talking animatedly, and I look around the room. We are all here to learn how we can help our clients and, nine times out of ten, at the core of their issues it always comes back to the parents. I should have been prepared that today's lecture would likely start with the mother and readied myself for the fact it might make me question my own history. I know nothing really about my mother; about her life or the things that shaped her. How, in turn, they may have shaped me.

The thought stays with me, and I find I am stuck on the fact that I barely even remember my mum. I have fragmented memories of her, but I find it hard to distinguish which memories of mine are real and which are pieced together from the occasional photos of her I've seen or from the few stories Dad has shared.

I was only four years old when she left us. Dad says she simply walked out of our house, trailing one suitcase behind her, and never came home. According to a letter Dad received a year later, she was living halfway across the world in Florida. She didn't leave a return address. Dad says it wasn't us who made her leave but that it was her; a pattern my mother had; that she ran away when things got too difficult. Apparently, she'd always liked to reinvent herself and leave her old world behind. He's told me she'd also done it with her parents – cutting ties with them before she met him. He always says that his mistake was to believe he was different.

I've never got to the bottom of why exactly she left. I understand it's painful for Dad to talk about, and as a child I accepted his answers as enough. *Your mother always ran away, why did I think we'd be the exception? She was flighty. She didn't love us enough. She was selfish.* But as I've grown older, I recognise those reasons for what they are – an angry and hurt partner left behind. They don't tell a full story.

In my child's mind, one day she was there and the next she was gone. There were no long days of wondering when she'd return. I don't remember the period of time which could be classified as 'coming to realise that my mum had left me behind'. Through my work as a therapist, I know our minds can be kind like that, blanking out memories that are too painful to help us cope and move on. It's an incredibly clever way of protecting ourselves.

Recently though, I've been finding myself wanting to fill in the blanks and to know more about who she was and why we weren't good enough to stay for, because no matter how much Dad asserts that Mum was the problem, not us, it doesn't feel that way to me. I look back at the board, this time staring purposefully at the thick black letters lining the top. BIOLOGICAL MOTHER .

My mother is Penelope Hawksmoor.

Chapter Four

Penny, 1990

As the train hurtles closer to her hometown, Penny is transported back to sitting round the dinner table as their mum had finally revealed the big family secret. The reason why she'd taken to bed for so much of their early childhood. That day, Chrissy told them how she'd fallen asleep at the wheel when they were only eleven months old. The sound of a blasting horn had jolted her awake and she'd swerved so hard to avoid an oncoming van that they'd crashed through the railings of a bridge and plummeted into a freezing cold river below. Chrissy had managed to get only one of them out of the car at the same time as herself, while the other was rescued by one of the men from the van who'd witnessed the accident. That day had been the trigger for a depression her mum couldn't ever fully recover from.

'Which one?' Rosey had demanded.

'Pardon?'

'Who did you save first? Me or Penny?'

'Well, you're identical and in the moment, I didn't know which baby was which. I was running out of time, there was only so much I could do and so I grabbed the baby closest to me.'

'You couldn't tell us apart?' Penny asked, latching on to this piece of information and turning it around in her mind.

'You left one of us to drown and you don't even know which?'

Penny had looked over to see Rosey sticking out her chin. It was starting to wobble and she realised they'd taken different points from their mother's story.

'I-um-I—'

'That's enough,' their dad, Patrick, cut in, protecting Chrissy just like he always did. 'No more questions. You might have been too young to remember the accident but your mother wasn't. It was a terrible thing to go through and very traumatic. Let's just be grateful that in the end everyone got out alive. Now, who wants trifle?'

That conversation had started the wheels turning in both Rosey and Penny's minds and Penny wonders who they'd be today – the things they might have done differently – if the accident had remained a secret. Because two things took root and grew from that day onwards.

The first, was the idea that Rosey and Penny were in some way interchangeable. The thought hadn't really crossed their minds before, what with them being so different in character to each other, and yet they first decided to swap identities for a day only two weeks after their mum's confession.

It wasn't for anything more than an experiment, at least not that first time, they just wanted to see if they could get away with it. They went through the day as normal, but with Penny role-playing Rosey and vice versa. Come night-time, they were kissed goodnight in each other's beds with their parents none the wiser. As soon as the lights were out, they swapped over again, gleeful in their deception. It made them feel powerful. That day was also Penny's first taste of the freedom playing someone else gave her, and it became addictive.

The second idea to take root, was the disappointment in their mother for not knowing which baby was which. It led to a competitiveness between the sisters that flowed through everything. Penny knows that while they love each other, there is also a constant humming resentment and a need to prove they are different from each other – that they can exist as separate people. That they are enough on their own. Though sometimes even she finds it hard to distinguish herself from her twin. It's a strange thing, having a mirror held up to yourself. It is hard to understand exactly where you stop, and they begin.

Patrick is already waiting for her at the station when she arrives. She thinks he looks tired and older than when she last saw him. Is that even possible? To age so visibly in the space of less than two months? On seeing her, he jumps out of the car and hauls open the boot of his Vauxhall Astra. They've had that car for as long as Penny can remember and there's something comforting about being greeted by it now: it has ridden the waves with them through the years and yet it is still here.

It makes her think more optimistically about the next two weeks and she reminds herself that no matter how claustrophobic it gets being back with Rosey, or how many arguments erupt between them over the next few days, they will survive it and move on. They will weather the storms, just like the car has. Patrick rushes to take the small wheelie from her and loads it into the boot.

'Good journey?' he asks and Penny feels something is off. She's not sure if it's just in her imagination but it feels as though he's avoiding looking at her. Penny knows he does that when he's nervous.

'Yes thanks, all OK with you?' she replies politely, watching as he nods repetitively. 'Is Rosey back yet?' she can't help but ask, kicking herself for it.

'She arrived last night. You know, she says she's missed you.'

'We've both been working hard.' Penny shrugs it off. Her and Rosey live in London, only twenty minutes away from each other by bus, yet they haven't seen each other since Penny moved to the city eight months ago.

'Well, I'm just so happy to have you both home. So happy,' he repeats. Penny notes a sadness creeping into his voice and the worry that has started to build since she laid eyes on him at the train station starts to swell.

The feeling grows as her dad makes small talk the entire journey home. He doesn't even pause to take in the magnificent sight of driving across the causeway on to the island, which in Penny's mind only cements further that something is wrong. Patrick is normally charmingly awkward rather than the type of person who tries to fill every silence with mindless chit-chat and observations about the weather. He is nervous, Penny notes. But what about? It is only when he lets her into their holiday home with an exaggerated air of delicacy that it dawns on Penny his behaviour has something to do with her mother.

She hears Chrissy before she sees her. Even her voice sounds smaller. Rosey appears behind, standing in the kitchen doorway just off the narrow hall. Her eyes look puffy and Penny is sure she's been crying. No one says anything, but her mother's small, resigned shrug of her shoulders tells Penny everything she needs to know.

'It's back?' she asks, and her mum begins to cry, stepping forwards to embrace her. 'Is it bad?'

'We don't know for certain, but the signs aren't good. We should get the results back soon.'

'How soon?'

'By the end of the week. The consultant said she'll likely ring on Thursday,' she sniffs.

Penny steps back and looks over her mum's shoulder to where Rosey is still hovering in the kitchen doorway. 'Why didn't you tell us you were having tests?' Penny asks abruptly and notices Rosey turning away, hurrying out of sight, clearly unable to bear it any longer.

'Penny,' Dad interrupts, as if on cue, because Penny is not allowed to talk this way to her mother. She never has been. Even when Chrissy's body wasn't ravaged with cancer, they still tiptoed around her.

'I'm just looking forward to spending the next two weeks together,' her mum answers meekly, and Penny uses all her strength to swallow her feelings back down, just as she has done so many times before. She is an expert at keeping her hurt tucked out of sight where it belongs. Other people's emotions are not welcome here. Instead, just like the good daughter she's learnt to be, she concedes.

'So am I,' she says, although every part of her is telling her to turn around and leave.

Penny can already feel the cottage has become consumed with sadness. It's carried in the air; the rooms feel smaller; the ceiling lower; and the colours darker. Usually, the cottage feels homely and cosy, but all Penny feels standing here between her parents is tension and pent-up grief. It is oppressive.

Chrissy's results – and ultimately the verdict on whether Penny's mother will live or die – are due in six days. Until then, Penny realises she is stuck on this island, forced to endure the worst countdown of her life. They are living in a pressure cooker.

Chapter Five

Lily, now

Back home from the conference, I kick off my trainers and hang my key on the brass hook next to Dad's. I think about the fact there are only two keys hanging here, not three. That it has always, more or less, been just Dad and me. The feeling tugs at my stomach and I close my eyes, breathe in deeply as though I'm back swimming in the pool, and as I exhale I try to visualise the sadness leaving my body.

Instead of letting the anxiety control me, I try to concentrate on the delicious, familiar smell of Dad's cooking.

'Lily, I'm in here,' Dad calls warmly and I follow his voice into the kitchen. 'Good swim this morning?' he asks, as I watch him expertly pouring red wine into a casserole dish. No need for measurements – Dad's cooking is always sublime.

'It was a hard one today,' I say, hopping on to one of the kitchen island's barstools. I swipe the bottle of wine from Dad as he walks past and indicate for him to pass me a glass. He takes two from the shelf and places them in front of me. One for each of us.

'Oh yeah? Is everything OK? You know, I won't be gone long,' he adds, and I nod appreciatively. Dad knows that often the intensity of my sessions reflects the way I'm feeling.

'I'm fine,' I shrug, trying to seem confident about the fact he is going away for a few days.

He looks at me for a beat too long, as if considering arguing with me, and I can see the concern etched across his forehead. The way his eyebrows knit closer together and the flex of his jaw as he wrestles with what to say next. I'm fully aware that at the age of twenty-five it's unusual for me to feel so fiercely uncomfortable about being in our house alone, and yet it is something I cannot seem to grow out of.

The last time Dad was away with work for a few days, I became so overwhelmed with anxiety that by the third day I wasn't capable of leaving the house. I couldn't explain why or what I was so afraid of, and yet I had absolutely no control over the physical or mental effects of being alone. The night sweats, the feeling that something catastrophic was about to happen and the pounding headaches. It's been the same all my life. Quite simply, I've never been able to be left home alone.

All I know, is that I end up afraid. Terrified, even. Dad is leaving again for work tomorrow, this time for five days. It doesn't happen often, he tries to be selective about which projects he takes on and which he doesn't, but according to him this one was worth accepting. My anxiety seems directly linked to being in the house alone. I'm OK if I'm elsewhere – alone for a walk, or in my office. But alone in our house? I can't do it.

I watch as he tastes the dinner from the wooden spoon, and I feel a surge of love for him. He has raised me all by himself. A single dad. Both his parents died when he was a teenager. Mum had a strained relationship with her family and so we've never met them. He's told me that according to her she was adamant they weren't people she wanted me to be around and so, even after she left us, he never tried to find them. He assumes that Mum, for all her faults, must have had her reasons for wanting to protect me from them. It means he has taken on all the different parenting roles through the years and, while nothing is ever perfect, he has always been present. Showed up in his own way and done the best he can.

'If you say so,' he relents, letting it go and changing topic. 'So remind me what your conference today was about?'

'Inherited trauma,' I reply blithely, and he whistles.

'Well actually,' I broach the subject hesitantly, 'I did want to talk to you about something.'

'Of course, anything.'

I take a deep breath, bracing myself for what I know will happen next. I'll mention Mum and the whole atmosphere will change. Dad will shut off with his answers becoming abrupt and sharp, as if I have done something wrong. I know it is just his grief and that he doesn't know how to handle his emotions or how to share them, but his silence about her is too constricting and I can feel myself outgrowing it. I need to speak about Mum as if she was real – her leaving us no longer something we pretend never happened.

'Today was about how much of your parents' past can influence your DNA. The way it is read and whether our cells have memory.'

'Sounds confusing. You're far too clever for me,' he says, not yet catching on to where I'm going with this.

'Well, essentially, some research suggests that our parents and what they experienced in their lives can influence who their children are. And, well—' I pause, briefly, summoning up the courage, 'spending a whole day listening to Dr Higham has made me think again about how little I know about Mum.' I rush the last part of my sentence. Forcing the words out quickly before I can change my mind.

'I see,' he says slowly and then turns his back to me. Rummages in a cupboard but I'm unsure if he is really looking for something or simply giving himself a moment before having to face me again.

'I wondered if maybe we could talk about her some more?' My voice climbs higher.

'What is it you want to know?' He still has his back to me but the cupboard door shuts a little too loudly when he closes it.

'I don't know. What she was like? The things she loved?'

'The things she loved?' He spins to face me. 'She should have loved us, but she left and she isn't coming back.' There's a forcefulness to his tone that takes me a little by surprise.

'I know,' I whisper, just as the cooker timer sounds loudly, making me jump. I've never liked loud and unexpected noises. Dad has made is very clear he isn't prepared to talk about Mum, and normally that would be enough for me to back down, but Dr Higham's presentation has wedged itself in my mind and I can't let go of it so easily.

'If you don't want to talk about Mum then what about her family instead? You never talk about them either.'

'That's because I don't know much. Your mum lost contact with her family long before she met me.'

'But she must have told you something. What happened between them? Why did they fall out?'

I can tell I'm pushing him too far. The air feels as though it has frozen around us. It is something Dad manages to do – to dictate the feel of the entire room with a change in his moods.

'Please. Just give me something,' I press. I've come this far, summoned this much courage, I can't give up yet. 'Please.' I am begging now, but before I can finish my sentence he turns sharply to face me. Eyes so wide it's impossible to miss his anger.

'Osea Island,' he spits out impatiently. I know I've tipped him over the edge, but at least it's worked. 'All I know is that your grandparents owned a holiday cottage there. One summer they had a falling out and Penny never spoke to them again. Are you happy now?' He is shouting but I'll take it. He has given me something, a golden nugget, and it's more than I've ever managed to get out of him before.

'Thank you,' I say quietly, keeping my eyes low. Without saying anything else, Dad ladles out the casserole into both dishes and then takes his through to the lounge to watch television, just as he does every evening. Sometimes I join him, but most of the time I don't – our tastes in television have never really aligned. According to him, I'm *delicate*.

I've known from a very young age that he's felt this way about me – as if I'm broken and he has to try and fix me. To stop me cracking apart completely. If I'm honest, I think I feel it too. I think that, within the fabric of me, there is something very wrong. I feel it in the way a feeling of fear never quite leaves the bottom of my stomach.

I eat my dinner in record speed and pour myself another glass of wine before lowering myself off the stool. I pad through the house, wine glass still in hand. Anyone would think we are rich, living in a house like this. It is a beautiful Victorian house in an up-and-coming part of North London, with big bay windows and a dark green Aga to die for. The kitchen extension Dad built all by himself really adds the wow factor, but it's all a façade.

Dad's money is all tied up in this house. He inherited it from his parents after they died. I know that nothing in this world could ever make him sell it. Just like with Mum leaving us, Dad also won't talk about his parents. Instead, he pushes it all deep down inside him with no room for his grief to go. Men of his generation were never taught that it's OK to show their emotions and Dad is the epitome of that, but I know he is a lot more sentimental than his silence allows for. I see it in his stoicism.

He's told me before, when some months have been tighter than others, that he'd rather go down swinging than lose this house. It is the house he grew up in, and the place he lived with my mother – something I wonder if he clings on to it in the hope that one day she might return. Not that he tells me those are the reasons he feels so strongly about this house. Rather, he simply states it is his and that he won't ever leave, but I'm sure I know what he really means; he belongs here with them, it is our family home.

As I walk past the lounge, I peer through the open door and see Dad is watching another true crime documentary. The image on the screen shows a yellowish staircase, with blood splattered all over the walls and floor. I look away quickly, but then surprise myself by hesitating. I hover in the doorway and before I leave, I turn my eyes back to the screen, this time lingering a little longer than normal.

The Palace

The Palace may be small but it is mighty. That's what Mum says. With its sloping roof and exposed wooden beams. Apparently, it's *majestic*. A big word I'm not exactly sure the meaning of. But she smiles as she says it, won't look away, and I know it means this place is special. We've lived in The Palace for as long as I can remember.

'Does that mean Father is the king?' I ask and watch as the shine behind her eyes turns to stone. She doesn't answer my question. Instead, she wraps her arms around me, her rough woollen cardigan scraping against my cheek, and kisses me hard on the forehead. It's a sloppy one and I laugh as I wriggle away.

'So, where are we going today, little one?'

I think hard. These are my favourite times of the day. When Father is out and The Palace is ours and ours alone.

'Horse riding,' I exclaim, already jumping up and down with excitement.

She kneels down on the floor. 'OK then your majesty, it's time to climb aboard.'

I clamber on to her back, wrapping my fragile thin arms around her neck, and then we're off galloping and trotting around the room. Mum describes everything we can see; the green leaves turning orange and yellow as they prepare to fall to the ground; the sound of birds from above us in their nests; a flock of geese flying overhead; the wind racing past our ears and the feel of it through our hair; she even describes the sounds of a young family having a picnic in one of the fields. I close my eyes and let it all come to life.

It's fun but we don't last long before my arms get too tired to keep holding on and she needs a break. She says it's the 'light' causing us to be so weak. Well, the lack of it. I only know this because I heard her talking to Father about it last time he visited. She'd never say something like that to me, but I'm not sure why she seems more afraid of me than she does of him. What makes her think she can tell *him* we need more light but not me? I wouldn't have got cross at her. Not like Father. She made a mistake there.

Mistake.

Yes, that was the word he'd used. '*It would be a mistake to complain. I provide you with everything you need. Ungratefulness is not a good trait for a mother. You need to do better.*' That's what he'd said.

'Mistake' and 'ungratefulness'. Two more big words. But I'm getting older now. Beginning to understand that we live here, in The Palace, but it isn't really ours. He just keeps us here.

Chapter Six

Lily, now

I know Dad will have already left by the time I make it back from my client meetings, yet I still find myself calling 'Hello?' as I let myself in. After last night's argument, he hadn't popped by the office to say goodbye. For the first few hours I fool myself that it's the same as any other day when I might be in the house by myself for a short period of time. It's not ideal, but I've built up a small level of resilience over the years. Now, it's mostly only the nights that have the worst effect on me. I order in pizza and watch reality TV with a glass of wine and chocolate for after. As I'd expected, when it comes to going to bed, my anxiety ramps up. It fizzes through my veins and I struggle to turn the television off.

I push the palms of my hands into my eyes and the action feels comfortingly familiar. It's something I do when I'm overwhelmed, I push the base of my hands hard against my eyes until all I see is a burst of colour. It soothes me. Helps to reset my anxiety, if only for a few brief blissful moments. Dad always tells me to stop. He hates it when I do it. At least that's one silver lining to him not being here. I glance at my phone and sigh deep in the knowledge that I can't put it off any longer. It's almost midnight.

As I switch the television off, I steady myself by repeating out loud that I am a grown woman and plenty of people live on their own. I am perfectly safe. This is my home. The house I've grown up in. Nothing bad has ever happened here. I make sure to force the words out even though no one is listening. It's a technique I teach my clients. Our brain is more likely to listen to us if we actually hear the words rather than just think them, and then I force my feet one in front of the other.

I tread up the stairs, my bare feet numb after all these years to the seventies carpet with its awful spiky texture. If you were to ask me, I'd say it is more suitable for a doormat than a carpet – but Dad never has been interested in my thoughts on redecorating. The only part of the house he has touched since he inherited the place is the kitchen extension. Now that really is beautiful, with its cool stone hexagonal tiles providing a sweet relief from the harshness of the rest of the house.

I usually wouldn't think twice as I move through our home, but today the very fact I'm on my own is making me hyper-aware of my surroundings. I feel the roughness of the wooden stair banister against my skin as I run my palm along it. Linger at the top of the stairs and look out of the circular window, taking a few seconds to watch the square below. Our house runs parallel to a good-sized communal garden, with terraces of eight Victorian houses along each of its four sides.

As I pass Dad's bedroom, I feel overwhelmed with the urge to go in. I never usually venture into his room, it's sort of an unspoken rule, but tonight I can't resist. Perhaps it's simply procrastination – my unwillingness to go to bed in this silent, empty house – or maybe it's been brought on by Dr Higham's lecture earlier. Whatever the reason for it, I find myself pushing open the door.

I kneel down by the side of his bed and extend my arm underneath until I feel what I'm looking for. It's a sleek, dark wooden box. A memory chest. I haven't looked in here for years and doing so now without Dad's permission feels like a violation.

My guilt swirls and yet it's not enough to make me stop. I click open the box's small metal clasp. Inside, it is half empty. It is indicative, I note with a pang of sadness, of a life abandoned. The role of 'mother' simply left behind.

I curl my fingers around the photograph lying on the top of a small pile and carefully pick it up. I bring it closer, staring at it as intensely as I can; somehow hoping that if I look closely enough it may conjure a real memory. I study the shape of her face, the lines of her eyebrows, the Cupid's bow and every freckle that delicately lines her nose as they sweep across her extraordinarily high cheek bones. Her smile is so wide and warm, it's unlike any smile I've seen in real life before. It is 'Hollywood model wide'. She reminds me of Julia Roberts.

This woman in front of me does not feel like my mother, but a stranger. A beautiful, selfish stranger. Even from just looking at this photo I can tell I'm nothing like her, I am nowhere near as remarkable. I don't replace the photo before shutting the lid and pushing the box back where it belongs – out of sight. Instead, I hold it against my chest as I make my way out of his bedroom, along the corridor and into mine.

I place it under my pillow before climbing into bed. At least I don't feel as alone now. Closing my eyes, waiting for sleep to come to me, I try to control the anxiety which is burning its way through my stomach by retracing every line of my mother's face in my mind. I try to imagine how she would look now, twenty-one years after she left us.

I am somehow both conscious of my own thrashing and yet also unable to make it stop. My top, wet with sweat, clings to me and I am aware that the sheets below me are also soaked through. There is a sweet smell. It is coming from me. Still, I cannot drag myself out of the nightmare which is holding me in a vice. All I know is the fear has finally arrived and I cannot break free.

There are no images and no sounds to this nightmare. It is pure panic. I hear myself screaming and feel my hands pounding at my own eyes, pushing even harder than usual into them. I haven't done it on purpose, had not thought the action through, but as light bursts across my eyelids I can feel the nightmare loosen its hold slightly and, as I fight to control my breathing, I can feel my body is at last responding to me – doing as I want it to and no longer being controlled by my fear.

Finally, I slowly open my eyes and blink into the darkness.

It feels as though I have lost and the knowledge that I couldn't even make it through one night alone sinks down deep inside of me. I wonder what my clients would think if they knew. I suppose they would all leave and find someone more 'capable' and 'stable'. The kind of therapist who has their own shit together before advising other people on how to fix theirs.

Glancing at my phone, bright digits tell me it's only 6.20 a.m. I take my time getting out of bed, slowly swinging my legs over the side and being careful not to sit up too quickly. My whole body feels delicate, as if it's been in an accident, and I know from experience to treat myself kindly today because this isn't the first time that something like this has happened to me.

As a child, I would be gripped by these blank night terrors frequently. I say 'blank', because there is nothing I ever remember from them. No images, no words, no scenes playing out in front of my eyes. I would simply be filled with pure terror and find myself thrashing until I finally woke up. Over time, they became less frequent, until they were a distant memory – something I'd left behind in my childhood. Until today.

I run the shower over my body, and scrub furiously to get the sweet stench of sweat off me, wondering why I had another nightmare now after all these years. Yes, I've struggled with my anxiety with being left alone in the house as an adult, but it's never resulted in one of these night terrors before. So what was different about it this time that triggered one? I scrub harder, my skin turning bright red beneath the white sponge. I don't have the answer, but I know that it's the exact question I'd be asking a client.

I tilt my head up towards the shower head, screw my eyes shut and hold my breath for as long as I can. I try to block everything else out as I soak in the force of the water pounding against my face, but I can't shut my mind off. No matter how much I try to let the rhythm of the shower numb me, I keep thinking about the fact I now have something tangible and new to link my mum to – Osea Island.

Quickly, I twist the knob turning the shower off and, wrapping myself in a towel, I head straight to my desk and flip open my laptop. Osea Island may be a private luxury island but a quick Google search tells me you can also book to stay there, either in their boutique small hotel or a holiday let of one of the owned cottages. Luckily for me, there's last-minute availability. I select to book and smile to myself – it's a perfect plan. I'll be no good to my clients in this state anyway, I might as well go away and escape the house for a few days. The confirmation email pings in my inbox with details of how to get to the island. The journey is all part of Osea's allure, as it is only accessible by boat or by car across the causeway twice a day at low tide. There's a number to call to arrange the crossing and as I reach for my phone a text pings up on the screen. It's from Dad.

I hope all is OK. Any plans today? X

I bite the side of my cheek. I don't normally lie to him, we aren't the type of family to have secrets, but I know how much going to Osea Island might upset him and I don't want him thinking I'm chasing after Mum. I'm not. I know she won't be there – she's estranged from her parents so there's absolutely no chance of bumping into her. I don't even know if her family still owns their holiday home. And yet, deep down I know I am chasing after *something*. And so I reply, **All fine, thanks. Nothing much. Hope work goes well**, and then I throw the phone down on to my bed as if by not looking at the lie, it means it doesn't exist.

Chapter Seven

Penny, 1990

The holiday cottage is quaintly named Chapel House and is one of only twelve holiday homes on Osea Island set in a big square formation. There is also a small hotel with a bar and restaurant, along with a communal swimming pool. It's just the right balance between being private and escapist but without being too far away.

Proximity has always been the main thing for the Taylor family; Chrissy's illness the puppeteer in the shadows, controlling every decision and every move they make. Even if it's unspoken. Osea provides the feel of a luxurious, rural getaway but without putting too many miles between Chrissy and her local hospital. Their very own Essex enclave of luxury. Penny's mother's Maldives.

Although their mum's results loom over them, Penny is hoping the island will work its magic where she and Rosey are concerned. Her relationship with her twin is complex. Deep-seated resentments, comparisons and competitiveness pretty much define everything about them. There is something both special and also unsettling about being one of a pair. They've always been able to read each other's minds and what once seemed like a secret skill pitting the two of them against the rest of the world, has in recent years felt more of a frustration.

She's anxious about spending so long together again, but she's also hoping that the freshness of the sea air and the simplicity of island life, might make room for a little more light to flood back into their relationship. Osea tends to have that effect on people. They haven't stayed here for a while and Penny wonders now if perhaps that's why recently they've seemed more distant from each other than ever. Maybe they're simply in need of the island's magic.

Penny wonders if their parents have noticed it too, how once again their relationship is breaking down. Is that why they are here? Is that the purpose of the trip, all but forced upon them? No room given to decline the invitation.

'Do you know why we're here?' Rosey asks, barging into Penny's room.

'No more than I'm guessing you do.' Penny barely looks up from her suitcase as she carries on unpacking.

'I thought we were done with this place.' Rosey flops on to Penny's bed and pulls out a cigarette.

'Don't smoke in here.'

'God, not you, too.'

'Seriously, Rosey, let's try and not argue.'

'I'm not arguing.'

'Not yet. But you've clearly come in here looking for a fight.'

'How?'

'You knew I'd tell you not to smoke. Seriously, get out of my room.'

'We're not fourteen anymore, Penny. We're adults.'

'Exactly, start acting like one.'

'Me? Start acting like one? What about you? You bury your head in the sand and don't come home for months. That's why we're here. You know that, don't you? Because of you. Because you keep pushing everyone out and never see us anymore. You don't make any effort and now Mum is dying—'

'She's not dying.'

'She might be. And so Mum and Dad are intervening, forcing us to spend two weeks together, because they know you wouldn't show up if they didn't. Because you run, Penny. That's what you do when things get tough. You disappear and leave everyone else to pick up the pieces. It's why you love swimming so much, because you can just pretend nothing else exists outside of that bloody lane you're swimming in. So they've brought us to this island for Mum to get her results here and to deal with it as a family. Together.'

'I thought you didn't know why we were here, but good to hear you have all the answers after all.' Penny slams the suitcase shut.

'Fuck you,' Rosey says quietly, hauling herself up off the bed and marching downstairs. The front door crashes behind her. Penny thinks it's ironic, given Rosey is doing exactly what she just accused Penny of – running. *I couldn't tell which twin was which.* Her mum's words from all those years ago echo through her mind.

Penny pauses where she's still kneeling on the floor. She knows what comes next; their dad's heavy footsteps up the stairs followed by his resigned sigh of disappointment. And so, she decides to save everyone the hassle and, before he has time to start the usual song and dance from their teenage years, Penny hauls herself up from the floor and follows Rosey down the stairs, shoving her feet into her sling-back sandals. She shouts, 'I'll go after her,' before opening the arched wooden cottage door, as if they aren't on a tiny island where it's almost impossible to get lost.

It's humid and Penny can't remember the last time it rained in Essex. It must have been weeks. It needs to rain, she can feel it. The humidity feels close against her skin. *Let it pour*, she thinks.

Penny looks up to the sky but once again all she sees is blue expanse. When the heatwave started it was welcome, but now, weeks on, they are tiring of it. England is not built for this intensity of heat, Penny muses. Now, she thinks the blue sky seems more ominous than anything else. It is threatening to bring the whole country to a standstill.

There aren't many places to hide on Osea – at least, none that Penny doesn't know of after spending the past fifteen years exploring every inch of the island. Wherever Rosey has run to, Penny feels confident she can find her. It's as she walks closer to the hotel that she both hears and feels the bass. There is music and clapping.

Penny follows the noise to the hotel bar and thinks it looks busier than she's ever seen it before. Rosey is right slap-bang in the middle of a crowd in front of the small stage. A drink already in her hand, swaying in time to the music.

'Pretty good, eh?' a voice says and a figure falls comfortably in step alongside Penny. Her body immediately senses that it's Joe even before she turns to face him, and she can't resist wrapping her arms around him tightly. Penny didn't want to come to Osea, she would have preferred to spend the time almost anywhere else than in a small, confined space with her family, but there have been small things that she's allowed herself to look forward to. Joe, the hotel manager, is one of them.

She's never clicked so well with someone older than her but, although Joe has years on her dad, he has an energy about him that's all-consuming. Warm and comforting. He's loud and charming. A real charismatic grandad figure. Typically Irish. To Penny, he represents everything her father isn't. Her dad is slight and small. Both in stature and in presence. Often, Penny wishes she knew if he had always been this way, or if it has happened to him slowly, like a disease.

'Easy Penn,' Joe laughs, while also pulling her tighter. A bear hug. *There is still magic to be found here*, she thinks. And then he gently pushes her away, surveying her as though she were still a young child who he is proudly watching grow up. 'Well look at you. I was wondering when you'd grace us again with your presence. We've missed you on the island these last few years.'

Penny twirls in response; giving the crowd what they want. It's something Rosey would do and she finds herself embarrassed by it. 'And how about our lovely Rosey, is she here too?'

Penny's face must give her away as Joe raises his eyebrows, knowingly.

'Not still arguing, are you?'

'Not an argument, not really,' she says uncertainly, and Joe pulls a face as if he doesn't believe her.

'Go. Find your sister and make up. She's family and believe me when I say that life is far too short to be arguing with the people who love you most.'

Later, Penny will wish that she'd listened harder to the words of this wise, kind older man and taken them more seriously. She will wish, with every part of her, that her and Rosey's argument that day had been their last. That the worst was not yet to come. But how was she to know that Joe's warning about life being too short would turn out to be painfully true? A premonition, of sorts.

Chapter Eight

Lily, now

Heybridge Basin Lock is picturesque with plenty of moorings along the estuary. Cute tearooms and pubs line the walk from the car park to the main docking area and, in the distance, I can see colourful beach huts on stilts lining the sea wall.

I'm greeted by a man in a black anorak with a cap pulled low over his eyes. He waves from where he's preparing a small boat, signalling for me to join him. The journey to reach the island takes close to half an hour and the man who I've come to know as Alan delights in giving me a running commentary about the area as we make the crossing. It is clear how much he lives and breathes this place, and how comfortable he is being out on the water. It is his life. His passion. There is something very endearing about it.

As we approach Osea, I am struck by how beautiful the island is and the way its colours become increasingly vibrant the closer we get to it. In the background the mainland further away remains looking grey and dull. I know it's only perspective, but the juxtaposition of colour gives Osea a kind of magical quality. It certainly stands out against the rest of the landscape. Given how little I remember or know about my mum, I can feel a warm glow of anticipation as we head someplace I know she once spent so much of her time.

Family. I've never had a family before – it's been just me and Dad for such a long time. But this beautiful island in front of me, it feels a part of my history, and that's something I've been craving more and more recently. To know who I am and where I'm from. This island is a slice of my mum's past.

'It's beautiful,' I say and Alan puffs his chest out, proudly.

'See over there?' he says loudly above the boat's humming engine. 'That green buoy is called the Doctor because when this used to be a rehab, the people would kayak or swim out to that buoy and leave money taped to it. Then, people from Heybridge would come by boat and take the money in exchange for leaving booze. And there, is a lookout tower from the Second World War,' he says, pointing towards a large structure in the distance on the other side of the island.

Not long after, we're pulling into the island pier and Alan jumps off the boat quickly to tether us to it. There are a few other boats but not many. He helps me off and on to the wooden slats of the pier. I feel my legs sway beneath me, not yet used to being back on solid ground.

'I told you she's a beauty,' Alan beams. I haven't even seen the resort yet, but he's right that even from here this place feels special. Before I can respond, Alan is proudly continuing his tour. 'And over there,' he says, pointing to the right of us, down the beach, 'you see those railway tracks?'

I don't clock them immediately but then I see two rusty tracks only about one metre long. It's clear they must have been here for a long time. Alan waits before carrying on, which feels very theatrical to me, so I nod to let him know I've spotted them.

'Well, they were used in the Second World War when Osea was a motor torpedo base. They used to haul the torpedoes along the railways to hide them in the middle of the island. This was back when it was all overgrown forest.'

'That's so cool,' I reply a little too robotically, never very good at small talk.

I tip him for the journey and then I wait, out of politeness perhaps, and watch as he climbs back into his boat. Wave as he steers away, back to mainland, but as he leaves me standing on the pier, I am hit once again by the memory of this morning's terror. Panic overwhelms me as I am all alone once again.

Rationally, I know it's just the leftover anxiety from this morning making me feel like catastrophe is just around the corner and yet, despite all my rationalising, as I walk inland I think again about the hidden torpedo base and the Doctor buoy, and I am left with the unsettling feeling that this island was made for keeping secrets.

Chapter Nine

Penny, 1990

Rosey's eyes are fixed upon the stage. The band is undeniably mesmerising; their energy magnetic. It's not the usual vibe here. Normally it's washed-up wannabes who get contracted to stay on Osea for weeks at a time, but the two young men on stage seem different.

'Finally, something a bit sexy around here,' Penny says, as she comes to stand shoulder to shoulder with Rosey.

'Thank God for that,' she replies. 'You should get a drink,' Rosey adds and the awkwardness between the two of them evaporates. They are well-rehearsed in arguing. Plus, the music seems to wash everything else away. Penny doesn't recognise the song and she realises with admiration that it must be an original.

She studies the two men up on the stage and finds it slightly amusing how different they seem. The lead singer is full of confidence, as you'd expect, but he seems to be in his own world with it. It doesn't come across showy or over the top, it's like he's drawing you in rather than projecting outwards. He is wearing skinny black jeans and his white open-necked shirt reveals a chest covered in tattoos. Penny notices how they snake down his forearms, vines of black ink continuing from his rolled-up sleeves down to his wrists.

The bassist is quite a bit taller than the main singer. His style is what you usually see from the bands that perform here. He's loving the crowd and putting on his best performance. At the end of the set, Rosey turns to Penny with a glint in her eye. 'You can take the bassist if you like. He's pretty cute. Broad, chiselled and confident. You like that kind of thing.'

'He's not yours to offer me.' Penny rolls her eyes although she knows Rosey is trying to apologise for earlier by sweeping everything under the carpet and finding new, lighter ground. Rosey shrugs as if that's only a matter of semantics and the two sisters laugh although, knowing Rosey, Penny can't help but wonder if it's also meant as a challenge: she's set the target, now who will he choose? Penny or her? Because that's the only way they know how to exist.

Their relationship has festered into being one big competition ever since their mother blurred the lines between them. While at times they've leant into that, used it for their own gain, it's always been laced with an edge. As they hit their teenage years, when they swapped identities, they began pushing those boundaries too – taking it a little too far. Seeing how much they could get away with while being each other.

Penny knows that they do it to themselves. Or at least, she is aware of them perpetuating the cycle. But she also knows it didn't start out that way. It started with their mum and the day she picked one of her daughters to save, leaving the other strapped in a sinking car, without even stopping to see which was which twin. As if it didn't matter.

Penny wonders if it would be better or worse if they knew which one of them their mum had saved? Would they have found a way of moving on or would their relationship be even worse? She suspects worse, though at times it's felt pretty fucking bad between them. And yet it is Chrissy who has always been considered the victim. They all survived after all, but some traumas take time to fester, to take seed and grow their own vines. To morph into something no one saw coming.

* * *

Before Penny registers it, the two young musicians are standing right in from of them.

'Hey there, double trouble,' the lead singer says, using a worn-out reference to them being identical twins. Penny smiles, deciding he's too handsome to call up on it. Besides, she's too entranced by his speaking voice, which sounds as rich in tone now as it did when he was singing. It matches the tapestry of his tattoos. Intricate and intriguing. 'I'm Mike and this is Robbie.'

Robbie – the bassist – gives a small tilt of his head in acknowledgement.

'Hi, I'm Rosey and this is Penny.'

'And how do we tell you girls apart, then? Both as beautiful as each other, of course,' Robbie says, eyeing them from head to toe, 'but can you give us any tips?'

'Sure. I wear this "R" necklace,' Rosey says, thumbing the delicate silver chain and letter hanging round the nape of her neck, 'and Penny's has a "P". Simple,' she grins.

'There are more differences between us than that though,' Penny adds.

'Obviously,' Rosey scoffs and looks at her in a way that is quite clearly telling Penny to lighten up. 'But for now, while you get to know us, it's an easy way to tell.'

'Amazing. Would you girls like a drink? On us of course.'

Smug bastard, the thought flashes through Penny's mind but she can tell Rosey's lapping it up.

'Gin and tonics, please. We'll go grab a table,' Rosey replies without even consulting Penny, and raising her eyebrows at her as soon as the guys' backs are turned. All tension from before has now been replaced with excitement and the fizz of possibilities. They find a small wooden table in a corner of the hotel bar and wait for them to return with their drinks.

'So, have you been on the island long?' Penny asks as soon as they're back, deciding she wants to find out more about them before they can steer the direction of the conversation.

'This is our third and final week,' Robbie replies and his relief that the end is in sight is palpable.

'Don't you like it here? You sound desperate to escape.'

'I suppose it's all right. The first few days were fun, but three weeks is a long time to stay in a place so small.'

'Tell us about it, darling,' Rosey interjects. 'We spent almost every holiday here growing up. We must have stayed on the island at least fifteen times.'

'So you reckon you can show us a thing or two around here we haven't yet found ourselves? We're running out of ideas and we still have five more days to fill. We leave on Friday.'

'Sure. We have a few tricks up our sleeves, don't we, Penny?'

'Oh, that we do.' Penny plays along, although she's not sure how much she really wants to commit to spending time with two guys who are all but strangers.

'It's a deal. Tomorrow, midday? Show us what we're missing?' Robbie holds his glass out towards them. A chinking to seal the deal. Mike copies, although it's not lost on Penny that he's stayed silent for most of the conversation.

Penny is still enthralled by their surprising dynamic; she's always loved watching people and yet she still hasn't worked out how the two guys work together. What their rhythm is. Because that's the thing her relationship with her own family has taught Penny; we don't exist or operate alone. We feed off other people. Find our place in a group and stick to it. But she finds the two of them surprising. There's no clear alpha – at least, not yet. Both men are charismatic in their own contrasting ways.

'Maybe you've already found it,' Rosey says before bursting out in self-deprecating laughter. Penny reflects on how she's always been so good at that; the way in which Rosey is able to take everything a little too far and push the boundaries, before reeling it all back in suddenly. It makes her exciting and intoxicating. It also helps people to relax around her. Except, with Penny it is different – she'll push the boundaries and then leave them there. A test to see how she'll react. To see if she can get away with it.

How closely bound are the two of them?

How far can she push Penny before she'll snap?

Only what Rosey doesn't realise, is that it's also something Penny has been wondering about herself. Because yes, she's a 'good girl' in that she's respectful and does as her parents ask. She is focused, ambitious and a successful competitive swimmer, but she can feel something else fizzing through her. It is a need to break free. To change who she is and what she's become. What they've made her.

The world has seemed to always assume that because she has Rosey, she's fine. It has always been about Chrissy and the pressing need to look after their mum. To put her feelings first. They have been moulded by the palpable fear that has emanated from their father ever since depression swamped their mum in the years after the accident. Shaped by a constant need to not rock the boat. They have been taught to scream silently behind closed doors. To plaster smiles on their faces and nod in all the right places.

But how long can someone keep that up? Because what scares Penny the most is that she's not sure how much longer she can keep this feeling inside – this impatience she feels running through her veins – and the more it boils through her, the more she recognises it as anger.

Chapter Ten

Lily, now

The second-storey apartment I'm staying in is called The Observatory and, as expected, the views across the island from the balcony are simply stunning. The building is part of the island's 'village'; a collection of houses all very charmingly named round a big village green.

It reminds me of our small tree-lined square in London, only the landscape is incomparable. From here, I can see the coast glistening boldly in every direction. The island is small, the village collection even smaller, but it is beautiful. It is exactly what I need these next few days to help the effects of this morning's nightmare to leave my body and my mind. I roll back my shoulders and try to relax. Try to imagine the tension I'm still feeling exiting my body and drifting out to sea.

I tell myself that this is why I'm here, simply to enjoy some time to myself and escape the loneliness of being in the house, but deep down I know it's not quite true. I don't know anything about Mum's family and nor does Dad – she was estranged from them before she even met him – but Mum abandoned her parents and then she abandoned me, and Osea Island was the last place she saw her family. If I'm honest with myself, I think I'm here to try and find a reason for it all. If I can find out why she first left them, will it help me understand why she left me too?

A flock of geese flies overhead, and I notice how loud the island sounds. I allow myself a small smile. It is hope. Usually I live my life feeling displaced but here, standing on this balcony, I feel comfortable; as though for the first time in as long as I can remember, I'm exactly where I'm meant to be.

I make myself an ice coffee using the fancy gadget in the apartment kitchen, fetch my book and then take a seat on the sun lounger on the balcony overlooking the village square. I try to concentrate on reading, but my eyes keep flitting down to the houses below. I can't help but wonder which one was theirs – my allusive grandparents. Do they still own it? Could they be here? And there it is – the real reason I am here. A need to connect with my mum in some way, a desire to find my family. Anything that might help me feel more tethered to her. Because I have been floating. Feeling like a ghost, for far too long now.

I give up on my book, and instead decide that a walk might do me good. I step out of the building and peer down at the island map in my hand. To the left of me is a sandy lane leading to the beach and the right path should lead on to a woodland trail that curves inland, cutting away from the resort to the other side of the island. It is supposed to be a much more rugged landscape with a marshy coast round the west of the island, compared to the beach-donned east where the resort is based. Yes, this is a good plan, I'll explore before making my way back around ready to spend the rest of the day at the resort with its sandy beach, Insta-worthy snack bar and saltwater pool.

I look back up from the map when the front door of the cottage on the end of the row adjacent to us. I know from looking at the resort website last night that it is called Chapel House, situated on the far-right corner of the village square. A woman steps out from the arched wooden door of the cottage. She is wearing a stylish all-white long cotton dress and wide-rimmed sun hat. She catches my eye, and waves. Awkwardly, I wave back.

I can't see her in much detail from where I'm standing, but I can already tell she's exactly the type of person who is used to being on holiday in luxurious, exclusive places such as this. I start walking down the path, already feeling socially awkward about the fact it's going to take me right past the corner of the woman's cottage, but it would be worse to stand still and stare.

As I walk past, she turns with a confidence I can only wish to emulate. A polite smile begins to spread across her face as her eyes drift towards me. And then, something in her expression changes. It only lasts a millisecond before she recovers, but I spot it. I am convinced that something about me made her falter.

I spend the rest of the walk across the island trying to forget about her, telling myself that I'm paranoid – which is something I'm definitely prone to – but an hour later, despite my very best efforts, I'm still replaying it in my mind. Who is she and why can't I stop thinking about her?

Chapter Eleven

Penny, 1990

Their dad has asked them to have a family breakfast every day before they go their separate ways. Penny knows the intention is to spend quality time together, but as they all sit at the table in silence it feels more awkward than anything. Their cutlery is too loud as it clangs against the table and plates. Penny's own chewing even sounds obnoxious in her ears. She can tell they were all watching Chrissy that bit more closely than usual. Slightly unsure of what to say next. Yes, small talk would feel pointless, but it has to be better than this silence. It is unbearable.

The need to put her mum's feelings before her own is something Penny had learnt was necessary long before Chrissy was first diagnosed with breast cancer, though that then amplified everything. But no, their emotional entrapment has nothing to do with her mum's diagnosis. Instead, it had taken root because of Chrissy's depression and her inability to be consistent or reliable after the accident.

Although her depression has improved in recent years, particularly after the news she was in remission, there are still moments – phrases even – that send Penny hurtling back to the more unsteady years of her childhood. Back to the nights her and Rosey would need to supervise getting her mum into bed while their dad was at work, making sure she'd eat dinner and helping her into her pyjamas. They had been as young as seven years old back then. This childlike behaviour, this vulnerability and instability, had caused them all to place Chrissy at the centre of the family. To put her feelings before everyone else's, and even as she'd improved, the fear that she could be sent back to that place at any moment had meant those habits remained.

The cancer had made things worse for a while. But who could blame her for that? In a way, that had made it even harder. Even more reason to squash your own feelings down. And then after, once they'd been told she was in remission, Chrissy had seemed a little more stable.

I'm grateful, she'd say. And things had improved. But how would she cope now the cancer was back? Would one wrong word be enough to send her over the edge again? Penny can feel it isn't just her feeling afraid and anxious about what is heading their way. How aggressive is the cancer this second time round? Has it already spread too far? How will their mum cope with it all mentally?

It feels selfish of Penny to feel sorry for herself in the face of her mum's news and yet every time she closes her eyes all she can picture is her seven-year-old self, trying so hard to push aside every emotion inside of her in case saying the wrong thing would mean her mum didn't get out of bed for three days.

And so, although it makes Penny want to scream, she spends the majority of their first family breakfast in silence. Small smiles exchange over passing the orange juice. Once the plates are cleared, Penny finds herself back to old habits, racing to her room and shutting the door behind her. Pulling at her own hair silently where no one can see her and letting it all out before plastering back on a serene, supportive face ready to emerge again.

She is already regretting agreeing to spend the day with the musicians from the bar before she even realises Rosey is unwell. As she marches downstairs, she sees Rosey lying across the sofa.

Normally Rosey would be up at the crack of dawn with her nose in a good book and a cup of steaming hot coffee beside her. Instead, she is lying horizontally with her eyes firmly shut, her eyebrows visibly knitted together. She'd been quiet at breakfast, they all had, but this was unlike her.

'Are you OK?' Penny asks.

'I'm fine,' Rosey groans, peeling one eye open to look at Penny.

'Yep, you look it. Really full of energy.'

'Shut up. I've got a migraine coming on.'

'That's OK, we'll just cancel.' Penny shrugs.

'We can't. We told them we'd be there and it's rude to go back on a promise.' Penny pulls a face, as if Rosey ever cared before about being rude. 'Come on, Penny, don't be a bore. God, we need something exciting around here to take our minds off everything else.'

Penny has to admit that she is right. Being in the house with Chrissy's impending results hanging over them feels horribly depressing. Anything has to be better than how she'd felt sitting round that breakfast table. Besides, Penny knows Rosey always loves a distraction. She needs life to be loud and fun, where otherwise she'd be hurting.

'Fine. But for the record, this is your plan, not mine. And when they turn out to be massive weirdos, it's on you.'

'Very funny. Just lighten up and have a little fun. I *dare* you.'

The four of them seem to have fallen into a quiet rhythm as they walk from one side of the island to the other. Joe has grand plans of creating a path cutting through the middle, but for now they have to traipse around the edge of the island. Their profiles cutting dark figures against the coastline.

The further away from the main resort, the wilder the island gets. There's no beach on the west side, it's just forest, rocks and marshland, meaning it's much quieter too. Not many people venture this way, the walk too uninviting as they clamber over rocks and through long, unkempt grass. They've already been walking for over an hour and the line of trees marking the abrupt and grand entrance into the denser forest is only a little way ahead of them.

They're isolated out here and Penny suspects they won't see anyone else until they return. She also knows the summer wind carries noise in the direction away from the resort. There's no chance of anyone hearing you from the den. She knows this because one summer, she and Rosey had conducted their own experiments. When they were younger, it felt thrilling to know you could do whatever you wanted and no one could hear you. No parents would come running telling you to stop. It's the main reason why they made the den in the first place, but now returning here as young women, no longer innocent teenagers, she's more aware of its isolation. Of the fact they only met these two men yesterday. Who really are they? She's trailing behind when Robbie slows his stride and falls into step alongside her.

'So this place we're going, Rosey said you made it?'

'Yep. It took us a few summers, but we did it.'

'Are you going to kidnap us and keep us captive in your secret wicked lair?'

'He wishes,' Rosey calls over her shoulder and the four of them laugh, but Penny is still feeling uneasy about bringing them here. This is meant to be their place; a safe space to escape from it all. They've never shown it to anyone before.

Finally, they reach the entrance to the forest. *You can't go over it. You can't go under it. Come on Penn, we've got to go through it.* Rosey's childhood chant springs to mind. Back then they used to joke that there might be a monster lurking within the trees.

Penny has always been the more risk-averse of the two, and in some ways that was part of the thrill on the days they'd decide to play each other. To make it believable, Penny would have to push her own limits to make herself that bit louder and more boisterous than she normally was. By contrast, she always wondered if sometimes Rosey's desire to be her for the day was because it gave her a bit of relief from playing the part she'd created for herself.

Penny understands that for both of them, having a mum like Chrissy has shaped who they've become: Penny continues to keep her emotions locked inside even when she isn't at home, whereas Rosey lets it all out in other ways. When they were younger, being Rosey for the day would give Penny an excuse to play up and get rid of some of that pent-up energy she shoved down inside her. For Rosey – being Penny gave her a rest.

Already, being back on Osea is starting to have an effect on the twins. Penny can feel herself warming back up to her sister. Yes, she is an absolute pain in the arse most of the time, but the island holds so many good memories of the two of them that it is hard not to feel a pull towards each other again.

It has been three years since they last swapped places. Their eighteenth birthday signalling the end – they'd agreed it was time to grow up and find their place in the world as themselves. Given just how different they have become as adults, she wonders if she could even still pull it off if she wanted to. Instinctively, Penny reaches for the delicate chain around her neck, feels the sharp corners of the 'P' and pushes them between her fingers.

Chapter Twelve

Lily, now

It happens again. The way the darkness pulls at my eyes only to be replaced with a hot white panic. It doesn't feel exactly the same as before, it is less like a nightmare. Is this what lucid dreaming is? I can feel my fists thrashing at the mattress underneath me and I try to open my eyes but terrifyingly they stay glued together.

Then, as I let rip a scream, a new feeling settles over me. It's no longer fear. It's as though I realise something; that there's no point in screaming anymore. *There's nothing more I can do. This is the end*, I think. But the end of what? None of it makes sense. Finally, my fists slacken and I slowly prise my eyelids apart.

I'm shocked it's happened again and this time I wasn't even in our house. I'd come here to escape the panic of being alone there, but it hasn't worked. It's followed me here. Why is it happening again? I know I should be trying to figure it out, but instead I do a professional job of pushing the problem away and heading out early to make the most of the day.

The beach is a long narrow strip of beautiful golden sand that curves round half of the island. I knew Osea boasts five miles of beach, but I hadn't been expecting it to be so stunning. My arms are starting to ache from where I'm holding my book while lying on my back. I roll over to change position and see that finally more people are starting to arrive.

By noon, there are now a number of families set up on the beach prepared to spend the whole day here, and as I order my first Aperol Spritz of the morning – telling myself that it's five p.m. someplace else – she arrives. A flutter in my stomach tells me that subconsciously I have been waiting for her. She's closely followed by a large man around the same age who I assume must be her husband and a young woman who looks in her early twenties, maybe a little younger. A daughter, perhaps. I sit up to get a better view of them, shading the sun from my eyes with my hand.

The woman is wearing the same wide-brimmed hat as yesterday. I feel a little guilty about how closely I'm watching them. 'We are not rude people, Lily.' Dad's voice bounces round my mind. It has always been important to him for us to act appropriately, but I'd argue that I'm currently simply people-watching which, in my opinion, is a perfectly acceptable holiday pastime. It doesn't matter that it's the woman from yesterday. She could be anyone.

And yet, it's her out of the three of them whom I am watching the most intensely. Observing her every move. A gust of wind blows her hat off and I can hear her laughter from here. She spins, jogging after it down the beach towards me. She sweeps it up in one hand and as she rises again, she looks at me and smiles. This time, it's me who falters. Maybe it's the angle, or the way the sun is shining on half her face, but if I didn't know any better, I'd swear the sight of her made my heart stop for a beat.

I scramble to my feet, grabbing my bag and sun towel, then hurry back towards the apartment. I know I'm probably getting carried away, letting my imagination get the better of me like always. It's easy to overthink when you only have yourself for company. But this? I can't pretend I haven't seen it. What if I'm right?

My hand is shaking as I unlock the front door of the apartment and run into my bedroom. I pull the suitcase out from the wardrobe and fling it open. Finally, I let myself pause and try to catch my breath. Sat on my knees, I count back from five as I always do to calm myself and then I pick up the photo. I drop it immediately again, as though it's so hot it's burning my fingertips.

Bracing myself for what I already know to be true, I pick it up again. Study it. Of course, it's hard to tell for certain given the years that must have passed, but their profile – the woman in white and my mother – there is a similarity between the two which I cannot unsee. Quickly, I pull my mobile phone out of my pocket and call Dad. I don't even know what I plan to say or ask, but the urge to speak to him takes over.

'Hi Dad, it's me.'

'Is everything all right?' His voice sounds comforting and I feel the tightness in my chest ease a little.

'I'm fine. But Dad, there's a – there's . . .' All of a sudden I find I can't bring myself to tell him. What exactly would I say? *Hi Dad, I booked a trip to Osea Island without telling you and there's a woman here who looks like the photo of Mum from twenty-five years ago?* God, what is wrong with me? Dad doesn't like me to make plans without telling him. *We're a team*, he says. Which really just means he likes me to tell him everything and to have a say. It's difficult but he's also had a lot to deal with and I know I should come clean about where I am. And yet, the words will not come. Instead, I find myself avoiding the question: 'Dad, do you know the name of the holiday house Mum's family owned on Osea?'

'Not this again, Lily,' I hear him groan.

'Do you know it?'

'Why are you asking?'

'I'm just wondering. I'm looking at the map on their website and each house has its own name. I thought you might know, that's all.' The lie slips out easier than I'd expected.

'I don't understand why you're so interested all of a sudden. Come on, Lily. You know what you're like, let's not get fixated on this.'

'It's not all of a sudden for me. I've wanted to know about Mum and her family for years, but you never say anything.'

'That's because she left us. We loved her and she left. That was her choice, not mine.'

'I know, I'm sorry. I really want to know more about who I am and where I come from. I just thought it might help.'

Dad sighs and there's a pause as I clench my teeth together waiting for him to speak. He doesn't. I look back at the photograph in my hand and decide to have one last go. I don't normally push Dad as much as I have been these past few days, but this feels worth it.

'So Mum told you about Osea Island but she never mentioned the name of their cottage. Are you sure? Please just have a think. It's important.'

'No. I've already told you. Now I really have to go.' I can hear how much me bringing her up again is hurting him. He's never been good with talking about her, the pain of it always cracking him open. I learnt young to stop asking about her. But I'm older and now I've started, I cannot stop.

'What about Chapel House? Was that it?'

'What did you say?' His voice is sharp and clipped.

'Chapel House. Does it ring a bell?'

'Maybe. I guess.' Every word is strained as if there's an echo of shock running through them. I've caught him by surprise.

'Does that mean yes?' I ask, and his silence tells me I'm right. Just then, another flock of birds flies overhead. They are loud. I try to cover the phone with my hand.

'Darling, where are you?'

'I'm in the garden,' I lie again. 'Got to go. Bye, Dad,' and I hang up quickly before he can explode at me. Because he is angry, that much I'm certain of. Dad never calls me darling. At least, not in an endearing way. He used to save it for when he would be disappointed with me. Much like how some parents utilise their child's full name, Dad would call me 'darling'. It always sounded cruel, using it in that context. His tone doesn't sound angry on the other end of the phone, but 'darling' is his giveaway. Without thinking, I push the palm of my free hand firmly into my left eye until the colours burst.

Chapter Thirteen

Penny, 1990

The den is, essentially, a wigwam with a little tyre hung up with thick blue rope in a nearby tree to make a swing. You have to cross a small ditch to reach it and Penny and Rosey had spent hours building a platform from one side to the other out of wooden pallets, which they'd spent the first half of the summer begging Joe to get for them.

Built into the thick forest lining the perimeter of the island, they'd chosen to build their own hideout towards the marshy side of the island. It is here, in the trees, where they would come as teens to escape their mum's emotional dependency and the impossible expectations put on them to be perfect.

A feeling of calm descends on Penny as the den comes into view. She and Rosey had spent a whole two weeks the summer they'd turned fourteen building it from scratch. It had weathered the years with them well, always providing an escape – a place to breathe and to be themselves – when they needed it. Somewhere they could scream and not be told to hold it in. In front of her, Robbie is exclaiming loudly how great it is. A clunky silver camera hangs round his neck, the same as her father owns, and he reaches for it now, taking photos of them. He is all limbs with his tall lanky frame and Penny can't help feeling he takes up too much space – that taking pictures somehow feels like a violation of the den's privacy.

'So, now we're here, what do we do?'

'Anything. That's the beauty of it. Freedom,' Rosey says lightly, but the truth of it is much heavier than she sounds. Penny wonders if Mike or Robbie pick up on it. The undertones that they'd needed this place so much as children.

'Well then, who's up for a game of two truths one lie?' Robbie claps, grinning.

'This guy loves a game. I'm sorry, he is the epitome of organised fun,' Mike says with a hint of exasperation, but once again Rosey is already lapping it up. Robbie is as loud and boisterous as she is. Mike on the other hand is much more reserved. He has a presence about him, but he is less try-hard than Robbie. Penny finds herself drawn to him.

She's noticed him watching her, too. His eyes keep flitting to her necklace, as if checking she is Penny and not Rosey. In truth, it makes her slightly uncomfortable, but she can't blame him for it, it takes some people months before they can tell them apart – and even then, the necklaces are always a helpful prompt. She catches it in the small flicker of an eye when people think she's not watching.

'Penny's a beautiful name,' Mike says suddenly, catching her by surprise.

'Thanks,' she blushes, as for a small moment his attention blocks out the noise of Rosey and Robbie; and in that precise moment, she feels seen.

Chapter Fourteen

Lily, now

I spread the weight evenly through my toes as I stand slightly over the edge of the glimmering outdoor pool, take a deep breath and then spring through every muscle in my feet, diving headfirst into the water. Even before I feel the shock of cold on my face, I know it is everything I need in this moment. The freefall of gliding through the air for a split second before submerging feels like nothing else. I need to gather my thoughts and reorder them. There is nothing better at focusing the mind than counting laps.

As I swim, I wonder if Dad is right about my over-active imagination. I have always projected Mum on to other women, it's something I've done for as long as I can remember. Only a few days ago I was doing exactly that with Dr Higham. Yes, sometimes it's gotten out of control, but I've never lost sense of the fact they aren't really her.

At the beginning, it's just me in the fitness lane, with families playing in the other area of the swimming pool, but I soon become conscious of someone else right behind me. Whoever they are, they are fast. I didn't see them enter the pool, they must have slipped into the lane just as I pushed off the side, but I can sense them behind me. They're in my slipstream. I can almost imagine their fingertips brushing my ankles. I pull harder through the water. Breathe quicker. I'm not used to someone being as fast as me. Faster, even.

I tumble-turn and try to catch sight of who my chaser is. I can't distinguish much, their face distorted by goggles, but it's a man and he is hot on my heels. Back at the shallow end I feign needing to stop for a drink, though truthfully I just want to suss out the competition and watch their stroke. Will they speed up without me in front, or will their pace drop without someone to chase? What is the game at play here?

The man glides past me smoothly and as he continues swimming my pride takes a hit. I watch him effortlessly speed up without me in front holding him back. He is strong. And fast. Incredibly fast. I watch in awe as he glides beautifully through the water. His shoulder muscles rippling with his stroke just above the surface. I realise that this man was not competing with me. In fact, when I think about it more, I am surprised he'd made no attempt to overtake me despite being so much faster. *There is no threat here*, I consciously tell my body and force my shoulders to relax.

It's a reminder that not everyone is as dangerous as I expect them to be. That I need to give people the benefit of the doubt more and not be so on-edge constantly. Sometimes, my suspicion feels so much a part of me that I think I must have come out of the womb anxious.

Pulling my goggles back over my eyes, I begin swimming again and we continue with him in front and me trailing behind, pulling ahead a little with every stroke, until he overtakes me on the sixth length and we begin again. We do this for the best part of half an hour. I'm red-faced and sore but it is exhilarating. I can feel the rhythm of my strokes taking control of my anxiety, helping to order my thoughts and create a safe space around them.

Finally, with every sinew in my body burning, I decide it's

time to stop and release my hair from its blue swim cap. Sensing I'm finished with the session, the other swimmer also stops when he gets to the end of the lane, where I'm now stretching against the side. There isn't much room for both our bodies and, instinctively, I step away.

'Giving me a run for my money out there, aren't you?' He grins and I'm surprised to hear a lyrical Irish accent as he talks. He is tall and broad. Muscular – a swimmer's physique. And he has blue eyes. The bluest eyes I think I've ever seen.

'Not really!' I say awkwardly. I'm not usually one to strike up conversation with strangers but it's only the two of us in our lane.

'Come now, don't be modest. Not many people are as fast as you.'

'Thanks,' I say reluctantly and my body reels backwards slightly. I can feel myself grimacing at the compliment, but if any topic is going to get me talking, it's swimming. 'I was trailing behind you though.'

'Well, that's to be expected.'

'Cocky, aren't you,' I quip back, surprising myself. He laughs and I notice how nice it sounds. Melodic, almost. 'So are you a professional swimmer?'

'No, I'm not good enough for all that. But I'm a surfer. I spend my days swimming in the sea against currents. I tell you, it makes a pool like this seem easy.'

'Surfer boy, I see,' I say, my voice tinged with judgement and I cringe at calling this man in front of me a 'boy'.

'Judgemental girl, I see,' he shoots back, but he's laughing again and I hold my hands up in apology. 'I know, we get a certain rep but—'

'But you're an exception?'

'No, not an exception. It's just a bullshit reputation in the first place. I'm Owen, by the way.'

'Lily.'

'Well, Lily, it's nice to meet you. Have you finished your session? Fancy grabbing some food with me?'

Like a date? I can feel my face reddening.

'Erm, thanks, but I really need to be heading back.' I'm worried about offending him but, even with his soft voice and piercing blue eyes, I can't think of anything worse than heading off spontaneously with a stranger.

'Shame, but it's been nice meeting you and I'm sure I'll bump into you later,' Owen smiles before hauling himself out of the pool and walking away to where his things lie on a sun lounger. It strikes me that he has taken the rejection on the chin and that I hadn't been expecting it. Readying myself for a fight even when there is none to be found.

I lie back in the water, letting myself float there for a while. While the swim has calmed my anxiety, it hasn't changed how I feel about the woman from the beach and the photograph of my mother. From my dad's silence earlier I'm pretty certain that my grandparents owned Chapel House and now there's a woman there who looks exactly like the photo of my mum from twenty-five years ago.

The swim has helped me think it through and I'm pretty sure it can't be her. Mum is estranged from her family so it wouldn't make any sense for her to come back here. But what if her parents do still own the cottage and the woman in white is a relation of some sort? Might she know what happened here the summer before Mum left? And then the reality of my situation crashes into me and I realise that maybe I don't want to find the truth.

Mum must have had her reasons for going her separate way. For not even introducing me, her daughter, to them. Do I really want to get close to people like that? To go against my mum's wishes? I'm not sure the answer should be yes, but at the same time I know with every bone in my body that there is no way I am leaving this island until I know who the woman is and anything she might know about my mother, Penny.

Chapter Fifteen

Penny, 1990

Thankfully, the next evening, the cottage felt a little less claustrophobic as they all got ready for what promised to be the biggest event of their week: Osea's Bonfire BBQ Ball. Having something to concentrate on and proactively do, instead of just sitting around trying to think of something to say, helped lighten the atmosphere. It was a welcome distraction for them all.

Penny had always thought it quite a bizarre theme, mixing a ball (something traditionally thought of as being refined) with things so naturally rugged – bonfires and barbecues. But that was the joke of it. According to their dad it was precisely what made it *such jolly good fun*. And so, every summer of their childhood they'd been forced to dance out on the beach, tearing into chicken wings and drinking out of paper cups, all while donning ballgowns.

As teenagers, they would spend weeks, months even, before the trip carefully selecting their outfits for this evening's annual event. They needed to find something that passed as a ball dress but also played into the vibe of the night – it had to be unique enough to pull off looking chic while dancing barefoot and drinking out of red plastic cups. Over the years, the bonfire night was one that always promised to bring drama, late-night drinking on the beach and plenty of flirting. As teens, they'd thrived off it.

Admittedly, Penny had approached packing with less childlike excitement than previous years, but still, the event hadn't slipped her mind. She'd packed a sage green satin halterneck dress with a ruffle hem, split to the knee for this evening's event. Now they're here, Penny buries her toes into the sand as she finds herself, once again, standing on the beach while wearing diamond earrings and holding a clutch bag under her arm. She has to admit that the sheer ridiculousness of the whole event still feels somewhat charming.

Rosey is also dressed as fabulously as expected. Always peacocking. Her yellow satin dress shimmers against the bonfire blaze as she air-kisses everyone she meets. Penny rolls her eyes. She's noticed since they arrived on the island that Rosey's speech has become sprinkled with 'darlings' and 'loves' – an affect, Penny presumes, of trying to reinvent herself in London these past eight months. It doesn't sound like her at all. But it isn't *unlike* her either – to pretend to be someone she isn't. To put on a façade. Yes, it is always the Rosey-Show. At least that much is consistent.

Patrick has sidled up to Joe over by the barbecue and she knows it is where he'll stay, sweltering in his black tie, for the majority of the night. Chrissy sits a little further away, her deck-chair strategically placed facing away from the wind, which carries with it the smoke from the bonfire. She has a tartan blanket folded over her knees to keep warm and Penny thinks it a shame it covers most of her beautiful dress.

Chrissy had been adamant not to miss out, even with her results on the horizon, just two days away now. 'And miss the look on your dad's face all night? Absolutely not. You'd have to bury me first,' she'd said while applying her lipstick to her thinning purpling lips in the mirror earlier that night. They'd all laughed in response, but it had been a soft hesitant laugh, none of them wanting to tempt fate.

Even Mum notices it then, Penny had thought, *that Dad transforms into someone else on these nights*. A little louder. A little more carefree. And she, too, likes to watch him like that. It makes Penny wonder if they are all feeling just as trapped as she is – that it isn't just Penny who feels like a prisoner in this picture-perfect family, but that they all do.

As she stands round the fire, for the first time in a while, Penny looks at her parents and sees them not as the grown-ups who she feels let down by, but past that. Her parents, Chrissy and Patrick, are just two people as insecure and vulnerable as she is, who are also going through life for their first time. Of course, they are going to have made mistakes. Does she have it in her to forgive them?

She wonders if the rage about it all boils inside them as hotly as it does her. Or is it just Penny who has all this anger fizzing around? She is fighting to keep it inside. She glances back to where Patrick stands next to Joe. He is looking noticeably thin in his slightly too big suit, and she can't imagine it. Does it make her a terrible person to feel so much anger towards her mum for taking so much of her childhood away from her? Where do the lines blur between victim and villain?

She takes them all in, the way they spread out away from each other as soon as they arrived, and thinks about how they have splintered. A family broken at its very core; so far down that most people miss it, unable to see the rot that has cracked them open. But it's there. Twisting and cracking. Chrissy is possibly dying and all Penny keeps finding herself doing is re-examining their past: the mistakes made along the way and the resentments against her parents that have built up over the years.

Penny is torn about how to be both devastatingly sad about her mum's possible prognosis, and yet angry with her, all at the same time. What kind of daughter does that make her? Certainly not the 'perfect one' she's expected to be.

She knows she needs to keep her anger pushed down inside of her. Her mother is unwell, there is nothing good that can come from bringing up the past. But what if she dies? The fear that these feelings will never get to be resolved swell inside of her and she can feel her anger rising.

Penny focuses on the stage and feels the music humming through her body, hoping it'll drown out her thoughts. There is no denying that both Mike and Robbie belong on the stage. Each of them is mesmerising in their own way. They have 'it', whatever 'it' is. A magnetic force. Charisma. A whole lot of arrogance. And as a result, the beach is pulsating with energy. She finds herself glad she'd bothered to dress up for the evening.

'Come on, come dance,' Rosey insists, sashaying over to where Penny stands a little further back from the rest of the crowd. 'You know you want to. Don't be a bore.'

There it is again, Penny thinks. Rosey always manages to lace everything with a little meanness before her laugh quickly paints over it, abruptly leaving you with no room to react. To accuse her of it. It is an art she has perfected. Penny wonders whether it is all part of her feeling insecure. If, in fact, she is just pushing the boundaries.

One of Penny's friends has a little boy aged two. She saw them not long ago and at one point the little boy hit his mum in the face. Later, when he was asleep, the mum had told Penny that once toddlers realise they exist in the world and can cause reactions, they go through a phase of testing the boundaries. He hit his mum to check it would get a reaction. That it's a way of affirming they exist and have consequence. It makes Penny wonder if that's why Rosey is the way she is. At eight years old, their mum made them question their own existence as an individual person with consequence. Just how far have those roots tangled and shaped them? She looks over to Chrissy, still sat in her chair and sees her looking straight at them.

'Go,' she mouths while shooing her from afar with her hands. The feeling catches in the back of Penny's throat. The sadness that gets stuck there makes her want to turn around and leave. Walk off that beach and not take part. Crawl under her duvet and scream into her pillow. How do their parents expect them to take part in this final show for their mum? Is this really what this holiday is supposed to be? She doesn't think she can do it. Is no longer up to playing the part. This time, Penny thinks they are asking too much of her.

But then again, what is Penny supposed to do? And so, just as her mum has instructed her to, she finds herself nodding and following Rosey towards the main group which has formed, dancing around the bonfire. She twirls when Rosey tells her to twirl and, on cue, she shimmies to the ground to see how low she can go.

After a while, Penny is surprised to feel herself starting to relax. She stops constantly thinking about her mother's eyes boring into her; the fact she is no doubt committing the scene to memory, just in case there are no more Bonfire BBQ Balls. The truth of it hums around them and yet Penny manages, eventually, to start pushing it away.

She isn't sure if it is whatever they've put in the punch bowl or if it's the magic of the sand between her toes, but for the rest of the band's set, their past seems to slowly melt away with each new song; the rivalry, the resentment, the insecurities that at times have threatened to boil over into hate. They dance around the flames, unaware that they are dangerously close to getting burned.

Chapter Sixteen

Lily, now

'You have got to be kidding me,' I exclaim as the guy manning the little water sports wooden hut looks up. He grins and it is annoyingly smug yet sexy. I shake the thought away. Remind myself I don't know him. Owen is a stranger.

'Found me so soon?'

'Don't flatter yourself, I have a kayak booked. You didn't mention you worked here.'

'I don't normally, but the guy who does has called in sick so I'm doing my grandad a favour.'

'Your grandad?'

'Joe. He's the hotel manager and has been for years. Though I haven't stayed here for a while, not since I was a little boy.'

My mind whirs as I turn this information over. I wonder what the likelihood is of Joe knowing my mum and her family. Has he worked here long enough? Did he know them back then? My skin starts to tingle with the possibility of it. Could Owen's grandad hold the answers about that final summer my mum spent here, and what happened to make her lose contact with her own family?

'Do you think I could speak with him?'

'Is everything OK with your room? He's off today but I can help with anything if you need.'

'Oh, no, it's nothing like that. My place is great. But thanks.'

'Sorry, he'll be back at work tomorrow. It's not a good idea to talk to him today. He takes the same day off every year.'

'How come?' I ask and then immediately regret it. I'm being rude and intrusive. 'Sorry, don't answer that,' I rush, but Owen gives a wide smile and shrugs it off.

'No need to apologise. My aunt died here when she was only a teenager. My grandad takes off the anniversary of her death every year and spends it on the other side of the island.'

'Oh shit. I'm sorry.'

'It's OK. Truthfully. I never knew her, she died twenty-six years ago. Summer of nineteen-ninety.'

1990. My throat goes dry.

'She died on the island?' I ask, reminded of how I'd felt on the approach by boat. The way I'd been sure this place was made for keeping secrets.

'Yes, they found her on the west side. That's why Joe spends the day there. I think it makes him feel closer to her. He's never gotten over her death. What's weird is that she wasn't the only person who died that year – another girls fell from a boat. I think it was even the same day, or close enough. In fact, I think I'm right in saying the other young woman who died, her sister, is staying here at the moment.'

'She is?'

'Yes, I'm sure she's here with her husband and daughter. They own Chapel House. I can't remember her name, but I helped Joe set up their breakfast bundle on arrival. Sometimes they rent it out but Joe definitely told me they were the owners. From what I can gather, that summer was pretty rough for everyone.'

The floor feels like it gives way beneath me, and I have to check I'm still standing.

'Do you know anything more about the family?' I ask, unable to stop myself. 'Were there any other children or was it just the two girls?'

'I don't really know. I don't think so, though. Joe has never mentioned anyone else but them.'

My head begins to swirl and instinctively I feel my hands reaching for my eyes as I try to fit it all together. Mum's family owned Chapel House. Clearly, if Joe told Owen that one of the daughters died back in 1990 then they must be the same owners now as back then. Which means if one of their daughters died before I was even born, leaving only one left, then the woman staying there now *has* to be Penny, my mum. Why did Dad never even mention Mum had a sister who died? Did she keep that a secret from him too?

'Are you OK?' Owen asks and I realise he's reached out to steady me.

'My mum,' I say shakily, deciding to test how it sounds out loud this time. 'She left my dad when I was young. I've never seen her since, but her family owns Chapel House,' I say, watching Owen's expression change with the realisation that my own mother abandoned me. I watch a shadow of sympathy cross his face but, to give credit where it is due, it's gone almost as quickly as it arrived.

'Is that why you're here?'

'Honestly? Yes. Although I didn't know which cottage it was when I first arrived and I never imagined there would actually be someone here at the same time. I never thought that she . . . she . . . I don't understand why she would be here. It doesn't make sense.'

'But you still came.'

'I did. If only to see somewhere Mum had spent so much of her life. I came to feel closer to her, I guess. Maybe in the same way that Joe spends today on the west side.' I can't believe how open I'm being with this man, but talking with him feels different. I realise I feel safe.

'Do you still want that kayak?' he says and I'm grateful for the change in topic.

'Yes, please. I think being out on the water will do me good. I need to work out what to do next.'

Owen leads me behind the shed to collect a bright orange kayak. He hands me a life jacket and for a moment I'm transfixed by his stare. He is ruggedly handsome. It's annoying. I snatch the life jacket from him. As I put it on, I can't help wondering if my feeling about the island is right and this holiday is going to be the thing that helps heal whatever is wrong with me – if it will save me.

The Palace

It's Wednesday today, which means that after we've finished what Father calls our 'family breakfast', he stays a little longer. Mondays, Wednesdays, Fridays and Saturdays are always the same. I don't know why he doesn't make Mummy lie down again on a Tuesday or Thursday, but I'm not going to ask him in case it makes him change his mind. On a Sunday he leaves early for church so we get the whole day to ourselves. That's our favourite day, closely followed by the two T's (that's what we call Tuesdays and Thursdays).

Mummy never says anything about the other days to me, but her hands shake for the rest of the morning after he's gone. Even when we're playing our favourite games. That's how I know it's bad, because Mummy loves our games too, but those mornings always feel different compared to the times when he eats and then simply leaves again. They feel heavier. Sadder. Mummy tries extra hard to hide it from me but I see it there in her louder voice and her stretched smile: she hates those mornings just as much as I do.

The divider between my bed and Mum's is pulled across so I can't see anything. It's the only time I'm ever alone. When he isn't here, I sleep in the bed with Mum. Hers is bigger than mine. It can fit the two of us. I know the rules, I have to stay exactly where I am. Sit on my mattress, and not make a sound. *Remember, not even a peep*, Mum says to me without fail every morning before he arrives for breakfast. I know his lines by heart now: 'Bad behaviour must not go without punishment, that's how people get away with doing terrible things. An ordered house is a respectable house. There can be no order without consequences.' Sometimes he even makes me say them back to him. When I get it right, I get a treat.

'Thank you,' I hear Mum say from the other side of the divider and I know it is almost over. One time not too long ago she didn't say it and he started all over again. That was a bad day. She hasn't forgotten again since. I know what will happen next. He'll appear on my side at the foot of the mattress, still tucking his T-shirt into his trousers, and say goodbye to me. I know he likes me to wish him a good day, so I will. But to my surprise, that isn't what happens. Instead, I hear Mum speaking. I freeze, too afraid even to breathe.

'I want to talk to you about school,' she says, and I know she must mean for me. She told me not long ago that other children my age would be starting school soon.

'It's not happening, don't be ridiculous.'

'But it's what children do,' she says, and I know she's trying to make him listen, because Father likes things to happen the way they're supposed to. It doesn't work.

'And how would I explain it? Don't be so naïve and never make me feel like a bad father again,' he says slowly, before adding, 'or I promise you. You will regret it.' With that he leaves – there is no 'goodbye' for me today. Did I do something wrong?

I unfold my legs from where I've been sitting on the mattress and climb on to Mum's bed instead. Lie down next to her. She is crying. She never cries. At least, not that I can remember. She told me once that she was all out of tears. And then she presses her forehead against mine.

'I'm going to think of something,' she whispers, 'I promise you. I'll figure it out.'

But I'm with Father on this one. How does she think she's going to get me to school when I've never even been outside before?

Chapter Seventeen

Lily, now

I'm scheduled to leave on a boat this morning, but I've been up all night panicking about leaving before I've had chance to delve deeper. To meet her. The woman in white. Is she really my mum? It sounds impossible as I churn it round in my mind, but I can't think of another explanation. There's no way I can leave Osea yet. I'm only just getting started.

I wait anxiously, my legs folded in on myself on the armchair in the apartment, until the clock turns to nine a.m. on the dot. And then I pick up the phone and call the resort's reception. There is only one more night's availability in a room in the small hotel, which means I need to still pack and leave The Observatory, but one night is better than nothing. It gives me twenty-four more hours to summon the courage to speak to the woman, and to find out as much as I can about my mother and her family. Why did they hate each other so much? And then before I can stop it, the child inside me asks, *Did she hate me, too? Is that why she left?*

Typically, I spend the rest of the morning regretting my decision to stay. Have I got carried away? The fact I'm all alone on this island has started to press in on me. What am I going to say to her? I've no idea where to begin. The reality that this woman chose to leave me is making me feel a lot less confident than I had been earlier. Yes, I think I've found Penny – but I'm pretty sure she doesn't *want* to be found.

Perhaps I'll just keep out of her way for the rest of the day and then go home tomorrow as planned and she'll stay none the wiser. I haven't seen her this morning yet and the idea is growing on me. I'm losing my nerve. To pass the time I try to find Owen. Figuring he might be at the pool, I pack my things and then step out of the apartment. It is still scorching and the humidity is almost unbearable now.

Disappointingly the pool area is empty and, more than ever, I wish I'd left on the boat this morning. But then I catch a glimpse of her exiting the hotel lobby. She's all billowing skirt and silk scarf. She's by herself and before I realise it, I'm following her. I'm too far behind to call out but I also don't want to lose sight of her. For a moment, as we follow the path back to the village green, my heart sinks as I assume she's going to go back inside her cottage, but she keeps walking, straight along the path I know takes you across the island to the west side. I follow behind, trying to catch up with her but it's impossible to do so without running.

Suddenly, she turns around and faces me. We're in the middle of nowhere, the path stretching out in front and the village green now far behind us. Shit. She stands, unwavering, waiting. There's no other option but to keep walking towards her. I have never felt so awkward in all my life, and that's saying something. What should I do? Should I keep walking past her and pretend like I'm just out here for a walk, too? Make out as though she's misinterpreted things.

'I know you're following me,' she calls before I quite reach her. I can feel the heat rush to my cheeks. Well, that's that plan out the window then.

'I'm sorry,' I start. 'I think I know who you are.'

'Are you a writer?' she says with a sigh and the question stops me in my tracks. What's she on about? 'Because if you are then you can just email me. I'm much more likely to read something that way than if you try to pitch to me now.'

'No, erm, I'm not a writer.'

'Oh. Then who are you?'

She doesn't know who I am. The thought pierces my heart and I can feel myself having to hold back tears.

'I'm Lily,' I say, waiting for the penny to drop, but she carries on staring at me with a blank expression.

'Are . . . are you Penny?' I add.

'Is this a joke?' the woman asks, but I can see she's looking at me differently now. Afraid, even.

'I'm sorry, maybe I've got it all wrong. I thought you were someone else – I'm sorry.' I turn and start rushing away back where we've come from. How have I made such a terrible mistake? I don't understand.

'Wait,' she shouts after me. 'Penny was my twin. I'm Rosey.'

I spin on my heel. 'What? No, that doesn't make any sense.'

'Why not?'

'I was told one of you drowned here in nineteen-ninety?' It sounds brash and rude of me to say it so plainly, but I'm confused. How can she be Rosey? Rosey died.

'Yes, that was Penny.'

'But – but, that's impossible.' I shake my head.

'Who are you? Why are you saying these things?'

'I'm Lily and Penny is my mum.'

Rosey's face visibly changes colour with the news and for a second I wonder if she's about to faint.

'That's not, that's just not possible,' she says, taking a step towards me. I can see she's studying me now, taking in the contours of me. Judging for herself the likelihood that I'm her niece.

'Here,' I say, pulling out the photograph I have of Mum stuffed in my pocket and shoving it towards her. I'm grateful I thought ahead to bring it with me this morning. 'This is my mum. That's Penny, right? Penny . . .' I go to say her surname and realise I don't know it. I've always thought of her as Penny Hawksmoor but it strikes me now that Mum and Dad never actually married.

'Oh my God,' she gasps and I reach out to steady her. 'When's this picture from? Where is she?'

'Just before I was born, I think. She's at my dad's house. That's our lounge.'

'I don't understand. When were you born?'

'Fourteenth of September 1991,' I state and I see the disbelief cemented on her face.

'But Penny died in August nineteen-ninety. She drowned. Right here on this island. I watched it happen.'

'I'm sorry. I didn't mean to upset you. I thought you must be her and that Rosey was the one who died.'

She shakes her head at me and the realisation that I have an aunt settles on me. Suddenly my family of two is expanding. I feel dizzy with it. It is both incredible and also terrifying. Who is she? Why do I know nothing about her?

'So I take it you don't know where Penny is now then either?' I know it's a stupid question even as the words leave my mouth, but I am full of disappointment. This woman isn't my mum. Sure, she's family, but she isn't her. I haven't found her. After my conversation with Owen, I'd been so certain.

'Lily, why don't you know where your mum is?' Rosey asks, finding her voice again.

'She left. She walked out on my dad when I was four and I haven't seen her since.'

Rosey nods slowly. 'Yes, she does that – runs away. Leaves people behind.' And I hear there is anger behind her words. It reminds me of Dad's warning, that Mum didn't want me to meet her family. That she was estranged from them by choice. But here we are.

'I can't believe you exist,' she says and for an awful moment I think she's going to reach out and touch me. I take a step back.

'What happened the night of the boat accident? Owen said one of you fell from a boat?'

'Who's Owen?'

'Joe's grandson.'

'Ah, yes,' Rosey says, nodding again, as if it's all starting to make sense to her. I wish it would all fit together for me, too. I'm feeling increasingly left behind. And then she begins to speak.

'I'm sorry, I just can't believe you exist. That she survived. You see, there was a storm. It had been building for days but it hit that night. We couldn't find Penny. We were supposed to be on a boat for the night but we didn't go because of the weather. We . . . we . . .' her voice catches and she places her hand against her chest as she pauses for a moment. 'We were too late. We watched from the pier. I've no idea why she was on the boat by herself, let alone why she was standing on the railing when we found her. I shouted at her to get down but she didn't listen. I don't even know if she could hear me above the storm. And then before we could make it on board, we watched as she fell.' She stops, as if caught in a daydream she can't pull herself from, and then she looks at me with an expression I can't quite work out etched upon her face. Is it disbelief?

'We thought she'd drowned. We held a memorial for her. But you're here,' she says again, as if by repeating it aloud helps her come to terms with it. 'Which means there is no way she could have died that night, is there? Not if you were born a whole thirteen months after she fell from the boat. It doesn't make any sense. Why didn't she come home?'

'So you never found her body then.' It's not a question, more a statement of fact as I try to piece all the information together.

'No, but the police told us it wasn't a surprise for that part of the sea, where the currents are notorious for how strong they are. They said it wasn't a stretch to believe they would be capable of pulling Penny's body far away quickly.'

'And you don't know why she was standing on the railing in the first place?'

Rosey shakes her head slowly and confirms that the question of why she was standing on that railing, why she took it upon herself to venture on to the boat in the first place when everyone else had decided against it, has been left unanswered all these years. The only thing they had been sure of was that they'd watched her fall from the boat and never resurface. At least, that's what she'd believed until now. Until I turned up, proving everything they thought had happened that summer had been a lie. Because for me to exist, Penny must have survived. Which begs the question, why did she let everyone believe she'd drowned? It's a bigger question than I'd ever imagined. What had happened that was so awful Penny chose to let her family believe she'd died, to put them through that, rather than return home?

Chapter Eighteen

Penny, 1990

Rosey isn't there at breakfast the next morning. It is just Penny and her parents sat round the breakfast table. Although she stayed in her chair the entire evening of the bonfire ball, Chrissy had exuded a glow about her that Penny realised she hadn't seen in her mother for years. There had been a sparkle in her eye as she took it all in. She'd delighted in the evening. But now the adrenalin has worn off it seems as if that burst of energy she'd found has left, leaving less than had been there before. She looks tired; her skin paler than in recent days, and her movements are noticeably slower. Her smile, though she tries, never quite reaches her eyes as she laughs weakly at their dad's retelling of the past evening's events.

Penny has also noticed the way Chrissy keeps looking around her surroundings wistfully, just as she had done at the BBQ Ball. Her gaze keeps lingering on things a moment longer than usual and it strikes Penny that she is taking it all in and trying to commit it all to memory – that she is preparing herself for the end. Readying herself for this to be her last ever holiday here. The thought catches Penny with such emotional force that she has to stand up and move her legs. What she really needs is a swim. The feeling of needing to scream and run from it all – from the sadness that is filling up their cottage – makes her think of Rosey. Because if Penny is struggling, then she knows Rosey will be too.

At first, when Rosey doesn't join them for breakfast, Penny doesn't think too much of it. She assumes that Rosey has simply already made her escape. Neither of them are rushing to spend time as a family – it is too much. Too painful. And on top of it all, they aren't expected to show any of it. Supposed to find the strength to continue being the perfect daughters. Everyone is, as usual, too worried about Chrissy to stop and think about them. It is the way it has always been, for as long as Penny can remember. It is mid-afternoon by the time she really starts to worry and Rosey's absence begins to press unusually into her skull. The island is small. It is more normal than not to end up seeing everyone multiple times a day, but she still hasn't seen Rosey.

She marches to the den, certain that must be where she is, but Rosey isn't there. The place is empty. Penny tries not to overreact – that is Rosey's energy, not hers – but the island feels too small this year, as though their mum's illness is taking up too much space. Her chest feels hot inside her almost all of the time. And now Rosey is nowhere to be found.

She's searched everywhere. The only place left she can think of is the sea. Rosey loves the water – as if her determination to spend time on it and master it is a fuck you to the way the car having plunged into the river as children has shaped their whole lives. Penny tries to reassure herself that it's likely she'll have taken out a paddleboard or jumped on someone's boat, but the need to scream is rising up and taking over. She can't help but imagine Rosey out on the water, but in this scene she is no longer laughing happily on a boat; instead she is face down, her body crashing into the rocks surrounding the western part of the island. The most dangerous side.

Penny knows it is only in her imagination but the need to let it all out is taking over. She closes her eyes and takes a deep breath in, filling her lungs with as much air as she can until it becomes painful. In the den, no one is going to hear her anyway.

She doesn't have to pretend to be OK out here or to put other people's feelings first. That was the whole reason for them building this place. It is theirs.

And so, finally, when she can hold it in no longer – Penny allows herself to scream. It doesn't simply exit her body and take the pain and fear with it. Instead, it seems to take over her whole body. It amplifies everything she is feeling, and as the scream rises up and morphs into rage, she lets it control her. All she wants to do is destroy everything around her. She pulls at the branches twined together. Her frustration building as they stay steadfastly in place, so she starts kicking at them instead. Screaming and kicking. The sound echoes through the den.

'Hey, hey,' a voice shouts forcefully. She can hear movement through the trees and realises that whoever it is is running towards her. Charging like a bull. Penny freezes. No one else is meant to be out here. To witness her. She was supposed to be alone. She feels an immediate need to hide. As teens, she and Rosey had taunted each other that a monster lurked in the surrounding trees and somehow that childhood joke has ingrained itself into her core.

'What's going on here? Are you OK?' the voice asks as the person it belongs to finally breaks through the edge of the trees and steps into the clearing.

Penny should be relieved to see a familiar face. Confirmation that there is no monster. But instead, she simply has a new target to direct her rage towards.

'You! Are you following me? Why are you out here?'

'Hey, calm down,' Mike says, holding his hands up as if to show her he means no harm. But he should have known better than to tell a woman to calm down.

'Calm down? How did you even know to find me here?'

'Firstly,' Mike smirks, 'I'm afraid to break it to you that me being here has nothing to do with you.'

'Then why are you looking at me like that?'

'Like what?'

'You're smirking.' Penny folds her arms and stares at him.

'I don't know,' he says, his smirk changing to an open smile. 'I quite like this side of you, I guess. A bit feistier. Less in your sister's shadow.'

'You can tell us apart?' Penny blurts out before she even registers what she's asking. She left her necklace at home this morning. It makes her cringe. She likes to tell herself she's grown-up and carved out her own identity over the past few years, but she's just exposed the truth – she's still exactly the same.

'Of course I can,' Mike says in a tone that shows he doesn't realise how momentous this news feels to Penny. 'You look the same but you stand differently, talk differently. I don't know, I guess the air around you *feels* different.'

Penny stares at him briefly, lost for words. She hadn't been expecting such a thoughtful response from the man with his tattoos and too-tight trousers. He has been watching her, that much is clear.

'Well, I am currently trying to find the louder, more annoying version of me,' she says finally.

'What do you mean?'

'Rosey's missing. I haven't seen her since yesterday and in case you haven't noticed, this is a pretty small island to be able to get lost on.'

'Are you worried?'

'Do I look worried?' Penny spits back at him sarcastically.

'Well then, let's go find her,' he states, devoid of emotion as if it were that simple.

'OK, Einstein, where do you think she is that I haven't already looked?'

'Just trust me.'

'Trust you? How do I know you weren't following me out here?' She feels mean as soon as it leaves her lips.

'Why would I be following you?'

'I don't know,' she says, feeling a little more unsure of herself.

'Are you going to come with me to find Rosey?'

'Fine,' Penny relents. Mike had seemed to act as though he knew where Rosey might be, and so she has no option other than to trust him. He'd appeared when she needed him and he'd offered to help her – and besides, it isn't really Mike she is angry with. It's her own family.

It's hot, the kind of hot that clings to you. Normally, there's a breeze from the coastline but, unusually, today the air is still. Penny thinks it is, quite literally, the calm before the storm.

'She could have picked a better day to make me traipse around the island after her,' Penny complains, as they march through the long grass back to the resort paths.

'Are you always this mad at your sister?' Mike raises his eyebrows at her, letting her know he's noticed that not everything is smooth sailing between them. How much does he watch them? she wonders but then pushes the thought away.

'It's complicated.'

'Isn't everything?'

'I don't know. I think some things are more difficult than others.'

'Do you want to talk about it?' he asks, but this time he doesn't look at her. He keeps his head forwards and his stride steady. It makes Penny feel safer opening up to him. It feels less confrontational or direct than having to look at the person you're talking to. And so, she finds herself starting to tell him everything.

She starts at the very beginning – which surprises her. He's made it so easy to talk to him that she ends up telling him things she's kept from even her closest friends. This band singer who she is certain is destined one day for worldwide fame. This almost-stranger. Maybe that's all part of his appeal.

'It's not that we hate each other, we don't, but it's because of the crash. There's this competitiveness to our relationship that seems to define everything. When we were eleven months old, our mum drove into a river by accident. At the time, she thought she could only save one of us. Which she did. Two builders in the van she'd swerved to avoid saved the other. Mum never knew which one of us she'd chosen to save, as if it didn't matter to her. That we were much of a muchness.'

'Fuck,' he says.

'Yep. Fuck.'

'And so now you're constantly competing to prove you're different?'

'Something like that. It's complicated,' Penny says, brushing it off. They are skirting dangerously close to the truth, but she and Rosey have a pact. It is their secret to keep.

'I can't imagine how that must have felt, or still feel. To think even your own mum found you interchangeable. As if you don't exist as a person by yourself,' he says and the ease with which he understands surprises Penny. 'I think I can maybe empathise a little though,' Mike adds, keeping his eyes fixed forwards.

'You can?'

'Not that it's a competition,' he jokes, and Penny jabs him in the side but she's grateful for his ability to lighten the mood a little without invalidating what she's just revealed. 'When I was six, my younger brother died. He was three. It was a congenital heart condition that hadn't been diagnosed. I spent my whole life feeling like my parents would rather it had been me who had died, and not him. I don't know how much was in my head, and how much was real. You can't work the truth of it out, right? Drive yourself mad.'

'I'm so sorry,' Penny says.

'Thanks.'

'Does that mean you're not close to your parents now then?'

'My parents actually died when I was fourteen.'

'Oh my God, that's so awful. Sorry, I didn't know.'

'We were on holiday at a caravan park. I was at the beach with friends when there was a fire in the caravan. My parents were asleep at the time. They never stood a chance.'

'I can't even imagine going through that,' Penny stutters, almost lost for words. She feels a shift inside of her as she starts to see him in a different light. You don't go through something like that unchanged. She reaches out and brushes her fingers against his.

'Thank you. It feels like a long time ago now and I don't like talking about it much. What about your relationship with your parents?' Mike asks, changing topic and she doesn't blame him for wanting to move on. 'You're here with them, aren't you? So I imagine it must be OK. Better than mine was, anyway.'

'Well, for a start, she's dying,' Penny whispers, feeling more confident about letting him in now he's shared his own story.

'That's very sad,' he says, softly, though it doesn't seem a shock. As though it's information he's already aware of.

'Thanks. She'd been in remission for a while but it seems to have come back with a vengeance this time. I think they've brought us here as a kind of goodbye. She's supposed to get her results tomorrow, but no one is expecting good news. Which makes me even more annoyed at Rosey and this bloody disappearing act.'

'Speaking of—' Mike says, stopping abruptly, 'we're here.'

They've stopped outside a white-cladded, two-storey cabin set on its own a little away from the main resort and built off the end of a walkway over the water. It looks to Penny almost like a houseboat, and it reminds her of similar ones she's seen lining the beach in Mersea. It is completely unlike the other cottages and hotel from the main resort. This one, she assumes, must be reserved as accommodation for the 'entertainment'. Mike leads her down the small wooden walkway and Penny notices it looks as though he is fumbling in his pocket for a key.

'What's going on?' she asks, more warily now. He puts his finger over his lips conspiratorially, indicating for her to stay quiet. She does as he says and they tread lightly into the cabin, as if this is suddenly all just a game and they haven't just opened up to each other in a way that now makes this seem abrupt and out of place.

It's two p.m. and yet when Mike throws open the brown door at the top of the staircase, there are two bodies lying on the bed. Penny screams before she can stop herself.

What the hell is Rosey doing in bed with Robbie?

And although Penny had a bad feeling about it from the start, none of them could ever have imagined that this was only the beginning. That in less than twenty-four hours' time, she would never see her family ever again and that one of them would have almost killed the other. Because if Rosey hadn't slept with Robbie, would he have held as much power over her? Over both of them? Or would they have done things differently? It was the butterfly effect, and it was deadly.

Chapter Nineteen

Lily, now

'You what? She's coming here now?' The man's voice travels through the open window in the front of the cottage and it's clear he isn't best pleased at the news of my imminent arrival. Rosey has told me she's here with her husband and daughter, Stef, who is a couple of years younger than me.

Feeling even more awkward having witnessed the disbelief in the man's voice, I almost turn around, but then I conjure up the image of Rosey's smile. I remember how it was just as wide and open as my mum's is in the photograph, as she'd hugged me goodbye yesterday and asked to meet with me again. I think about all my unanswered questions and the shock on Rosey's face when I'd told her Penny is my mum. The realisation that Penelope must have lived. I force one foot in front of the other as I edge closer to the front door.

'And what if she isn't who she says she is? You don't know the girl isn't lying about Penny. Where's the proof?' The man's voice sounds even more urgent than before.

'And why would she lie?' I hear Rosey's voice float through the window.

'You tell me,' he hisses back, quieter now and my fist hovers in front of the door. I wait, hoping to glean a bit more from their conversation before I interrupt it. 'Do you really want to go over everything again? To have the past laid out and re-examined?'

'I know what you're saying but I can handle it.'

'She's going to ask questions, Rosey. You do realise that?'

'Of course.'

'And you're up to it?'

'Perfectly capable, as always.'

'I hope you know what you're doing.'

Sensing their conversation has come to a natural ending, I rap my fist on the door and paint a serene expression on my face, as if I certainly haven't just overheard them talking about me and that it hasn't left me with even more questions than when I first arrived.

Rosey opens the door with gusto and I realise that there's a lot about this woman – my aunt – that is a performance. Not least, the way she smiles at me without a single trace of the argument she's just had with her husband. I tilt my chin with the knowledge of it and store it away. Some say I'm paranoid but, on the days when I feel most confident about myself, I think I'm observant.

If my work has taught me anything, it's that most people have secrets and everyone is hiding something. The question is whether Rosey's performance is purposefully deceiving or if it's an innocent social trait to make herself more *appealing*. Either way, it's a performance I have not yet mastered for myself.

'See you later,' Rosey calls over her shoulder before stepping out of the cottage and shutting the door firmly behind her. It strikes me as odd that I haven't yet met her husband, having heard he's definitely in the cottage but hasn't come to introduce himself. Isn't he curious about his wife's newfound niece?

'So, you said you're heading back today?' she asks as we head off down the path leading around the perimeter of the island. The wind has picked up a little and I note how susceptible this part of the island must be to the weather, with no trees to shield or protect it.

'Yes, there was only one night available in the hotel so I've booked a boat back for early this evening.'

'Well, we better make the most of this time then. I suppose you have plenty of questions for me after yesterday, but I think I probably have just as many for you, if not more.' She stops and looks at me. 'We really thought Penny was dead, and now here you are saying she didn't drown that night and, well, you – you can't be that much older than she was the last time I saw her.'

'I'm twenty-five,' I say and Rosey gives a small sad nod.

'We were only twenty-one.'

'If she didn't drown, like you all thought, what do you think happened to her? I don't understand why she didn't make it home?'

Rosey takes a deep breath and I sense she's reluctant to answer my question, but there's no time to take things slowly. I need answers and I need them now.

'I've been up all night asking the same question. Why did she never come back to us? My own sister, my identical twin. We were always a part of each other, and then now I find out that she didn't die but she chose, she—' Rosey falters, 'she chose to leave me.'

'But why? What happened?' I press her, harder now.

'I don't know, our mum was unwell and maybe it was all too much for her,' Rosey answers, but I'm reminded of the conversation I overheard earlier. Of her husband's warning, *she'll ask questions about the past*. Did something happen that summer between my mum and Rosey that meant she ran away?

I find myself both curious and also relieved. Dad has always told me that Mum loved to run when things got tough, but I'd never known if it was just something to say to make me feel less awful about the fact she abandoned us, or if he was telling the truth. It's comforting to hear it's not just a story Dad spins to try to keep me happy.

'I'm sorry she left you too,' Rosey adds, and I realise I've not said anything for a while.

'Are you angry at her?' I ask and Rosey let's out a laugh. It's not one that reaches her eyes, sounding hollow and exasperated rather than genuine.

'I think I'm too in shock right now to feel anything. You know we held a memorial for Penny on the island? Would you like to see it?' It hits me then, just how much my very existence has changed everything Rosey has believed for the last twenty-six years. What must have been an overwhelming grief at losing her twin – all of that now needs to be reframed.

'Yes please,' I say. I know it might be strange, visiting a grave for someone who never really died, but I wonder if there might be something about having a place to visit and mourn the loss of my mum that might feel cathartic. Someplace tangible to grieve her leaving us.

'OK then, let's go. I haven't been yet this holiday and I usually visit every year,' Rosey says matter-of-factly and I am once again struck by just how composed she seems after such a huge revelation that Penny is in fact still alive. Where's the screaming, the anger, the emotion? Is it simply shock, like she said, or has putting on a cloak of armour, hiding from reality, become a little too easy for her?

I can handle it, she'd said. The hairs stand up on the back of my neck and I feel a sudden urge to push the palms of my hands into my eyes.

'Actually,' I say, jogging to catch up with her where she's strode on ahead, 'would you mind if I go alone?'

'Oh.' She turns, wide-eyed, and I can see I've taken her by surprise. 'Absolutely. Of course. So sorry, darling, I wasn't thinking.'

I note that she recovers fast and well. An expert.

'Thank you. I know it's not really her grave, but I think I'd like to visit it by myself first. If that's OK. It still feels important, somehow, like it represents her leaving. In our own way, we grieved her too.' I leave out the fact that I have a sudden urge to not let Rosey get too close. To have a few moments to myself and try to process it all.

'It makes perfect sense,' she says with a sympathetic smile, and I realise that perhaps I'm better at putting on a front than I'd given myself credit for.

I glance again at the hand-drawn map I am clutching, even though by now I've looked at it so many times I'm sure I could recite the route from memory. At the end of this path on the right there should be a stile. If I go over it and follow the path up the hill, at the top there should be an old, small church. It is there that a gravestone was erected for my mother in 1990. A grave, without a body beneath it.

The island is only small, and it doesn't take long before I reach the top of the hill. In front of me stands a crooked stone church. It is quaint and extraordinarily beautiful. It looks gentle and kind, if a building can ever be described that way. There are pretty stained-glass windows and a modest steeple and bell. The grass here is overgrown and I have to push the blades away to read some of the engravings.

Eventually, I find what I'm looking for and am surprised to see it's been well-kept despite not having family permanently on the island. There are freshly laid flowers on the ground beside it. All purples and pinks. Rosey already admitted she hadn't visited yet, so if she didn't lay the flowers, then who did? The feeling of being here alone, surrounded by strangers, closes in on me and I begin to panic. I glance around, trying to see if there's anyone here with me, but all I see and hear are the birds. There are so many birds on this island.

I tell myself that I'm being paranoid, reverting to my normal state of play of catastrophising, and pull my shoulders back before looking again towards the gravestone in front of me.

Penelope Elspeth Taylor
A loving daughter, sister and friend.
9th August 1990
Always in our thoughts. For ever in our hearts.

I read the markings over and over, unable to peel my eyes away from the date, the ninth of August 1990. A new feeling creeps over me. As I stand facing what for years has been considered her grave, I am no longer filled with sadness for her absence throughout my life. Instead, that sadness has taken on a different form – it is rage and injustice that fills me now. How dare she be so cowardly? Not only did she run away from me, but by running away from her family – in letting them believe she'd died – she also took them away from me. I have an aunt. A cousin. And they never even knew I existed.

This grave, it doesn't just represent my mother. It is proof of a lie. Penny Taylor lived. And she gave birth to me. Suddenly the date in front of me feels as though it eradicates my very existence and I feel the pressing need to find out the truth even more acutely than before. What really happened here all those years ago? Why did she let everyone believe such an awful lie?

A sound jolts me from my anger. It is the crunch of footsteps. The noise seems to reverberate off the hilltop and I watch as the geese above me scatter. I look back down at the fresh flowers on my mother's grave and before I realise I'm even doing it, I swoop down and pick them up. Hold them close to my chest, taking in the smell of them, as if they were always intended for me.

'Hello?' I call. 'Rosey?' I'm sure I hear another crunch from a footstep, but no one answers. Whoever they are, they remain hidden. I may not be able to see them, but the hairs standing up on my arms tell me I am not alone. Carefully, gently, I lay the flowers back down on the ground and try to keep control of my breathing, which sounds louder now. Panic thrumming in my ears.

I turn and start back down the hillside, letting the momentum take over. My legs gaining speed as fast as I can run; from whoever was watching me; from the faux grave at the top; from all the different stories that keep spinning together in a way that seems impossible to unscramble.

As my feet pound the floor as fast as they can, the thought hits me: what if the reason Penny never returned home wasn't just because of a family argument that went too far and couldn't be forgiven? What if she was running away from something or someone? Was she in danger?

And then a new question forms, swirling round and round in my mind: *and if so, are they still here?*

Chapter Twenty

Penny, 1990

The thing about Rosey is that she always manages to convince Penny to do anything she wants. Today is no exception, which is exactly how the morning after finding Rosey in bed with Robbie, the three of them have ended up out on the water together. Rosey and Robbie paddle side by side as if they are a proper couple, with Penny reduced to being the third wheel. Robbie still has his clunky camera he's so proud of hanging round his neck, and Rosey is wearing a delicate red summer dress – which in Penny's opinion is ridiculous attire for kayaking and stinks of trying too hard. Rosey has always been one to dive into things headfirst, but this feels especially fast even for her. Penny puts it down to her need to escape the reality of their mum's illness; the need to have something else to channel her emotions into, but it leaves an uncomfortable feeling.

Out on the water, trailing behind, Penny realises she's slightly disappointed they haven't been joined by Mike. She'd assumed he'd be here, too. The currents are strong around the island, and although there are lots of pretty little enclaves to explore, it's also dangerous. The tranquil beauty of the landscape gives way to the deadly dangerous water just below the surface. It's when the surface is calm and still, the sun rays reflecting off it, that most accidents happen. People forget what lurks beneath. They are taken in by the serene surface. Of what it looks like, not what it's capable of. Which is why the rule has always been that if they go exploring along the western side of the island, where the currents are at their strongest during the summer months and where the edge is mostly black jagged rocks, then they stay together.

Of course, it's the western side that Rosey leads them to, today. She claims it's because there's more to find – and although it's true that the landscape this side offers a particularly expansive view – the way her stroke is that bit faster than normal as she presses forwards, makes Penny wonder how much it has to do with impressing Robbie and how much it really has to do with leaving their mum's fragility as far behind as possible. Because while Rosey accuses Penny of running when things get tough – she's not the only one.

The air is muggy today with a level of humidity that tells you a storm is on its way. It's been building for a few days now. Penny stops paddling for a moment, resting her oars against her lap and allowing herself to drift with the ocean. She tilts her chin upwards and watches the birds. Always so many birds. She notices that finally the storm clouds seem to be rolling in, scattering the blue light and casting a yellow hue across the sky. Change is on its way. Not just in the weather but within their family too. The consultant should be calling with Chrissy's results tomorrow. Have they arrived early? Has the timer already been set? How long does her mum have left?

When she looks forwards again, Penny has drifted further from Rosey and Robbie than she'd realised. It was a silly mistake, the currents here are notorious. In the distance she can see Rosey gesticulating towards her. She squints and makes out that she's pointing to the left. Penny sighs. Of course, Rosey would want to show Robbie the wrecks further offshore. Penny should have known this would have been her plan; always looking to impress. Penny paddles faster, regretting pushing herself this morning in the pool, for she can feel the burn in her arms.

By the time she reaches the wreck, she realises she hasn't seen the others for a while. She's always found the rotten shipwrecks eerie. They used to frighten her and after they'd first found them around the age of twelve, she'd had a nightmare so awful that she'd wet herself. She's always remembered the shame of it – she'd been far too old to be wetting the bed, but she'd been so incredibly frightened by the wrecks and the visions she kept having of the people on them drowning, that she'd had the most vivid and terrible nightmare about them. Even when her dad had told her time and time again that they likely hadn't been on the boats when they'd become stuck, that they'd probably become wrecks over time simply from being abandoned, she still hadn't been able to let go of the idea that people had been stranded out here. Surrounded by water. Unable to call for help until it had been too late.

'Hello?' she calls across the water, drifting closer towards the wrecks.

'Rosey? Robbie?' She shouts for them again but there is only the sound of geese above her.

Penny can feel the heat of anxiety working its way across her skin. Rosey has always known how she feels about the wrecks. Why would she leave her alone?

'Rosey?' This time she's screaming.

Penny can feel tears swelling so she closes her eyes and counts backwards from five, desperately willing them not to fall. Eventually she hears a splash, and then another. She is certain someone is close and then finally from round the grassy corner in the distance she sees the tip of a kayak.

Penny squints, waiting for a second kayak, but there's only the one and she realises that the figure heading in her direction isn't Rosey but another girl. As her kayak comes closer, she notes the girl is younger than she'd been expecting. Only a teenager.

'Hi,' the blonde, freckled girl says. 'Are you out here on your own too?'

'I wasn't, but it looks like I am now.'

'Are you lost?'

'No, not lost, just been left by my sister and her apparent new boyfriend.'

'God, the worst,' the girl says dramatically, letting her kayak float so close to Penny's the noses are almost touching. 'I was going to do another loop of the island if you want to come with me?'

'Thanks, but I'm going to head back in.'

'Oh, OK.' She sounds disappointed. 'Can I join you?'

'I thought you were staying out here?'

'Looks like I've changed my mind, if you'll have me.' The girl shrugs, her expression full of hope, and Penny realises that she hasn't seen many other teenagers on the island the past few days. There are lots of much younger children. This girl must be bored out of her mind.

Penny starts to head back towards Osea and the girl follows alongside her. It's not like she can tell her to leave her alone, at least not without sounding incredibly rude.

'If you're following me, are you going to tell me your name?'

'I'm Eloise Manning.'

'And how old are you, Eloise?'

'Old enough to be bored on this tiny island. I'm sixteen.'

'Your parents make you come?'

'Something like that. My uncle is hotel manager.'

'Joe's your uncle?' Penny asks, suddenly a little more interested in the teen who won't leave her side.

'He is. And yes, he's great, whatever, I know everyone loves him,' she reels off as if she's fed up of hearing everyone tell her how brilliant Joe is, 'but I'm bored out of my mind and I'm hoping you can help with that.'

'Sure, OK. You can hang with us,' Penny relents, feeling more obliged to keep the girl company now she knows who she is.

Penny suspects she knows where to find them, heading straight across the island to the den. She is striding so fast that she can hear Eloise panting to keep up with her. She hears her exclaim 'wow' under her breath as the den's clearing comes into view. Penny ignores her, instead calling across to the three bodies she sees sat on a picnic blanket at the entrance of the wigwam.

'Hey, arseholes,' she shouts. 'Remember me?'

'Sorry, who are you?' Rosey calls back and Eloise laughs.

'Don't laugh. You'll only encourage her,' Penny warns.

'Wait, is she? Are you?' They're closer now and Eloise has a better view of Rosey sitting only a few metres away. Penny wonders if she should have told her first, although this part is always quite fun – the surprise and shock when people realise there are two of them.

'Identical? Yes, we are. Though she's more annoying than I am. Meaner, too.'

'Who's this then?' Robbie says, jumping to his feet and shading his eyes from the sun.

'Hi, I'm Eloise.'

Penny watches as the young girl becomes nervous in front of the guys, and has horrible flashbacks about what it was like being a teenager.

'She's Joe's niece,' Penny adds, meaning it as a warning to the others to be nice. Robbie and Mike are older than her and Rosey, in their mid-twenties, and she realises Eloise must seem even more like a child to them. Almost half their age.

'Well, in that case take a seat.' Mike gestures to the blanket laid out on the forest floor.

'So what are you doing out here? Pretty sweet place you have,' Eloise says, looking round the den in wonder and taking it all in. There's an old mattress inside for comfort and fairy lights adorning the entrance.

'Just chilling. Me and Penny made this place when we were around your age,' Rosey chimes in, never one to miss an opportunity to place herself back at the centre of attention.

'Nice,' Eloise exclaims, and you can tell she's impressed. Then she looks around at them again and begins tapping her foot on the floor.

'You bored?' Mike asks, looking at the ground where she is tapping her foot and it feels a little to Penny like he's challenging Eloise. She likes Mike, she finds the way he is quiet and yet imposing all at once intriguing. Attractive, even. But there's something about his tone of voice that feels a little icier than she's come to be used to. It seems to Penny more likely that Eloise is just nervous.

'I don't know. Maybe. A little,' Eloise says, but Penny doesn't believe her. It just sounds cooler than admitting she's intimidated.

'Well, we can't be having that,' Mike declares a little more theatrically than usual. He cracks open a bottle of beer and Penny's eyes fall to the cluster of bottles already gathering at the side of the den. It hits her that he wasn't kayaking with them because he was here, drinking alone. 'You want a beer?'

And as Eloise takes one from him, Penny starts to think that maybe it wasn't the smartest idea letting her join them after all.

Chapter Twenty-One

Lily, now

I don't stop running until I'm in the hotel lobby. Wait impatiently as they fetch my suitcase from the storage room.

'Is everything OK?' a skinny teenager sat behind the lobby desk asks.

'Can I get a taxi off the island, please? I have a boat booked for later but I need to leave now instead,' I say trying to keep my voice level.

'I'm afraid not, miss. It's high tide. No cars can access the causeway until tomorrow.'

'What about the boat then? When does it next leave?'

'It doesn't,' he replies, already sounding bored of the conversation. 'You're right bang in the middle of no boat or car being able to get to or off the island.'

'You're telling me that I'm trapped here until my boat later?'

'About that,' he says, drawing the words out slowly, and my stomach drops, 'I'm afraid we just got a call to say all boat rides have been cancelled until the incoming storm has passed.'

'Right. And when is that going to be?'

He shrugs noncommittally. 'Dunno. But they're usually overnight, aren't they. Storms, I mean. Look it up on your phone.' He waves his at me and I realise it's actually quite a sensible suggestion. A quick check on my weather app tells me the storm isn't going to be a case of it quickly rolling in and out. It is forecast to weather through the night.

'What time can I call a boat for tomorrow then?' I'm getting desperate now.

'Depends on the weather,' he replies and I feel the need to press my palms into my eyes. Since meeting Rosey the urge is almost constantly there, pulsing through my body.

'Thanks very much,' I retort sarcastically, snatching the handle of my suitcase and turning quickly on my heel. I can feel it now, the storm that's brewing, as I march towards the seafront and stare out at the ocean. Usually so beautiful, this island and the glimmering sea surrounding it have turned into my captor. I'm stuck here for at least another night. Where am I going to stay?

The feeling of being trapped hits me all at once. It doesn't creep up on me, or build slowly, but instead I feel the full force of it and my legs buckle under me. My chest is tight. The kind of tense where I can barely breathe. I screw my eyes shut, although I don't know what it is I'm trying to block out.

And then, it happens again.

The tingling builds and the blood pounds. I feel totally disconnected from where I am standing, barely able to see the ocean that only moments ago was right in front of me. Again, I feel both angry and terrified, but this time the whole episode feels even more vivid than before. The terror is no longer entirely blank. To my surprise, there are images flashing through my mind. They are coming thick and fast, but frustratingly I can't quite make the shapes out. It's strange, as though I know I'm seeing something but my brain can't compute the images. It's like someone is talking really fast but in a different language. And then someone is shouting. Screaming. And I am afraid. This is the third time something like this has happened to me now over the past few days and the only constant seems to be that I am always afraid in them. Then, for the first time, I see something clearly enough that I can make it out. Green tiles. Square porcelain tiles. And all of a sudden, I know that in my mind I'm in a very small kitchen.

Their hand feels like an electric shock as they place it on my shoulder. It does the job of jolting me out of wherever I've been, and I'm flooded with relief when I realise I can see again. To my surprise, it's Rosey. Her firm hand grips me and she's looking at me in shock, but I can't work out why. I still feel half in my nightmare and half in reality. Her mouth is moving but I can't hear her. Somebody is screaming. It is too loud. And then, as I link the noise to Rosey's expression, and as my senses return to me, I realise that the person screaming is me.

'Lily,' she's repeating, and as I feel more control seeping into my own body, I force myself to stop. But my body keeps shaking.

'What's happened? What's wrong?' she asks, but I truly, honestly, don't know the answer.

'I-I-,' I stutter. How can I explain how lost I feel? That I think something very strange has started happening to me? It's as though I'm being transported to another body in another time. Watching something awful happen, but I can't yet fit the images together. So I say something else, something more solid. Something which I know to be true. 'I need to get off this island, but they've cancelled my boat.'

'OK,' Rosey says calmly, but she's using the kind of voice I've heard parents utilise to placate their toddlers. It is as though she's worried I'm a bomb about to go off if handled incorrectly. 'I hear there's a storm approaching so that will be why. While we wait for that to pass, how about you come with me? You're welcome to stay with us until the boat is running again. We have a spare room. How does that sound?'

I look at her, adrenalin still coursing through me, and everything is telling me to run. To not trust this woman. *Your mother didn't want them to be a part of your life.* Dad's words echo through my mind. But where else am I supposed to go?

'Darling, come with me,' Rosey says again and holds out a hand.

Although my instinct is to brush her hand away and remind myself that she is practically a stranger, my legs still feel like jelly and so, reluctantly, I close my fingers around hers and she leads me away.

I wasn't expecting there to be a nice atmosphere to the cottage. In my mind, I've built my estranged family up to be so awful that I'm thrown a little at how welcoming the space feels. Certainly, Rosey has been nothing but kind to me so far.

The place is small but it exudes character. Books line every shelf and there are piles of them on the floor in every room. I shouldn't be surprised. Rosey has already told me she's a literary agent. She's pretty successful too, from the sound of things. I looked her up last night and she represents some of the biggest names in fiction. Everything about Rosey oozes personality and, with it, success.

If I look past the books, from the look of the furniture and prints on the wall, I presume much of it has remained the same for many years. It strikes me then that I am looking at the same walls and furnishings as my mother once had. I am quite literally standing in her footsteps. If only I knew more about the person to whom they belong. Why did she stop seeing her family, and what really happened here? Because whatever people thought they saw that night, they were wrong. She survived. But she didn't return.

The truth of it shivers through me and I make a note not to trust anyone while I'm here. It's a small island, where I've been told most people return year on year. It feels safe to presume that most of the people staying on the island will at some point in their lives have met my mother or have links to people who had. Something happened to her here, that much is for certain.

'Lily,' Rosey calls from the top of the stairs, 'your room is ready for you.' She's needed a few minutes to make it presentable, unprepared for my sudden appearance – apparently it has become something of a 'storage room' over the last few years.

I make my way upstairs, past the hanging photographs lining the stairway and breathe in deeply halfway up. My feet stay frozen where they are. It's like she is looking straight at me. Whereas the other photos are group ones, this is just of her. My mother. Portrait style. The photo has a border and a label beneath the picture reads, PENNY TAYLOR.

She's slightly younger than the photos my dad has of her. She looks mischievous. It's caught me by surprise. There's something different about her. Is it just the innocence of youth? I'm trying to work out how old she is when Rosey appears above me at the top of the stairs.

'I know, it's a lovely photo. It was always Mum's favourite one of Penny. She had a copy of it on their fireplace at home. Dare I say I used to be a little jealous.'

'Do you remember how old she is?'

'She's ten. Come, I'll show you to your room,' Rosey nudges me and I force my feet to start moving again. 'It's your mother's old room, I hope that's OK.'

'Of course. More than fine, thank you.'

I thought it might feel a bit strange staying in my mum's old room for the night but instead, as I step inside, I feel a jolt of emotion and it dawns on me that there is very little of Mum left around our house. Dad has cleared her out; his pain too big to keep her there. But in this bedroom, she is everywhere. She feels real; from the ballerina jewellery box on the windowsill to the pen marks on the doorframe detailing her age and height.

'Thank you,' I repeat. I am both happy to have something tangible to link to my mum and also desperately sad that she didn't want to stay a part of my life.

'I'll leave you to get settled, then,' Rosey says, before marching downstairs and allowing me some privacy.

It's only mid-afternoon and I'm not at all tired, yet I find myself clambering into what was once Mum's bed. Logically, I know these are likely different bedsheets and they are most certainly – Rosey has assured me – freshly washed. But still, I envelop myself in the duvet and then pull it up to my face and breathe it in. I imagine I am breathing her in. That she never left me. That I was enough for her to stay.

Chapter Twenty-Two

Eloise, 1990

The twins had disappeared into the forest together when Rosey declared she needed a change of scenery, dragging Penny along with her – leaving Eloise alone with the guys. Rosey and Penny hadn't been gone long but it was enough time for Mike and Robbie to concoct a plan. One that if Eloise hadn't been so much younger, she would have told them was a ridiculous idea. Even at sixteen she knew that. Instead, she'd gone along with it. Helping Mike – who she thought was incredibly handsome (and was perhaps one of the main reasons she'd not objected to the idea in the first place) – to haul the old mattress from inside the den out on to the forest floor. Now, the mattress is balanced on top of their heads as she follows Mike along the forest path.

'It's just round this bend,' he says, leading the way confidently.

They dump the mattress at the foot of the lookout tower. Robbie is already waiting for them, rushing forwards with excitement when he sees them. Eloise is relieved when Mike finally slides the mattress off his head and lets it drop to the floor. She cricks her neck, which is hurting from the weight of it, and silently watches as Robbie takes her place. He helps Mike to haul it off the ground once again and they shove it hard and fast on to the flat roof of a stone outhouse. The small building stands only a few metres to the side of the tower.

'What about Rosey and Penny?' Eloise asks.

'They'll find us,' Robbie replies flippantly. 'So, who's going first?'

'Ladies first,' Mike says, looking towards her.

'I'm not sure I—'

'Oh, come on. You can do it. I believe in you,' he presses, though Eloise can see Robbie looking at her more warily.

'Don't be a dick,' Robbie says eventually, and Eloise lets all her breath out.

'Fine. I'll go first. But Eloise, if you're with us, you have to be *with* us. You get me? You're hanging out with the big boys now,' Mike calls to her, heading towards the ladder and beginning to climb up the tower.

She nods, telling herself to be braver. Cooler. To grow up.

'Seriously, it's just a bit of fun. A game. You like games, don't you, Eloise?' And with that, Mike launches himself off the first platform of the tower on to the mattress on the flat roof of the outhouse.

'Oh my God,' shrieks a voice from behind them and Eloise spins on her heels to see the twins have found them. Rosey is leading the way in her red dress, excitement spreading across her face. 'This is insane. I fucking love it!'

'Good. It's our guest's turn next. Go on, Eloise. You've got a full audience now,' Mike says, giving her a slight push on her lower back. Eloise swallows hard, waiting to see if anyone will object, but no one does. She looks to Penny but she just shrugs, though Eloise is sure she looks apologetic about it. But still, she says nothing.

And so, Eloise follows suit, hauling herself up the ladder and stepping on to the wooden platform. *OK, it's not actually too bad*, she thinks to herself. From up here, the mattress doesn't seem too far away. She can make it, she thinks. And then they'll let her hang out with them for the rest of the holiday. She just needs to prove she can keep up. That even though she's so much younger than them, she's still fun enough to keep around. God knows, they are more interesting than hanging out with the younger kids for the next few days. Climbing over the metal railing, but still keeping hold of it behind her, she balances with her toes over the edge.

'Just count back from five and then jump,' she hears Penny instructing her from below.

Five, Four, Three, Two, One.

She leaps.

And she makes it. She fucking makes it. The cheers from the group below rush through her, filling her up, and Eloise punches the air.

'My turn!' she hears Robbie declaring from the ground.

The game has well and truly begun.

Finally, it has started to rain. When the first drops had fallen, they'd looked up at the sky, thrown back their heads, spread their arms wide and howled with laughter. The alcohol racing through them keeping them warm. The mattress is soaked through, but still they carry on jumping.

Eloise has never felt more alive. She thinks this group of adults are electrifying. The twins have an enigmatic quality about them, helped by them being identical and the fact there are two of them, both as beautiful as each other. And then there are the guys. Robbie and Mike. Musicians. Now this, right here, in the rain with alcohol coursing through her, is something she can go home and tell her friends about.

'Hey, anyone want to join me?' The voice sounds as if it is coming from above her, but there is no one on the first platform of the tower.

'I'm up here,' the voice calls again and this time Eloise squints to spot a figure through the trees. They are wearing a red dress and she realises with a jolt that Rosey has climbed up to the second platform above the trees. Much higher than the first. It must be at least ten metres off the ground.

Looking around, Eloise sees how Rosey has caught the attention of the rest of the group. Robbie and Mike are looking up, wide-eyed. Impressed. Maybe it is the beer, or perhaps it's simply the thrill of being included in their group, but it is Eloise's feet, no one else's, which start moving towards the cold and wet ladder.

'I'm coming,' she shouts, her voice getting lost in the rain. They've been waiting for a storm to come for a while, but it isn't meant to hit until tomorrow. This rain is only the very beginning of it, she knows it's going to get a hell of a lot worse before it gets better.

Holding on to the ladder, she begins to climb, up past the first platform, higher and higher. The higher she climbs, the louder the wind and rain roars in her ears. Rosey is waiting for her at the top. They are all soaked through, clothes clinging tight to their bodies.

'Hold on to the railing as you walk round,' Rosey instructs. 'It feels a bit rocky up here but it's only because we're higher and the wind has picked up. You can see for miles in every direction. It's incredible. Come,' she says as she starts to walk round the platform.

Eloise spots the dodgy plank too late, the crack of it taking them both by surprise. Eloise freezes with panic as she hovers for a second before the wood splinters completely in half and she shoots through it. Rosey lunges just in time, grabbing her by the arm before she disappears completely. And now they are stuck there, with Eloise's legs dangling into nothingness as she hangs suspended ten metres above ground, Rosey's hand gripping tightly around her wrist.

The force of Eloise's fall has pulled Rosey to the floor and she's now lying on her stomach across the wooden platform.

Thinking fast, she wraps her ankles around the poles of the outside railing, anchoring herself in place. All she needs to do is keep hold of Eloise.

'It's OK,' Rosey tells her firmly, rain running down her face and off her chin as she stares at Eloise. 'I can see they're getting the mattress off the roof. Yes, great idea. OK, it's OK. Just hold on.'

'I can't, Rosey, I'm slipping.' Every word is punctuated with fear.

'I know, darling. I've got you. I promise.' As she says it, Eloise slips lower down Rosey's grip. The rain is making it hard to keep hold of her.

'They've almost done it. They're just dragging the mattress to us now, they just need to—'

But Eloise never hears the end of Rosey's sentence. She only hears the screams – her own and everyone else's – as she tumbles to the hard ground below.

She doesn't hear the flutter of wings as the birds descend high into the sky at the sound of her body cracking against the forest floor.

She doesn't see what the others see – the angle of her neck, her glassy eyes, the blood running out of her nose and ears.

Eloise doesn't feel the loss of hope nor the horror that replaces it as reality sets in, because she is already dead.

Chapter Twenty-Three

Lily, now

When I wake, the cottage smells of bacon. Eggs, too. According to the island's website, you can arrange for them to be delivered every morning along with a whole hamper of wholesome goods. Pure luxury.

Not only does the cottage smell amazing but it's noisy too. There are loud voices. Back home it is always so quiet. Just me and Dad. But today, I wake up and this place sounds *busy*. I tread downstairs and as soon as my toes graze the hallway a tall figure appears next to me.

'Good morning, Lily. It's great to finally meet you. I'm Rosey's husband, Robert,' his voice booms.

I take in the full stature of him. I've only seen him from a distance before. He seems friendly enough as he holds out a large hand, but I have not forgotten the conversation I overheard yesterday. Despite his welcome, I know he doesn't trust me, which makes two of us – both as distrusting of each other. I shake his hand.

'Come, we're through here,' he says, ushering me through the door at the far end of the narrow hallway. 'Can I get you a bacon roll? It is our holiday tradition. Always start each day the way you mean to go on. With good food and plenty of coffee.' He laughs – well, it's more of a bark – and manoeuvres around me to start plating up the food. The cottage feels even smaller now there are more of us here. Last night when I arrived it had only been me and Rosey. The others had been out enjoying the hotel's entertainment for the evening.

Rosey is already out of her chair, coming towards me with what I realise a little too late were intended to be air-kisses, and my face bumps awkwardly with hers. This is not my world.

'Morning, darling. This is Stefanie, who I've told you about already.'

'Hey,' she says with a small smile that is laced with judgement as her eyes flit over me.

I take the spare seat at the table and in return I study Stef from where I am sitting. I already know she's younger than me. Rosey told me she's twenty, in her second year of university at St Andrews. Everything about her stinks of privilege and private education. I wonder if she's aware of it – how she gives her background away even in the way she sits. She takes up space with no concern for those next to her. I imagine she feels she's earnt the right to spread out and spill over into other people's spaces. Or perhaps she isn't even aware she's doing it – used to other people always making room for her. Never being told to make herself smaller.

There is a confidence that comes from being rich; one you can spot a mile off. I think it comes from a sense that everything will be OK. That life will work out, in the end. It's a confidence you can't fake. Even with my clients, who have explicitly acknowledged they need my help, they still smell of the stuff – entitlement.

Stefanie is reading a worn-looking paperback – something classic, from the looks of it, and Rosey has a manuscript printed out in front her. Is Mum intelligent too? Does she like reading? We have very few books back home.

I'm about to ask when Stefanie says, 'I'm taking the boat out this morning with my friend Amber, and you're welcome to join us if you'd like?' She says it as though she doesn't really care if I join or not, but it's a surprisingly kind offer. Have I got her wrong?

'That sounds great. Thank you.'

'Lovely idea, Stef,' Aunt Rosey chimes in. 'Just, maybe not the boat today.'

'But why? We always go on the boat.'

'I know but . . . I just think . . . Perhaps.'

'They'll be fine,' Robert cuts in, firmly. 'Let them go.'

'Is there an issue with the boat? Is it broken? It seemed fine yesterday.' Stef pushes the issue. She's clearly taken aback by the idea we shouldn't go on it today. Not used to being told no.

'No, nothing like that,' Robert reassures her, looking quickly and purposefully towards Rosey. A look that says, *be careful what you say next.*

'I checked the weather and the storm isn't meant to hit until this evening.' God, Stefanie really can't let it drop. Clearly, my first impression was the right one – Stef seems so unused to being challenged. There's no way Dad would ever let me speak to him this way.

'I know they've stopped the crossings ahead of tonight but it is currently quite calm out there and if you don't go out for long, and stay close to the island I think you'll be fine,' Robert agrees with her.

'Exactly, so why did you say we can't go on it?' Stef asks Rosey directly.

She sighs, lowering her glasses further down her nose, 'I never said you can't go on it. I simply suggested that you didn't go on it *today*.'

'You're being weird. We always sail every morning. It's like some unspoken family holiday ritual – that and bacon rolls. If it's not broken, we're going on the boat. It would be mad not to make the most of it while we can.'

'I actually had the idea of us doing something together, given this is Lily's first day with us. Lily,' she says, turning to face me, 'do you play tennis?'

'I'm not great but I can play,' I say hesitantly, feeling like I'm caught in the middle of something I don't fully understand.

'Well I can't let Amber down, we said we'd hang out, so there's an odd number of us,' Stef says defiantly.

'What about that man you know here, Lily. Owen, that's his name, isn't it? Joe's grandson?'

'I can ask him.'

'Perfect. In that case, let's play tennis this morning and if the weather is still calm then you and Amber can take the boat out after.' Rosey says it more firmly than before and despite the scowl plastered across Stef's face, this time she stays silent. Clearly, the idea of playing tennis doesn't seem like too awful an alternative.

Well played, Rosey.

With that, the issue seems to be resolved, except that if the boat isn't broken and they usually take it out every morning, then why should today be any different? Is there a reason why Rosey doesn't want me on that boat?

Chapter Twenty-Four

Penny, 1990

No matter how hard Penny tries to focus on counting her strokes, she cannot erase Eloise's fall from her mind; every splash sounds like the crack of bone; every tumble-turn punctuated by the vision of her body freefalling through the air. Penny opens her mouth and screams underwater.

Normally, swimming in an outdoor pool while it's raining is one of Penny's favourite things to do. She loves the feel of raindrops on her back as she swims. But there is nothing about this session that is enjoyable. Pain radiates through every muscle as she pushes herself harder and faster. Punishing herself.

Why did she go along with it?

The question turns over and over in her mind. The decision to leave Eloise and clear away any trace of them ever being there with her had been made so fast and convincingly that she'd found herself nodding along. She'd watched on in silence as Mike and Robbie had carried the mattress back to the den. Had followed their instructions to gather up all the drink bottles and empty cans.

She's dead. Whether we were with her or not doesn't change that, they'd said. But it does change the truth. It twists the story Eloise's family and friends will know about how and why she died. Yes, they'd all been in shock, and certainly a little drunk, but what about the truth? What about their culpability? After all, it was them who'd supplied her with alcohol when she was underage. Their stupid game to climb the tower in the first place. They should have been looking out for her. Instead, their recklessness killed her.

She wonders how long it will take for anyone to find Eloise's cracked and bloodied body. People don't venture to the west side of the island very often. The urge to tell someone burns through her. She wonders how the others are feeling. Are they all coming to the same conclusion? They'd acted too quickly. Made the wrong choices. Yes, there was most definitely nothing more that could be done to save Eloise, they'd all agreed on that, but her body now lay out there exposed to the elements. Alone. And no one would ever know why she'd climbed the lookout tower in the first place. Her death would never make any sense to her family. Penny knows it is going to rip them apart.

It feels like there is no escape. Death lingers everywhere. It is among the trees with Eloise's body, and it is inside their own cottage – carried on the stagnant air surrounding their mother's illness. Penny stops swimming and lets herself simply float face down. She holds her breath as she stares at the pool floor. Wonders what the point of it all is. Perhaps even more painful is the question racing through her mind asking what the point of *her* is? If all she ever does is nod and go along with everyone else's plans.

Gasping for breath, Penny finally surfaces. She can feel her muscles protesting even at the very thought of swimming another length, so she hauls herself out instead. It is pouring now and the wind whips around her body painfully, yet she doesn't even reach for a towel. She lets herself feel the pain. *She deserves it*, she thinks, *we all do*.

As she turns, she notices that Rosey and Robbie sit watching her from a seat under the pool bar canopy. How long have they been there? She looks towards Robbie's hand, resting on Rosey's knee. It makes her blood boil. How are they sitting so calmly? Touching each other when Eloise's body grows colder by the minute? More self-conscious now under the gaze of Robbie, Penny gives in and grabs her towel off a nearby lounger.

'What do you want? Have they found her yet?'

Robbie shushes her and looks around making sure no one has heard. But it's just them there, no one else is crazy enough to venture out in this rain. Penny is getting tired of Rosey clinging on to Robbie as though he's her prized possession. She also doesn't like the way Robbie looks at her as he holds Rosey close. She doesn't trust him. It was his and Mike's suggestion that they leave Eloise, bloodied and broken, in the first place. Though if she's honest, she can't remember which of them first took the lead.

'Look, I think we all need to get off this island for a bit. Before . . . before—' Robbie doesn't finish his sentence before skipping ahead, 'Mike and I always said that on our last night we'd hire a catamaran for the evening. Go out in style. I know it seems a bit—'

'Inappropriate? Thoughtless?' Penny offers and he has the audacity to smirk.

'We just think that maybe it would do us all some good,' he replies, but his measured response only infuriates Penny even more.

'We?' she spits back, looking towards Rosey. Does she really agree with him, that after Eloise's death they should go on to party?

'What else do you suggest? Would you really rather spend the evening with Mum and Dad?'

And then it hits her that today is Thursday, day four, and she knows Rosey will do anything and everything in her power to avoid going home.

'There's a storm coming. It's a ridiculous idea,' Penny says, looking up to the sky which is even darker today than yesterday.

'There's been a storm brewing for days. Are you really afraid of a bit of rain?' Rosey challenges her.

'You're wrong, the storm is coming and I think it's going to hit sooner than they predict,' Penny says. 'Thanks for the offer, but no.'

'Why are you being so ungrateful? Robbie's already paid for the boat,' Rosey whines, and Penny can hear that really she's pleading with her sister to change her mind. To not leave her alone.

'It's not safe. Stay away from the water tonight, Rosey. I'm telling you. It's not a good idea.'

'You're just like Dad,' Rosey spits at her, before dragging Robbie away from the poolside. The comment cuts Penny deep, as it was intended to. Their Dad is small and quiet. He lets life pass him by, acting as though he is afraid of it. As though by enjoying anything too much, it means he becomes too afraid of losing it. As though if he stays quiet, life might forget about him. Might forget to take Chrissy away from him.

Penny's usually good at letting Rosey's fiery words roll off her, but today they stick. Today, she can't help but agree with her. Because she stayed quiet, didn't she, when they told her to. Lost her own voice. And it makes her afraid. She can feel it through the very core of her; she is petrified of who she has become. Of what they've done and what she let them do.

Chapter Twenty-Five

Lily, now

Owen's silhouette cuts an athletic shape as I watch him lead the way across the island to the tennis courts. I always feel more comfortable at the back, watching and listening, taking in other people rather than putting myself out there. Observing people is what drew me to becoming a therapist.

It is Dad who first taught me to sit back and glean information from others. How to read posture, facial expressions and to look out for intonation changes. He always used to say that if you look hard enough then no one can ever surprise you. Knowledge is power and power is control. And so, I learnt to judge others from a young age. This idea that if you don't watch out then people will reveal their true colours, also made me feel as though I should always be watching to anticipate who would eventually let me down. As though there is, inherently, something to be afraid of within everyone.

Was that what Dad had meant or have I picked this up from elsewhere? Was Mum also naturally fearful and distrustful of people? Over the past few days, I feel like I've been spun around and hung upside down. It's amazing to have found my aunt and cousin, having dreamt about having a larger family for so long, but it's all wrapped up in so much hurt and confusion. I knew mum was estranged from her parents but I didn't even know she had a twin sister, and I certainly never would have imagined they believed Penny had died. Surely Rosey must feel just as shaken up by it all as me? If not more? And yet as I watch her striding on ahead, clad head to toe in tennis attire, it strikes me again just how expertly she seems to be handling it all.

'*Your mum didn't want them to be a part of her life anymore. She said they weren't the type of people she'd want around her child and so I've respected that, even after she left us.*'

Dad's words circle round my mind. Admittedly, I've not known any of them for long, but from what I've seen they are nothing like I'd expected. They are clearly well educated and well-off. They've welcomed me into their home and told me more about my mother than Dad ever has. But Mum must have had her reasons for choosing to allow everyone to believe her dead. Whatever it was that severed the bond between Mum and Rosey so irrevocably that she left them for good, must have been of a certain magnitude. It's the only thing that makes sense.

I never professed to be a brilliant tennis player and yet the way Stef rolls her eyes when I miss the ball you would have thought I'd claimed I once competed at Wimbledon. The ball is heading towards my face at a speed I cannot match, and I know before I've hit the ground that I've stretched a little too far.

Although I skid to a halt, my momentum carries me forwards. There's no chance of me saving face and turning it into an elegant and impressive ninja roll. Instead, I hear myself cry out as I tumble to the ground and feel a hot burn down my leg as it scrapes along the surface. I feel the wet, warm blood oozing down my shin. I'm not too hurt, but it sure as hell stings.

I hear Stef calling that there's probably a medical kit in the clubhouse. She doesn't offer to come with me, but that suits me fine. I'm reminded again how only a few days ago I didn't even know these people.

The clubhouse has a picturesque view through a glass wall out to the sparkling sea in the distance. Behind it, I can see across to Mersea. I watch the rest of the group carry on playing from where I'm sitting until Robert raises his racket in the air, excusing himself, before heading towards me and the clubhouse.

'Mind if I take a look?' he asks, pointing towards my injured leg.

'Why, are you a doctor?' I quip back, but at the same time I lift away the ice pack I've been holding over it and let him peer closer. He takes my leg in his hands and I'm conscious of his touch. I'm sure he's just being kind, but it feels strangely intimate. I go to pull my leg away but he's holding it tight around my ankle.

'I just want to check you're OK. I promise I won't hurt you,' he says, smiling, as he tugs my leg back towards him. After a minute or so more he lets go, announcing, 'I don't think you need stitches, you'll be fine.' And then his eyes travel up my body.

'You're a lot like Penny, you know,' he says, which strikes me as an odd thing to say given he's married to her identical sister. If I remind him of my mum, then I must also remind him of Rosey. I wonder what it is about me specifically that makes me more like Penny. The question gets stuck on the tip of my tongue. For some reason it feels too confrontational. Too personal a question. But it also makes me wonder how well he really knew my mum before her accident. Rosey had told me she was with Robert when they watched Penny fall from the boat. But is that the truth?

A small warning echoes again in the back of my mind, *everyone has secrets*.

It's a lesson Dad has impressed on me all my life – to never trust anyone. That it's just the two of us against the world. 'Trust needs to be earnt, not given,' he often says. I don't trust Robert or Rosey and I certainly don't trust anything they tell me. Still, I can't stop myself from asking more questions. The need to find out what happened that summer burns bright inside me.

I figure that even if Robert spins me a story, which I'm sure he will given his warning to Rosey about raking over the past again, that there still might be some clue to help point me towards the truth. Anything, even lies, must be better than nothing.

'Did Penny and Rosey argue that evening on the boat?'

'Of course not,' he says so seriously I find myself believing him. 'What happened to Penny had nothing to do with me or Rosey.'

'But there must have been a fight or something more that happened, otherwise why wouldn't she have gone back home. Why did she jump off the boat and choose to let everyone believe she was dead? It makes no sense. Please, help me understand.'

'We don't know that she jumped. No one was with her on the boat. We'll never know why she was up on the ledge or how exactly she ended up in the water.'

'But you watched her, didn't you? With Rosey from the pier.'

'I did. But all we know is what we saw. She was there, and then she wasn't.' He rubs the bridge of his nose and I can see he's feeling uncomfortable. 'That summer was hard for everyone. A lot happened. I don't know why Penny let us all think she'd died. It seems like a bit of an overreaction.'

'An overreaction? To what?' I ask and Robert snaps his head towards me, regret plastered across his face.

'Nothing,' he says firmly.

'You're lying. Something did happen, didn't it?'

'Your grandma was dying of cancer. Did Rosey tell you that? It put a lot of strain on the family. Maybe Penny just couldn't handle it any longer and so she ran away. Perhaps she saw her opportunity to leave it all behind, and she took it.' I stare at him, waiting for him to go on. Is that it? Is that all he has for me? Vague assumptions? 'What I was trying to say, was that I think she must have overreacted to her mum's diagnosis,' he adds, and it confirms my suspicion that he is clutching at straws, trying to cover up the fact he has said too much.

'And you're sure they hadn't argued that day?'

'Lily, I really think you're going too far. I understand wanting to find out what happened to Penny, but you need to stop asking so many questions.'

'Are you threatening me?'

'Absolutely not,' he says, standing up tall. Looming over me. Is it a deliberate power move? 'But you'd be wise to listen to me. I'll see you back at the cottage,' he adds, before walking away.

I mutter *arsehole*, under my breath, and then pull out my phone and text Owen, letting him know I'm in no fit state to keep playing and asking to meet up with him later. I need help figuring out what my next move should be because I may not have been told much of the truth by Robert, but I'm confident that something more than they are letting on happened that day. And whatever it was, my mother must have felt it was unforgivable.

I watch Robert disappear round a corner and let the sound of birds settle over me. It reminds me of being in the cemetery only a couple of days ago and I remember the fresh flowers on Mum's grave. The way I'd felt certain someone was watching me. And I realise that while Rosey had admitted to me she'd not yet been to see Mum's grave, there is nothing to say Robert hadn't already made his way there. What if all this time I've been focusing on the wrong person? Trying to work out what had happened between Mum and Rosey, when in fact I should have been looking into Robert?

The sun has started to set by the time I approach Chapel House. My pace is slower than usual and I've walked a longer way than necessary back from the clubhouse, making several detours and loops on my return. I needed space and time away from everyone before rushing back to them – to Robert. The cut on my knee throbs with every step and I have a slight limp. But I force myself to quicken now, the hair rising on the back of my neck, because for the past ten minutes I've had a strange feeling as if I'm being followed.

Who is watching me? Is it the same person from the church yesterday? Whoever they were, they'd kept themselves concealed among the trees even when I called out for them. Perhaps even more than the question of who, I should be asking why?

The cottage is empty when I get back. Discarded tennis rackets by the front door tell me they've already been home and gone out again, no doubt to the hotel bar. I need to get changed out of my sportswear and clean myself up. The blood has started to crust down my leg. And so I head straight upstairs.

I notice it immediately. The door to my bedroom is open. I shut it when I left. No question about it in my mind. Dad always drilled into me that doors were to be shut, and not left open. If I left my door open growing up, he'd threaten to take it off its hinges. Not that he ever went through with it, of course. But he'd always spout the same parent-crap about respecting the house and keeping it looking presentable. That the things in my room were mine, and not to just let the whole world in to see. *A proud home is a tidy one*, he'd say. *Family needs to be respected and this is our family home*. Another of his favourite quotes. And although I'd roll my eyes and always knew it was overkill, I understood that he was just doing his best to fill Mum's empty shoes. To run a home.

Which means there is no way that after twenty-five years of Dad's mantra having been drilled into me, that I would have left the door open. Not in my own home and certainly not somewhere I'm staying as a guest.

Someone has been in my room.

I tell myself there could be all kinds of reasons for it. Perhaps Rosey had left something of hers in there and needed to go get it? But as I round the doorframe, the feeling stays heavy in my stomach. I am certain that someone has been through my belongings. It's not obvious, no clothes strewn across the floor, but it is in the details. And, as someone who has always needed to control their environment, the room no longer feels right. Whoever has been through my things has tried hard to make it look like they were never here at all. Or maybe I'm just being paranoid and seeing things that aren't really there; nothing seems to be missing, and why would anyone want to go through my stuff anyway? I can't think of anything I have, that someone on this island might want – so I realign my notebook which is now at an unpleasant angle on top of the desk, kick the corner of my suitcase back further underneath the bedframe out of sight, and push the feeling away.

The Palace

Today it's my turn to be sick. Last week, it was Mum's. I hate it but Mummy says it's important. Gets me to repeat 'I'm strong, brave and proud,' and then wraps me up once again in the duvet cover. Calls me her little burrito and then tells me to tip my head back to make sure I can breathe. The cover is over the top of my head and I'm sweating. I know that's meant to be a good thing, but it makes me feel sick. I am hot and sticky and although I am trying my hardest to be brave for Mummy, I feel a tear rolling down my cheek.

'You're doing so well, darling, I'm proud of you, he'll be back soon,' Mum says and I can see her looking at me through the gap in the duvet above my head. 'Slow breaths, that's it, you don't have much longer to go.' And then she must hear him returning, as suddenly she's unwrapping me as fast as she can. She places a hand quickly on my chest and nods. 'Good, well done, I'm sorry,' she whispers and I lie back down on the bed. She places the duvet over me but lays it in its normal position this time, just as he'd expect.

Father has already visited once this morning, which was the first time today Mum had unwrapped me and pretended I had a temperature. He'd gone to get me my medicine – he keeps it with him, we aren't allowed any here in The Palace.

I'm not sure why it's so important that we keep pretending we're unwell but Mum says to trust her. 'It's because it gets so cold in here,' I hear her telling him, exactly the same as she had last time. 'If only we could keep ourselves warm with water bottles and hot drinks, I think we would do better through the winter months.'

Once again, Father doesn't answer her. 'I'll be back in eight hours to give another dose,' he says gruffly. And then he leaves. I kick the duvet off me as fast as I can and strip off.

Mum rushes to me with a cold wet cloth. 'You did so well.'

'Did it work?'

'We'll see.'

'Do I have to do it again?'

'Maybe baby, maybe.'

Chapter Twenty-Six

Penny, 1990

Penny sees him from the end of the road, which she's thankful for because it gives her time to step out of view. He's staring out of the window. One hand against the glass. Even from where she hovers behind a tree, she can see that he's crying. In his other hand, the cottage's phone is clutched to his chest. The results must have come in and from the expression on her dad's face, there can be no other answer: her mother is dying.

Penny feels frozen, stuck where she is. The wind is whipping up around her. There's no doubt about it, the storm is coming tonight just as she'd warned Rosey and Robbie. She knows she needs to move, that her dad is likely waiting to deliver the news. No doubt he is staring out the window watching for his two daughters to come back home to them. It's why they brought them here, after all. And yet she cannot move an inch. At least, not in the direction of the cottage. Not towards all the sadness and pain that awaits her there.

She closes her eyes and sees Eloise's broken body lying on the forest floor. Hears the crack of bones. The scream as she fell through the air now seems to howl through the wind. Haunting her. How is she supposed to face her parents now? To pull herself together and pretend everything is fine? There is no way she can be who they need her to be, not tonight.

Penny turns, and she runs. It's raining harder, and she can feel her clothes are soaked through but she keeps on running away from the cottage. Away from having to face the fact her mum is going to die. Away from her own guilt and all their secrets.

You always run away.

Rosey's voice taunts her. Is she really so predictable? And yet she doesn't stop. Not until she's down at the harbour, standing in front of Joe's boat. It's a terrible idea, she said so herself, but she's desperate to escape. To pretend none of it is true, even if just for a little while.

And so, she climbs the cold steel ladder up to the deck and runs towards the cabin door. Knocks hard and shouts, 'Hey, I'm here,' until Robbie throws it open, smiling at her like he'd always known she'd turn up. As if they haven't just killed a teenage girl. The thought sends an icy chill through her and yet, despite the warning signs and knowing it is a terrible idea, she steps inside.

Chapter Twenty-Seven

Lily, now

It was Owen's suggestion to meet here though the cinema is currently closed until the first showing of the day which is later this evening. I look at the neon sign above the door and the bright lights make me wonder how much of this island has changed since Mum was last here, and how much has stayed the same. I know the cinema was built in recent years. What did the island feel like all those summers ago?

'I'm afraid a film isn't exactly what I have in mind,' I say, giving Owen a rough and awkward hug. It feels strange to me but I am pleased to see him.

'I didn't imagine it was, but from the sounds of things I thought we could do with some privacy,' he says, opening the cinema door with a flourish.

'They don't lock it?'

'Nope. This is the kind of place where luxury also buys you trust.'

The very notion of it – trust – makes the hairs stand up along my arms. I just hope my instincts about Owen are correct. He flicks the lights on from the corner of the room and in front of us I see six rows of sofas leading up to a huge screen.

'So do you want to tell me what's going on?' he asks, standing closer to me now. 'You disappeared from tennis. Is your leg all right?'

'I'm fine. But how did you know the door would be unlocked? You said before that you haven't come to Osea for years.' My dad's voice whispers in my mind. *Trust no one.*

'I haven't, but when I was a boy, I used to hide out in here all the time. Joe used to let me put extra films on. There's not exactly loads to do for an eight-year-old on a small island. I figured old habits die hard and tried the door the first night I arrived. What can I say? I'm sentimental like that. But I like it in here. So? Are you going to tell me what's wrong?' Owen prompts again, and I decide to try and trust him.

'I think Robert and Rosey are lying to me about the night Mum died. I have this feeling that they argued about something and whatever really happened was bad enough Mum chose to let her own family – her twin and her dying mum – believe she was dead. What made her so determined to never return? And how did she get off the island without being seen?'

'Have you asked them directly about it?'

'I just asked Robert and, well, I think he threatened me.'

'He what?'

'Maybe I misinterpreted it, I don't know, but I hate being here not knowing who I can trust and who I can't. It's all too much. My mum didn't want me to ever meet Rosey and I guess I'm only really understanding that she must have had her reasons about why. What if she wasn't safe here? I should have gone home as planned. But—' I sigh exaggeratedly and theatrically, 'the storm tonight means I'm still stuck here until tomorrow.' I stop, finally taking a breath.

'OK,' Owen says nodding slowly. 'Silver lining,' he says suddenly, his head snapping up towards me with a glint of mischief in his eyes, 'that means you have at least twelve hours to get to the bottom of this and I'm going to help you.'

I jump as I hear the door of the cinema creak open and watch as Joe steps into view. How did he know we were here?

'Someone told me the lights were on, I thought I'd come and check it out myself.'

'Sorry, it's my fault,' I say, but Joe swipes the apology away.

'No need to say sorry. I figured it would be Owen up to his old tricks again, but thought I better come check it out for myself. Is everything OK?'

'We're just trying to figure out why Penny let everyone think she'd died instead of going home,' I say, defeatedly. 'And I'm pretty sure Robert and Rosey aren't telling me the whole truth about the night they thought she'd drowned.'

'Have you been on their boat yet?' Joe asks.

'I was meant to go on it this morning but Rosey suggested tennis instead. Why?'

'Well, it's the same boat that Penny fell from.'

'How? They didn't own a boat back then. Rosey told me they bought it after the accident.'

'Yes, they bought it from me. And it was me who Robert hired it from all those years ago.'

'Can you show us which one it is?' Owen asks.

'Of course. Come with me. But Lily, I think perhaps you should also tread carefully when it comes to Robert and Rosey.'

'You don't trust them either?'

'All I know is that I don't believe in coincidences, and two accidents in one night? Penny's and Eloise's?' His voice catches as he says his niece's name. 'I've always thought they must be linked.'

'But no one was with Eloise when she fell.'

'And no one was on the boat with Penny either,' he says, cocking his head to one side, waiting for me to catch up with him. My head swirls and I push my palms against my eyes. Like Joe, I also don't believe in coincidences. And as a therapist, I believe that all behaviour is led by patterns. Formed through experience. Behaviour is repetitive.

'Why didn't you say anything earlier?' I ask, trying to sound less angry with Joe than I feel for keeping me in the dark before. *Trust no one.*

'I wanted you to reach this point by yourself,' he says, almost apologetically. 'You came to Osea a few days ago having only just learnt your family once owned a holiday home here. You've had a lot to take in and, I suppose, I didn't want to scare you off too soon or for you to think I was just some crazy old man with an overactive imagination.'

I laugh, knowing too well what that feels like. 'It's OK,' I reassure him with a smile, 'I'll help you find the truth about Eloise's death, and I think we should start by getting on that boat.'

It has started to rain and the wind lashes round our shoulders as we haul ourselves up the ladder and on to the deck. We duck down low hoping no one will spot us. I can feel the adrenalin pumping through me. I've never been one to sneak around or break the rules and yet here I am.

I follow Owen as he darts across to the cabin door leading to the living quarters and watch as he scoops up a boat hook from the deck. He indicates for me to stay low out of sight, and I watch in awe as he uses the hook to pick the overhead hatch of the cabin door. Of course, I knew we'd have to find a way in somehow so I can't pretend to be completely naïve, but it's the way in which he does it so confidently, without hesitation, which fills me with more unease than I was prepared for. How well do I really know him? He must be able to tell from the way I'm staring, mouth slightly agape that I have questions, but he just shouts above the rain, 'Go, quick,' as he pushes the door wide open and we dart inside. It slams shut behind us and it's a relief to no longer be fighting against the biting wind. The boat rocks and I take some deep breaths trying to keep my travel sickness at bay.

'Thanks.'

'No problem. So, what now?'

'I've got no idea but there must be a reason why Rosey didn't want me on this boat.'

'OK, let's start looking.'

Before I begin, I take the time to try and get my bearings. This is the boat my mother was on the night she fell into the water. The last time she ever saw her family again. I look around, trying to commit every detail to memory. *My mum was here.*

At the very end of the galley, there's a small snug area with brown leather sofas and a television. Between us and the snug, there's a wooden table that looks worse for wear, as though it's been here for ever. We're standing in front of the kitchen area. The small wooden ladder from the deck has taken us straight into the middle of the space that makes up the lower deck, I spin three-hundred-and-sixty degrees to take in the full view of the kitchen behind me, and that's when the air gets sucked out of me. I reach out and grab for Owen. My fingers clenching desperately. Because here in this kitchen, I see something I recognise:

Green tiles above the units.

They are small squares with a rustic texture. Are they exactly the same as the ones I saw in my panic attack? I screw my eyes shut and try to remember, but I can't conjure the image clearly enough to be sure. They're the same colour, that's for certain, but why – how – could I have known? I've never been here, and I've certainly never seen this kitchen before.

'Are you OK?' Owen asks.

'Yeah, I just think we should hurry up,' I force myself to say, unable to tell him that my whole body is now filled with a mix of dread and anticipation. That somehow I know we're on the right track.

We look in all the cupboards and throw the cushions off the sofas. There are some Fortnum and Mason hampers used as storage to the side of the snug, which we empty before dragging them away from the wall. Disappointingly, all we find are cosy knitted blankets.

There's nothing here.

'I'm sorry,' Owen says, 'I really thought we'd find something. We should go though, Lily. The weather's getting worse.'

He's right, of course – the loose trinkets on a shelf along the kitchen wall are sliding up and down with the waves. I really don't want to have broken Rosey's trust for nothing. My suspicions began when Rosey seemed reluctant for me to ever board this boat, so if I was wrong about this, did I fabricate everything else?

'One minute,' I say, and then in one last attempt to make sure I have searched this boat as thoroughly as I can, I lower myself on to my hands and knees and crawl under the old table in the centre of the room.

I see it, scratched under the table just above the right leg.

The dread I felt only moments before is now replaced with relief, and I can't help but smile; it's better than letting the fear creep in, because at least I now know I'm right.

They've been lying to me from the very beginning.

The Palace

Mum isn't well but it isn't a game. Not part of a plan. I can't yet tell the time, but my stomach is grumbling so it must be way past lunch. Mum still hasn't gotten out of bed. She isn't hurt; not like sometimes. Luckily it's a Sunday, so we don't need to worry about Father coming, or we'd be in trouble. He doesn't like it when she's this way.

This morning, I'd checked her all over as she lay completely still, eyes open but not moving. There were no new marks. The map of her body the same as it had been for a while. I placed my hand on her chest checking for a temperature, the way she has done plenty of times recently to make sure I'm hot enough for when Father arrives, but it didn't feel unusually warm. 'What's wrong, Mum? What's hurting?' I asked and she'd closed her eyes and whispered in a tiny voice, 'It's just my heart.' And then I'd known she'd be staying in bed all day, that any playing or stories would have to wait until tomorrow. That's what happens when it's her heart that's hurting.

My stomach makes another loud noise and I take two plates out of the cupboard. I make up our usual lunch; an energy bar, apple, yoghurt and a packet of crisps. I already know she won't touch it, but I'll leave it by the bed just in case.

Father brings us a hot dinner twice a week. Other than that we have food from the fridge and a sandwich. Avocado and cheese wrap is my favourite, but we are only allowed one avocado a week. Father says it's expensive, and that we are lucky he buys it for us at all. We always save it for our favourite day of the week – a Sunday. The day that is all ours.

I feel sad for Mum that her Sunday is ruined. That she'll have to wait a whole seven days until she can enjoy a Sunday again. Mum says it's Father who broke her heart and I believe her, because who else could it have been? It's just me, Mum and Father. So if it wasn't Father, then it would have been me who hurt her. And that can't be right because Mum tells me I'm her shooting star. She says that without me, her heart would stop beating entirely. And so I eat, and I wait, hoping that tomorrow she'll be well enough to tell me a story again.

Chapter Twenty-Eight

Penny, 1990

Penny's stomach lurches with the boat. She is used to being on the water, but the storm is creating huge swells and the boat rocks viciously along with the waves. They'd remained moored to the pier, they weren't that reckless, but as the sea violently throws the catamaran around, it still feels like they'd have been safer staying on land.

Robbie's arm is looped round Rosey as she pours herself another glass of prosecco. The drinking feels more frenzied than it has any other night. They are all drinking to forget. It is not only alcohol filling their cups, but their guilt too. Overflowing and spilling on to the floor. Except for Penny, who feels so sick from her guilt that there's no room for anything else. And so she watches them, as they ramp the music up and paint smiles on their faces; as they pretend the storm isn't ravaging Eloise's body while they drink and party.

Mike proposed a game of dares which so far has seen Robbie downing a pint of milk. They've agreed to go round the table clockwise with the person to their left making up the challenge, which means it is Penny's turn next and Rosey's chance to come up with a dare for her.

'I dare you to graffiti Joe's boat,' Rosey smirks, crossing her arms and leaning back smugly. She knows Penny is always a stickler for the rules and is most likely counting on her refusing.

It would help Rosey cement her role as the cooler one of the two. Besides, deep down they aren't really that dissimilar. She's sure Rosey doesn't really want her to upset Joe. She loves him as much as she does.

'I'm not doing that,' Penny retorts and, on cue, Rosey raises her eyebrows smugly.

'Come on,' Robbie jeers as though they are all back at university and this is some kind of fresher's rite of passage she's failing.

'Don't bother,' Rosey says. 'She won't do it.'

'Get me a kitchen knife then,' Penny snaps, nodding towards the wooden block of knives behind them in the kitchen. Rosey jumps up in delight and fetches her one. She slips slightly as she sits back down and then she passes the small sharp knife across the table.

It is trickier than Penny had anticipated but she manages to scratch their initials under the table, the markings just about legible. She starts with an E for Eloise. The need to honour her in some way. To mark the day and what they did. And then she adds the rest of their initials. *E M P R R*. Dates it underneath 09/08/1990. It feels like a confession and the relief fills her for a moment.

It starts a trail of thought that she can't stop.

'Right, my go then,' Rosey sings, moving the focus away from Penny and back on to herself. This time, it is Robbie's turn to come up with the dare.

'I dare you to streak naked on the top deck.'

'No way, that's ridiculous,' Penny starts, but Rosey is already grinning wildly as she stands up and then slowly removes her top as though it is part of a striptease.

'That's enough,' Penny shouts above Robbie's jeers and Rosey's singing. 'It's chucking it down out there. Don't be stupid.'

'Fine, fine,' Robbie holds his hands up. 'Just the top off is fine.'

Rosey winks, carrying on the show, and then takes it up a notch as she dances towards the ladder and climbs out into the storm above them. Entranced by her boldness, they all follow – which of course is exactly what Rosey always craves. An audience. Affirmation. Proof of her own existence.

'Like this?' she says as she dances her way seductively in the storm across the deck. She raises her arms above her head, but as Penny watches her all she can see is Eloise's arms cracked at unnatural sharp angles laid out on the floor, framing her lifeless body.

And Penny finds she can't hold it in any longer. The anger she feels. The scream that's been building inside of her for days. The hatred; towards her family for being stuck on this island and towards Rosey – for everything she has done and everything she is; for the things she's made Penny do; and most of all towards herself. Every fibre of her body is screaming with the responsibility of Eloise's death. A young girl who had simply wanted to hang out with them for the day. She'd ended up dead for it. And then they'd left her. Wiped their hands clean of it. She can't take it any longer. She needs to let it out and this time, unlike a few days ago at the den, she doesn't care who is here to witness it.

'What the fuck is wrong with you?' she screams at her sister – at all of them. Because Rosey is just as guilty as the rest of them. Although Rosey's way of dealing with everything first appears loud and carefree – it's all a façade. She's being loud in all the wrong places; it's simply her own way of silencing the cracks. Of burying everything. Hiding the pain – the truth – away. But Penny has decided there comes a point where that is no longer an excuse. When you are no longer the victim – the sum of the things that have shaped you – but when you become the villain. Just like their mother. And here Rosey is, half-naked in a storm putting on yet another show to quiet the truth of what they have done and of what's still waiting for them back at the cottage – their mother's illness.

'Eloise is dead, Mum is dying and you're acting like you don't have a care in the fucking world. Is this what you want? Is it?' Penny shouts above the wind. She's climbing now, up on to the railings of the boat. She's lost control – no way of pushing it all back inside of her.

'Everyone look at me, I'm Rosey and I am always the centre of attention. Love me. Love me,' she mocks, her voice escalating higher as she starts to dance on the side of the boat. Imitating Rosey perfectly in the way she moves and talks. She's holding on to a rope that's attached to a sail, but it's raining hard and the surfaces are slippery. The stormy waves thrash in the darkness below her.

'Don't be a bitch,' Rosey shouts back, but she's edging closer and Penny delights in being able to detect that she's afraid. It seeps in around the corners of her voice. She doubts Robbie or Mike can hear it, but it's there all right. *Good. Finally. Show me you feel it*. 'Come down from there, Penny, you're acting weird,' Rosey shouts again.

'I'm acting like *you*. This is what you do. You act up and people get hurt. It's your fault she died, Rosey. Yours.'

'What? You have to be kidding me,' Rosey shouts back, furious now. 'How is what happened to Eloise anything to do with me?'

'Because this is what you do. It's always the Rosey-Show.'

'And you blame me for that? What about you?'

'I blame us all. We have to tell someone she's out there. In this fucking storm,' Penny roars. She is no longer dancing but she is still up there on the catamaran's ledge. Standing with her toes too close to the edge. One hand on the railing, the other on the rope to keep herself steady as the boat rocks with the waves.

Rosey edges her way across the deck closer to her.

'Just come down, Penny. You're making a scene and it really doesn't suit you. We can decide what to do about Eloise once you're off that stupid ledge.'

'I'm not coming down until we agree to tell everyone what really happened. You're the one saying I always push everything aside. Pretend nothing is wrong. Well, this is me refusing to do that any longer. So, who's the most like Dad now?'

It gets Rosey's attention, just as it was intended to, but as Rosey whips back to face Penny, she loses her balance on the slippery deck and grabs for the closest thing to help steady herself. Her hands scramble, clutching the rope between them. Her body weight swings with it as she fights to find her footing again. It's a natural instinct. Survival.

She hadn't thought it through.

Had never meant to knock Penny off the boat into the deadly water below.

Chapter Twenty-Nine

Lily, now

After breaking into the catamaran and finding the graffiti, my plan had been to crash at Owen's and sleep on my anger. To work out how it all fit together before facing Robert and Rosey again. I had wanted to confront them once I felt more prepared, but I should know by now that things never go to plan. Instead, Rosey is hurling herself towards me the moment my feet hit the dock.

'Lily, are you out of your mind? There's a storm coming!' She is shouting at me and it's the first time I've ever seen her looking like she's fully lost control. Other times, when I've caught her off guard, she's seemed prickly and wide-eyed, but this is different. It's as though all the façade, all the defence mechanisms, have been dropped and she's one big ball of emotion. It's so unlike the woman I've come to know over the past few days and it's a stark reminder of the fact she's been painting over the truth. Presenting herself as one thing to me, but none of it has been true. She's been wearing a mask. Yes, she's my aunt, my mum's identical twin, but she's also a liar.

I go to answer, to apologise and make up an excuse for having been on her boat without permission, when I stop myself. I realise that she hasn't even mentioned the boat. Her anger isn't about me breaking and entering – it's about the fact I'm out in a storm. And it hits me, then, that the emotion hurled at me might not only be anger. She'd lost Penny in a storm just like this one. I let her hug me. The wind is roaring round us, there's no point trying to get the truth out of her now; I wouldn't even be able to hear her lies.

'Come,' she says, taking charge and leading me away to her jeep. 'And you.' She turns sharply towards Owen. 'You should go, too.' He lowers his head like a told-off schoolboy but looks at me first, checking I'm OK and waiting for me to signal for him to go.

'I'm assuming Joe told Owen which boat is ours,' Rosey says, keeping her eyes firmly on the road ahead. The windscreen wipers working overtime.

'Yep. I know you bought it off Joe after you thought Penny died.'

'I see. Do you care to explain why you were on it in a storm without my permission?'

'I was looking for something,' I reply vaguely, suddenly compelled to play her at her own game.

'Did you find it?'

'I did.'

The car screeches to an abrupt stop and I'm flung forwards in my seat until my seatbelt jars. Through the hammering rain, I can see we've arrived back at the cottage. We sit side by side in silence, staying in the warmth of the car for as long as we can.

'Does Joe know?'

'Not yet.'

'Well then, I guess we have a lot to discuss,' Rosey says, finally turning to look at me.

There's an apprehensive but resigned look in her eyes – much like a deer frozen in headlights – and it's clear she knows exactly what I found on the boat. I've uncovered the truth and it means the story they've been spinning everyone for all these years is, and always has been, a lie. The graffitied table with their initials and the date of her accident means I don't believe for a second longer that Robert and Rosey weren't with Penny that night. She was not by herself when she decided to climb on to the ledge of the boat. They did not watch her fall from where they stood helplessly on the pier. Quite the opposite, they were right there with her. More than that, it's a lie I'm convinced they've spun not once but twice.

Because from the *E M* initials etched under the table alongside theirs, they also met Eloise that summer. From the date scratched next to their initials, I'm pretty certain they were with her the day she died.

E M P R R

Eloise Manning, Penny, Rosey, Robert.

And they've been lying about it ever since.

The log burner is lit and Chapel House oozes cosiness. I assume Stef must be upstairs as it's just Robert in the front room with his slippers on, reading a book by the fire. It is so fucking cute and homely. It makes me sick and I feel the urge to push my palms into my eyes. To feel the sharp pain of the pressure and the flash of light.

It makes me think about all the winters I've spent with Dad in our big house, frozen to the core. A big house with only the two of us to fill it and not enough money to keep the heating on every day. No family to help us after she'd left. The anger writhes through my body. Rosey and Robert drove her away and whatever happened on that boat, whatever they're lying about, it has shaped my whole life. I hate them for it. Just as Penny must have done.

Chapter Thirty

Rosey, 1990

Rosey hears the chorus of screams – Rob's, Mike's, Penny's – carried on the wind. But she doesn't see what has happened until she's regained her balance. She looks towards the ledge where Penny had last been standing and sees she is no longer there. In the space she filled mere moments before, there is now only rain and darkness. No small furious figure shouting at her from the ledge.

It's a silent scream that rips its way out of Rosey's body when she realises what's happened. The pain and fear so big it forces its way out of her body silently. She's only seen it happen this way before in babies. The way their cry can escalate through the volumes until they emit a purple silent scream. She hadn't known it was possible for an adult, too, to produce such a terrifying cry.

After what realistically must only be a second or two of feeling paralysed – though it felt like a lifetime to her – Rosey is rushing forwards and scanning the sea below for any sign of Penny. Just as she already knew it would be, the sea thrashes unwelcomingly below them. It is too dark and the waves too impossibly ferocious to see much of anything.

Soon, Robbie is right there next to her and Mike arrives on the other side. She must be trying to climb up on to the ledge herself now as she can feel someone – she thinks it's Robbie – pulling her down, shouting at her, 'Stop, you can't, I'm sorry.' She is clawing at them. Half aware of what she's doing, half existing someplace else.

All three of them are leaning so far over the edge she thinks she might be sick. Worried another of them might fall into the sea next. But still, despite the pain and the cold and the rocking, they can't look away.

Eventually, the knowledge takes over and she no longer fights the need for her legs to buckle underneath her. There is no sign of Penny. No head bobbing. No arms flailing. She's simply disappeared. The sea angry and swollen beneath them.

Surely no one could survive it.

'I killed her,' Rosey wails and Robbie is holding her again. She's sure he's crying too. She feels his body heaving in rhythm with hers. At some point, Mike must have slipped below deck as he is now wrapping them both in a thick tartan blanket.

'It was an accident,' Robbie reassures her.

'She's dead though, isn't she?' Rosey looks at Robbie and Mike with childlike hope, desperate for them to tell her she's wrong.

'She must be,' Mike agrees. 'There's no sign of her and the sea is too rough.'

'We need to call someone.' Rosey suddenly leaps into action.

'I've already called them. I used the boat's emergency phone as soon as she fell,' Robbie reassures her, pulling her in to him even closer. 'They'll be here soon.'

'And my parents? Can you call them too?' Rosey asks and he nods. Kisses her forehead. This evening has solidified the two of them as a team.

'You should get out of the rain,' Rosey hears Mike call as he heads back down the deck away from them. She assumes he's gone below deck to wait out of the storm for everyone else to arrive. Rosey can't find the strength to move, and so she stays sat on the floor, half-naked, with Robbie's arms wrapped round her tightly for a little while longer. And then Robbie whispers in her ear, 'We don't have to tell them why she was up on the ledge in the first place if you don't want to. It doesn't change what happened. It wasn't our fault.'

She thinks of Eloise and her own sister, now both dead within the space of hours. And then there are her parents, waiting for them to come home. The whole reason they came to this bloody island in the first place was to face Chrissy's diagnosis together as a family, and she finds she can no longer breathe. Penny's death is going to kill her mother before the cancer will. Does she really need to die thinking her daughters are responsible for the death of a teenage girl, too? She tries to catch her breath, gasping to maintain control.

Rosey needs to decide what the best thing to do is, for her, but also for her family. If they tell people they were with Penny when she fell, there will be all sorts of questions about why she was up on the ledge in the first place. She's sure that eventually one of them would crack and tell them they'd been with Eloise. They can't take back the fact they'd left her there, dead in the forest. Alone. Even if her mum could ever forgive them for their role in Eloise falling, she knows they will never be forgiven for leaving her. Perhaps Robbie is right, she decides. They can't change the past, they just have to live with it.

'OK, we need to get off this boat,' she says.

Chapter Thirty-One

Lily, now

As soon as we are through the door, Rosey declares to Robert firmly and matter-of-factly that we all need to talk. I imagine it's the same tone she uses at work when calling a client with bad news.

'Oh good, you found her,' Robert says, hauling himself up out of the chair at Rosey's orders and following her through into the kitchen.

'She knows we were on the boat.' Rosey cuts to the chase and immediately Robert's shoulders drop.

'I see.' He rubs his brow the same way he had done when I'd challenged him in the clubhouse earlier. 'Coffee, anyone?'

'No, I don't want more of your coffee. I just want the truth. I know you were both on the boat the night Penny went overboard, so why have you lied about being there? Was Eloise with you?' I ask, slamming my hands against the table and, as I do so, something jolts through me. It's pure terror. But it's fleeting and then it's gone again. Yes, I'm filled with anger. But that, that was something different.

'Eloise? No, she was long dead by the time we were on the boat,' Rosey says simply and both Robert and I turn to her in shock. No, that's not quite right. I am shocked but Robert looks disappointed. At least I know she's telling the truth this time.

'Let's sit down first, shall we?' he says slowly, and I see his bluster and politeness for what it really is – he is playing to control the situation. Has he always been this way? A master manipulator?

'We really did think Penny had drowned,' Rosey says and her whole body looks punctuated by grief and regret. 'That part we've never lied about. You have to believe me, Lily. The decisions we made next, they were all mixed up in grief and fear. As I said before, our mother received news that day that she was dying.'

'I don't understand how this has anything to do with—'

'Please,' she says softly and reaches out to place a hand over mine. I snatch it back. 'Just, listen. That's all I'm asking of you.'

I relent. I did ask her for the truth, after all. But is that what she's giving me? I suppose I have to at least listen in order to find out. To gather enough information to decide what I believe and don't believe.

'I'm assuming by now that you know Penny wasn't the only accident that day?'

'You mean Eloise?'

'Yes.' Rosey closes her eyes and Robert reaches for her hand as she pauses. Regains control. 'We were with Eloise when she fell from the lookout tower and we told no one. We just left her there. They found her body during the sweep of the island the next morning while looking for Penny. You're right that we did argue on the boat. You have to understand that Eloise's death was a complete accident, but we were older and it was our stupid game that got her killed. We were afraid. We were drunk and we acted stupidly. That night on the boat, Penny was so angry about what had happened. She wanted to tell the truth about Eloise and about us being with her.'

'And you didn't agree?'

'I don't know what we would have decided to do. We never got that far before she fell.'

'But you were fighting about it?' I ask, taking a step back from Rosey and trying to digest it all.

'We were.'

'Did you push her? Try to silence her?' I force my voice to sound louder and more confident than I'm feeling. Why hadn't I thought of it before? I'd always assumed they'd had a terrible fight. It hadn't crossed my mind that Rosey might be guiltier of something much worse; that she might have tried to kill my mother.

'No! Oh my goodness, absolutely not.'

'It was an accident!' Robert cuts in, always defending Rosey; always needing his voice to be heard. But this time it doesn't make me believe her, it makes me doubt the story she's spinning.

'It was my fault she went into the water, but none of it was on purpose. The storm had made the deck slippery and I lost my balance. I grabbed on to the nearest rope to steady myself. The problem—' Rosey pauses and sniffs before forcing herself to continue, 'the problem was that Penny had also been holding on to that same rope. And so, the momentum of my falling and grabbing it, well it knocked her overboard.' Her voice catches in her throat with almost every syllable and I can see she's turned grey at the memory of it.

'We searched for her, Lily,' she presses on. 'We watched from the boat the whole time. We were so sure she'd drowned. That's not a lie.'

'But you've been covering your tracks because you're the reason she fell off the boat? The two of you conspiring to sanitise your part in it? Just like you did with Eloise? You are cowards. Both of you.' I can hear the venom in my voice as I spit the words at her.

'I know you must think that, but the truth is more complicated. We were on that boat with Penny, but I was afraid they'd ask me what we were arguing about and I was so confused about what to do. We couldn't explain it to anyone without telling them we were also to blame for Eloise's death. Her fall was an accident but she was a child and we were the adults. We supplied her with alcohol, and it was us who goaded her into climbing that tower. It was our fault. And then all of a sudden Penny was gone too, and that also was my fault. I didn't think anyone would believe both things could have been accidents. You have to understand we were afraid and most certainly also in shock. Drunk, too. So we told them we watched her fall but we said we saw her from the pier. That we didn't know why she was on the ledge. I knew that the last thing our mother needed, on top of everything else just before she died, was to think that her daughters were responsible for Eloise's death.'

'You erased your part in it all once again. How convenient.'

Rosey takes the criticism silently, folding her hands across her knees and looking me directly in the eye.

'Did they not question how you'd seen her in the dark? In the storm?'

'The dock is lit and it was just before the power cut hit the island. We told them we'd purposefully gone out in the storm to try and find her. That we suspected we might find her there because Robert had originally paid Joe to use the boat for the night, but that we'd changed our minds because of the storm. We said we guessed that was where she might have been.'

'And they just believed you?'

'Not necessarily. But they also had no reason to probe further. I've never forgiven myself. I was in shock and panicking and I couldn't work out how I could explain Penny falling, without telling them the whole truth. Nothing I said was going to change the fact Penny and Eloise had died. But I could change how Mum felt about it all.'

'But Penny didn't die.' I can't help myself and Rosey gives a small reluctant smile.

'No, but we honestly believed that she had. That was our reality. We have lived for more than twenty-six years believing she did. I didn't want our mum going to her deathbed thinking that at the crux of it all, Penny was guilty of Eloise's death. I was trying to protect everyone.'

'And yourself.'

'You have to try and understand how our whole lives had been moulded around Mum's feelings. Putting her first and squashing everything else. You can't just break a pattern overnight. I did what I thought was best at the time. I'm sorry.'

'It's all just very convenient.' It's all I can find to say. It's a lot to take in and frankly I'm not sure how much I believe, or forgive – and clearly, my mother had never forgiven Rosey either or she'd have made contact.

Had Mum known it was an accident, or did she believe her sister had purposefully hurled her off the side of a boat in order to keep her quiet? It's almost too hard to imagine how she must have felt, and I find myself crossing my arms and folding myself inwards. Trying to keep the feelings locked inside. *You can't just break a pattern overnight*. Rosey's words echo through me.

'I'm sure it sounds that way right now, but it's the truth.'

'So how did she get off the island without anyone noticing?'

'Now that, I have absolutely no idea about. I've been thinking it through since you turned up and the only explanation would be that she washed up someplace else, not on Osea, so she never needed to get off the island in the first place,' she says.

'I'll leave first thing tomorrow morning,' I state.

'I doubt there will be a boat able to cross after the storm until the afternoon. Let me drive you at low tide,' Robert offers but there is nothing I want less than to spend time enclosed in a car with this man. It would be naïve of me to think I've suddenly got the whole story from them both, and there's still the matter of who has been through my things and why? But I've had enough of dissecting the past for today. I have no energy left.

'No. I'll get Owen to take me,' I reply curtly and then scrape my chair back against their tiles. I see Rosey flinch. I don't even bother trying to stop myself from looking happy about it.

The Palace

I stare at the present, still wrapped up in shiny pink paper, the whole way through breakfast. Father hasn't mentioned it, just placed the gift in the middle of the table when he first arrived. We know better than to be the first ones to say anything. Don't want to seem greedy. It's Mum's birthday today, and we've been counting down to this moment. Everything is riding on it. I've felt Mum becoming more nervous the last few days, wondering if we've done enough. I can feel my palms beginning to itch and all I want to do is snatch the present and tear the paper off. Instead, I sit quietly until my bowl of cereal is finished and then I place my hands carefully in my lap. Waiting. Silent. I am a good daughter.

After what seems like for ever, as though time has stood still, finally Father slams his hands down on the table. The sound is too loud, the movement purposefully abrupt, and it makes me jump. 'And now, for the birthday girl,' he says and pulls the present towards him slowly and dramatically before handing it to Mum. 'For you.'

'Thank you,' she says, keeping her eyes low.

'Well, don't you want to open it?'

'Yes, yes of course.'

I see her take a deep breath and wonder if it's everything we've been wishing for these past few weeks. Did it work? Have we done it?

She's careful not to rip the wrapping paper, knows Father thinks it's unattractive to seem desperate, but her eyes meet his and I see a small smile at the corner of her mouth. 'Thank you, I'm sure this will help.'

I squeeze my fingernails against my thighs, knowing I need to behave, but inside I am whooping for joy.

'At first I thought about a kettle, so you can heat up hot water bottles, stop you getting so cold, but it's true that you have been good for a while now. And just as bad behaviour has consequences, good behaviour should also be rewarded. We are a fair family. Besides, this way you can also make yourself some hot meals instead of me having to bring everything to you.'

'Thank you,' Mum repeats and then, all of a sudden, he is grabbing her wrist.

'You are welcome. But you need to remember that anything given can be taken away. Do I make myself clear? I am trusting you with this. Do not disappoint me.'

'I won't. I promise.'

'Good. A mother should be able to cook for her child. And now, I know it's a Tuesday, but I cleared my morning because it's your birthday,' he says, and my stomach drops.

Chapter Thirty-Two

Lily, now

It feels strange leaving the island by a different mode of transport to when I arrived. This time, we drive off Osea using the causeway at low tide instead of by boat.

The strip of road is surprisingly narrow, not much leeway either side of the car until it gives way to the thick mud of the seabed. As we reach the end of the causeway, which marks our return to Heybridge, I remember Alan telling me that some of the rocks at the start of the causeway had come from London Bridge after it was bombed in the war.

As we drive away, leaving the island trailing behind us, I think about how the island itself seems to have been fated in bloodshed – how poetic it feels that the very route you have to drive to reach Osea has been paved from something so cruel and steeped in death. How, even centuries before that, it is recorded in the Doomsday Book that the Battle of Maldon was even fought along the causeway. Now packaged as a luxury escape, I can't help but wonder if in reality the island is cursed.

Dad's van isn't on the driveway when Owen drops me home. I feel a bit guilty when I'm relieved he isn't here. The past few days have been emotionally draining and the last thing I need now is a run-in with Dad. If he were here, it would mean I'd need to decide to continue lying or to tell him the truth about going to Osea. To try to explain everything I've learnt about Mum and how she let everyone believe she'd drowned and that was why they were no longer in her life.

Neither are particularly appealing options and I'm pleased not to have to decide yet about how I'm going to handle it. I hadn't thought this far ahead when I first decided to go to Osea Island. I'd been excited and optimistic about learning more about my family but the reality is that I've come home with more questions than answers. Did Mum ever tell Dad about what happened that summer? How much does he already know and how much has he kept from me?

As I let myself into the house, Mum's absence feels louder than ever. She is nowhere to be found. I cannot stay here, the blank walls where photos of us as a family ought to be feel like a harsh reminder that, in the end, she left us too.

I couldn't think of anyone else to call. When I asked Owen to drop me home he decided to cut his trip short and go back to his place in South London. It's unlike me to reach out to someone, but a lot has happened over the past week and I feel that, as my understanding of my mum's past is deepening, I'm changing with it. We've arranged to meet halfway in a small pub in central London. My social anxiety means I arrived far too early and I'm already one glass of wine down. While I've been waiting, I've been mulling over my last conversation with Rosey and her supposed confession, but something still doesn't add up. As I swirl my wine, making waves around the glass, I can't shake the feeling I am still missing a crucial piece of the puzzle.

Rosey said they combed the island top to bottom for days. According to her, the first group gathered at six a.m. the next day, a long line of them, and they moved along the coast inch by inch. They never found any sign of Penny, but came across Eloise's body instead. But the island is exactly that – an island. Penny didn't own a car back then, and Alan stopped any boat trips for three days after the accident until the search for Penny ceased. Yes, she could have washed up off the island like Rosey suggested, but that means the currents would have pulled her far and for a long time. What's the chance of her surviving in the sea that long compared to if she'd washed up closer to where she fell? So, if that's the case, then how did she slip past them all? There's no way she could have done it alone, and especially not after such a traumatic accident. She must have been weak and most likely badly hurt.

A breeze signals the pub doors have opened and I look over to see Owen has finally arrived. An unfamiliar feeling settles across my stomach as he walks towards me and I realise it's excitement. I am pleased to see him. I stand and Owen hugs me tightly before clocking the almost empty glass of wine.

'Another?' he asks and I nod.

I watch him returning from the bar with a bottle wine, a small smile on my lips, when I hear the background music switch. I don't know the last time I heard this song but every single muscle in my body feels as though it suddenly seizes up. I feel frozen for a couple of seconds as Owen sits down in front of me and watch as he starts singing along to 'Visions of Love' which is now playing.

'Nineties music is simply the best,' he says, pouring me a glass of wine, but I can't find the words to answer him. Cannot make my mouth move the way I want it to. I'm looking at him, but my vision is narrowing. The flash of green tiles swirls back into my mind, and before long I can no longer see Owen. It's like I'm no longer in the pub, I'm transported somewhere else. I can no longer feel the seat beneath me, but I can hear something. It's a loud, repetitive banging. Thump, thump, thump.

'Lily, Lily.' Slowly I hear Owen's voice piercing through the terror and his face comes back into view. 'Are you OK? What's wrong?'

I realise I've never seen him scared before and it dawns on me that the source of the banging is me. He is afraid of me. I am smashing my head on the wall behind me over and over again. I force myself to stop but it takes more effort to control my body than I'd anticipated. I am fighting to be present.

'Shit. I'm sorry,' I croak, unsure what else there is to say. I can't believe how violent this episode was.

'Was it another panic attack?'

'I don't know what they are. Each one feels different. I don't know if they're flashbacks or some kind of nightmare. I know this is going to sound crazy, but I don't even know if whatever is happening even belongs to me,' I add, hesitantly, unsure it's a sensible decision to admit this to anyone.

'What do you mean?'

'Well, I saw these green tiles in one of them and I think they were the same green tiles from the boat, only I saw them in an episode I had before I'd ever even been on the boat. How is that possible?' I'm on a roll now and can't stop. I think of Dr Higham's conference on how trauma may be inherited. 'What if they're Penny's memories, passed down to me?' It's the wine talking but still it feels a relief to share my fear with someone.

'If that's what's happening here, that would be a huge deal – people would want to study you. So, just bear with me. What if they *are* your memories, Lily, but you have blocked them out and now, for some reason, something has triggered them to resurface. Finding out you have an aunt, for example. That your mum has an identical twin sister. That's huge. Something that big could have a massive effect on the subconscious.'

'But what would I have to block out?' I ask and I can hear the desperation in my voice. *Help me.*

'I don't know. But whatever is happening to you, it can't carry on.'

'Then what should I do? I have no idea what I'm meant to be remembering.'

Owen takes a few minutes and I know he's thinking it all through carefully before giving me an answer. Instead of saying something for the sake of it, he's taking his time and I appreciate him for it.

'I'm not the therapist here but let's do some role-play for a moment. Pretend this isn't happening to you. Can you do that?'

'I can try.'

'Great. So just imagine I'm the client and you're the therapist. What would you say to me?'

'First, I'd tell you to slow down on the wine.'

'Touché. What next?'

'OK, well let's say your mind has erased something from your memory. It won't have erased every single link to that event. It's too big a task and it would leave you with too little – there are always ripple effects. You need to find the ripples that still remain in your consciousness, and then we would go from there to address them and bring more of that memory to the forefront.'

'And how would I find those ripples?' he asks, fully embracing his role as client.

'I would say you need to think about certain things, times, events, phrases, books, songs – anything – that hold a particular significance or feel notably impactful to you, and go from there.'

'That's where you start then,' he says, as if it really is that simple. But he's looking over his glass at me in a way that reminds me how messed up what just happened is. Embarrassment swamps me. Fuck, I need to sort myself out. 'Just write down everything you can think of, even if it doesn't feel related to triggering the flashbacks – and see what you come up with.'

'If they even are my own flashbacks,' I shoot back defensively.

'Exactly,' he says, but I can tell it's just to placate me. That there's no part of Owen that thinks these memories aren't my own.

He's wrong. I'm sure he's wrong, but at least it's a starting place. The one thing that's for certain is that I can't go on like this. When I first found Rosey on Osea, I was convinced I was finally going to get the closure I need to heal and move on, but I've come back more broken than I was before. The question is, why?

Chapter Thirty-Three

Penny, 1990

Salt. Too much salt. Penny's body doubles over as she throws up again. She hasn't been able to control it – the body will always prioritise breathing, even when it's underwater. And now that same body is expelling the seawater it forced her to swallow.

She cannot believe she is alive. She can't even put it down to her strength as a swimmer. There was no chance of swimming against those waves. It was pure luck that had saved her. Nothing else. All she remembers about being in the water is how the cold had felt like knives and how disorientated she'd been under the surface. Pitch-black with no idea which way was up, and which way was down.

The gasp for breath when she'd broken the surface had been quickly followed by being crashed into, wave after wave. Each breath she managed to catch felt like a small miracle, only too short-lived. And then without any sense of where she was, she found her body hitting against something hard. In then out, in then out, she'd crashed against it repeatedly before she managed to summon all her strength and claw her way up the rocky side. She'd had no idea where she was. This could have been Mersea, Northey Island, or someplace else entirely. She'd lost sense of how long she'd been in the water or which direction the currents had swept her. How far from Osea had she been tossed?

Finally, she is out of the water, resting on her hands and knees.

She is aware of blood streaming down her but from where, and from how many places, she can't tell. It is dark, almost pitch-black, but miraculously as she gains her bearings between the flashes of lightning, she realises she hadn't drifted very far at all. From the distinguishable single line of trees that she can make out when the lightning comes, she must have washed up on Osea but on the west side.

Has there been a power cut? *Oh good lord, please don't let there have been a power cut*, she prays. The island is dark at night at the best of times, but if all the streetlamps are out then she'll have no hope of finding her way back to the main paths. It is cold and she is soaked through. The sea hasn't killed her, but Penny knows that staying out in this storm all night most definitely will.

She can feel all hope flooding from her body, so much so that she thinks she must be imagining it when she first sees the flicker of light.

A flashlight.

'Hey, here! I'm over here!' she calls, when it shines in her direction for a third time, but her voice is hoarse from the seawater. The ocean has stolen almost every last bit of her strength. It has even taken her voice. And yet, the light keeps getting closer. Brighter. Until it is almost upon her, and finally she can make out the shape of the man holding it.

He isn't even wearing a coat and is still in exactly the same clothes as he'd been wearing on the boat the last time she'd seen him. But he's come for her. And he's found her. It is as though the knowledge that she is finally safe gives her body permission to shut down and she feels herself falling to the floor. Penny doesn't protest when Mike picks her up, nor does she ask him where Rosey is. She simply closes her eyes and lets him carry her away.

* * *

Penny must have fallen asleep – or perhaps passed out would be more accurate – as Mike strode heroically through the storm with her in his arms, because when she next becomes aware of her surroundings she is lying on the sofa in his and Robbie's cabin. A thick duvet has been placed over her and Mike is sitting in a chair in the corner of the room, watching her.

'Hi, you're safe. I've got you,' he reassures her in a soothingly calm voice. 'Our cabin was closest so I brought you here to get out of the storm and dry as quickly as possible. I hope you don't mind.'

'Do they know you found me?' she croaks, her throat still sore and hoarse.

'Not yet, there's a power cut across the whole island. The phone lines aren't working.'

'Good. I don't want to see them,' she says and closes her eyes, shutting it all out again.

Everything feels too overwhelming. The argument with Rosey and the fact she'd almost drowned. She is sure it had been an accident, Rosey wouldn't have purposefully tugged on that rope, and yet the more she replays it in her mind, the more she becomes unsure of exactly what she saw. It is as though with every memory of it, she can rewrite it a little more each time. She is losing her sense of reality. Starting not to trust her own memories. She is tired.

'Did you see her grab on to the rope?' she asks Mike, looking for him to reassure her.

Mike takes a deep breath, seeming to carefully consider what to say next. 'I didn't. I just know that one minute you were there, and the next you weren't.'

'So you don't know if it was an accident or not?'

'I'm sorry.'

She lets a silence settle between them. Her whole body still hurts from the physicality of being tossed around in the sea, and she is bone-deep tired. Emotionally and physically.

'Thank you for finding me,' she says, and he looks at her with such an intensity it makes her hairs stand on end. She feels it across her arms and even down her legs.

'What do you want to happen now?'

'Have they found her yet?' Penny croaks. It's the only thing whirling through her mind.

'I don't think so. But I'm sure her family have raised the alarm she hasn't been home. They'll find her soon.'

'We need to tell them what happened. You agree with me, don't you?'

'Say we do tell them. What next? We didn't mean for her to die. They'll understand it was an accident. Us telling them changes nothing.'

'She shouldn't have been drinking. We gave her the alcohol. It's our fault,' Penny says, breaking into a painful coughing fit.

'OK. You're right. We all panicked and we made the wrong decision. I'm with you, Penny. But we can't go out in this storm again and the phone lines are currently down. It'll have to wait. I'm sorry.'

It all becomes too much for her then, and she starts to cry. Her whole body shaking as all the emotions she'd been holding inside – about her childhood, her mum's cancer and now Eloise's death – it all spills over and she can't push it back inside. And what about her argument with Rosey? Did she really mean to hurt her? She tries to catch her breath but her chest feels like it's being squeezed too tight. She feels Mike's hand upon her back and he is telling her it's going to be OK, urging her to relax. She lets the warmth of his hand spread through her and slowly it starts to calm her.

'I've got an idea,' he says. 'You've been through a lot and clearly you need some space. How about as soon as the storm eases a little, I go tell your parents about Eloise and let everyone know that you're OK, and then let's get off this island for a couple of days? I'm meant to be leaving anyway. And then once you're recovered, we can come back and face the fire.'

'I can't. My mum's ill. She'll have got her results yesterday.'

'Of course. I understand. Let me tell everyone you're OK and then we'll decide what to do next. For now, you need to rest.'

'Thank you,' Penny relents, pulling the duvet up closer underneath her chin. They've been through a lot but she is warm and safe.

It is barely morning when Penny is woken again by Mike letting himself back into the cabin. It is light outside but the clock on the wall tells her it is only 4.30 a.m. It is the height of summer, after all. Yet, true to his word, Mike must have slipped out at first light as soon as the weather had improved and spread the news that she was safe.

'I told them.' He keeps his voice quiet, allowing Penny time to slowly work her way through the haze of that place that exists between being asleep and awake. 'They said they'll come over in a few hours.'

'And what about Eloise?'

'They know,' he confirms and Penny feels the huge weight at the bottom of her stomach leave her body.

'I've been thinking about what you said. I'm not sure I can face it all yet,' Penny admits, knowing that as soon as she goes home, they'll have to talk about her mother's illness. About what happens next. The image of her dad standing broken by the cottage window is still etched painfully across her memory. And then she'll watch them break apart further when they learn more about Eloise's death. How their daughters are responsible not only for a young girl's death, but also the terrible selfish decisions they made after.

'The offer still stands. We can leave right now if you want?' Mike suggests hesitantly. 'It's low tide – the causeway will be clear. You could hang at my place for the weekend and then I'll drive you back?'

'We can't. We have to face what we did.'

'I didn't need to tell them about Eloise because Rosey already had. She clearly listened to you, after all.'

'Well, that's a fucking first.'

'It was Rosey anyway who was at the top of the tower with Eloise and she's already talking. Are you sure you don't want to just disappear for a couple of days? I'm already packed.' Penny looks around, noticing a suitcase now standing by the front door. 'Or we can wait, if you really want. Talk to your parents and Rosey first. But last night was pretty rough for you and if you're not ready to talk to Rosey yet and face your parents, then I have some money and we can grab you some clothes nearer mine. We can come back soon.'

Penny churns it over, plays the different scenarios in her mind of all the ways the next couple of days will look like for her. She knows she'll have to face what happened one day, but the idea of unpacking everything about their family, the resentments that have finally spilled out into the open, her lies, the events of last night and on top of all that face the news their mum is dying – it all feels too much for her then, and she starts to cry. First, she needs a little more time to stuff it all back inside of her again.

'OK, let's just go. If Rosey is talking then that's good enough for me. I'm not ready to face Mum or Rosey yet. I'm sure the police will want to talk to us anyway, but they can do that from yours, right?'

'Exactly.' Mike grins back at her. This man, who had faced the storm without even a coat on in order to find her. To save her. And now here he is, leaving at the drop of a hat to help her yet again. She leans forwards and places her lips firmly against his. He pulls her closer and Penny thinks how special it is the way their bodies seem to fit together. As if they are made for each other, even among the chaos around them. And right then, given everything that has happened over the past week, Penny truly feels like it is the two of them against the world.

Chapter Thirty-Four

Rosey, now

It takes Rosey by surprise how much she misses Lily now that she's gone. The niece she never knew she had. For the past twenty-five years, Rosey hadn't known Lily even existed, and yet here she is, three days after Lily left, feeling like she has lost one of her limbs.

Rosey is self-aware enough to know she hadn't been the most welcoming to Lily when she stayed with them. Slightly cagey. Fighting against her own guilt and secrets. The fact she reminded her so much of Penny didn't help with things, either.

Rosey finds herself feeling completely lost now that Lily's gone. To fill the silence, she has roped Stef into helping her sort through the things she'd quickly moved out of Penny's old room to make it more presentable for Lily. Most of these boxes have remained untouched for years. But, instead of simply shoving them back, this time Rosey has a desperate urge to sort through them.

'I don't have long,' Stef declares as she helps open the first box.

'That's fine, darling. I'll take any help I can get.'

Only two of the boxes contain Penny's old things and so that's where they start – with the belongings that Penny had accumulated over the years of holidaying on the island. The first box contains a stack of A3 coloured scrapbooks and Rosey remembers how up until their teenage years, their parents would insist on them filling out holiday scrapbooks. Inside, there are drawings of shells and sharks' teeth they'd found on the beach.

'So this is why you always tried to get me to make scrapbooks on holidays,' Stef marvels, but she says it fondly.

'It's a childhood rite of passage,' Rosey laughs, remembering the days when Stef was young, her hand so small in hers. She fit perfectly.

'What are these?' Stef says, putting the scrapbook down and delving deeper into the box. She pulls out a fat envelope. The kind that's instantly recognisable to the older generation but now very rarely seen. Inside must be hundreds of photographs – a mix of Robert's and Patrick's from that summer. She pulls the wad of photos out and the very top picture sends her hurtling back in time. It shows Rosey and Penny, standing awkwardly in the cottage's too-narrow hallway. Rosey is wearing a yellow satin dress and Penny is dressed in the most beautiful green halterneck. Rosey remembers it vividly – the way she'd been jealous at just how gorgeous Penny had looked. It had been the night of the BBQ Bonfire Ball. The last one they ever went to together.

Stef must sense the affect the photos have on Rosey; how still her body has become as she fights not to let the emotions overwhelm her, because Stef looks at her and then she asks ever so softly – in a tone she rarely uses – 'Are these from that summer?' But Rosey can't bring herself to reply, instead closing her eyes as Stef flicks through them – unable to bring herself to look. To remember.

'Mum, I think you should give these to Lily,' Stef says at last.

'She isn't answering my texts. She doesn't want to hear from me.'

'But she deserves to have these. If I lost you, I'd want to keep every part of you I could find.'

Stef's honesty and vulnerability knock the air out of Rosey's lungs making her head spin with it. She stares at her, this child of hers who is now an adult. She is spiky and loud. Obnoxious and cruel. But it's all a front. A defence mechanism. *Yes, she is just like me*, the thought creeps up on Rosey. *Just as Lily is a part of Penny.*

'Then you should ask Owen to give them to her. He drove her home the other day, right? I'm sure she'll answer to him, the little slut-bag,' Stef continues facetiously, and Rosey lets it slide. Stef's guard firmly back in place.

'No, no, I'll go myself,' she says resolutely, because honestly, she's been looking for an excuse to have to find Lily again. To apologise. Maybe, to even tell her the truth this time. It is something she is mulling over. Does she have it in her? Penny was always the more courageous one.

Rosey is busy making a separate pile of the photos to give to Lily when the doorbell rings. When she opens it, she is not entirely surprised to find two police officers standing there. She knew that Lily would have told Joe everything before she left the island and that he'd report it. Even after all these years he's never given up hope of finding out the truth about Eloise's death, and Rosey feels a strange sense of relief for him that he's got it. Well, a version of it anyway. A version that puts Rosey on the top of that lookout platform along with Eloise, with her hand wrapped round her wrist, until she fell.

She smiles and invites them in, asks Stef to make them a cup of tea.

It has been twenty-six years since Rosey has seen her sister, but she's not about to go spilling all their secrets now. Yes, the two of them fought like hell most of the time, but it wasn't as simple as that. They are identical twins. They have exactly the same DNA – shared a sac in their mother's womb. When they were younger, everyone seemed fascinated by the pair of them. The girls were constantly asked what it was like being identical. But how could they ever explain that while they were fighting so hard to be their own selves, they were also always a part of each other. That there are some bonds that can't be broken. Some lines that are forever blurry? Rosey knows that no one else will ever understand. Only Penny, and the thought brings with it an urgent need to speak to her again. Lily doesn't know where she is, but she is still out there. Somewhere. And Rosey is going to find her.

Rosey is sitting in her car outside number 78 Bishop Road, Islington, which is where Owen has told her she can find Lily. She's been here for at least an hour but is yet to catch sight of her. Given they didn't leave things on good terms last time they spoke, Rosey hadn't wanted her to know she was coming in case she would purposefully avoid seeing her, so Rosey hadn't texted ahead.

She'd left Osea as soon as the officers were satisfied that she'd answered all their questions. She'd told them everything they'd wanted to know; that the four of them had been with Eloise when she fell and they had left her body broken and bruised. Clarified she'd been dead beyond any doubt. That they'd supplied the alcohol she'd been drinking underage. *Thank you for your co-operation*, they'd said and it had sent a small, unexpected thrill through her as she walked a delicate balance between fact and fiction.

Rosey turns the ignition to start the engine, ready to drive to get some food, when a grey van pulls into the driveway. It reads SOS PROPERTY MAINTENANCE across the back in shiny black letters and she remembers Lily telling her that her dad was a handyman – *a jack of all trades, master of none*, she'd joked. Intrigued by the man Penny had ended up with, Rosey waits and watches as two brown boots swing to the ground. The man shuts the door behind him and frustratingly she doesn't catch a glimpse of his face.

That is, until he drops his keys on the floor as he strides towards the house. He turns, bends down to grab them and as he stands up again, Rosey is surprised to realise that she already knows him. The shock of seeing him again after all these years makes her drop the envelope of photos she is holding, and they scatter to the floor around her feet. Under the car pedals and seat.

If he's Lily's dad, then that means Rosey hasn't been the only one keeping secrets about that summer, nor the night Penny supposedly drowned and the days that followed. How can this be true? When Robert told Mike he was no longer able to be in the band because he wanted to focus on supporting her through Penny's death and Mum's illness, Mike had never mentioned anything. He let them all go on believing that she'd drowned. And yet here he stands, the father of Penny's child.

When did they find each other again? And why did he never tell them?

The revelation has thrown Rosey, and she needs to regather her thoughts. She doesn't understand how this is possible. Maybe it's not him and she's mistaken? Robert and Mike kept in touch over the years. Sporadically – but still. Enough that this was clearly meant to be one big fucking secret. Rosey suddenly feels terrified he's going to see her – though what she's afraid of exactly she's no idea. Still, Rosey slams her foot on the accelerator a little too hard and the car lurches forwards, loudly. As quick as she can, she speeds away, with the photos she'd intended on giving to Lily still lying scattered at her feet.

Rosey passes her on the corner of the street. Lily doesn't see her, but Rosey does a double-take – with a swim bag slung over one shoulder, her wet hair hanging down her back and a tell-tale red pinch to her cheeks, she is transported back in time to Penny's training days. The way she always smelled of chlorine.

Before she was gone.

Chapter Thirty-Five

Penny, 1990

She knows she is running away but as Mike leads her up the stairs of his home, back on mainland, and spins her round to face him, she does not care. She lets him kiss her neck, his fingers entwined with hers; lets him lift her up, legs wrapped round his waist, and lower her gently on to his bed.

She sinks into it, the weight of his body pushing her down, and it feels comforting – as if he is pushing out everything else. She needs to get lost in him. She keeps having flashbacks to being tossed around in the sea; to the look of anger on Rosey's face as they argued. She is sure that Rosey had hated her on the boat. And maybe she was right to? But Penny also blames Rosey; for everything she's done and everything she hasn't. Ever since they were eight years old they've had their secrets. But what now? Will Rosey tell the truth or will she bear it, silently, as they'd always promised to do?

Thinking about it makes her dizzy. Over the years it has become hard to distinguish exactly where Penny stops and Rosey begins. Because although it was Mike and Robbie's idea to keep their involvement in Eloise's fall secret, Penny and Rosey have even more reason to avoid talking about that day. To keep the lid on their own secrets firmly shut.

Now their involvement is out there, how long will it be until the truth of everything is prised open? In part, that is really what their argument on the boat had been about. Rosey's resistance to telling the truth. Penny stands by the fact it was the right thing to do, but she is also in no rush to face the consequences. She decides she'll take the weekend, gather some courage, and then head back.

For now, she is exactly where she wants to be – and it feels good. She arches her back and reaches out a hand to pull Mike even closer into her. She cups his face and whispers, 'I wish I could stay here for ever.' She hears 'Vision of Love' playing in the background and smiles, knowing that she'll remember this day for ever. It is a perfect moment in time.

Afterwards, they lie there entwined for hours. Him, stroking her hair.

'You said you didn't want to go back,' Mike says finally, clearing his throat first as though he is nervous.

'No. But I have to. I need to go back for Mum and to sort things out with Rosey.'

'I get that. But I lied to you before,' he says and Penny hears how anxious he sounds.

'About what?' Penny raises her head from his chest and pushes away from him slightly. She studies him but realises he doesn't look guilty, instead he seems protective and apologetic. Soft with it.

'You'd been through so much, what with the accident, I didn't want to upset you more but . . . well . . . I'm really sorry, Penny. Fuck.' This time he runs a hand through his hair.

'What is it? Just tell me!'

'I'm not so sure that you falling off the boat was an accident. I'm pretty certain Rosey purposefully swung the rope. She was so angry, Penny. I saw it.'

The pain is excruciating.

Rosey had hurt her on purpose? They'd always argued, but they'd also fiercely loved each other. But this? This was too far. How were they meant to come back from this? Did she even want to? She finds it hard to believe but then she thinks of everything they've done over the years and of all the reasons why Rosey might want to keep the truth hidden more than most. What would their parents think?

She pounds a fist into Mike's chest and can't stop herself from crying. As children, tears were only reserved for her mother, with the rest of them expected to play their parts as her unwavering support system.

But here, in Mike's arms, she sobs.

'I have to go back though,' she says when Mike suggests she stays with him longer than they'd originally planned. 'Mum needs me. I don't even know how long they've given her.'

'I'm sorry, I wanted you to hear it from your parents, not from me, but when I told them you were safe after the boat accident they also told me Chrissy's results. Do you want to know?' he asks, giving her a moment to take it all in and to decide for herself.

'How long?' she whispers.

'Six months to a year. I'm so sorry.'

But surprisingly Penny finds herself sighing, almost with relief. The fact her mum is dying is no longer news, they'd all been expecting it from the translucency of her skin and how much weight she'd lost, but six months is longer than she'd imagined. She thought it would be a matter of weeks, a couple of months at best.

'We can head back now if you want?' Mike offers, but Penny rolls on top of him and kisses him hard.

'No. We have more time than I thought. I want to spend it with you.'

She knows she's putting it off, but she has time. She'd rather lose herself here with Mike for as long as she can. Besides, surely the police will force them back to reality soon. No doubt they'll come knocking with questions shortly. For the time being, she's exactly where she wants to be and she'll make the most of it for as long as she can.

Chapter Thirty-Six

Lily, now

I'm almost embarrassed to admit how excited I feel to be seeing Owen again. When we'd been on Osea I'd presumed all contact would cease once we were off the island, but we keep finding ourselves drawn back together. I realise I like it.

The heaviness hits me hard when I arrive and the wave of disappointment almost makes me cry. But then the anger kicks in, taking over. Because as the bell chimes loudly above the coffeeshop door when I push it open, it isn't Owen who is sitting waiting for me, it is Rosey. She has her hair pulled back in a tight neat bun, her glasses balanced delicately on the bridge of her nose, and she looks worried. Deep in thought.

'Please stay,' she calls in a high shrill voice when she sees me enter, as if she can read my mind and knows that all I want to do is turn straight back around and march out the door. *Your mother always ran.* I clench my jaw and the pressure pounds in my ears. But – ever the good girl – I predictably end up doing as she asks and slide into the bamboo slatted seat opposite her.

'First Robert, now Owen. Who are you going to recruit next to play along with your games? Help you spin your lies?' I smile, sarcastically, and she stays quiet, letting me have my moment. It is so unlike her. 'Why are you here?' I cut to the chase.

'I wanted to give you these,' Rosey says, producing an envelope thick with photographs from her lap. But before she hands them over, she pauses. 'First I need to tell you something.' She hesitates again, as if waiting for my permission. But what is it I'm meant to be giving her permission for? I've no idea. Instead, I resolutely stare back at her until she decides to continue.

'That summer, there was a group of four of us before we met Eloise,' she says and this new information swirls around my mind. I think of the etchings under the table on the boat and how I'd jumped to conclusions. *E M P R R*. I'd assumed the first two stood for *Eloise Manning*. It had fit. But if there were five of them then it stands to reason it was just Eloise, the same as the others, and that M was not for Manning but for the fourth person. So who is M?

'There was me, Robert, your mum and another young man,' Rosey continues, and I see something I wasn't expecting in her expression. Sympathy. 'I hadn't seen him since your mum's accident. Well, not until recently. This isn't the first time I've come here, Lily. I tried to give you these photos three days ago. I sat outside your house, waiting for you. I missed you – I think you'd been swimming,' she smiles affectionately, as if lost in a memory. 'But then I saw him. I'm sure of it. Tell me, Lily, what's your dad's name? I realise you've never told me before.'

'It's Mike. Why, do you know him?' I ask, and I can feel my mouth has turned dry. Why is she looking at me with such a worried expression plastered across her face? Why has she made me meet her so far from the house?

As she finally passes me the photos, she says, 'I think these will answer that for you. Yes, you look ever so like your mum. But I see it now. I don't know how I missed it before. You have his teeth.'

I frown and open the envelope. The first is a beautiful photo of my mum and Rosey. Their initial necklaces hanging delicately round their necks. R and P.

'That was the night of the BBQ Bonfire Ball,' she tells me. I place it down on the table and beneath it the next photo shows a group of four people sat outside a wigwam in the forest. I look closely at the figures. There's Mum, Rosey, and then there's Robert. I study the fourth person. The other man, and I notice his crossover teeth and the tattoo vines down his arms.

I hear my own gasp before I realise that I'm doing it.

It's Dad, there's no doubt about it.

'You're telling me that my dad was also on Osea Island with you that summer in nineteen-ninety? This can't be right. He told me he'd never been.'

'He was definitely there. And after the accident, he left and I never saw him again. But Robert has seen him a few times over the years. I don't understand, Lily, why did he never tell us Penny survived?'

All of a sudden, my veins feel like they're flooded with ice. It runs through me. Top to bottom, even though it's still summer outside.

'Mum must not have wanted him to. She clearly didn't want to see you ever again, not after you pushed her off the boat and left her to drown to keep your own guilty secret.'

'I didn't push her. It was an accident,' Rosey says, but she lowers her eyes. I realise that without Robert here to back her up, now might be my only chance to get the truth out of her.

'Was it? There's something you aren't telling me still. I know it. And until you tell me the truth, I'm not interested in anything else you have to say.'

'I would never have intentionally hurt my sister,' Rosey hisses back ferociously. 'I'm sorry you don't trust me. This has been hard for me too, you know. Learning that Penny didn't drown and that I have a beautiful niece.'

I try not to scoff.

'I slipped. That much is true. But you're right I've not told you the whole truth. I thought maybe Penny had told your dad about

Eloise and our fight on the boat. And so, I went through your belongings to see if you had a diary or anything you might have written in about it. I'm sorry.'

'It was you? I knew I wasn't imagining it.'

'It was me. I'm sorry about that.'

'And at the cemetery, was that you watching me then, too?'

Rosey nods.

'So why now? Why are you telling me all this? You've spent years spinning your own version of events. And now all of a sudden here's a full-on confession? I'm not buying it.'

'It's because of Mike,' she says quickly and firmly. 'I don't trust him.'

'Fuck you,' I hiss. 'That's my dad you're talking about and he has done nothing but protect me.'

'And what about Penny? Was he just protecting her too?'

I stand up to leave when she calls after me, 'What if *he's* the reason she never came back to us?'

'They loved each other. She didn't want you. She wanted him. Accept it. She never forgave you, Rosey. And nor will I. I wish I'd never met you.'

'Did she though?' Rosey says quietly.

'Did she what?'

'Love him. Penny left him, remember.'

'She left you too.'

Rosey lets out a small sad laugh. 'Yes, but she thought I'd thrown her over the side of a boat and left her to drown. So my question, Lily, is what did Mike do that was so bad it made her leave him too?'

I grit my teeth, my jaw tightening, and then I turn my back on her and walk away quickly. I force myself to keep my eyes looking ahead. But her words have hit harder than I let on. Because yes, Rosey had lied to me from the very beginning about being on that boat with Penny when she fell, had covered up their part in Eloise's death, but Dad lied to me too. He told me he'd never been to Osea Island but the photos in my pocket prove otherwise.

Was he also involved in Eloise's death and the cover-up after? I realise I haven't asked Rosey enough questions about it all, too angry with her accusations towards him to stop and think things through. Is that why he didn't tell me the truth? But if that's the case, then how did Mum end up in a relationship with Dad? Did she change her mind about coming clean?

Chapter Thirty-Seven

Lily, now

I wait until later that night to bring it up with Dad. I know that if I rush it, go in there fuelled by too much emotion and hurt, that he'll shut down. He never copes very well if he doesn't feel in control of a situation and he's reluctant to talk about Mum at the best of times. So I play the game, and take my time. I wait while he serves up dinner – a dish he has prepared especially for me as we've not seen each other for a few days. It smells incredible.

'Please don't get mad,' I start, changing the subject with about as much grace and tact as a bull in a china shop. 'I didn't stay home while you were away. I couldn't get Osea Island out of my head and so I found some last-minute accommodation there. That's where I was the days you were away. I'm sorry I lied, but Dad, I found Aunt Rosey and she says she knew you.'

He puts down his wine glass slowly and carefully. I watch as his chest heaves with a purposeful intake of air. He is controlling his emotions. Trying hard not to explode.

'How is she?' he asks and I'm relieved that at least he's decided not to deny it all, not pretending he doesn't already know who Rosey is.

'Worried about me. She came to our house a couple of days ago,' I say and at that his head snaps towards me. A little less calm and collected than before. 'She saw you and it seemed to rattle her. She gave me these photos,' I say, placing a couple on the kitchen table. The rest are in my room. *Safe.* The word appears in my mind without warning. I press it down inside of me. 'Why did you pretend you'd never been before? And why did you never tell Rosey and Robert that Mum was still alive? You knew they thought she was dead. There's even a grave on Osea Island for her. They thought she'd died one whole year before I was even born. Why was it this big secret? Why was I this big secret? Is it all to do with keeping quiet about Eloise?' I ask and his eyes grow larger with the shock of just how much I know.

Of course, I care about what happened to Eloise and keeping the promise I made to Joe to find out the truth, but more than anything I also care about me in this situation. About how I came to be erased from history. Because I am here. I exist. I am real.

'I lied because I wasn't ready to talk about it. She broke my heart.'

'I know, but—' He holds up a hand, palm facing me, and I stop abruptly.

'As for your mum's relationship with her family. With Rosey—' and as he says her name, I watch his eyes narrow, a sneer appearing on his lips, 'Penny didn't want them to know. Lily,' he turns towards me now and places my hands in his. Leans in. Looks at me intently. 'We loved each other very much. Your mum, she had a lot going on at home and it wasn't healthy for her there. At first it was just a game, really, in a way. We were running away from it all but we did mean to go back. Everything was so perfect, just the two of us. And then, magically, there were going to be three. And we decided why would we go back, back to all that which was so rotten and hard and painful, when we could stay here and be happy? We could be better. Purer. A real family.

'We realised that we'd escaped everything awful that had happened in Osea, and we wanted it to stay that way. So, we made a new start. A fresh one. No longer tainted by the past or what had come before. You were our future, Lily. We wanted to be a family. To create a safe environment for you. For us to be the best parents to you that we could be.'

I take it in and feel his fingers squeezing mine.

'I promise you,' he says again, 'it was the three of us against the world. That was all that mattered. Until she left, we were a family. In my eyes, up until that moment we'd been a perfect family.'

Chapter Thirty-Eight

Rosey, now

Rosey lowers the phone down and presses it against her chest. Her heart beating too fast.

'Rob, darling? Do you have a minute?'

'Of course,' he says, striding into the lounge. For a moment, she takes in her surroundings. Their house is bigger than the holiday cottage. It's grand and it's fancy. They have, after all, prioritised status over truth. There is a feature wall with a fireplace where interesting trinkets adorn the mantelpiece; alcove bookshelves either side are lined with books from top to bottom. A velvet orange reading chair sits by the window with a leopard print cushion and a big gold lamp stands next to it in the shape of a giraffe. A gorgeous Aztec rug covers most of the wooden floor and on one wall is an enormous print of a book cover showing the silhouette of a woman. Opulent and audacious, it is all a show.

Rosey used to think the cottage in Osea was so small that it was suffocating, but now she can see the charm in it. What's the point in having a big house if there aren't plenty of people to fill it? Chrissy. Patrick. Penny. They're all gone.

And now she's found Lily and she is desperate not to lose her too.

Lily had been ignoring Rosey again since she'd practically accosted her in the coffeeshop, which meant she'd been particularly surprised when her number flashed up on her phone.

She'd needed to take a few breaths to steady herself before rushing to answer it.

Lily had explained that she was calling because she wanted to tell Rosey she'd spoken with her dad and that there was no reason for her to worry. Penny and Mike had been in love. According to him, when Penny fell pregnant, they decided to stay away from all the drama and pain back home. She said her mum couldn't face going back to unpack everything that had happened surrounding Eloise's death.

So Penny was being selfish, Rosey had thought, but she stayed quiet, careful not to push it too far. The fact that Lily had called her – even if it was to try and prove her wrong about Mike – was a step in the right direction. So, she'd listened and then said, *OK, love, thank you for calling*, as sweetly as she could before hanging up. But nothing about this feels right to Rosey.

'What did you think of Mike?' she asks Robert, who is now standing in front of her, expectantly. 'Did you trust him?'

He blows the air out through his lips, making them vibrate and Rosey is filled with the desire to punch him in the face. Does he not understand that this is urgent?

'I guess. We were very different but we got on. Worked together as a team, musically. We were in our twenties back then, I don't really think I ever got to know him, to be honest. This was the nineties we're talking about. Men didn't exactly talk. Not about real stuff. I barely knew anything about him. I just knew that he could make anyone fall in love with him, with his quiet charm, whereas my intensity and brashness made me the less likeable one of the two. That and my lanky height.'

He pauses, as if waiting for Rosey to jump to his defence – which she doesn't. This isn't about his ego. Nor hers. Not anymore. They've grown up since then. At least, Rosey likes to think so. She's found revisiting their past this summer full of unpleasant truths about the people they once were. But aren't all people some kind of terrible in their twenties? Desperate to prove they're adults and independent? Rosey has come to think that your twenties are for pretending to be who you want to be – or perhaps pretending *not* to be who you are; your thirties are for learning and accepting who you really are; and then you're ready to actually *be* that person in your forties.

And now here they are, in their fifties, totally different people to who they were back in 1990. Robert has learnt to smooth over his intense edges with a little more charm, and Rosey has learnt to direct her showmanship into her career. Publishing is, after all, full of theatrics. Authors and editors have certain ideas of what they think an 'agent' should be and Rosey enjoys putting on that mask. Admittedly it's still pretending to be someone she isn't, but this time it's directed in a healthier way. No harm done.

But what about Mike? Rosey can't even imagine who he might have turned into, because they have no idea who he was trying so hard not to be back when he was in his twenties. He was there, but he also kept himself to himself. His cards kept close to his chest, but he was just as much a part of it all as they were.

There's something about the memory of him that makes her eye twitch. She feels her jaw stiffen with stress. She clicks it and, as she does, she notices the pounding in her ears. The blood is rushing round her body too ferociously. The dread that's filling her up feels so visceral it is physically painful. Because no matter what Mike has told Lily about how much the two of them were in love, the fact remains that he knew Penny was alive yet let everyone go on believing her to be dead. Even if that was Penny's idea, what kind of person can keep a secret like that? How did he look Robert in the eye and never say a word?

Her mind races back to the summer of nineteen-ninety and she tries to recall every detail. She wants to remember everything about Mike, but it was such a long time ago and she was always more preoccupied with Robert. Quickly, she rushes upstairs and pulls out the box of photographs she'd sorted through with Stef. Flicks through them again, looking more closely this time. She doesn't know what she's looking for, is probably clutching at straws, but still she has to try something. And then she sees it.

The photograph was taken by their dad at the breakfast table in the cottage. She remembers how that year he'd asked for them all to have a family breakfast every morning – the rest of the day was theirs to spend how they liked. It was always just the four of them. But there, in the corner of the photo, through the window, is a figure that doesn't belong. He's in the distance, across the path, but there's no doubt he's looking straight at the cottage. She squints and brings it closer, but she's sure she's not mistaken. The man watching through the window is Mike. Was it a coincidence that he was passing at the time of the photo, or was he watching them? And if so, for how long and why?

'I need the car keys,' she says suddenly and urgently. Robert automatically abides, pulling them from his trouser pocket and throws them to her.

'Where are you going?'

'To get some answers.'

'Do you want me to come too?'

'Absolutely not,' she calls over her shoulder and Robert stops following her like a lost puppy. 'I love you. But I need to do this on my own.'

Because this is between Penny and Rosey. No one else.

Twenty-six years ago, the last conversation she had with Penny was an argument. They both did things wrong back then. Perhaps, finally, it's time to get the full story. Not Mike's version of events. And, most importantly, to try and make amends. To listen this time.

Chapter Thirty-Nine

Lily, now

Dad's quieter this morning than usual, as if the frostiness of last night has settled over the house. It feels icy. I tell myself that there's no way he could have heard my call with Rosey before I came down, but still I find myself feeling guilty about it. I know Dad would have considered my calling her a betrayal – going against his and Mum's wishes. Especially now I know the truth about what Mum really wanted and why. Yet I felt the need to explain Dad to her. It hadn't sat well with me when we last met the way she'd painted him to be so untrustworthy.

Of course, I haven't told Dad that part of the story – want to avoid angering him unnecessarily. For now, I'm back hiding out in my bedroom, avoiding the awkwardness that has settled between us, when I hear the front door close and watch out my window as he pulls away in the van.

Suddenly, my phone vibrates with a message, and a quick glance shows it's Owen checking in on me, asking how I'm doing. The subtext of course is that he's asking if I've made any progress with the task we came up with. I'm meant to be making a list of anything that holds a particular significance to me. Something that sparks any strong emotion when I think about it. The idea is that we'll meet again soon and go through it all together.

The truth is that I have been too preoccupied the last couple of days with Rosey to think about it, but he's right – I do need to turn my attention to sorting this out and I'm thankful to him for checking in on me. I sit for a while in my room, but my brain remains completely blank. So, I decide to walk around the house instead, hoping for inspiration to strike. I make my way downstairs, thinking I'll start there. And as I walk through the house, I think about my childhood memories. The time I cut my knee learning to ride a bike and Dad hoisted me on to the side in our kitchen. Blood running down my shin. How he told me he'd never let me fall again. That his job as a father was to protect me at all costs.

I remember the way every Sunday when I was young, we'd cook a roast dinner together. As I got older, I began asking if I could go out with friends shopping or to the cinema instead, but he'd always shake his head and say *Sundays are for family*. Of course, I'd slink away annoyed, but actually when it came to sitting down together at the table, I always ended up having a good time with him. Just the two of us.

They're strong, nice memories, and they don't evoke that something else, that emotional tug I know I must be looking for. There's no edge to the memories. Nothing that indicates they're linked to something bigger. I'm starting to think about giving up and am heading back to my room upstairs when I pass Dad's bedroom. I never spend much time in there and can't imagine what use it would be to go in, but I know I need to be thorough otherwise there is no point in doing the exercise at all, and so I open the door and step inside. I'm standing in the middle of the room when a memory hits, unexpectedly.

It's something Dad would say often. This particular memory though is from a time when I was young. I must have been around seven, maybe a little younger, and I was refusing to go to bed. Too afraid of monsters. I asked Dad to check under my bed, refusing even to step into my bedroom until he did so. He'd given in and had reluctantly knelt down, burying his head under the bed before shaking it at me, exasperated.

'No monsters. You know, Lily, everyone always thinks the monsters are under the bed. Nobody ever thinks to look up, they always look down. But all monsters must know by now that people check under things for them. I'm sure the clever ones have found new places to hide.' He grinned at me, but I found myself more scared than I had been before calling him in. 'Of course, there are no monsters. Not really – not even high up,' he'd added. But it was too late, and I remember having awful nightmares that night.

Nobody ever thinks to look up.

I freeze where I'm standing and slowly, ever so slowly, as if subconsciously my mind is trying to stop me – prolonging it – I lift my head to see I'm standing directly under the loft hatch.

I stand for a moment, frozen to the spot, unable to work out how exactly to get into the loft, but also unsure why I feel a desperate urge all of a sudden to do so. My body is buzzing with the need to get into that loft. At the same time, I don't want to. I find myself desperately wanting to walk away and to never think about it again. Self-preservation tells me to pretend it doesn't exist.

A loft is a loft is a loft.

Until it's not.

I don't know where the thought comes from – nor the dread that seems to run through me – but this feels important somehow, so I force myself to shake the feeling away. A quick Google search tells me that there should be a pole which releases the hatch and a ladder that then swings down. Somehow, I know before I even try it, that this won't be the case. That there will be no pole tucked away in a cupboard somewhere. No ladder waiting to invitingly spring down. The feeling is so certain that I don't even bother trying. Instead, I head straight out to the shed next to my office. Dad's a workman, I'm sure I'll be able to find something to help me out there.

With surprising ease, I find a few different tools which might do the job. They're all long and thin and each have slightly different shaped ends. I'm hoping one might fit the hatch lock. I tuck the tools – four in total – under my arm and march back into the house. They clang against each other loudly and the sound feels aggressive against my eardrums. I feel on edge as if my senses have been turned up on a dial somewhere. My whole body is churning with anticipation and dread.

I lay the tools down more carefully than I probably need to, on the old brown carpet under the hatch and then I head outside for a second time. With every step I find myself having to fight against the urge that is sitting heavy in my stomach telling me to simply walk away. That feeling is swelling now. Filling me up. Shouting at me to run.

This time, I struggle back into the house and up the stairs carrying a folding ladder I'd once seen Dad use to rescue an injured bird from a tree in our garden. We'd brought it in and put it ever so carefully into a shoebox before taking it to the vet. I'd loved him for that.

By the time I try the fourth and final pole-like tool that I'd retrieved from the shed, I am sweating. The back of my neck is hot and aching from looking up for too long. I pick up the silver tool – my last attempt – and feel strangely hopeful. It has a small square end and when I feed it through the hatch's hole, I feel it slot in snugly. My shoulders slouch with the knowledge it's worked and slowly I roll my neck out. Stretch one way, then the other. A moment of light relief before the next part. Push the palms of my hands into my eyes and wait for the flash of light.

Am I buying for time?

I force myself to clasp the tool in my hands once more and then I twist until the opening creaks. It's stiff. Clearly no one has been up here in years. As I pull it down, thick dust covers me.

Just as I'd expected, no ladder magically swings down so I set up the one I've already brought in from the shed, and then I stand at the bottom looking up into the gaping black hole now open above me. My hands are cold against the ladder and my heart is beating so fast it doesn't seem beyond the realm of possibility that it might rip through my chest.

People never look up.

I can't do it. I can't move. And so, I do what I always do when I feel anxious. I count, resolutely, back from five.

Five, four, three, two, one.

And then I climb the creaky steps. Up into the darkness above.

Up high, where the monsters have learnt to live.

Chapter Forty

Rosey, now

Rosey isn't usually one to speed, not since a police officer stopped and breathalysed her on the way to her friend's wedding eighteen years ago. She was a bridesmaid and had been so overexcited that she'd bombed it down the motorway without even realising, apparently hitting ninety-six miles an hour according to the surprisingly friendly male police officer who'd pulled her over on the M25. But now Rosey finds herself pushing the speedometer up higher and higher again. Way past seventy. Yet she can't stop.

The more she remembers about that week on Osea all those years ago, the more dread floods into her. Fills her up and threatens to pour back out again. When Lily had first turned up and proven that their belief that Penny had drowned was wrong, Rosey had assumed that Lily must believe she'd intentionally hurt her mum that night on the boat and had come looking for proof. Revenge even.

But since learning that Penny ended up in a relationship with Mike and that he'd purposefully kept the fact she was alive from them, she hasn't been able to think about anything else. Mike's reasoning that she'd wanted to create a perfect family away from Rosey and her parents, away from all the death that surrounded them – their mum's and Eloise's – doesn't sit well with her and she can't shift the feeling that it just isn't right. That it doesn't fit. Not with the Penny she knew. And Rosey knew Penny as well as she knew herself.

This idea that Lily has spun her, of Penny having stayed away because she wanted to have an idyllic family – her, Mike and a baby – well, there's just no way. No way that Penny would have chosen him. Mike. Over them. Over being there for their mum. Penny had always been the better daughter out of the two of them. When she'd first met Lily, she'd assumed Penny must have fallen in love with someone so captivating she never came back to them.

But for that person to have been Mike?

Yes, she admits he was charismatic. And yes, being a musician gave him a certain allure. But aside from all that? He was quiet. Unassuming. There but not there. Frankly, she'd always thought him a little unusual.

And then there's the photo of him watching them at breakfast. There's something about his pose that unsettles her. It doesn't look casual, but instead static, as if he had been standing there a long time. It makes her feel uncomfortable and the more she thinks about that summer as she speeds towards London, the more she remembers. She is certain that although they'd all gone along with it initially, it was Mike who'd first suggested they left Eloise's body alone in the forest. That it was him who'd offered her that first underage beer. It was Mike who'd made the first jump from the lookout tower.

Rosey thinks about the moments where Mike was with them and by extension the moments when he wasn't. Looking back on it now with more distance between her and the past helps her re-examine their actions in a clearer light, with less guilt and fear skewing everything in the way it had at the time. And it strikes fear through her as she realises just how expertly Mike had managed to manipulate them into everything without them even realising he was doing it. In particular, she remembers the night of the boat. How, when the rescue team arrived and they'd asked her and Robert countless questions, that Mike had already vanished.

Lily had told her on the phone earlier that Penny found Mike after washing up on the island and asked him to help her leave. But what if that isn't the whole truth and is simply another one of Mike's expertly woven manipulations? There is the possibility that the reason Mike disappeared before the rescue team had even arrived was because he knew where to find Penny but didn't tell anyone.

That possibility strikes fear into Rosey, because often it's the things we don't say rather than the things we do, that tell us the most about who someone is and what they're capable of – that have the biggest ripple effect. And if Mike had chosen to let them believe Penny had drowned before he'd even had the chance to talk to her, then does that mean it had all been part of a grand plan to convince her to leave with him? And if so, what kind of man would that make him?

Not a man.

A monster.

Rosey calls Lily, willing her to pick up but it rings out to voicemail. *Fuck*.

The dread inside Rosey swirls and morphs into guilt. If her suspicion that Mike cannot be trusted is correct, then it won't just be the boat accident Penny has never forgiven her for, but also what came after.

Lily is right about Rosey still spinning lies and reframing her own guilt in ways that make it more palatable. She still hasn't told her everything – old habits die hard, after all. The person she really needs to talk to now is Penny. To hear her out this time. But no one knows where she is, so she's heading to the next best thing: Mike. She needs answers and she needs to find her sister.

Chapter Forty-One

Lily, now

I don't know why, but I find myself automatically reaching to the right of me at the top of the hatch opening, as if somewhere deep down inside of me I already know that I'll find a long fraying cord to turn the lights on.

I pull on it until I hear a click. Close my eyes as I do, somehow aware that when I open them again my world will have changed. I force them open and see the whole space is filled with an orange glow.

Usually when someone is shocked by something they might gasp, or perhaps take a step backwards, reaching out for something to steady them – but in this moment, I stay completely still. No noise emits from my body. My conscious mind is shocked – confused even – by what I see, but my body isn't. My subconscious already aware of what I would find. Of what it has been hiding from me all these years.

Dad has never mentioned a loft conversion, and certainly there are no windows up here, but there is no doubt that this is what the space is. It's a mini studio, in fact. The area is clearly divided into three sections. There's a double mattress on the floor in one corner with a single mattress at the foot of it, a free-standing shutter is placed to the side as a way to divide the beds from the rest of the living area. Then there are two wooden chairs in the middle of the room with a stack of books in front of them and a very old-fashioned dusty television balanced on top.

I scan further to the left and see a small kitchenette area. There's a small block of units that have been fitted along one side with a camping gas stove on top of one cupboard and a CD player on a shelf. The wall behind has been tiled. In front of the units is a small wooden table. The care with which someone must have created this space is more than evident. For all intents and purposes, it has been built beautifully.

Lovingly, even – if a stranger were to observe it. If it wasn't for the colour of the green tiles and the small textured shape of them – exactly like those in my flashbacks. For that is what I know they are now – my memories. Yes, the tiles on Rosey's boat were similar and it threw me off for a while, but these ones are larger and slightly shinier. I once knew these tiles like the back of my hand. I know that for sure now. Just as I know this place was not lovingly built. Not in the true sense of the word – though perhaps that's what he convinced himself of at the time.

Because I am no stranger to this place. I know that love is not all that this loft encompassed. I remember it now. All of it. This time it's not just a disjointed flashback that I'm hit with, it's a whole, fully formed memory. Not one, not two, but thousands of them. I am filled with memories of my mum as I saw her through my child's eyes. She was *beautiful*.

And I feel it, the thing I'd been searching for this whole summer, I finally feel it – my mother's love. Yes, my mum loved me with every single bone in her body and she was my entire world. It is both beautiful and devastating all at once and I am overwhelmed by the gravity of it. Of what I've remembered. It is a past that my childhood brain had tried so hard to protect itself from. Because this was not a normal loft conversion. This place was not built only out of love. Bad things happened here.

Once upon a time, it was our prison. We called it The Palace.

My mum was beautiful. I'd cup my small hands around her face and tell her that I never wanted her to leave me. In return she'd laugh and kiss my nose. Tell me she wasn't going anywhere. That she'd always be with me, no matter what.

And then one day, tucked up in her bed, my body curved against hers, she'd told me that we had to leave. The words she'd used were 'go down the hole'. She was crying, the tears rolling off her nose making our pillow wet. But I remember how she was smiling too, delicately stroking along my eyebrows following the shape down my nose.

'I love you, Lily. And I'll always be with you. Even when I'm not around anymore you'll find me right here,' she'd said, poking me right by my heart and then turning it into a tickle to make me laugh. But I could hear in her voice that this was serious. I was only four, but I knew that leaving meant we had to get past him, first. And that was never going to be easy.

We'd made a plan and practised it for weeks. Mum had scratched a countdown on our wall, back from five, and she said once she'd crossed through all the marks that meant the day had arrived and that we had to go through with it. I think it was as much for her as it was for me. To prepare us. To help give us the courage for when the moment came. To make it feel as if there was no other choice, once the final mark had been struck through – we were committed.

Five, Four, Three, Two, One.

That morning – it had to be morning, Mum insisted, *so we just wake up and we do it* – we knew that at 7.15 a.m. on the dot, Mike (or Dad as he made me call him, though when it was just us we never called him that), would open the hatch. Six days a week we had breakfast together. This was something Mike used to refer to Mum as a 'non-negotiable'. It was, apparently, something that families did together. I never understood why that meant he had to join us.

Right on time, at 7.15 a.m. on the dot, we heard the clatter of the ladder being unfolded below us. Mum counted down from five in a whisper, reinforcing that it was now or never, and I knew that this was it. She squeezed my hand and then broke free confidently, indicating it was time to get in position. I tiptoed behind the entrance to the loft so that Mike wouldn't immediately see me as he ascended the ladder. Under my arm, I clutched one of Mum's jumpers. It had been folded carefully, so it was just the right thickness. We figured a jumper wouldn't make a sound.

Mum had taken up her position in the kitchenette next to a saucepan of water that had been boiling for a while. The gas stove had been a birthday present the week before. It had taken a while to pull it off, but this escape plan hadn't been formed overnight. It had taken months to put together – for Mum to prove her trustworthiness to Mike. To explain that the loft got cold during the winter months and that we kept getting sick from it. That a way of boiling water to have hot drinks and fill up water bottles through the night would help keep us safe. It had involved a number of feigned temperatures – mine and Mum's – for Mike to eventually relent and one day enter the loft with the camping stove wrapped in pink wrapping paper.

With me in position and the water now boiling in the pan, the plan was well and truly under way. And so, just as Mike lifted up the hatch, Mum pressed play on the CD player. The idea was that it would provide a distraction. We had never played music during one of his visits before, we reserved that just for us. Mum had told me how the CD player had been a gift the very first birthday she had spent up here (because families give presents on birthdays, he'd told her).

He'd only provided one CD with it, but we loved dancing along to it when we were able to. There were strict rules about when we could and couldn't make any noise. Generally, Mike never had any visitors, but still if he was in the house he liked to not be disturbed. When he was out, we could make as much noise as possible. No one ever heard us.

With Mike almost completely through the opening, and with his back still to me, I placed the jumper as precisely as I could so that when the hatch dropped closed below him it wouldn't catch completely, the jumper stopping it from closing.

Mum was singing loudly to the music, drawing his attention away from me. Miraculously, this part worked. He hadn't noticed there was no secure click behind him. As she sang, Mum caught my eye and I could see she was proud of me. A glint. *We are going to do this, Lily*, she'd promised me the night before as we lay in bed, and I remember thinking at that moment – with the jumper in place and Mike's attention solely on Mum – that she was right.

And then, just as I knew would happen, Mum moved on to the next part of the plan and I remembered her instruction to keep well away. She placed two mugs on the unit and dropped a tea bag into each. Then, she calmly picked up the saucepan. She'd told me it was important Mike didn't suspect anything too early but still I was impressed with how steady she managed to keep her movements.

'You're in a good mood this morning,' Mike said, now only a couple of steps away from her.

'Am I?' Mum replied before, without any warning, suddenly everything changed. It all sped up. She lunged at him, throwing the boiling water in his direction. He screamed in pain as the scorching water poured across his body. And then Mum was running past him towards the chairs. She picked the nearest one up and swung it at him. But Mike had been less injured from the boiling water than we'd hoped. The water had hit him, but it hadn't drenched him the way we'd planned.

He'd avoided it across his face, and crucially it seemed mostly to have hit where he was wearing clothes. The chair crashed into him, but he was coming for Mum now. 'You bitch,' he screamed at her, his hand whipping up to crack against her cheek, before punching her straight in the stomach.

I watched as Mum fell to the floor and without even thinking about Mike, I ran to her. She was my whole world. I grabbed hold of her hand where it was stretched out, her arms flung wide where she had fallen. My fingers felt small interlaced in hers and when I looked, the glint I'd seen earlier in her eyes had been replaced with fear. 'Go,' she shouted at me as Mike lunged for her again, pulling her up from the floor by her dress's collar. The movement ripped my fingers from hers.

'Go,' she screamed again, one last time.

I darted away from them back across to the hatch where I'd slid the jumper earlier. I tried over and over again to lift it, but I could not pull it hard enough. My skinny, weak, malnourished four-year-old body unable to help us escape.

Desperately, I turned to see that Mum was now lying on the floor. Mike's form was heavy and large on top of her. He had his hands twisted around her neck and he was shaking her so viciously that her head kept hitting the floor. As he moved, I kept watching the tattoos around his wrists look like they were writhing. Dancing to my mum's death. The song 'Vision of Love' was blasting in the background as the CD continued to play – the soundtrack to my mother's murder.

With no strength left to keep trying the hatch, I'd backed away, pushing myself into the furthest corner of the loft wall away from them and sank down against it until I was sitting. Curled tight into a ball. I could not tear my eyes away.

I watched, terrified, as Mike drained the life out of my beautiful mum. My own head hit the wall in time to the rhythmic bangs coming from where he smashed her head against the floor. Over and over again. Finally, he stopped, resting his knees on the floor where he still sat across her stomach. He'd wiped the sweat away from his brow with his sleeve. Mum's head was turned to the side, as if looking at me. Only, even at four, I knew she wasn't there anymore. That she'd left and flown someplace else. Somewhere better than here. I didn't want to see her looking at me like that any longer, and so I'd pushed the palms of my hands as hard as I could into my eyes. Kept them there, blocking her lifeless body out, for as long as I possibly could.

Eventually he'd hauled himself off her body and trodden heavily over to me. I'd heard him, rather than seen him. My palms still pushed firmly across my eyes. He hadn't said a word but he picked my curled body up, hooking an arm under my bent knees, and then marched across the room. He placed me down carefully on the mattress. 'You can take your hands away now,' he said. 'Wait here until I come back. Do not move,' he'd ordered, before pulling the shutter divider across so I couldn't see him – or perhaps it was him who didn't want to see me.

It must have been hours later, maybe even the next morning – keeping track of time had been Mum's job – when he pulled the divider back and revealed there was no trace of Mum left. No body lying in the middle of the floor. Had I imagined it? My four-year-old self wished so hard that it had all been a terrible nightmare. The truth of it too hard to process.

'It's just you and me now, kid,' he'd said matter-of-factly, as though he hadn't just killed my whole world right in front of my eyes. I'd stared blankly at him, unable to form any words. It was as though my conscious mind was no longer able to function.

'She always wanted you with her. A child belongs with its mother, it's only natural. But she's gone now. She left us. Which means, you belong with me.' Then he held my hand and pulled me up from the bed. Carried me down the ladder over his shoulder and asked if I would like a mug of hot chocolate.

Finally, I remember it all.

Chapter Forty-Two

Penny, 1990

Penny can't believe how fast time has flown. It has been two weeks since they left Osea, which is much longer than she'd thought she'd have before someone came knocking about Eloise's death. She'd been sure they'd want to talk to her and Mike about it. Had Rosey really told them everything?

Even more pressing, was the fact she needed to get back to Chrissy. She is surprised they haven't dragged her home already. Mike had called her parents the first day they'd arrived home to give them his address and tell them where she was. Were they really so angry at her for leaving? The past couple of weeks had been great but the bubble had burst and reality was pushing its way back in. She'd pushed it all away for long enough.

Penny walks into the kitchen where Mike is preparing a cooked breakfast. It smells amazing. 'Morning,' she says, wrapping her arms around his waist and giving him a quick kiss. She isn't particularly in the mood but she knows Mike gets upset if he feels she's ignoring him. She's learnt he's a lot more sensitive than she'd realised on the island.

She tells herself it's a good thing, to have a man so in touch with his own emotions. Someone who isn't afraid to talk about how they feel – unlike her own dad, who always pretends everything is fine. He holds her close for longer than she'd expected.

Eventually he lets her go and she walks towards the landline, hanging on the wall.

'What are you doing?'

'I've had a great time here, thank you, but I need to go home,' she says confidently and picks up the phone. She's surprised and disappointed to hear it's disconnected.

'Sorry, it's broken.' He doesn't say so, but she can tell he's angry with her. That she's made him cross. She feels it in the way the whole room suddenly feels icier.

'Since when?'

'Since yesterday.'

'OK. Well, can we leave today? Would you mind driving me home?'

'I can't today. I've taken on some work with a friend.'

'What kind of work?'

'He's a builder. They need an extra pair of hands and they're expecting me this afternoon. But I'll take you tomorrow.'

'Do you promise?'

'Of course. I promise.'

'Thank you,' she says, placing the cord phone back in its cream-coloured holder on the wall. When she walks past him again, he grabs her wrist and pulls her towards him. Kisses her firmly on the lips. Her wrist stings as he holds it, and she realises it must be bruised from last night.

At first, their sex had felt special. Intense, certainly, but in a way that had made her feel loved and needed. It had shut out the rest of the world, which is exactly what she'd wanted it to do. But over the past two weeks there have been small changes. It doesn't feel as special anymore. Maybe she's just a prude, not as experienced as Mike. Rosey would know these things, if only she could speak with her. Iron things out and make things right.

Chapter Forty-Three

Lily, now

I race down the ladder into the bedroom, not wanting to spend a minute longer back up in the loft than I need to. I reach under Dad's bed and pull forwards the small wooden memory chest. I already know that everything he has told me is a lie; that my mum never abandoned us but that he killed her. And yet it's like I need more proof. To keep affirming it. To solidify my memories now that they're back and to make sure my brain doesn't hide the truth from me again. I need to face this.

Just like I thought, under the pile of photos I find no birth certificate with my name on it. No death certificate for Mum. I look through the photos again. I'd always thought she looked so happy in them. Wide-open smile. Bright eyes. She'd looked free. But as I look through them again, I realise that every photo must have been taken in a very short space of time: there aren't many, and she looks exactly the same in all of them. There are no photos of her pregnant. No photos of me as a newborn. Of my first birthday. No cheesy Christmas photos with me dressed up as an elf or mini reindeer. Of course, there are other photos of me framed throughout the house. Proudly laid out – the perfect image of a single father and his only daughter. A perfect family. Just as Dad always wanted. But I'm older in those.

They came after.

Because that's what there was: a before, a during and an after.

All my life, I've felt like something was missing. That I couldn't fully understand who I was or why sometimes the different parts of me didn't seem to make sense. Why I always felt afraid and lost, less trusting of other people.

I realise now that it's because I was missing 'the during'. Only living in the 'after'. I only ever had access to part of myself. It was self-preservation, but my barriers have been cracking for a while. Now, I'm old enough for the truth and this knowledge of who my dad is and what he has done – well, it's power. Somehow, I feel bigger. Taller. Stronger. I am no longer hiding from the truth. I'm exactly who I'm meant to be.

I am my mother's daughter.

I stay sitting curled up on his bedroom floor, repeatedly thumbing through the few belongings I've found, as the memory of those early years in the loft reframes my whole childhood. I no longer see an overprotective Dad all consumed by responsibility of single-parenting, but instead I see all the ways in which he has exerted control over my life.

He has always kept me on a short string: I don't have friends because I was never allowed any, always made to decline invitations for play dates or going out at weekends. He has always moulded me into his doing – the office at the bottom of the garden and working for myself was originally his idea. And as for his idea on family values, something which has always been so prevalent and provided a clear structure to our life, well I now see it as nothing more than a twisted fantasy. Something he is clinging on to. Is it his rule book? Is it the way in which he justifies his own actions? Because we are not family. Mum and I, we were his captives.

Finally, I hear the van return and Mike's heavy work boots approaching the house. Inside, he calls out for me. I roll back my shoulders and tell myself there's no way he can know I've been in the loft or that I've remembered. Not yet. I force myself to stay where I am until he finds me, letting the moment build and giving my courage the chance to swell. I want to catch him unaware. Count back from five as I hear him climbing the stairs.

'Lily? What are you doing?' he asks, rounding the door and taking in the mess around me. The photos. The look on my face. The hatred in my eyes. I stand up then, my knees cracking from how long I've been sitting on the floor, and take a small step towards him.

'I remember,' I say and, although I'm trying to be confident, I can hear my voice sounds shaky. 'Why did you do it? Why did you keep us up there?'

'Now Lily, calm down. All I wanted was for us to stay together. Your mum, she was going to leave me.'

'So, what, you kidnapped her? Kept her in a prison?'

Dad's head twitches to the side and I can tell he's angry. Holding it all in. He takes a tentative step towards me as if I'm a live wire. The next thought that hits, makes me want to be sick.

'Was I . . . ? Did you . . . ?' I find I can't even form the words. Too afraid to say my fears out loud. 'Was Mum already pregnant when you locked her in the loft?'

He doesn't speak.

'Answer me,' I yell, surprising even myself with my own confidence.

'No,' he says, and although I'd already guessed that the timings didn't add up, that Penny was being held up there by the time I was conceived, it still feels catastrophic to have it confirmed.

Dad goes to open his mouth, but I can't stand to hear one more word from him. Instead, I run as fast as I can past him and out of the room and down the stairs. My heart is thumping, expecting him to chase after me. To attack me just like he did my mother. Perhaps, even, to force me back up into the loft.

He doesn't.

I grab the keys to his van on my way out and as I pull away with a screech of the tyres, I look up to see him standing completely still; he is watching me out of his bedroom window.

What happens now? What will his next move be?

I speed towards the police station in his van, but there are other ways he can try and run. I'm just hoping the police can get to him before he makes it too far. He deserves to be punished for what he has done. My dad the murderer. The thought pounds against my head and I can barely make any sense of it. I feel myself wanting to push the truth away again, deep down inside of me and to pretend it never happened. But I remember, and I need to never forget it. For Mum and for what he did to her.

I've only been driving for ten minutes when it hits me that this plan of mine isn't going to work. I always thought Dad swearing blind that he would never leave our house was because it held too much sentimental value for him. But it strikes me now that he *couldn't* leave, rather than him not wanting to. The house is in fact a crime scene. There is too much evidence there; Mum's blood would have soaked into the floorboards. And then it dawns on me, and I slam the brakes with the force of it. Relish the pain as the seatbelt cuts into me.

It isn't just the memories of her – of what he did – that he can't leave behind, it is her. Because she didn't leave. There was no letter sent a year later from Florida. He killed her. And, I realise, my hands gripping the steering wheel, that means there's a body.

Dad can't leave, won't leave, because he can't *physically* leave her behind. And knowing Dad, knowing how much he has always fought for perfection and to control things, I realise that there's no way he would ever flee, but I'm also sure that there's no way he'd let them catch him either. All those times he said he'd rather die than leave the house, suddenly it all takes on a whole new meaning.

I make a U-turn, and speed back the way I've come.

I call 999 from the car.

I'm aware of my knuckles turning white against the steering wheel as I shout 'Police' followed by 'Ambulance'. I hurtle back the route I've just come along, praying I'm not too late.

Chapter Forty-Four

Penny, 1990

Mike has been gone a while already and although Penny wants to believe that he'll take her tomorrow, she also can't quite shake an odd feeling about the phone being disconnected. She rubs her wrist, the bruise that's emerging there is a physical reminder of all the things she's not so sure about when it comes to Mike anymore. The longer she waits in that empty house while he's away, the more desperate she grows to leave.

She finds a plastic bag in the kitchen and packs her few belongings in it before slipping out the front door. She walks hurriedly down the road and keeps walking until she finds a coffeeshop. Inside, she asks the kind old lady behind the counter if she can use their phone. Shakily, she dials the only number she knows off by heart and waits for someone to answer. She isn't sure what to say, other than that she's sorry and she wants to come home now, please.

It is Rosey who answers and at the sound of her voice the memories of their last fight on the boat come flooding back. Penny's chest tightens. So much happened that day, will they ever be able to forgive each other? To untangle the blame and guilt?

'Hello?' Rosey repeats from the other end of the phone.

'Hi, it's me,' Penny answers, her voice crackling with the shame of having disappeared on them all.

'Penny? Really?'

'Yeah, sorry I've been gone a while.'

'You're *alive*?' Rosey sounds shocked and Penny is thrown. What does she mean, she's alive?

'Of course I'm alive. What are you on about?'

'You fucking selfish bitch.' The insult is hurled at Penny with such venom it takes her a minute to even register the words.

'I don't—' she starts, trying to work out what on earth is going on. Why Rosey is acting so weirdly.

'She's dead, you know. Mum. She died and you fucking missed it.'

No, no, no. This can't be right. She's got it all wrong. Why is she lying? Mike told her their mum had months. It's only been a couple of weeks. What is she talking about? The shock paralyses Penny, unable to get her words out as she listens helplessly to Rosey's hatred on the other end of the phone.

'You ran away, let us believe you were dead. You left me! Where have you been?'

'I don't understand. I've been—'

'Actually, fuck it. I don't care where you are. I just care that you haven't been here. I hate you, Penny. I fucking hate you. We thought you'd drowned and you're still dead to me. Don't bother coming back. There's nothing to come back to.'

And then Rosey hangs up on her, leaving Penny standing alone in the coffeeshop with tears streaming down her face. Her whole body feels like it has been cracked open. Their mum has died? Gone. And Penny never said goodbye. And what on earth was she on about saying they thought Penny had drowned? Mike told them he'd found her. He'd even rung them from his house to give them his address. Why hadn't they come for her? Why did they let her mum die without her? None of it makes any sense. She can barely control her breathing, let alone work any of it out.

Still clutching the plastic bag with her sparse belongings in, she walks slowly in a daze of confusion and grief, back to Mike's house. As she walks, she feels like she's lost her mind. None of it can be true. She walks, watching the world go by as if she no longer exists in it. Floating along. She needs to get back to Mike. He'll be able to explain it all. And then he'll take her home. He promised.

Chapter Forty-Five

Lily, now

I see his shoes first. Brown leather work boots. Normally so rooted to the floor, earthy and dependable, they are Dad's trademark look. In stark contrast to how I'm used to observing them, I watch as they swing freely above me. Left, right, left, right.

A pendulum of pain. His. Hers. Mine.

I heave myself up into the loft as fast as I can, a splinter catching in the palm of my hand. He has wrapped his belt around a low beam across the ceiling.

I am shouting. Pleading. But of course, there's no answer. It's just me and him here, in this part of our house no one else knows even exists. He hangs just to the side of one of the wooden chairs, and I imagine him teetering on its edge only moments earlier. It feels inevitable that he would end up choosing to die here, in the place where he murdered my mother, rather than leave it all behind.

Coward.

I wonder, as I rush to support his legs, hoisting them up on to my shoulders as much as possible, if he was thinking of her when he stepped off. Of Mum and of what he did to her. Or perhaps he was thinking of me. The good times we had together and the way it's all come crashing down. Because that's one thing I hate myself for – how when my memories of the past came flooding back, my good ones didn't immediately leave. I would have preferred it if they'd replaced them. Instead, they stand side by side, jostling for attention.

As I continue to hold his weight where he hangs, as I feel the tears rolling down my cheeks, hear the sobs crack me open, I know that I'm crying for my father. The one who I have loved deeply, despite our difficulties. Not the one who kept me here in this awful place. Nor the one who killed my mother. But for the dad who made me hot chocolate. Who read me books at night, bought me a fairy house light for by my bed and a dreamcatcher for my wall. The dad who, once I was a teenager, on the few occasions I did go out, would always make me text him whenever I arrived somewhere, so he'd know I was safe, and who'd without exception always wait downstairs until I came home – no matter what time of day it was. And I hold his body close. Because that's the thing about monsters – they haven't just learnt to hide, they've learnt to camouflage themselves.

Finally, there are shouts from downstairs letting me know they've arrived. Their tone sounds urgent yet authoritative and immediately I feel some of the responsibility pass from me on to them. They are the professionals. *But this?* A small voice inside of me whispers. *You really think they've seen this before?* The gravity of what they're about to discover hits me and I wonder if it'll change them too, working on a case like mine. How far does this thing spread? How far do the ripples flow and where did they begin? Because everything is connected, it is the law of cause and effect. Of course, some consequences are bigger and more devastating than others, but nothing happens independently. It makes me question what it was about Mum that made their paths collide so catastrophically that summer? Why her? Where did this all start?

As I hear them marching up the stairs, I strain to hold his body even further off the ground. Bear the weight even more for as long as I can, even though my arms and back are hot with pain. I find myself weeping harder now. I cry because he is gone. That dad I loved needs to no longer exist and all my good memories of him need to die with him. How else will I survive everything that is bound to come next? Soon the whole world will know, and then there's no going back. It is impossible to undo the past. There can be no more hiding from it. That dad who I loved so much? I can't let myself love him anymore.

For a split second I can feel myself losing the battle. The urge to sink back into obliviousness, rising within me. I force myself to look around me. To remember racing round the room on my mum's back pretending we were horse riding out in the wild. The breakfasts we were forced to endure in silence at the wooden table. *I remember*, I remind myself. I have to keep remembering.

'Save him,' I plead with the people in uniform who are now swarming into the loft. I know from my work in mental health that the statistics for failed self-strangulation are high. I pray that Dad fits in to that category.

Have they noticed yet the lack of windows, or the blood-splattered stain on the side of the wooden chair, where Dad clearly hadn't quite managed to eradicate every last trace of Penny and what happened here? The small details that are out of place. If they look closely enough, they'll see that violence is imprinted all over.

For now, as the pace of everything moves so fast and the emergency team's focus remains zoomed in on the body swinging in the middle of the room, I'm sure they simply take my words and tears at face value. They probably think I fully embody the distraught daughter desperate for them to save their father – that they've witnessed this a thousand times. Because yes, my tears are for the man I loved. But my desire for them to save him? That's not for him. This man who now hangs from the ceiling? He needs to live so that he can face the consequences.

He doesn't get to die.

Not now. Not just as I've relearnt the truth. I want him to survive so that he can live locked in a cage just like he made us; so that I can watch as the whole world judges him for murdering my beautiful mother.

'You don't understand. You have to save him,' I repeat, as I lower myself down the ladder I'd fetched from the garden earlier – a kind-faced officer leading me away. I'm craning my neck for one last view when it happens. I suppose you could call it the beginning of the end.

'Sir?' I hear one of the female police officers say to whom I assume must be in charge.

'What is it?' the man answers abruptly, unaware of what is about to unfold.

'There's a chain with a handcuff on the wall next to the mattress, sir.'

And then I disappear from view.

Chapter Forty-Six

Rosey, now

Rosey slams the brakes as soon as she sees the police car and ambulance parked outside the house. *Please let Lily be OK*, she prays, and then she runs as fast as she can, pushing her way past the officer who is guarding the front door.

'Miss, you can't come in here,' they call after her, but she doesn't look back.

'Lily! Lily!' she shouts frantically. Her heart feels as though it might explode at any moment.

What has happened here? She races up the stairs where she can hear a hum of activity above her.

And then she sees her, face ghostly white with an officer guiding her gently through a doorway. Behind her, Rosey can see a ladder. She's almost unrecognisable. Her skin translucent. She looks physically and mentally ravaged. Blank, haunted eyes stare out at her. An officer follows behind. Rosey rushes up the last few stairs and grabs hold of her tightly. Lily barely moves, hardly acknowledging she's even there.

'Is she hurt? Who is the ambulance for?' Rosey shouts at the officer who'd followed Lily down the ladder. 'Who's up there?'

'Miss, I need to you calm down. Are you the mother?'

'No, I'm her aunt. I'm Rosey. Please, tell me what's going on?'

'Do you know where the mother is? We need to contact her.'

'I don't. I think Lily said she was in Florida. Why? What's happened?'

'No,' Lily croaks, her head shaking slowly. 'She's not. She's dead. He killed her.'

Rosey looks at Lily and sees in her eyes the devastating truth of it. Her entire body folds into itself as she collapses to the floor. What does she mean Penny is dead? Surely she'd have known? Wouldn't she have felt it somehow? The pain rips its way out of her and she howls. Because this is all her fault, isn't it?

The call from Penny had come through to Rosey's landline. She'd only returned to the flat that morning, having stayed at her parents' house since they'd left Osea. Rosey had almost let it ring out. She was exhausted. The previous two weeks had been like nothing she'd ever experienced before – the Taylor family of four suddenly down to two. And the guilt. She remembers how the guilt had been twisting constantly inside her gut. Writhing. Constantly asking herself how could she carry on living this way? The night of the boat accident on loop in her mind. If she just hadn't slipped. Hadn't reached out for the rope. The 'what ifs' were too much to bear.

Their mum shouldn't have had to pass away while grieving for her youngest daughter. She'd never seen her so small and fragile before. They'd thought she was delicate growing up, but they hadn't realised how much worse it could get. How skeletal, both mentally and physically, a person could become while still remaining alive. Cancer and grief did not mix well together.

After she died, Rosey found herself left with all this pain and anger, and no one to direct it towards. So, when she heard the familiar voice on the other end of the phone line, it hadn't sunk in immediately. Surely it wasn't possible? She'd needed to release some of her anger. To be able to let it out. To hurl her hatred towards someone.

She'd wanted to know what had kept Penny from coming

home, but there was too much hurt and too much grief to allow for a more considered conversation. *There will be time to get to the bottom of it*, Rosey thought as she'd hung up on her. Yes, she'd told Penny to never see her again, but she had never expected her to follow through with it. Had never thought that the last thing she'd ever say to her sister was that she hated her.

That phone call has haunted her ever since and now she knows it will never leave her. She will never be able to make amends. It is a guilt she cannot escape from. At the time she'd known she needed to tell their dad that Penny was still alive, but first of all she wanted to fix it; to find Penny and bring her home to him. Their argument on the phone had been so heated, her hurt towards Penny so visceral, that she'd never even asked where she was. And then, she'd had no way of finding Penny again.

The number Penny had dialled from only showed up in the Yellow Pages as being the main call centre for a large chain of coffeeshops. She had no idea where to find her. It was up to Penny to come home – something she never did – and their dad died five years ago not knowing his daughter was still out there somewhere. For a brief moment Rosey is relieved he is not here to witness this. Patrick does not have to bear the unimaginable pain of knowing his daughter was murdered. If she's going to get through this feeling of guilt, which is threatening to weigh her down, then she needs to find the light. Needs something to keep the faith alive in herself. This is it, and she clings to it as hard as she can.

Chapter Forty-Seven

Lily, now

I squint and shield the sun from my eyes as my body takes a little while to adjust to being outside again. Yesterday, I followed the ambulance and spent hours in the artificial hospital light sitting outside Dad's bay before due process caught up with me and, as they started to piece the puzzle together, a team of four officers escorted me to the police station. It was never going to be a quick thing to explain and, in the end, they put me up in a hotel overnight before taking the rest of my statement this morning. I have a headache from all the harsh ceiling lights and the lack of fresh air. Over the course of the past twenty-four hours, I have watched as disbelief turned to horror and then to full-blown urgency as the officers unravelled our story. My mother's and mine.

I arch my back after hours of sitting down and tug the small plaster from my skin where they took my blood – to verify who my parents are – as I begin to walk back home. I already knew that everything was going to change the moment I looked up to see the loft hatch. The quiet life my dad had made us lead is now gone. No doubt, we will be a news story the whole world will consume for years to come.

This feeling is cemented as I round the corner and see that the stream of uniforms charging into the house yesterday had only been the start. The whole road is now full of police vehicles and vans. People walking in and out of the house like a colony of ants. Only these ants are wearing white suits.

Forensics.

They are looking for my mother.

Have they found her yet?

I realise then that I haven't just lost my dad – replaced now by what the whole world will deem a monster even as he recovers from his hospital bed with one hand already chained to the railings and officers guarding his room – but I have also lost my home. It is now a crime scene. Part of a gruesome horror story.

Once again, I feel lost. Displaced. I set out only a few weeks ago thinking I was finally going to find out more about who I am and where I came from, but in doing so it hits me that I've lost everything I thought I ever had. Yes, I know who I am. What I am: I am a victim and a survivor. No doubt, I'll become the main character in a true crime podcast. But I realise, as I stare at my house from across the street, that in doing so – in uncovering the truth – I have lost everything I once was or had.

I'm alone. Still stuck feeling separated from everyone else.

I push my palms into my eyes and try to pull myself together: no, I am a survivor. I must remember that. I repeat the words to myself and slowly feel the knowledge of it unlock a new strength inside of me. I feel it ignite; a flicker of power and strength. Something I haven't felt before. He had taken that from me, but I can feel it seeping back in. I am not his victim. I am a survivor. I have carved that identity out for myself – my mind protecting myself from the truth until I was ready to step into the role.

I use one of the exercises I sometimes set my clients and tell myself to take the emotion out of it. To simply recite the facts of my situation. The idea is that it helps remove the insecurities and vulnerabilities which often cloud a situation; all the things that can stop someone from seeing the good in their life as their own insecurities obscure the positives. I also need to do something to try and reframe Dad away from the man who raised me and instead for who he really is – my captor – because right now my heart feels ripped in two. It is almost unbearable. Shakily, I begin:

'Mike Hawksmoor – the man who kidnapped my mum and then killed her – lies in his hospital bed, being watched over by two police officers at any one time with one wrist chained to the frame, until he is well enough to answer for what he has done. Meanwhile, I stand here alive and free.

When I first arrived on Osea I had this overwhelming feeling that it was going to heal whatever was wrong with me. To fix the thing setting me apart from everyone else. In the end, the feeling I had was right. I found out who and what was making me feel constantly afraid, keeping me as a mere shadow of myself. The answer was him: Mike Hawksmoor.'

But he can no longer hurt me.

I am set free and that means I no longer need to feel alone. That sense of myself – that I never fit in – it was his doing. His manipulation. The trauma he imparted on me and my need to hide from the truth to protect myself. But I'm no longer under his spell nor his grasp. Maybe it can be different now? I want to hope it can be. That this marks the end.

The grief of losing my dad is still heavy, but there's also the spark of a newfound strength inside of me. Still, one thing is for certain – I'm not yet ready to step inside that house. The place I used to call home. It all feels like one big joke now. Was he laughing at me for playing along all those years? Why did he do it and why did he bring me down from the loft after she'd died? I still have so many questions, but until he's well enough the doctors won't allow for him to be questioned. At least he didn't get to die and take the answers with him.

* * *

Owen slows his car down as he approaches the house. I presume he needs a minute to process everything he's seeing: the ants in their white suits; the police tape; me, most likely looking completely shell-shocked and worse for wear. He stops just in front of me and jumps out the car, rushing towards me.

'Lily, what's going on? Are you OK?' He is still looking from me to the house, then back to me, on repeat.

'Not really.'

'What happened?'

'I remembered,' I say quietly. It is all I can manage. After hours at the police station, I've got nothing left to offer.

'Remembered what?'

'My mother,' I tell him plainly.

'I don't understand.' Concern oozes from him and I imagine it's taking all of his resolve not to shake me, but I can no longer care about what anyone else needs from me. I just have to get away from here. 'Why are the police swarming your house? What's going on?' He continues to fire questions at me.

'Can you take me home?'

'Home? I'm worried about you, Lily. Maybe you should go to the hospital.'

'No. I've just come from there,' I say more firmly this time. 'Well, there and then the police station. Can you take me to Aunt Rosey's place? Please, Owen, I want to go home.'

Because somehow Rosey now feels like the closest thing to home. To where my mum would want me to go. It had always been her plan, to escape and go back to her family. Back home.

'But you live here,' Owen answers, as if talking to a delicate child, still as confused as he was when he first arrived.

'No, I don't.' I shake my head fiercely and my eyes snap up towards his. I feel the fire inside of me burning brighter now. I am alive and I am free. 'It was never my home. It was my prison.'

I see the colour in his face change. I'm sure all sorts of things are racing through his mind, but I stay quiet and instead simply open the passenger seat to his car and climb in. For now, the conversation is over. He'll find out more soon enough, no doubt it'll be all over the news by the end of the day.

On the journey to Rosey's in Surrey, I'm grateful for the fact Owen doesn't try asking any further questions; though he steals any and every opportunity to look in my direction. After a while, I pretend to fall asleep. I am exhausted, the kind of tired I didn't know it was possible to feel. And yet, sleep evades me.

It had been the same last night in the hotel room the police organised for me. It makes me wonder if I'll ever sleep again. How can I be so tired and yet remain wide awake? I find it is the same set of questions running through my mind and keeping me up now, as it was last night. I know it will likely be a few weeks until Mike has recovered enough for the doctors to allow him to be questioned, but I can't push it from my mind. I need answers:

Where is my mother's body?

And how did we end up in the loft in the first place?

Chapter Forty-Eight

Penny, 1990

The tears are still pouring down Penny's cheeks, flowing freely, as she arrives back at the house. She sees Mike's van is back in the driveway and she realises that she is both afraid and relieved all at once. Surely, he will help make sense of it.

She's still all colours and emotions, unable to understand how this has happened. What had Rosey been talking about? Where had all her hate come from? Wasn't it Rosey who was to blame for Penny falling into the sea in the first place? She'd been expecting an apology, not this.

Penny had been in shock immediately after the call, walking back to the house slowly as though her legs could barely carry her there, but now she's back in the house the urgency to get answers takes over. She races through the house trying to find Mike. Was Rosey lying? Was she just being spiteful? Please, oh God, please, don't let her mum have died without saying goodbye.

On the second floor at the top of the stairs she sees a step ladder under an open hatch and realises he must be in the loft. She can feel her chest heaving and is finding it difficult to catch a breath. She climbs up the ladder and pulls herself into the loft above her.

She doesn't see it coming. The pain hits her back before she registers what's happening. She falls, smashing her head on the floor as she does. She's lying there, blinking hard, trying to gain some understanding of what on earth is going on. Who just hit her? Are they being burgled?

But then he comes into view. His head looming high above where she lies, and she realises that the object used to hit her was the loft hatch pole. Long and thin. And that the person who wielded it is no intruder. It's Mike.

'What's going on?' she stutters, her eyesight still blurry from where she's hit her head.

'You think I don't know you were going to leave?' he snarls. 'You are mine, Penny. Do you understand? Mine. I saved you from them. How dare you want to go back.'

Slowly, even though she still feels dizzy, her head heavy with pain, it starts to fit together. The lies. The stories he has masterfully woven to lure her away. To isolate her.

'I won't let you leave,' he states, in a tone that is so matter-of-fact it sends shivers across her skin and down her spine. It fills her with fear.

Slowly and painfully, Penny manages to pull herself up to a sitting position. Mike is still blocking the hatch opening and with the way she's feeling, there's no chance of battling her way past him.

'You let them think I was dead,' she says. 'You never told them you'd found me, did you? It was all a lie.' It's not even a question, she already knows it to be true. It's the only way any of it makes sense. Mike never slipped out of the cabin and visited her parents like he claimed. That he had, in fact, manipulated her off the island before the search party had even had time to begin.

'You were better off without them.'

Penny looks at him and realises with a jolt of pure terror that he actually believes what he's saying.

'I never got to say goodbye to my mum.' *Surely he'll apologise for that? He can't be pure evil?* Penny thinks. But he barely reacts.

'Watching someone die isn't all it's cracked up to be,' Mike bristles, clearly uncomfortable about something, but there is no apology. It dawns on her the gravity of his delusion; that Mike believes he is somehow saving her. From what they've done and from what awaits her back home.

'What about Eloise? Did Rosey really tell them the truth?'

'That's enough,' he says abruptly, and Penny can tell from the tone of his voice that he is losing control. He is furious with her. 'After everything you did, you should be grateful I took you away before anyone found out. Do you really think Rosey will keep your little secret?'

'What?'

Mike laughs. But it no longer sounds kind or soft, not the way she'd first thought of him only a few weeks before. 'You really thought you'd gotten away with it? Of course I knew it was you and not Rosey up there with her. I'd been watching, remember. I'm good at reading people. And you, Penny Taylor, are not as much like your sister as you might think. I know you and I know what you've done.'

'I didn't do anything. It was an accident.'

'You think they'll really believe that? No one else was up there with her when she fell. Just you.'

'I tried to save her.'

'Not from where I was standing.'

'You're lying. It was Rosey. Why are you saying this?'

'Because you need to understand that you owe me, Penny. I've kept your secret. I know it was you, not Rosey, who lured Eloise to the top. You are responsible for her death. You killed her, Penny. You did that. Not us.'

'You've got it wrong, I didn't. That's not what happened.'

'Are you sure? What will the police think? And who will they believe when they learn you and Rosey have been lying to people your entire lives? Not very trustworthy of you, is it? I doubt they'll believe anything you say once they know all about your swapping of identities. Have you done it all your life? Did you fuck Robbie, too?'

'Fuck you.'

'No, Penny. Fuck you. Fuck you and your perfect little family. You hate your parents, but all they're guilty of is loving you too much and trying to protect you. Boo-fucking-hoo. Welcome to the real world. I'll be back tomorrow.'

'What? No!' she roars, looking around frantically. She spots the mattress on the floor and thinks she's going to throw up.

'I know there's more to do to the place, but I'll make it beautiful for you, don't worry,' he says, suddenly dropping all his anger and actually sounding apologetic about it. This version of him is even more frightening than when he was angry. How does he switch so easily? Who even is the real Mike?

'You can't keep me here,' Penny screams at him, forcing herself up on to her feet. But her head is hurting so badly that standing up makes her feel even weaker. Her back is definitely bruised from where he hit her. Did he break her rib?

'You've proven I can't trust you. Actions have consequences, Penny. Despite everything you've done, I still love you and I know you love me. That makes us family and family don't leave each other. We stick together.'

'You're not my family, and I haven't done anything.'

'You're just upset. Every family argues, that's normal.'

'Who are you?' she screams as he turns his back on her. 'You can't keep me up here. This can't last for ever. I'll never love you. I'll kill you,' she shouts after him as he lowers himself through the hatch.

Before he disappears out of sight completely, he replies calmly, almost sweetly even, 'You're upset and afraid, but family don't kill each other, Penny. You'll forgive me eventually. People who love each other always do,' and then he pulls the hatch closed and she hears him lock it from beneath.

Chapter Forty-Nine

HM PRISON BELMARSH
THIRD INTERVIEW RECORDING
WITH MICHAEL HAWKSMOOR
28th September 2016

Mike: The truth is, they weren't looking out for her. Not really. Still the centre of their own universes, even in the face of Penny drowning, Robert and Rosey allowed their own emotions to cloud their judgement. They missed it. All wrapped up in each other. They didn't look hard enough, and they missed her.

But I've always been good at looking out. For myself. For others. It's a skill I have, a way my brain works that's different to everyone else's. Better. I can read people. Work out what they want, what they need, and then I can help them get it. If I want to. It helps to gain their trust. And once you've got people's trust, well, you can get them to do pretty much anything you want. What can I say? I'm a people person.

Officer: Is that what you did to Penny? Why you chose her? Tell us, what was it you felt she needed that you could use against her?

Mike: I didn't use anything against her. I loved her. We were going to be a real family.

Officer: I see this idea of 'a real family' has come up a lot in interviews so far. Tell me, what is it about family that is so important to you?

Mike: I don't know. It's just life, isn't it? Family. It's good. The ways things are meant to be.

Officer: Now, we know a bit about your own parents, Mike. A report I have here says they died in a caravan fire when you were a boy on holiday.

Mike: That's right.

Officer: And you were out at the beach at the time?

Mike: Correct.

Officer: Conveniently, perhaps?

Mike: Well, I didn't die, did I?

Officer: Can you tell me about them? Were you a happy family?

Mike: Not particularly.

Officer: Can you elaborate for us?

Mike: I don't want to.

Officer: And after their death, you were taken into foster care until you turned eighteen and inherited the house. Is that correct?

Mike: You already know these answers so why are you asking me all this?

Officer: We're just trying to understand, Mike. It would help you, to help us.

Mike: I don't want to talk about my parents.

Officer: What about any siblings?

Mike: I'm an only child. I'm sure you already know that.

Officer: We do. But what's interesting to us is that we asked the victim's sister to write a statement with everything she knew about you. In it, she writes that Penny once told her you had a little brother who'd died. Maybe you can help us out here, Mike, because as you just told us, there never was a little brother, was there?

Mike: No comment.

Officer: No comment? It was just another lie, wasn't it? You see, we're trying to understand you, Mike. Paint a picture. Was changing yourself and lying about who you are simply a way to gain trust? Would you say you're a pathological liar?

Mike: Go to hell.

Officer: OK, let's go back to Penny then, shall we? At what point did you realise she was still alive and hadn't drowned on the ninth of August nineteen-ninety, like everyone else believed?

Mike: I saw her from the boat. A flash of white. She could have been mistaken for a wave breaking but it was in the wrong place. It didn't fit with the pattern of waves around it. I couldn't be certain what I'd seen, of course, but I had to know if she'd made it out alive. So I went looking for her.

Officer: But you didn't tell anyone else what you saw?

Mike: No. They weren't looking hard enough. I saw her. Not them. I saved her. And she loved me for it. For a while at least.

Officer: What about later? What happened next? Did she ever want to leave?

Mike: Eventually, but by then there was no going back. I loved her and she loved me. In my eyes that made us family, and real family don't abandon each other, even when things get tough. They don't turn on each other. They love, unconditionally.

Officer: See, Mike, this is what I mean. Everything always comes back to this idea of what a family is and how it functions.

Mike: And?

Officer: For the sake of the recording, I'm now presenting Exhibit C. We found this book in your bedroom. It struck the officer searching as slightly strange to have a children's book by your bed when there are no young children living in the house. Again, for the record, the title of the book is *My Dad and Me* by Charlotte Rice. Now, Mike, what's really of interest here are the hand-drawn pictures and notes written on the pages. Is that your handwriting and did you draw the pictures?

Mike: It is and yes, I did.

Officer: For the record, the pictures show numerous illustrations of a man and a woman with their faces mutilated in different ways, and there are a number of notes around the text written about supposed rules of family. Can you tell me who the drawings are of?

Mike: My parents.

Officer: Your mum and dad?

Mike: Yes. Obviously.

Officer: Can you tell me their names?

Mike: Frank and Penny Hawksmoor.

Officer: See, that's very interesting, don't you think? Your mum's name was Penny, just like Penny Taylor. Is that why you picked her? Did she remind you of your mother, Mike? Did you want to recreate with her a love that your mum never showed you?

Mike: Fuck off.

Officer: OK, OK, let's take a beat. If we go back to the book, it's clear that the idea of family is an important one to you. Something, I think it's fair to say from the notes in the margins, you became obsessed with. Was being a dad important to you? Is that why you brought Lily down from the loft?

Mike: A child needs its parent.

Officer: And she could no longer be with her mum, could she, because you'd killed her?

Mike: Penny forced me do it. She was trying to leave me. Again.

Officer: And where is she now? Can you tell us what you did with her body? We have officers combing your property for her. It would save everyone a lot of trouble if you could just answer the question.

Mike: You've taken everything from me. My daughter. My house. My family. So I'm afraid, my answer is no. I won't let you take Penny, too. She's mine.

Eleven Months Later

Chapter Fifty

Rosey, now

It has taken months for Mike to finally add Rosey to his visitor list – although from her understanding of the situation, she will be the first visitor he's had since his arrest. Rosey can't believe it's actually happening, she's feeling a weird mixture of emotions about it all. Excited is the wrong word – she has nothing but hatred for the man – but she wants the opportunity to speak with him. To look him in the eye and demand answers. In truth, what she's excited for, is to gain some closure. She hopes he gives it to her. In a somewhat full circle moment which she hadn't planned, the visitation date she was given has fallen on the day before she's arranged to holiday back on Osea Island with everyone again, Lily and Owen included. It feels like fate, as if this meeting is meant to be. That everything will work out.

The drive to the prison takes two hours, and she can feel her nerves building all the way there. She'd checked before leaving that the visit was still scheduled to happen, but in prison, two hours is a long time. Things change quickly. She's desperate to be allowed in and hopes nothing has occurred during her drive to get it cancelled. She's been careful about what she's wearing too, as the prison has strict rules for visitors. Nothing low cut and no midriff on show. No sportswear. The simplest thing can mean they turn you away.

When she arrives, she shows her passport and is given a white card to transfer a small amount of money on to for the vending machines inside the prison. It's the only form of money allowed through the prison barriers at the front. Once she's been allowed through, she's escorted along a grey drab corridor into a large room with no windows. Two long tables have been set up and she's told they are all to sit along the right side. Once they're allowed in, the inmates will sit along the left. As she enters the room, she gives Mike's surname to the officer on the door, and he ticks her name off his list before giving her a number. Seat 13.

Before finding her place at the table she heads over to the vending machine and buys food and drink for their meeting. The last thing she wants is to be kind to the man who killed her sister, but she also wants to do anything and everything she can to increase his willingness to talk. To give her the answers she so desperately wants. After stocking up, she finds her seat, and she waits.

Everything about him is the colour grey. Greying hair, grey skin a symptom of being deprived of enough natural light, grey sweater and grey jogging bottoms. Everyone else around them takes advantage of the brief physical interaction that is allowed at the start of each meet, but the two of them remain on their opposite sides of the table. There is no love here. Mike looks at the food and drink planted on their table and raises his eyebrow at her. Smug bastard. She wants to punch him in the face. Instead, she digs her fingernails into the palm of her hand and stays seated. It takes all of her strength to remain in control of her anger. It has been eleven months, but nothing has erased the grief of knowing Penny was murdered. That perhaps she could have saved her.

'Thank you for meeting with me,' she forces herself to say, digging her nails harder into her palms. He doesn't say anything and when she forces herself to raise her eyes and finally look at him straight on, she realises that he is staring at the necklace hanging around her neck. It is her 'R' necklace. The matching one to Penny's, 'P'.

She supposes it must be strange for him to face her now – the mirror image of the woman he killed. Older, sure, but she's certain it won't be lost on him that she is the spitting image of the life he cut short. But Rosey detects no sense of remorse. In its place, she is surprised to see the shape of a cruel smile spreading across his lips.

'Why do you still wear that?' he asks her, a glint of something in his eye. What game is he playing here?

'Out of habit, maybe. I don't know. It reminds me of Penny.' Rosey watches as Mike flinches at the use of her name.

'It's not like you need it anymore though, is it?' he says and Rosey's shock deepens. Is he really boasting about killing Penny?

'I suppose not.' She forces the words out, twisting her ankles around each other trying to force herself to remain in control. To stay sitting and not lunge across the table towards this monster. She came with an agenda, and that means keeping him talking.

'I mean,' he continues, spreading himself wider, lounging on his chair as if suddenly he holds all the power. 'It's not like you need a prop anymore. Is it? Something to help you pull off your sick little game.'

Rosey freezes.

'I don't know what you're talking about,' she says, instinctively reaching for the necklace and holding it tightly between her finger and thumb.

'Oh, I think you do.'

'You knew? Did Penny tell you?'

'She didn't have to. I saw you. I was watching. When you went off into the forest on your little walk, I followed you. I saw what you did. Heard everything you said and realised this was more than a one-off party trick.'

Rosey folds her hands in her lap and closes her eyes as he speaks. Concentrates on her breathing. It may not be what she expected to hear, but it is, after all, what she has come for. The truth.

'Did you watch us a lot?' she asks, thinking back to the photo she found all those months ago showing him in the background. Watching. Hunting his prey.

'I was more interested in Penny than you. I like watching people. It's what I do.'

'Do you get off on it?' She regrets it as soon as the words leave her mouth. Curses her stupid attitude. It has always gotten her – and Penny – into trouble. He looks at her, bemused, as though it makes him feel powerful to see he's elicited a reaction from her. It strikes her then that Mike has also approached their meeting with an agenda. He wants to let her know that he still has something over her and Penny. That although he is the one behind bars, he still has some power.

'Did you use it against her?'

'No, I'd never do such a thing. But I told her that I knew it was her, not you, at the top of that lookout tower with Eloise when she fell.'

'Did you threaten her?'

'Me? I just pointed out that it wouldn't exactly look good on you both if people found out about your game. Untrustworthy. I think that was the word I used.'

'It wasn't her fault. Eloise died because Penny was trying to act like me. If I wasn't so – I don't know, me – then she never would have climbed that tower in the first place. She was showing off. Making it the Rosey-Show. She was trying to show me how much of an arsehole she thought I was. And then she couldn't face her own guilt and that's why she so desperately wanted to go to the police and to tell the truth. She felt responsible and she wanted to make it right. But you preyed on that vulnerability, didn't you? You knew she felt guilty, couldn't live with what she'd done, and you manipulated her into leaving Osea. Then you never let her come home. You took her from us. From me.'

'That's a vivid imagination, Rosey. You've been reading too many books in that job of yours.'

'I'm right though, aren't I? She was vulnerable and you took advantage of her. You lied and you pretended to be someone you weren't. You pretended to be helping her when in fact you were doing the very opposite. And then you killed her. You killed my sister!'

'But I wasn't the only one pretending, was I? Can you really sit there and judge me for lying? For putting on a mask?'

Rosey falls silent, because what else is there to say when you're confronted with the uncomfortable truth of it? Penny and Rosey had been lying to people ever since they were eight years old. Before that summer, they hadn't swapped identities since they were eighteen years old and had gone to separate colleges, but that day with Eloise in the woods, Rosey had convinced Penny to do it one last time.

She'd been reluctant at first, keen not to have to pretend to fancy Robbie, but Rosey had assured her they wouldn't switch for long. That he wasn't going to expect anything of her while they were all together in a group, and that they could swap back at any time if she felt too uncomfortable. *Please*, she remembers begging, *you are clearly moping about feeling left out, so let's do something that's just for us again. You and me, back together. Come on, Penny. Besides, I'm curious if we can even do it still. Aren't you?*

In the end, Penny had agreed and the two of them had swapped clothes, and necklaces, right there in the forest. And then they'd marched through the trees back to the group, with Penny wearing Rosey's red dress, fully committed to putting on one last performance.

Instinctively, Rosey reaches again for her necklace as she gets lost in the memory. The guilt swirls inside of her. Was it all her fault? Right from the very beginning? She wipes away a tear before it can fall, determined not to let the monster sitting in front of her see her cry.

'Oh come on now, Rosey, don't be too hard on yourself. We all have our little secrets. Life would be no fun, if we didn't,' he says, mocking her from where he leans back in his chair. Legs splayed wide. He is enjoying this, and it hits Rosey that of course a man like him – the man who murdered Penny and kept his own child locked up for years – must have other secrets. That acts of evil aren't just committed suddenly with no warning signs, and as the thought settles over her, she wonders what else he might be guilty of.

Chapter Fifty-One

Mike, 1976

The smoke was thick and black as it curled and danced its way up towards the sky. Mike didn't stay long, had to reach the beach before anyone saw him, but he couldn't stop himself from glancing behind him to watch it every now and then. It was beautiful, and it was the end.

He hadn't planned to kill them, but now that he had, he felt something he rarely ever did. Joy. Earlier that day, his dad had warned him they were on holiday, which meant while they had brought him with them, they wanted to see as little of him as possible. Mike knew his best bet was to stay out of their way, but that day the winds were strong and he'd forgotten to bring a hoodie with him to the beach. He'd stuck it out as long as he could, but eventually he'd headed back.

Letting himself into the caravan quietly, he'd hoped he could sneak in to grab a jumper and then leave again without being seen. Usually, his parents spent most of their holidays getting high, drinking or fighting. It was late afternoon, which meant there was a good chance they were both passed out by now. As the door creaked open and he stepped inside, he could see his mum lying on the small two-seater sofa. Through the crack of a door, his dad's shoes could be seen on top of the bed in the bedroom off the main living space.

His black hoodie was over the back of the sofa where his mum was sleeping and, feeling a little braver and safer now, Mike edged his way closer. It happened just as he leant over her, his face horribly close to hers. It made him jump. The way her body had started jolting and frothy white sick started leaking from the corners of her mouth, but her eyes had stayed shut. She was on her side, and he knew she would have positioned her body that way purposefully to avoid choking on her own vomit.

All it took was one small push on her shoulder to roll her on to her back. One push and a little patience as he waited and watched; it really had been that easy. He stood over her until the shuddering stopped and then he knew he needed a plan. There was no way Mike could let his dad find his mum. Everything would just get worse for him. He would have solved nothing. And so, he'd acted quickly, with his dad still asleep in the other room.

He'd slid the cigarette packet and lighter out of his mother's bag, but not before removing the battery in the fire alarm. He'd heard it only takes sixty seconds for a caravan to become fully engulfed by flames, so he'd waited until the very last second to strike it. Dropped it from the top of the caravan steps, and then he'd run as fast as he could back the way he'd come.

Fourteen years of hell, and it really had been that easy to end it all and take back control. His father had always said he was a coward; that Mike didn't have it in him to be a man. Well, if only they could see him now, he thought, as he made it back to the beach, picked up a stone and skimmed it across the sea's surface triumphantly. He'd only gone and fucking done it. *I'm the king of the world*, he'd howled at the top of his voice.

Chapter Fifty-Two

Lily, now

It took a couple of months of careful forensic work, combing the house and its foundations inch by inch, but eventually they found Penny in the kitchen. No, not in it. Under it. Along with her body they found the original pole used to open the loft hatch. Now, rebranded as 'the murder weapon'.

Mike Hawksmoor had buried her in the concrete floor of the kitchen/diner extension he'd built – the part of the house which had become the centre of our lives. Rage boils inside of me when I think about all the family occasions we'd celebrated in that part of the house, specifically. The way Mum's absence would be particularly present in those moments, and how often I'd think to myself how lucky I was to have Dad. All the Christmas dinners, the birthday meals, the Friday night takeaway tradition we'd upheld for years; had it made him feel powerful? Knowing he'd encased her under the very floor we were standing on? Was he gloating?

The police helped set me up with my own therapist and for the past eleven months I've had almost daily sessions with her to help reclaim my memories and process them. Not that it would have been possible to hide from the truth again; only a few days after Dad had tried to hang himself, I'd become spotlight news on television. My face was published on the front page of newspapers for months. I'd had to delete my social media – the comments were mostly empathetic, but it was the vile ones that I couldn't push from my mind. The ones who said they bet my mother deserved it. Or even insinuated that I had known and been complicit in my silence for all these years.

Reading those comments, I'd found myself wanting to defend Dad – to say we'd actually been happy for most of those years. That in some ways, he'd been a great dad. But when I think about it more carefully, knowing what I now know, I don't think that's true either. He was controlling and possessive. His moods dictated our days, and it was never, ever, worth rocking the boat. It's hard to remember sometimes. To not let the good memories make me doubt the bad ones. The psychiatric report ahead of his trial used words like 'narcissist', 'delusions of grandeur' and 'psychopathic traits possibly as a result of childhood trauma'. Was all of it a lie? Was his love and kindness towards me simply part of his own trauma? His delusions and obsessions about family and his strict rules about what was right and wrong? Or was some of it real? I know I have to accept the fact I'll never know. My dad, the monster.

I'm still experiencing flashbacks, although they're not as violent as before; my subconscious is no longer having to fight for the memories to burst through. Instead, I experience them more as nightmares again. It's frustrating, to still feel I haven't moved on and that there's a part of what Mike did to us that has changed me for ever, but I know not to expect too much of myself. Trauma doesn't leave you: it burns a mark deep on to your soul and, while it may heal, it never disappears.

I can at least convincingly say it is starting to fade. No longer a raw purple angry scar, it is transitioning into a calmer, fainter mark. Still, even I was surprised that I accepted when Aunt Rosey invited us all back to Osea Island this summer. That's what I call her now – not just Rosey, but Aunt. It's hard to explain to others how in hindsight my week there is something I can now look back on almost fondly. Without it, I don't know how much longer it would have taken me to uncover the truth again. Most importantly, it brought me back to my mum. Now, when I close my eyes, I can see her. I can smell her. It feels almost as though I should be able to reach out and touch her. For that, I will always be grateful. Even if by remembering, the rest of my world shattered around my feet.

The car rumbles loudly across the causeway and Owen drives with one hand upon my knee, eyeing me cautiously the closer we get to the island. I kiss him softly to let him know I'm OK. My relationship with Owen has been another surprising thing since last summer. Whether or not I will ever be able to fully trust a man again, I don't know, but I sure as hell can try to rewrite my own script. To not let Mike and his abuse dictate every part of me for the rest of my life. I am trying my best to take back control. That's what Mum wanted us to do so it's what I'm going to try and achieve, for the both of us. She wanted me to be happy. To live.

Owen reaches for the radio, cranking the music up, and then he opens the roof of his convertible. I look at him and see the glint in his eye. I don't even have to say anything for him to read my mind and he gives me a nod. That's how close we've become over this past year. I remember last summer when he'd handed me a life jacket and how I'd felt that my trip to Osea might one day save me – I never could have guessed how accurate that feeling would become.

I undo my seat belt and stand up, letting the wind race through my hair as we speed along the causeway. Now this is what freedom tastes like. I throw my arms wide open and look up towards the sky. A large flock of brent geese are flying right above us as if escorting us towards the island. In the distance, I see a tiny figure waiting for us on the pier and I know it will be Joe, ready to welcome us back to the island with open arms.

While I am struggling to come to terms with the acceptance of who Mike really was and what he was capable of – as I try to pick up the pieces of my shattered life – out of the debris I have also found a new family; one which is full of people who once also loved my mother. There is something precious about that fact.

I did it Mum, I think, *I really did it. I escaped.* And I know that she would be proud of me. Glad that, in the end, she didn't die for nothing.

Chapter Fifty-Three

Rosey, now

They'll be arriving any minute, but first, Rosey has one last thing she needs to do. So, while Stef and Robert have taken the boat out for the morning, she takes the opportunity to walk up the small hill to the church and cemetery where Penny's grave still stands. Once they'd exhumed her body, she'd asked, with Lily's permission, to have her remains brought to Osea for a proper funeral. At last, she's at peace.

As is usual, Rosey is the only one in the cemetery today. It is just her and the birds. She kneels in front of Penny's gravestone and places fresh flowers on the ground. Rosey is tired. So tired. She is still keeping so many secrets; no one else apart from Mike knows about how they used to trade places with each other. How deep their deception was woven. And she certainly hasn't told anyone that while she didn't know Mike was the one behind Penny's disappearance, or that she had been in danger, she did know she hadn't drowned. She can't forgive herself for that, let alone expect forgiveness from anyone else.

She tells herself that admitting it all to Robert or to Lily will achieve nothing. In telling them, she'd stand to lose everything she has. And then what will it all have been for; the lies upon lies to protect herself, if only to burn it all down? Yet, there is one secret that it's time to finally let go of. If Penny deserves something from Rosey even after death, it's this. And so, she sits in front of Penny's grave, and she begins.

Rosey thinks back to their eighteenth birthday, which was the day so much had changed for her. Penny had left early in the morning for a swim and Rosey had sauntered downstairs to make a cup of coffee, excitement fizzing through her for the celebrations ahead, when she'd heard Chrissy out in the garden through the kitchen window. She was alone and sat at the small white garden table with her head bent over. It sounded to Rosey as if her mother was praying. She'd listened, quietly, careful not to disturb, and that's when she heard it. Her mother's confession. Asking for forgiveness on her children's eighteenth birthday and thanking God for allowing her to celebrate both her daughters' birthdays, not just one. Quietly muttered but clear as day, Rosey listened as Chrissy asked for forgiveness for choosing to save Penny that day.

Those were the words she used. *Choosing.* It swirled round Rosey's mind and the pain of it cracked her open. She knew she'd become even louder and more ostentatious in the years that had followed. Desperate to be seen. To be heard. To be worth something. She wonders now if perhaps that's where her guilt begins and where the threads of Eloise's death had started to be sewn. Because, in the end, if she had been different, more muted, then Penny might never have thought to climb the tower to the top while pretending to be her.

'I'm sorry,' Rosey says out loud. 'I'm sorry I never told you Mum chose you.' She is crying now, tears rolling off her nose and chin. Carefully, she undoes the clasp of her 'R' necklace round her neck. She digs a small hole in the ground beside Penny's gravestone, and she drops it in. She doesn't need it anymore. That part of their life is over. Penny is dead. There's only Rosey left.

'I'm sorry. It was meant to be you who lived, not me.'

She piles dirt back on top of it, closes her eyes, counts back from five just as Penny always told everyone to do when they were feeling overwhelmed, and then she walks away.

She knows Lily and the rest of the group will have arrived by now and be waiting for her at the cottage when she gets back. If she'd escaped Mike and survived, would Penny ever have forgiven her for everything that had happened that summer? For leaving her on the other end of the phone line when she'd asked for help? For letting everyone believe she was dead even when Rosey knew that no longer to be true? She very much doubts it. She doesn't deserve forgiveness. But luckily for Rosey, Lily can't forgive, nor resent, what she doesn't know.

And so, she plasters a smile on her face, and marches back to the cottage ready to be greeted as Aunt Rosey. It's like she's always said, patterns are hard to break and old habits die hard. We are all products of what came before us and what happens next is a result of what we do now; it is almost impossible to avoid the butterfly effect. Once again, Rosey tries to find the light in it all – a way to keep going – and she wonders to herself, does it make us all less guilty?

Chapter Fifty-Four

Chrissy, 22 January 1970

Chrissy was the kind of tired you can feel in your bones. She'd wound all the car windows down, not just because it was too hot in the car but also because the wind on her cheeks was keeping her awake. Usually, at least one of the girls would have been causing enough noise to help her stay alert, but by some kind of miracle they were both fast asleep in their car seats.

After it had happened, she was certain she hadn't fallen asleep. That she'd fought against the need to blink and simply not open her eyes again. But the headlights in front of them had seemed to appear out of thin air. Where had the van come from and why was it on the wrong side of the road? Too late, she'd realised with a jolt of fear that it wasn't the van that was on the wrong side, it was her. She must have closed her eyes for longer than she'd realised and drifted lanes.

Chrissy didn't scream at first. She was too shocked to make a sound. Instead, she swerved. Hard and fast. *Too fast*, she realised, as she lost complete control of the car. The scream finally arrived and poured out of Chrissy's body as they smashed through the bridge railings, and it continued to pierce the air as they landed in the river below; as the nose of the car dipped below the surface.

She was still screaming even as water began to leak through every crevice in the vehicle's body. The water swirled around her ankles and she felt the flow of the river trying to pull the car back towards the low bridge.

The one good thing was that the feel of the water shocked her out of her fear and finally she stopped screaming. There was no time for that anymore. Without hesitation, Chrissy's protective instincts kicked in. She dived into the backseat and undid Penny's belt. Told her as firmly and stoically as possible that it would all be OK. That she was safe. They were all going to be OK. But no matter how many times she said it, she couldn't convince herself it was the truth. She knew, deep down, that nothing about their situation was OK.

Both children were now awake, screaming. Purple faces. Snot and tears. They were only eleven months old, but Chrissy could feel their fear expanding. It felt to her as though it were filling the car – making them even bigger and heavier, as if their fear alone was enough to sink them.

Chrissy knew there was no way she could get both children out of the car at the same time. It was simply impossible. They were too young. There was no way she could hold them both and swim at the same time. How long did she have until the car would be submerged completely?

She turned, kissing Rosey on the forehead and promising her that Mummy would be back. Then, she scooped up the child closest to her and, pushing with all her might, she squeezed through the open window into the freezing cold water.

By now the water inside the car was level with the seats. Chrissy had never known fear like it but imagined that this was what the end of the world felt like. Her world, certainly. Because she knew it would end right here, right now. It felt black, but not in an empty vacuum way. It was a blackness that felt overwhelmingly sad. Painful and all-consuming, as she knew she'd just made a promise she wasn't going to be able to keep.

It took a while for her to recover from the shock of the cold, which felt like knives against her skin as she swam to the riverbank. It was only once she became aware again of her surroundings that she registered their movements. Heard their shouts. It was as though until then, her brain had drowned out everything else other than the car and her children inside it. She'd only been able to concentrate on the freezing water that was going to kill one of them.

But now she saw that the van she'd swerved to avoid was parked on the other side of the bridge. Its doors had been flung open and two men hung over the side. She realised, incredulously, that they were using ratchet straps they must have had inside their van to secure the car to the bridge, preventing it from being pulled further underwater.

'She's still in there,' Chrissy screamed as loudly and wildly as she possibly could, still swimming to the side. 'You need to get her out. Please. Please save her,' she pleaded over and over again.

Finally, after what felt like for ever, she reached the bank of the river and hurled Penny on to the grassy side. She turned, ready to swim back, but saw the splash of one of the men jumping in. They'd heard. Thank God. They were going to save Rosey.

The other man was running towards her. She was still in the river, unable to bring herself to get out. He reached her and began trying to pull her out. Telling her she needed to get out of the cold. She refused, pushing his hands away from her. There was no way she was leaving the water before she knew what had happened to her child still trapped in the car. It would feel too final to be on dry land while she was still stuck in the water, drowning.

Chrissy screamed with relief as she watched the man who had jumped into the water finally haul himself and Rosey's small frame out of the car window. He swam on his back, with her daughter on his chest, to the bank on the opposite side of the river.

They were safe.

Chrissy no longer resisted as strong hands hurled her out of the water. It was OK. The world was going to keep turning. They were alive. All three of them.

And then the guilt washed over her with such force that she screamed so hard it made her throw up. She'd only been able to save one of them. If the men hadn't had the ratchet straps in their van, her decision would have saved one of her children and killed the other.

She was a mother. How was she supposed to live with that?

They had all survived, but for months, years even, she'd lie in bed each night replaying every thought that had raced through her mind that day. She'd try to remember it differently, but the truth of it always played out exactly the same. Her guilt wouldn't let her remould it or make it more palatable.

Because as she'd laid on the grass waiting for the paramedics, miraculously clutching both babies safe at her side, she'd decided never to tell the truth. How could she admit she'd consciously chosen one child over the other? No, she'd thought, it would be best if she pretended that in the chaos of it all, she hadn't known which identical twin was which.

And so that was the story she'd told, right from the very start. But inside, the truth of it had slowly killed her. Yes, their story had a happy ending – both children were saved – but in that moment, she had consciously saved one daughter and believed she'd knowingly condemned the other. It was a truth that could not be sugar-coated and that decision haunted Chrissy – it changed her. It made her smaller. She may have survived the crash, but she'd still lost part of herself that day.

A mother should never have to choose one child over the other; it was simply unnatural. The ripple effects would have devastating consequences and in the end, years later when the worst had happened, Chrissy believed it could all be traced back to the accident. To the decisions she'd made that day.

She believed that finally, fate had served up her punishment.

THE END

Acknowledgements

A huge thank you for choosing to read *One Dark Summer*. I hope you've enjoyed reading about Lily and Penny. One thing I want to acknowledge is that, whilst I've taken the real setting of Osea Island and drawn on the atmosphere and essence of this beautiful place with its unique location, I have also made it my own and used a certain degree of creative license! That creativity doesn't come without time or effort, and there is a whole team of people supporting me and making it possible for me to exist for hours at a time in my own head.

The first thanks has to go to my incredible agent, Juliet Mushens, who has continued to shower me with unwavering support. If Carlsberg were to make literary agents, Juliet is who they'd come up with.

Thanks to my editor, Phoebe Morgan, for her amazing editorial eye and guidance. I am eternally grateful to Phoebe for holding on to my vision for the story through the whole process and for her kindness, too.

Huge thanks to the team at Hodder for their hard work and support; Ross Jamieson, Jo Dickinson, Niamh Anderson, Alainna Hadjigeorgiou, Jake Carr, Kate Norman and Lisa Horton.

Thank you to my little army of friends and family who believe in me without fail. To Fran, Sophie, Lottie, Becky, John, Mum and Dad. To Luke and our two girls, Hazel and Florrie – this book has been written through some of our hardest times as a family. There were moments I could never imagine myself capable of writing . . . But here it is, and here we are. I love you all.

READ ON FOR AN EXTRACT OF
SARAH HORNSLEY'S DEBUT NOVEL

BAD BLOOD

Chapter One

I was seven when I learned aloe vera plants are the best remedy for burns. I'd been watching my mother from the kitchen doorway as she sliced the plant in half with a knife before scooping out its wet flesh and applying it to the top of her arm. Her burn had taken almost three weeks to heal, first turning a sloppy yellow in the middle before leaving a perfect circular scar I noticed every summer after. I never mentioned it; had jumped out of sight when she turned from the kitchen counter.

This is how I know the defendant is lying about the burn. I scribble it down on a piece of paper and pass it to where Charles Cole is standing midway through his cross-examination. He glances at it and then to me. I can see he's confused but he trusts me. I am his rising star and so, after only a moment's deliberation, he indicates for me to stand and makes his way back to the prosecution desk.

He is handing the court – our stage – over to me.

'Mr Jackson.' I smile at the defendant, though it isn't a friendly one. I am a wolf in a barrister's robe. 'I want to take a minute to go over the information you just gave the court.' I gesture towards the jury, making sure they understand I am about to reveal how he has lied to them. I want it to feel personal. 'On the twenty-second of November last year did you expect Peter Taylor to be in his home when you entered it?'

'I did not.' He shakes his head and I can tell he has no idea where I'm going with this. He thinks I am lost and playing for time.

‘When Peter did indeed turn out to be home, and he confronted you in his kitchen, can you tell the court again what transpired?’

‘Sure.’ He shrugs. ‘He attacked me.’

‘Can you describe the attack for the court?’

‘He rugby-tackled me to the floor and we fought a while, he kept trying to grab me round the neck but I managed to get away. I was trying to leave, had my back to him, when he must have grabbed the iron from its board where it stood at the side. The next thing I knew, I felt a searing hot pain on my left shoulder.’

‘He burnt you with the iron?’

‘Yes.’

‘But he didn’t hit you with it? It’s a heavy object.’ I watch his eyes flit to his defence barrister, Rose Ballard, before answering me. She hadn’t prepared him for this line of questioning.

‘Well, he was quite far away from me at this point. I was trying to leave. I guess he lunged and it caught me.’

‘And what happened next?’

‘I spun around. He was much closer to me by then. He had the iron swung back as if he was about to whack me with it again.’

‘Can you tell me what was going through your mind when you realised he’d burnt you and was still holding the iron?’

‘I thought he was going to kill me.’ He looks over to the jury as he says it, all sad and forlorn-looking. What he doesn’t realise is he’s just delivered me the perfect answer.

‘And how exactly did you react to this?’

‘I stabbed him.’

‘How many times?’

‘Five. In self-defence.’

I pause, letting it sink in. Not just once, but five times. ‘OK. Can you confirm for me that the reason you stabbed Mr Taylor in self-defence was because he burnt you with the iron?’

'That's right. I had my back turned and was leaving. I'm telling you, he came for me.' I try not to smile, keeping my cards close to my chest for just a little while longer.

'Did you have any injuries as a result of Mr Taylor's assault?'

'We've been over this already,' he sighs, clearly tiring of my questioning. Good. The more frustrated they are, the more likely they are to make mistakes. We wear them down.

'Humour me,' I say, gesturing theatrically and making some of the jurors snigger.

'I have a scar on the back of my shoulder.'

'And this scar was there when the police arrested you one week after Peter Taylor was killed in his kitchen. Correct?'

'That's right. They have photos and everything. I ain't lying.' I raise my eyebrows. He is starting to sweat.

'So you were caught by the iron badly enough for it to scar. And that same burn had healed one week after the injury was first sustained, allowing the police to take photos of the area as shown during the trial when you were arrested one week after the attack?'

'Erm.'

'Just answer the question please. It's a simple yes or no.'

'Yes.'

'During the period of time between the burning and your arrest – just one week – did you receive any medical advice or treatment? Did you google how to treat a burn? Was there anything you did to help it heal?'

'Not that I can remember.'

'The thing is, Mr Jackson, a second-degree burn, which is what you would need to have sustained for it to scar as shown in the photos, takes at least two to three weeks to heal and that's even using the best treatments around.'

'Well not for me,' he says forcefully, the puppy-dog eyes from earlier turning into something a little more threatening. *That's right, I'm on to you.* The adrenalin is pumping faster through my veins now. This feeling, it is addictive.

'I put it to you that it did in fact take precisely the normal two to three weeks for the burn on the back of your shoulder to scar. It could not have been sustained during the alleged assault you were subjected to by Mr Taylor but must have happened before you even entered his home, otherwise it would still have been an open wound at the time of your arrest.

'To be clear, whatever caused you to get that scar must have been inflicted at least – and I repeat, at least – one week prior to the incident you're currently on trial for. In fact, I think given this scar is the only injury you can point to having sustained from Mr Taylor, that there was no attack at all from the victim and you killed him in his home without being provoked.

'Importantly, you killed him not as an act of self-defence but simply because you could.' He doesn't say anything, just gawps looking like a rabbit caught in headlights. 'Mr Jackson,' I raise my voice, 'am I correct? Did you sustain your burn before the night in question?'

I watch as he rubs his hands over his face, leaving red finger marks trailing down his cheeks. He is cracking.

We are going to win.

The robing room sounds a lot more majestic than it is, but the romance of it is not to be underestimated. I always find that I need this time and the camaraderie found here, even between opposing sides, to make the transition from hard-nosed barrister back to functioning human. Without it, I wonder if my marriage would have survived this long. If I'm honest, I highly doubt it. The two sides of me, constantly pulled in opposite directions. One part doggedly determined to win no matter the cost; the other desperate to find stability. I can't seem to make my mind up on what exactly I define as 'success'.

That's why, as Rose asks if I'm joining them in The Ship for Lara's birthday drinks later, I hesitate. Lara works for the same chambers as Rose and I first got to know her from frequenting the well-known barrister haunts of London, such as The Ship, after work hours. Our paths have crossed a couple of times in the courtroom, too. I would bet the majority of people I work with will be out tonight.

Everyone knows that important work still gets done during the hours spent at the pub. As old-school as it sounds, it is still our reality. The problem is that you never know quite when those important conversations will take place, so it's not like you can strategically show up then make a speedy exit. They could happen at ten p.m. Maybe one a.m. Frequently at three a.m. Never before nine. You're in it for the long haul or you might as well not go at all.

And so, instead, I make my excuses, offering my biggest smile to the woman I just spent the past six hours up against in court. I remove my wig that is the same off-white colour as the worn walls and gather my things before heading home. I tell her it's my and Noah's fifth wedding anniversary but decide to leave out the fact he isn't even home for it because he is away on business in Paris; that my evening will be spent sharing a dinner hundreds of miles apart relying on a dodgy Wi-Fi connection to summon some kind of romantic atmosphere.

It's a far-cry from how we spent last year's anniversary – mostly with our bodies entwined at a hotel in Oxford, where they serve only locally sourced produce and have large fireplaces in every room. I smile back at the memory of it – it really was the perfect weekend, spent with my perfect husband. Absurdly expensive for one night, I admit – but given this year is a bit of a miss, maybe next year I'll suggest we stay there again.

'Well done today, Justine,' Rose calls after me, 'formidable as always, but next time I'll win.' I can hear the smile in her voice. Any trace of bitterness is gone. You can't hold a grudge in this business. Not if you want to survive.

'We'll see about that,' I call over my shoulder and smile to myself as I push open the door, though I make sure it doesn't linger too long. I have always made a point not to celebrate my court successes. There's something a little distasteful about being responsible for locking someone up. That's not to say they don't deserve it or that it isn't the right thing to do, but over the duration of a case you get to know the defendant. Not personally of course, but it feels like I become them.

I like to think of it as a character study, doing what I do. You simply can't ignore the nuances of it all, how each event in someone's life has shaped them. What if you could unshackle them from all of it? Start again, reborn. Do people deserve a second chance?

In my line of work the answer is no, but I spend one hour a week with my therapist, Aya, convincing myself that I am deserving of exactly that. Rationalising that I am worthy of spending luxurious weekends away in fancy hotels with my loving husband.

The thing about red wine is that no matter how earthy or smoked it supposedly is, all I can smell as it swirls around my glass is the distinct iron zing of blood.

'Cheers,' we say in unison, all smiles as we pretend to clink our glasses together.

I look at the image of Noah over the rim of my glass; his suit is still on from a long day at the office but his shirt is now open at the collar, his tie discarded, and I think about how different he is to the husband I'd always imagined myself to have. I push it away. Allow myself to be happy. He is handsome, very handsome, and he is kind.

The two don't normally go hand in hand, count yourself lucky, my mother's voice echoes.

And, while my skin crawls at the double standard of it – that a woman should, without exception, be always both beautiful and likeable – she is right. I am lucky. From the moment I opened the front door this evening, Noah has clearly been on a mission to make tonight feel special. A bottle of champagne – Bollinger, no less – delivered to the house along with a bunch of white roses (my favourite), and instructions to turn on a new Spotify playlist he has made with songs from our wedding.

I'm allowed to be happy. I am worthy. Do not push Noah away.

It's a trait of mine, when things feel like they are spiralling out of my control, to push Noah away. As though the easiest way to deal with my fear of losing him is to not have him in the first place. That way no one can take him away from me. Or, worse, him decide he no longer wants me. The problem is, I have been feeling overwhelmed a lot recently.

I hear a knock on his hotel room and a small voice announces room service.

'Ah ha! The pièce de résistance,' he exclaims before dashing off-screen to open the door and retrieve his apple crumble. Noah is not normally the type of man to exclaim, nor dash, and I can tell he's trying to make an effort, even though we are apart.

While he is away, I sneak a look at my phone. I'd promised him a phone-free (meaning work-free) evening and true to my word had put my work phone in the office drawer, but I'd kept my personal one tucked under the screen, out of sight. I'm not sure why – I suppose I've fallen victim to constantly needing to feel connected to people rather than happy in my own company.

Aya suggests the noise of social media helps keep my own

thoughts at bay. She labels it 'unhealthy'. I feel the itch creep along my fingers and before I realise I'm doing it, I've logged on to Instagram to see how my colleagues are getting on at Lara's birthday drinks. There's nothing on my newsfeed. In fact, there's nothing new at all since the last time I looked, and I find myself absent-mindedly typing into the search bar at the top of the app.

Jake Reynolds.

It's a habit I haven't been able to shift. Nearly eighteen years ago, it was only Facebook I would find myself searching through but now there's Instagram and Twitter too. Each time, I'm presented with a long list of Jake Reynoldses but not one of them is him.

I don't know why I still do it. It's not like I expect him to suddenly show up at the top of my screen after all these years. But just like unlocking your phone or checking your emails become habits, typing his name into search bars has become ingrained in my muscle memory. I don't consciously do it, but I can't stop either.

I feel the guilt worm its way in, that on my anniversary it is Jake who I am searching for. I love my husband, I really do, but your first love never leaves you. And Jake was no normal first love. He saved me. And then he left me. I suppose that's one of the reasons the next guy I fell in love with was Noah. In some respects, the two of them are similar; they both made me feel safe, but the ways in which they achieved that were entirely different.

Jake made me feel safe enough to be myself, to let loose, to free myself from any shackles of expectation. I was allowed to feel big. Being with Jake was like putting loud music on and finding yourself dancing to it without a care in the world.

With Noah it is different. He is steady. Secure. I feel safe he will not abandon me. It isn't an explosive kind of love – we aren't the most flamboyant couple in the world – but it is just as strong in a different way. It is secure. Steadfast. Real.

We've even started thinking about trying to get pregnant. Well, Noah has. The thought of being a mother doesn't feel the most natural thing for me. That title, 'mother', and everything it would mean. It's not an easy thing to be.

What if I fail? Not everyone is cut out to be a mother. I know the harm that can be done if you don't do it well. Would I be a good one? I'm not so sure. If I'm honest, I think Noah talking about having a baby soon has fed into my feeling overwhelmed recently. It has reminded me of my own mother. Of her shortcomings. Of everything I would hope not to be.

Noah returns to his laptop full of gusto as he shows me his plate of food from across the ether and I push my phone further out of sight. Take a large gulp of my red wine and tell him it looks delicious. That I wish I were there sharing it with him. He smiles back at me and I push away the encroaching doubt; the voice inside my head asking, 'But is that really true?'.

LIFE IN ENGLAND non-stop through the 1970s

▪ News ▪ Football ▪ TV ▪ Cinema ▪ Pop Music
▪ Cars ▪ Beer ▪ Cigarettes

A Chronicle of Memories.

Ian Palmer

First edition published 2024

Gift Book For Dad
Rugeley
Staffordshire

ISBN 978-1-840-41038-9

The information in this book has been compiled from numerous sources over many years. The final text is arranged as a chronological review, designed to evoke memories of a time long past and to aid study of that era. This book describes events and popular culture from a particular time in history and reflects the values of those times. Readers might find some of the material offensive when judged by modern day standards.

All phrases, slogans and lyrics quoted are for study and review purposes.

The author and publisher cannot be held responsible for any errors or inaccuracies.

One or two fictional snippets may have been added for devilment.

Christmas 1969

Morecambe & Wise TV Christmas special

Monarch:	Queen Elizabeth II (aged 43)
Prime-minister:	Harold Wilson (aged 53)
Chancellor:	Roy Jenkins (aged 49)
Home Secretary:	James Callaghan (aged 57)
Foreign Secretary:	Michael Stewart (aged 63)
Football Manager:	Alf Ramsey (aged 49)
Radio 1 Breakfast DJ:	Tony Blackburn (aged 26)
New car reg. suffix:	'H'

▪ The nation prepares for Christmas ▪ The *TV Times* costs 1s/6d, has a fourteen day schedule showing ITV television programmes and features 37-year-old Des O'Connor (in a red Santa hat and white beard) on the front cover ▪ The *Radio Times* costs 1s/6d, has a fourteen day schedule showing BBC programmes and features an artful yule-tide collage (which includes images of Tommy Steele, Jimmy Tarbuck, Elvis Presley, Rolf Harris, three of the seven dwarfs, a wild stag, Eric Morcambe, Ernie Wise and 43-year-old Jimmy Savile) on the front cover ▪ There's thick fog across much of the country ▪ Three people are killed and dozens more injured in multiple crashes on the M6 motorway ▪ 53-year-old Labour prime-minister Harold Wilson chairs a Cabinet meeting at Number 10 Downing Street, with 59-year-old Barbara Castle (Secretary of State for Employment and Productivity) and 39-year-old Shirley Williams (Minister of State for Home Affairs) in attendance ▪ 44-year-old Conservative MP (and Shadow Education Secretary) Margaret Thatcher tells her Finchley constituents, "No woman in my time will be prime-minister or foreign secretary - not the top jobs. Anyway, I wouldn't want to be prime-minister" ▪ "Something in the way she moves, attracts me like no other lover"

- The double A sided single *Something / Come Together* by The Beatles moves down the hit parade to number eight ▪ 38-year-old Bert Foord presents the weather forecast on BBC One ▪ Dense fog gives way to brisk winds and sharp, clear skies ▪ Mao 'flu sweeps the South East of England, with tens of thousands of people suffering headaches, pain behind the eyes and violent coughing ▪ 'It's groovy, baby' - 42-year-old Roger Moore and 25-year-old Claudie Lange star at cinemas in *Crossplot* - a film with a story based around a modelling agency in Swinging London ▪ 29-year-old Robin Phillips plays the title role in *David Copperfield.* The all-star supporting cast includes: 46-year-old Richard Attenborough, 32-year-old Susan Hampshire, 45-year-old Ron Moody, 62-year-old Sir Laurence Olivier, 61-year-old Michael Redgrave and 66-year-old Sir Ralph Richardson ▪ "You've painted up your lips and rolled and curled your tinted hair. Ruby, are you contemplating going out somewhere?" - *Ruby Don't Take Your Love To Town* by 31-year-old Kenny Rogers and the First Edition climbs to number two in the pop chart and stays there for six weeks ▪ *Sugar Sugar* ("... you are my candy girl, and you got me wanting you") by The Archies remains at number one for one more week before being replaced by *Two Little Boys* by 39-year-old Rolf Harris ▪ Children are excited - Christmas is coming! ▪ Schoolboys crave a die-cast model of the *Batmobile* (manufactured by *Corgi Toys*) for 13s/6d ▪ Schoolgirls crave a *Sindy* doll (manufactured by *Pedigree*) for 25s/3d ▪ Housewives crave a seasonal tipple ▪ A bottle of *Harvey's Bristol Cream* sherry is 24s/11d ▪ A bottle of *Warnink's* advocaat is 32s/- ▪ The Smith family from Chigwell hires a new-fangled colour TV set from *Radio Rentals* ▪ Two more commercial television companies begin broadcasting in full colour and viewers in the Southern TV region and in Scotland can now watch their favourite programmes in colour ▪ "We are the Diddymen, itsy-bitsy Diddymen" - *Ken Dodd and the Diddymen* is hugely popular with younger viewers ▪ Teenagers enjoy listening to music on portable HMV record players ▪ *Abbey Road* by The Beatles is top of the album chart ▪ Hallmark Records release *The Best of Top of the Pops "69"* - a budget priced, cover-version pop compilation LP with pretty girls on the sleeve ▪ *Wonderful World Beautiful People* ("... you and your girl, things could be pretty") by 25-year-old

Jimmy Cliff is number six in the pop chart ▪ *The Liquidator* by The Harry J Allstars is number nine ▪ In an act of frustration, 23-year-old footballer 'super' Georgie Best knocks the ball from the hands of referee Jack Taylor after a League Cup semi-final defeat to Manchester City. Best will now face FA disciplinary action for his petulance ▪ 36-year-old Frank Bough introduces *Grandstand* on BBC One on Saturday afternoons ▪ 42-year-old Sam Leitch previews the football ▪ 25-year-old Franny Lee (of Manchester City) misses a penalty and 34-year-old Jack Charlton (of Leeds Utd) heads a goal from his brother's corner kick, as Sir Alf Ramsey's England team (Bonetti, Reaney, E Hughes, Mullery, J Charlton, Moore, F Lee, Bell, Astle, R Charlton, Ball and substitute, Peters) beats Portugal 1-0 on a rain sodden Wembley pitch ▪ In Division One, 19-year-old Alan Whittle scores for top-of-the-table Everton in a 0-1 victory over West Ham Utd at Upton Park ▪ 31-year-old Wimbledon tennis champion Ann Jones is voted BBC's 'Sports Personality of the Year' ▪ 33-year-old Gordon Honeycombe reads the news for ITN ▪ The Troubles prevail in Northern Ireland ▪ Sectarian violence is commonplace as skirmishes continue between Loyalists, Nationalists and the Royal Ulster Constabulary ▪ The Provisional Irish Republican Army (a splinter group of the IRA) is formed ▪ Back in England - people enjoy an evening at the cinema ▪ 30-year-old George Lazenby is the new James Bond (aka 007) in *On Her Majesty's Secret Service*. 31-year-old Diana Rigg captures Bond's heart and becomes his screen wife - but with tragic consequences. 45-year-old Telly Savalas plays master criminal Ernst Stavro Blofeld. 61-year-old Bernard Lee is M. 55-year-old Desmond Llewelyn is Q. 42-year-old Lois Maxwell is Miss Moneypenny ▪ 35-year-old Alan Bates and 31-year-old Oliver Reed wrestle naked in front of the fire in *Women In Love* ▪ "If you're looking for trouble, I'll accommodate ya" - 62-year-old John Wayne stars in *True Grit* ▪ The abolition of the death penalty is made permanent by 57-year-old Home Secretary Jim Callaghan ▪ "I have been a rover, I have walked alone. Hiked a hundred highways, never found a home" - *Love's Been Good To Me* by 54-year-old Frank Sinatra from New Jersey is number eight on the hit parade ▪ *Without Love (There Is Nothing)* by 29-year-old Tom Jones from Pontypridd is number ten ▪ A fire at the Rose and Crown

in Saffron Walden kills eleven people ▪ The outbreak of Mao 'flu spreads from the South East to other areas of the country. People take to their beds with extra blankets and hot water bottles ▪ An eighteen mile stretch of dual carriageway opens between Horwich and Preston in Lancashire ▪ 'Well off' young men drive their cars, hard and fast, on the country's ever-expanding network of motorways ▪ A brand new 'H' reg Ford *Escort Twin Cam* costs £1,242, has a 1600cc engine (manufactured by Lotus), a top speed of 113 mph and accelerates from 0-60 mph in 9.9 seconds ▪ The latest *Mini 1275GT* costs £834, has a redesigned front end and 'go-fast' stripes, a top speed of 91 mph and accelerates from 0-60 mph in 14.5 seconds ▪ A Singer *Chamois Sport* costs £779, has twin headlights, a top speed of 90 mph and accelerates from 0-60 mph in 16.3 seconds ▪ 'Here we go! Morning ray-dee-oh!' - 26-year-old Tony Blackburn presents the breakfast show on Radio One ▪ *Two Little Boys* ("... had two little toys. Each had a wooden horse") by 39-year-old Rolf Harris from Australia stays at the top of the pop chart for six weeks ▪ "The world is just a great big onion" - *The Onion Song* by 30-year-old Marvin Gaye and 24-year-old Tammi Terrell reaches number nine ▪ *Green River* by Creedence Clearwater Revival peaks at number nineteen ▪ Schoolboys read comics ▪The Christmas edition of *Whizzer and Chips* (with 'Sid's Snake' and 'Me and My Shadow') is on sale at newsagents for 6d ▪ 53-year-old prime-minister Harold Wilson and 49-year-old Chancellor of the Exchequer Roy Jenkins are relieved to see significant improvement in Britain's economy ▪ The balance of payments has moved into a surplus of £100 million - it's the first time in ten years that the value of exports has been greater than the value of imports ▪ More than 300,000 men are employed in the coal industry - many working long, hard shifts in dangerous conditions. 156 million tonnes of coal have been produced in 1969 - that's 54 million tonnes fewer than ten years ago ▪ Working-class families gather around black and white television sets ▪ Affluent, middle-class families gather around colour TV sets ▪ Just under 100,000 colour TV licenses have been issued this year, compared to over 15 million black and white licenses ▪ Morecambe & Wise feature in their first ever Christmas Day TV 'special' - Frankie Vaughan, Nina, Sacha Distel and 42-year-old Fenella Fielding are the

guest stars ▪ 20-year-old model Twiggy appears on ITV's *This Is Your Life* ▪ "All my sorrow, sad tomorrow. Take me back to my old home" - ***R**eflections Of My Life* by The Marmalade climbs to number three in the pop chart ▪ 44-year-old Pete Murray and 48-year-old Jimmy Young spin records and chat to their devoted listeners on Radio One on weekday mornings ▪ 11-year-old Simon Mayo from Southgate in Middlesex dreams of one day becoming a famous DJ ▪ 18-year-old footballer Steve Perryman scores his first league goal for Tottenham Hotspur in a 2-0 victory over Crystal Palace ▪ 23-year-old 'super' Georgie Best plays for Manchester Utd on Boxing Day (in front of 52,732 spectators at Old Trafford) in a 0-0 draw against Wolverhampton Wanderers in Division One ▪ 18-year-old Kevin Keegan plays for Scunthorpe Utd (in front of 7,796 spectators at London Road) in a 2-2 draw against Peterborough Utd in Division Four ▪ Schoolboys update their football 'League Ladders' each week ▪ Just one point separates Harry Catterick's Everton (with West, Labone, Kendall, Ball, Morrissey and Royle) from Don Revie's hard-tackling Leeds Utd (with Sprake, Charlton, Bremner, Giles, Lorimer and Clarke) at the top of Division One ▪ 22-year-old Peter 'Ossie' Osgood scores four goals as third placed Chelsea thrash Crystal Palace 1-5 at Selhurst Park ▪ *Yester-Me, Yester-You, Yesterday* by 19-year-old Stevie Wonder is number two in the pop chart ▪ "Take a pinch of white man, wrap it up in black skin, add a touch of blue blood, and a little bitty bit of Red Indian boy" - *Melting Pot* by Blue Mink is number three ▪ Motoring technology moves on apace ▪ More and more cars are being fitted with an electronically heated rear window ▪ Middle-class men visit car showrooms ▪ A fabulous new Saab *99* has a top speed of 102 mph and costs £1,295 from the Gunner & Allen dealership at Lee-on-Solent ▪ A wonderful new Volvo *144* has a top speed of 88 mph and costs £1,515 from Swanswell Garage in Coventry ▪ Working-class men stand together on football terraces and cheer on their local team ▪ 19-year-old centre-forward Malcolm Macdonald bags a hat-trick as Luton Town thrash Bradford City 5-0 in front of 11,857 spectators at Kenilworth Road in Division Three ▪ 32-year-old Bobby Charlton is on the score-sheet as Manchester Utd beat Liverpool 1-4 in front of 47,682 spectators at Anfield in Division One ▪ Bill Shankly sells 31-year-old striker

Roger Hunt to Bolton Wanderers for £30,000 ▪ "I wish to complain about this parrot what I purchased not half an hour ago from this very boutique" - 30-year-old John Cleese and 26-year-old Michael Palin perform the 'dead parrot sketch' on *Monty Python's Flying Circus* ▪ "This is the planet Earth. Our planet. It is a small planet, wrapped in clouds" - The *Clangers* is new on TV for children ▪ Families listen to music on Ferguson *Solid State* radiograms ▪ "We can't go on together, with…" *Suspicious Minds* by 34-year-old Elvis Presley climbs to number two in the pop chart ▪ "I've got to leave old Durham Town, and that leaving's gonna get me down" - *Durham Town (The Leavin')* by 33-year-old Roger Whittaker is number twelve ▪ The Kinks play gigs in Canada ▪ The Rolling Stones play to three hundred-thousand people in California - with Hells Angels providing security around the stage ▪ 18-year-old Meredith Hunter is stabbed and killed ▪ Back in England - The Who play non-stop, two-hour concerts at Liverpool (Empire), London (Coliseum) and Newcastle-upon-Tyne (City Hall) ▪ Construction work is nearing completion on the new Strensham to Tewkesbury section of the M5 motorway ▪ The weather turns cold and frosty ▪ Families huddle together in small living rooms - watching TV ▪ *The Rolf Harris Show* - starring 39-year-old Rolf and featuring dance troupe The Young Generation (which includes 23-year-old Lesley Judd) is enjoyed by millions ▪ 43-year-old Jimmy Savile introduces *Pop Goes The 60s* - a look back at the music of the last decade. The programme features music from: The Bachelors, Kenny Ball and his Jazzmen, The Beatles, Cilla Black, Adam Faith, The Hollies, Horst Jankowski, The Kinks, Lulu, Cliff Richard, The Rolling Stones, The Shadows, Helen Shapiro, Sandie Shaw, Dusty Springfield, The Tremeloes and The Who ▪ 53-year-old Labour prime-minister Harold Wilson sits in an armchair, studying official papers and smoking his pipe ▪ At midnight on the thirty-first of December, crowds of people in clubs and pubs all across the country celebrate the new year - and the dawning of the 1970s ▪ Millions of men enjoy a beer and a smoke ▪ A pint of bitter is 2s/2d ▪ A pack of five Castella cigars is 9s/8d ▪ Adverts say, 'Castella. The man-sized cigar for the man who likes his pint.'

New Year 1970

Raindrops keep falling on my head

Monarch:	Queen Elizabeth II (aged 43)
Prime-minister:	Harold Wilson (aged 53)
Chancellor:	Roy Jenkins (aged 49)
Home Secretary:	James Callaghan (aged 57)
Foreign Secretary:	Michael Stewart (aged 63)
Football Manager:	Alf Ramsey (aged 50)
Radio 1 Breakfast DJ:	Tony Blackburn (aged 27)
New car reg. suffix:	'H'

▪ A groovy new decade begins ▪ The weather is cold and frosty ▪ Families gather around coal-effect, two-bar electric fires ▪ "My love, the days are colder. So let me take you by your hand and lead you through a snow white land" - *Winter World Of Love* by 33-year-old Engelbert Humperdinck is number eight on the hit parade ▪ *Tracy* ("... you're gonna be, happy with me. I'll build a world around you") by The Cuff Links is number nine ▪ Trade unions push for higher wages for their members ▪ Heading off a possible 'avalanche' of pay claims, 59-year-old Barbara Castle MP (Minister for Employment in Harold Wilson's Labour government) warns union leaders that any demands for wage increases has to match productivity otherwise retail prices will rise ▪ 53-year-old prime-minister Harold Wilson leaves the UK and flies across the Atlantic Ocean ▪ "We are together, and being together a great deal is possible" - 57-year-old US president Richard Nixon greets Mr. Wilson with warm words as the two leaders meet for talks at the White House in Washington ▪ Back in Britain - the half-crown coin is no longer legal tender. (Money is set to be decimalised one year from now) ▪ "Oh, Arr-thur!" - a new TV series of *On the Buses* begins, with 33-year-old Anna Karen as Olive, 39-year-old Michael Robbins as Arthur, 53-year-old Reg Varney as Stan, 37-year-old Bob Grant as Jack and 43-year-old Stephen Lewis as Blakey ▪ 'X' certificate films are popular at the cinema ▪ Crowds flock to see *A Promise of Bed* - a 'far out' sex comedy, starring 40-year-old Victor Spinetti, 21-year-old Dennis Waterman, 33-year-old John Bird and 21-year-old Vanessa Howard ▪ 42-year-old Sam Leitch reports on football matters for BBC One's

Grandstand TV programme ▪ 51-year-old Arsenal manager Bertie Mee signs 19-year-old striker Peter Marinello from Hibernian for £100,000 ▪ 34-year-old Derby County manager Brian Clough signs 27-year-old defender Terry Hennessey from Nottingham Forest for £110,000 ▪ 23-year-old Manchester Utd star 'super' Georgie Best is fined £100 and suspended for four weeks by an FA Disciplinary Committee ▪ 26-year-old rock star Mick Jagger is fined for possession of cannabis ▪ 23-year-old Keith Moon accidently drives his Bentley over his chauffeur, Neil Boland, and kills him ▪ "When I was just a little boy, you know my one and only joy was list'nin' to that..." *Good Old Rock'n'Roll* by The Dave Clark Five is number seven on the hit parade ▪ "No one ever seems to care, just as long as they were there. Friends beside you..." *Friends* ("... to guide you") by Arrival climbs from number eighteen to number eleven ▪ 11-year-old Simon Le Bon from Bushey dreams of one day becoming a famous pop star ▪ Elvis Presley, Tom Jones and Led Zeppelin feature on the front cover of the latest *New Musical Express* ▪ The first jumbo jet (a Boeing *747*) lands at Heathrow airport, carrying 324 passengers from New York ▪ 47-year-old Eamonn Andrews surprises 43-year-old Jimmy Savile on ITV's *This is Your Life* ▪ "Did you think I would leave you crying, when there's room on my horse for two?" - *Two Little Boys* by Rolf Harris remains at number one in the pop chart ▪ *Let It All Hang Out* by 25-year-old Jonathan King is number thirty-one ▪ 53-year-old leader of the Tory opposition Edward Heath and his shadow Chancellor, Iain Macleod, begin devising economic strategies based on a free-market economy - where 'consumer choice' is key ▪ A 22-inch colour *PYE* TV set costs £249 ▪ An *Electrolux* fridge costs 31 guineas ▪ A plain coloured *Bri Nylon* shirt is 32s/11d ▪ A striped *Bri Nylon* shirt is 35s/11d ▪ A pack of twenty Player's *No. 6* cigarettes is four shillings ▪ A pack of twenty menthol-fresh Consulate cigarettes costs 5s/5d ▪ 26-year-old boxer Smokin' Joe Frazier becomes the undisputed heavy-weight champion of the world - after beating Jimmy Ellis by a Technical Knock Out at Madison Square Garden in New York ▪ Back in England - 29-year-old footballer Jimmy 'Greavsie' Greaves scores a goal for Bill Nicholson's Tottenham Hotspur in a 2-1 victory over Brian Clough's Derby County ▪ 21-year-old goalkeeper Ray Clemence makes his league debut for Bill Shankly's Liverpool in a 1-0 defeat against Not-

tingham Forest ▪ 21-year-old Prince Charles joins the Royal Navy ▪ "Oh..." *Love Grows (Where My Rosemary Goes)* ("... and nobody knows like me") by Edison Lighthouse climbs to number one in the pop chart - and stays there for five weeks! ▪ "So kiss me and smile for me. Tell me that you'll wait for me. Hold me like you'll never let me go. 'Cause I'm..." *Leavin' On A Jet Plane* ("... don't know when I'll be back again") by Peter, Paul and Mary is number two ▪ *Skippy* - 'The Bush Kangaroo' is new on ITV ▪ 23-year-old footballer 'super' Georgie Best returns from suspension and scores six goals as Wilf McGuinness' Manchester Utd thrash Northampton Town 8-2 in the fifth round of the FA Cup ▪ 20-year-old Joe Royle scores twice, and 23-year-old Howard Kendall scores once, as Harry Catterick's high-flying Everton defeat Bobby Robson's Ipswich Town 3-0 at Goodison Park in Division One ▪ Aston Villa (currently struggling at the bottom of Division Two) sack manager Tommy Docherty and appoint 38-year-old Vic Crowe as his replacement ▪ "Oh baby, give me one more chance" - *I Want You Back* by The Jackson Five reaches number two in the pop chart ▪ "If you want it, here it is..." *Come And Get It* ("... But you'd better hurry 'cause it's goin' fast") by Badfinger reaches number four ▪ 24-year-old midfielder Alan Ball scores twice, and 23-year-old striker Peter 'Ossie' Osgood makes his international debut, as Sir Alf Ramsey's England team (G Banks, T Wright, Cooper, Moore, Labone, E Hughes, F Lee, Ball, Osgood, G Hurst, Peters) beats Belgium 1-3 in Anderlecht ▪ 35-year-old Johnny Haynes plays his final match for Fulham before retiring ▪ 'Billy's Boots' - schoolboy Billy Dane wears Dead-Shot Keen's old football boots in a fantastic new sports comic for boys called *Scorcher* ▪ 'People are the ultimate spectacle' - 32-year-old Jane Fonda, 29-year-old Michael Sarrazin and 31-year-old Susannah York star at cinemas in *They Shoot Horses Don't They* - a film directed by 35-year-old Sydney Pollack ▪ 'Not that it matters, but most of it is true' - 44-year-old Paul Newman and 33-year-old Robert Redford star in *Butch Cassidy and the Sundance Kid* ▪ "Raindrops keep falling on my head, and just like the guy whose feet are too big for his bed, nothing seems to fit" - 37-year-old Sacha Distel sings *Raindrops Keep Falling On My Head* - and the song climbs to number ten in the pop chart ▪ "Come on, come on..." *Let's Work Together* by Canned Heat is number two ▪ The Hillman *Avenger* motorcar,

with distinctive 'hockey-stick' shaped rear lights, is launched. The *de Luxe* model costs £766, the *Super* is £811 and the *Grand Luxe* is £903. Top speed of the *Avenger* (with 1500cc engine) is 91 mph ▪ The latest Alfa Romeo *Spider* now has a square tail instead of a rounded tail ▪ Prime-minister Harold Wilson returns from a visit to Canada, New York and Washington ▪ Labour MPs claim that Anglo-American relations are stronger than ever, in stark contrast with some of the rows that had developed between the two countries when Sir Anthony Eden and Harold Macmillan were prime-ministers ▪ "He'll never love you, the way that I love you" - *Na Na Hey Hey Kiss Him Goodbye* by Steam is number nine in the pop chart ▪ "Sing a song of…" *Temma Harbour* ("… climb a coconut tree. Catch a fish and light a fire, drink some wine with me") by 19-year-old Mary Hopkin is number six ▪ 25-year-old Cyd Hayman stars alongside Robert Hardy on ITV in *Manhunt* ▪ 50-year-old Jon Pertwee is the new *Dr. Who* on BBC - taking over from 49-year-old Patrick Troughton. In this new series, entitled 'Spearhead from Space', the newly regenerated Doctor is on planet Earth, helping Brigadier Lethbridge-Stewart (played by 40-year-old Nicholas Courtnay) investigate a mysterious meteorite shower ▪ Actor Jimmy Hanley dies of cancer aged 51 at Fetcham in Surrey ▪ Schoolboys accidentally break miniture plastic footballers when playing *Subbuteo* ▪ A tube of *Bostik* costs 1s/6d ▪ 7-inch vinyl pop records cost 3s/11d ▪ The double A sided single *The Witch's Promise / Teacher* by Jethro Tull is number four in the pop chart ▪ *Led Zeppelin II* is top of the album chart ▪ The sun shines in late February ▪ People feel good about the future and book their holidays for the summer ▪ *SkyTours* offer low priced package holidays abroad ▪ Eight days in Majorca costs around £29 ▪ Fifteen days in Corfu is £70 ▪ New housing estates with modern semi-detached, three-bedroomed homes are springing up all around the country - some of the new properties come with gas central heating already installed! ▪ The average price of a house in the UK is £4,300 ▪ With the economy now in a healthy state, 53-year-old Labour prime-minister Harold Wilson considers calling a general election - but doesn't do so yet ▪ "Instant Karma's gonna get you. Gonna knock you right on the head" - *Instant Karma!* by Lennon/Ono with the Plastic Ono Band peaks at number five in the pop chart.

Spring 1970

Harry Catterick's Everton are Champions!

Monarch:	Queen Elizabeth II (aged 44)
Prime-minister:	Harold Wilson (aged 54)
Chancellor:	Roy Jenkins (aged 49)
Home Secretary:	James Callaghan (aged 58)
Foreign Secretary:	Michael Stewart (aged 63)
Football Manager:	Alf Ramsey (aged 50)
Radio 1 Breakfast DJ:	Tony Blackburn (aged 27)
New car reg. suffix:	'H'

▪ 46-year-old Jack Scott presents the weather forecast on BBC One ▪ Unexpected snowstorms arrive. Depths of up to twelve inches are reported in the Midlands - and traffic grinds to a halt ▪ Roads are impassable - clogged by snow and ice ▪ An ERF *LV* six-wheeler truck ('F' reg) is stranded on the A65 near Otley ▪ A Foden *S40* eight-wheel tipper ('G' reg) is stuck on the A523 at Macclesfield ▪ People stay indoors and watch television ▪ A new series of *Steptoe and Son* begins (with 44-year-old Harry H. Corbett and 57-year-old Wilfrid Brambell) and now it's in colour! ▪ *The Adventures of Parsley* (a spin-off from popular children's programme *The Herbs*) is on TV for the first time ▪ The commercial television company HTV begins broadcasting in full colour and viewers in Wales and western England can now watch their favourite programs in colour ▪ *Magpie* (with 31-year-old Susan Stranks) is popular with teenage boys ▪ A repeat of *The Saint* (with 42-year-old Roger Moore) is popular with women of a certain age ▪ 54-year-old Labour prime-minister Harold Wilson welcomes 66-year-old West German Chancellor Willy Brandt for talks at Number 10 Downing Street ▪ "Wheels are made for rollin'. Mules are made to pack. I've never seen a sight that didn't look better looking back. I was born under a..." *Wand'rin Star* by 46-year-old Lee Marvin is number one in the pop chart ▪ *Gimme Dat Ding* by Pipkins is number four ▪ *All I Have To Do Is Dream* by 27-year-old Bobbie Gentry and 33-year-old Glen Campbell reaches number three ▪ The *Apollo 13* spacecraft develops a serious technical hitch on its voyage to the Moon and astronauts Jim Lovell, John Swigert and

Fred Haise radio through to Mission Control with the message, "Houston, we have a problem" ▪ Back in England - the weather clears and 34-year-old jockey Lester Piggott rides *Nijinsky* to victory in the Two-Thousand Guineas at Doncaster ▪ Don Revie's hard-tackling Leeds Utd football team beats Standard Liege 2-0 (on aggregate, over two matches) in the quarter-final of the European Cup and will now face Celtic in the semi-finals ▪ Revie fields an under-strength Leeds team in a First Division match against Brian Clough's Derby County - and loses 4-1 ▪ 42-year-old Alan 'Fluff' Freeman presents *Pick of the Pops* on Sunday afternoons on BBC Radio One ▪ "When all the broken hearted people living in the world agree, there will be an answer..." *Let It Be* by The Beatles (29-year-old John Lennon, 27-year-old Paul McCartney, 27-year-old George Harrison and 29-year-old Ringo Starr) is number two in the chart ▪ "But she can really do the..." *Brontosaurus* ("... and she can scream the heeby jeebies for us") by The Move (with, lead singer 23-year-old Roy Wood, drummer 25-year-old Bev Bevan and newly recruited guitarist 22-year-old Jeff Lynne) is number seven ▪ *Be Young, Be Foolish, Be Happy* by The Tams is number thirty-eight ▪ *Till* ("... the moon deserts the sky, till all the seas run dry. Till then, I'll worship you") by 54-year-old Dorothy Squires is number forty-four ▪ 42-year-old actor Roger Moore is on set in London, filming Basil Dearden's new movie, *The Man Who Haunted Himself* ▪ 33-year-old Gordon Honeycombe reads the news for ITN ▪ Production workers at car windscreen manufacturer Pilkington Glass go on strike ▪ British Leyland staff are on a go-slow. The corporation's chairman, Lord Stokes, says, "We don't control our factories, the work people do. People these days just walk out because a place is too hot, or too cold" ▪ 'D-Day. One Year From Now' - a short TV information film explains the new decimal currency system which will begin next year ▪ 23-year-old star footballer 'super' Georgie Best opens a fashionable new clothes boutique in Manchester called *George Best Rogue* ▪ "I still get..." *That Same Old Feeling* ("... tearing at this heart of mine") by Pickettywitch is number five in the pop chart ▪ "Like a..." *Bridge Over Troubled Water* ("... I will lay me down") by Simon and Garfunkle is new at number one ▪ 35-year-old writer David Nobbs pens humorous scripts and one-line gags for Les Dawson and other comedians ▪ 'The Carry On team in Starkest Africa' -

Carry On Up the Jungle is now showing at cinemas, with 53-year-old Frankie Howerd as Professor Tinkle, 56-year-old Sid 'Ha-ak-ak' James as Bill Boosey, 42-year-old Terry Scott as Ug and with 26-year-old Valerie Leon (36-26-36) as leader of the all-women Lubby-Dubby tribe ▪ *You're Such A Good Looking Woman* by 30-year-old Joe Dolan is number seventeen on the weekly hit parade ▪ "Wise men say, 'Only fools rush in.' But I..." *Can't Help Falling In Love With You* by 42-year-old Andy Williams is number three ▪ The legal voting age in Britain is lowered from 21 to 18 ▪ Younger people vote for the first time at a by-election in Bridgwater - where Tom King is elected for the Conservatives ▪ The bodies of 11-year-old Susan Blatchford and 12-year-old Gary Hanlon are found in woodland at Lippitts Hill in Epping Forest. Police begin a manhunt for the murderer, but despite numerous public appeals, the perpetrator cannot be found ▪ Cambridge win the Boat Race for a third consecutive year ▪ *L'Escargot* wins the Cheltenham Gold Cup, at odds of thirty-three to one ▪ 18-year-old Dana wins the Eurovision song contest for Ireland, singing *All Kinds Of Everything* ("… remind me of you") - and the record reaches number one in the pop chart ▪ *Knock, Knock Who's There?* by 20-year-old Mary Hopkin is number two ▪ 'M*A*S*H gives a D*A*M*N' - Robert Altman's dark comedy *M*A*S*H* (starring 34-year-old Donald Sutherland, 31-year-old Elliott Gould, 36-year-old Tom Skerritt and with 32-year-old Sally Kellerman as Major 'Hot Lips' Houlihan) is at cinemas ▪ 37-year-old Ray 'Dracula' Reardon wins the Player's *No.6* World Snooker Championship - beating 46-year-old John Pulman by 37 frames to 33 in the final ▪ 23-year-old winger Glyn Pardoe scores the winning goal as Joe Mercer's Manchester City beat Alan Ashman's West Bromwich Albion 2-1 in the League Cup final at Wembley ▪ 30-year-old Jimmy 'Greavsie' Greaves plays his final game for Tottenham Hotspur before transferring to West Ham Utd in an exchange deal for 26-year-old Martin Peters ▪ Peters scores on his debut for Spurs in a 1-2 defeat against Coventry City at White Hart Lane ▪ Greavsie scores twice on his debut for 'The Hammers' in a 1-5 victory over Manchester City (on a quagmire pitch) at Maine Road ▪ 23-year-old 'super' Georgie Best is sent off for Northern Ireland (in a match against Scotland) for throwing mud at referee Eric Jennings ▪ 41-year-old racing driver Graham Hill makes his return to Formula One

(in the South African Grand Prix) after breaking both legs five months ago ▪ Schoolboys keep up to date with the escapades of Skid Solo in *Tiger and Jag* comic - on sale at newsagents every Monday for 7d ▪ Don Revie's hard-tackling Leeds Utd lose a two-legged European Cup semi final against Celtic. The first leg is a 0-1 defeat in front of 46,381 spectators at Elland Road. The second leg is 2-1 defeat in front of 136,505 spectators at Hampden Park ▪ 'He's not my daddy. He's my husband' - 19-year-old Susan George stars alongside 48-year-old Charles Bronson in the movie *Twinky* ▪ "Oh, mother tell your children not to do what I have done. Spend your lives in sin and misery in the..." *House Of The Rising Sun* by Frijid Pink is number four on the hit parade ▪ *Who Do You Love* by Juicy Lucy is number fourteen ▪ Arsenal beat Anderlecht 3-0 on a muddy Highbury pitch to turn around a 1-3 deficit from the first leg - and win the Inter Cities Fairs Cup 4-3 on aggregate ▪ Manchester City beat Gornik Zabrze 2-1 in the European Cup Winners Cup final in Vienna - with goals from Neil Young and Franny Lee ▪ Back in England - 32-year-old Bobby Charlton and 23-year-old 'super' Georgie Best score the goals as Manchester Utd draw 2-2 with Sheffield Wednesday in front of 36,649 at Old Trafford ▪ Harry Catterick's Everton beat West Bromwich Albion 2-0 in front of 58,523 at Goodison Park - to clinch the First Division title, with two games of the season still remaining. Gordon West, Tommy Wright, Keith Newton, Howard Kendall, Brian Labone, Tommy Jackson, Colin Harvey, Jimmy Husband, Alan Whittle, John Hurst, John Morrissey, Sandy Brown, Alan Ball and 21-year-old top scorer Joe Royle have all been outstanding for 'The Toffees' ▪ Don Revie's hard-tackling Leeds Utd (with Sprake, Reaney, Cooper, Bremner, Charlton, Hunter, Madeley, Lorimer, Jones, Clarke, Giles, Gray, Yorath, Hibbitt and Bates) are runners-up ▪ Dave Sexton's Chelsea (with Bonetti, Webb, McCreadie, Hinton, Dempsey, Harris, Osgood, Hollins, Hutchinson, Hudson, Cooke, Baldwin and Houseman) are third ▪ 21-year-old Mick Channon has scored fifteen goals (in thirty-seven matches) for Ted Bates' Southampton - and 'The Saints' avoid relegation at the expense of Sunderland and Sheffield Wednesday ▪ "Prepare yourself. You know it's a must. Gotta have a friend in Jesus" - *Spirit In The Sky* by 27-year-old Norman Greenbaum reaches number one in the pop chart ▪ "They call me..." *The Seeker* ("... I've been searchin' low and

high") by The Who is number twenty-four ▪ Chelsea's Ron 'Chopper' Harris nobbles Leeds Utd's Eddie Gray early on in the FA Cup final (on a heavily sanded Wembley pitch) and the match finishes 2-2 after extra-time. (6-year-old Ged O'Brien from Reading attends the match with his dad). A ticket for the standing enclosure at the Empire Stadium costs 12s/6d. A seat in the South Terrace is twenty-five shillings ▪ Chelsea win the replay 2-1 at Old Trafford, with 23-year-old Peter 'Ossie' Osgood scoring a diving header ▪ Vic Crowe's Aston Villa and Alan Ball Sr.'s Preston North End are relegated to the Third Division for the first time in their histories ▪ *Farewell Is A Lonely Sound* by 34-year-old Jimmy Ruffin is number eight in the pop chart ▪ "To be…" *Young, Gifted And Black* by Bob Andy and Marcia Griffiths is number five ▪ Radio One's weekday schedule is - Tony Blackburn (7 a.m. to 9 a.m.), Pete Murray (9 a.m. to 10 a.m.), Jimmy Young (10 a.m. to 12 noon), Johnnie Walker (12 noon to 2 p.m.) and Terry Wogan (2 p.m. to 4.15 p.m.) ▪ Speculation in the media is rife: The Beatles are about to split up!? ▪ The group's latest LP, *Let It Be*, is number one in the album chart ▪ *McCartney*, the debut solo LP from 27-year-old Paul McCartney, is number two ▪ *ABC* ("… it's easy as 1, 2, 3") by The Jackson Five is number eight in the singles chart ▪ *Do The Funky Chicken* by Rufus Thomas is number eighteen ▪ Hollywood disaster movie *Airport*, starring 56-year-old Burt Lancaster, 52-year-old Dean Martin, 25-year-old Jacqueline Bisset and 69-year-old Helen Hayes, goes on general release at cinemas ▪ 'Dice was his vice. Men hers' - 33-year-old Warren Beatty stars alongside 38-year-old Elizabeth Taylor in *The Only Game in Town* ▪ Children watch *Play School*, *Jackanory* and *Marine Boy* on BBC One television at tea-time ▪ The four-wheel drive *Range Rover* 'off road' motorcar is launched. This wonderful new luxury car has a V8 engine and returns around 15 mpg ▪ Also new is the Triumph *Stag* sports car - a stylish convertible with a top speed of 115 mph and capable of accelerating from 0-60 mph in 11.6 seconds ▪ Adverts warn of the dangers of smoking in bed ▪ A pack of twenty Benson & Hedges *Gold Bond* cigarettes costs 4s/6d ▪ Tens of thousands of people are shocked and controversy ensues when *Oz* magazine publishes an image of Rupert the Bear with an erect penis ▪ 59-year-old Mrs. Mary Whitehouse is outraged ▪ Young people in denim jackets and flared jeans hang around on high streets ▪ A *Wimpy* hamburger

costs two shillings ▪ A King Size *Wimpy* is 3s/9d ▪ The average weekly wage in the UK is £31/4s ▪ Great excitement is building in the country ▪ There's huge expectation for England's world-champion footballers to perform well in the upcoming FIFA World Cup tournament in Mexico ▪ "We'll fight until the whistle blows, for the folks…" *Back Home* by the England World Cup Squad climbs to the top of the hit parade - and stays there for three weeks ▪ Players: Banks (Stoke City), Newton (Everton), Cooper (Leeds Utd), Mullery (Tottenham Hotspur), Labone (Everton), Moore (West Ham Utd), Lee (Manchester City), Ball (Everton), R. Charlton (Manchester Utd), Hurst (West Ham Utd), Peters (Tottenham Hotspur), Bonetti (Chelsea), Stepney (Manchester Utd), Wright (Everton), Stiles (Manchester Utd), Hughes (Liverpool), J. Charlton (Leeds Utd), Hunter (Leeds Utd), Bell (Manchester City), Osgood (Chelsea), Clarke (Leeds Utd) and Astle (West Bromwich Albion) carry the hopes and dreams of the entire nation ▪ *Daughter Of Darkness* ("… stay out of my life, my life") by 29-year-old Tom Jones is number five ▪ 54-year-old Labour prime-minister Harold Wilson calls a general election for the eighteenth of June and campaigning begins ▪ Anti-immigration parties are hoping to win plenty of votes ▪ John O'Brien succeeds Arthur K. Chesterton as chairman of the National Front ▪ 11-year-old schoolboy Steven Patrick Morrissey from Manchester sits in his bedroom writing clever lyrics ▪ "And when you stop and think about it, you won't believe it's true; that all the love you've been giving, has all been meant for you" - *Question* by The Moody Blues is number two in the pop chart ▪ "It was back in Louisiana, just about a mile from Texarkana, in them old…" *Cottonfields* ("... back home") by The Beach Boys is number five ▪ 71-year-old businessman Sir Jack Cohen retires from his position as chairman of *Tesco* ▪ 23-year-old footballer Keith Weller transfers from Benny Fenton's Second Division Millwall to Dave Sexton's First Division Chelsea for £100,000 ▪ 50-year-old wartime football legend Tommy Lawton is currently out of work and claiming unemployment benefit ▪ Men visit the off-license ▪ A (non returnable) bottle of *Skol* lager is 1s/4d ▪ A (non returnable) bottle of *Worthington* light ale is 1s/3d ▪ Adverts for stout say - '*Mackeson* - Taste the goodness!'

Summer 1970

Back home, they'll be thinking about us

Monarch:	Queen Elizabeth II (aged 44)
Prime-minister:	Edward Heath (aged 54)
Chancellor:	Anthony Barber (aged 50)
Home Secretary:	Reginald Maudling (aged 53)
Foreign Secretary:	Alec Douglas-Home (aged 67)
Football Manager:	Alf Ramsey (aged 50)
Radio 1 Breakfast DJ:	Tony Blackburn (aged 27)
New car reg. suffix:	'J'

▪ The sun shines ▪ Boys climb trees ▪ Children take their buckets and spades to the seaside ▪ Families enjoy picnics on the beach ▪ Everything is 'groovy' ▪ 58-year-old Jimmy Chipperfield opens a new safari park at Woburn Abbey and families travel from all around to see the monkeys ▪ The Pier Head building at Brighton Beach is deemed to be unsafe and is closed to the public ▪ Lester Piggott rides *Nijinsky* to victory in the Epsom Derby ▪ *Yellow River* ("… yellow river, is in my mind and in my eyes") by Christie is new at number one in the pop chart ▪ *Goodbye Sam Hello Samantha* ("… Goodbye Lou. Hello Louise") by 29-year-old Cliff Richard is number six ▪ *The Green Manalishi (With The Two-Prong Crown)* by Fleetwood Mac is number ten ▪ Deep Purple (Ritchie Blackmore, Jon Lord, Ian Paice, Roger Glover and 24-year-old, lead singer, Ian Gillan) feature on the front cover of the latest *New Musical Express* ▪ A fortnight later, Led Zeppelin (Jimmy Page, John Paul Jones, John Bonham and 21-year-old, lead singer, Robert Plant) are the 'heavy rock' stars on the cover of the popular weekly music paper ▪ Reports of friction between members of The Beatles continue and there's speculation that the band may soon split-up ▪ 25-year-old DJ Kenny Everett is sacked by Radio One ▪ 24-year-old footballer 'super' Georgie Best moves into a 'futuristic' £30,000 house at Bramhall in Cheshire ▪ 'Space! The final frontier' - *Star Trek* (with 39-year-old William Shatner as Captain Kirk and 39-year-old Leonard Nimoy as Spock) is on BBC One on Monday evenings ▪ 46-year-old Robin Day presents *Panorama* straight afterwards ▪ Millions of viewers tune-in for *It's A Knockout* on Wednesday evenings. (In one exciting contest, a

team from Margate plays its joker in the ‘Tea for Two’ event and goes on to beat a team from Ramsgate by eleven points to ten) ▪ *In The Summertime* by Mungo Jerry (with, lead singer, 24-year-old Ray Dorset) climbs to number one in the pop chart - and stays at the top for seven weeks! ▪ *Groovin’ With Mr. Bloe* by Mr. Bloe is number two ▪ *Honey Come Back* by 34-year-old Glen Campbell is number four ▪ ‘For safety learn the new wiring colours’ - there’s a change to the wire colours in 3-pin electrical plugs. ‘Live’ is now brown. (Previously it was red). ‘Neutral’ is now blue. (Previously it was black). ‘Earth’ is now green and yellow. (Previously it was green) ▪ The Reliant Motor Company launches the *Bond Bug*. The sporty ‘three-wheeler’ comes in bright orange, has a top speed of 75 mph and costs £629 ▪ *Everything Is Beautiful* (“… in its own way. Like a starry summer night or a snow covered winter’s day”) by 31-year-old Ray Stevens is number six in the pop chart ▪ *Sally* (“... Sally, pride of our alley”) by 37-year-old Gerry Monroe is number four ▪ Hundreds of workers at Lucas in Birmingham go on strike, demanding higher pay ▪ Thousands of workers at British Leyland are laid-off ▪ ‘When it comes down to it, aren’t Labour’s ideals yours as well?’ - campaigning is underway for the general election ▪ ‘For a better tomorrow, Vote Conservative’ ▪ “And I mean that most sincerely, folks” - 50-year-old Hughie Green presents a new series of *Opportunity Knocks* on ITV ▪ Long haired kids in flared jeans and tight fitting T shirts ‘hang loose’ and smoke weed ▪ *Alright Now* (“… baby, it’s alright now”) by Free climbs to number two in the singles chart ▪ Teenage rock band Stray release their eponymous debut album. *All In Your Mind* is the opening track on side one. *Only What You Make It* is the opening track on side two ▪ 41-year-old Leonard Parkin reads the news for ITN ▪ Politics and international sport are at odds ▪ A planned tour of England by the South African cricket team is cancelled. England’s captain Ray Illingworth scores 94 runs in a hastily arranged match against a Rest of the World XI at Lord’s ▪ 34-year-old children’s entertainer Rod Hull decides to move back to Britain (from Australia) and develop his popular act with an uncontrollable puppet called Emu ▪ *Up The Ladder To The Roof* by The Supremes is number six in the pop chart ▪ *I Will Survive* by Arrival is number sixteen ▪ There’s a flurry of activity on football’s transfer market ▪ Chelsea players, 24-year-old midfielder Alan Birchenhall and 28-year-old

striker Bobby Tambling leave Stamford Bridge and transfer to Bert Head's Crystal Palace for £140,000 ▪ 23-year-old striker Bobby Gould leaves Arsenal and joins Wolverhampton Wanderers for £55,000 ▪ 19-year-old goalkeeper Phil Parkes leaves Walsall and joins Queens Park Rangers for £15,000 ▪ 21-year-old midfielder Brian Horton leaves non-league Hednesford Town and joins Port Vale for the price of a pint of shandy ▪ Adverts say: 'He's only here for the beer - it's *Double Diamond*' ▪ 46-year-old Leslie Phillips stars at cinemas in *Doctor in Trouble* ▪ "Come on the rising wind, we're going..." *Up Around The Bend* ("... yeah!") by Creedence Clearwater Revival is number three in the pop chart ▪ "Many a tear has to fall, but..." *It's All In The Game* ("... All in the wonderful game that we know as love") by The Four Tops is number five ▪ The catchy pop song *Back Home* ("... they'll be watching and waiting and cheering every move") by the England World Cup Squad crackles from transistor radios all across the country ▪ 29-year-old England football captain Bobby Moore is arrested on suspicion of stealing a bracelet in Colombia and detained by police for four days ▪ Prime-minister Harold Wilson intervenes and Moore is set free and allowed to join his team-mates in Mexico ▪ Alf Ramsey's reigning world champions are poised and ready ▪ The FIFA World Cup tournament gets underway ▪ Referees use red and yellow cards for the first time ▪ *Adidas* introduces the iconic *Telstar* football ▪ England qualify for the knock-out stages by beating Romania (1-0) and Czechoslovakia (1-0) but losing to Brazil (0-1) - in a match where 32-year-old England goalkeeper Gordon Banks pulls off an incredible save from a header by 29-year-old superstar Pele. On the fourteenth of June at the Estadio Leon, 28-year-old Alan Mullery and 26-year-old Martin Peters score the goals to put England 2-0 up against West Germany in the quarter finals. Then disaster strikes. Late goals from Beckenbauer, Seeler and Muller secure a 3-2 victory for the Germans (after extra time) and England are out. Gordon Banks, Peter 'the cat' Bonetti, Keith Newton, Terry Cooper, Brian Labone, Bobby Moore, Alan Ball, Franny Lee, Bobby Charlton, Colin Bell, Geoff Hurst, Martin Peters and Alan Mullery all return home disappointed ▪ Back in England - the sun is shining ▪ 24-year-old footballer 'super' Georgie Best takes a spin in his *E-Type* Jaguar with model girlfriend Siv Hederby at his side ▪ "When the weather's fine, you got women,

you got women on your mind. Have a drink, have a drive. Go out and see what you can find" - *In The Summertime* by Mungo Jerry remains at number one in the pop chart ▪ "She walked up to me and she asked me to dance. I asked her name, and in a dark brown voice she said 'Lola'. L-O-L-A Lola, lo-lo-lo-lo..." *Lola* by The Kinks is number two ▪ 'Vice. And versa.' - *Performance* (starring 31-year-old James Fox, 27-year-old Mick Jagger and 28-year-old Anita Pallenberg) goes on general release at cinemas across the country ▪ *You Can't Win 'Em All* (starring 45-year-old Tony Curtis and 48-year-old Charles Bronson) is also now showing ▪ All around the nation, large outdoor posters convey messages from the big two political parties ▪ 'Now Britain's strong let's make it great to live in - Vote Labour' ▪ 'Labour's let you down. You'd be better off Conservative' ▪ The day of the general election arrives and 28 million people cast their votes ▪ 53-year-old Conservative Edward Heath is the surprise victor and takes over from Harold Wilson at Number 10. (Conservatives: 330 seats, Labour: 288 seats, Liberals: 6 seats) ▪ 44-year-old Margaret Thatcher is appointed Minister for Education and Science in the new government ▪ 56-year-old Chancellor of the Exchequer Iain Macleod dies after just one month in office and is replaced by Anthony Barber ▪ 43-year-old Conservative Geoffrey Howe is the new MP for Reigate ▪ 39-year-old Conservative Norman Tebbit is the new MP for Epping ▪ The film *Cromwell* is at cinemas - 39-year-old Richard Harris and 56-year-old Alec Guinness are the stars ▪ "Rainbow, look me up, look me down. Rainbow, you were fun to have around" - *Rainbow* by The Marmalade is number three in the pop chart ▪ *Signed, Sealed, Delivered, I'm Yours* by 20-year-old Stevie Wonder is number fifteen ▪ 32-year-old Caroline Thorpe (wife of Liberal party leader Jeremy Thorpe) dies in a car crash ▪ Jack Walker, landlord of 'The Rovers Return' in ITV's popular soap-opera *Coronation Street*, dies of a heart attack and his widow Annie is now in sole charge of the famous Weatherfield pub ▪ 24-year-old Douglas Fielding plays PC Alec Quilley in BBC's long-running police drama *Z Cars* ▪ 'Stalked by fear and terror ... night and day!' - 42-year-old Roger Moore stars at cinemas in *The Man Who Haunted Himself* ▪ 41-year-old George Peppard and 37-year-old Joan Collins star in *The Executioner* ▪ "But I'm doing all right now, rolling..." *Down The Dustpipe* ("... Na-na-na-na, nana-na-nana-na") by Status Quo

is number twelve in the pop chart ▪ "They paved paradise and put up a parking lot" - *Big Yellow Taxi* by 26-year-old Joni Mitchell peaks at number eleven ▪ Dock workers go on strike for higher pay - raising fears of possible food shortages in shops ▪ At the Wimbledon tennis championships, there's a double Australian victory with 26-year-old John Newcombe taking the men's singles title and 27-year-old Margaret Court taking the women's title ▪ 41-year-old racing driver Graham Hill (in a Lotus) finishes sixth in the British Grand Prix at Brands Hatch. 28-year-old Jochen Rindt from Austria (also in a Lotus) is the winner. 31-year-old Jackie Stewart (in a March) retires on lap 52 with clutch problems ▪ Young boys push toy cars across the carpet at home, or send them speeding down slopes of plastic track on the stairs ▪ *Matchbox* bring out *Superfast* die-cast model cars with new improved wheels ▪ The *Matchbox* model of a BP Service Station and Forecourt is extremely popular ▪ 'J' reg cars go on sale ▪ The new V6 Ford *Capri 3000GT* has a top speed of 122 mph and can reach 60 mph in 8.4 seconds ▪ A Gilbern *Invader* (manufactured in Wales) has a top speed of 124 mph and accelerates from 0-60 mph in 7.7 seconds ▪ Princess Anne is presented with a Reliant *Scimitar GTE* for her 20th birthday ▪ A new elevated section of M6 motorway opens between Walsall and Great Barr in the Midlands ▪ Four-star leaded petrol has risen in price to 6s/6d a gallon ▪ A leaflet called, 'Your Guide To Decimal Money' is widely available ▪ Heavy rain leads to flash floods in the middle of August ▪ A Vauxhall *Viva Estate* is submerged beneath water at Spon End in Coventry ▪ *In The Summertime* by Mungo Jerry remains at number one in the pop chart ▪ *Black Night* ("... is not right. I don't feel so bright") by Deep Purple climbs to number two ▪ "Like, crazy man! That's far out" - Jimi Hendrix, The Who and The Doors play the Isle of White festival, where 600,000 people attend (over five days). 27-year-old festival compare, Rikki Farr, addresses the crowd and tells them to, "Go to hell!" when some people break through the security barriers - in an attempt to gain free entry ▪ Elsewhere in the country, industrial unrest prevails and new prime-minister Edward Heath is under intense pressure ▪ Dock workers continue their strike ▪ Troops are put on standby and a State of Emergency is declared ▪ Production workers at Pilkington Glass in St. Helens have been on strike for two months ▪ Car production at British Leyland, Rover and

Jaguar has slowed because of a shortage of windscreens ▪ The commercial television company Tyne Tees begins broadcasting in full colour and viewers in the North East can now watch their favourite programs in colour ▪ Younger viewers in the region enjoy a repeat run of *Thunderbirds* on Fridays at teatime ▪ "That's the wonder…" *The Wonder Of You* by 35-year-old Elvis Presley climbs to number one in the pop chart - and stays there for six weeks! ▪ "I'm a Neanderthal man. You're a Neanderthal girl. Let's make Neanderthal love in this Neanderthal world" - *Neanderthal Man* by Hotlegs peaks at number two ▪ *Love Is Life* by Hot Chocolate reaches number six ▪ *Ace of Wands* is a new TV program for teenagers ▪ Millions watch as Elsie Tanner (played by 46-year-old Pat Phoenix) marries Alan Howard (played by 44-year-old Alan Browning) in ITV's *Coronation Street* ▪ 46-year-old Kenneth Kendall reads the news on BBC One ▪ The dock strike comes to an end after two weeks of disruption when union leaders accept a 7% pay rise ▪ Repeats of last year's series of *Dad's Army* are transmitted on BBC One on Saturday evenings ▪ 37-year-old Freddie Goodwin is the new football manager at Second Division Birmingham City ▪ 37-year-old John Bond is new at Fourth Division Bournemouth ▪ 24-year-old 'super' Georgie Best scores a goal as Manchester Utd lose 4-1 to Brian Clough's Derby County in the final of the Watney Invitation Cup at the Baseball Ground ▪ 25-year-old Everton captain Alan Ball wears trendy white football boots as 'The Toffees' beat Dave Sexton's Chelsea 2-1 in the Charity Shield at Stamford Bridge ▪ 23-year-old John Radford bags a hat-trick as Bertie Mee's Arsenal thrash Manchester Utd 4-0 at Highbury in Division One ▪ "That's the wonder…" *The Wonder Of You* by Elvis Presley remains at number one in the pop chart ▪ *Mama Told Me (Not To Come)* ("... That ain't the way to have fun, son") by Three Dog Night is number three ▪ New Conservative prime-minister Edward Heath takes a short holiday in Scotland ▪ 44-year-old Queen Elizabeth II spends time at Balmoral Castle ▪ 44-year-old Peter Sellers and 22-year-old Sinead Cusack star at cinemas in the dark and sinister *Hoffman* ▪ After weeks of speculation, 27-year-old Paul McCartney confirms that he has left The Beatles - and the 'Fab Four' are no more ▪ All around the world, pop music fans are devastated.

Autumn 1970

Pilton Pop Festival

Monarch:	Queen Elizabeth II (aged 44)
Prime-minister:	Edward Heath (aged 54)
Chancellor:	Anthony Barber (aged 50)
Home Secretary:	Reginald Maudling (aged 53)
Foreign Secretary:	Alec Douglas-Home (aged 67)
Football Manager:	Alf Ramsey (aged 50)
Radio 1 Breakfast DJ:	Tony Blackburn (aged 27)
New car reg. suffix:	'J'

▪ 54-year-old Edward Heath's Conservative government introduces the Industrial Relations Bill - triggering a wider rift with the unions ▪ Workers at Pilkington Glass in St. Helens continue their strike ▪ With no wind-screens being produced, thousands of men at British Leyland's Cowley and Longbridge factories are idle ▪ 29-year-old John Lennon and 37-year-old Yoko Ono record songs at Abbey Road Studios in London for their new album: *Lennon/ Plastic Ono Band* ▪ "Now if there's a smile on my face, it's only there trying to fool the public" - *Tears Of A Clown* by Smokey Robinson and the Miracles is new at number one in the singles chart ▪ The commercial television companies Ulster and Anglia begin broadcasting in full colour and viewers in Northern Ireland and in the east of England can now watch their favourite programs in colour ▪ *Magpie* (with 28-year-old Pete Brady, 26-year-old Tony Bastable and 31-year-old Susan Stranks) is a popular ITV tea-time show on Tuesdays and Thurs-days ▪ *Please Sir!* (with 29-year-old John Alderton and 56-year-old Dery-ck Guyler) is popular on Sunday evenings ▪ A new series of *Dad's Army* (with 55-year-old Arthur Lowe as Captain Mainwaring, 58-year-old John Le Mesurier as Sergeant Wilson, 50-year-old Clive Dunn as Lance-Corpo-ral Jones, 74-year-old Arnold Ridley as Private Godfrey, 73-year-old John Laurie as Private Fraser, 41-year-old James Beck as Private Walker and 24-year-old Ian Lavender as Private 'stupid boy' Pike) begins on BBC One on Friday evenings ▪ 'They had a message for the Army: Up the Brass!' - *Kelly's Heroes* is at cinemas. 40-year-old Clint Eastwood and 48-year-old Telly Savalas are the stars ▪ *War* ("... what is it good for? Ab-solutely nothing") by 28-year-old Edwin Starr climbs to number three in

the pop chart ▪ *It's Wonderful* by 34-year-old Jimmy Ruffin peaks at number six ▪ Children are back at school after the summer holidays ▪ Boys play conkers on the playground ▪ 11-year-old Robert Mortimer from Middlesbrough plays kiss-chase with the girls ▪ Footballers, Ray Kennedy, George Graham and George Armstrong score the goals for Arsenal as Bertie Mee's team thrashes West Bromwich Albion 6-2 at Highbury in Division One ▪ 20-year-old centre-forward Malcolm MacDonald bags a hat-trick for Luton Town in a 1-5 away win against Sheffield Wednesday in Division Two ▪ *Give Me Just A Little More Time* ("… and our love will surely grow") by Chairman of the Board climbs to number three in the pop chart ▪ "And if you're wondering what this song is leading to, I want to..." *Make It With You* by Bread is number five ▪ 42-year-old Alastair Burnet reads the news for ITN ▪ A *BOAC* passenger plane is hijacked en-route to Heathrow and forced to land at Dawson's Field in Jordan ▪ Back in England - David Lean's latest movie, *Ryan's Daughter* (starring 53-year-old Robert Mitchum and 57-year-old Trevor Howard), goes on general release at cinemas ▪ 43-year-old Don Revie's hard-tackling Leeds Utd are the early league leaders in Division One ▪ 23-year-old Peter Lorimer scores twice as Leeds beat newly promoted Huddersfield Town 2-0 at Elland Road ▪ 32-year-old Bobby Charlton of Manchester Utd makes his 500th league appearance for the club as Utd lose 0-1 at home to Crystal Palace ▪ 27-year-old Ernie Hunt of Coventry City scores an amazing goal from a free-kick twenty yards out, when his team mate Willie Carr flicks the ball into the air (using both of his heels) and Hunt volleys into the net. The 'Sky Blues' defeat Everton 3-1 and climb to fourteenth in the table ▪ Gerry Summers' Oxford Utd move to the top of Division Two with a 0-2 victory over Bolton Wanderers. (31-year-old Big Ron Atkinson is on the score-sheet for Oxford) ▪ *Something* ("... in the way he moves attracts me like no other lover") by 33-year-old Shirley Bassey reaches number four in the pop chart ▪ *It's So Easy* by 42-year-old Andy Williams is number thirteen ▪ 34-year-old jockey Lester Piggott rides *Nijinsky* to victory in the St. Ledger at Doncaster - and *Nijinsky* is the first racehorse to win 'the triple crown' since *Bahram* in 1935 ▪ Jimi Hendrix dies aged 27 at Notting Hill in London ▪ The Kinks pull out of a new pop festival at Pilton in Somerset ▪ Festival organiser 34-year-old Michael Eavis books Tyrannosaurus

Rex (with, lead singer, 22-year-old Marc Bolan) instead ▪ "Ooh, baby, baby it's a... *Wild World* by 22-year-old Jimmy Cliff climbs to number eight in the pop chart ▪ "Here's one I made earlier" - 33-year-old Valerie Singleton, 36-year-old John Noakes and 31-year-old Peter Purves present *Blue Peter* on BBC One ▪ A new series of *The Flaxton Boys* (a gripping drama for children, set in Yorkshire in the year 1870) is on ITV ▪ 56-year-old Robert Dougall presents the first *Nine O'Clock News* program ▪ Concorde (the supersonic passenger plane) reaches a speed of 1,135 mph during a test flight from Scotland to Cornwall ▪ *You Can Get It If You Really Want* ("... but you must try, try and try") by 29-year-old Desmond Dekker and the Aces is number two in the pop chart ▪ "Whoa-oh, whoa-whoa, whoa-whoa-whoa. Whoa-oh, whoa-whoa, whoa-whoa-whoa Come sing me loud. Come sing me..." *Montego Bay* by 24-year-old Bobby Bloom is number three ▪ 24-year-old Manchester Utd footballer 'super' Georgie Best glides past Chelsea's hard man defender Ron 'Chopper' Harris and rounds goalkeeper Peter Bonnetti to score the winning goal for Utd in a 2-1 victory in the fourth round of the League Cup ▪ 24-year-old striker Keith Weller scores five goals in three matches for Dave Sexton's Chelsea in League Division One ▪ Derby County manager Brian Clough signs 23-year-old midfielder Archie Gemmill for £50,000 from Preston North End ▪ 45-year-old Richard Baker reads the news on BBC One ▪ For the third year running - the clocks do not get 'put back', as the government continues to assess the benefits of moving to a 'British Standard Time' ▪ Children wear orange reflective armbands on their way into school - as the mornings stay darker for longer ▪ 'Doing Their Bit for Laughter! In a Tale of Love, Lust and of course a Perfect Pair' - *Carry On Loving* is now showing at cinemas, with Kenneth Williams as Percival Snooper, Sid 'Ha-ak-ak' James as Sidney Bliss and with 28-year-old Imogen Hassall (aka the Countess of Cleavage) as Jenny Grubb ▪ 'Taste the Deadly Passion of the Blood Nymphs!' - 57-year-old Peter Cushing, 28-year-old Jon Finch and 32-year-old Ingrid Pitt star in 'X' rated Hammer horror film *The Vampire Lovers* ▪ Stephanie Rahn is the first topless page three girl in *The Sun* ▪ Women's Liberation activists throw flour at Bob Hope during the annual Miss World contest - pretty little 22-year-old Jennifer Hosten (36-24-38) is the eventual winner ▪ "Beryl, we live in a permissive society / Not on

this street we don't / Everybody's at it / Not with me they're not / All girls are supposed to be crying out for it / Not this one Geoffrey, I'm the silent majority" - 20-year-old Paula Wilcox is Beryl and 23-year-old Richard Beckinsale is Geoffrey in ITV's new sit-com *The Lovers* ▪ 39-year-old blonde sex-siren Diana Dors stars in *Queenie's Castle* ▪ "Now that you're gone, all that's left is a..." *Band Of Gold* by Freda Payne is top of the hit parade for five weeks! ▪ "Finished with my woman 'cause she couldn't help me with my mind. People think I'm insane because I am frowning all the time" - *Paranoid* by Black Sabbath climbs to number four ▪ *(They Long To Be) Close To You* by The Carpenters reaches number six ▪ BP discovers a large oil field in the North Sea ▪ The fabulous new Ford *Cortina MkIII* goes on sale with a range of models comprising of *L*, *XL*, *GT and GXL* ▪ British Leyland makes improvements to the *Maxi* - upgrading the seats, introducing a new fascia and making the gear change much smoother ▪ Production staff return to work at Leyland's Cowley and Longbridge factories ▪ The 'jam sandwich' police car is new as motorway patrol vehicles get a coat of white paint and a broad horizontal orange/red luminous stripe ▪ A new forty mile stretch of M6 motorway between Lancaster and Penrith (crossing the summit at Shap) is now open to motorists ▪ "Goodies! Goody, goody, yum, yum" - 27-year-old Graeme Garden, 29-year-old Bill Oddie and 30-year-old Tim Brooke-Taylor debut as *The Goodies* on BBC Two ▪ England's fast bowler Fred Trueman makes a guest appearance in *Dad's Army* - playing in a cricket match between the Home Guard platoon and the ARP wardens. The episode ends with 71-year-old Private Godfrey (played by 74-year-old Arnold Ridley) scoring the winning runs for Captain Mainwaring's Home Guard team ▪ "Papa was a great old man. I can see him with a shovel in his hands, see" - *Patches* by Clarence Carter climbs to number two in the pop chart ▪ "We are stardust, we are golden, and we've got to get ourselves back to the garden" - *Woodstock* by Matthews' Southern Comfort is number one ▪ 38-year-old Ray Illingworth leads England's cricketers, down-under, on a seven match Ashes series against Australia. 30-year-old Geoffrey Boycott and 31-year-old Brian Luckhurst stride out together to open the batting for England at Brisbane in the first Test. Boycott scores 37 runs. Luckhurst makes 74 (before being run out) and the match ends in a draw ▪ Back in England -

Technicians at ITV go on strike - refusing to work with new-fangled 'colour' equipment ▪ 26-year-old maverick footballer Rodney Marsh scores a hat-trick as Queens Park Rangers defeat Birmingham City 5-2 in front of 13,074 spectators at Loftus Road. (27-year-old Terry Venables is also on the score-sheet for QPR) ▪ 24-year-old Bobby Gould scores a hat-trick as Wolverhampton Wanderers beat Manchester Utd 3-2 in front of 38,692 spectators at the Molineux ▪ 21-year-old John Toshack leaves Cardiff City and joins Liverpool for £110,000 - Toshack makes his debut in a 0-0 draw against Noel Cantwell's Coventry City in front of 50,503 spectators at Anfield ▪ 17-year-old winger Leighton James makes his debut for bottom-of-the-table Burnley in a 2-1 victory over Nottingham Forest in front of 13,036 spectators at Turf Moor ▪ "Oh, me and my life..." *Me And My Life* by The Tremeloes is number four in the pop chart ▪ *Ain't No Mountain High Enough* ("... Ain't no valley low enough. Ain't no river wide enough, to keep me from you") by 26-year-old Diana Ross is number six ▪ 'Get there early before the police do' - *Perfect Friday* (a bank heist film), starring 34-year-old Ursula Andress (38-25-35), 42-year-old Stanley Baker and 29-year-old David Warner, goes on general release at cinemas ▪ 21-year-old goalkeeper Peter Shilton makes his debut for Sir Alf Ramsey's England football team (Shilton, Hughes, Cooper, Mullery, Sadler, Moore, F Lee, Ball, G Hurst, A Clarke, Peters) in a 3-1 victory over East Germany at Wembley. 26-year-old Franny Lee, 27-year-old Martin Peters and 24-year-old Allan 'sniffer' Clarke score the goals for England ▪ *Baby I Won't Let You Down* by Pickettywitch is number twenty-seven in the pop chart ▪ *Whole Lotta Love* by CCS is number eighteen ▪ "Goodbye..." *Ruby Tuesday* ("... who's gonna hang a name on you?") by 23-year-old Melanie peaks at number nine ▪ 15-year-old Claire McAlpine is invited to be part of the studio audience for a recording of popular TV show *Top of the Pops* ▪ 58-year-old Gordon Wilkins presents *Wheelbase* - a motoring programme on BBC Two ▪ 'A fine range of cars - now better than ever' - Vauxhall promotes its stylish new *Viva HC*. A standard two-door saloon costs £701. A four-door *SL* is £844. A *de Luxe Estate* is £851 ▪ Production of the hugely successful Morris *Minor 1000* motorcar comes to an end. Approximately 1.6 million *Minors* have been built since the model was introduced in 1948.

Christmas 1970

A Raleigh Chopper for Christmas

Monarch:	Queen Elizabeth II (aged 44)
Prime-minister:	Edward Heath (aged 54)
Chancellor:	Anthony Barber (aged 50)
Home Secretary:	Reginald Maudling (aged 53)
Foreign Secretary:	Alec Douglas-Home (aged 67)
Football Manager:	Alf Ramsey (aged 50)
Radio 1 Breakfast DJ:	Tony Blackburn (aged 27)
New car reg. suffix:	'J'

▪ It's a white Christmas for most of the UK ▪ "Innit marvellous!?" - a new series of *On the Buses* is on TV, with 43-year-old Stephen Lewis as Blakey, 54-year-old Reg Varney as Stan, 38-year-old Bob Grant as Jack, 40-year-old Michael Robbins as Arthur and 34-year-old Anna Karen as Olive ▪ Happy and smiling, 15-year-old Claire McAlpine dances with the crowds on *Top of the Pops*. 44-year-old DJ Jimmy Savile takes his turn to present the show on the third of December ▪ "Oh, oh, oh, oh..." *When I'm Dead And Gone* ("... I wanna leave some happy woman living on") by McGuinness Flint climbs to number two on the hit parade ▪ *You're Ready Now* by 36-year-old Frankie Valli is new at number twenty-nine ▪ *Blue Peter* presenters - 36-year-old John Noakes, 31-year-old Peter Purves and 33-year-old Valerie Singleton urge people to send in old spoons and forks to raise money to provide suitable holiday homes for disabled children ▪ "I don't believe in Beatles. I just believe in me" - *God* is one of the songs to feature on *John Lennon/Plastic Ono Band* - the first solo album from 30-year-old John Lennon ▪ *Led Zeppelin 3* is top of the LP chart ▪ "'Cause I'm a voodoo chile. Lord knows I'm a..." *Voodoo Chile* by the late Jimi Hendrix reaches number one in the singles' chart ▪ "Cherokee people, Cherokee tribe. So proud to live, so proud to die" - *Indian Reservation* by 27-year-old Don Fardon from Coventry is number three ▪ *Breakaway* is a new type of chocolate bar ▪ 11-year-old schoolboy Simon Cowell from Elstree in Hertfordshire annoys his teachers with glib comments and an unjustified sense of self importance ▪ "Bah, humbug" - 34-year-old Albert Finney

stars at cinemas, playing the role of *Scrooge* in a musical version of Charles Dickens' *A Christmas Carol.* 56-year-old Alec Guinness is Jacob Marley. 56-year-old Kenneth More is the Ghost of Christmas Present ▪ 48-year-old Christopher Lee stars in the latest Hammer production, *Scars of Dracula.* 50-year-old Patrick Troughton, 22-year-old Dennis Waterman and 23-year-old Jenny Hanley are in the cast ▪ 'She's every girl who has said, "Oh well ... just this once..."' 20-year-old Robin Askwith and 21-year-old Janet Lynn star in *Cool it, Carol!* - a sex comedy from director Pete Walker ▪ 37-year-old Frank Bough presents *Grandstand* on BBC One ▪ 23-year-old footballer Archie Gemmill scores his first league goal for Derby County as Brian Clough's team defeats Matt Gillies' Nottingham Forest 2-4 at the City Ground ▪ 33-year-old Brentford goalkeeper Chic Brodie is badly injured after colliding with a dog on the pitch in a match away against Colchester Utd ▪ Reports in newspapers suggest that football has become 'dirty' ▪ Three players are booked in a First Division match between Everton and hard-tackling Leeds Utd ▪ Five players are booked in a Second Division match between Middlesbrough and Hull City ▪ Four players are booked and a fifth is sent-off in a Second Division match between Orient and Blackburn Rovers ▪ 11-year-old Uriah Rennie from Sheffield in Yorkshire plays out with his friends ▪ *Cracklin' Rosie* ("... get on board. We're gonna ride till there ain't no more to go. Takin' it slow") by 30-year-old Neil Diamond is number three in the pop chart ▪ *My Prayer* by 37-year-old Gerry Monroe is number nine ▪ Conservative prime-minister Edward Heath continues to push his Industrial Relations Bill through parliament - the proposed new legislation will restrict trade unions from calling instant walk-out strikes ▪ British Leyland announces that five-thousand jobs are to be axed from its Austin-Morris manufacturing division ▪ NCB coal production is at its lowest level since 1926. Just 147 million tonnes have been mined in 1970 and the number of mine workers has fallen below 300,000 ▪ *You've Got Me Dangling On A String* ("... Please don't let me drop, my life will surely stop") by Chairman of the Board reaches number five in the pop chart ▪ "Sad and lonely, only myself to blame..." *Broken Hearted* by 43-year-old Ken Dodd peaks at number fifteen ▪ Wilf McGuinness' Manchester Utd football team loses 4-1 at home

to Joe Mercer's Manchester City - and 'super' Georgie Best is booked for a dangerous tackle on Glyn Pardoe ▪ A week later, Utd lose again (this time 3-1 at home to Bertie Mee's Arsenal) and slip down to eighteenth position in Division One ▪ The winter mornings remain dark until around 9 a.m. - as an experiment continues to assess if a new 'British Standard Time' should be established ▪ 'Always Use The Green Cross Code' - the Green Cross Man warns children to be safe when crossing the road ▪ 20-year-old David 'Kid' Jensen spins discs on Radio Luxembourg ▪ "Julie, Julie..." *Julie Do Ya Love Me?* ("... Julie, Julie, Julie do you care?") by White Plains is number eight in the pop chart ▪ "This feeling inside me could never deny me, the right to be wrong if I choose. And this pleasure I get from say, winning a bet, is to lose" - *Nothing Rhymed* by 24-year-old Gilbert O'Sullivan climbs from number thirty to number eight ▪ Comedians, 37-year-old Leslie Crowther and 61-year-old Jimmy Jewell feature in a one-off edition of *The Black and White Minstrel Show* on BBC One ▪ "Rupert, Rupert the bear. Everyone knows his name" - *The Adventures of Rupert Bear* is on ATV ▪ 28-year-old actress Julie Goodyear plays Bet Lynch (a new barmaid in 'The Rovers Return') on *Coronation Street* ▪ 'De-de-der-der-de-de-de-de-de-de-de-der-der, der-der-de-de-de-de-de' - 45-year-old comedian Benny Hill stars in *The Benny Hill Show* - the program is broadcast in black and white due to the ITV technicians' strike ▪ Popular 36-year-old boxer Henry Cooper (aka Our 'Enry) is BBC's 'Sports Personality of the Year' - for the second time in his career ▪ Excitement builds for Christmas ▪ 'It's Here!' - 40-year-old Rolf Harris promotes the amazing *Stylophone* - a Pocket Electronic Organ ▪ A GAF *Talking-Viewmaster* (batteries not included) is also popular ▪ Children go crazy for the new Raleigh *Chopper* bicycle which costs £34/19s/- ▪ The latest 'World Cup' edition of the table-top football game from *Subbuteo* is popular with young boys - and their dads! ▪ Hallmark Records release *The Best of Top of the Pops '70'* - a budget priced, cover-version pop compilation LP with pretty girls pictured on the sleeve ▪ "You went away and left me, long time ago" - *I Hear You Knocking* by 26-year-old Dave Edmunds from Cardiff climbs to number one in the pop chart - and stays there for six weeks! ▪ "You and I must make a pact, we must bring salvation back. Where there is love..." *I'll Be There* ("... I'll be there") by The Jackson

Five is number four ▪ People write out Christmas cards before sending them in the post to family and friends ▪ All Christmas mail is postmarked with 'Remember to use the Postal Code' ▪ 27-year-old Cilla Black introduces *Christmas Night With The Stars* on BBC One ▪ Programs on ITV are broadcast in black and white due to on-going industrial action by technicians ▪ Public Information programs explain the new decimal currency system - which is to be introduced soon ▪ A bottle of *Harveys Bristol Cream* costs 24s/11d ▪ The Gay Liberation Front marches through London ▪ "Wear a tall hat like a druid in the old days. Wear a tall hat and a tattooed gown. Ride a white swan like the people of the Beltane. Wear your hair long babe, you can't go wrong" - *Ride A White Swan* by T-Rex is number six in the pop chart ▪ *Home Lovin' Man* by 43-year-old Andy Williams is number seven ▪ Don Revie's hard-tackling Leeds Utd football team (with Gary Sprake, Billy Bremner and 24-year-old Peter Lorimer) and Bertie Mee's Arsenal (with Bob Wilson, Frank McLintock and 23-year-old John Radford) battle it out for top spot in Division One ▪ Manchester Utd sack 33-year-old Wilf McGuinness after a poor run of results in Division One and a League Cup semi-final defeat to Third Division Aston Villa ▪ 61-year-old Sir Matt Busby returns to Old Trafford as Utd manager ▪ Ten football league matches are postponed on Boxing Day because of snow ▪ Ray Illingworth's England cricket team draws the second Test down-under in Perth, Australia. Brian Luckhurst scores 131 runs and Geoffrey Boycott scores 70 and 50 ▪ Adolescent boys hang around outside the newsagents ▪ 'Would You Believe I'm A Virgin Witch?' - a Bumper 100-page edition of *Mayfair* magazine is on sale ▪ 'The railway, the children … and the wonderful secret they'll share with you!' - 18-year-old Jenny Agutter stars at cinemas in *The Railway Children* (along with 16-year-old Gary Warren, 20-year-old Sally Thomsett and 41-year-old Bernard Cribbins) ▪ 24-year-old Hayley Mills and 32-year-old Oliver Reed star in *Take a Girl Like You* ▪ "Scooby! Dooby! DOO!!" - *Scooby Doo Where Are You?* is on TV ▪ The snow thaws ▪ Children play out ▪ The future seems bright ▪ Cadbury's launches the *Curlywurly* chocolate bar ▪ Men spend an evening in the pub ▪ A pint of bitter in the Red Lion costs 2s/2d ▪ Housewives go shopping ▪ A loaf of bread costs one shilling ▪ Adverts say, '*Wonderloaf* is wonderful every day of the week'.

New Year 1971

Curlywurly

Monarch:	Queen Elizabeth II (aged 44)
Prime-minister:	Edward Heath (aged 54)
Chancellor:	Anthony Barber (aged 50)
Home Secretary:	Reginald Maudling (aged 53)
Foreign Secretary:	Alec Douglas-Home (aged 67)
Football Manager:	Alf Ramsey (aged 51)
Radio 1 Breakfast DJ:	Tony Blackburn (aged 28)
New car reg. suffix:	'J'

▪ The weather is dry and mild, turning wet and windy at the end of January ▪ 47-year-old Richard 'Dicky' Attenborough, 22-year-old Judy Geeson and 30-year-old John Hurt star at cinemas in *10 Rillington Place* - the grim tale of mass murderer John Christie, who was convicted and hanged in 1953 ▪ Millions of TV viewers tune into BBC's long-running police drama *Z Cars* on Monday and Tuesday evenings ▪ Regulars of 'The Rovers Return' pub in ITV's popular soap-opera *Coronation Street* are shocked to learn that they're drinking watered down gin ▪ "But..." *It's Only Make Believe* by 34-year-old Glen Campbell is number four in the pop chart ▪ "It's a little bit funny, this feeling inside" - *Your Song* by 23-year-old Elton John is number seven ▪ Manchester Utd footballer 'super' Georgie Best is in trouble after failing to turn up for a match against Chelsea. Utd Manager Sir Matt Busby bans the 24-year-old from the club for fourteen days. Best is also summonsed to appear before an FA Disciplinary Committee - where he receives a record fine of £250 and a six week suspended ban ▪ 30-year-old Jimmy 'Greavsie' Greaves spends an evening drinking in a Blackpool nightclub until the early hours. The next day, Greavsie plays for West Ham Utd in a 4-0 defeat against 'The Seasiders' ▪ *Grandad* ("... grandad, you're lovely. That's what we all think of you") by 51-year-old Clive Dunn is number one in the pop chart ▪ "There's nothin' I can do if it don't get through, just..." *Blame It On The Pony Express* by Johnny Johnson and the Bandwagon is number seven ▪ 'Love means never having to stay you're sorry…' *Love Story*, starring 31-year-old Ali MacGraw and 29-year-old Ryan O'Neal, draws crowds to cinemas ▪ 26-year-old Hywel

Bennett stars in *Percy* - the story of a man who undergoes a penis transplant ▪ *Growing Up* - a new sex-education film for school children causes outrage as the graphic colour images show a couple engaged in the act of love making ▪ 65-year-old Earl of Longford describes the film as pornographic ▪ Millions of people complete a pools coupon each week (and say a prayer) in the hope of winning a fortune ▪ Father James Curtin from Walsall wins more than £100,000 on *Vernons* ▪ The new decimal currency system gets underway on Monday the fifteenth of February, with the introduction of three bronze coloured coins - the ½p (with the Royal Crown on the front), the 1p (with portcullis and chains) and the 2p (with the 'three feather' emblem of the Prince of Wales). The silver coloured 5p, 10p and 50p coins have been in circulation for a few years - serving respectively as one shilling, two shilling and ten shilling coins. Under the new system - one old penny is equal to ½ new pence and one shilling is equal to 5 new pence ▪ Travelling sales representatives (driving white Hillman *Hunter* estate cars) stop for lunch at *Little Chef* cafés ▪ A plate of sausages, eggs and French fried potatoes costs 27½ new pence (was previously 5s/6d) ▪ A side order of buttered bread is 3 new pence (was previously 7d) ▪ A cup of tea is 4 new pence (was previously 9d) ▪ A cup of coffee is 6 new pence (was previously 1s/3d) ▪ Men enjoy an evening in the pub ▪ A pint of bitter is 12½p (was previously 2s/4d) ▪ A pint of lager is 16½p (was previously 3s/2d) ▪ Fashions are changing ▪ Young people apply brightly coloured make-up to their eyelids and spray glitter on their faces ▪ Happy and smiling, 15-year-old Claire McAlpine dances with the crowds on *Top of the Pops* ▪ 12-year-old Deborah Meaden dances with her friends at boarding school ▪ *Ride A White Swan* by T-Rex (with 23-year-old Marc Bolan) climbs back up the pop chart to number two (after previously peaking at number six) ▪ *Resurrection Shuffle* by Ashton, Gardner and Dyke is number three ▪ School children are mesmerised as *Mr. Benn* (of number fifty-two Festive Road) makes his debut on television ▪ Fred the *Homepride* flour character is a popular new kitchen accessory ▪ *Apollo 14* (with astronauts: Alan Shepard, Stuart Roosa and Edgar D. Mitchell) lands on the Moon and sends back colour photographs ▪ 'Kill the Bill' - the TUC holds a demonstration against Edward Heath's Industrial Relations Bill - 170,000 people march through London ▪ Thousands of British Leyland car work-

ers stage a 24-hour walk-out ▪ Postal workers go on strike after their demand for a 15% pay increase is rejected ▪ Richard Branson's mail-order music business grinds to a halt because of the strike - and so, the 20-year-old entrepreneur sets up a retail operation instead ▪ *Virgin Records* (a small shop) opens on Oxford Street in London ▪ 44-year-old DJ Jimmy Savile presents *Top of the Pops* on BBC One ▪ "Doesn't matter what you do, girl. Ooh girl, want you" - *No Matter What* by Badfinger climbs to number five in the pop chart ▪ *It's The Same Old Song* ("... but with a different meaning since you've been gone") by The Weatherman (aka Jonathan King) is number nineteen ▪ *Baby I Won't Let You Down* ("... when you call, I'll be 'round") by Pickettywitch is number twenty-seven ▪ A bomb explodes at Hadley Green near Barnet - outside the home of government minister Robert Carr. A group called The Angry Brigade claims responsibility ▪ Scotland Yard sets up a specialist Bomb Squad division ▪ The Troubles escalate in Northern Ireland - a British soldier is killed in Ulster for the first time in fifty years ▪ "I don't feel safe in this world no more, I don't want to die in a nuclear war, I want to sail away to a distant shore, and make like an…" *Apeman* by The Kinks (led by 26-year-old Ray Davies) is new at number five in the pop chart ▪ Parents and children enjoy matinee screenings at the local cinema ▪ 'Meet the cats who know where it's at … for fun, music and adventure!' - Walt Disney's *The Aristocats* is now showing ▪ 28-year-old Desmond Lynam presents *Sport on 2* on BBC Radio Two on Saturday afternoons ▪ England's cricketers are in action in Australia ▪ 30-year-old batsman Geoffrey Boycott scores a century in each of the Test Matches at Sydney and Adelaide. Brian Luckhurst, John Edrich and Basil D'Oliveira also make centuries during the seven match series. 21-year-old fast-bowler Bob Willis makes his debut for England - and takes the wickets of Marsh, Chappell and Lillee in the final Test at Sydney. Ray Illingworth's team is triumphant - England regain the Ashes from Bill Lawry's Aussies - winning the series by two Tests to nil. G Boycott, B W Luckhurst, A P E Knott (wk), J H Edrich, M C Cowdrey, K W R Fletcher, B L D'Oliveira, R Illingworth (cpt), J H Hampshire, J A Snow, D L Underwood, K Shuttleworth, P Lever and R G D Willis are all buoyed by this historic Ashes victory - the first since 1956! ▪ Rock music fans queue outside record shops ▪ Black Sabbath (with, lead singer, 22-year-old Ozzy

Osbourne) release their *Paranoid* album ▪ Stray (with, drummer, 19-year-Ritchie Cole) release their *Suicide* album ▪ "Now behave yourself" - 37-year-old Michael Caine stars at cinemas as Jack Carter in *Get Carter* ▪ "Are you dancin'? / Are you askin'? / I'm askin' / I'm dancin'" - A new series of *The Liver Birds* begins on BBC One, starring 29-year-old Polly James as Beryl and 29-year-old Nerys Hughes as Sandra ▪ "Get on board. Get on board. Come and join the Double Deckers. Take a ticket for a journey, on our double decker London bus" - excited children watch TV on Fridays at teatime, transfixed by Doughnut (12-year-old Douglas Simmonds), Scooper (17-year-old Peter Firth), Brains (14-year-old Michael Audreson), Billie (15-year-old Gillian Bailey), Sticks (12-year-old Bruce Clark), Spring (17-year-old Brinsley Forde) and Tiger (10-year-old Debbie Russ) in fabulous new show *Here Come The Double Deckers!* ▪ The ITV technician's strike comes to an end and programs are broadcast in colour once more ▪ 57-year-old Sid 'Ha-ak-ak' James, 42-year-old Diana Coupland and 20-year-old Sally Geeson star in new sit-com *Bless This House* ▪ The first edition of *Look-In* ('a great new TV magazine for boys and girls') is published for 5 new pence ▪ "Oh, my..." *Candida* ("... we could make it together") by Dawn (with, lead singer, 26-year-old Tony Orlando) is number nine on the hit parade ▪ *Amazing Grace* by 31-year-old Judy Collins is number five ▪ Derby County football manager Brian Clough signs 22-year-old defender Colin Todd from Sunderland for £175,000 ▪ Norman Hunter and Johnny Giles score late goals for Don Revie's hard-tackling Leeds Utd, but the 'all-whites' crash out of the FA Cup in a shock 3-2 defeat against Fourth Division Colchester Utd ▪ 25-year-old Martin Chivers scores twice as Bill Nicholson's First Division Tottenham Hotspur defeat Vic Crowe's Third Division Aston Villa 2-0 in the League Cup final at Wembley ▪ 20-year-old Charlie George is on the score-sheet as Arsenal beat 38-year-old Bobby Robson's Ipswich Town 3-2 at Highbury ▪ Big band leader Harry Roy (aka the King of 'Hot-Cha') dies in London aged 71 ▪ "My sweet Lord. Oh, my Lord. My sweet Lord..." *My Sweet Lord* by 27-year-old George Harrison spends five weeks at the top of the pop chart ▪ *Black Skin Blue Eyed Boys* by The Equals peaks at number nine ▪ West Ham Utd football manager Ron Greenwood drops 22-year-old Trevor Brooking from the team ▪ 30-year-

old footballer Jimmy 'Greavsie' Greaves scores the only goal as 'The Hammers' beat Coventry City 0-1 to remain third from bottom in Division One ▪ 16-year-old apprentice footballer Trevor Francis scores all four goals as Second Division Birmingham City thrash Bolton Wanderers 4-0 at St. Andrew's. In the next game, young Francis scores twice as 'The Blues' beat Swindon Town 1-2 at the County Ground ▪ "Riding along on my pushbike honey, when I noticed you" - *The Pushbike Song* by The Mixtures enters the pop chart at number twenty-four ▪ Prime-minister Edward Heath meets with 55-year-old Minister of Aviation Fred Corfield to discuss the future of Rolls Royce - the iconic company is in grave financial difficulties ▪ 'A Great Guy with his Chopper!' - *Carry On Henry* is now showing at cinemas, with Sid 'Ha-ak-ak' James as King Henry VIII, 45-year-old Kenneth Williams as Thomas Cromwell and 33-year-old Barbara Windsor (36-24-34) as Bettina - a buxom serving wench ▪ 'Mirror, mirror, on the wall, who's the most terrifying of them all?' - 33-year-old Ingrid Pitt and 16-year-old Lesley-Anne Down star in 'X' rated Hammer horror *Countess Dracula* ▪ "There's a little bear like you've never seen before, who's a lot of fun. Children everywhere grow to love him more and more, he's the number one" - *Rupert* by Jackie Lee is number fourteen in the pop chart ▪ "Don't ya hear the wind a-blowing..." *Stoned Love* ("... Oh, yeah") by The Supremes is number three ▪ 35-year-old writer David Nobbs pens humorous scripts and one-line gags for a new TV show called *The Two Ronnies* ▪ BBC One TV programs on a Saturday evening include: *Dr. Who* - with 51-year-old Jon Pertwee as the Doctor; *Here's Lucy* - with Lucille Ball; *It's Cliff Richard* - hosted by 30-year-old pop star Cliff; and *Dixon of Dock Green* - with 75-year-old Jack Warner in the title role ▪ Families enjoy an evening in, playing records on teak-effect *PYE* stereograms ▪ "You looked so pretty as you were riding along. You looked so pretty as you were singing this song" - *The Pushbike Song* by The Mixtures climbs to number two on the hit parade ▪ *It's Impossible* ("... tell the sun to leave the sky") by 58-year-old Perry Como is number four ▪ Kids hang about near shopping precincts ▪ Fish and chips wrapped in newspaper costs 25 new pence ▪ A Cadbury's *Curlywurly* chocolate bar is 3 new pence ▪ A pack of twenty *Park Drive* tipped is 20½p.

Spring 1971

It's a 'Double' for Bertie Mee's Arsenal!

Monarch:	Queen Elizabeth II (aged 45)
Prime-minister:	Edward Heath (aged 54)
Chancellor:	Anthony Barber (aged 50)
Home Secretary:	Reginald Maudling (aged 54)
Foreign Secretary:	Alec Douglas-Home (aged 67)
Football Manager:	Alf Ramsey (aged 51)
Radio 1 Breakfast DJ:	Tony Blackburn (aged 28)
New car reg. suffix:	'J'

▪ Trade union leaders organise a day of industrial action ▪ Across the country, one-million workers 'down tools' on Monday the first of March - protesting against the government's Industrial Relations Act ▪ 54-year-old Robert Carr (Employment Secretary in Edward Heath's Conservative government) is critical of the strike and says the unions seem to be "determined to use their power to bring to a halt key sectors of industry upon which the well-being of all was finally dependent." ▪ Postal workers return to work after being on strike for seven weeks ▪ Rolls Royce goes into liquidation and the government buys up the company's assets ▪ Thousands of British Leyland car production workers are sent home due to a shortage of component parts ▪ Production of Ford's new *Cortina MKIII* motorcar is slowed by an unofficial strike at the Dagenham factory ▪ "And if you can't be with the one you love, honey…" *Love The One You're With* by 26-year-old Stephen Stills enters the pop chart at number thirty-seven ▪ "She's a lady. Woah, woah, woah…" *She's A Lady* by 30-year-old Tom Jones moves down to number thirty after peaking at number thirteen ▪ Northern counties are hit by snow storms in March. Up to a foot falls in Northumberland and Yorkshire, with light snow and slush covering Cheshire, Derbyshire and Nottinghamshire ▪ There's bad news for shoppers ▪ 43-year-old Agriculture Minister James Prior announces in the House of Commons that bread, butter, milk and cheese are all set to go up in price. Milk will go up in July by half-a-penny a pint. Bread will go up at the same time, with increases in butter and cheese to come shortly afterwards ▪ Unemployment in the country reaches 815,000 and Edward Heath's new Conservative government is under pressure to take immediate action to im-

prove the economy ▪ 50-year-old Chancellor of the Exchequer Anthony Barber delivers his first Budget ▪ It's announced that a new value added tax (VAT) will come into effect in 1973 ▪ Trade and Industry Secretary John Davis unveils government plans to build a new international airport at Maplin Sands in Essex ▪ Kentish Town West Railway Station closes down after a serious fire ▪ The Tower Restaurant opens in Liverpool, offering its diners steak and chips and panoramic views across the city ▪ 23-year-old Marc Bolan (lead singer from T-Rex) features on the front cover of the latest *New Musical Express* ▪ Happy and smiling, 15-year-old Claire McAlpine dances with the crowds on *Top of the Pops* ▪ "Baby, baby..." *Baby Jump* ("... into my dreams") by Mungo Jerry (with, lead singer, 24-year-old Ray Dorset) is new at number one in the pop chart ▪ *Sweet Caroline* ("... de-de-der. Good times never seemed so good") by 30-year-old Neil Diamond is number eight ▪ 24-year-old cricketer David Lloyd (an opening batsman for Lancashire) scores 54 runs as his team defeats Gloucestershire by an innings and 24 runs in the opening match of the County Championship ▪ 'The Fight of the Century' takes place at Madison Square Garden in New York, where 27-year-old heavy-weight boxer Smokin' Joe Frazier beats 29-year-old Muhammad Ali in fifteen rounds ▪ Back in England - 21-year-old Joe Bugner defeats 36-year-old Henry Cooper (aka Our 'Enry) by ¼ point at Wembley ▪ 43-year-old Andy Williams is number four in the pop chart with *(Where Do I Begin) Love Story* ▪ 36-year-old Waldo de los Rios is number five with an arrangement of *Mozart's Symphony No. 40 in G minor K550 1st Movement (Allegro Molto)* ▪ 24-year-old footballer 'super' Georgie Best scores twice as Manchester Utd beat Stoke City 1-2 at the Victoria Ground - Utd climb up to ninth position in Division One ▪ 31-year-old Jimmy 'Greavsie' Greaves scores twice as West Ham Utd draw 2-2 against Ipswich Town - 'The Hammers' stay just above the relegation zone ▪ 21-year-old Tony Currie scores the only goal as Sheffield Utd beat Bristol City 0-1 at Ashton Gate - 'The Blades' move up to second in Division Two ▪ 25-year-old Steve Earle scores the goal as Fulham beat Rotherham Utd 1-0 at Craven Cottage - 'The Cottagers' stay second in Division Three ▪ 19-year-old Kevin Keegan scores a goal as Scunthorpe Utd beat Southport 2-0 at the Old Show Ground - 'The Iron' climb up to fourteenth in Division Four ▪

33-year-old Anthony Hopkins and 60-year-old Jack Hawkins star at cinemas in *When Eight Bells Toll* - a film based on a novel by 48-year-old Alistair McLean ▪ 18-year-old Jack Wild, 12-year-old Mark Lester and 11-year-old Tracy Hyde star in *S.W.A.L.K.* ▪ 28-year-old Radio One DJ Tony Blackburn enjoys a romantic night out with his beautiful blonde girlfriend, 22-year-old actress Tessa Wyatt ▪ Boys and girls sit together in youth club halls, listening to pop records on the ITT *KP-820* stereo record player ▪ Glam rock is exciting and new ▪ "Well she's faster than most and she lives on the coast, a-ha-ha" - *Hot Love* by T-Rex (with 23-year-old Marc Bolan) climbs to number one in the chart - and stays there for six weeks! ▪ *Bridget The Midget (The Queen Of The Blues)* by 32-year-old Ray Stevens is number two ▪ 'Devils in Female Bodies' - 31-year-old Ralph Bates and 24-year-old Yutte Stensgaard star at cinemas in the latest 'X' rated Hammer horror film, *Lust for a Vampire* ▪ TV viewers are shocked when Valerie Barlow (wife of Ken and mother of 5-year-old twins Peter and Susan) dies from an electric shock caused by a faulty power socket at number 14 *Coronation Street* ▪ 36-year-old Wendy Craig stars in a new sit-com called *And Mother Makes Three* ▪ "It's just..." *Another Day* by 28-year-old Paul McCartney is number two in the pop chart ▪ "I beg your pardon. I never promised you a..." *Rose Garden* by 23-year-old Lynn Anderson is number three ▪ 34-year-old Glenda Jackson wins an Oscar for her performance in *Women in Love* ▪ Racehorse *L'Escargot* (ridden by 29-year-old Tommy Carberry) wins the Cheltenham Gold Cup for the second year running ▪ *Specify* (ridden by 33-year-old Johnny Cook) wins the Grand National ▪ Bertie Mee's Arsenal and Don Revie's hard-tackling Leeds Utd are neck and neck at the top of Division One ▪ 19-year-old Ray Kennedy scores twice for Arsenal as 'The Gunners' defeat Chelsea 2-0 in front of 62,087 spectators at Highbury ▪ 24-year-old Alan 'sniffer' Clarke scores all four goals for Leeds as the 'All Whites' thrash Burnley 4-0 in front of 31,192 at Elland Road ▪ "Say we want a revolution, we better get on right away" - *Power To The People* by 29-year-old John Lennon and the Plastic Ono Band is number seven in the pop chart ▪ "Well, my little girl is a sweet little girl, but she does things that make your eyebrows curl" - *Rosetta* by Fame and Price Together (27-year-old Georgie Fame and 29-year-old Alan Price) peaks at number eleven ▪ "Balderdash" - the

65-year-old Earl of Longford storms out of a preview screening of Dr. Martin Cole's sex education film, *Growing Up* ▪ "It's good-night from me / And it's good-night from him" - *The Two Ronnies* debuts on TV, with 41-year-old Ronnie Barker and 40-year-old Ronnie Corbett ▪ "Hannibal Heyes and Kid Curry, the two most successful outlaws in the history of the West. And in all the trains and banks they robbed, they never shot anyone" - the American 'Western' series *Alias Smith and Jones* begins on BBC Two, with 31-year-old Pete Duel and 28-year-old Ben Murphy ▪ "They don't like it up 'em!" - a film version of *Dad's Army* is now showing at cinemas. 55-year-old Arthur Lowe (as Captain Mainwaring), 58-year-old John Le Mesurier (as Sergeant Wilson), 51-year-old Clive Dunn (as Lance-Corporal Jones), 75-year-old Arnold Ridley (as Private Godfrey) and 25-year-old Ian Lavender (as Private 'stupid boy' Pike) are the stars ▪ *Hot Love* by T-Rex remains at number one in the weekly pop chart ▪ Adolescent boys and girls pin glossy posters of 23-year-old Marc Bolan to their bedroom walls ▪ BBC's One *Top of the Pops* television program is presented by 44-year-old Radio One DJ Jimmy Savile ▪ Keen dancer and regular *Top of the Pops* audience member 15-year-old Claire McAlpine takes an overdose of pills and ends her own life ▪ *There Goes My Everything* by 36-year-old Elvis Presley is number six in the pop chart ▪ *Remember Me* ("... as a sunny day that you once had along the way") by 27-year-old Diana Ross peaks at number seven ▪ 43-year-old Sam Leitch presents the weekly Football Preview every Saturday on *Grandstand* on BBC One ▪ Leeds Utd fans invade the pitch at Elland Road when Jeff Astle's goal for West Bromwich Albion is allowed to stand, even though the off-side flag was raised. Leeds lose the match 1-2 and slip down to second place in Division One, behind Arsenal ▪ *Match of the Day* shows slow motion action replays for the first time ▪ "I'm just your..." *Jack In The Box* ("... you know when ever love knocks, I'm gonna bounce up and down on my spring") by 24-year-old Clodagh Rodgers finishes fourth in the Eurovision Song Contest (held in Dublin) - and climbs to number four in the UK pop chart ▪ *If Not For You* ("... my sky would fall, rain would gather too") by 22-year-old Olivia Newton-John is number seven ▪ The football season draws to a close ▪ Johnny Carey's Blackburn Rovers and Jimmy Meadows' Bolton Wanderers are relegated to the Third Division for the first

time in their histories ▪ 21-year-old centre-forward Malcolm MacDonald scores a hat-trick as Luton Town beat Cardiff City 3-0 at Kenilworth Road in Division Two ▪ The names 'Best, Charlton, Law' feature together on the same score-sheet as Sir Matt Busby's Manchester Utd beat Joe Mercer's Manchester City 4-3 on the final day of the season - to finish in eighth position in Division One ▪ Bertie Mee's Arsenal pip Don Revie's hard-tackling Leeds Utd to the title with a 0-1 victory over Tottenham Hotspur at White Hart Lane. Arsenal players, Bob Wilson, Pat Rice, Bob McNab, Frank McLintock (captain), Peter Storey, John Roberts, Peter Simpson, Jon Sammels, Eddie Kelly, John Radford, George Armstrong, Charlie George, George Graham and 19-year-old, top scorer, Ray Kennedy have all been outstanding ▪ 'The Gunners' also clinch the FA Cup - and achieve a wonderful 'double' - when 20-year-old Charlie George scores the winning goal in extra-time to snatch a 2-1 victory over Bill Shankly's Liverpool. A ticket for the standing enclosure at the Empire Stadium in Wembley costs £1.00 ▪ Dave Sexton's Chelsea draw 1-1 against Real Madrid in the UEFA Cup Winners Cup final in Greece. Chelsea go on to win the replay 2-1 - with John Dempsey and Peter 'Ossie' Osgood scoring the goals ▪ *Indiana Wants Me* ("... Lord, I can't go back there") by R Dean Taylor is number three in the pop chart ▪ "I said Jake, now won't you wait? What's got into you?" - *My Brother Jake* by Free climbs nine places to number eleven ▪ 54-year-old prime-minister Edward Heath travels to Paris for a summit meeting with 59-year-old French President Georges Pompidou over Britain's entry into the European Economic Community. The meeting is a success - France agrees to lend its support to Britain joining the Common Market ▪ 27-year-old rock star Mick Jagger marries 26-year-old model Bianca De Macias in Saint-Tropez ▪ *Hot Love* by T-Rex continues to occupy top spot in the weekly pop chart ▪ *Strange Kind Of Woman* by Deep Purple is number eight ▪ 60-year-old Mrs. Mary Whitehouse claims that Dr. Martin Cole's graphic sex education film, *Growing Up*, reduces humans "to the level of animals" ▪ 'Sex King Cole!' - *The Sun* newspaper publishes an article - with 39-year-old Dr. Cole defending his film and saying he has no regrets ▪ Wearing tight fitting vest tops and tiny pairs of shorts, 16-year-old Josephine Howard from Essex and 25-year-old Penny Dainton from Sussex take part in the 'Miss Hot Pants, 1971' contest in

London ▪ In a splendid wide brimmed hat, 45-year-old Mrs. Margaret Thatcher MP (Minister for Education in Edward Heath's Conservative government) opens Netherley Community Comprehensive school in Liverpool ▪ 36-year-old writer David Nobbs pens humorous scripts and one-line gags for comedian Les Dawson ▪ 20-year-old Richard Branson (boss of *Virgin Records*) is arrested for purchase-tax fraud and ordered to pay costs of £60,000 ▪ 24-year-old footballer 'super' Georgie Best kicks the ball cheekily from the hands of goalkeeper Gordon Banks and then heads into the net, only for the goal to be disallowed, in a match between England and Northern Ireland in Belfast. (England go on to win the tie 0-1, with a goal from Alan 'sniffer' Clarke) ▪ 57-year-old Bill Shankly (manager of Liverpool Football Club) signs a promising young midfielder called Kevin Keegan from Scunthorpe Utd for £35,000 ▪ 22-year-old Trevor Brooking is on the transfer list at West Ham Utd (at his own request) after being dropped from the team ▪ "I am double-U O-O-O, and I'm still up here again!" - *Double Barrel* by Dave and Ansil Collins is the new number one record ▪ "Gotta pay your dues if you wanna sing the blues, and you know..." *It Don't Come Easy* by 30-year-old Ringo Starr is number four ▪ Production of the Triumph *Herald* motorcar comes to an end after twelve years ▪ The all new Triumph *Toledo* is launched, with a choice of two or four doors, a 1300cc engine and a top speed of 85 mph. Prices for the new saloon start at £926 ▪ 11-year-old schoolboy Jeremy Clarkson from Doncaster flicks through the pages of a car magazine in his bedroom ▪ 31-year-old racing driver Jackie Stewart wins the Monaco Grand Prix in a blue Tyrrell-Ford (number 11). 42-year-old Graham Hill finishes in ninth position. 37-year-old John Surtees is tenth ▪ 41-year-old pop star Dickie Valentine dies in a car crash (travelling in a Hillman *Avenger*) at Crickhowell in Wales ▪ The new British Leyland *Morris Marina* goes on sale. The *1.3 De Luxe Coupe* costs £923, has a top speed of 82 mph and accelerates from 0-60 mph in 17.5 seconds ▪ The *1.8 TC* costs £1,177 has a top speed of 100 mph and can reach 60 mph in 12.5 seconds ▪ 44-year-old Jimmy Savile says, "Clunk, click, every trip." ▪ "Scarred old slaver knows he's doin' alright, hear him whip the women just around midnight..." *Brown Sugar* ("... how come you taste so good?") by The Rolling Stones is number two on the hit parade.

Summer 1971

Ford Cortina Mk III

Monarch:	Queen Elizabeth II (aged 45)
Prime-minister:	Edward Heath (aged 55)
Chancellor:	Anthony Barber (aged 51)
Home Secretary:	Reginald Maudling (aged 54)
Foreign Secretary:	Alec Douglas-Home (aged 68)
Football Manager:	Alf Ramsey (aged 51)
Radio 1 Breakfast DJ:	Tony Blackburn (aged 28)
New car reg. suffix:	'K'

▪ The sun shines ▪ "Blackpool Tower isn't as big as I thought it would be either!" - saucy postcards continue to sell well at seaside resorts ▪ "By Jove, Missus!" - 43-year-old entertainer Ken Dodd appears in summer season at the Opera House in Blackpool ▪ 31-year-old Jimmy Tarbuck is on stage at Coventry ▪ Groovy kids wear flared jeans and platform shoes and sit together in the park drinking alcohol ▪ 'Pull a bird tonight. Woodpecker for the wild life' - *Woodpecker* cider is available from the 'off-licence.' A litre bottle is 12½p plus deposit ▪ *I'm Gonna Run Away From You* ("... A-hoo") by 32-year-old Tammi Lynn is number four in the pop chart ▪ *Let Your Yeah Be Yeah* by The Pioneers is number five ▪ 27-year-old Julie Edge is Voluptua, 21-year-old Adriene Posta is Scrubba and 54-year-old Frankie Howerd is Lurcio in *Up Pompeii* - now showing at cinemas across the country ▪ *Die Screaming, Marianne* (with 21-year-old Susan George) is coming soon ▪ "Oh my darling, knock three times on the ceiling if you want me. Twice on the pipe, if the answer is no" - *Knock Three Times* by Dawn spends five weeks at number one on the hit parade ▪ *I Am... I Said* by 30-year-old Neil Diamond peaks at number four ▪ Dennis Filkins wins the annual *News of the World* darts tournament at the Ship Inn in Weymouth - beating Derek White by two legs to nil in the final ▪ 10-year-old schoolboy Phil Taylor from Burslem in Staffordshire enjoys a game of 'arrows' with his mates ▪ Schoolboys kick orange *Wembley Trophy* footballs in the park ▪ 10-year-old Gary Lineker from Leicester scores a hat-trick, then goes home for a packet of crisps ▪ "Glory, glory, glory. Listen to the band" - *Banner Man* by Blue Mink is number three in the weekly pop chart ▪ *Don't Let It Die* ("... Don't let it die, or say goodbye.

Amen") by 47-year-old Hurricane Smith climbs to number two ▪ 36-year-old jockey Geoff Lewis from Wales rides *Mill Reef* to victory in the Epsom Derby ▪ Kenneth Kendall from Cornwall reads the news on BBC One ▪ Production at British Leyland car factories remains slow - with many workers idle due to a lack of component parts ▪ 38-year-old businessman James Goldsmith buys the Bovril company for £13 million - and begins selling off the assets ▪ Conservative MPs are split on the issue of Europe ▪ A number of Tory back-benchers inform 54-year-old prime-minister Edward Heath that they will not support his plan to take Britain into the Common Market ▪ 'The Milk Snatcher' - thousands of protestors take to the streets as 45-year-old Education Secretary Margaret Thatcher ends the provision of free milk for children in primary schools ▪ "Wanna thank you for the joy you brought me. Thank you for the things you taught me" - *Heaven Must Have Sent You* by The Elgins is number three in the pop chart ▪ "Take an eye for an eye and a life for a life. And somebody must die for the death of my wife. Yes..." *I Did What I Did For Maria* by 28-year-old Tony Christie peaks at number two ▪ People enjoy a night in, watching television on rented *PYE CT-71* (22-inch) sets ▪ *The Black and White Minstrel Show* is broadcast on BBC One on Saturday evenings - followed by *A Man Called Ironside*, starring 54-year-old Raymond Burr ▪ 36-year-old Michael Parkinson hosts *Parkinson* a brand new, late night chat show. 27-year-old tennis player Arthur Ashe, 36-year-old jazz singer Marian Montgomery and 59-year-old actor Terry-Thomas are the first guests to be interviewed ▪ 40-year-old comedian Les Dawson appears in a new series of *Sez Les* on ITV ▪ "£6.30 a day plus expenses" - 53-year-old Alfred Burke stars as Private Investigator Frank Maker in a new series of *Public Eye* ▪ 35-year-old Glenda Jackson stars at cinemas in *Sunday Bloody Sunday* - a tale of bisexual love ▪ 47-year-old Marlon Brando and 24-year-old Stephanie Beacham star in *The Nightcomers* - a movie from 35-year-old director Michael Winner ▪ 17-year-old Rosemary Letts murders 8-year-old Charmaine West in Gloucester ▪ 29-year-old Fred West (recently released from prison) murders his former wife, Rena Costello, and buries her body in a field near Kempley in Gloucestershire ▪ *Girls Are Out To Get You* by The Fascinations stalls at number thirty-two in the pop chart ▪ *Me And You And A Dog Named Boo* ("... how I love being a free

man") by Lobo climbs to number four ▪ Don Revie's hard-tackling Leeds Utd win the Inter Cities Fairs Cup by beating Juventus (with 24-year-old midfielder Fabio Capello in their team) on the away goals rule ▪ 23-year-old winger Ray Graydon transfers from Third Division Bristol Rovers to Third Division Aston Villa for £50,000 ▪ 21-year-old striker Malcolm MacDonald transfers from Second Division Luton Town to First Division Newcastle Utd for £180,000 ▪ *Good Old Arsenal* by The Arsenal First Team Squad reaches number sixteen in the pop chart ▪ "Gonna stamp out your fire. He can change your desire" - *He's Gonna Step On You Again* by 25-year-old John Kongos is number four ▪ 64-year-old E. W. Swanton, 59-year-old Brian 'Johnners' Johnston and 52-year-old John Arlott commentate on cricket for BBC radio's *Test Match Special* ▪ John Edrich and Brian Luckhurst stride out together to open the batting for England at Edgbaston in the first Test against Pakistan. Edrich is out for a duck. Luckhurst makes 35. 25-year-old wicketkeeper Alan Knott (batting at number seven) scores a century and the match ends in a draw. 30-year-old Geoffrey Boycott scores 121 not out in the second Test at Lord's and England win the series, 1-0 ▪ The sun shines ▪ Girls wear hotpants ▪ "Welcome to *Top of the Pops*. Lots of nice young ladies about with us this evening" - 44-year-old disc jockey Jimmy Savile introduces *Top of the Pops* from a crowded TV studio ▪ "Where's your mamma gone? Where's your mamma gone? Far, far away. Far, far away" - *Chirpy Chirpy Cheep Cheep* by Middle of the Road (with vocalist, 26-year-old Sally Carr) moves up sixteen places to number one - and stays at the top for five weeks! ▪ "I once knew a girl who was very, very shy. She never ever seemed to catch any boy's eye" - *Leap Up And Down (Wave Your Knickers In The Air)* by St. Cecilia is number twelve ▪ 23-year-old Gyles Brandreth and the 65-year-old Earl of Longford travel to Copenhagen to take part in a fact-finding mission looking into pornography ▪ Back in England - *Up the Chastity Belt* (with 54-year-old Frankie Howerd and 23-year-old Anne Aston) goes on general release at cinemas ▪ 'It's Scrumdidilyumptious!' - 38-year-old Gene Wilder stars in *Willy Wonka and the Chocolate Factory*. 13-year-old Peter Ostrum plays the role of Charlie Bucket. 64-year-old Harold Albertson is Grandpa Joe ▪ 59-year-old Jimmy Chipperfield opens a new safari park at Knowsley on Merseyside and families travel from all around to see the

monkeys ▪ 45-year-old Queen Elizabeth II opens the Kingsway tunnel under the River Mersey between Liverpool and Wallasey ▪ "Co-Co would dream of dancing at midnight beneath the stars" - *Co-Co* by The Sweet (with vocalist, 25-year-old Brian Connolly) climbs to number two in the pop chart ▪ "Tom-Tom lived for all he could give" - *Tom-Tom Turnaround* by New World is number six ▪ 'K' reg cars go on sale on the first of August ▪ There's a four-month waiting time (due to a shortage of cars) at Morris and Austin dealers ▪ Ford promote the new *Cortina MkIII* with an advertising strap-line that claims the new model, 'takes motoring to a new peak' ▪ Sales of foreign cars are increasing ▪ The new Datsun *100A Cherry* has a top speed of 87 mph and can reach 60 mph in 14.6 seconds ▪ The latest BMW *2002tii* has a top speed of 115 mph and can reach 60 mph in 9.8 seconds ▪ Four star leaded petrol is 34 new pence a gallon ▪ 32-year-old racing driver Jackie Stewart wins the British Grand Prix at Silverstone in a blue Tyrrell-Ford (number 12) and goes on to be crowned Formula One world champion for a second time ▪ "I'll tip my hat to the new constitution, take a bow for the new revolution" - *We Won't Get Fooled Again* by The Who (with 27-year-old Roger Daltrey, 26-year-old Pete Townshend, 26-year-old John Entwistle and 24-year-old Keith Moon) climbs to number nine in the pop chart ▪ "But what can a poor boy do, except to sing for a rock'n'roll band? 'Cause in sleepy London town there's just no place for a..." *Street Fighting Man* by The Rolling Stones (with 28-year-old Mick Jagger, 27-year-old Keith Richards, 30-year-old Charlie Watts and with the late Brian Jones on sitar) peaks at number twenty-one ▪ 43-year-old Frank O'Farrell leaves Leicester City to take over from Sir Matt Busby as manager of Manchester Utd ▪ 31-year-old Denis Law scores for Utd in a 2-2 draw against Derby County on the opening day of the season ▪ 20-year-old Kevin Keegan scores on his debut for Bill Shankly's Liverpool in a 3-1 win against Nottingham Forest ▪ A week later, 21-year-old Malcolm MacDonald scores a hat-trick as Newcastle Utd beat Liverpool 3-2 at St. James' Park ▪ A pale-blue, three-wheeled AC*70 Invacar* is parked at the side of the football pitch at Highfield Road as Coventry City draw 2-2 with Derby County ▪ "I 'ate you, Butler!" - 44-year-old Stephen Lewis is Inspector Blake (aka Blakey) and 55-year-old Reg Varney is Stan Butler in a cinema film version of popular TV show *On the Buses* ▪ 31-year-old

George Lazenby and 32-year-old Germaine Greer star in *Universal Soldier* ▪ Uncouth show jumper 32-year-old Harvey Smith causes an outrage at Hickstead by making a 'V' sign at Douglas Bunn - one of the judges ▪ "W'alright everybody!" - *Get Down And Get With It* by Slade (with 25-year-old Noddy Holder) is number sixteen in the pop chart ▪ "This is! A heavy, heavy monster sound" - *Monkey Spanner* by Dave and Ansil Collins is number seven ▪ *Apollo 15* (with astronauts: David Scott, Alfred Worden and James Irwin) lands on the Moon and stays for three days ▪ Back in England - Ron Greenwood's West Ham Utd lose their opening three matches of the football season and recall transfer listed 22-year-old Trevor Brooking to the team ▪ Manchester Utd's 25-year-old 'super' Georgie Best is sent off for swearing at the referee in a match against Chelsea ▪ 19-year-old goalkeeper John 'Budgie' Burridge transfers from Fourth Division Workington Town to Second Division Blackpool for £10,000 ▪ 'Strange, savage and terrifying things happen on a Walkabout' - 19-year-old Jenny Agutter swims naked in *Walkabout* - now showing at cinemas ▪ 22-year-old Gillian Blake stars on TV in *Follyfoot* ▪ "You're dirty, sweet and you're my girl. Get it on. Bang a gong ..." *Get It On* by T-Rex (with 23-year-old Marc Bolan) is new at number one - the song is the group's second number one hit ▪ "The world is black, the world is white, it turns by day and then by night" - *Black And White* by Greyhound is number six ▪ *What Are You Doing Sunday* ("... baby? Would you like to marry me?") by Dawn (22-year-old Telma Hopkins, 24-year-old Joyce Vincent and 27-year-old Tony Orlando) is number thirteen ▪ Adolescent boys browse the top shelf at their local newsagents ▪ *Parade* is on sale for 8 new pence. Pretty 24-year-old Doris Arden is topless on the front cover ▪ *The Daily Mirror* publishes the headline, 'Longford Porn Team Split' when 23-year-old Gyles Brandreth decides pornography isn't so bad afterall and quits the commission headed up by the Earl of Longford ▪ 'Keep your eyes on what she cannot see' - 26-year-old Mia Farrow plays the role of a terrified blind woman in *See No Evil* - a psychological thriller from Richard Fleischer ▪ 'Hate. Terror. Fear' - 38-year-old Joan Collins and 43-year-old James Booth star in *Revenge* ▪ Shoppers visit *Green Shield Stamps* catalogue stores ▪ Modern household gadgets are in vogue ▪ A Goblin *Teasmade* costs thirty-two books (or £27.50).

Autumn 1971

Spaghetti Junction

Monarch:	Queen Elizabeth II (aged 45)
Prime-minister:	Edward Heath (aged 55)
Chancellor:	Anthony Barber (aged 51)
Home Secretary:	Reginald Maudling (aged 54)
Foreign Secretary:	Alec Douglas-Home (aged 68)
Football Manager:	Alf Ramsey (aged 51)
Radio 1 Breakfast DJ:	Tony Blackburn (aged 28)
New car reg. suffix:	'K'

▪ The Troubles continue in Ireland ▪ A school girl is fatally wounded in crossfire between British soldiers and the IRA ▪ The Democratic Unionist Party is founded by 45-year-old Rev Ian Paisley ▪ A bomb explodes at the Post Office tower in London - there are no casualties ▪ 10-year-old schoolboy Jonathan Ross from Leytonstone stays up late to watch telly ▪ 50-year-old movie star Dirk Bogarde is a guest on BBC One chat show *Parkinson* ▪ 30-year-old John Alderton (as teacher, Mr. Hedges) 56-year-old Deryck Guyler (as Potter, the caretaker) and 22-year-old Carol Hawkins (as a pupil from Class 5C) star at cinemas in *Please Sir!* - a film spin-off from the popular TV series telling of the shenanigans at Fenn Street School ▪ 31-year-old Julie Christie and 37-year-old Alan Bates star in *The Go-Between* ▪ "I remember when I was five and you were ten, boy. You knew that I was shy, so you teased and made me cry, but I loved you" - *I'm Still Waiting* by 27-year-old Diana Ross climbs to number one in the pop chart - and stays there for four weeks ▪ "I've got a never ending love for you" - *Never Ending Song Of Love* by the New Seekers spends five weeks at number two ▪ 'The Festival of Light' takes place in Trafalgar Square - and 50,000 people turn up to hear 61-year-old Mrs. Mary Whitehouse and 68-year-old Malcolm Muggeridge deliver speeches denouncing pornography and violence in the mass media ▪ 30-year-old Cliff Richard and 20-year-old Dana perform Christian songs in Hyde Park ▪ *Back Street Luv* by Curved Air is number four in the pop chart ▪ *Soldier Blue* by 30-year-old Buffy Sainte-Marie is number seven ▪ "That's made my day, that has!" - a new series of *On the Buses* begins on ITV, with 44-year-old Stephen Lewis as Blakey, 55-year-old Reg Varney as Stan, 39-year-old Bob Grant

as Jack, 40-year-old Michael Robbins as Arthur and 35-year-old Anna Karen as Olive ▪ *I Believe (In Love)* by Hot Chocolate is number eight in the pop chart ▪ "Yes, I'm being followed by a moon shadow. Moon shadow…" *Moonshadow* by 23-year-old Cat Stevens stalls at number twenty-two ▪ 29-year-old Geoff Hurst and 26-year-old Martin Chivers score the goals as Sir Alf Ramsey's England football team (G Banks, Lawler, Cooper, Mullery, McFarland, Moore, F Lee, Madeley, Chivers, G Hurst, Peters and substitute, Radford) beats Switzerland 2-3 in Basel ▪ Back in Britain - the political battle between Left and Right intensifies as Edward Heath's new Industrial Relations Act becomes law. Defiant union leaders say they will not comply with its conditions ▪ Thirty-four football hooligans are arrested at a First Division match between Huddersfield Town and Leeds Utd ▪ Triumph car workers at Speke and Coventry are on a go-slow in an effort to avoid being laid-off due to a shortage of components ▪ Thousands of workers are also idle at British Leyland's Longbridge factory ▪ Civil servants begin working on Mr. Heath's plans for a new airport at Maplin Sands in Essex ▪ *And Now For Something Completely Different…* the Monty Python team (30-year-old Graham Chapman, 31-year-old John Cleese, 28-year-old Eric Idle, 29-year-old Terry Jones, 28-year-old Michael Palin and 30-year-old Terry Gilliam) makes cinema audiences laugh with a collection of wacky sketches and crazy animation ▪ "You just call out my name, and you know wherever I am, I'll come running (oh yeah, baby), to see you again" - *You've Got A Friend* by 23-year-old James Taylor is number four in the pop chart ▪ *Bangla-Desh* by 28-year-old George Harrison is number ten ▪ Thieves break into Lloyds Bank on Baker Street in London and steal cash and valuables from over two-hundred safe deposit boxes ▪ Thick fog descends on the North West of the country ▪ A motorway pile-up (involving two-hundred vehicles) on the M6 at the Thelwall Viaduct near Warrington claims the lives of ten people and injures dozens more ▪ 45-year-old Queen Elizabeth II cuts the ribbon to open (officially) the new section of M62 motorway across the Pennines ▪ "Well I just wonder…" *Did You Ever* ("… all the time") by 31-year-old Nancy Sinatra and 42-year-old Lee Hazelwood is number two in the pop chart ▪ *Tweedle Dee, Tweedle Dum* by Middle of the Road is number four ▪ Yellow 'smiley face' images are seen everywhere. Boys wear T shirts

with the happy symbol emblazoned on the front. Girls sew 'smiley face' badges onto their jeans ▪ A new series of *The Flaxton Boys* (a drama for children, set in Yorkshire in the year 1928) is on ITV ▪ *Blue Peter* is on BBC One on Monday and Thursday evenings. 37-year-old presenter John Noakes introduces a new pet - a young border collie - and viewers are asked to send in postcards with suggestions of a name for the puppy ▪ 25-year-old footballer 'super' Georgie Best bags a hat-trick for Manchester Utd in a 4-2 victory over West Ham Utd at Old Trafford ▪ 33-year-old centre-forward Derek Dougan bags a hat-trick for Wolverhampton Wanderers in a 4-2 victory over Nottingham Forest at the Molineux ▪ In Division Three, 25-year-old Alf Wood scores five as Shrewsbury Town thrash Blackburn Rovers 7-1 at Gay Meadow ▪ "You never wrote me, you never called..." *Nathan Jones* ("... you've been gone too long") by The Supremes is number five in the pop chart ▪ *Keep On Dancing* by The Bay City Rollers is number nine ▪ The *Daily Mail* reports, 'Wild scenes as MPs take big step into Europe' ▪ 50-year-old Roy Jenkins and many of his fellow Labour MPs defy a party whip by voting with Edward Heath's Conservative government - to approve Britain's entry into the Common Market. (A number of disgruntled Tory back-benchers are still hoping to scupper the deal before it becomes law) ▪ Queen Elizabeth II welcomes 70-year-old Emperor Hirohito of Japan on an official state visit to Britain ▪ 21-year-old Princess Anne wins the three-day horse trial event at Burghley House on *Doublet* ▪ 26-year-old disc jockey Dave Lee Travis presents the weekday lunch time show on Radio One ▪ *Hey Girl Don't Bother Me* ("... stay out of my arms, don't use your charms. Don't bother me") by The Tams spends three weeks at number one in the pop chart ▪ *Tap Turns On The Water* by CCS is number five ▪ Radio One DJ's take turns to present *Top of the Pops* on BBC One television at 7.25 p.m. on Thursday evenings ▪ 28-year-old Tony Blackburn hosts the show on the fourteenth of October ▪ 44-year-old Jimmy Savile hosts the show the following week ▪ Pan's People (Felicity 'Flick' Colby, Barbara 'Babs' Lord, Louise Clarke, Dee Dee Wilde, Andi Rutherford and Ruth Pearson) are the resident dancers ▪ For the first time since 1967, the clocks are moved back by one hour - as the government ends its experiment into 'British Standard Time' and reverts to 'Greenwich Mean Time' ▪ 30-year-old Ed 'stewpot' Stewart presents *Junior*

Choice on Radio One at the weekend ▪ "To Bombay, a travelling circus came, they brought an intelligent elephant, and Nellie was her name" - Mandy Miller sings *Nellie The Elephant* ▪ All sixty-three people on board BEA Flight 706 are killed when the plane crashes to the ground in Belgium ▪ The Troubles continue in Northern Ireland ▪ 'Super' Georgie Best receives death threats from Irish Nationalists ▪ Police detectives from Special Branch are assigned protection duties to the star footballer ▪ A boardroom power struggle at Manchester City results in 44-year-old Malcolm Allison taking over from 57-year-old Joe Mercer as manager ▪ John Harris' Sheffield Utd lead the way in Division One after beating Jimmy Bloomfield's Leicester City 1-0 at Bramall Lane ▪ The names 'Best, Charlton, Law' appear together on the same score-sheet for the final time as Manchester Utd beat Huddersfield Town 3-0 with goals from 25-year-old George, 33-year-old Bobby and 31-year-old Denis ▪ 21-year-old actress Susan George plays a terrified babysitter in the horror film *Fright* ▪ "Marie, Marie da voodoo veau, she'll put a spell on you" - *The Witch Queen Of New Orleans* by Redbone climbs to number two in the pop chart ▪ "We are all the same and life is just a..." *Simple Game* ("De-de-der!") by The Four Tops is number three ▪ *For All We Know* by 34-year-old Shirley Bassey is number six ▪ "Wake up Maggie I think I got something to say to you. It's late September and I really should be back at school" - *Maggie May* by 26-year-old Rod Stewart is new at number one ▪ The new 100 mph Triumph *Dolomite* motorcar is on display at the Earls Court Motor Show - but after recent industrial action, orders for the new car will take up to two-months to fulfill ▪ 41-year-old Steve McQueen stars at cinemas in *Le Mans* ▪ 25-year-old Bruce Robinson and 22-year-old Susan Penhaligon star in *Private Road* - a gritty new drama written and directed by Barney Platts-Mills ▪ "Good game, good game!" - 43-year-old Bruce Forsyth presents the *Generation Game* on BBC One ▪ ITV broadcasts the first episode of *Upstairs Downstairs* (with 37-year-old Jean Marsh as Rose, 67-year-old Angela Baddeley as Mrs. Bridges and 47-year-old Gordon Jackson as Hudson) ▪ "It really doesn't matter if it's raining or it's fine, just as long as you've got time, to P-L-A-Y, play-away-away-way, play-away-play-play, away-way, play-away, play-away" - 38-year-old Brian Cant introduces the first *Play Away* for younger viewers on BBC Two ▪

Crystal Tipps and Alistair is also new ■ "Reggae, Reggae, Reggae. Here comes Johnny Reggae. Johnny Reggae Reggae. Lay it on me" - *Johnny Reggae* by The Piglets (with, lead singer, Barbara Kay) reaches number three in the pop chart ■ "I won't laugh at you when you boo hoo hoo..." *Coz I Luv You* by Slade (with 25-year-old Noddy Holder) spends four weeks at number one ■ John Lennon and The Plastic Ono Band are number one in the album chart with *Imagine* ■ Tape cassettes and 8-track cartridges are in demand at *The Tape Revolution Store* ■ 21-year-old Richard Branson's *Virgin Records* on Oxford Street is thriving ■ *The Old Grey Whistle Test* begins on late-night BBC Two ■ "Don't cry. Don't raise your eye. It's only teenage wasteland" - *Baba O'Riley* by The Who plays on a transistor radio ■ 33-year-old purple-shirted Jake Thackray appears on TV show *Braden's Week* ■ 38-year-old Peter Wyngarde drives a Bentley *S2 Continental* and stars as *Jason King* on ATV ■ The second, third, fourth, fifth and sixth episodes of *Upstairs Downstairs* are all transmitted in black and white due to last year's strike by ITV technicians ■ Children read *Mr. Tickle* - the first of *The Mr. Men* books by Roger Hargreaves ■ "There's a farmer down there with a purple face / I expect it's all that sun and the open air life, Joe / Now he's doing one of those country dances / Well, I don't think he looks very friendly / Aye, maybe you're right. 'Though it can't be anything we've done" - cartoon couple Joe and Petunia star on TV in a short public information film telling people to follow the Country Code - and close gates behind them ■ There's a flurry of activity on football's transfer market ■ 25-year-old striker Keith Weller leaves Dave Sexton's Chelsea and joins Jimmy Bloomfield's Leicester City for £100,000 ■ 25-year-old playmaker Tony Green leaves Bob Stokoe's Blackpool and joins Joe Harvey's Newcastle Utd for £150,000 ■ 19-year-old midfielder Martin O'Neill leaves Distillery in Ireland and joins Matt Gillies' Nottingham Forest for £15,000 ■ The proposed transfer of Asa Hartford from West Bromwich Albion to Leeds Utd is called off when a medical reveals that the 21-year-old has a hole in his heart ■ 'Super' Georgie Best scores a hat-trick as Frank O'Farrell's league-leaders Manchester Utd win 2-5 at Southampton ■ 30-year-old centre-forward Andy Lochhead scores a hat-trick, and 24-year-old midfielder Bruce Rioch nets twice, as Vic Crowe's Aston Villa thrash Oldham Athletic 0-6 in Division Three ■ 24-year-old

Ted MacDougall scores nine goals as Bournemouth thrash Margate 11-0 in the first round of the FA Cup ▪ "I'm so..." *Tired Of Being Alone* ("... I'm so tired of on my own") by 25-year-old Al Green is number four in the pop chart ▪ *The Night They Drove Old Dixie Down* by 30-year-old Joan Baez is number six ▪ The national road network continues to develop and grow ▪ A section of the new Gravelly Hill Interchange (aka 'Spaghetti Junction') opens - and the M6 motorway links up seamlessly with the A38(M) to form a brand new express-way into Birmingham city centre ▪ The stylish new Vauxhall *Viva* motorcar is available as a saloon, estate or coupe. The 1100cc base model has a top speed of 78 mph and accelerates from 0-60 mph in 20 seconds ▪ A new television series called *The Onedin Line* (with 40-year-old Peter Gilmore, 32-year-old Anne Stallybrass and 60-year-old Howard Lang) begins on BBC One on Friday evenings ▪ "Goodies! Goody, goody, yum, yum" - *The Goodies* episode 'Kitten Kong' airs for the first time, with a giant pussy cat terrorising the city of London ▪ TV presenter Eamonn Andrews surprises 25-year-old footballer Georgie Best on *This is Your Life* ▪ Hilda Ogden (played by 45-year-old Jean Alexander) wins £500 of premium bonds in ITV's popular soap-opera *Coronation Street* ▪ 'De-de-der-der-de-de-de-de-de-de-de-de-der-der, der-der-de-de-de-de-de' - 47-year-old Benny Hill stars in a new edition of *The Benny Hill Show*, with 48-year-old Nicholas Parsons, 61-year-old Patricia Hayes and 24-year-old Jenny Lee-Wright in the supporting cast ▪ 43-year-old John Collin plays DS Cecil Haggar in BBC's long-running police drama *Z Cars* ▪ 21-year-old Susan George from Surbiton stars alongside Dustin Hoffman in *Straw Dogs* - a sinister and thrilling new film from Sam Peckinpah ▪ 19-year-old twins Mary and Madeleine Collinson from Malta star alongside Peter Cushing in *Twins of Evil* - an 'X' rated horror film from Hammer ▪ Miss Marple features in *Nemesis* - the latest 'whodunit' novel from 81-year-old crime-writer Agatha Christie ▪ "Till the moon deserts the sky, till all the seas run dry, till then I'll worship you" - *Till* by 31-year-old Tom Jones is number two in the weekly pop chart ▪ *Banks Of The Ohio* by 23-year-old Olivia Newton-John is number six ▪ Modern food branding takes a step forward ▪ *Wotsits* crisps are new ▪ *Golden Nuggets* breakfast cereal is new ▪ Conservative prime-minister Edward Heath expells 105 Russian diplomats from Britain over allegations of spying.

Christmas 1971

A Space-Hopper for Christmas

Monarch:	Queen Elizabeth II (aged 45)
Prime-minister:	Edward Heath (aged 55)
Chancellor:	Anthony Barber (aged 51)
Home Secretary:	Reginald Maudling (aged 54)
Foreign Secretary:	Alec Douglas-Home (aged 68)
Football Manager:	Alf Ramsey (aged 51)
Radio 1 Breakfast DJ:	Tony Blackburn (aged 28)
New car reg. suffix:	'K'

▪ 'Everybody Out!' - Strikes at British Leyland ▪ Strikes at Ford ▪ Strikes at hundreds of engineering factories across the country ▪ Armitage Shanks launches a trendy new bathroom suite called the *Sheraton* ▪ 'Flushed with Success! The Carry On team carries on round the bend!' - *Carry On at Your Convenience* is now showing at cinemas, with 45-year-old Kenneth Williams as W.C. Boggs, 58-year-old Sid 'Ha-ak-ak' James as Sid Plummer and with 39-year-old Kenneth Cope as Vic Spanner - shop steward of the National Union of Chinaware Industrial Employees (aka NUCIE) ▪ *Diamonds Are Forever* ("... They are all I need to please me. They can stimulate and tease me") - 34-year-old Shirley Bassey sings the theme song as 41-year-old Sean Connery returns as James Bond (aka 007) in the movie *Diamonds Are Forever.* 43-year-old Jimmy Dean plays Willard Whyte. 31-year-old Jill St John is (Bond girl) Tiffany Case. 22-year-old Lola Larson is Bambi. 23-year-old Trina Parks is Thumper ▪ Prime-minister Edward Heath accuses Opposition Leader Harold Wilson of failing to take action against Soviet spies when Labour was in power. Mr. Heath refutes the claim and says he always "took immediate action" to have spies ousted ▪ "They'd call us..." *Gypsies, Tramps And Thieves* ("... but every night all the men would come around, and lay their money down") by 25-year-old Cher is number four in the pop chart ▪ "You're so sweet, you're so fine. I want you all and everything just to be mine, 'cause you're my babe" - *Jeepster* by T-Rex (with 24-year-old Marc Bolan) is number two ▪ *Four Symbols (Led Zeppelin 4)* by Led Zeppelin (27-year-old Jimmy Page, 23-year-old John Bonham, 25-year-old John Paul Jones and 23-year-old Robert Plant) is top of the album chart ▪ Emerson, Lake &

Palmer, comprising of 27-year-old Keith Emerson (keyboards), 24-year-old Greg Lake (guitar/vocals) and 21-year-old Carl Palmer (drums) feature on the front cover of the latest *New Musical Express* ▪ 35-year-old Gordon Honeycombe reads the news for ITN ▪ Inflation is rising - it now stands at 8.6% ▪ 55-year-old prime-minister Edward Heath is under severe pressure due of the weak economy, rising unemployment and poor relations with the unions ▪ 37-year-old *Blue Peter* presenter John Noakes announces to viewers that the show's new border collie puppy will be called 'Shep' ▪ Stan and Hilda Ogden (played by 56-year-old Bernard Youens and 45-year-old Jean Alexander) are proud owners of a new miniature cocktail bar, now placed in the living-room of their house at number 13 *Coronation Street* ▪ A bottle of *White Horse* whisky costs £2.55 ▪ A bottle of *Martell* brandy is £3.30 ▪ A bottle of *Warninks* advocaat is £1.60 ▪ A bottle of *Harveys Bristol Cream* is £1.25 ▪ 23-year-old footballer Trevor Brooking scores a goal for West Ham Utd in a 3-3 draw against Southampton at The Dell. 23-year-old Mick Channon is on the score-sheet for 'The Saints' ▪ 21-year-old Malcolm MacDonald scores twice as Newcastle Utd beat West Bromwich Albion 0-3 at the Hawthorns ▪ Retail prices are rising ▪ A ticket for a seat in the circle at the local cinema costs around 40p. A seat in the stalls is 30p ▪ 'The sleuth, the whole sleuth and nothing but the sleuth' - *Gumshoe* is now showing, with 35-year-old Albert Finney - playing the role of a bingo caller turned private detective in Liverpool ▪ 'Hell will hold no surprises for them' - 34-year-old Vanessa Redgrave and 33-year-old Oliver Reed star in *The Devils* - a film from 44-year-old director Ken Russell ▪ *Softly Whispering I Love You* by The Congregation is number four in the pop chart ▪ *It Must Be Love* ("... love, love") by 26-year-old Labi Siffre is number fourteen ▪ Freezing fog rolls across the Midlands and South-East ▪ The commercial television companies Westward, Border and Grampian are all now broadcasting in full colour ▪ 600,000 colour TV licenses have been issued this year ▪ 44-year-old Roger Moore plays Lord Sinclair and 46-year-old Tony Curtis plays Daniel 'Danny' Wilde in *The Persuaders!* on ITV ▪ 37-year-old Wendy Craig stars in a new series of *And Mother Makes Three* ▪ 21-year-old Princess Anne is voted BBC's 'Sports Personality of the Year', after winning a major equestrian event at Burghley House ▪ 12-year-old Neil Reid from Glasgow scores the highest

number of points on the 'clapometer' and also obtains the most public votes to win ITV's popular talent show *Opportunity Knocks* - singing *Mother Of Mine* ▪ Comedians, 45-year-old Frank Carson, 40-year-old Les Dawson and double act Little and Large all appear on the Christmas special *Opportunity Knocks - All Winners Show* ▪ 'Very Urgent' - Monty Python's *Big Red Book* is on sale in all good bookshops ▪ Hallmark Records release *The Best of Top of the Pops '71* - a budget priced, cover-version pop compilation LP with a buxom girl pictured on the sleeve ▪ "Ch-ch-ch-ch, changes" - 24-year-old David Bowie releases the *Hunky Dory* album with the tracks *Changes* and *Life On Mars?* on side one ▪ "If I were a rich man" - 36-year-old Topol stars at cinemas in a film version of *Fiddler on the Roof* ▪ 'The time is just right for an out and out thriller like this' - 41-year-old Gene Hackman, 54-year-old Fernando Rey and 39-year-old Roy Scheider star in *The French Connection* ▪ 'I lay awake at nights, thinking of my next victim!' - 35-year-old Hal Reed stars in *The Zodiac Killer* ▪ "Do you want pasteurised, 'cause pasteurised is best? She said 'Ernie, I'll be happy if it comes up to me chest'" - *Ernie (The Fastest Milkman In The West)* by 47-year-old Benny Hill climbs to number one on the hit parade - and stays there for four weeks ▪ "When the day is dawning, on a Texas Sunday morning" - *Is This The Way To Amarillo* by 28-year-old Tony Christie is number eighteen ▪ The Troubles continue in Northern Ireland ▪ A bomb explosion kills fifteen people in a Belfast bar ▪ Footballers, 29-year-old Geoff Hurst and 26-year-old Martin Chivers score the goals for Sir Alf Ramsey's England team (G Banks, Madeley, Hughes, Bell, McFarland, Moore, F Lee, Ball, Chivers, G Hurst, Peters) in a 2-0 victory over Greece ▪ Frank O'Farrell's Manchester Utd remain top of Division One with a 3-2 victory over Nottingham Forest ▪ 36-year-old Brian Clough's Derby County move up to second with a 2-0 win against Everton ▪ 27-year-old Franny Lee scores for Manchester City in a 1-3 away win at Stoke City ▪ 26-year-old Alan Ball leaves Everton and joins Arsenal for a new record transfer fee of £220,000 ▪ Parents take their kids to the cinema to see the latest Disney film, *Bedknobs and Broomsticks*, and to eat snacks ▪ *Hula-Hoops* from KP are new ▪ Christmas morning arrives ▪ *Klackers*, *Lego*, *Etch-A-Sketch*, *Shaker Makers*, *Fuzzy-Felts* and orange bouncy *Space Hoppers* (retailing at £1.50 each) keep the children happy ▪

The new *Mastermind* board game (where the aim is for one player to deduce the correct sequence of colours of his opponents four hidden pegs) is also popular ▪ Excited schoolboys play with Matchbox *Superfast* 'double-loop' race sets and Corgi *Whizzwheels* 'rockets' tracks - with a 'Super Booster' black, plastic launch tunnel ▪ Some children make themselves sick before dinner is even on the table ▪ A *Cadbury's* Selection Box costs 20p ▪ Millions watch TV ▪ 41-year-old Rolf Harris *Meets the Kids in Hospital* on BBC One ▪ 42-year-old pianist and conductor Andre Previn is a guest star on the *Morecambe & Wise Show* in the evening. During the program - Previn criticises Eric Morecambe for playing all the wrong musical notes. The 45-year-old comedian responds by saying, "I am playing all the *right* notes, but not *necessarily* in the right order" ▪ 52-year-old Sir Derek Ezra is the new chairman of the National Coal Board ▪ Production has risen slightly in 1971 with 154 million tonnes of coal being mined, but there's unrest within the National Union of Mineworkers ▪ A demand for a 25% pay increase is rejected and miners embark on an overtime ban ▪ Development of the new Concorde supersonic airplane has been a success ▪ Airline BOAC is expected to place a £65 million order for five new Concordes in the next few months ▪ Young men get ready for a night out on the town ▪ A new-fangled Remington *Lektro Blade* electric shaver costs £10.50 ▪ 'The Mark of a Man' - a cask of *Old Spice* origial aftershave is 90p ▪ 'Shaft's his name. Shaft's his game' - 29-year-old Richard Roundtree stars at cinemas as funky detective John Shaft ▪ "Who's the black private dick that's a sex machine to all the chicks? (Shaft!) You're damn right" - The *Theme From 'Shaft'* by 29-year-old Isaac Hayes is number four in the pop chart ▪ *No Matter How I Try* ("... I just can't say goodbye") by 25-year-old Gilbert O'Sullivan is number five ▪ "Now Ernie had a rival, an evil looking man, called Two-Ton Ted from Teddington and he drove the baker's van" - *Ernie (The Fastest Milkman In The West)* by Benny Hill remains at number one ▪ Young boys lie on the floor at home, pushing *Tonka* toys over the carpet - imagining that they're *really* driving the large, metal, yellow tipper truck or dark green army Jeep ▪ Families sit on three-piece suites, watching telly and eating food snacks ▪ A packet of *Golden Wonder* crisps costs 3 new pence ▪ A bar of Cadbury's *Old Jamaica* is 9 new pence ▪ The average price of a house in the UK is now over £5,000.

New Year 1972

Ronnie Radford's screamer for Hereford Utd

Monarch:	Queen Elizabeth II (aged 45)
Prime-minister:	Edward Heath (aged 55)
Chancellor:	Anthony Barber (aged 51)
Home Secretary:	Reginald Maudling (aged 54)
Foreign Secretary:	Alec Douglas-Home (aged 68)
Football Manager:	Alf Ramsey (aged 52)
Radio 1 Breakfast DJ:	Tony Blackburn (aged 29)
New car reg. suffix:	'K'

▪ "Coo-ee! Mr. Shifter!" - the chimpanzees move a piano in a TV advert for *PG Tips* ▪ The coal miners overtime ban escalates into a full-blown strike ▪ Nationwide power cuts plunge the country into darkness ▪ Schools and businesses are forced to close ▪ 55-year-old prime-minister Edward Heath declares a State of Emergency ▪ Three-thousand workers are laid-off at British Leyland's Longbridge factory after two-hundred engine inspectors walk out on strike ▪ Unemployment tops one million for the first time in thirty years ▪ Frugal housewives carry out the 'weekly shop' at supermarkets ▪ A loaf of bread is 10p ▪ A pint of milk is 5p ▪ A small jar of *Maxwell House* coffee is 25p ▪ A tub of *Stork* margarine is 11½p ▪ A can of *Coca-Cola* is 6½p ▪ *I'd Like To Teach The World To Sing (In Perfect Harmony)* ("... I'd like to hold it in my arms, and keep it company") by The New Seekers spends four weeks at the top of the hit parade ▪ Families book their summer holidays at the travel agents ▪ 'Go Pontin!' - a chalet at one of *Pontin's* thirteen holiday centres around Britain is available from just £13.50 per person, per week ▪ 'Well-to-do' middle-class families also book their summer holidays at the travel agents ▪ 'Pontinental' - a week in Torremolinos costs £55 per person ▪ "Mother of mine, you gave to me, all of my life to do as I please. I owe everything I have to you, mother, sweet..." *Mother Of Mine* by 12-year-old *Opportunity Knocks* winner Neil Reid is number two in the pop chart ▪ *Softly Whispering I Love You* ("... Echoes of your voice are calling") by The Congregation is number four ▪ 'A screwball comedy, remember them?' - 29-year-old Barbra Streisand and 30-year-old Ryan O'Neal star at cinemas in *What's Up, Doc?* ▪

63-year-old Bette Davis and 41-year-old Robert Wagner star in *Madame Sin* ▪ 58-year-old Sid 'Ha-ak-ak' James, 43-year-old Diana Coupland and 21-year-old Sally Geeson star in a new series of sit-com *Bless This House* on ITV ▪ "What's got four legs, walks peculiar, talks with all the choicest words? What's got four arms, loves to grab you? Answer is, two Liver Birds" - 30-year-old Polly James and 30-year-old Nerys Hughes star as Beryl and Sandra in a new series of *The Liver Birds* on BBC One ▪ 46-year-old Richard Baker presents the *Nine O'Clock News* ▪ Prime-minister Edward Heath travels to Brussels to sign a treaty binding Britain to Europe - and gets doused in ink by a German protestor ▪ Accompanying the premier on his trip are former prime-minister 77-year-old Harold Macmillan and 63-year-old Duncan Sandys MP, son-in-law of the late Sir Winston Churchill and co-founder of Britain's European Movement ▪ 'End the Common Market!' - demonstrators take to the streets of Britain urging the government to think again and alter its course ▪ 11-year-old public schoolboy Ian Hislop reads the Sunday newspapers ▪ *Something Tells Me (Something Is Gonna Happen Tonight)* by 28-year-old Cilla Black is number three in the pop chart ▪ *Tokoloshe Man* by 26-year-old John Kongos moves down four places to number eleven ▪ The miners' strike continues ▪ 37-year-old picket Freddie Matthews is killed when a lorry mounts the pavement outside a power station in Lincolnshire ▪ 34-year-old Arthur Scargill leads thousands of miners against the police at Saltley in Birmingham - and forces the closure of a large coke depot ▪ Power cuts continue and families huddle around candles in cold, dim living rooms ▪ The Troubles in Northern Ireland reach a tragic low point on Bloody Sunday when soldiers of the British Army kill thirteen unarmed people in Derry. A fourteenth person dies four months later ▪ 48-year-old Jack Scott presents the weather forecast on BBC One ▪ It's generally cold, wet and windy ▪ A film version of Dylan Thomas' *Under Milk Wood* (starring Richard Burton, Peter O'Toole and 39-year-old Elizabeth Taylor) is at cinemas ▪ 'Being the adventures of a young man whose principle interests are rape, ultra-violence and Beethoven' - Stanley Kubrick's ('X' rated) *A Clockwork Orange* is also now showing ▪ 61-year-old Mrs. Mary Whitehouse launches a national petition for improved standards in public decency - which she plans

to present at the door of Number 10 Downing Street ▪ 30-year-old Fred West marries 18-year-old Rosemary Letts at Gloucester Register Office ▪ "Ohhh..." *Soley Soley* by Middle Of The Road is number five on the hit parade ▪ "I can't remember if I cried, when I read about his widowed bride. Something touched me deep inside, the day the music died" - *American Pie* by 26-year-old Don McLean is number two ▪ 25-year-old Manchester Utd footballer 'super' Georgie Best fails to turn up for training after his team loses 3-0 to West Ham at Upton Park and manager Frank O'Farrell drops him from the side ▪ Best spends the evening at *Tramp* discotheque in London - drinking Champagne with his girlfriend, 19-year-old Carolyn Moore (aka Miss Great Britain) ▪ 36-year-old writer David Nobbs pens humorous scripts and one-line gags for the new series of *Sez Les* on ITV ▪ 5-year-old Sean O'Hara spends his first day at St. Joseph's school in Rugeley ▪ Many school children are now being taught with 'The Wide Range Readers' blue and green books ▪ *Ken Dodd and the Diddymen* and *The Basil Brush Show* keep young TV viewers entertained on Sunday afternoons - before *Songs of Praise* begins ▪ *Morning Has Broken* ("... like the first morning. Blackbird has spoken, like the first bird") by Cat Stevens is number nine in the pop chart ▪ "I've been through the desert on a..." *Horse With No Name* by America is number three ▪ 25-year-old footballer 'super' Georgie Best returns to the Manchester Utd team and scores twice in a 4-1 win victory over Southampton at Old Trafford ▪ 28-year-old footballer Ronnie Radford scores a 'screamer' as non-league Hereford knock First Division Newcastle Utd out of the FA Cup ▪ 21-year-old Charlie George scores twice as Bertie Mee's Arsenal beat John Harris' Sheffield Utd 0-5 at Bramall Lane ▪ 29-year-old Alan Hinton scores twice as Brian Clough's Derby County thrash Matt Gillies' Nottingham Forest 4-0 in front of 31,801 at the Baseball Ground ▪ *I Just Can't Help Believing* ("... when she's lying close beside me, and my heart beats with the rhythm of her sighs. This time the girl is gonna stay. This time the girl is gonna stay, for more than just a day") by 37-year-old Elvis Presley is number six in the pop chart ▪ "Oh, I got a brand new pair of roller skates, you got a..." *Brand New Key* by 24-year-old Melanie is number four ▪ 45-year-old disc jockey Jimmy Savile is awarded an OBE ▪ Seven people are killed when

an IRA car-bomb explodes at an army base in Aldershot ▪ 22-year-old Alex 'Hurricane' Higgins wins £400 in the *Park Drive* World Snooker Championship - beating John Spencer by 37 frames to 32 in the final at Selly Park British Legion in Birmingham ▪ The Beehive department store on Albert Street in Birmingham closes down ▪ 49-year-old Nicholas Parsons presents *Sale of the Century* - an exciting new game-show from Anglia TV in Norwich ▪ ITV's hugely popular *Upstairs Downstairs* (with 37-year-old Jean Marsh as Rose, 67-year-old Angela Baddeley as Mrs. Bridges and 48-year-old Gordon Jackson as Hudson) is now being broadcast in colour ▪ 38-year-old Joan Collins makes a guest appearance in *The Pursuaders* - starring alongside Tony Curtis and Roger Moore ▪ A new series of *Steptoe and Son* begins on BBC One, with 46-year-old Harry H. Corbett and 59-year-old Wilfrid Brambell. 45-year-old Leonard Rossiter makes a guest appearance in episode seven - playing an escaped convict ▪ "Yoffy lifts a finger, and a mouse is there"- *Fingerbobs*, with 34-year-old Rick Jones (aka Yoffy), is new for the children ▪ Glam rock blares out (in stereo) from ITT *KP-821* record players ▪ "Telegram Sam, Telegram Sam, you're my main man" - *Telegram Sam* by T-Rex (with 24-year-old Marc Bolan) is top of the pop chart - it's the group's third number one hit ▪ "Hey, hey, hey, hey what you doin' to me? Hey, hey, hey…" *Look Wot You Dun* by Slade (with 25-year-old Noddy Holder) is number four ▪ 'An absolute ball' - 38-year-old Michael Caine stars on the big screen (alongside 39-year-old Elizabeth Taylor and 33-year-old Susannah York) in *Zee and Co.* ▪ 27-year-old footballer Franny Lee scores a hat-trick for Malcolm Allison's high-flying Manchester City in a 5-2 victory over Wolverhampton Wanderers at Maine Road. The win keeps City at the top of Division One, closely followed by Leeds Utd, Derby County and Liverpool ▪ 20-year-old Steve Perryman is on the score-sheet for Tottenham Hotspur in a 2-0 win against Manchester Utd ▪ 21-year-old Malcolm 'Supermac' MacDonald is on the score-sheet for Newcastle Utd in a 2-0 win against Leicester City ▪ A top-of-the-table Third Division clash between Vic Crowe's Aston Villa and John Bond's Bournemouth draws a crowd of 48,110. Villa achieve a 2-1 victory with goals from 30-year-old Geoff Vowden and 30-year-old Andy Lochhead ▪ "I, I'm so in love with you" -

Let's Stay Together by 25-year-old Al Green is number seven in the pop chart ▪ *Sleepy Shores* by 46-year-old Johnny Pearson is number eight ▪ Queen Elizabeth II arrives in Thailand on the first stage of a six-week tour of South East Asia. The 45-year-old monarch is accompanied by 50-year-old Prince Philip, the Duke of Edinburgh, and 21-year-old Princess Anne ▪ Back in England - Power cuts continue ▪ High streets are in darkness ▪ Shops run out of candles and paraffin ▪ 54-year-old Joe Gormely of the National Union of Mineworkers negotiates with 55-year-old prime-minister Edward Heath (over beer and sandwiches) at 10 Downing Street ▪ After seven weeks of strike action - the miners return to work with a 20% pay rise and a 'shopping list' of other demands fully met ▪ 35-year-old burglar Donald Nielson (aka the Black Panther) breaks into a sub-post office at Haywood in Lancashire and guns down postmaster Leslie Richardson ▪ Queen Elizabeth and her royal party continue their overseas tour, moving onto Singapore, Malaysia, Brunei, the Maldives and the Seychelles ▪ Back in London - Chelsea football supporters invade the pitch at Brisbane Road when 21-year-old Barry Fairbrother scores a last minute winner for Orient in the fifth round of the FA Cup ▪ In Division One, 21-year-old Kevin Keegan scores a goal as Bill Shankly's Liverpool move to the-top-of-the-table with a 3-0 victory over Manchester City ▪ 22-year-old centre-back Martin Buchan transfers from Aberdeen to Manchester Utd for £125,000 ▪ "Son of my father, molded I was folded I was preform packed. Son of my father, commanded I was branded in a plastic vac. Surrounded and confounded by statistic facts" - *Son Of My Father* by Chicory Tip (a group from Maidstone, comprising of Rick Foster, Barry Mayger, Brian Shearer and 26-year-old, lead singer, Peter Hewson) is new at number one in the pop chart ▪ *Have You Seen Her* ("... Tell me, have you seen her?") by The Chi-Lites is number three ▪ "Pitter patter, pitter patter, pitter patter, pitter patter. One drop of rain on your window pane, doesn't mean to say there's a thunderstorm comin'" - *Storm In A Teacup* by The Fortunes is number seven ▪ Families gather around the kitchen table at breakfast time to eat cereal ▪ Tony the Tiger advertises *Frosties* on TV - "They're g-r-r-r-eat!"

Spring 1972

Cloughie's Derby County are champions

Monarch:	Queen Elizabeth II (aged 46)
Prime-minister:	Edward Heath (aged 55)
Chancellor:	Anthony Barber (aged 51)
Home Secretary:	Reginald Maudling (aged 55)
Foreign Secretary:	Alec Douglas-Home (aged 68)
Football Manager:	Alf Ramsey (aged 52)
Radio 1 Breakfast DJ:	Tony Blackburn (aged 29)
New car reg. suffix:	'K'

▪ The Troubles continue in Northern Ireland ▪ 55-year-old prime-minister Edward Heath imposes direct rule on the province and sends more troops to patrol the streets of Belfast. Protestant leaders in Ulster are critical of Mr. Heath's decision and condemn the shut down of Stormont as a victory for IRA terrorists ▪ In other news, 14-year-old schoolboy Timothy Davey is jailed in Turkey for conspiring to sell cannabis ▪ *Got To Be There* ("... in the morning") by 13-year-old Michael Jackson is number five in the pop chart ▪ "You know, I'll..." *Beg, Steal Or Borrow* ("... to give you sunny days") by The New Seekers climbs to number two ▪ Tony Waddington's Stoke City football team (with Mike Pejic, Denis Smith, Terry Conroy, Jimmy Greenhoff, John Ritchie and 34-year-old goalkeeper Gordon Banks) defeats Dave Sexton's Chelsea (with Ron 'Chopper' Harris, John Hollins, David Webb, Peter 'Ossie' Osgood, Alan Hudson and 30-year-old goalkeeper Peter 'the cat' Bonetti) by two goals to one in the League Cup final ▪ "Blue is the colour. Football is the game. We're all together and winning is our aim" - *Blue Is The Colour* by The Chelsea Football Team moves down the pop chart ▪ 18-year-old office junior Matthew Harding runs errands at a firm of insurance brokers in London - young Harding holds ambitions to become a successful businessman ▪ 11-year-old schoolboy William Hague from Rotherham completes his homework - young Hague holds ambitions to become a politician ▪ 46-year-old Margaret Thatcher (Education Secretary in Edward Heath's Conservative government) orders an inquiry into the reading standards of schoolchildren ▪ "No, I can't forget this evening or your face as you were leaving, but I

guess that's just the way the story goes. You always smile but in your eyes your sorrow shows, yes it shows" - *Without You* by 30-year-old Nilsson climbs to number one in the pop chart - and stays there for five weeks! ▪ "But the..." *Mother And Child Reunion* ("... is only a motion away") by 30-year-old Paul Simon reaches number five ▪ *Until It's Time For You To Go* by 37-year-old Elvis Presley also peaks at number five ▪ Middle-class families listen to radio programs on the transistor radio placed on the kitchen window sill ▪ A Bush *Automaster 2* (mains or battery operated) with VHF/MW/LW wavebands costs £25.95 ▪ 29-year-old Radio One DJ Tony Blackburn marries beautiful blonde actress 23-year-old Tessa Wyatt at Caxton Hall in London ▪ *I'm Sorry I Haven't A Clue*, a brand new comedy show begins on Radio Four. 29-year-old Graeme Garden, 34-year-old Jo Kendall, 30-year-old Bill Oddie and 31-year-old Tim Brooke-Taylor are the stars. 37-year-old Barry Cryer is chairman for the first show. 50-year-old Humphrey Lyttelton then takes over in the hot seat for subsequent programs ▪ 29-year-old Norman Lamont is elected as a new Conservative MP after winning a by-election at Kingston-upon-Thames ▪ "Hey Mr. Dream Seller, where have you been?" - *Meet Me On The Corner* by Lindisfarne is number five in the pop chart ▪ *It's One Of Those Nights* by The Partridge Family (with 21-year-old heart-throb David Cassidy) climbs to number eleven ▪ A craze for yoga sweeps the nation ▪ Middle-aged folk sit cross legged on the floor and contemplate life ▪ Fashionable young people head off to the pub wearing flared jeans and cheese-cloth shirts - many with a yellow 'smiley face' badge sewn onto the rear pocket of their denim jeans ▪ Star footballer 'super' Georgie Best scores in a 2-1 win for Manchester Utd against Huddersfield Town. 28-year-old winger Ian Storey-Moore (making his debut for Utd) is also on the score-sheet ▪ 23-year-old Trevor Brooking, 30-year-old Geoff Hurst and 26-year-old Pop Robson (2) score the goals for West Ham Utd in a 4-2 victory over Nottingham Forest ▪ The race to become champions of Division One is being contested by four teams: Manchester City, Derby County, Leeds Utd and Liverpool. Just three points separates the clubs with six games still to play ▪ Eamonn Andrews surprises 34-year-old England goalkeeper Gordon Banks on ITV's *This is Your Life* ▪ 47-year-old Kenneth Kendall reads the news on BBC One ▪ A motorway pile-up involving two-hundred vehicles on the

M1 near Luton claims the lives of nine people and injures dozens more ▪ 27-year-old Detective Sergeant Derek Ridgewell of the British Transport Police arrests four innocent black men at Oval tube station in London ▪ *All Coppers Are ...* - 27-year-old Martin Potter, 26-year-old Nicky Henson and 28-year-old Julia Foster star at cinemas in a gritty B-movie filmed in Battersea ▪ "I can't live, if living is..." *Without You* by Nilsson remains at number one in the pop chart ▪ *What Is Life* by 23-year-old Olivia Newton-John is number sixteen ▪ 'Dirty little devil' - Crowds flock to cinemas to see a new feature-length film version of the popular comedy *Steptoe & Son* - in which Harold (Harry H. Corbett) marries a stripper, and Old Man Steptoe (Wilfrid Brambell) does his best to break up the happy couple ▪ "Get off your horse and drink your milk" - 64-year-old John Wayne berates a young actor during filming of *The Cowboys* - a 'Western' from 42-year-old director Mark Rydell ▪ 30-year-old Anne Raitt and 32-year-old Eric Allan star in *Bleak Moments* - a simplistic and compelling new movie from 29-year-old director Mike Leigh ▪ Noisy schoolboys spend Saturday mornings in the stalls at the local *Odeon* ▪ 'Guns, grenades and an army of men roar through the jungle to destroy the most dangerous animal alive ... TARZAN!' - 33-year-old Ron Ely stars as Tarzan, and 16-year-old Manuel Padilla Jr. is Jai, in exciting new movie *Tarzan's Deadly Silence* ▪ 19-year-old Nina Carter (34C) from Solihull is a popular new page three girl in *The Sun* newspaper ▪ *Cosmopolitan* magazine is new - and contains the feature, 'How to turn a man on when he's having problems in bed' ▪ 51-year-old Chancellor of the Exchequer Anthony Barber delivers his second Budget for Edward Heath's Conservative government ▪ Sweeping cuts are made in income tax ▪ Huge tax concessions are given to industry ▪ It's a high-risk budget designed to deliver immediate growth in the economy and to reverse rising unemployment ▪ Builders and labourers go on strike demanding higher pay and better conditions ▪ Flying pickets move in - and occupy construction sites around the country ▪ *Hold Your Head Up* ("... high") by Argent is number five in the pop chart ▪ "I want to live. I want to give. I've been a miner for a heart of gold. It's these expressions I never give, that keep me searchin' for a..." *Heart Of Gold* by Neil Young is number ten. The talented 26-year-old singer / songwriter from Toronto, Canada features on the front cover of the latest *New*

Musical Express ▪ American spacecraft *Apollo 16* (with astronauts: John Young, Tom Mattingly and Charles Duke) lands on the Moon and stays for three days ▪ "And I think it's gonna be a long, long time, till touch down brings me round again to find, I'm not the man they think I am at home. Oh, no, no, no" - *Rocket Man* by 25-year-old Elton John reaches number two in the pop chart ▪ *Apollo 16* makes a safe return to Earth - splashing down successfully in the Pacific Ocean ▪ Back in England - Don Revie's high-flying Leeds Utd football team records two remarkable league victories: thrashing Manchester Utd 5-1 (with Mick Jones bagging a hat-trick) and Southampton 7-0 (with Peter Lorimer bagging a hat-trick) ▪ In the following game, 36-year-old Jack Charlton makes his 600th appearance for Leeds (and scores the goal) in a 1-0 victory over Coventry City at Elland Road ▪ 27-year-old maverick footballer Rodney Marsh transfers from Queens Park Rangers to high-flying Manchester City for £200,000. (Marsh scores his first two goals for City in a 3-1 win against West Ham Utd) ▪ With just four matches remaining, City are equal on points with Liverpool, one point behind Leeds Utd and two points behind Division One leaders, Derby County ▪ New TV drama *The Brothers* (with Jean Anderson as Mary Hammond, Glyn Owen as Edward Hammond, Richard Easton as Brian Hammond, Robin Chadwick as David Hammond and 27-year-old Gabrielle Drake as Jill Williams) grips the nation on Friday evenings ▪ Emily Nugent (played by 40-year-old Eileen Derbyshire) marries Ernest Bishop (played by 46-year-old Stephen Hancock) in ITV's popular soap-opera *Coronation Street* ▪ "You bloody nig-nog!" - 40-year-old Jack Smethhurst is Eddie 'Honky' Booth and 32-year-old Rudolph Walker is Bill 'Chalky' Reynolds in *Love Thy Neighbour* ▪ *To Kill a Mockingbird* (starring Gregory Peck as Atticus Finch) is broadcast on BBC One ▪ The *Black and White Minstrel Show* is broadcast on BBC Two ▪ "Oh, come on. Stop messin' about" - 46-year-old Kenneth Williams, 50-year-old Hattie Jacques and 34-year-old Barbara Windsor (36-24-34) star at cinemas in *Carry On Matron* ▪ "Ask yourself one question, 'Do I feel lucky?' Well do ya punk?" - 41-year-old Clint Eastwood stars in *Dirty Harry* ▪ *Saturday Night At The Movies* (" .. who cares what picture you see?") by The Drifters is number three in the pop chart ▪ *Sweet Talking Guy* by The Chiffons is number four ▪ Footballers, 25-year-old 'super' Georgie Best and

34-year-old Bobby Charlton are on the score-sheet for Frank O'Farrell's Manchester Utd in a 3-0 victory over Stoke City. Utd finish the season in eighth position ▪ Brian Clough's Derby County defeat Liverpool 1-0 in their final game of the season and 'The Rams' are champions of Division One - but only just! Colin Boulton, Ron Webster, John Robson, Roy McFarland, Colin Todd, Alan Durban, Terry Hennessey, Archie Gemmill, John O'Hare, Kevin Hector, John McGovern and 29-year-old top scorer Alan Hinton have all been outstanding. Just one point separates Derby from three other teams: Don Revie's hard-tackling Leeds Utd (with Sprake, Reaney, Charlton, Hunter, Cooper, Bremner, Madeley, Lorimer, Clarke, Giles, Jones and Gray); Bill Shankly's Liverpool (with Clemence, Lawler, Lloyd, Hughes, Lindsay, Smith, Ross, Hall, Whitham, Keegan, Heighway, Toshack and Callaghan); and Malcolm Allison's Manchester City (with Corrigan, Book, Doyle, Booth, Oakes, Donachie, Summerbee, Bell, Davies, Lee, Mellor, Towers and Marsh) ▪ 31-year-old John Craven presents *John Craven's Newsround* - a new (twice-weekly) TV program for sensible children ▪ 11-year-old schoolboy William Hague from Rotherham watches avidly, before completing his homework ▪ *Amazing Grace* by The Pipes and Drums and Military Band of the Royal Scots Dragoon Guards spends five weeks at number one on the hit parade ▪ People purchase the latest 7-inch singles at *Woolworths* for 50 new pence ▪ "Could it be forever, or is my mind just rambling on? Touched you once, kissed you once, now I feel like you're mine" - *Could It Be Forever / Cherish* by 22-year-old heart-throb David Cassidy is number two in the pop chart ▪ "We may as well go home, as I did on my own…" *Alone Again (Naturally)* by 25-year-old Gilbert O'Sullivan is number three ▪ Bomb disposal experts from the SAS and Royal Marines are scrambled to deal with a bomb scare on board the *QE2* ocean liner as the luxury vessel is sailing between New York and Southampton. No explosives are found. The incident is a hoax ▪ 25-year-old footballer Allan 'sniffer' Clarke scores the only goal as Leeds Utd beat Bertie Mee's Arsenal 1-0 in the FA Cup final. 29-year-old Billy Bremner (captain of the 'All Whites') lifts the famous silver trophy. A ticket for the standing enclosure at the Empire Stadium in Wembley costs £1.00 ▪ "There's a red headed tiger known as Billy and he goes like a human dynamo" - *Leeds United* by Leeds United FC is number

ten in the pop chart ▪ *Oh Babe What Would You Say* by Hurricane Smith is number four ▪ 41-year-old footballer Roy Sproson plays his final game for Port Vale - a 1-2 defeat against Rotherham Utd in Division Three ▪ Martin Chivers scores twice, and Alan Mullery scores once, as Bill Nicholson's Tottenham Hotspur beat Bill McGarry's Wolverhampton Wanderers 3-2 on aggregate over two legs to win the UEFA Cup ▪ People enjoy an evening of entertainment at the cinema ▪ 29-year-old Britt Ekland and 34-year-old Susan Hampshire star in *A Time for Loving* ▪ 38-year-old Alan Bates and 33-year-old Janet Suzman star in *A Day in the Death of Joe Egg* ▪ 'You're looking at an animal!' - 34-year-old Oliver Reed stars in *Sitting Target* ▪ "Wake up, meat head. Don't pretend that you are dead. Get yourself up off the cart" - *Back Off Boogaloo* by 31-year-old Ringo Starr is number two on the hit parade ▪ "The..." *Young New Mexican Puppeteer* ("... he saw the people all lived in fear. He thought that maybe they'd listen to a puppet telling them what to do") by 31-year-old Tom Jones is number six ▪ "You are a child of the universe, no less than the trees and the stars. You have a right..." *Desiderata* by 38-year-old Les Crane is number seven ▪ 27-year-old maverick striker Rodney Marsh, 26-year-old Colin Bell and 24-year-old Emlyn Hughes score the goals (and 22-year-old centre-forward Malcolm 'Supermac' MacDonald makes his debut) for Sir Alf Ramsey's England team in a 0-3 victory over Wales at Ninian Park. England's full line-up for the match is: G Banks, Madeley, Hughes, Storey, McFarland, Moore, Summerbee, Bell, MacDonald, Marsh and Hunter ▪ *Stir It Up* ("... little darling") by 31-year-old Johnny Nash is number thirteen in the pop chart ▪ "Oh..." *Deborah* ("... always look like a zeb-o-ra") by Tyrannosaurus Rex is number seven ▪ 40-year-old Secretary of State for the Environment Peter Walker opens the final section of the Gravelly Hill Interchange (aka 'Spaghetti Junction') - linking the carriageway up with the M6 motorway and motorists can now travel uninterrupted for 226 miles between Rugby and Carlisle ▪ The Triumph *Dolomite* 1850cc motorcar has a top speed of 100 mph and accelerates from 0-60 mph in 11.3 seconds. The popular saloon (known affectionately as the 'dolly') costs £1,399 (plus delivery) and comes with fully reclining front seats as standard ▪ More and more foreign cars are being sold in the UK ▪ The latest

Datsun *100A Cherry* (manufactured at Tochigi in Japan) costs £765.63 (plus delivery) and comes with hazard warning lights and two speed wipers ▪ The Wartburg *Knight* (manufactured at Eisenach in East Germany) costs £719.13 and comes with a two-stroke engine and electric windscreen washer ▪ Fashion conscious home owners install multi coloured 'crazy paving' on their driveways ▪ 33-year-old disc jockey Terry Wogan leaves Radio One to become the new host of Radio Two's breakfast show ▪ 44-year-old Alan 'Fluff' Freeman replaces Wogan at Radio One ("Not 'arf!") ▪ *Come What May* ("… I will love you forever, and forever my heart belongs to you") by 22-year-old Vicky Leandros is number two in the pop chart ▪ "You can't see it with your eyes, hold it in your hand, but like the wind it covers our land. Strong enough to move the heart of any man, this thing called love" - *A Thing Called Love* by 40-year-old Johnny Cash is number four ▪ A tragic road accident at Armitage in Staffordshire takes the life of 7-year-old schoolgirl Vanessa Pope ▪ 25-year-old Lesley Judd is a new presenter on BBC One's children program *Blue Peter* ▪ Ford launches the *Consul* and *Granada* range of motorcars as a replacement for the ageing *Zephyr* and *Zodiac*. The new 2000cc *Consul* has a top speed of 92 mph and accelerates from 0-60 mph in 16.5 seconds. The new 2500cc *Granada* has a top speed of 106 mph and accelerates from 0-60 mph in 11.6 seconds ▪ "All right…" *Lady Eleanor* ("… I'm all right where I am") by Lindisfarne (with, lead singer, 27-year-old Alan Hull) is number three in the pop chart ▪ "Got to roll me, got to roll me, yeah" - *Tumbling Dice* by The Rolling Stones (with, lead singer, 28-year-old Mick Jagger) is number five ▪ *Don't Let Him Touch You* ("… He's playing the game of love and he's trying to see how much you'll let him have") by The Angelettes stalls at number thirty-five ▪ Prince Edward, Duke of Windsor, dies aged 77 in Paris. The Duke's wife, 75-year-old Wallis, Duchess of Windsor, is at his side ▪ Back in England - a twenty-foot tall statue of King Kong is erected near the Bull Ring in Birmingham ▪ Recently married couple Fred and Rosemary West move into a house at 25 Cromwell Street in Gloucester ▪ *Texas Homecare* 'Do-It-Yourself' stores are new ▪ Woodchip wallpaper is all the rage ▪ "Can you ride tandem?" - The *PG Tips* chimpanzees are back on ITV.

Summer 1972

Jesus Christ, Superstar

Monarch:	Queen Elizabeth II (aged 46)
Prime-minister:	Edward Heath (aged 56)
Chancellor:	Anthony Barber (aged 52)
Home Secretary:	Robert Carr (aged 55)
Foreign Secretary:	Alec Douglas-Home (aged 69)
Football Manager:	Alf Ramsey (aged 52)
Radio 1 Breakfast DJ:	Tony Blackburn (aged 29)
New car reg. suffix:	'L'

▪ The sun shines ▪ Boys strip to the waist and go swimming in rivers ▪ Girls in hot-pants and brightly coloured bikini tops sunbathe on the bank ▪ *Shandy Bass* is a refreshing new drink ▪ Discarded ring-pulls from drinks cans litter public parks and communal spaces ▪ "He rocks in the tree tops all day long, hoppin' and a-boppin' and singing his song" - *Rockin' Robin* by 13-year-old Michael Jackson is number three in the pop chart ▪ *Oh Babe, What Would You Say* by 48-year-old Hurricane Smith is number four ▪ The funeral of Prince Edward, the Duke of Windsor, takes place at the Frogmore burial ground near Windsor Castle. Queen Elizabeth II, the Duke of Edinburgh, Prince Charles, Edward Heath and a small number of other distinguished guests gather to pay their respects - alongside 75-year-old Wallis, the Duchess of Windsor ▪ 60-year-old Ronnie Delderfield (better known as the writer R. F. Delderfield) dies of lung cancer, in Sidmouth ▪ 'From the Master of Shock, a Shocking Masterpiece!' - 72-year-old Alfred Hitchcock draws crowds to the cinema with his latest thriller, *Frenzy* ▪ 23-year-old Judy Geeson and 39-year-old Joan Collins star in *Fear in the Night* - a terrifying new film from 44-year-old director Jimmy Sangster ▪ "All my life's a circle" - *Circles* by The New Seekers is number four in the pop chart ▪ "So, look away, look away, look away, Dixieland" - *An American Trilogy* by 37-year-old Elvis Presley is number eight ▪ Children break up from school ▪ *The Adventures of Robinson Crusoe* - a black and white TV program (first shown in 1965) is broadcast during the summer holiday ▪ "Down in the meadow where the wind blows free, in the middle of a field

stands a lightning tree. Its limbs all torn from the day it was born, for the tree was born in a thunderstorm. Grow, grow, the lightning tree. It's never too late for you and me" - a second series of *Follyfoot* is on ITV ▪ "I 'ate you, Butler!" - 45-year-old Stephen Lewis is Blakey and 55-year-old Reg Varney is Stan Butler in *Mutiny on the Buses* - the second feature length cinema film spin-off from the popular TV show ▪ The sun continues to shine ▪ White dog poo is seen on pavements ▪ Boys play with pen-knives ▪ Girls play with *Klackers* ▪ Raleigh introduces the *Tomahawk* children's bicycle. Available in Red or Ultra Violet, the arrow-wedge shaped bike comes with a 16-inch rear wheel, an 11-inch front wheel, high handle-bars and costs £25.05 ▪ "Metal guru is it you? Metal guru is it you? Sitting there in your armour plated chair" - *Metal Guru* by T-Rex (with, lead singer, 24-year-old Marc Bolan) is top of the pop chart - the record is the group's fourth number one hit ▪ *Song Sung Blue* ("... everybody knows one") by 31-year-old Neil Diamond is number fourteen ▪ David Bowie releases *The Rise and Fall of Ziggy Stardust and the Spiders from Mars* album, which peaks at number five ▪ Manchester Utd's 26-year-old 'super' Georgie Best announces his retirement from football, whilst on holiday in Marbella. Six weeks later, Best changes his mind and says he'll continue playing for Utd ▪ 36-year-old jockey Lester Piggott rides *Roberto* to victory in the Epsom Derby ▪ "Down, doobie-doo, down-down" - *Breaking Up Is Hard To Do* by The Partridge Family is number three in the pop chart ▪ Retail prices continue to rise ▪ 51-year-old Chancellor of the Exchequer Anthony Barber decides to float the pound. Almost immediately, sterling plummets in value ▪ Long-term price inflation has become a major threat to the economy ▪ The House of Commons votes in favour of Britain's entry into the European Common Market - membership will begin at the start of next year ▪ Industrial disputes continue ▪ More than two-thousand production workers walk out at British Leyland's Morris engine plant in Coventry ▪ Flying pickets hold up construction work as the builders' strike continues ▪ Dockworkers also come out on strike and there's fear of food shortages in shops ▪ 56-year-old Conservative prime-minister Edward Heath declares a State of Emergency - it's the second in just eight months ▪ 41-year-old Peter Woods reads the news on BBC One ▪ 14-year-old schoolgirl

Judith Roberts is battered to death at Tamworth in Staffordshire ▪ "Starry, starry night. Paint your palette blue and grey. Look out on a summer's day, with eyes that know the darkness in my soul" - *Vincent* by Don McLean is new at number one in the pop chart ▪ *I Can See Clearly Now* ("… the rain has gone") by Johnny Nash is number five ▪ Rain delays the finals at the Wimbledon tennis championships - the matches are played on a Sunday for the first time in the tournament's history ▪ 29-year-old Billie Jean King (from America) beats 20-year-old Evonne Goolagong (from Australia) 6-3, 6-3 in the women's singles final on centre-court ▪ 25-year-old Stan Smith (from America) beats 25-year-old Ilie Nastase (from Romania) 4-6, 6-3, 6-3, 4-6, 7-5 in the men's final ▪ Conservative prime-minister Edward Heath (a keen sailor) skippers his yacht *Morning Cloud* in the Cardonnet Race at the Royal Albert Yacht Club in Southsea ▪ 24-year-old footballer Trevor Cherry leaves Huddersfield Town and joins Don Revie's hard-tackling Leeds Utd for a fee of £100,000 ▪ 30-year-old Geoff Hurst leaves West Ham Utd and joins Tony Waddington's Stoke City for £80,000 ▪ 41-year-old Richie Benaud commentates on cricket matches for BBC One television ▪ 31-year-old Geoffrey Boycott and 34-year-old John Edrich stride out together to open the batting for England in the first Test against Ian Chappell's Australia at Old Trafford. Boycott scores 8 runs. Edrich makes 49 before being run out. 25-year-old all-rounder Tony Greig makes a half-century and England win the match by 89 runs. 27-year-old bowler Derek Underwood takes 6 for 45 in the fourth Test at Headingley and 40-year-old captain Ray Illingworth scores 57 runs, as England gain the victory needed to retain the Ashes. G Boycott, J H Edrich, B W Luckhurst, B Wood, M J K Smith, P H Parfitt, B L D'Oliveira, K W R Fletcher, A W Greig, J H Hampshire, A P E Knott (wk), R Illingworth (cpt), J A Snow, N Gifford, G G Arnold, J S E Price and P Lever have all contributed to keeping the Ashes in England ▪ Conservative prime-minister Edward Heath makes changes to his Cabinet - Robert Carr takes over from Reg Maudling as Home Secretary ▪ Trade unions reject the prime-minister's wage restraint plan ▪ One-hundred and eighteen people die when BEA Flight 548 crashes near the town of Staines after taking off from Heathrow - an investigation into the accident concludes that pilot error was partly to blame ▪

The Smith family from Chigwell enjoys a motoring holiday in France - after crossing the Channel on British Rail's *Seaspeed* hovercraft ▪ 'The beast is out of its cage. These will be bloody times" - 40-year-old Elizabeth Taylor stars at cinemas alongside her husband, 46-year-old Richard Burton, in *Hammersmith is Out* - the movie is not a huge success ▪ 39-year-old Michael Caine and 51-year-old Mickey Rooney star in *Pulp* - a comedy thriller from director Mike Hodges ▪ A repeat of *The Monkees* is broadcast on BBC One television on Friday evenings ▪ 8-year-old Jarvis Cocker from Sheffield dreams of one day becoming a famous pop star ▪ "Can you still recall, in the juke box hall, when the music played. And the world span round to a brand new sound in those far off days. In their blue-suede shoes they would scream and shout, as they sang the blues, let it all hang out. Rock 'n' ro-o-oll, rock 'n' roll!" - *Rock And Roll (Parts 1 & 2)* by 28-year-old Gary Glitter is number two in the pop chart ▪ "And it was alright, yeah it was alright" - *Take Me Bak 'Ome* by Slade (with 26-year-old Noddy Holder) spends a week at number one ▪ 29-year-old entertainer Freddie Starr makes the nation laugh with his hilarious impersonations of Elvis Presley, Mick Jagger, Norman Wisdom and Adolf Hitler, on ITV's *Who Do You Do?* ▪ Window cleaner Stan Ogden (played by 57-year-old Bernard Youens) is accused of being a Peeping Tom in ITV's popular soap-opera *Coronation Street* ▪ Sandy Richardson (played by 26-year-old Roger Tonge) is in a coma after being critically injured in a car crash in *Crossroads* ▪ "'Cause Little Willy, Willy won't go home! But you can't push Willy 'round, Willy won't go" - *Little Willy* by The Sweet is number four in the pop chart ▪ 42-year-old Stuart Hall is the new presenter of *It's a Knockout* on BBC One. 57-year-old referee Arthur Ellis ensures fair play between the teams and keeps order with his dipstick. Millions tune-in on Friday evenings to watch as a team from Salisbury gains a victory over a team from Exeter (by twelve points to nine). In the following weeks, a team from Banbury beats a team from Congleton (by twelve points to ten). A team from Folkestone beats a team from Canterbury (by thirteen points to seven). A team from Dalkeith beats a team from Lanark (by thirteen points to eight). A team from Lincoln beats a team from Nottingham (by fourteen points to eight). A team from Luton thrashes a team from Watford

(by sixteen points to four) ▪ The Troubles continue in Northern Ireland ▪ The IRA plants twenty-two bombs at various locations around Belfast on Friday the twenty-first of July - killing nine people and injuring one-hundred and thirty ▪ "I've got a..." *Silver Machine* by Hawkwind reaches number three in the pop chart ▪ *10538 Overture* by the Electric Light Orchestra is number nine ▪ 'L' reg cars go on sale ▪ An Austin *Mini 1000* costs £797 ▪ A sporty *Mini 1275 GT* costs £973 ▪ The new Ford *Consul 2000L* saloon costs £1.350 - a vinyl roof is extra ▪ Jaguar announces the *XJ12* with a 5.3 litre engine and a top speed of 140 mph ▪ Four star leaded petrol is 35 new pence a gallon ▪ Racing driver Jackie Stewart finishes second in the British Grand Prix at Brands Hatch in a Tyrrell-Ford. Emerson Fittipaldi from Brazil wins the race in a Lotus ▪ 45-year-old Jimmy Savile OBE is back on TV reminding motorists - "Clunk, click, every trip" ▪ "And they called it puppy love, I guess they'll never know" - *Puppy Love* by 14-year-old Donny Osmond is a smash hit - the song stays at the top of the pop chart for five weeks! ▪ "Sylvia's mother says, Sylvia's busy, too busy to come to the phone. Sylvia's mother says, Sylvia's tryin' to start a new life of her own" - *Sylvia's Mother* by Dr. Hook and the Medicine Show is number two ▪ 32-year-old disc jockey John Peel presents *Sounds of the Seventies* on Radio One on Tuesday nights ▪ "There's a starman waiting in the sky, he'd like to come and meet us, but he thinks he'd blow our minds" - 25-year-old David Bowie performs *Starman* on *Top of the Pops* and becomes an instant figure of inspiration to thousands of confused teenagers ▪ 48-year-old Larry Grayson stars in *Shut That Door!* ▪ It's estimated that there are now 1.5 million colour TV sets in the UK. Most families rent from *Visionhire*, *Rediffusion*, *Radio Rentals* or the *Co-op* - where it costs around £80 a year to hire a 22-inch set ▪ 39-year-old Frank Bough presents *Grandstand* on BBC One ▪ 39-year-old Dickie Davies presents *World of Sport* on ITV ▪ The Munich Olympics are marred by a terrorist attack - which leads to the death of seventeen people including five Israeli athletes ▪ The Games continue ▪ 33-year-old Mary Peters from Halewood wins a gold medal in the pentathlon ▪ 21-year-old Alan Minter from Crawley wins a bronze in boxing ▪ 25-year-old Brian Jacks from London wins a bronze in judo ▪ 18-year-old David Wilkie from Scotland wins a silver in swimming ▪ David Hemery, David Jenkins, Alan Pascoe

and Martin Reynolds win silver in the 4x400m relay ▪ The musical *Jesus Christ Superstar* ("… do you think you're what they say you are?") debuts in the West End, with 27-year-old Paul Nicholas in the title role ▪ 46-year-old Rock Hudson stars on TV alongside 26-year-old Susan Saint James in *McMillan and Wife* ▪ 24-year-old footballer David Nish leaves Jimmy Bloomfield's Leicester City and joins Brian Clough's Derby County for a new record transfer fee of £225,000 ▪ 39-year-old Graham Parker presents the weather forecast on BBC One ▪ The sun shines ▪ A fresh breeze keeps temperatures cool ▪ "School's out for summer..." *School's Out* ("... for ever") by 24-year-old Alice Cooper moves to the top of the pop chart - after 62-year-old Mrs. Mary Whitehouse calls for the record to be banned from *Top of the Pops* ▪ "Sunbathe now on the beach. Here is the man who sells ice-cream" - *Sea Side Shuffle* by Terry Dactyl and the Dinosaurs is number two ▪ The infectious instrumental *Popcorn* by Hot Butter climbs to number five ▪ 43-year-old Leonard Parkin reads the news for ITN ▪ Prisoners stage a protest at Albany Jail on the Isle of Wight - setting fire to bedding and demanding better living conditions ▪ The protest spreads to other prisons, with inmates rioting and staging roof-top vigils ▪ Home Secretary 55-year-old Robert Carr is currently on holiday in Greece ▪ "Come on and ..." *Join Together* ("... with the band") by The Who slides down the pop chart after peaking at number nine ▪ *Ain't No Sunshine* ("... when she's gone") by 13-year-old Michael Jackson is new entry at number forty-one ▪ Teenagers hang out at fun-fairs and queue for a turn on the Parachutes ▪ Candyfloss costs 6p ▪ A toffee-apple is 8p ▪ The new football season gets underway ▪ 20-year-old centre-forward Joe Jordan scores his first league goals for Don Revie's hard-tackling Leeds Utd - netting twice in a 3-3 draw against Bobby Robson's Ipswich Town ▪ 27-year-old Alan Ball scores from the penalty spot as Bertie Mee's Arsenal defeat Ron Greenwood's West Ham Utd 1-0 at Highbury ▪ Adolescent boys find discarded pornographic magazines in the bushes near canal tow-paths ▪ 'New Andrex goes a long, long way' - The 'Andrex' Labrador Retriever puppy is used for the first time in television adverts ▪ Men enjoy a drink and a smoke in the pub with their friends ▪ A pint of mild in the Red Lion costs 12p ▪ A pack of twenty Player's *No. 6* is 20½p ▪ A pack of twenty *JPS* is 30p.

Autumn 1972

Mrs. Slocambe's pussy

Monarch:	Queen Elizabeth II (aged 46)
Prime-minister:	Edward Heath (aged 56)
Chancellor:	Anthony Barber (aged 52)
Home Secretary:	Robert Carr (aged 56)
Foreign Secretary:	Alec Douglas-Home (aged 69)
Football Manager:	Alf Ramsey (aged 52)
Radio 1 Breakfast DJ:	Tony Blackburn (aged 29)
New car reg. suffix:	'L'

▪ *School's Out* by 24-year-old Alice Cooper remains at number one in the pop chart ▪ *Ain't No Sunshine* by 14-year-old Michael Jackson climbs to number eight ▪ 32-year-old John Craven presents *John Craven's Newsround* on BBC One on Tuesday and Thursday evenings ▪ The prison riots continue and Conservative Home Secretary Robert Carr is forced to cut short his holiday in Greece and return to the UK for meetings with senior prison staff ▪ Prisoners remain on the roof at Gartree, Camp Hill, Parkhurst, Risley Remand Centre and Stafford ▪ Unemployment continues to rise and so does inflation ▪ A *Mars* bar costs 5 new pence ▪ A packet of spicy tomato *Snaps* (crisps) is 2 new pence ▪ A can of *Coca-Cola* is 7 new pence ▪ Property prices have also increased, with the average cost of a house now standing at over £6,000 ▪ 56-year-old prime-minister Edward Heath and his 52-year-old Chancellor of the Exchequer Anthony Barber call for a 'national crusade' against inflation ▪ Despite pressure from the unions, the government introduces statutory controls to restrict pay increases and hold retail prices ▪ Wages are frozen for ninety days ▪ Workers at Jaguar's car factory in Coventry go on strike for more money ▪ The builders' strike continues ▪ Twenty-four flying pickets are arrested in Shrewsbury and two of the men (34-year-old Des Warren from Chester and 33-year-old Ricky Tomlinson from Liverpool) are given prison sentences ▪ "Last night we broke up. This morning I woke up"- *It's Four In The Morning* by 40-year-old Faron Young is number three in the pop chart ▪ *Sugar Me* by 24-year-old Lynsey de Paul is number five ▪ "The closer you get, the better you

look, baby. The better you look, the more I want you" - *I Get The Sweetest Feeling* by 38-year-old Jackie Wilson is number nine ▪ 'The Greatest Family Comedy Team Now on the Big Screen!' - 59-year-old Sid 'Ha-ak-ak' James', 44-year-old Diana Coupland, 22-year-old Sally Geeson and 21-year-old Robin Askwith star at cinemas in *Bless This House* - a feature length film spin-off from the popular TV show ▪ 55-year-old Frankie Howerd and 64-year-old Bill Fraser star in *Up the Front* - the third feature film spin-off from TV show *Up Pompeii!* ▪ 20-year-old Scottish footballer Gordon McQueen transfers from St. Mirren to 'high-flying' Leeds Utd for £30,000 ▪ 25-year-old Newcastle Utd footballer Tony Green is badly injured in a match against Crystal Palace - and the playing career of a talented young winger comes to a premature end ▪ 26-year-old striker Pop Robson scores his eighth goal in nine games as West Ham Utd thrash Norwich City 4-0 at Upton Park. 23-year-old Trevor Brooking and 20-year-old Tommy Taylor are also on the score-sheet for 'The Hammers' ▪ A linesman is injured in a match between Arsenal and Liverpool at Highbury and 44-year-old football pundit Jimmy Hill (in a fetching pale blue tracksuit) is called into action to 'run the line' ▪ *You Wear It Well* ("... a little old fashioned but that's all right") by 27-year-old Rod Stewart spends a week at number one in the pop chart ▪ "Right now is where you are..." *In A Broken Dream* by Python Lee Jackson is number three ▪ "I'm..." *Standing In The Road* ("... a man without a home") by Blackfoot Sue is number four ▪ *Layla* ("... you've got me on my knees") by Derek and the Dominoes is number seven ▪ 'Keep Britain White' - 38-year-old John Tyndall becomes leader of the National Front. 28-year-old Martin Webster organises rallies for the extreme right-wing fascist group ▪ A new series of *Till Death Us Do Part* is on BBC One, with 46-year-old Warren Mitchell as Alf Garnett ▪ A new series of *Love Thy Neighbour* is on ITV, with 40-year-old Jack Smethurst as 'Chalky' and 33-year-old Rudolph Walker as 'Honky' ▪ Winston Trew, Sterling Christie, Omar Boucher and George Griffiths (aka 'The Oval Four') are sentenced to two years in prison after being 'fitted-up' by bent copper DS Derek Ridgewell ▪ *Come On Over To My Place* ("... Hey girl, we're havin'a party") by The Drifters is number nine in the pop chart ▪ "Black pussy, white pussy, pink pussy, blue. The

name of the game is-a Little Boy Blue" - *Big Six* by Judge Dread (aka Alexander Hughes) reaches number eleven - despite being banned by the BBC ▪ 62-year-old moral campaigner Mrs. Mary Whitehouse continues to collect signatures for a petition calling for improved standards in public decency ▪ *The Ruling Classes*, starring 40-year-old Peter O'Toole, 72-year-old Alastair Sim and 57-year-old Arthur Lowe, is now showing at cinemas ▪ 56-year-old prime-minister Edward Heath meets with 55-year-old Irish taoiseach Jack Lynch to discuss the on-going Troubles in the North ▪ 21-year-old footballer Kevin Keegan scores a penalty (and is man-of-the-match) as Bob Shankly's Liverpool move to the top of Division One by thrashing John Harris' Sheffield Utd 5-0 at Anfield. Phil Boersma, Alec Lindsay, Steve Heighway and Peter Cormack are also on the score-sheet for the high-flying 'Reds' ▪ 19-year-old Leighton James scores a goal as Jimmy Adamson's Burnley remain at the top of Division Two with a 4-3 victory over Harry Potts' Blackpool ▪ *All The Young Dudes* ("… carry the news. Boog-a-loo dudes, carry the news") by Mott the Hoople is number three in the pop chart ▪ "What's her name..?" *Virginia Plain* by Roxy Music climbs to number four ▪ A new series of *The Onedin Line* (with 41-year-old Peter Gilmore, 33-year-old Anne Stallybrass and 61-year-old Howard Lang) begins on BBC One ▪ Comedians, 42-year-old Ronnie Barker and 41-year-old Ronnie Corbett play the roles of bumbling private detectives, Piggy Malone and Charley Farley, in the latest series of *The Two Ronnies* ▪ A new series of *Upstairs Downstairs* (with 38-year-old Jean Marsh as Rose, 68-year-old Angela Baddeley as Mrs. Bridges and 48-year-old Gordon Jackson as Hudson) begins on ITV ▪ 38-year-old Wendy Craig stars as Sally Harrison in *And Mother Makes Three* ▪ 19-year-old student Tony Blair goes up to Oxford to read Jurisprudence ▪ Girls (and boys!) wear glittery make-up and outlandish clothes - flares and platform shoes are very much in vogue ▪ "Don't stop now, ah c'mon. Another drop now, ah c'mon. I wanna lot now, so c'mon. That's right, that's right. I said… *Mama Weer All Crazee Now* by Slade (with 26-year-old Noddy Holder) is new at number one in the pop chart ▪ *Wig-Wam Bam* ("… gonna make you my man. Wam-bam bam, gonna get you if I can") by Sweet (with 26-year-old Brian Connelly) is number four ▪ 33-year-old racing driver Jackie Stewart wins the Canadian Grand Prix in a Tyrrell-Ford. 43-year-old Graham Hill

is eighth in a Brabham-Ford ▪ Back in Britain - 22-year-old footballer Malcolm 'Supermac' MacDonald scores a hat-trick as Newcastle Utd beat Coventry City 0-3 at Highfield Road ▪ 28-year-old Martin Peters scores all four goals for Tottenham Hotspur in a 1-4 victory over Manchester Utd at Old Trafford ▪ 23-year-old centre-forward Stuart Pearson scores four goals as Hull City thrash Portsmouth 5-1 in Division Two ▪ 20-year-old goal-keeper John 'Budgie' Burridge keeps a clean sheet as Blackpool gain a 0-0 draw away at Aston Villa in Division Two ▪ 20-year-old goalkeeper David Icke keeps a clean sheet as Hereford Utd beat Aldershot 1-0 in Division Four ▪ Teenage boys play football in the park ▪ A pair of Gola *Champion* football boots (with moulded sole) cost £4.95 ▪ A pair of Gola *International* (with screw-in studs) cost £5.50 ▪ Teenage girls hang glossy posters of David Cassidy on their bedroom walls ▪ *How Can I Be Sure* ("... I really, really, really wanna know. I really, really, really wanna know") - the latest single from the 22-year-old heart-throb climbs to number one - and stays at the top of the pop chart for two weeks ▪ *John, I'm Only Dancing* ("... She turns me on") by 25-year-old David Bowie peaks at number twelve ▪ 32-year-old inventor Clive Sinclair launches the Sinclair *Executive* - a 'new fangled' pocket calculator, costing £79 ▪ 25-year-old entrepreneur Alan Sugar changes the name of his thriving electrical company to A. M. S. Trading (Amstrad) ▪ *Access* credit cards are new ▪ A Hoover Automatic washing machine costs £105 ▪ Conservative prime-minister Edward Heath meets with his ambitious Minister for Education and Science, 46-year-old Margaret Thatcher, at Number 10 Downing Street ▪ The school leaving age is raised from 15 to 16 ▪ "Up above the streets and houses, rainbow climbing high. Everyone can see it smiling over the sky. Paint the whole world with a..." *Rainbow* (with Bungle the Bear and 32-year-old David Cook) is a new program for children on ITV ▪ The fifth series of *Dad's Army* begins on BBC One on Friday evenings. The opening episode sees Captain Mainwaring's home-guard platoon trapped inside a pumping station ▪ Television soap-operas are hugely popular ▪ Sandy Richardson comes out of his coma in ATV's *Crossroads* - but is now confined to a wheelchair ▪ Yorkshire Television broadcasts the first episode of *Emmerdale Farm* and introduces the characters Annie Sugden (played by 53-year-old Sheila Mercier), Joe Sugden (28-year-old Frazer Hines) and Amos

Brearly (52-year-old Ronald Magill) ▪ *Mouldy Old Dough* by Lieutenant Pigeon climbs to number one in the pop chart - and stays at the top for four weeks ▪ "No, you won't fool the..." *Children Of The Revolution* by T-Rex (with 25-year-old Marc Bolan) reaches number two ▪ Thomas and Peggy Gallagher of Longsight in Manchester are proud parents of a newborn son, Liam - a little brother for 5-year-old Noel ▪ 47-year-old Richard Baker reads the news for BBC ▪ 17-year-old soldier Andrew Evans is charged with the murder of schoolgirl Judith Roberts in Tamworth ▪ Forty-two football hooligans are arrested at a Second Division football match between Nottingham Forest and Aston Villa ▪ Seventy-five football hooligans are arrested at a First Division match between Manchester Utd and Liverpool ▪ "Clair, the moment I met you, I swear. I felt as if something, somewhere, had happened to me, which I couldn't see" - *Clair* by 25-year-old Gilbert O'Sullivan is top of the hit parade ▪ *Donna* ("… I love you") by 10cc peaks climbs to number two ▪ 40-year-old Reginald Bosanquet reads the news for ITN ▪ Iceland extends its territorial fishing waters around its shoreline to fifty nautical miles. (Previously, it was twelve). British trawlers continue to operate in the disputed zone and political tensions rise between prime-minister Edward Heath and Kristjan Eldjarn the president of Iceland. The 'Cod Wars' begin when an Icelandic gunboat chases sixteen British and German trawlers from the area ▪ "I've started so I'll finish" - 42-year-old Magnus Magnusson presents *Mastermind* on TV ▪ 39-year-old Barry Norman presents the late night movie review program *Film 72* on BBC One ▪ "I'm gonna make him an offer he can't refuse…" 48-year-old Marlon Brando stars at cinemas as Don Vito Corleone in *The Godfather* ▪ "Your kisses lift me higher, like the sweet song of a choir. You light my morning sky with…" *Burning Love* by 37-year-old Elvis Presley moves up to number seven in the pop chart ▪ "Your little heart desires these things I do, 'cause… *I'm Stone In Love With You* by The Stylistics is number nine ▪ *The Joy Of Sex* - a gourmet guide to lovemaking is now available in book shops - the popular publication features graphic lined-drawings of a bearded (ape-like) man performing sex acts with a dark haired woman ▪ Mrs. Slocombe tells tales about her pussy in a new TV comedy called *Are You Being Served?* ▪ 49-year-old Eric Sykes and 50-year-old Hattie Jacques star in a new series of *Sykes* on BBC One ▪ *The*

Adventures of Black Beauty (with 18-year-old Judi Bowker as Vicky) begins on ITV ▪ Children play out - spending hours on end, racing around on bicycles ▪ The wonderful Raleigh *Chopper* costs £35.99 ▪ A Raleigh *Chipper* is £23.65 ▪ Many adults relax at home, with a cup of tea and a good book ▪ A quarter pound pack of *Ty-phoo* loose-leaf tea costs 7½ p ▪ Popular fictional detective Hercule Poirot features in *Elephants Can Remember* - the latest 'whodunit' novel from 82-year-old crime-writer Agatha Christie ▪ Labour MP Jack McCann dies aged 61 - triggering a by-election in Rochdale. 44-year-old Liberal Cyril Smith (29 stone) wins the seat, with a five-thousand majority over Lawrence Cunliffe the Labour candidate. Jim Merrick (chairman of the British Campaign to Stop Immigration) comes last ▪ "My ding-a-ling, my ding-a-ling, I want you to play with..." *My Ding-A-Ling* by 46-year-old Chuck Berry is new at number one in the pop chart ▪ "Crazy horses (Wah! Wah!)" - *Crazy Horses* by The Osmonds (a group comprising of five brothers: 23-year-old Alan, 21-year-old Wayne, 19-year-old Merrill, 17-year-old Jay and 14-year-old Donny) is number two ▪ 33-year-old Jackie Stewart wins the American Grand Prix in a dark blue (Elf sponsored) Tyrrell-Ford racing car ▪ *Matchbox* die-cast model toys bring out a futuristic wedge shaped car called the *Soopa Coopa* ▪ 22-year-old boxer Joe Bugner defeats Jurgen Blin in eight rounds at Wembley to become the new European heavy-weight champion ▪ 34-year-old Stoke City and England goalkeeper Gordon Banks is injured in a car crash after losing control of his Ford *Consul* at Hanchurch in Staffordshire. (24-year-old Ray Clemence of Liverpool will take over the green number one shirt for England in the next international game) ▪ 23-year-old striker Mick Channon makes his debut for Sir Alf Ramsey's England team against Yugoslavia - the match ends in a 1-1 draw ▪ 21-year-old Kevin Keegan makes his debut for England against Wales - the match ends in a 1-0 victory to England with Colin Bell scoring the winning goal ▪ 24-year-old Stan Bowles transfers from Second Division Carlisle Utd to Second Division Queens Park Rangers for £110,000 ▪ 22-year-old speedy winger Dave Thomas also joins QPR - signing from Burnley for £165,000 ▪ "I'll say... *Goodbye To Love* ("... No one ever cared if I should live or die. Time and time again the chance for love has passed me by, and all I know of love, is how to live without it") by The Carpenters (a pop duo comprising of

22-year-old Karen Carpenter and her 26-year-old brother, Richard) is number nine in the pop chart ▪ "I met him at the candy store. He turned around and smiled at me. You get the picture? That's when I fell for the…" *Leader Of The Pack* by The Shangri-Las is number three ▪ Frank O'Farrell's Manchester Utd football team (with 35-year-old Bobby Charlton, 32-year-old Denis Law, 26-year-old 'super' Georgie Best and new signings 30-year-old Wyn Davis and 25-year-old Ted MacDougall) is struggling near the bottom of Division One after a 3-0 defeat to Malcolm Allison's Manchester City ▪ Bill Shankly's Liverpool are top, after 26-year-old Peter Cormack scores the only goal in a 1-0 victory over Harry Catterick's Everton ▪ Second Division Sunderland sack manager Alan Brown and appoint Bob Stokoe ▪ "If you're the tallest, the smallest, if you beat them all" - *Record Breakers* with 40-year-old Roy Castle and 47-year-old twin brothers Norris and Noel McWhirter is on TV ▪ Hartley the Hare is up to no good in *Inigo Pipkin* ▪ Cheeky 41-year-old comedian Les Dawson is up to no good in the latest series of *Sez Les* ▪ "You made me sing…" *Loop Di Love* by Shag (27-year-old Jonathan King) is number five in the pop chart ▪ *Let's Dance (1972)* by 29-year-old Chris Montez climbs to number nine ▪ Sunday drivers take to the roads at weekends as families enjoy a spin in the motorcar ▪ A new Hillman *Avenger 1500* hs a top speed of 87 mph and accelerates from 0-60 mph in 14.9 seconds ▪ A new Austin *1100* has a top speed of 80 mph and accelerates from 0-60 mph in 19.7 seconds ▪ "If you mix cross-ply and racial tyres on the same axel, or use cross-ply on the rear, when you've radials on the front, you might not live to regret it!" - a short, hard-hitting public information film for motorists is shown on TV ▪ 33-year-old Roger Clark wins the RAC Rally in a Ford *Escort* (registration LVX 942J) ▪ 'You can buy an Ford Escort for £848. We'd like to sell you one for £1,212' - a sporty new *Escort Mexico* costs £1,212, has a 1600 GT engine, a top speed of 103 mph and accelerates from 0-60 mph in 10.7 seconds ▪ The three-millionth *Mini* rolls off the production line at Longbridge and British Leyland chairman, Lord Stokes, drives the super little car to the Earls Court Motor Show as a publicity stunt ▪ Conservative Prime-minister Edward Heath travels to Leicester by helicopter to visit the new Wreake Valley Upper School and two old people's homes ▪ 45-year-

old Sir Geoffrey Howe MP is appointed Minister of State for Trade ▪ 47-year-old Minister for Education and Science Margaret Thatcher breezes past Sir Geoffrey (ignoring him, completely) in a crowded corridor at Westminster. Sir Geoffrey remains calm and doesn't react to the snub ▪ 'You're Mine' - *Love Hearts* (sweets) from Swizzels are popular ▪ "I remember when rock was young. Me and Susie had so much fun" - *Crocodile Rock* by 25-year-old Elton John is number five in the pop chart ▪ *Gudbuy T'Jane* ("... Gudbuy t' Jane. She's a dark horse, see if she can") by Slade (with 26-year-old Noddy Holder) is number two ▪ Schools organise coach trips for pupils ▪ Children (with packed lunches) trudge around Blackpool Zoo, looking at the monkeys ▪ 26-year-old footballer 'super' Georgie Best scores a goal for Manchester Utd in a 2-2 draw against Leicester City. Frank O'Farrell's Utd team remains at the bottom of the league and relegation is looking increasingly likely ▪ Millions of people enjoy a night in, watching telly ▪ Eamonn Andrews surprises 49-year-old Pat Phoenix (who plays Elsie Howard in ITV's soap-opera *Coronation Street*) on *This is Your Life* ▪ Upper middle class families flock to the theatre ▪ 37-year-old Rod Hull and his uncontrollable puppet, Emu, appear in front of the Queen Mother at the Royal Variety Show ▪ Lower middle class men spend hours washing and polishing their cars on Sunday mornings ▪ Neighbours walk past, on their way out for a newspaper, and say cheerfully, "Hope you're going to do mine next?" ▪ "I'm your top prime cut of meat. I'm your choice, I wanna be..." *Elected* by 24-year-old Alice Cooper climbs to number four in the pop chart ▪ *There Are More Questions Than Answers* by 32-year-old Johnny Nash is number nine ▪ Working class men enjoy an evening out at the cinema ▪ 'They came to make the beds … and made everything else!' - 28-year-old Gabrielle Drake and 20-year-old Me Me Lay appear stark naked in *Au Pair Girls* ▪ A pair of *Wilkinson Sword* garden shears cost £2.75 at hardware shops ▪ 62-year-old moral campaigner Mrs. Mary Whitehouse continues to collect signatures for a petition calling for improved standards in public decency ▪ "She flies like a bird in the sky" - adverts say, '*Nimble* - real bread but lighter' ▪ A return flight from London to New York on *BOAC* costs £85.05.

Christmas 1972

Weebles wobble but they don't fall down

Monarch:	Queen Elizabeth II (aged 46)
Prime-minister:	Edward Heath (aged 56)
Chancellor:	Anthony Barber (aged 52)
Home Secretary:	Robert Carr (aged 56)
Foreign Secretary:	Alec Douglas-Home (aged 69)
Football Manager:	Alf Ramsey (aged 52)
Radio 1 Breakfast DJ:	Tony Blackburn (aged 29)
New car reg. suffix:	'L'

▪ "It's late and she is waiting, and I know I must go home" - The double A sided single *Angel / What Made Milwaukee Famous (Has Made A Loser Out Of Me)* by 27-year-old Rod Stewart is number four in the pop chart ▪ "There ain't no place to run…" *Shotgun Wedding* by 33-year-old Roy C is number eight ▪ Mornings are cold and frosty ▪ Green 'snorkel' parker coats, with fur-lined hoods, keep schoolboys warm and dry ▪ TV adverts say, '*Ready Brek* - central heating for kids' ▪ "Get down, Shep!" - 38-year-old John Noakes, 33-year-old Peter Purves and 26-year-old Lesley Judd present *Blue Peter* on BBC One. Viewers are asked to donate old watch straps and key-rings to help raise money for specially equipped vans to deliver hot dinners to elderly people ▪ 33-year-old Olympic champion Mary Peters is BBC's 'Sports Personality of the Year' ▪ "I'll be your…" *Long Haired Lover From Liverpool* ("… and I'll do anything you say") by 9-year-old Little Jimmy Osmond climbs to number one in the pop chart - and stays there for five weeks! ▪ *Ben* ("... the two of us need look no more") by 14-year-old Michael Jackson is number seven ▪ "You better watch out, you better not cry" - *Santa Claus Is Comin' To Town* by The Jackson Five is new at number forty-three ▪ Schoolboys run to the shops, eager to spend their pocket-money ▪ *The Beano Book* (with Biffo the Bear on the front cover) costs 50p at newsagents ▪ The Christmas edition of *Mayfair* magazine (featuring a bare Benny Hill Show 'bird') also costs 50p ▪ Football matches draw crowds of men to the terraces on Saturday afternoons ▪ 25-year-old right-winger Ray Graydon scores twice for Aston Villa in a 2-2 draw away against Sheffield Wednesday in Division Two ▪ 26-year-old left-winger Tony Field scores twice for Blackburn Rovers in a

2-1 victory over Southend Utd in Division Three ▪ Industrial unrest prevails as powerful trade unions fight for the rights of their members ▪ Eleven-thousand British Leyland car workers at Cowley join a national strike of engineers - protesting against a fine imposed on the AUEW ▪ Coal production is at an all time low, after recent strike action by the NUM. Just 127 million tonnes have been produced in 1972 ▪ NCB chairman Sir George Ezra seeks to improve industrial relations and increase production ▪ Approximately one-million people in the UK are unemployed ▪ The individual weekly dole payment currently stands at £6.75 ▪ A pack of twenty *Benson & Hedges* is 22½p ▪ The Troubles continue in Northern Ireland ▪ 54-year-old Secretary of State for Northern Ireland Willie Whitelaw holds top-secret meetings with IRA representatives ▪ The 'Cod Wars' continue in the seas off the coast of Iceland ▪ Icelandic patrol boats cut the lines of nets on British trawlers and valuable hauls of cod and other fish are lost ▪ *Stay With Me* ("... lay with me, love me for longer than just your goodbye") by Blue Mink is number eleven in the pop chart ▪ *Keeper Of The Castle* ("... so be a good man to your lady") by The Four Tops is number eighteen ▪ K-tel's compilation *20 All Time Hits of the 50s* is the number one LP ▪ Hallmark Records release *The Best of Top of the Pops '72* - a budget priced, cover-version pop compilation record with a pretty blonde girl pictured on the sleeve ▪ "And so this is Christmas, and what have you done? Another year over, and a new one just begun" - John and Yoko and the Plastic Ono Band sing *Happy Xmas (War Is Over)* ▪ "You're everywhere and nowhere, baby. That's where you're at" - a re-release of *Hi-Ho Silver Lining* by Jeff Beck is number seventeen in the pop chart ▪ 'I'd Love a Babycham' - Ladies accompany their men to the pub ▪ *Bontempi* electronic organs (retailing at around £18.50) are popular gifts for lucky children ▪ Also in demand is the wonderful game of *Crossfire* (from Ideal) and the new *Big League* table-top football game (from Chad Valley) ▪ A *Shaker Maker* costs £1.99 ▪ Soap-on-a-Rope is a common stocking filler ▪ 34-year-old Tony Lewis is England's cricket captain for a tour of India and Pakistan ▪ New BBC drama series *Colditz* (with 42-year-old Jack Hedley and 39-year-old David McCallum) grips the nation for an hour on Thursday evenings ▪ 18-year-old actress Anne Kirkbride makes her first appearance as Deirdre Hunt in ITV's popular soap-opera *Coronation Street* ▪

26-year-old footballer 'super' Georgie Best walks out on struggling Manchester Utd and is seen in the early hours in a London nightclub ▪ "But I can't get no satisfaction, all I want is easy action!" - *Solid Gold Easy Action* by T-Rex (with, lead singer, 25-year-old Marc Bolan) is number two in the pop chart ▪ "I'll never let you go. Why? Because I love you" - *Why* by 15-year-old Donny Osmond is number three ▪ Bill Shankly's Liverpool are three points clear at the top of Division One. 23-year-old John Toshack scores twice, and 21-year-old Kevin Keegan is man-of-the-match, as 'The Reds' beat Coventry City 2-0 at Anfield ▪ *Apollo 17* (with astronauts: Eugene Cernan, Ron Evans and Harrison Schmitt) lands on the Moon and stays for three days. (This will be the final moon landing of the Apollo space program) ▪ "A jumped up pantry boy, who never knew his place" - 39-year-old Michael Caine and 65-year-old Lord Olivier (Laurence Olivier) star at cinemas in *Sleuth* ▪ Men in long, grubby 'macs' loiter outside seedy picture houses ▪ 'How far does a girl have to go to untangle her tingle?' - 23-year-old Linda Lovelace stars in *Deep Throat* ▪ 'The savage revenge of a young bride ravaged on her wedding night!' - 18-year-old Maribel Martin and 26-year-old Alexandra Bastedo star in *The Blood Splattered Bride* ▪ 62-year-old moral campaigner Mrs. Mary Whitehouse continues to collect signatures for a petition calling for improved standards in public decency ▪ 39-year-old Frank Bough presents *Nationwide* on TV ▪ 'The Holiday of a Laugh time!' - 59-year-old Sid 'Ha-ak-ak' James is Vic Flange and 35-year-old Barbara Windsor (36-24-34) is Sadie Tomkins in *Carry On Abroad* - a low-budget film, with tropical Mediterranean scenes shot on a car-park at Pinewood Studios near London ▪ ITV television programmes on Friday evenings include: *Danger Man* (a repeat) - starring Patrick McGoohan; *The Forest Rangers*; *Magpie* - presented by 34-year-old Susan Stranks, 25-year-old Douglas Rae and 26-year-old Mick Robertson; *The Flintstones*; *Crossroads* - with 26-year-old Roger Tonge as Sandy Richardson, 53-year-old Noele Gordon as Meg Richardson and 69-year-old Ann George as Amy Turtle; *The Sky's the Limit* - hosted by 52-year-old Hughie Green; and *The Protectors* - starring 40-year-old Robert Vaughn ▪ "Jack be nimble, Jack be quick. Jack jumped over the candle stick. Silly boy should have jumped higher; goodness gracious great balls of fire. Hey, hey, diddle dumb day, ie-ie ie-er" - *Big Seven*

by Judge Dread (aka Alexander Hughes) reaches number eight in the pop chart - despite being banned by the BBC ▪ "Take the ribbon from my hair. Shake it loose and let it fall" - *Help Me Make It Through The Night* by 28-year-old Gladys Knight and the Pips is number eleven ▪ 22-year-old footballer Malcolm 'Supermac' MacDonald scores a goal for Newcastle Utd in a 4-1 victory over Sheffield Utd - and 'The Toon' move up to fifth in Division One ▪ Manchester Utd are second from bottom after losing 5-0 against Crystal Palace ▪ 26-year-old 'super' Georgie Best is no longer in the Utd team and has been placed on the transfer list ▪ Utd sack manager Frank O'Farrell and appoint 44-year-old Tommy Docherty as replacement ▪ 'The Doc' immediately signs 29-year-old George Graham from Arsenal, 20-year-old Alex Forsyth from Partick Thistle and 23-year-old Lou Macari from Celtic ▪ Groovy teenagers listen to the latest pop tunes on Ferguson Thorn *3052* stereo record players ▪ "The Jean Genie lives on his back. The Jean Genie loves chimney stacks. He's outrageous, he screams and he bawls. Jean Genie, let yourself go, woah" - *The Jean Genie* by 25-year-old David Bowie jumps from number sixteen to number four in the pop chart, before peaking at number two ▪ *Getting A Drag* by 24-year-old Lynsey De Paul is number eighteen ▪ *Don't Do That* by Geordie is number thirty-two ▪ Private Pike and Private Walker (played by 26-year-old Ian Lavender and 43-year-old James Beck) cause a large radio-controlled wheel (loaded with explosives) to go out of control in *Dad's Army* on BBC One ▪ 'De-de-der-der-de-de-de-de-de-de-de-de-der-der, der-der-de-de-de-de-de' - 48-year-old Benny Hill stars in a new edition of *The Benny Hill Show* on ITV ▪ 'Weebles wobble but they don't fall down' - is the advertising strap-line for a range of new toys ▪ 'If you like a lot of chocolate on your biscuit join our club' - is the advertising strap-line used by Jacobs *Club* ▪ 56-year-old prime-minister Edward Heath gives his authorisation for construction work to begin on a new airport at Maplin Sands in Essex ▪ Children buy *Fruit Salads*, *Black Jacks* and *Drumsticks* from the sweet shop ▪ House-wives stay at home and do the dusting ▪ 'The polish that cleans' - *Mr. Sheen* is new ▪ The cost of living is on the increase ▪ The average price of a house in the UK has risen to £7,400 ▪ A Ford *Cortina* motorcar costs over £1,000 ▪ A pint of milk is 5½p ▪ A loaf of bread is 11p ▪ A dozen large white eggs are 22p ▪ A bottle of *Harveys Bristol Cream* is £1.29.

New Year 1973

Underground, overground, Wombling free

Monarch:	Queen Elizabeth II (aged 46)
Prime-minister:	Edward Heath (aged 56)
Chancellor:	Anthony Barber (aged 52)
Home Secretary:	Robert Carr (aged 56)
Foreign Secretary:	Alec Douglas-Home (aged 69)
Football Manager:	Alf Ramsey (aged 53)
Radio 1 Breakfast DJ:	Tony Blackburn (aged 30)
New car reg. suffix:	'L'

▪ There's snow across much of the country, with the heaviest falls occurring in East Anglia, the Midlands and the Home Counties ▪ Traffic is disrupted and some schools and factories close temporarily due to the cold weather ▪ An Austin *1100* ('J' reg) is stranded on the A11 near Thetford ▪ A *Co-op* electric milk-float ('H' reg) is stuck on the Pear Tree housing estate in Rugeley ▪ Milk bottles freeze on doorsteps and silver tops are pushed upwards by the iced milk ▪ The European community expands from six member states to nine - as Britain, Ireland and Denmark join West Germany, France, Italy, the Netherlands, Belgium and Luxembourg in the Common Market ▪ The value of the (recently floated) pound falls against other currencies - such as the franc, the deutsche mark and the lire ▪ Conservative prime-minister Edward Heath and his Chancellor of the Exchequer, Anthony Barber, are forced to defend their economic record, in the House of Commons ▪ "You better beware. You better take care. You better watch out if you've got long black hair. He'll come from behind, you'll go out of your mind. You'd better not go, you never know what you'll find" - *Blockbuster* by Sweet is a number one smash hit - the record stays at the top of the pop chart for five weeks! ▪ "You walked into the party, like you were walking onto a yacht. Your hat strategically dipped below one eye, your scarf it was apricot" - *You're So Vain* by 27-year-old Carly Simon is number three ▪ *Hi Hi Hi / C Moon* by Wings (with, lead singer, 30-year-old Paul McCartney) is number five ▪ Steeleye Span (with, lead singer, 25-year-old Maddy Prior) feature on the front cover of the latest *New Musical Express* ▪ 'Waiting for Baby' - Celebrity couple (and expectant parents) 29-year-old DJ Tony Blackburn and 24-year-old ac-

tress Tessa Wyatt are pictured on the front cover of the latest *TV Times* magazine ▪ 21-year-old footballer Kevin Keegan scores a goal for Bill Shankly's high-flying Liverpool in a 0-1 victory over West Ham Utd ▪ The 'Cod Wars' continue in the seas off the coast of Iceland ▪ British trawlers are forced to retreat from the disputed waters after Icelandic patrol boats successfully cut the fishing lines on eighteen vessels ▪ Back in England - A national strike by BRS lorry drivers disrupts the supply of components to British Leyland car factories ▪ Production of *Minis*, *1100s*, *1300s* and *1800s* at Longbridge in Birmingham comes to a halt ▪ Production of Jaguar *XJ6s* and *XJ12s* comes to a halt in Coventry ▪ Adverts say 'Move over to BMW' ▪ A new BMW *2002* (with a top speed of 113 mph) costs £2,145 ▪ A new BMW *2002tii* (with a top speed of 119 mph) costs £2,499 ▪ "Take off your hat. Kick off your shoes. I know you ain't goin' anywhere" - *Wishing Well* by Free is number seven in the pop chart ▪ "Very superstitious, writing's on the wall" - *Superstition* by 22-year-old Stevie Wonder is number eleven ▪ 59-year-old Sid 'Ha-ak-ak' James, 44-year-old Diana Coupland and 22-year-old Sally Geeson star in the third series of sit-com *Bless This House* on ITV ▪ The second series of family drama *The Brothers* grips the nation on Sunday evenings on BBC One. 65-year-old Jean Anderson (as Mary), 38-year-old Patrick O'Connell (as Edward), 39-year-old Richard Easton (as Brian) and 28-year-old Gabrielle Drake (as Jill) are the stars ▪ 'Hell, Upside Down' - cinema goers flock to see 43-year-old Gene Hackman, 30-year-old Carol Lynley and 20-year-old Pamela Sue Martin in Hollywood disaster movie *The Poseidon Adventure* ▪ 42-year-old Sean Connery and 59-year-old Trevor Howard star in *The Offence* ▪ 16-year-old Fiona Fullerton stars in *Alice's Adventures in Wonderland* ▪ 19-year-old Jilly Johnson (34A) from Woking is a popular new page three girl in *The Sun* ▪ "What a fool I've been to fall in love again. Love, love, when will it ever end?" - *Ball Park Incident* by Wizzard is number six in the pop chart ▪ "Daniel my brother, you are older than me. Do you still feel the pain of the scars that won't heal?" - *Daniel* by 25-year-old Elton John climbs to number four ▪ 22-year-old boxer Joe Bugner defeats Rudi Lubbers in fifteen rounds at the Royal Albert Hall to retain his European heavy-weight title ▪ 24-year-old American George Foreman knocks out Smokin' Joe Frazier in Jamaica to become the new heavy-weight champi-

on of the world ▪ Back in England - 11-year-old Frank Bruno from Wandsworth plays out with his friends ▪ 51-year-old Raymond Baxter and 29-year-old Michael Rodd present *Tomorrow's World* on BBC One ▪ A new concept called the 'digital watch' will soon be available, but at around £150, is far too expensive for most people ▪ "Does anyone know the way? There's got to be a way, to..." *Blockbuster* by Sweet remains at number one in the pop chart ▪ *Sylvia* (a progressive rock instrumental) by Focus reaches number four ▪ *Looking Through The Eyes Of Love* by The Partridge Family (with 22-year-old heart-throb David Cassidy) is number nine ▪ "A house - with a door. One-two-three-four. Ready to play - what's the day?" - 39-year-old Brian Cant and 32-year-old Toni Arthur present *Play School* on BBC Two ▪ Children have hours of fun playing out on pogo-sticks ▪ England football manager Sir Alf Ramsey loses patience with 29-year-old maverick striker Rodney Marsh in a match against Wales and threatens to "pull him off" at half-time. Marsh tells Sir Alf he only gets an orange when he plays for Manchester City ▪ Troublesome footballer 26-year-old 'super' Georgie Best remains on the transfer list at Manchester Utd ▪ Manager Tommy 'The Doc' Docherty says he'll consider offers of around £300,000 for Best ▪ 35-year-old Bobby Charlton scores twice for Utd in a 2-1 win over Wolverhampton Wanderers - and 'The Reds' begin to climb the league table ▪ "Would you like to ride my..." *Paper Plane* by Status Quo reaches number eight in the pop chart ▪ "Wack for my daddy-oh, there's..." *Whisky In The Jar* ("...oh") by Thin Lizzy peaks at number six ▪ Alan Ball and John Radford score the goals as Bertie Mee's Arsenal defeat Bill Shankly's Liverpool 0-2 at Anfield in a top-of-the-table clash ▪ Don Revie's hard-tackling Leeds Utd lose 2-0 at Filbert Street against Jimmy Bloomfield's Leicester City ▪ 27-year-old West Ham Utd striker Pop Robson scores twice in a 3-1 victory over Chelsea at Upton Park - Robson is the leading goal scorer in Division One ▪ 24-year-old Mick Channon scores his first international goal in England's 0-5 victory over Scotland at Hampden Park - the other four goals come from 26-year-old Allan 'sniffer' Clarke (2), 27-year-old Martin Chivers and an own goal by Peter Lorimer. England's full line-up for the match is: Shilton, Storey, Hughes, Bell, Madeley, Moore, Ball, Channon, Chivers, Clarke and Peters ▪ "On Wimbledon Common, where the Wombles live, Bungo and Orinoco

are tidying up" - 44-year-old Bernard Cribbins narrates *The Wombles* - a new teatime TV show for children on BBC One ▪ 26-year-old Bob Harris presents *The Old Grey Whistle Test* on BBC Two on Tuesday nights at 10.45 p.m. ▪ "Yo-de-oh-da-dodie, oh-da-dodie, oh-da-dodie, oh-da-dodie, oh-da-dodie, oh-da-um-ba-bah!" - *Hocus Pocus* by Focus climbs to number twenty in the pop chart ▪ 38-year-old American pop legend Elvis Presley and his wife, 27-year-old Priscilla, announce their separation ▪ The obscene and gratuitous French movie *Blow Out* is banned at many cinemas throughout the UK ▪ Mrs. Mary Whitehouse describes the film as "degrading" and the 62-year-old campaigner (from rural Worcestershire) continues to collect signatures for a petition calling for improved standards in the levels of public decency ▪ "Do you wanna touch? (Yeah). Do you wanna touch? (Yeah). Do you wanna touch me there?" - *Do You Wanna Touch Me? (Oh Yeah)* by 28-year-old Gary Glitter reaches number two on the hit parade ▪ 36-year-old Gordon Honeycombe reads the news for ITN ▪ BRS lorry drivers continue their industrial action ▪ The distribution of goods to shops and factories slows down ▪ Rail workers come-out strike ▪ 3,800 Liverpool dockers come-out on strike ▪ 400 men at GEC come-out on strike ▪ "You don't get me, I'm part of the union. You don't get me, I'm part of the union. You don't get me, I'm part of the union. Till the day I die, till the day I die" - *Part Of The Union* by The Strawbs (with 24-year-old John Ford on lead vocals) reaches number two on the hit parade - and stays there for three weeks ▪ Civil servants go on strike ▪ Prime-minister Edward Heath spends a couple of days in the West Midlands. As part of his visit, the 56-year-old premier unveils a memorial to herald the start of construction of the new National Exhibition Centre - at Bickenhill in Birmingham ▪ "Oh, what happened to you? Whatever happened to me? What became of the people, we used to be? " - 37-year-old James Bolam and 35-year-old Rodney Bewes return to TV screens after a gap of six years in *Whatever Happened To The Likely Lads* ▪ "Oooh, Betty" - 30-year-old Michael Crawford (Frank Spencer) and 24-year-old Michele Dotrice (Betty) star in *Some Mothers Do 'Ave 'Em* ▪ "I'll 'ave you, Butler!" - 46-year-old Stephen Lewis (Inspector 'Blakey' Blake) and 56-year-old Reg Varney (Stan Butler) star in the seventh, and final, series of *On the Buses* ▪ A 22-inch *PYE* colour TV set costs £258 ▪ The average price of a house in

the UK has risen to £8,500 ▪ The number of *Wimpy* hamburger bars has risen to one-thousand ▪ Prime-minister Edward Heath and his Conservative government set up the Maplin Development Authority - a new body to oversee the construction of an international airport on the Essex coast ▪ 22-year-old boxer Joe Bugner takes on Muhammad Ali in Las Vegas - Bugner loses by a unanimous decision after twelve rounds ▪ 40-year-old Stan Anderson resigns as football manager of Second Division Middlesbrough ▪ 28-year-old defender Cyril Knowles scores a 'nice one' as Tottenham Hotspur beat non league Margate 0-6 in the FA Cup third round ▪ 23-year-old winger Don Givens is on the score-sheet as Queens Park Rangers defeat Burnley 2-0 in a top-of-the-table clash in League Division Two ▪ 19-year-old midfielder Graeme Souness transfers from Tottenham Hotspur to Middlesbrough for £30,000 ▪ 21-year-old midfielder Terry McDermott transfers from Bury to Newcastle Utd for £25,000 ▪ 35-year-old Stoke City and England goalkeeper Gordon Banks remains optimistic of making a return to football after his recent car accident ▪ "The... " *Look Of Love* ("... is in your eyes, a look your smile can't disguise") by Gladys Knight and The Pips enters the pop chart at number forty-nine ▪ "People all over the world, join hands, start a love train..." *Love Train* by The O'Jays is new at number forty-six ▪ *Blockbuster* by Sweet is still number one ▪ Prime-minister 56-year-old Edward Heath works late into the night at Number 10 Downing Street ▪ Chancellor of the Exchequer 52-year-old Anthony Barber works late into the night at Number 11 Downing Street ▪ The government imposed wage restraint program continues ▪ Working families begin to feel the pinch ▪ A loaf of bread goes up in price to 12p ▪ A quater pound pack of Co-op *99* Tea is 7p ▪ A black and white TV linsense (of which 15 million were issued in 1972) is £7 ▪ A colour TV licence (of which 1.6 million were issued) is £12 ▪ The clocks go forward an hour - and the evenings stay lighter for longer ▪ Youngsters congregate on street corners ▪ The sound of glam-rock blares from transistor radios ▪ The LP *Slayed?* by Slade, with the tracks: *Gudbuy T'Jane*, *Mama Weer All Crazee Now* and *Let The Good Times Roll*, is currently number nine in the album chart (after peaking at number one in January) ▪ Freaky people in tanktops and loons 'score' gallons of juice in the pub, man ▪ A pint of *Skol* lager in the Red Lion is 17p ▪ A pint of Ansell's *King-Pin* bitter is 14p.

Spring 1973

The 'all new' Austin Allegro

Monarch:	Queen Elizabeth II (aged 47)
Prime-minister:	Edward Heath (aged 56)
Chancellor:	Anthony Barber (aged 52)
Home Secretary:	Robert Carr (aged 56)
Foreign Secretary:	Alec Douglas-Home (aged 69)
Football Manager:	Alf Ramsey (aged 53)
Radio 1 Breakfast DJ:	Tony Blackburn (aged 30)
New car reg. suffix:	'L'

▪ "So, cum on feel the noise. Girls grab the boys. We get wild, wild, wild" - *Cum On Feel The Noize* by Slade (with 26-year-old Noddy Holder) enters the pop chart at number one - and stays there for four weeks ▪ *Nice One Cyril* ("… nice one son. Nice one Cyril, let's have another one") by the Cockerel Chorus is number fourteen ▪ "In the…" *Avenues And Alleyways* by 29-year-old Tony Christie is number twenty-seven ▪ 26-year-old David Bowie features on the front cover of the latest *New Musical Express* ▪ 40-year-old Robert Vaughn and 37-year-old Nyree Dawn Porter star in *The Protectors* on ATV ▪ 54-year-old Patrick Cargill stars in *Father, Dear Father* on LWT ▪ Approximately 18 million people watch *Coronation Street* each week. In the current storyline, Hilda Ogden (played by 47-year-old Jean Alexander) is embarrassed because her house (at number 13) requires fumigation ▪ Millions also tune-in to see *It's A Knockout* on BBC One on Friday evenings. Presenter Stuart Hall laughs so much as he's describing events in a contest between Bicester and Woodstock, that he's unable to speak - 62-year-old co-commentator Eddie Waring steps in when needed. (Bicester win by fourteen points to eight) ▪ 'The antidote to panel games' - a new series of *I'm Sorry I Haven't A Clue* begins on Radio Four, with panelists Graeme Garden, Jo Kendall, Bill Oddie and Tim Brooke-Taylor and with 51-year-old Humphrey Lyttelton in the chair ▪ "Oh…" *Cindy Incidentally* ("… Baby, I ain't puttin' you on") by The Faces (with, lead singer, 28-year-old Rod Stewart, and guitarist 25-year-old Ronnie Wood) is number two in the pop chart ▪ *Killing Me Softly With His Song* by 36-year-old Roberta Flack is number six ▪ Retail prices continue to rise ▪

Prime-minister Edward Heath and his Cabinet are under severe pressure ▪ The Trade Union Congress calls for a one day strike to protest against the government's pay restraint program ▪ The manufacturing sector, rail travel and postal service are all severely affected ▪ Construction work begins on the new airport at Maplin Sands - 60,000 tonnes of stone and gravel are deposited on the mudflats of the Thames estuary to create a protective bank for the new complex ▪ Harold Wilson (leader of the opposition Labour Party) is against the multi-million pound project ▪ 54-year-old Shadow Environment Secretary Anthony Crosland describes Maplin as a "thoroughly bad site" to build a new international airport ▪ A national environmental campaign encourages people to 'Plant a Tree in '73' ▪ A witty horticulturist does so and pledges to 'Plant Some More in '74' ▪ 30-year-old former Beatle Paul McCartney is charged with growing cannabis on his farm in Scotland ▪ Celebrity couple, 30-year-old DJ Tony Blackburn and 24-year-old actress Tessa Wyatt are proud parents of a new born baby boy, Simon ▪ 11-year-old schoolboy Richard Coles from Northampton plays out with his friends, before going to church ▪ "Feel…" *Feel The Need In Me* by The Detroit Emeralds climbs to number four on the hit parade ▪ *Roll Over Beethoven* ("… tell Tchaikovsky the news") by the Electric Light Orchestra is number six ▪ *Baby I Love You* ("…Come on, baby") by 28-year-old Dave Edmunds is number eight ▪ 41-year-old football reporter Brian Moore presents *On the Ball* on Saturday lunchtimes on ITV. 44-year-old football pundit Jimmy Hill chips in with a weekly talking point ▪ 35-year-old centre-forward Derek Dougan bags a hat-trick (and his strike partner John Richards scores twice) as Wolverhampton Wanderers thrash Manchester City 5-1 at the Molinuex ▪ 27-year-old Pop Robson bags a hat-trick (and 24-year-old Trevor Brooking is also on the score-sheet) as West Ham Utd beat Southampton 4-3 at Upton Park ▪ 45-year-old Malcolm Allison resigns as football manager of Manchester City and takes over at Crystal Palace - on a salary reputed to be £13,000, plus bonuses. Allison's first game in charge produces a 2-0 victory over Chelsea - but Palace remain near the bottom of the First Division table ▪ "I…" *Never, Never, Never* ("… want to be in love with anyone but you") by 36-year-old Shirley Bassey is number eight in the pop chart ▪ "Take

away a…" *Heart Of Stone* by 23-year-old Tony Kenny is number eleven ▪ 48-year-old Kenneth Kendall reads the news on BBC One ▪ Two IRA bombs explode in London killing two people and injuring hundreds ▪ Edward Heath's Conservative government brings in 'trial without jury' for terrorist offences in Northern Ireland ▪ 46-year-old Queen Elizabeth II opens the new London Bridge. The splendid new construction, designed by 65-year-old architect William Holford, has three spans (the central span measures 341 ft) and cost £4 million to build ▪ Retail prices go up again, as a 10% Value Added Tax comes into effect ▪ The 'Cod Wars' continue in the seas off the coast of Iceland ▪ Royal Navy frigates escort British trawlers back into the disputed waters so that fishing can be resumed ▪ Icelandic people are angered by the Royal Navy's intervention. The British Embassy in Reykjavic is attacked and its windows smashed ▪ Back in England - 31-year-old Fred West and his wife, 19-year-old Rosemary, murder 19-year-old Lynda Gough and bury her body beneath their house at 25 Cromwell Street in Gloucester ▪ "Hey! Hey! Hey! And it's…" *All Because Of You* ("…baby") by Geordie is number six in the pop chart ▪ *Hello Hurray* ("… Let the show begin") by 25-year-old Alice Cooper is number six ▪ "I may seem a fool to you, for everything I say or think or do" - *Pyjamarama* by Roxy Music (featuring 27-year-old Bryan Ferry) is number ten ▪ 'Introducing Allegro. The new driving force from Austin' - after eleven years in production, Austin *1100* and *1300* motorcars are replaced by the all new *Allegro*, with its revolutionary hydragas suspension and a 'Quartic' (square-shaped) steering wheel. A new *Allegro 1100 De-luxe* costs £1,009 and has a top speed of 83 mph. A new *Allegro 1500 Super De-luxe* costs £1,200 and has a top speed of 92 mph ▪ BMW launches the all-new *520* - an outstanding, large, up-market saloon costing £2,999 and with a top speed of 106 mph ▪ The *Red* and *Blue* albums from The Beatles are released - three years after the 'Fab Four' went their separate ways. The *Red* album comprises of Beatles' songs from the years 1962 to 1966. The *Blue* album comprises of Beatles' songs from the years 1967 to 1970 ▪ *The Dark Side Of The Moon* (with tracks *Breathe*, *Time*, *Money*, *Us And Them* and *Brain Damage*) by Pink Floyd moves down to number eleven in the LP chart, after peaking at number two ▪ *Hickory House* (fea-

turing 36-year-old Alan Rothwell and a talking cushion called Humphrey) is new on TV for children ▪ The fourth series of *The Flaxton Boys* (a drama set in Yorkshire in the year 1945) is broadcast on Sunday afternoons on ITV ▪ "It's Friday. It's five o'clock and it's..." *Crackerjack* (hosted by 40-year-old Michael Aspel and featuring, comedians, 29-year-old Don MacLean and 55-year-old Peter Glaze) is on BBC One ▪ 26-year-old footballer Ralph Coates comes on as a substitute to score the only goal as Bill Nicholson's Tottenham Hotspur beat Ron Saunders' Norwich City 1-0 in the League Cup final at Wembley ▪ Joint favourite *Red Rum* (ridden by Brian Fletcher) makes a late run to win the Grand National at Aintree ▪ Cambridge win the Boat Race for the sixth consecutive year - beating Oxford by thirteen lengths ▪ "You ask how long I'll love you. I'll tell you true. Until..." *The Twelfth Of Never* ("... and that's a long, long time") by 15-year-old Donny Osmond spends a week at number one ▪ "Yeah, I'm your toy, your..." *20th Century Boy* by T-Rex reaches number three ▪ 32-year-old Cliff Richard competes in the Eurovision song contest in Luxembourg and finishes third singing *Power To All Our Friends* ("... to the music that never ends. To the people we want to be. Baby, power to you and me") ▪ 62-year-old Mrs. Mary Whitehouse delivers a petition to Number 10 Downing Street - with 1.35 million signatures of people calling for improved standards in public decency ▪ *Doctor Who* (played by 53-year-old Jon Pertwee) fights the Daleks on BBC One ▪ *Tarzan* (played by 34-year-old Ron Ely) fights crocodiles on ITV ▪ 40-year-old Ray 'Dracula' Reardon wins the *Park Drive* World Snooker Championship - beating Graham Miles from Birmingham by 22 frames to 12 in the final at Belle Vue in Manchester ▪ 59-year-old Alec Guinness chills cinema audiences with his performance as Germany's war time Fuehrer in *Hitler: the Last 10 Days* ▪ "Told you once before, and I won't tell you no more. Get down, get down, get down. You're a bad dog baby, but I still want you around" - *Get Down* by 26-year-old Gilbert O'Sullivan spends two weeks at the top of the pop chart ▪ "Tweedle, tweedle, tweedle doh. I'm a lucky so and so' - *Tweedle Dee* by 9-year-old Little Jimmy Osmond is number four ▪ 56,202 football spectators are at Anfield on Saturday the twenty-eighth of April to see Bill Shankly's Liverpool gain a point (from a 0-0 draw against Leicester City) and become the new champions of Division One. Ray Clemence,

Chris Lawler, Alec Lindsay, Tommy Smith, Larry Lloyd, Phil Thompson, Emlyn Hughes, Brian Hall, Steve Heighway, John Toshack, Peter Cormack, Ian Callaghan, Phil Boersma and 22-year-old Kevin Keegan have all been outstanding for 'The Reds' ▪ Bertie Mee's Arsenal (with Bob Wilson, Geoff Barnett, Pat Rice, Bob McNab, Peter Storey, Frank McLintock, Jeff Blockley, Peter Simpson, Alan Ball, George Armstrong, John Radford, Eddie Kelly and 21-year-old Ray Kennedy) are runners-up ▪ Don Howe's West Bromwich Albion finish bottom of the table and are relegated along with Malcolm Allison's Crystal Palace ▪ After serving his club for twenty years, 35-year-old Bobby Charlton makes his final appearance for Manchester Utd in a 1-0 defeat against Chelsea ▪ Crowds flock to the cinema to see 25-year-old David Essex, 26-year-old Keith Moon and 32-year-old Ringo Starr in *That'll Be The Day*, a new film from Claude Whatham ▪ "And..." *My Love* ("... does it good") by 30-year-old Paul McCartney and Wings is number nine in the pop chart ▪ 27-year-old Bob Harris, 34-year-old John Peel and 33-year-old Annie Nightingale take turns presenting *Sounds of the 70s* on Radio One at 10 p.m. on weekday nights ▪ "It's a crash course for the ravers. It's a..." *Drive-In Saturday* by 26-year-old David Bowie is number three in the singles chart ▪ Bowie's new LP, *Aladdin Sane*, is number one in the album chart ▪ "Rhododendron! Is a nice flower!"- *Do The Strand* is the opening track on *For Your Pleasure*, the latest LP from Roxy Music - which peaks at number four in the album chart ▪ Jimmy Adamson's Burnley football team (with Keith Newton, Martin Dobson, Paul Fletcher and 20-year-old Leighton James) finishes top of Division Two and gains promotion to Division One alongside Gordon Jago's Queens Park Rangers (with Gerry Francis, Dave Thomas, Don Givens and 24-year-old Stan Bowles) ▪ 27-year-old midfielder Ian Porterfield scores the only goal as Bob Stokoe's Second Division Sunderland shock the football world with a surprise FA Cup final victory over Leeds Utd of the First Division. A ticket for the standing enclosure at the Empire Stadium in Wembley costs £1.00 ▪ "Oh, I was just a boy..." *Giving It All Away* by 29-year-old Roger Daltrey is number five in the pop chart ▪ *I'm A Clown / Some Kind Of Summer* by 23-year-old heartthrob David Cassidy is number three ▪ 38-year-old Jack Charlton is the new football manager of Second Division Middlesbrough ▪ 35-year-old

Bobby Charlton is the new football manager of Second Division Preston North End ▪ 32-year-old Esther Rantzen presents the first edition of *That's Life* on TV ▪ 37-year-old John Inman (aka Mr. Humphries) declares, "I'm Free!" in *Are You Being Served?* 73-year-old Harold Bennett (aka Young Mr. Grace) informs the staff, "You've all done very well" ▪ Alf Roberts (played by 41-year-old Bryan Mosley) and Annie Walker (played by 74-year-old Doris Speed) are the new Mayor and Mayoress of Weatherfield in ITV's popular soap-opera *Coronation Street* ▪ 60-year-old Jimmy Chipperfield opens the West Midland Safari Park near Kidderminster and families travel from all around to see the monkeys ▪ The 'C' reg Ford *Zephyr 4* belonging to David Lovell breaks down and the 32-year-old lorry driver from Armitage, Staffordshire purchases a 'J' reg Hillman *Avenger* (in Tangerine Metallic) for £595 as a replacement ▪ "I'm coming home, I've done my time, and I've got to know what is and isn't mine" - *Tie A Yellow Ribbon Round The Old Oak Tree* ("... it's been three long years, do you still want me?") by Dawn is new at number one in the pop chart ▪ "Hello, hello. It's good to be back. It's good to be back. Did you miss me (yeah) while I was away?" - *Hello Hello I'm Back Again* by 29-year-old Gary Glitter is number two ▪ "She knows what she wants. Crazy..." *Crazy* "... You amaze me") the debut single from Mud (with 27-year-old, lead-singer, Les Gray) reaches number twelve ▪ Bill Shankly's Liverpool football team wins the UEFA Cup - defeating Borussia Monchengladbach 3-2 on aggregate (over two legs). 24-year-old goalkeeper Ray Clemence saves a penalty and 22-year-old Kevin Keegan and 24-year-old Larry Lloyd score the goals for high-flying Liverpool ▪ 29-year-old outside-left Martin Peters scores the only goal as England (with Peter Shilton, Emlyn Hughes and 32-year-old Bobby Moore) beat Scotland (with Ally Hunter, Lou Macari and 30-year-old Billy Bremner) 1-0 in front of 95,950 spectators at Wembley ▪ 'Nothing says goodbye like a bullet' - 34-year-old Elliott Gould stars at cinemas in *The Long Goodbye* ▪ 'Best of Enemies. Deadliest of Friends' - 44-year-old James Coburn, 36-year-old Kris Kristofferson and 32-year-old Bob Dylan star in *Pat Garrett and Billy the Kid* ▪ 55-year-old bussinesman Tiny Rowland, chief executive of the conglomerate Lonrho, is ousted from his position after a High Court rules that he

concealed financial information from other members of the board. Subsequently, shareholders step in to support Mr. Rowland and he is able to continue as Lonrho's chief exectutive ▪ 56-year-old Conservative prime-minister Edward Heath describes the unsavoury affair as the "unpleasant and unacceptable face of capitalism." ▪ Petrol prices are rising ▪ A gallon of four-star costs 37p ▪ The fuel economy of motorcars is becoming more and more important ▪ A Jaguar *XJ12* returns around 10 miles per gallon ▪ A Morris *Marina 1.8TC* returns 19.6 mpg ▪ A Hillman *Imp* returns 32.4 mpg ▪ An Austin *Allegro 1100* (which has just been launched) returns 33 mpg ▪ "Look out! Look out! Your mamma will shout, you might as well go home" - *See My Baby Jive* by Wizzard (with, lead singer, 26-year-old Roy Wood) reaches number one in the pop chart ▪ "Plucked her eyebrows on the way, shaved her legs and then he was a she. She said, hey babe, take a..." *Walk On The Wild Side* by 31-year-old Lou Reed peaks at number ten ▪ The new LP *Tubular Bells* by 20-year-old Mike Oldfield is the first release on 22-year-old Richard Branson's *Virgin Record* label ▪ Sally Harrison (played by 38-year-old Wendy Craig) marries David Redway (played by 43-year-old Richard Coleman) in a new series of *And Mother Makes Three* on ITV ▪ 41-year-old Jack Smethurst and 33-year-old Rudolph Walker star as 'Chalky' and 'Honky' in a new series of *Love Thy Neighbour* ▪ "Ain't no difference if you're black or white. Brothers, you know what I mean" - *Brother Louie* by Hot Chocolate (with, lead singer, 29-year-old Errol Brown) is number seven in the pop chart ▪ John Tyndall's National Front party takes 16% of the vote at a by-election in West Bromwich, but 43-year-old Betty Boothroyd manages to hold the seat for Labour ▪ "She's a hell raiser, star chaser, trail blazer, natural born raver, yeah! Yeah! Yeah! Yeah! Yeah!" - *Hell Raiser* by Sweet (with, lead singer, 27-year-old Brian Connolly) is number two on the hit parade ▪ *And I Love You So* ("... The people ask me how, how I've lived till now") by 60-year-old Perry Como is number three ▪ 'Admittance Restricted' - 49-year-old Marlon Brando and 21-year-old Maria Schneider get raunchy in a new movie called *Last Tango In Paris* ▪ Half a pound of *Lurpak* butter costs 11p at *Fine-Fare*.

Summer 1973

Secret lemonade drinker

Monarch:	Queen Elizabeth II (aged 47)
Prime-minister:	Edward Heath (aged 57)
Chancellor:	Anthony Barber (aged 53)
Home Secretary:	Robert Carr (aged 56)
Foreign Secretary:	Alec Douglas-Home (aged 70)
Football Manager:	Alf Ramsey (aged 53)
Radio 1 Breakfast DJ:	Noel Edmonds (aged 24)
New car reg. suffix:	'M'

▪ The sun shines, but temperatures remain cool ▪ 'Stop Me and Buy One' - children purchase *Screwballs*, *Funny Feet* and *99s* from the ice-cream man ▪ The brand new BMW *2002 Cabriolet* (a convertible, 4-seater motorcar with a sporting pedigree) is in showrooms now. Retail price of this shiny new model is £3,299 and top speed is 110 mph ▪ A re-issue of *Albatross* by Fleetwood Mac climbs to number two in the pop chart ▪ "Like…" *Walking In The Rain* ("… and wishing on a star") by The Partridge Family, starring 23-year-old heart-throb David Cassidy, is number ten ▪ The first edition of *Why Don't You Just Switch Off Your Television Set and Go and Do Something Less Boring Instead?* is on TV ▪ Children play out ▪ Girls wear cheese-cloth tops with tie waists ▪ Boys ride bikes ▪ A Mark II Raleigh *Chopper* costs £33.75 and is available in three colours: Infra Red, Ultra Violet or Fizzy Lemon ▪ 11-year-old schoolboy Phillip Schofield from Oldham stays in to watch telly ▪ "Oooh, hello honky tonks" - 58-year-old Dick Emery stars in *The Best of Dick Emery* on BBC One ▪ 'They had the perfect love affair. Until they fell in love' - 39-year-old George Segal and 37-year-old Glenda Jackson star at cinemas in *A Touch of Class* ▪ 45-year-old Robert Shaw and 31-year-old Sarah Miles star in *The Hireling* ▪ 36-year-old Edward Fox stars in *The Day of the Jackal* - a film based on the novel of the same name by 34-year-old Frederick Forsyth ▪ "One and one is one, little darling, now…" *One And One Is One* by Medicine Head is number three in the pop chart ▪ *Honaloochie Boogie* by Mott the Hoople is new at number thirty-eight ▪ The first ever Radio One Roadshow is broadcast from Fistral Beach at Newquay in Cornwall - 46-year-old disc

jockey Alan 'Fluff' Freeman is the host ("Not 'arf!") ▪ "So make a stand for your man honey, try to can the can. Put your man in the can honey, get him while you can…" *Can The Can* by 23-year-old Suzi Quatro is new at number one in the pop chart ▪ "Clowns to the left of me, jokers to the right. Here I am…" *Stuck In The Middle With You* by Stealers Wheel is number eight ▪ 40-year-old Dickie Bird stands as umpire for the first time in an international cricket Test Match - Ray Illingworth's England team beats Bevan Congdon's New Zealand by 38 runs ▪ The 'Cod Wars' continue in the seas off the coast of Iceland ▪ Icelandic patrol boats employ a new tactic of ramming into British Royal Navy frigates ▪ Back in England - heated debate takes place in the House of Commons over the high inflation rate and rising food costs ▪ Harold Wilson's Labour opposition pushes for food subsidies to be given to the less well off, but Conservative Chancellor of the Exchequer Anthony Barber resists ▪ 'Maxi. It Goes With a Way of Life.' - The versatile Austin *Maxi* motorcar is in showrooms. A top-of-the-range *1750HL* model costs £1,358.50 ▪ 'Skoda - the complete car' - A Skoda *S100L* (manufactured in Czechoslovakia) costs just £796 ▪ The number of road accidents in the UK is on the increase ▪ It's now compulsory for motorcyclists to wear crash-helmets ▪ The latest Suzuki *GT250* has a top speed of 90 mph ▪ The wonderful new Yamaha *FS-1* moped can reach 55 mph - travelling downhill, with a following wind ▪ 'The old man didn't die laughing but you will' - Crowds flock to cinemas to see *Steptoe & Son Ride Again* - in which Old Man Steptoe (Wilfrid Brambell) fakes his own death so that son Harold (Harry H. Corbett) can cash in on a life insurance policy ▪ A film version of the hugely popular TV series *Love Thy Neighbour* - with 41-year-old Jack Smethurst as Eddie 'Honky' Booth and 33-year-old Rudolph Walker as Bill 'Chalky' Reynolds is also now showing ▪ *You Are The Sunshine Of My Life* ("... That's why I'll always be around") by 23-year-old Stevie Wonder is number seven in the pop chart ▪ *Hallelujah Day* by The Jackson Five is number twenty ▪ Don Revie's hard-tackling Leeds Utd are fined by the Football Association for their poor disciplinary record last season ▪ Derby County's outspoken manager Brian Clough says Leeds' punishment should have been relegation to Division Two ▪ 28-year-old Alan Ball is sent-off for fighting as Sir Alf Ram-

sey's England team (Shilton, Madeley, Hughes, Storey, McFarland, Moore, Ball, Bell, Chivers, A Clarke, Peters) loses 2-0 in Poland ▪ "It's seven o'clock and I wanna rock, wanna get a belly full of beer" - *Saturday Night's Alright For Fighting* ("... get a little action in") by 26-year-old Elton John is number seven in the pop chart ▪ *Give Me Love (Give Me Peace On Earth)* by 30-year-old George Harrison is number eight ▪ *No Sex Please, We're British* is at cinemas, with 57-year-old Arthur Lowe, 54-year-old Beryl Reid, 29-year-old Ian Ogilvy, 23-year-old Susan Penhaligon and 42-year-old Ronnie Corbett in the cast ▪ 25-year-old Brendan Price stars in *Secrets of a Door to Door Salesman* ▪ 42-year-old Richie Benaud commentates on cricket matches for BBC One television ▪ 32-year-old Geoffrey Boycott and 30-year-old Dennis Amiss stride out together to open the batting for England against the West Indies at the Oval. Boycott scores 97 runs. Amiss makes 29. Clive Lloyd hits 132 and Alvin Kallicharran scores 80 as the touring West Indians triumph by 158 runs. In the third Test at Lord's, an IRA bomb scare halts play for almost two hours before the West Indians complete an easy 2-0 series victory over Ray Illingworth's team ▪ "Load up, load up, load up with..." *Rubber Bullets* by 10cc spends a week at the top of the pop chart ▪ "Ten, twenty, thirty, forty, fifty or more. The Bloody Red Baron was rollin' out the score. Eighty men died tryin' to end that spree, of the Bloody Red Baron of Germany" - *Snoopy vs The Red Baron* by The Hotshots is number four ▪ 42-year-old Peter Woods reads the news on BBC One ▪ 22-year-old David McGreavy is sentenced to life imprisonment for the brutal murders of three young children in Worcester ▪ 18-year-old Andrew Evans is sentenced to life imprisonment for the brutal murder of schoolgirl Judith Roberts in Tamworth ▪ 'M' reg cars go on sale ▪ 'Well-to-do' young men drive fast on motorways in sporty saloons ▪ 'The new Triumph Dolomite Sprint is a nice, quiet, luxurious utterly civilized car. And laps at 116mph' - The wonderful Triumph *Dolomite Sprint* has a top speed of 116 mph and accelerates from 0-60 mph in 9.1 seconds ▪ The Vauxhall *Firenza 2300 SL* has a top speed of 120 mph and accelerates from 0-60 mph in 8 seconds ▪ Sensible family men consider the options for a new motorcar ▪ More and more foreign cars being purchased in Britain each year ▪ Economical hatchbacks are popular ▪ A Datsun *Cherry* costs £884 and consumes fuel

at a rate of 34.8 mpg ▪ A Fiat *127* costs £978 and returns 32 mpg ▪ The new Renault *5TL* costs £929 and returns 26.5 mpg ▪ Four star leaded petrol has risen in price to 39p a gallon ▪ "I hear you talking..." *Alright Alright Alright* by Mungo Jerry is number three in the pop chart ▪ "Goin' home, goin' home..." *Goin' Home* by The Osmonds is number four ▪ Actor James Beck (who plays Private Walker in the hit television comedy *Dad's Army*) dies aged 44 in Roehampton ▪ 43-year-old Ronnie Barker is Fletcher and 50-year-old Fulton Mackay is Mr. Mackay in *Prisoner and Escort* - a one-off comedy written by Dick Clement and Ian La Frenais for BBC's *Seven Of One* series ▪ 26-year-old footballer Fabio Capello scores a goal past goalkeeper Peter Shilton, as Italy beat Sir Alf Ramsey's England 2-0 in Torino. England's full line-up for the match is: Shilton, Madeley, Hughes, Storey, McFarland, Moore, Currie, Channon, Chivers, A Clarke and Peters ▪ 33-year-old Denis Law leaves Manchester Utd and joins Manchester City on a free transfer ▪ 28-year-old Peter Noble leaves Swindon Town and joins Burnley for £40,000 ▪ 24-year-old Noel Edmonds takes over from Tony Blackburn as presenter of Radio One's breakfast show. 30-year-old Blackburn moves to the mid-morning slot ▪ "You know how to skweeze me. Whoa-ah! You know how to pleeze me. Whoa-ah!" - *Skweeze Me Pleeze Me* by Slade (with 27-year-old Noddy Holder) comes straight into the pop chart at number one - and stays at the top for three weeks ▪ Slade's drummer Don Powell is badly injured and his girlfriend Angela Morris is killed in a car crash ▪ "They call me..." *The Groover* ("... when I'm on the floor") by T-Rex (with, lead singer, 25-year-old Marc Bolan) is number four on the weekly hit parade ▪ "C'mon..." *Take Me To The Mardi Gras* by 31-year-old Paul Simon is number seven ▪ 23-year-old boxer Joe Bugner loses to former world champion Smokin' Joe Frazier in a closely fought contest at Earls Court ▪ 31-year-old tennis player Roger Taylor from Sheffield loses to Jan Kodes in the semi-finals of the men's singles championship at Wimbledon ▪ 28-year-old Virginia Wade from Bournemouth loses to Evonne Goolagong in the quarter-finals of the ladies' singles ▪ Nine racing cars crash at Woodgate Corner on the first lap of the British Grand Prix at Silverstone - and the race has to be restarted. Peter Revson (from the USA) is the eventual winner ▪ Two weeks later, 34-year-old Jackie Stewart wins the Dutch Grand Prix and

extends his lead to ten points over Emerson Fittipaldi in the drivers' championship ▪ "Good evening. The name's Bond, you have a reservation for me" - The film *Live And Let Die* is now showing at cinemas, with 45-year-old Roger Moore as the new James Bond (aka 007). 22-year-old Jane Seymour plays the role of Solitaire. 65-year-old Bernard Lee is M. 46-year-old Lois Maxwell is Miss Moneypenny ▪ "When you were young, and your heart was an open book, you used to say, live and let live. (You know you did - you know you did - you know you did). But in this ever changin' world in which we live in, makes you give in, and cry. Say…" *Live And Let Die* by Paul McCartney and Wings is number seven in the pop chart ▪ "Welcome home. (Welcome). Come on in, and close the door" - *Welcome Home* by Peters and Lee (41-year-old Lennie Peters and 24-year-old Dianne Lee) is number one for a week ▪ "So I gave her up for music and..." *The Free Electric Band* by 28-year-old Albert Hammond peaks at number nineteen ▪ Families sit together and watch TV ▪ An *ITT CK702* 26-inch colour set costs £292.00 including VAT ▪ A *Ferguson* 12-inch portable black and white set costs £56.05 including VAT ▪ *Man About the House* is a great new sit-com - starring 23-year-old Paula Wilcox, 23-year-old Sally Thomsett and 29-year-old Richard O'Sullivan ▪ Rita Littlewood (played by 39-year-old Barbara Knox) and Mavis Riley (played by 44-year-old Thelma Barlow) serve customers at 'The Kabin' - a brand new newsagents - in *Coronation Street* ▪ Children enjoy a new show called *Michael Bentine's Potty Time* ▪ 21-year-old Hereford Utd goalkeeper David Icke is forced to retire from football because of arthritis in his knees ▪ "Oh man, wonder if he'll ever know, he's in the freakiest show. Is there..." *Life On Mars* by 26-year-old David Bowie is number three on the weekly hit parade ▪ "Come on - come on! Come on - come on! Come on - come on - come on! D'ya wanna be in my gang, my gang, my gang?" - *I'm The Leader Of The Gang (I Am)* by 29-year-old Gary Glitter is number one for four weeks ▪ Teenage tearaways smoke cigarettes in the park ▪ A pack of twenty Player's *No. 6* cigarettes is 21p ▪ "48 crash, 48 crash. Come like a lightning flash, a lightning flash. And it's a silk sash bash, a silk sash bash. That's the..." *48 Crash* by 23-year-old Suzi Quatro reaches number three in the pop chart ▪ "Every sha-la la-la, every wo-oh wo-oh still shines. Every shing-a-ling-a-ling, that they're starting to sing's so fine. When they

get to the part, where he's breaking her heart, it can really make me cry, just like before. It's..." *Yesterday Once More* by The Carpenters (with, lead singer, 23-year-old Karen Carpenter) peaks at number two ▪ Veteran singer Donald Peers dies aged 65 in Hove ▪ Ace racing driver Jackie Stewart wins the German Grand Prix at the Nurburgring - and extends his lead to fifteen point in the Formula One drivers' championship ▪ Back in England - the new football season gets underway ▪ 23-year-old Malcolm 'Supermac' MacDonald scores twice as Newcastle Utd beat West Ham Utd 2-1 in front of 28,169 spectators at St. James' Park ▪ Billy Bremner, Johnny Giles and Mick Jones are on the score-sheet as Leeds Utd beat Everton 3-1 in front of 39,325 at Elland Road. (Leeds' players have a new club badge on their jerseys - the letters L and U joined together in a yellow bubble, reminiscent of the ubiquitous 'smiley face' symbol) ▪ "Blue..." *Spanish Eyes* ("... Prettiest eyes in all of Mexico") by 45-year-old Al Martino is number five in the pop chart ▪ "Ying tong, ying tong, ying tong, ying tong, ying tong, iddle I po" - *The Ying Tong Song* by The Goons is number nine ▪ 57-year-old Conservtive prime-minister Edward Heath visits Northern Ireland and makes a speech at Stormont Castle saying that the British Army will remain in the provence to back up the Royal Ulster Constabulary until the terrorists are overcome ▪ Back on the mainland - A bright new *British Home Stores* shop opens at Worthing in Sussex. Shoppers queue to try out the wonderful, modern, 350-seater, self-service restaurant - which has air-conditioning ▪ 41-year-old Elizabeth Taylor and 44-year-old Lawrence Harvey star at cinemas in *Night Watch* ▪ *Jollees* nightclub opens in Stoke-on-Trent. Customers enjoy chicken-in-a-basket whilst being entertained by upcoming comedians Little & Large ▪ 35-year-old Stoke City and England goalkeeper Gordon Banks announces his retirement from football after being blinded in one eye in a car accident last year ▪ *Touch Me In The Morning* ("... Then just walk away") by 29-year-old Diana Ross is number nine in the pop chart ▪ *TBad Bad Boy* by Nazareth is number ten ▪ Energetic people don *Bri-Nylon* tracksuits and play table tennis together around the dining table - it's a sport that's currently 'all the rage' ▪ "I'm a secret lemonade drinker. R Whites. R Whites. I've been tryin' to give it up but it's one of those nights" - *R Whites* advertise lemonade on TV.

Autumn 1973

Gary Glitter v Alvin Stardust

Monarch:	Queen Elizabeth II (aged 47)
Prime-minister:	Edward Heath (aged 57)
Chancellor:	Anthony Barber (aged 53)
Home Secretary:	Robert Carr (aged 57)
Foreign Secretary:	Alec Douglas-Home (aged 70)
Football Manager:	Alf Ramsey (aged 53)
Radio 1 Breakfast DJ:	Noel Edmonds (aged 24)
New car reg. suffix:	'M'

▪ 47-year-old Queen Elizabeth II opens Sydney Opera House in Australia - the impressive new building has taken fourteen years to complete ▪ Back in Britain - inflation is rising and 57-year-old prime-minister Edward Heath and his Chancellor of the Exchequer 53-year-old Anthony Barber are forced to take action ▪ Mr. Heath holds three days of meetings to devise an anti-inflation policy. On day one, the prime-minister meets with representatives of the Confederation of British Industry. On day two, he meets with senior people from the Retail Consortium. On day three, he meets with leaders from the Trade Union Congress ▪ " Goodnight, thank you and may your God go with you" - 37-year-old comedian Dave Allen stars in *Dave Allen at Large* on BBC One television on Friday evenings ▪ 39-year-old Jean Marsh (Rose), 69-year-old Angela Baddeley (Mrs. Bridges) and 49-year-old Gordon Jackson (Hudson) star in a new series of *Upstairs Downstairs* on ITV on Saturday evenings ▪ "They say for every boy and girl, there's just one love in this whole world, and I-I-I know I-I-I've found mine" - *Young Love* by 15-year-old heart-throb Donny Osmond moves up to number one in the pop chart ▪ "Don't wanna say good night..." *Dancing On A Saturday Night* by 22-year-old Barry Blue is number two ▪ 29-year-old Michael Fish presents the weather forecast on BBC One ▪ The sun shines brightly in early September ▪ Tinted glass is an optional extra on Triumph *Dolomite* motorcars ▪ Ford introduces the wonderful new *Escort RS2000* - the sporty new model is in showrooms now, with a retail price of £1,442 plus VAT ▪ 35-year-old Barry Davies and 28-year-old John Motson commentate on football matches for BBC One's

Match of the Day program ▪ Manchester Utd's goalkeeper, 30-year-old Alex Stepney, scores a second half penalty as Utd lose 1-2 against Leicester City at Old Trafford in Division One ▪ Aston Villa's goalkeeper, 29-year-old Jim Cumbes, is knocked-out by a missile thrown from the crowd after Villa's 1-1 draw against Millwall at The Den in Division Two ▪ *Like Sister And Brother* ("… we'll wave to each other") by The Drifters is number seven in the pop chart ▪ *Say, Has Anybody Seen My Sweet Gypsy Rose* by Dawn featuring 29-year-old Tony Orlando is number twelve ▪ 11-year-old schoolboy Micky Flanagan from Whitechapel in East London plays out-out with his mates ▪ Children return to school after the summer holidays. All those aged ten or eleven with neat hand-writing are permitted to use an ink cartridge *Parker* pen instead of a pencil - in preparation for secondary school ▪ "You can do magic, baby..." *You Can Do Magic* ("... magic") by Limmie and the Family Cookin' is new at number three on the hit parade ▪ *The Dean And I* by 10cc is number ten ▪ After his recent visit to Northern Ireland, 57-year-old Conservative prime-minister Edward Heath is now back at Number 10 Downing Street ▪ The IRA steps up its bombing campaign in England ▪ There are explosions at King's Cross Station, Euston Station, Oxford Street, Sloane Square and also in Manchester ▪ Speaking of the terrorist outrages, Mr. Heath says "We shall relentlessly pursue and hunt down those who are responsible for violence in every part of the United Kingdom." ▪ In other news, an agreement over fishing rights is reached between Iceland and the UK and the 'Cod Wars' come to an end. A zone of fifty nautical miles from the coastline of Iceland is established, with British trawlers being granted limited rights to fish within the newly defined area ▪ 40-year-old Barry Norman presents the late night movie review program *Film 73* on BBC One ▪ 'As P. T. Barnum put it, "There's a sucker born every minute"' - *Paper Moon* is at cinemas, with 32-year-old Ryan O'Neal as Moses and 9-year-old Tatum O'Neal as Addie ▪ The late Bruce Lee stars in *Enter the Dragon* - a martial arts movie from Robert Clouse ▪ "Ha-ha-ha, hee-hee-hee, I'm a laughing gnome and you don't catch me" - *The Laughing Gnome* by 26-year-old David Bowie is number six in the pop chart ▪ *My Friend Stan* ("… 's got a funny old man. Oh yeah, oh yeah") by Slade is number two ▪ 25-year-old Cap-

tain Mark Phillips wins the three-day horse trial event at Burghley House on *Maid Marion* ▪ 23-year-old boxer Joe Bugner defeats Giuseppe Ros on points at the Royal Albert Hall to retain his European heavy-weight title ▪ Footballers, 27-year-old Billy Bonds and 25-year-old Trevor Brooking score the goals as struggling West Ham Utd come from 2-0 down to snatch a 2-2 draw against Sheffield Utd in Division One ▪ 20-year-old striker Paul Mariner scores twice on his debut for Plymouth Argyle in a 5-0 victory over Rochdale in Division Three ▪ "Are you ready Steve? Uh-huh. Andy? Yeah. Mick? Okay. Alright fellas, let's go!" - *Ballroom Blitz* by The Sweet (with, lead singer, 27-year-old Brian Connolly) is number two in the pop chart ▪ *Angie* ("… Angie, ain't it good to be alive?") by The Rolling Stones (with, lead singer, 30-year-old Mick Jagger) is number five ▪ Supersonic airplane Concorde makes its first non-stop crossing of the Atlantic - and completes the trip in a record breaking time of just 3 hours and 32 minutes ▪ Prime-minister Edward Heath and his Conservative government push ahead with plans for a new international airport at Maplin Sands in Essex - even though estimated costs for the project have risen to over £1,000 million ▪ Inflation stands at 8.8% ▪ Chancellor of the Exchequer Anthony Barber ignores calls to put the brakes on the economy and says, "I believe our present path of expansion is sustainable and my conclusion is that it would be wrong now to check it" ▪ Tensions are growing between the National Coal Board (led by 54-year-old Sir Derek Ezra) and the National Union of Mineworkers (led by 56-year-old Joe Gormley) ▪ Coal miners begin an overtime ban ▪ Housewives go shopping on crowded high streets ▪ *Green Shield Stamps* catalogue stores are now called *Argos* ▪ A *Russell Hobbs* electric kettle costs £6.10 ▪ A *Morphy Richards* hair-dryer costs £3.25 ▪ A red *Tonka Toy* fire-engine is £4.95 ▪ *Angel Fingers* ("… Angel fingers, how I sing for the things you do") by Wizzard (with, lead singer, 26-year-old Roy Wood) spends a week at number one in the pop chart ▪ "Hey kid, rock and roll…" *Rock On* ("… Ooh, my soul") by 26-year-old David Essex peaks at number three ▪ "When are you gonna come down? When are you gonna land?" - *Goodbye Yellow Brick Road* by 26-year-old Elton John is number six ▪ Fashions move on ▪ The Swinging Sixties seem like a distant memory ▪ Carnaby Street in London is pedestrianised ▪

26-year-old footballer Peter Lorimer bags a hat-trick as Don Revie's hard-tackling Leeds Utd beat Freddie Goodwin's Birmingham City 3-0 at Elland Road ▪ 51-year-old Raymond Baxter commentates on motor racing for BBC One television ▪ Ace racing driver Jackie Stewart is in blistering form! The 34-year-old Scot charges through a pack of cars at the Italian Grand Prix and moves up from twentieth position to fourth - gaining enough points to become Formula One world champion for the third time in his career ▪ Emerson Fittipaldi from Brazil is runner up in the drivers' championship and Ronnie Peterson of Sweden is third ▪ Back in England - young men dream of owning a fast car ▪ The wonderful new Ford *Escort RS2000* has a top speed of 108 mph and can reach 60 mph in 9 seconds ▪ The latest Hillman *Avenger Tiger* has a top speed of 106 mph and can reach 60 mph in 9.5 seconds ▪ Middle-aged men with limited budgets dream of owning a car ▪ The all new Reliant *Robin* 'three-wheeler' replaces the Reliant *Regal* ▪ The bright orange *Bond Bug* 'three-wheeler' (which was launched in 1970) now comes with a 750cc engine ▪ Schoolboys crave the new *Matchbox* die-cast model of the *Boss Mustang* car in yellow with a black (opening) bonnet ▪ "Der-de-de-der, de-de, de-de, de-de, de-de. Der-de-de-de-de-der" - *Eye Level* by The Simon Park Orchestra spends four weeks at number one in the pop chart ▪ 41-year-old actor Barry Foster plays Dutch detective *Van der Valk* on Wednesday evenings on ITV ▪ A new series of *The Onedin Line* (with 42-year-old Peter Gilmore, 34-year-old Anne Stallybrass and 62-year-old Howard Lang) is on BBC One on Sunday evenings ▪ The character Sgt Bert Lynch (played by 42-year-old Jimmy Ellis) is promoted to the rank of Inspector in long-running police drama *Z Cars* ▪ 15-year-old Stacy Dorning is Jenny Gordon in a new series of *The Adventures of Black Beauty* on ITV ▪ Elsie Howard (played by 49-year-old Pat Phoenix) and her husband Alan leave the popular soap-opera *Coronation Street* to begin a new life in Newcastle ▪ "A-G! A-G-R! A-G-R-O! AGRO!" - Angry football supporters chant from the terraces ▪ Don Revie's hard-tackling Leeds Utd are the early leaders in Division One ▪ 27-year-old striker Allan 'sniffer' Clarke scores twice for Leeds in a 1-2 away victory at Southampton - to make it seven consecutive wins for the 'All Whites' ▪ 45-year-old Jimmy Hill is the new presenter of *Match of the*

Day ▪ "I was working in the lab, late one night, when my eyes beheld an eerie sight. For my monster from his slab, began to rise and suddenly to my surprise, he did the mash. He did the…" *Monster Mash* by Bobby 'Boris' Pickett and the Crypt-Kickers reaches number three in the pop chart ▪ "'Ello darlin'!" - 32-year-old Ed 'stewpot' Stewart presents *Junior Choice* on weekend mornings on Radio One ▪ "Oh! The runaway train came down the track and she blew. The runaway train came down the track and she blew. The runaway train came down the track, her whistle wide and her throttle back, and she blew-oo-oo-oo-oo" - Michael Holliday sings *The Runaway Train* ▪ Sir Alf Ramsey's England football team fails to qualify for next year's world cup competition. Mistakes by 29-year-old defender Norman Hunter and 24-year-old goalkeeper Peter Shilton allow Poland to score a goal in a match at Wembley - and a sixty-third minute penalty equaliser by Allan 'sniffer' Clarke is not enough. The game ends in a 1-1 draw - and England needed to win. Shilton, Hunter and Clarke - along with Paul Madeley, Roy McFarland, Emlyn Hughes, Colin Bell, Tony Currie, Martin Peters, Mick Channon, Martin Chivers and Kevin Hector all miss out on the chance to play in the finals in West Germany ▪ 38-year-old manager Brian Clough shocks the football world by 'walking out' at Derby County ▪ "I'm just a daydreamer. I'm walkin' in the rain, chasin' after rainbows I may never find again" - *Daydreamer* by 23-year-old heart-throb David Cassidy is top of the hit parade ▪ "Come on sweet Caroline. You're my sweet…" *Caroline* by Status Quo (with, lead singer, 24-year-old Francis Rossi and guitarist 25-year-old Rick Parfitt) is number five ▪ 26-year-old Uri Geller bends spoons on TV - and the nation attempts to emulate him ▪ Captain Mainwaring says, "Don't tell him, Pike!", in the opening episode of a new series of *Dad's Army*. The recently deceased James Beck (who plays Private Walker) appears in six of the shows - which were recorded just weeks before his death ▪ "Don't look so sad, I know it's over" - *For The Good Times* by 61-year-old Perry Como is number seven in the pop chart ▪ "A church house, gin house. A school house, outhouse. On Highway Number Nineteen, the people keep the city clean" - *Nutbush City Limits* by 41-year-old Ike Turner and his wife, 33-year-old Tina, is number three ▪ 17-year-old footballer Liam Brady makes his de-

but for Arsenal - coming on as a substitute in a 1-0 victory over Birmingham City ▪ 23-year-old Malcolm 'Supermac' MacDonald scores twice as Newcastle Utd beat Chelsea 2-0 in front of 32,154 spectators at St. James' Park ▪ After a year out of the game, 27-year-old 'super' Georgie Best asks Manchester Utd manager Tommy 'The Doc' Docherty if he can return to the team ▪ 'Super' Georgie resumes training and is called up to play in a First Division match against Tottenham Hotspur at White Hart Lane - where he scores Utd's goal in a 2-1 defeat ▪ 23-year-old Terry Yorath scores a goal for top-of-the-table Leeds Utd in a 3-0 victory over Ipswich Town ▪ "With your long blond hair and your eyes of blue, the only thing I ever got from you was sorrow..." *Sorrow* by David Bowie is number three in the pop chart ▪ "And she walked in looking like..." *Dyna-Mite* by Mud is number four ▪ 18-year-old Penny Irving (34B) appears topless on page three of *The Sun* newspaper ▪ "Cheeky little thing! I'd like to put her across my knee" - *Carry On Girls* is now showing at cinemas, with 54-year-old Peter Butterworth as 'the old admiral', 60-year-old Sid 'Ha-ak-ak' James as Sidney Fiddler and with 36-year-old Barbara Windsor (36-24-34) as Hope Springs ▪ "I say. Ha-lo. Ding-dong" - 49-year-old Leslie Phillips stars in *Casanova '73* on television ▪ "We're still together, after all that we've been through. They tried to tell you, I was not the boy for you. They didn't like my hair, the clothes I love to wear. They didn't realise that I was strong enough for two" - *I Love, You Love, Me Love* by 29-year-old Gary Glitter enters the pop chart at number one - and stays there for four weeks ▪ "Ah-won't you be..." *My Coo-Ca Choo* by 31-year-old Alvin Stardust is number two ▪ 28-year-old maverick striker Rodney Marsh scores a goal for Manchester City and 24-year-old Mick Channon scores for Southampton in a 1-1 draw at Maine Road ▪ Millions fill in their weekly football pools coupon - hoping for eight score-draws ▪ *Littlewoods* introduce 'Spot the Ball' ▪ 21-year-old Steve Perryman is on the score-sheet for Tottenham Hotspur in a 1-1 against Everton at Goodison Park ▪ "Marching on together!" - Don Revie's hard-tackling Leeds Utd stay top of Division One with a 1-2 away victory over Chelsea at Stamford Bridge. Joe Jordan and Mick Jones score the goals ▪ 40-year-old John Bond replaces Ron Saunders as manager of Norwich City ▪ 32-year-old Fred West

and his wife, 19-year-old Rosemary, murder 15-year-old Carol Ann Cooper and bury her body beneath their house at 25 Cromwell Street in Gloucester ▪ "Won't you plea-ea-ease..." *Let Me In* ("... Let me in your arms again") by The Osmonds peaks at number two in the pop chart ▪ "I'm on top of the world looking down on creation and the only explanation I can find, is the love that I've found, ever since you've been around, your love's put me at the..." *Top Of The World* by The Carpenters is number five ▪ "Oooh, Betty" - 31-year-old Michael Crawford plays Frank Spencer in a new series of *Some Mothers Do 'Ave 'Em.* 25-year-old Michele Dotrice is Betty, Frank's long sufering wife ▪ Ken Barlow (played by 41-year-old Bill Roache) marries Janet Reid (played by 30-year-old Judith Barker) in *Coronation Street* ▪ 23-year-old Princess Anne marries 25-year-old Captain Mark Phillips at Westminster Abbey. The young Princess' wedding dress is designed by 52-year-old Maureen Baker. 9-year-old Lady Sarah Armstrong-Jones is bridesmaid and 9-year-old Prince Edward is page boy ▪ *Paper Roses* ("... Paper roses. Oh, how real those roses seem to me") by 14-year-old Marie Osmond climbs to number two in the pop chart ▪ "Every time I see your face it reminds me of the place we used to go" - *Photograph* by 33-year-old Ringo Starr is number eight ▪ "I love, you love. You love me too, love. I love, you love, me love" - *I Love, You Love, Me Love* by 29-year-old Gary Glitter remains at number one ▪ Nottingham city centre is pedestrianised ▪ Vauxhall launches the new *Magnum* motorcar (a sporty version of the *Viva*) with *Rostyle* wheels and a choice of 1800cc or 2300cc engine. Prices atart from £1,365 ▪ Travelling sales representatives (driving white Morris *Marina* estate cars) stop for lunch in 'greasy spoon' cafés ▪ Egg & Chips costs 22p ▪ Bread & Butter is 4p ▪ A mug of tea is 5p ▪ Children rush to the sweet-shop after school for a *Sherbet Fountain* before going home to watch *Animal Magic* on TV ▪ Heavy rain moves in across the country ▪ Families spend the weekend indoors ▪ There's very little to do on grey Sunday afternoons ▪ Mums polish the ornamental ceramic shire horse (with plastic cart) on the mantelpiece ▪ Dads carry out tricky DIY jobs ▪ A Black & Decker *D520* 2-speed electric drill costs £13.69 ▪ Adverts say, 'Do It Well With Polycell'.

Christmas 1973

Are you hangin' up your stocking on the wall?

Monarch:	Queen Elizabeth II (aged 47)
Prime-minister:	Edward Heath (aged 57)
Chancellor:	Anthony Barber (aged 53)
Home Secretary:	Robert Carr (aged 57)
Foreign Secretary:	Alec Douglas-Home (aged 70)
Football Manager:	Alf Ramsey (aged 53)
Radio 1 Breakfast DJ:	Noel Edmonds (aged 25)
New car reg. suffix:	'M'

▪ 'De-de-der-der-de-de-de-de-de-de-de-de-der-der, der-der-de-de-de-de-de' - 49-year-old Benny Hill stars in a new edition of *The Benny Hill Show* on ITV ▪ 'Flash, cleans without scratching' - 63-year-old Molly Weir advertises *Flash* scouring powder ▪ 50-year-old Jack Scott presents the weather forecast on BBC One ▪ There's snow in the air ▪ "Are you hanging up a stocking on your wall? It's the time that every Santa has a ball" - *Merry Xmas Everybody* by Slade (with 27-year-old Noddy Holder) enters the pop chart at number one! ▪ *When I Fall In Love* ("… it will be forever") by 16-year-old Donny Osmond is number four ▪ Christmas is coming ▪ Families stock up with essential supplies ▪ A bottle of *Teacher's* whisky costs £2.49 ▪ A bottle of *Gordon's* gin is £2.45 ▪ A bottle of *Martell* brandy is £4.19 ▪ A bottle of *Lamb's Navy Rum* is £2.69 ▪ A bottle of *Warninks* advocaat is £1.89 ▪ A bottle of *Harveys Bristol Cream* is £1.35 ▪ A four-pack of *Babycham* (small) bottles is 34p ▪ 32-year-old footballer Bobby Moore makes his 108th (and final) appearance for England in a 0-1 defeat against Italy at Wembley. (27-year-old Fabio Capello scores Italy's goal two minutes before full-time). England's line-up for the match is: Shilton, Madeley, Hughes, Bell, McFarland, Moore, Currie, Channon, Osgood, Clarke, Peters and substitute, Hector ▪ "Ooh, baby would I look right, climbing up the drainpipe? Baby, would it feel right, if I stayed all night?" - *Lamplight* by 26-year-old David Essex is number seven in the pop chart ▪ "Won't you..." *Roll Away The Stone* ("... Why be cold and so alone?") by Mott the Hoople (with 34-year-old, lead singer, Ian Hunter) is number eight ▪ 26-year-old footballer Peter 'Ossie' Osgood scores a goal

for Chelsea in a 3-2 victory over Leicester City at Stamford Bridge. (25-year-old Frank Worthington is on the score-sheet for Leicester) ▪ 34-year-old world champion racing driver Jackie Stewart is BBC's 'Sports Personality of the Year' ▪ People purchase colour TV licences for £12 ▪ 3.3 million colour licenses have been issued this year, compared to 13.8 million black and white permits ▪ Stan and Hilda Ogden celebrate their thirtieth wedding anniversary in ITV's popular soap-opera *Coronation Street* ▪ 31-year-old actor John Thaw marries 40-year-old Sheila Hancock in Cirencester ▪ People post their Christmas cards in plenty of time before the big day ▪ A first class postage stamp costs 3½p ▪ A second class stamp is 3p ▪ The IRA bombing campaign continues - a device is detonated outside the Home Office at Millbank in London and sixty people are injured ▪ Children rush to the cinema to see the matinee screening of *Digby the Biggest Dog in the World* - starring Jim Dale, Angela Douglas and 55-year-old Spike Milligan ▪ Walt Disney's *Robin Hood* is also now showing ▪ *The Golden Voyage of Sinbad* is coming soon ▪ 35-year-old disc jockey Terry Wogan attracts millions of listeners to his morning program on Radio Two ▪ 48-year-old Pete Murray entertains housewives on his mid-morning show, before *Waggoners' Walk* ▪ "Step into Christmas, let's join together, we can watch the snow fall for ever and ever " - *Step Into Christmas* by 26-year-old Elton John is number eleven in the pop chart ▪ "Truck on, truck on, truck on…" *Truck On (Tyke)* by T. Rex (with 26-year-old Marc Bolan) is number twelve ▪ Hallmark Records release *The Best of Top of the Pops '73* - a budget priced, cover-version pop compilation LP with a 'knowing' blonde girl on the sleeve ▪ Paul Heaton from Hull is involved in a murder. He keeps it to himself ▪ Coal miners hold firm with their overtime ban ▪ The Conservative government imposes restrictions on the 'non-essential' use of electricity ▪ 'This Christmas, with less energy available we must provide for essential services and hospitals who will be at risk. We can save most by heating one room only, so - Cut Down at Christmas' - a public information film is broadcast on TV ▪ Football clubs are banned from using floodlights - and all matches have to be played in daylight hours ▪ Jack Charlton's Middlesbrough are top of Division Two after a 3-0 win against Bobby Charlton's Preston North End ▪ *Do You Wanna*

Dance ("... and hold me tight?") by 23-year-old Barry Blue from London climbs to number seven in the pop chart ▪ *Amoureuse* by 26-year-old Kiki Dee from Bradford peaks at number thirteen ▪ 55-year-old Willie Whitelaw is the new Secretary of State for Employment in Edward Heath's Cabinet ▪ Francis Pym is the Secretary of State for Northern Ireland ▪ BBC One TV programs on a Saturday night include: *Dr. Who* - starring 54-year-old Jon Pertwee; *Wonderful World of Disney*; *Bruce Forsyth and The Generation Game* - with 45-year-old Bruce and 25-year-old Anthea Redfern; *The Harry Secombe Show*; and *Match of the Day* - introduced by 45-year-old Jimmy Hill ▪ 22-year-old Kevin Keegan and 26-year-old Steve Heighway score the goals as Bill Shankly's Liverpool beat Tommy 'The Doc' Docherty's Manchester Utd 2-0 at Anfield ▪ Opposing football fans taunt George Best with the chant, "Georgie Best. Superstar. Walks like a woman and he wears a bra" ▪ Don Revie's hard-tackling Leeds Utd remain unbeaten - and are seven points clear at the top of Division One ▪ 23-year-old Terry Yorath scores the only goal as Leeds achieve a 1-0 victory over John Bond's Norwich City in front of 34,747 at Elland Road ▪ 37-year-old Lawrie McMenemy takes over from Ted Bates as manager of Southampton ▪ 38-year-old Brian Clough is the new manager of Third Division Brighton and Hove Albion. 16,017 spectators turn out at the Goldstone Ground for Cloughie's first game in charge - a 0-0 draw against York City ▪ "Wish everybody would leave me alone, yeah" - *Street Life* by Roxy Music (with, lead singer, 28-year-old Bryan Ferry) is number nine in the pop chart ▪ "You're breaking my heart, just in case you didn't know..." *Why, Oh Why, Oh Why* by 27-year-old Gilbert O'Sullivan is number six ▪ 60-year-old Robert Dougall and 40-year-old Richard Whitmore read the news on BBC One ▪ 53-year-old Chancellor of the Exchequer Anthony Barber refuses to budge from the path he's set for speedy economic expansion ▪ Inflation has now rocketed to 10.6% and food prices are at an all-time high ▪ To compound the government's woes, the coal miners come out on strike leading to fuel shortages and power cuts ▪ The country is plunged into darkness ▪ Shops run out of candles ▪ Schools are without heating and are forced to close ▪ 57-year-old prime-minister Edward Heath introduces a three-day working week ▪ 132 million tonnes of coal have been mined in

1973 - just 5 million more than the all time low of last year ▪ The oil crisis escalates in the Middle East and petrol prices soar ▪ Four star is now 59p a gallon ▪ Two star is 57p ▪ Petrol supplies are scarce ▪ Lines of stationary Morris *1100s*, Ford *Escorts*, Hillman *Avengers* and Vauxhall *Vivas* clog the roads outside garage forecourts ▪ A 50 mph speed limit is imposed on motorists in an effort to conserve fuel ▪ A limited edition Ford *Capri RS3100* goes on sale - with a (petrol thirsty) V6 engine - and sales of the new car are slow ▪ A strike at British Leyland's car body factory at Llanelli affects production at Longbridge and Cowley - with many workers being laid-off ▪ The nights are cold and foggy ▪ Brave courting couples venture out for an evening at the local cinema ▪ 'Flesh to touch ... Flesh to Burn!' - 31-year-old Britt Ekland dances naked in *The Wicker Man* ▪ 41-year-old Elizabeth Taylor stars alongside Henry Fonda in *Ash Wednesday* ▪ 32-year-old Bill Oddie, 30-year-old Graeme Garden and 33-year-old Tim Brooke-Taylor star in *The Goodies and the Beanstalk* - a one-off TV special shown on Christmas Eve ▪ "So here it is, 'Merry Christmas', everybody's havin' fun. Look to the future now, it's only just begun" - *Merry Xmas Everybody* by Slade remains at number one in the pop chart ▪ "Oh, well..." *I Wish It Could Be Christmas Everyday* ("... when the kids start singing and the band begins to play") by Wizzard (with, lead singer, 27-year-old Roy Wood) is number four ▪ Competitive, energetic schoolboys ask Santa Claus for a 5-speed racer bicycle with *Huret* speedometer ▪ Cool, trendy schoolboys ask Santa Claus for a Raleigh *Chopper* ▪ Pocket calculators and a new board game called *Escape From Colditz* are also in demand ▪ 'You'll find what you want in a box of Week-End' - millions of people give Mackintosh's *Week-End* assorted chocolates as gifts ▪ 10-year-old James May from Bristol receives an *Airfix* model from his auntie ▪ The power cuts continue and families huddle around candles in cold, dim living rooms ▪ Don Revie's hard-tackling, top-of-the-table Leeds Utd football team beats Newcastle Utd 0-1 on Boxing Day, with a goal from 29-year-old Paul Madeley ▪ Bill Shankly's second placed Liverpool lose 1-2 at Burnley ▪ 57-year-old prime-minister Edward Heath and his Cabinet review their plans for a new international airport at Maplin Sands in Essex. The project now seems a little extravagant in light of the current economic climate ▪ "Charley and I were in the park. Then this

man came up and said would I like to see some puppies and I said 'yes,' and I was going to go, but Charley stopped me" - A cartoon cat called Charley tells the public not to go anywhere with men or ladies they don't know ▪ 47-year-old Jimmy Savile OBE presents *Savile's Travels* on Sunday afternoons on Radio One ▪ 44-year-old Stuart Hall presents *That Stuart Hall Show* on Friday afternoons on BBC One television ▪ 32-year-old Fred West and his wife, 20-year-old Rosemary, murder 21-year-old Lucy Partington and bury her body beneath their house at 25 Cromwell Street in Gloucester ▪ "We've got a thing that's called radar love. We've got a wave in the air..." *Radar Love* by Dutch rock group Golden Earring is number seven in the pop chart ▪ Men smoke cigarettes ▪ A pack of twenty king-size *John Player Special* costs 30p ▪ Housewives go shopping on Saturday afternoons ▪ There's 2p off *Vim* at *Fine Fare* ▪ Instant puddings sell well at *VG Food Stores* ▪ Banana flavour *Angel Delight* tastes great ▪ 'Stork SB margarine helps a good mum become a super mum' - 45-year-old Bruce Forsyth promotes margarine, on TV ▪ The energy crisis continues and many businesses and households are affected by power cuts ▪ Intense pressure is building on prime-minister Edward Heath and his Conservative government ▪ With a new year about to begin, 57-year-old Opposition Leader Harold Wilson says, "Britain faces its most forbidding year since the war. Economically, industrially and socially the outlook is grim, especially so because we have a demoralised Government at the helm." ▪ "I 'ate you, Butler!" - 47-year-old Stephen Lewis is Blakey and 57-year-old Reg Varney is Stan in *Holiday on the Buses* - the third feature length cinema film spin-off from the popular TV show ▪ 38-year-old David Vine introduces the first *Superstars* TV program - Bobby Moore (footballer), Joe Bugner (boxer), Jackie Stewart (racing driver), Roger Taylor (tennis player), David Hemery (runner), Tony Jacklin (golfer) and Barry John (rugby player) all take part. 29-year-old David Hemery is the eventual winner ▪ 24-year-old Derek Hobson introduces the *New Faces All Winners' Show* - the grand final for the popular talent program. 23-year-old vocalist Tom Waite is the eventual winner. Showaddywaddy (an eight-piece pop group from Leicester, fronted by 21-year-old Dave Bartram) are runners-up.

New Year 1974

Who rules Britain? Heath or the miners?

Monarch:	Queen Elizabeth II (aged 47)
Prime-minister:	Edward Heath (aged 57)
Chancellor:	Anthony Barber (aged 53)
Home Secretary:	Robert Carr (aged 57)
Foreign Secretary:	Alec Douglas-Home (aged 70)
Football Manager:	Alf Ramsey (aged 54)
Radio 1 Breakfast DJ:	Noel Edmonds (aged 25)
New car reg. suffix:	'M'

▪ Cold dark nights, miners on an overtime ban, power cuts, twenty per cent inflation and a three-day working week ▪ The country is in crisis ▪ Prime-minister Edward Heath appoints 53-year-old Lord Carrington as head of a new government department responsible for developing and expanding energy supplies ▪ 'Switch Off Something - NOW!" - householders are encouraged to save energy in order to keep vital industries going ▪ *You Won't Find Another Fool Like Me* ("… babe") by The New Seekers is new at number one in the pop chart ▪ "Baby! Although I chose this lonely life, it seems it's strangling me now" - *The Show Must Go On* by 25-year-old Leo Sayer is number two ▪ *Dance With The Devil* by Cozy Powell is number three ▪ "Oh, what happened to you? Whatever happened to me? What became of the people, we used to be? " - 38-year-old James Bolam (Terry), 36-year-old Rodney Bewes (Bob) and 33-year-old Brigit Forsyth (Thelma) star in a new series of *Whatever Happened To The Likely Lads* ▪ Tanktops are in fashion ▪ 35-year-old Barbara Edwards presents the weather forecast on BBC One ▪ It's generally cold, wet and windy with some sleet on high ground ▪ The energy crisis continues ▪ In between power cuts, housewives cook food (on low power) in the kitchen and distribute it to their waiting families through a 'serving-hatch' in the wall ▪ *Findus* Crispy Pancakes are delicious ▪ On behalf of the government, Lord Carrington urges people to go to bed early and switch off lights and heating ▪ Television channels shut down their programs earlier than usual ▪ 32-year-old Polly James, 32-year-old Nerys Hughes and a pregnant pet

hamster star in the first of a new series of *The Liver Birds* on BBC One ▪ 24-year-old Paula Wilcox, 23-year-old Sally Thomsett and 29-year-old Richard O'Sullivan star in a new series of *Man About the House* on ITV ▪ "If she'll put the hurt on me, forever..." *Forever* by 27-year-old Roy Wood climbs to number eight in the pop chart ▪ *Rockin' Roll Baby* by The Stylistics peaks at number six ▪ 29-year-old Kevin Hector bags a hat-trick, and 25-year-old Jeff Bourne scores twice, as Dave Mackay's Derby County football team thrashes Jimmy Adamson's Burnley 5-1 at the Baseball Ground ▪ 43-year-old Chelsea manager Dave Sexton falls-out with star players Alan Hudson and Peter 'Ossie' Osgood, and puts both men on the transfer list ▪ Eamonn Andrews surprises 35-year-old footballer Derek Dougan on *This is Your Life* ▪ 27-year-old 'super' Georgie Best plays his final match for Manchester Utd - a 3-0 defeat against Queens Park Rangers ▪ "That's neat, that's neat, that's neat, that's neat. I really love your..." *Tiger Feet* by Mud climbs to number one in the pop chart - and stays there for four weeks ▪ "So recognise your age it's a teenage rampage. Turn another page on the..." *Teenage Rampage* ("... now, now, now, now, now, now, now, now") by Sweet is number two ▪ The miners escalate their overtime ban into an all-out strike and production of coal ceases ▪ Ambulance workers and railway men also come out on strike ▪ The Triumph motor-cycle factory at Meriden near Coventry closes down with the loss of 1750 jobs ▪ Prime-minister Edward Heath holds crisis talks with 51-year-old Len Murray of the TUC. No agreement is reached and the country is plunged into yet more chaos ▪ Two large diesel generators are installed at Westminster, to ensure the government can continue working through the power cuts ▪ "I'm the red ball express of lovin'. Diesel powered straight to you" - *Keep On Truckin'* by Eddie Kendricks is number eighteen in the pop chart ▪ *Pool Hall Richard* by The Faces (with 29-year-old Rod Stewart and 26-year-old Ronnie Wood) is number eight ▪ For many people, a night at the cinema is a rare treat ▪ 43-year-old Clint Eastwood returns to the big screen as Dirty Harry in the movie *Magnum Force* ▪ 'The Greatest Adventure of Escape' - 43-year-old Steve McQueen and 36-year-old Dustin Hoffman star in *Papillon* ▪ A strike by British Leyland workers at Cowley brings production of the Austin *Maxi* motorcar to a halt

▪ More and more foreign cars are being sold in the UK ▪ The latest Renault *5TL* costs £1,086 and has a top speed of 87 mph ▪ A smart, new Volkswagen *Passat L 1300* costs £1,686 and has a top speed of 92 mph ▪ 37-year-old burglar Donald Nielson (aka the Black Panther) breaks into a post office at Harrogate in Yorkshire and murders sub-postmaster Donald Skepper ▪ BRMB radio station launches in Birmingham ▪ 38-year-old sports presenter Tony Butler keeps listeners up to date with the local football news ▪ 23-year-old striker Bob Latchford leaves Birmingham City and joins Everton for a new record transfer fee of £350,000 ▪ Second Division Aston Villa achieve a 2-0 victory over First Division Arsenal in an FA Cup fourth round replay at Villa Park - Alun Evans and Sammy Morgan score the goals ▪ "Bagpuss, dear Bagpuss, old fat furry Catpuss" - a children's TV show called *Bagpuss* is new on BBC One ▪ "Meet the gang 'cause the boys are here, the boys to entertain you" - *It Ain't Half Hot Mum* (a sit-com set in the Burmese jungle during World War II) is also new. 43-year-old Windsor Davies (as Sergeant Major), 40-year-old Don Estelle (as Lofty) and 38-year-old Melvyn Hayes (as Gloria) are the stars ▪ 60-year-old Sid 'Ha-ak-ak' James, 45-year-old Diana Coupland and 23-year-old Sally Geeson star in the fourth series of popular ITV sit-com *Bless This House* ▪ 51-year-old Denholm Elliot and 24-year-old Susan Penhaligon star in *The Last Chapter*, a disturbing new thirty-minute drama ▪ "So, come alive! Come alive! Down in..." *Devil Gate Drive* by 23-year-old Suzi Quatro climbs to number one in the pop chart ▪ "Underground, overground, wombling free. The Wombles of Wimbledon Common are we" - *The Wombling Song* by The Wombles is number four ▪ The energy crisis continues ▪ 47-year-old Patrick Jenkin (Minister for Energy in Edward Heath's Conservative government) considers shortening the opening hours for cinemas in an effort to conserve electricity ▪ '... all it takes is a little Confidence' - 48-year-old Paul Newman and 37-year-old Robert Redford star in Hollywood movie *The Sting* ▪ A shocking new movie called *The Exorcist* (starring 14-year-old Linda Blair as possessed schoolgirl Regan MacNeil) is banned in many cinemas, after public protests ▪ 45-year-old Alastair Burnet reads the news for ITN ▪ Industrial action continues and the three-day working week remains in place ▪ Nine British soldiers and three civilians lose their lives when an IRA bomb explodes on

a coach travelling on the M62 in Yorkshire ▪ 17-year-old cemetery keeper Stephen Downing is sentenced to life imprisonment for the brutal rape and murder of Wendy Sewell at Bakewell in Derbyshire ▪ Police detective Jack Slipper of the Yard meets 44-year-old fugitive Ronnie Biggs in Copacabana but is unable to extradite him back to the UK ▪ "Oh no, not me. I never lost control. You're face to face with…" *The Man Who Sold The World* by 25-year-old Lulu reaches number three in the pop chart ▪ "There was a man, a lonely man, who lost his love through his indifference" - *Solitaire* by 46-year-old Andy Williams peaks at number four ▪ 22-year-old footballer Joe Jordan scores twice as Don Revie's hard-tackling Leeds Utd defeat Arsenal 3-1 to stay seven points clear at the top of Division One ▪ Kevin Keegan and Alec Lindsay score the goals as Bill Shankly's Liverpool beat Joe Mercer's Coventry City 2-1 at Anfield to stay second ▪ 22-year-old Alan Hudson leaves Chelsea and signs for Stoke City for £240,000 ▪ Peter 'Ossie' Osgood remains on the transfer list at Stamford Bridge ▪ 26-year-old Ray Graydon scores the winning goal for Vic Crowe's Aston Villa in a 0-1 victory over Cardiff City in Division Two ▪ 'Today Is Saturday Watch and Smile' - 27-year-old Chris Tarrant presents a new program called *Tiswas* on ATV - and Saturday morning telly for children in the Midlands is never quite the same again ▪ "Goodnight John Boy / Goodnight Mary Ellen" - *The Waltons* begins on BBC Two on Monday evenings ▪ The third series of TV drama *The Brothers* grips the nation on Sunday evenings ▪ On-going industrial action by workers at British Leyland's Cowley factory slows production of *Maxi* and *Marina* motorcars ▪ The miners' strike continues ▪ The three-day working week prevails ▪ Power cuts are common and households are plunged into darkness with TV sets going off suddenly ▪ Families light candles and sit in the eerie gloom - wondering what was about to happen in *Play for Today* ▪ 'Who rules Britain? Heath or the miners?' ▪ A general election is called and people go to the polls on the twenty-eighth of February ▪ When all counts are completed, the Conservatives are four seats behind Labour. (Labour: 301 seats, Conservatives: 297 seats, Liberals: 14 seats). Sitting Conservative prime-minister Edward Heath fails to form a coalition with Jeremy Thorpe's Liberals ▪ Labour's leader, Harold Wilson, becomes prime-minister in a hung parliament ▪ 30-year-old Conservative candidate John Major

loses in St. Pancras North ▪ 43-year-old Douglas Hurd is the new Conservative MP for Mid Oxfordshire ▪ 41-year-old Nigel Lawson is the new Conservative MP for Blaby ▪ 48-year-old John Stonehouse is the new Labour MP for Walsall North ▪ 'Beyond 1984, Beyond 2001, Beyond Love, Beyond Death' - 43-year-old Sean Connery and 28-year-old Charlotte Rampling star in *Zardoz* - a science-fiction film from John Boorman ▪ "Living just enough, just enough for the city" - *Living For The City* by 23-year-old Stevie Wonder is number fifteen in the pop chart ▪ *All Of My Life* ("… there's a song to sing, a chorus for two") by 29-year-old Diana Ross is number nine ▪ "Sha-la-la-la-la-la-la-la, sho-be-do-ay. Remember all the little things we used to say" - *Remember (Sha-La-La)* by The Bay City Rollers (with, lead singer, 18-year-old Les McKeown) is number six ▪ Peter and Janet Williams from Stoke-on-Trent are proud parents of a newborn son, Robbie ▪ 'Where did it all go wrong?' - 27-year-old wayward footballer Georgie Best spends an evening drinking Champagne with Marjorie Wallace (aka Miss World) at his own nightclub, *Slack Alice*, in Manchester ▪ 25-year-old footballer Phil Boyer transfers from Third Division AFC Bournemouth to First Division Norwich City for £150,000 ▪ 26-year-old Bruce Rioch transfers from Second Division Aston Villa to First Division Derby County for £200,000 ▪ "The marching band came down along Main Street, the soldier blues fell in behind. I looked across and there I saw Billy, waiting to go and join the line" - *Billy Don't Be A Hero* by Paper Lace enters the pop chart at number thirty-eight ▪ *Love's Theme* by The Love Unlimited Orchestra moves down to number twelve after peaking at number ten ▪ Prime-minister Harold Wilson holds talks with 56-year-old NUM leader Joe Gormley, hoping to find a solution to the on-going miners' strike ▪ Dreaming of more prosperous times, working men flick through the pages of car magazines ▪ The Ford *Capri Mk II* (with a contemporary 'hatchback' boot design) is launched ▪ The *1300 L* model costs £1,731 and has a top speed of 87 mph ▪ The *3000 Ghia* costs £3,109 and has a top speed of 120 mph ▪ Inflation remains high under the new Labour government ▪ A loaf of bread is 13p ▪ A 12oz block of chedar cheese is 15p ▪ 'Bring Out the Branston!' - a 16oz jar of *Branston* pickle is 14p.

Spring 1974

Dirty Leeds, the champions!

Monarch:	Queen Elizabeth II (aged 48)
Prime-minister:	Harold Wilson (aged 58)
Chancellor:	Denis Healey (aged 56)
Home Secretary:	Roy Jenkins (aged 53)
Foreign Secretary:	James Callaghan (aged 62)
Football Manager:	Joe Mercer (aged 59)
Radio 1 Breakfast DJ:	Noel Edmonds (aged 25)
New car reg. suffix:	'M'

▪ Harold Wilson's Labour government and Joe Gormley of the NUM continue negotiations to find a solution to the miners' strike ▪ "Kids in water, they love it" - 43-year-old Rolf Harris presents a short public safety program on TV to promote 'Teaching children to swim' ▪ The *Double Top Ten Show* on Radio One is presented by 47-year-old Jimmy Savile OBE ▪ "Ma! Ma! He's makin' eyes at me. Ma, he's awfully nice to me" - 10-year-old Lena Zavaroni wins ITV's *Opportunity Knocks* for five weeks running. Zavaroni's song, *Ma He's Making Eyes At Me*, reaches number ten in the pop chart ▪ *Jet* ("… I can almost remember their funny faces") by 31-year-old Paul McCartney and Wings is number seven ▪ "Ah-oh! It's just my…" *Jealous Mind* by 31-year-old Alvin Stardust is number one ▪ 41-year-old Jack Smethurst and 34-year-old Rudolph Walker star as 'Chalky' and 'Honky' in the fifth series of *Love Thy Neighbour* on ITV ▪ "Hey! The sheriff's a nig… (bell chimes) / What did he say? / He said the sheriff's near" - 34-year-old Cleavon Little, 40-year-old Gene Wilder, 54-year-old Slim Pickens and 47-year-old Harvey Korman star at cinemas in Mel Brooks' shocking new comedy 'Western', *Blazing Saddles* ▪ 'The race against death!' - 23-year-old Scott Anthony, 39-year-old Michael Williams and 39-year-old Judi Dench star in *Dead Cert* - a film based on a novel by 53-year-old Dick Francis ▪ "Sometimes, all I need is…" *The Air That I Breathe* ("… and to love you") by The Hollies is number three in the pop chart ▪ *School Love* by 23-year-old Barry Blue is number eleven ▪ There's a flu bug going around ▪ Poorly children stay home from school, sipping *Lucozade*, drawing pictures with *Crayola* crayons and watching

television ▪ 31-year-old Geoffrey Hayes is the new presenter of *Rainbow* on ITV. Bungle, Zippy and George are Geoffrey's housemates ▪ 44-year-old Leonard Parkin reads the lunchtime news for ITN ▪ A *Turkish Airlines* flight from Istanbul to London crashes near Paris killing all 346 people on board - it's the world's worst aviation disaster ▪ The airlines *BOAC* and *BEA* merge to form *British Airways* ▪ French president Georges Pompidou dies aged 62 in Paris. Prime-minister Harold Wilson and Leader of the Opposition Edward Heath attend the funeral along with dozens of other political leaders including Willy Brandt of West Germany and Richard Nixon of the USA ▪ "The table is set, but something is missing" - *It's You* by 31-year-old comedian Freddie Starr climbs to number nine in the pop chart ▪ After surviving alone for twenty-nine years on the remote Lubang Island in the Philippines, an old Japanese soldier is rescued - and is surprised to find out that World War II has ended ▪ Back in Britain - striking miners return to work after an improved pay offer from Harold Wilson's Labour government ▪ The three-day working week comes to an end ▪ Full production resumes at British Leyland's Cowley plant - but Austin *Maxi* and Morris *Marina* motorcars remain in short supply ▪ The Reliant Motor Company ceases production of its bright orange *Bond Bug* 'three-wheeler'. Sales of the tiny, wedge shaped car have been disappointing since its launch four years ago ▪ 56-year-old Chancellor of the Exchequer Denis Healey delivers his first Budget ▪ The basic rate of income tax rises from thirty percent to thirty-three percent ▪ A pint of beer increases by one penny. Bitter now costs around 15p a pint. Lager is 19p ▪ Spirits are increased by twenty pence ▪ A new 'fly-on-the-wall' TV documentary called *The Family* begins on BBC One. The everyday lives of 39-year-old Margaret Wilkins and her husband, 40-year-old Terry, are recorded by a film crew at the family home in Reading ▪ 32-year-old Fred West and his wife, 20-year-old Rosemary, murder 21-year-old Therese Siegenthaler and bury her body beneath their house at 25 Cromwell Street in Gloucester ▪ "Goodbye Joe, you gotta go, me oh, my oh. He gotta go pole the pirogue, down the bayou" - *Jambalaya (On The Bayou)* by The Carpenters reaches number twelve on the hit parade ▪ "Emmalene..." *Emma* ("... Emmalene, I'm gonna write your name high on that silver screen") by Hot Chocolate is number three ▪ 27-year-old wayward footballer Georgie Best is charged

(and later acquitted) with stealing a fur coat from Marjorie Wallace (aka Miss World) ▪ 46-year-old Bill McGarry's Wolverhampton Wanderers defeat 41-year-old Ron Saunders' Manchester City 2-1 in the League Cup final at Wembley - with goals from 23-year-old Kenny Hibbitt and 23-year-old John Richards ▪ West Ham Utd defeat Chelsea 3-0 in a Division One tie at Upton Park - with 27-year-old Billy Bonds bagging a hat-trick ▪ "Billy don't be a hero, don't be a fool with your life. Billy don't be a hero, come back and make me your wife. And as Billy started to go, she said, keep your pretty head low, oh, oh…" *Billy Don't Be A Hero* ("… come back to me") by Paper Lace (with, lead singer/drummer, 25-year-old Phil Wright) climbs to number one in the pop chart ▪ "Fear me, you loathsome, lazy creatures. I descend upon your Earth from the skies" - *Seven Seas Of Rhye* by Queen (with, lead singer, 27-year-old Freddie Mercury) peaks at number ten ▪ "And it seemed to me, you lived your life like a..." *Candle In The Wind* ("... Never knowing who to cling to when the rain set in") by 27-year-old Elton John reaches number eleven ▪ The football season is drawing to a close ▪ Leeds Utd's captain, 31-year-old Billy Bremner, is on the score-sheet as the 'All Whites' defeat Dave Mackay's Derby County 2-0 at Elland Road to remain top of Division One ▪ Families enjoy a night in, watching TV ▪ ATV's programs on a Saturday evening include: *Reg Varney* - a musical variety show featuring 57-year-old Reg Varney, with Henry McGee and Pat Coombs; *Sale of the Century* - hosted by 50-year-old Nicholas Parsons; *Candid Camera* - with Peter Dulay and Arthur Atkins; and *The Saturday Night Film* ▪ Oxford win the Boat Race for the first time in seven years ▪ A naked 25-year-old Michael O'Brien streaks across Twickenham rugby pitch before being caught by a policeman - who covers the young man's embarrassment with his helmet ▪ *Rebel Rebel* ("… you've torn your dress. Rebel, rebel, your face is a mess") by 27-year-old David Bowie is number five in the pop chart ▪ "Let it rip! And then the cat crept in, and crept out again" - *The Cat Crept In* by Mud (with, lead singer, 28-year-old Les Gray) climbs to number two ▪ 25-year-old footballer Trevor Brooking of West Ham Utd makes his debut for England in a 0-0 draw against Portugal in Lisbon. The match turns out to be the last game in which 54-year-old Sir Alf Ramsey takes charge of the national team ▪ 'His brain came from a genius. His body came from a killer. His soul came

from hell!' - 61-year-old Peter Cushing stars at cinemas in *Frankenstein and the Monster from Hell* ▪ 'Evil Begets Evil on the Sabbath of the Undead!' - 51-year-old Christopher Lee stars in *The Satanic Rites of Dracula* ▪ 32-year-old footballer Bobby Moore leaves First Division West Ham (after eighteen years) and transfers to Second Division Fulham for £25,000 ▪ "I will love you all my life, just one thing I pray. When you dream of me each night..." *Remember Me This Way* by 29-year-old Gary Glitter is number three in the pop chart ▪ *Doctor's Orders* by Sunny is number seven ▪ 18-year-old striker Tony Woodcock makes his debut for Nottingham Forest in a 3-1 defeat against Aston Villa (Hamilton, Campbell and Graydon score the goals for Villa. Duncan McKenzie scores for Forest) ▪ 31-year-old Des Lynam presents *Sports Report* on Radio Two on Saturday afternoons ▪ Fans protest outside Stamford Bridge football ground when Chelsea manager Dave Sexton sells 27-year-old Peter 'Ossie' Osgood to Southampton for £275,000 ▪ "We're gonna win the league! We're gonna win the league! And now you're gonna believe us!" - Don Revie's hard-tackling Leeds Utd finish the season five points ahead of Bill Shankly's Liverpool to become champions of Division One ▪ 27-year-old Peter Lorimer scores twice as Leeds beat Sheffield Utd 0-2 and then two more victories over Ipswich Town (3-2) and Queens Park Rangers (1-0) ensure that Leeds finish top-of-the-table ▪ Liverpool are runners-up ▪ Dave Mackay's Derby County are third ▪ Leeds' players: David Harvey, Trevor Cherry, Paul Reaney, Paul Madeley, Gordon McQueen, Norman 'Bites Yer Legs' Hunter, Johnny Giles, Billy Bremner, Terry Yorath, Peter Lorimer, Mick Jones, Allan 'sniffer' Clarke and 22-year-old Joe Jordan have all been outstanding ▪ 34-year-old Denis Law scores in a 0-1 win for Manchester City at Old Trafford and Tommy 'The Doc' Docherty's Manchester Utd are relegated to Division Two ▪ "We had joy we had fun, we had seasons in the sun, but the hills that we climbed, were just seasons out of time" - *Seasons In The Sun* by 30-year-old Terry Jacks spends four weeks at number one in the pop chart ▪ *I'm Gonna Knock On Your Door* ("... ring on your bell, tap on your window too. If you don't come out tonight, when the moon is bright, I'm gonna knock and ring and tap until you do") by 11-year-old Little Jimmy Osmond is number eleven ▪ 54-year-old Sir Alf Ramsey is sacked as England manager and Joe Mercer is appointed to the

role on a temporary basis ▪ 25-year-old Mick Channon and 25-year-old Frank Worthington score the goals as England (with a line-up of: Shilton, Hughes, Lindsay, Todd, Watson, Bell, Keegan, Channon, Worthington, Weller and Brooking) draw 2-2 in a friendly against Argentina at Wembley. (19-year-old Mario Kempes scores both goals for Argentina) ▪ The Wonderloaf Gang charges down the grass bank on the playing field at St. Joseph's Junior School in Rugeley - in pursuit of the Freedom Fighter Gang. (Headmaster Mr. 'Percy' Edwards is not amused) ▪ "Angel face, angel face, you've got the cutest…" *Angel Face* by The Glitter Band is number four in the pop chart ▪ "So I hold back the tears until the movie's through, then…" *I Get A Little Sentimental Over You* by The New Seekers featuring 25-year-old Lyn Paul is number five ▪ Families gather together to watch television in the evenings, pleased that the power cuts have now ended ▪ 39-year-old Wendy Craig stars in *And Mother Makes Five* - a new sit-com from ITV which picks up the storyline from last year's *And Mother Makes Three* ▪ 49-year-old Kenneth Kendall reads the news on BBC One ▪ 58-year-old Labour prime-minister Harold Wilson and his Chancellor of the Exchequer, Denis Healey, discuss the problems of rising inflation ▪ A quarter pound pack of *Typhoo* loose leaf tea is 7p ▪ A pack of *Tate & Lyle* sugar is 9p ▪ A 10 oz tin of *Ambrosia* creamed rice is 7p ▪ A 15 oz tin of *Ambrosia* custard is 7 ½ p ▪ A tin of *Crosse & Blackwell* baked beans is 5p ▪ 17-year-old Timothy Davey is released from a jail in Turkey after serving two years for conspiring to sell cannabis ▪ Michael Barratt, Frank Bough, Bob Wellings and 27-year-old Sue Lawley present *Nationwide* ▪ A kidnap attempt is made on Princess Anne and Captain Mark Phillips - it fails ▪ 21-year-old Nina Carter (34C) appears topless on page three of *The Sun* newspaper ▪ "Hey, did you happen to see…" *The Most Beautiful Girl* ("… in the world") by 40-year-old Charlie Rich climbs to number two in the pop chart ▪ *Everyday* ("… when I'm away, I'm thinking of you") by Slade (with, lead singer, 27-year-old Noddy Holder) is number three ▪ *You're Sixteen* ('… you're beautiful, and you're mine") by 32-year-old Ringo Starr reaches number four ▪ *Red Rum* (ridden by Brian Fletcher) wins the Grand National at Aintree for the second year in succession ▪ The Eurovision Song Contest (with 47-year-old Katie Boyle as compare) takes place in Brighton on the sixth of April. Britain's entry, *Long Live Love* by

25-year-old Olivia Newton-John, finishes in fourth position. Sweden's entry, *Waterloo* by Abba, is the winning song ▪ The Lamborghini *Countach* sports car is launched, with a top speed of 192 mph and capable of 0-60 mph in just 5.4 seconds. On-the-road price for this wonderful new 'supercar' is £19,952 ▪ Citroen launches its range of *CX* executive cars, with hydro-pneumatic suspension and a top speed of 108 mph. ▪ "Waterloo, I was defeated, you won the war. Waterloo, promise to love you forever more" *Waterloo* by Abba (with 27-year-old Benny, 29-year-old Bjorn, 28-year-old Anni-Frid and 24-year-old Agnetha) moves up to number one in the pop chart ▪ *Remember You're A Womble* ("... Remember you're a Womble. Remember, 'member, 'member what a Womble, Womble, Womble you are") by The Wombles is number three ▪ *Homely Girl* by The Chi-Lites is number five ▪ 23-year-old footballer Kevin Keegan scores twice as Bill Shankly's Liverpool beat Joe Harvey's Newcastle Utd 3-0 in the FA Cup final. (26-year-old Steve Heighway is also on the score-sheet). 43-year-old Gordon Kew from South Shields is referee. A ticket for the standing enclosure at the Empire Stadium in Wembley costs £1.00 ▪ Relegated Manchester Utd sign 24-year-old centre-forward Stuart Pearson from Hull City for £200,000 ▪ Radio One DJs take turns to present *Top of the Pops* on Thursday evenings on BBC One television ▪ 18-year-old dancer Sue Menhenick replaces 24-year-old Louise Clarke in Pan's People ▪ "Sugar baby love..." *Sugar Baby Love* ("... Bop, showaddy. Bop showaddy waddy") by The Rubettes shoots up the pop chart from number twenty-seven to number two and moves up to top spot the following week ▪ "Well, we sang shang-a-lang as we ran with the gang, doin' doo wop be dooby do aye. We were all in the news with our blue suede shoes, and our dancin' the night away" - *Shang-a-Lang* by The Bay City Rollers reaches number two ▪ Glossy, colour posters of Eric, Les, Woody, Alan and Derek adorn the bedroom walls of teenage girls ▪ The older boyfriend is waiting outside in his 'F' reg Ford *Cortina MKII*, with chromium wing-mirrors and sheep-skin seat covers ▪ *The Wombles* are on TV ▪ Glossy, colour posters of Orinoco, Tobermory, Bungo, Wellington and Great Uncle Bulgaria adorn the bedroom walls of young school children ▪ Public Notices remind people to, 'Keep Britain Tidy'.

Summer 1974

Oh, this year we're off to sunny Spain

Monarch:	Queen Elizabeth II (aged 48)
Prime-minister:	Harold Wilson (aged 58)
Chancellor:	Denis Healey (aged 57)
Home Secretary:	Roy Jenkins (aged 53)
Foreign Secretary:	James Callaghan (aged 62)
Football Manager:	Don Revie (aged 47)
Radio 1 Breakfast DJ:	Noel Edmonds (aged 25)
New car reg. suffix:	'N'

▪ It's a dull and drizzly summer ▪ "It's the way I tell 'em" - 47-year-old comedian Frank Carson entertains holidaymakers at Scarborough ▪ 31-year-old Freddie Starr appears on stage at the ABC Theatre in Great Yarmouth ▪ 47-year-old Radio One DJ Jimmy Savile OBE takes his turn to present *Top of the Pops* on BBC One ▪ "Who's the girl dancing in the red dress? I want her for my lover" - *Red Dress* by 31-year-old Alvin Stardust is number seven in the chart ▪ "It's so sad to leave you crying in the rain" - *Rock 'n' Roll Winter* by Wizzard is number six ▪ School children break-up for six weeks of summer holiday ▪ Middle-class children attend the local cinema for a matinee screening of *Swallows and Amazons*, starring 43-year-old Virginia McKenna, 44-year-old Ronald Fraser and with 14-year-old Sophie Neville as Titty ▪ Working-class children stay at home, watching *Wacky Races*, *Whirlybirds*, *Adventures of Tintin* and *Daktari* on television ▪ "Heartbeat, increasing heartbeat" - *This Town Ain't Big Enough For The Both Of Us* by Sparks (with 28-year-old Ron Mael and 25-year-old Russell Mael) climbs to number two in the pop chart ▪ "Wo-oh, wo-oh. Jet plane flying high above me..." *Don't Stay Away Too Long* by Peters and Lee (with 42-year-old Lennie Peters and 24-year-old Dianne Lee) peaks at number three ▪ BBC One's fly-on-the-wall documentary *The Family* (detailing the life of the Wilkins family from Reading) grips television viewers on Wednesday evenings ▪ 44-year-old Stuart Hall presents *It's A Knockout* on Friday evenings. A team representing Skegness beats a team from Mablethorpe and Sutton-on-Sea, after competing in events: Canoe Race, Water Netball, Pyjama Race, Island Crossing, Boat Sinking, Netting

the Ball and Raft Pyramid ▪ 24-year-old boxer Joe Bugner defeats Piermario Baruzzi by a Technical Knock-out in round ten in Copenhagen to retain his European heavy-weight title ▪ "Baby…" *I'd Love You To Want Me* ("… the way that I want you") by Lobo is number five in the pop chart ▪ *Wall Street Shuffle* by 10cc is number ten ▪ 43-year-old Peter Woods reads the news on BBC One ▪ Hospital services are disrupted as disgruntled NHS staff stage a number of walk-outs, sit-ins and go-slows ▪ White collar workers go on strike at Triumph's car factory in Coventry ▪ Production workers walk-out at Rover's factory in Solihull ▪ "Come on follow the Geordie boys, they'll fill your heart with joy. They're marching for their freedom now" - *Jarrow Song* by 32-year-old Alan Price climbs from number eighteen to number eight in the pop chart ▪ *Judy Teen* ("... the queen of the scene") by Cockney Rebel is number seven ▪ Adverts for *Coca-Cola* proclaim, 'It's the real thing. Coke' ▪ Discarded ring-pulls from drinks cans litter public parks and communal spaces ▪ The campaign to 'Keep Britain Tidy' intensifies ▪ *Banana Rock* by The Wombles climbs to number nine in the pop chart ▪ Kids chase *Alpine* lorries down the road as the pop-man delivers bottles of limeade and lemonade to local houses ▪ Black-faced coal-men hump heavy bags from Bedford 'flat-bed' trucks ▪ 45-year-old Leonard Parkin reads the evening news for ITN ▪ Violence breaks out at Red Lion Square in central London when members of the National Front are confronted by demonstrators from the Liberation group ▪ Mounted police charge into the crowd ▪ 20-year-old student Kevin Gately dies after receiving a blow to the head ▪ "I heard my mama cry, I heard her pray…" *The Night Chicago Died* by Paper Lace is number three in the pop chart ▪ 'I'm in with…" *The 'In' Crowd* ("… I go where the 'in' crowd goes") by 28-year-old Bryan Ferry is number thirteen ▪ 41-year-old Reginald Bosanquet reads the *News at Ten* for ITN ▪ An explosion at a chemical plant in Flixborough on Humberside kills twenty-eight people ▪ Sugar is in short supply due to low stocks of sugar cane at refineries - long queues form outside shops ▪ The sun shines briefly in mid June ▪ 7-year-old Helen Hinks makes her First Holy Communion at St. Joseph & St. Etheldreda's church in Rugeley ▪ 42-year-old Elizabeth Taylor and 48-year-old Richard Burton divorce after ten years of marriage ▪ "Oh yes, they call him the streak. Bug-idee. Bug-idee" - *The Streak* by Ray Stevens is the new num-

ber one pop song ▪ *There's A Ghost In My House* ("… the ghost of your memories. The ghost of the love you took from me") by R Dean Taylor is number three ▪ Kids take to the streets, attempting to pull wheelies on Raleigh *Choppers* ▪ Parents spend the evening in, watching TV ▪ 46-year-old Terry Scott and 48-year-old June Whitfield star in *Happy Ever After* on BBC One ▪ 43-year-old Les Dawson from Manchester appears in ITV's hit comedy *Sez Les* - some of the show's jokes and sketches are written by 39-year-old David Nobbs ▪ "I know, you know, I'll never, never let you go" - *Always Yours* by Gary Glitter moves up to number one on the hit parade ▪ *Hey Rock And Roll* ("… Bring it to town, let's stroll!") by Showaddywaddy peaks at number two ▪ *Summer Breeze* ("… makes me feel fine, blowin' through the jasmin in my mind") by The Isley Brothers is number sixteen ▪ Cricketers, Geoffrey Boycott and Dennis Amiss stride out together to open the batting for England against India at Old Trafford. Boycott makes 10 runs. Amiss hits 56. 30-year-old batsman Keith Fletcher scores 123 not out. 25-year-old fast bowler Bob Willis takes 4 for 64 and England win the match ▪ 21-year-old Jimmy Conners uses a new-fangled metal framed tennis racket instead of the traditional wooden instrument as he defeats 39-year-old Ken Rosewall (6-1, 6-1, 6-4) in the men's singles final at Wimbledon ▪ *Kissin' In The Back Row Of The Movies* ("… on a Saturday night with you. Holdin' hands together, you and I, holdin' hands together") by The Drifters reaches number two in the pop chart ▪ *The Bangin' Man* by Slade peaks at number three ▪ 24-year-old racing driver Jody Scheckter wins the British Grand Prix at Brands Hatch, driving an 'elf' sponsored Tyrell Formula One car ▪ 25-year-old Tom Pryce from Ruthin (in a Shadow) is eighth, 28-year-old John Watson from Belfast (in a Brabham) is eleventh and 45-year-old Graham Hill from London (in a Lola) is thirteenth ▪ Chancellor of the Exchequer Denis Healey reduces the standard rate of VAT from 10% to 8%, but introduces a new higher rate of 12.5% on petrol ▪ An IRA bomb explodes at the Houses of Parliament - injuring eleven people ▪ 'N' reg cars go on sale ▪ High-flying businessmen in dark pinstriped suits (with wide lapels and flared trousers) order their brand new car from the showroom ▪ The new Ford *Capri MKII 3000 GT* costs £2,243, has a top speed of 120 mph and accelerates from 0-60 mph in 8.4 seconds ▪ The latest BMW *2002 Turbo* costs £4,221, has

a top speed of 130 mph and can reach 60 mph in 7.5 seconds ▪ A Jensen *Interceptor III* costs £8,334, has a top speed of 135 mph and can reach 60 mph in 7.5 seconds ▪ Families watch television together in the evenings ▪ 32-year-old Geoffrey Hayes makes his final appearance as DC Dave Scatliffe in BBC's long-running police drama *Z Cars* ▪ 16-year-old actress Helen Worth makes her first appearance as Gail Potter in ITV's popular soap-opera *Coronation Street* ▪ "She, may be the face I can't forget, a trace of pleasure or regret, maybe my treasure or the price I have to pay" - *She* by 54-year-old Charles Aznavour is new at number one in the pop chart ▪ "Well, I'm a one man band. Nobody knows nor understands" - *One Man Band* by 26-year-old Leo Sayer is number six ▪ Radio One's weekday schedule of disc jockeys is: Noel Edmonds (7 a.m. to 9 a.m.), Tony Blackburn (9 a.m. to 12 noon), Johnnie Walker (12 noon to 2 p.m.), 'Diddy' David Hamilton (2 p.m. to 5 p.m.) and 47-year-old Alan 'Fluff' Freeman (5 p.m. to 7 p.m.) ▪ 40-year-old actor Tom Baker takes over from 55-year-old Jon Pertwee as *Dr. Who* on TV ▪ 'All for one! One for all!' - 32-year-old Michael York is d'Artagnan playing alongside Oliver Reed, Frank Finlay and Richard Chamberlain in *The Three Musketeers* - now showing at cinemas ▪ 'Dick Turpin Carries On with his Flintlock Cocked!' - 61-year-old Sid 'Ha-ak-ak' James is 'Big Dick' Turpin and 36-year-old Barbara Windsor (36-24-34) is his partner-in-crime in *Carry On Dick* ▪ 32-year-old singer Cass Elliot (aka Mama Cass) dies of heart failure at Flat 12, Number 9 Curzon Place, Mayfair in London ▪ "Woman, take me in your arms…" *Rock Your Baby* by 29-year-old George McCrae spends three weeks at number one in the pop chart ▪ "I was…" *Born With A Smile On My Face* ("… the whole of my life's been a pantomime") by 25-year-old Stephanie de Sykes (with Rain) is number two ▪ *Beach Baby* ("… Beach Baby, give me your hand. Give me something that I can remember") by First Class is number thirteen ▪ A bomb explodes at the Tower of London - killing one person and injuring forty-one ▪ The chief of Scotland Yard's Bomb Squad says, "It was an indiscriminate attack designed to create as much trouble and injury as possible. It is the sort of target the IRA would pick" ▪ Fears are high that more terror atrocities are to follow ▪ 46-year-old Don Revie is appointed as the new football manager of En-

gland ■ 39-year-old Brian Clough takes over at Leeds Utd and tells his new players they can throw their medals in the bin because they've all been won by cheating ■ Bill Shankly retires as Liverpool manager and is replaced by 55-year-old Bob Paisley ■ 41-year-old Ron Saunders is the new manager of Second Division Aston Villa ■ 34-year-old John Lyall is the new manager of First Division West Ham Utd ■ Michael Barratt, Frank Bough, Bob Wellings and 28-year-old Sue Lawley present *Nationwide* on BBC One ■ Court Line (a charter airline company) goes into liquidation and 40,000 British holidaymakers are left stranded abroad ■ "Oh this year we're off to sunny Spain…" *Y Viva Espana* by Sylvia climbs to number four in the pop chart ■ "And you can run in the sun, having fun with the one that you really love. Walk in the sand, hand in hand, with the boy that you met on vacation. And on a warm summer night, it's alright when he says, 'Baby I love you'. Then, boy oh boy, you're enjoying that summer-love sensation" - Tartan-clad teenage girls go wild with joy as *Summer-love Sensation* by The Bay City Rollers reaches number two ■ 27-year-old cricketer David Lloyd scores an unbeaten 214 at Edgbaston and Mike Denness' England team goes on to win the Test series, 3-0, against India ■ 48-year-old Richard Baker reads the news on BBC One ■ Richard Nixon is forced to resign over the Watergate scandal. 60-year-old Gerald Ford becomes the new president of the USA ■ Back in England - The headless body of a woman is found near Swaffham in Norfolk ■ 33-year-old Esther Rantzen presents *That's Life* on TV - aided by reporters Glyn Worsnip, Kieran Prendiville and 61-year-old Cyril Fletcher - who delivers odd little odes at the end of the show ■ "H-ooh-ooh. H-aah-aah. H-aah-aah. H-ooh-ooh. Precious moments..." *When Will I See You Again* by The Three Degrees (26-year-old Fayette Pinkney, 26-year-old Valerie Holiday and 26-year-old Sheila Ferguson) reaches number one in the pop chart ■ *I Shot The Sheriff* ("... but I did not shoot the deputy") by 29-year-old Eric Clapton is number nine ■ 'He doesn't make friends - and all his enemies are dead!' - 44-year-old Edward Woodward stars at cinemas as *Callan* ■ There's a flurry of activity on football's transfer market ■ 23-year-old Ray Kennedy leaves Arsenal and joins Liverpool for £180,000 ■ 25-year-old Brian Kidd transfers from Manchester Utd to Arsenal for £110,000 ■

25-year-old Larry Lloyd leaves Liverpool and joins Coventry City for £240,000 ▪ 30-year-old Franny Lee leaves Manchester City and joins Dave Mackay's Derby County for £100,000 ▪ 28-year-old 'super' Georgie Best is released from his contract at Manchester Utd ▪ People buy the latest 7-inch singles at *W. H. Smith & Son* for 55p ▪ "Oh, Liverpool Lou, lovely…" *Liverpool Lou* by The Scaffold is number seven in the pop chart ▪ "Now..." *Rocket* ("... I'm gonna launch you soon") by Mud is number four ▪ "And the jailer man and sailor Sam were searching everyone, for the…" *Band On The Run* by Paul McCartney and Wings is number three ▪ *I'm Leaving It (All) Up To You* ("... ooh-ooh-ooh") by 16-year-old Donny Osmond and 14-year-old Marie Osmond is number two ▪ The new football season gets underway ▪ 31-year-old Billy Bremner of Leeds Utd and 23-year-old Kevin Keegan of Liverpool fight on the pitch in the Charity Shield at Wembley ▪ Football fans wear flared jeans, platform shoes, denim jackets; and tie their (club coloured) scarves around their wrists ▪ Hooligans run riot at Ashton Gate as Bristol City beat Cardiff City 2-1 in the League Cup ▪ Other instances of football violence occur throughout the country ▪ A tragic low point is reached when 17-year-old Kevin Olsson is stabbed to death at a match between Blackpool and Bolton Wanderers ▪ "Don't love me for fun girl, let me be the one girl. Love me for a reason, and let the reason be love" - *Love Me For A Reason* by The Osmonds is top of the pop chart ▪ *What Becomes Of The Broken Hearted* ("… who had love that's now departed") by 38-year-old Jimmy Ruffin is number four ▪ "Big wheels keep on turning, carry me home to see my kin" - *Sweet Home Alabama* by Lynyrd Skynyrd is number twenty-one ▪ 54-year-old wartime football legend Tommy Lawton is found guilty of obtaining goods by deception ▪ 54-year-old Bill Nicholson resigns as manager of Tottenham Hotspur. Nicholson has been with Spurs for thirty-eight years - serving first as a trainee, then as a player and finally as the manager ▪ 25-year-old Joe Royle scores twice for Billy Bingham's Everton in a 2-1 victory over Stoke City in a First Division match at Goodison Park ▪ 20-year-old Gerry Daly scores a hat-trick for Tommy 'The Doc' Docherty's Manchester Utd in a 4-0 victory over Millwall in a Second Division match at Old Trafford ▪ *Rock The Boat* ("… Don't rock the boat, baby. Rock the boat. Don't tip

the boat over") by The Hues Corporation reaches number six in the pop chart ▪ "I know..." *It's Only Rock And Roll* ("... but I like it, I like it, yes I do") by The Rolling Stones is number ten ▪ *Stop, Look, Listen (To Your Heart)* - a duet from 30-year-old Diana Ross and 35-year-old Marvin Gaye only makes it as high as number twenty-five ▪ A re-issue of *Baby Love* by The Supremes peaks at number twelve ▪ 21-year-old Mary Connors is fired from a cannon at Tewkesbury in a crazy attempt to cross the River Avon. She fails, and has to be rescued from the water by a diver ▪ Adolescent boys peruse the shelves at newsagents ▪ 'Our Barest Beach Girls' - *Mayfair* magazine costs 40p ▪ 'Knave Beauties: More of Them Than Ever Too!' - *Knave* is also 40p ▪ A pack of twenty Player's *No. 6* cigarettes is 25½p ▪ Prices continue to rise and people of Britain are becoming anxious ▪ 56-year-old Shadow Home Secretary Keith Joseph warns that, "Inflation is threatening to destroy our society" ▪ The average price of a house in the UK has now risen above £10,000 ▪ An Austin *Mini 850* motorcar costs £1,027 ▪ Industrial action continues to blight the car industry ▪ Production at the Austin-Morris factory in Longbridge, Birmingham comes to a halt when two-thousand workers walk-out at Leyland's transmission plant in Washwood Heath, Birmingham ▪ 58-year-old Prime-minister Harold Wilson takes a holiday in the Scillies and enjoys some down time, walking along the coastline and smoking his pipe ▪ 58-year-old Leader of the Conservative Opposition Edward Heath (a keen sailor) takes part in the Royal Temple Yacht Club Regatta ▪ 45-year-old Liberal leader Jeremy Thorpe campaigns for new votes, travelling by hovercraft and visiting packed holiday beaches ▪ "You..." *You Make Me Feel Brand New* by The Stylistics is number two in the pop chart ▪ *Mr. Soft* ("... believe everything they tell you and be damned if they'll thank you") by Cockney Rebel (with 23-year-old, lead singer, Steve Harley) is number eight ▪ "Last night I said these words to my girl" - *Please Please Me* by 24-year-old heart-throb David Cassidy is number sixteen ▪ 'The antidote to panel games' - a new series of *I'm Sorry I Haven't A Clue* begins on Radio Four, with panelists Graeme Garden, Barry Cryer, Willie Rushton and Tim Brooke-Taylor and with 53-year-old Humphrey Lyttelton in the chair ▪ Adverts say, '*Tetley* make teabags make tea!'

Autumn 1974

Who loves ya, baby?

Monarch:	Queen Elizabeth II (aged 48)
Prime-minister:	Harold Wilson (aged 58)
Chancellor:	Denis Healey (aged 57)
Home Secretary:	Roy Jenkins (aged 54)
Foreign Secretary:	James Callaghan (aged 62)
Football Manager:	Don Revie (aged 47)
Radio 1 Breakfast DJ:	Noel Edmonds (aged 25)
New car reg. suffix:	'N'

▪ The rain falls hard on humdrum towns ▪ 15-year-old Steven Patrick Morrissey sits in his bedroom in Manchester listening to *Kimono My House*, the new L.P. from Sparks ▪ 11-year-old Nick Robinson from Macclesfield rushes home from school to watch *John Craven's Newsroun*d on BBC One ▪ Labour prime-minister Harold Wilson returns from his holiday in the Scillies and resumes his work at Number 10 Downing Street ▪ Chancellor of the Exchequer Denis Healey doubles the higher rate of VAT ▪ Four star petrol rises sharply in price - it's now a staggering 75p per gallon! ▪ Sugar remains in short supply at shops ▪ *Baby Love* ("... My baby love, I need you, oh how I need you") by 30-year-old Diana Ross and the Supremes is number twelve in the pop chart ▪ "My darling, I..." *Can't Get Enough Of Your Love, Babe* by 30-year-old Barry White is number eight ▪ "She's the..." *Queen Of Clubs* ("... Woo!") by KC and the Sunshine Band is number seven ▪ 'Look Who's Up and at it Again!' - 64-year-old David Niven and 26-year-old Teresa Graves star at cinemas in *Vampira* - a new comedy horror film ▪ 'The comedy that rises to the occasion!' - 33-year-old Elke Sommer, 29-year-old Leigh Lawson and 49-year-old Harry H. Corbett star in *Percy's Progress* ▪ "You know I can't dance. You know I can't dance" - *Long Tall Glasses* by 26-year-old Leo Sayer from Shoreham is number four in the pop chart ▪ *You, You, You* by 32-year-old Alvin Stardust from Muswell Hill is number six ▪ A new ring-road opens in Coventry ▪ Resurfacing work takes place on the A41 in Wolverhampton ▪ Motoring technology moves on apace ▪ The traditional metal and chrome bumpers on the MG *B* and MG *Midget* sports cars are replaced by modern

rubber bumpers. The new *Midget* costs £1,350 and has a top speed of 101 mph. The new *B* costs £1,847 and has a top speed of 104 mph ▪ An unofficial walk-out by engineering inspectors at British Leyland's factory in Solihull leads to four-thousand workers being laid off ▪ 22-year-old aberrant footballer Robin Friday bags a hat-trick as Reading defeat Southport 4-1 in Division Four ▪ Fighting breaks out on the terracing at a Second Division football match between West Bromwich Albion and Manchester Utd ▪ Fighting breaks out on the terracing at a First Division football match between Chelsea and Arsenal ▪ "Everybody was…" *Kung Fu Fighting* ("… those kicks were fast as lightning. In fact it was a little bit frightening, but they fought with expert timing") by Carl Douglas is number one in the pop chart ▪ "She keeps the Moet et Chandon in her pretty cabinet. 'Let them eat cake' she says, just like Marie Antoinette" - *Killer Queen* by Queen climbs to number two ▪ Crowds flock to the cinema to see 27-year-old David Essex and 28-year-old Keith Moon in *Stardust*, a sequel to last year's hit movie *That'll Be The Day* ▪ *Rising Damp* is a brand new sit-com on ITV - with Frances de la Tour, Richard Beckinsale, Don Warrington and starring 47-year-old Leonard Rossiter as Rigsby ▪ The third series of *Man About the House* begins - starring 24-year-old Paula Wilcox, 24-year-old Sally Thomsett and 30-year-old Richard O'Sullivan as flat mates - with the Ropers (48-year-old Yootha Joyce and 42-year-old Brian Murphy) as nosy neighbours ▪ The latest series of *Upstairs Downstairs* (with 40-year-old Jean Marsh as Rose, 70-year-old Angela Baddeley as Mrs. Bridges, 50-year-old Gordon Jackson as Hudson and 20-year-old Lesley-Anne Down as Georgina Worsley) depicts life in an aristocratic London house during World War One ▪ "You fill up my senses, like a night in the forest, like the mountains in springtime, like a walk in the rain" - *Annie's Song* by 30-year-old John Denver spends a week at number one on the hit parade ▪ *Rock Me Gently* ("… Rock me slowly") by 27-year-old Andy Kim from Canada is number two ▪ 49-year-old Richard Baker and 50-year-old Kenneth Kendall present the *9 O'Clock News* on BBC One ▪ 38-year-old burglar Donald Nielson (aka the Black Panther) breaks into a post office at Baxenden in Lancashire and murders Derek Astin ▪ 54-year-old football legend Tommy Lawton carries out two-hundred hours of com-

munity service - after his recent conviction for obtaining goods by deception ▪ 32-year-old Terry Neill is the new manager at Tottenham Hotspur ▪ 22-year-old Nenad 'Pop' Popovic is the new PE teacher at Cardinal Griffin School in Cannock ▪ 18-year-old student Teresa Brasier from Eastbourne goes up to Oxford to read Geography ▪ *Sad Sweet Dreamer* ("… it's just one of those things we put down to experience") by Sweet Sensation spends a week at number one in the pop chart ▪ "And I'm..." *Far Far Away* ("... with my head up in the clouds") by Slade (with, lead singer, 28-year-old Noddy Holder) comes straight in at number three and climbs to number two the following week ▪ Seeking a stronger mandate, 58-year-old prime-minister Harold Wilson calls the second general election of the year ▪ Campaigning gets underway ▪ Conservative leader Edward Heath condemns Labour's achievements in office, pointing out that the rate of inflation has more than doubled from 9 per cent to 20 per cent, and strikes are also up on last year by more than a third ▪ Labour makes a manifesto pledge to give the country a referendum on membership of the European Common Market ▪ People cast their votes in a general election on the tenth of October and Mr. Wilson wins another term as prime-minister - gaining a small majority over Mr. Heath. (Labour: 319 seats, Conservatives: 277 seats, Liberals: 13 seats) ▪ 31-year-old Conservative candidate John Major loses for a second time in St. Pancras North ▪ One-thousand workers go on strike at British Leyland's factory in Castle Bromwich - slowing production of *Jaguar* and *Mini* motorcars ▪ "If you..." *Minuetto Allegretto* ("... you will live to be old") by The Wombles reaches number sixteen in the pop chart ▪ "I love you..." *I Honestly Love You* by 26-year-old Olivia Newton-John peaks at number twenty-two ▪ 39-year-old football manager Brian Clough is sacked after just forty-four days in charge at Leeds Utd ▪ 20-year-old striker Trevor Francis scores a hat-trick for Freddie Goodwin's Birmingham City in a 1-3 win over Harry Haslam's Luton Town ▪ Three days later, Francis scores again as Birmingham beat reigning champions Leeds Utd 1-0 in front of 36,513 at St. Andrew's ▪ 24-year-old Malcolm 'Supermac' MacDonald scores twice as Newcastle Utd thrash Chelsea 5-0 at St. James' Park ▪ 22-year-old midfielder Terry McDermott leaves Newcastle and joins Liverpool for £175,000 ▪ 25-year-old goalkeeper Peter Shilton leaves Leicester City and joins Stoke City for

£325,000 ▪ 19-year-old defender Sam Allardyce makes his debut for Second Division Bolton Wanderers in a 1-3 defeat against Notts County ▪ Pubs are forced to close and shops are boarded up as Millwall play host to Manchester Utd in Division Two - Gerry Daly scores in a 0-1 win for Utd ▪ 36-year-old Ian St. John is appointed manager of Portsmouth football club ▪ 51-year-old Larry Grayson appears on stage at the London Palladium in 'Grayson's Scandals' - a new all comedy spectacular! ▪ *The Bitch Is Back* by 27-year-old Elton John is number fifteen in the pop chart ▪ *Hang On In There Baby* ("… Hang on in there darlin'. I'm gonna give you more than you ever dreamed possible") by Johnny Bristol is number three ▪ "Who loves ya, baby?" - Telly Savalas is *Kojak* on TV ▪ 33-year-old Fred West and his wife, 20-year-old Rosemary, murder 15-year-old Shirley Hubbard and bury her body beneath their house at 25 Cromwell Street in Gloucester ▪ 51-year-old Eamonn Andrews surprises 78-year-old actor Jack Howarth (who plays the role of Grumpy Albert Tatlock in *Coronation Street*) on ITV's *This is Your Life* ▪ 'Rollermania' causes pandemonium as teenage girls 'go crazy' for their favourite pop star heart-throbs ▪ 14-year-old Kora Blake from Desborough faints in the crowd when The Bay City Rollers (20-year-old Eric Faulkner, 18-year-old Les McKeown, 17-year-old Stuart 'Woody' Wood, 26-year-old Alan Longmuir and 23-year-old Derek Longmuir) take to the stage at the Granada Theatre in Kettering ▪ "But I said it before, and I'll say it again, and again, and again, and again…" *All Of Me Loves All Of You* ("… and every little thing you do") by 'The Rollers' climbs to number four in the pop chart ▪ "And I would give anything I own. Give up my life, my heart, my home" - *Everything I Own* by 26-year-old Ken Boothe is number one ▪ The IRA's terror campaign intensifies ▪ Five people are killed and forty-four are injured in pub bombings in Guildford ▪ A British soldier and a civilian are killed by a bomb in Woolwich ▪ Another twenty-one people are killed and almost two-hundred injured by bombs detonated in two Birmingham pubs ▪ 54-year-old Home Secretary Roy Jenkins signs his approval for the Prevention of Terrorism Act - giving police the right to arrest, detain and question suspects for a period of up to seven days, with the further sanction of deportation back to Ireland ▪ Public outrage over the indiscriminate bombings leads to the ostracisation of many Irish people living in En-

gland, with some being abused in the street and refused service in shops, cafes and pubs ▪ *Let's Get Together Again* by The Glitter Band climbs to number eight in the pop chart ▪ *Too Good To Be Forgotten* by The Chi-Lites peaks at number ten ▪ 'Rumble in the Jungle' - 32-year-old boxer Muhammad Ali regains the world heavy-weight title by knocking out 25-year-old George Foreman in the eighth round in Kinshasa, Zaire ▪ Back in England - the High Street in West Bromwich is pedestrianised ▪ Crowds flock to the cinema for an evening of thrills and suspense ▪ 41-year-old Michael Caine, 65-year-old James Mason and 59-year-old Anthony Quinn star in *The Marseille Contract* ▪ 43-year-old Richard Harris, 42-year-old Omar Sharif and 36-year-old Anthony Hopkins star in *Juggernaut* - a movie billed as 'The Greatest Sea Adventure in History' ▪ 'Here Be Sea Monsters' - Back at home, before the news begins, young TV viewers are enthralled by a new colour version of the cartoon *Captain Pugwash*, with Willy and Barnabas (pirates), Tom (the cabin boy) and Captain Horatio Pugwash ▪ *Roobarb* - a crazy new psychedelic cartoon (voiced by 40-year-old Richard Briers) also grabs the attention of school children ▪ "Norman Stanley Fletcher, you have pleaded guilty to the charges brought by this court and it is now my duty to pass sentence" - *Porridge*, with 44-year-old Ronnie Barker as Fletcher and 27-year-old Richard Beckinsale as Godber, debuts on BBC One on Thursday evenings ▪ A new series of the hugely popular *Dad's Army* is broadcast on Fridays ▪ "We can rebuild him. We have the technology" - schoolboys all around the country try to emulate *The Six Million Dollar Man* - as 35-year-old Lee Majors stars as the bionic Steve Austin ▪ 27-year-old Jenny Hanley replaces 35-year-old Susan Stranks on *Magpie* ▪ 44-year-old Bernard Manning is compare at *The Wheeltappers and Shunters Social Club* - where 43-year-old Colin Crompton wears a flat cap and rings his bell… "On behalf of the committ-ee!!" ▪ 29-year-old house-keeper Sandra Rivett is found murdered in Belgravia and 39-year-old Lord Lucan disappears - never to be seen again ▪ *(You're) Having My Baby* ("… What a lovely way of sayin' how much you love me") by 33-year-old Paul Anka is number six in the pop chart ▪ "Don't want to know about anything, 'cause…" *All I Want Is You* by Roxy Music (with, lead singer, 29-year-old Bryan Ferry) is number twelve ▪ 41-year-

old Barry Norman presents the late night movie review program *Film 74* on BBC One ▪ "This is your life Timmy Lea" - 24-year-old Robin Askwith stars at cinemas as Timmy Lea in *Confessions of a Window Cleaner* ▪ Men in long, grubby 'macs' loiter outside seedy picture houses ▪ 22-year-old Sylvia Kristel stars in *Emmanuelle* - an erotic film made in France ▪ "Opal Fruits, made to make you mouth water" - *Opal Fruits* are advertised on TV ▪ The first *McDonalds* hamburger restaurant opens at Woolwich ▪ A *Big Mac* costs 45p ▪ 'Regular' *French Fries* are 12p ▪ "Say you'll meet me…" *Down On The Beach Tonight* by The Drifters is number seven in the pop chart ▪ *Let's Put It All Together* ("… 'cause lovin' is all there is") by The Stylistics is number nine ▪ Tottenham Hotspur footballers, Steve Perryman (aged 22) and Martin Chivers (aged 29) score the goals to give Spurs a 2-0 victory over North London rivals Arsenal in Division One ▪ 27-year-old Ray Graydon bags a hat-trick as Ron Saunders' Aston Villa beat Millwall 3-0 in Division Two ▪ 17-year-old violinist Nigel Kennedy busks on Fifth Avenue in New York ▪ "Well, I know I've been out of style for a short while, but I don't care how cold you are. I'm coming home soon. I'm…" *Gonna Make You A Star* ("Yeah!") by 27-year-old David Essex climbs to number one in the pop chart - and stays there for three weeks ▪ *No Honestly* ("… I know we were meant to be") by 26-year-old Lynsey De Paul is number seven ▪ Racial tensions remain high in London ▪ 40-year-old National Front leader John Tyndall is ousted as chairman and replaced by 38-year-old John Kingsley Read ▪ Right wing extremists harass people from ethnic minorities in the street ▪ Hundreds of council tenants in North Kensington return home from work each day to their new accommodation at Grenfell Tower - a modern 'hi-rise' tower block ▪ *(Hey There) Lonely Girl* ("... Lonely girl, let me make your broken heart like new") by 28-year-old Eddie Holman is number four in the pop chart ▪ The wild instrumental *Pepper Box* by The Peppers is number six ▪ A re-issue of, "I met him on a Monday and my heart stood still…" *Da Doo Ron Ron* ("…Ron. Da doo, Ron Ron") by The Crystals peaks at number fifteen ▪ 35-year-old Big Ron Atkinson is appointed manager of Cambridge Utd Football Club. Atkinson's first match in charge is a 0-0 draw against Rotherham Utd in Division Four ▪ Richard Baker and Kenneth Kendall

present the *9 O'Clock News* on BBC One ▪ 49-year-old Labour MP John Stonehouse goes missing and is presumed dead (by drowning) after his clothes are found on a beach in Miami ▪ 39-year-old writer David Nobbs works on his fourth novel - a dark comedy called *The Death of Reginald Perrin* ▪ 24-year-old teacher John Darwin and his wife, Anne, take a walk along the beach at Seaton Carew ▪ 38-year-old burglar Donald Nielson (aka the Black Panther) breaks into a post office at Langley in the West Midlands and shoots dead Sidney Grayland ▪ An evil rapist terrorises young women in Cambridge. Police are hunting for a short, stocky man who has struck three times in the past few weeks ▪ *The Wild One* by 24-year-old Suzi Quatro is number seven in the pop chart ▪ *Sound Your Funky Horn* by KC and the Sunshine Band is new at number thirty-one ▪ Austin launches a *Vanden Plas* version of the *Allegro* motorcar. The luxurious new model costs just over £2,000 and boasts Connolly hide seating and trim, deep carpeting throughout, additional sound proofing, a full-width burred walnut veneer dashboard with lockable glove box and more comprehensive instrumentation than the usual *Allegro* cars. This new top-of-the-range model also has a distinctive large style bonnet grill, similar to the ones usually seen on Jaguars and Daimlers ▪ 60-year-old British Leyland chairman Lord Stokes meets with Labour's 49-year-old Industry Secretary Anthony Wedgwood Benn to discuss a possible government bail-out for the ailing car manufacturer ▪ Workers from Leyland's Longbridge factory in Birmingham enjoy a night out, drinking beer and smoking cigarettes and cigars ▪ A pint of *M&B Mild* costs 12p ▪ A pint of *Brew XI* is 15p ▪ A pint of *Ansell's Bitter* is 15½p ▪ A pack of twenty *Rothmans* is 27p ▪ Five *Hamlet* panatellas are 26p ▪ Patient children sit at home chewing Anglo *BUBBLY* bubble-gum, watching TV and waiting for father to return from the pub ▪ 31-year-old Radio One DJ Tony Blackburn is conducting a secret and illicit love affair with his neighbour's wife. Blackburn's own wife, 26-year-old actress Tessa Wyatt, is doing similar with the neighbour's husband ▪ "On your last trip, did you discover what the Earth people eat? / They eat a great many of these. [Shows a potato] "They peel them with their metal knives. Boil them for twenty of their minutes. Then they smash them all to bits. (Ha-ha-ha). They are clearly a most primitive people" - 'For Mash Get *Smash*' - the Martians are on ITV.

Christmas 1974

Inflation rises to 17.2%

Monarch:	Queen Elizabeth II (aged 48)
Prime-minister:	Harold Wilson (aged 58)
Chancellor:	Denis Healey (aged 57)
Home Secretary:	Roy Jenkins (aged 54)
Foreign Secretary:	James Callaghan (aged 62)
Football Manager:	Don Revie (aged 47)
Radio 1 Breakfast DJ:	Noel Edmonds (aged 26)
New car reg. suffix:	'N'

▪ The weather is mild and breezy ▪ Aran jumpers and wide-flared jeans are in fashion ▪ Children devour *Fizzy Lemonade* flavoured *Spangles* ▪ 'Hai Karate - be careful how you use it' - Men douse themselves in *Hai Karate* aftershave, because, "just one whiff drives women wild" ▪ "We got it together didn't we? We've definitely got our thing together, don't we baby?" - *You're The First The Last My Everything* by 30-year-old Barry White is number one on the hit parade ▪ *Oh Yes! You're Beautiful* ("... Beautiful. Didn't I tell you?") by 30-year-old Gary Glitter is number three ▪ "'Ello, darlin'! Ha-ha-ha-hah" - 33-year-old Ed 'stewpot' Stewart presents *Junior Choice* on weekend mornings on Radio One ▪ "Three wheels on my wagon, and I'm still rollin' along. The Cherokees are chasin' me. Arrows fly right on by, but I'm singin' a happy song" - The New Christy Minstrels sing *Three Wheels On My Wagon* ▪ Rock band Stray play a one-off gig at the Oldham College of Technology - and go down a storm with the students ▪ 49-year-old Richard Burton and 40-year-old Sophia Loren star at cinemas in *Brief Encounter* - a modern day re-make of the highly acclaimed wartime film ▪ 23-year-old footballer Bob Latchford scores his seventh goal of the season as Billy Bingham's Everton beat Derby County 0-1 to remain top of Division One ▪ 25-year-old Stuart Pearson scores his eleventh goal of the season as Tommy 'The Doc' Docherty's Manchester Utd beat York City 0-1 to remain top of Division Two ▪ "Oh, oh, oh. It's magic, you know. Never believe it's not so" - *Magic* by Pilot is number eleven in the pop chart ▪ *How Long* ("... has this been going on?) by Ace is number twenty ▪ 38-year-old Gordon Honeycombe reads the news for

ITN ▪ The IRA's bombing campaign continues ▪ Seventeen people are injured when a device explodes amongst shoppers in Bristol ▪ Bombs are also detonated outside *Selfridges* and *Harrods* in London; and at the home of Edward Heath in Belgravia - thankfully, there are no casualties ▪ "Let's go, let's go, let's go, let's go, down to..." *Junior's Farm* ("... where I wanna lay low") by 32-year-old Paul McCartney and Wings is number sixteen in the pop chart ▪ *Only You* ("... can make this world seem right") by 34-year-old Ringo Starr is number twenty-eight ▪ The so-called Cambridge Rapist strikes again - breaking into the homes of two women in the city and committing savage and brutal attacks. Police continue their search for the evil perpetrator ▪ An industrial dispute at British Leyland in Coventry sees thousands of assembly workers laid-off ▪ Cash is tight for tens of thousands of parents in working-class families ▪ Those that can afford it take their children to matinee screenings at the local cinema during the Christmas holiday ▪ 'The Love Bug's back in a new hilarious adventure!' - Walt Disney's *Herbie Rides Again* is now showing ▪ "It's behind you!" - Middle-class families enjoy an evening at the Pantomime ▪ 59-year-old comedian Dick Emery appears in *Goldilocks and the Three Bears* at the Wimbledon Theatre ▪ 61-year-old Sid 'Ha-ak-ak' James, 46-year-old Diana Coupland and 24-year-old Sally Geeson star in the fifth series of popular ITV sit-com *Bless This House* ▪ "You are my life, my pride, my joy" - *My Boy* by 39-year-old Elvis Presley is number six in the pop chart ▪ "Picture yourself in a boat on a river" - *Lucy in The Sky With Diamonds* by 27-year-old Elton John is number ten ▪ 40-year-old John Noakes, 35-year-old Peter Purves and 27-year-old Lesley Judd present *Blue Peter* on BBC One. The Christmas Appeal is underway with thousands of children sending in old buttons, buckles and badges to help raise money for new guide dogs for blind people ▪ 26-year-old athlete Brendan Foster (world record holder in the 3000 metre running event) is BBC's 'Sports Personality of the Year' ▪ "It'll be..." *Lonely This Christmas* ("... without you to hold") by Mud (with 28-year-old, lead singer, Les Gray) spends four weeks at number one in the pop chart ▪ "We wish you a..." *Wombling Merry Christmas* by The Wombles is number two ▪ "At twelve o'clock on Christmas Eve she tiptoed up the stairs" - *The Inbetweenies / Father Christmas Do*

Not Touch Me by The Goodies is number seven ▪ *Christmas Song* by 28-year-old Gilbert O'Sullivan climbs to number twelve ▪ *Hey Mr. Christmas* by Showaddywaddy peaks at number thirteen ▪ A Thomas Salter *Adventure Kit* at £4.99 (including water bottle, torch, camera, compass and penknife) is an exciting Christmas gift for schoolboys ▪ A *Hornby* electric train set is £10.95 from *Argos* ▪ The 'World Cup Striker' table-top football game from *Palitoy* now comes with floodlights ▪ Families gather around television sets in their G-Plan furnished living rooms ▪ A 'room divider' unit (supplied as a 'flat-pack') costs £22.50 ▪ *The Likely Lads* Christmas TV special sees Bob and Thelma (played by 36-year-old Rodney Bewes and 34-year-old Brigit Forsyth) attend a fancy dress party with Terry (39-year-old James Bolam) as their mini cab driver ▪ "Who's going to see the Queen?" - In *Some Mothers Do 'Ave 'Em*, Frank and Betty (played by 32-year-old Michael Crawford and 26-year-old Michele Dotrice) spend their first Christmas with baby, Jessica ▪ 52-year-old Eamonn Andrews surprises 74-year-old entertainer Arthur Askey on ITV's *This is Your Life* ▪ The latest series of TV drama *The Brothers* continues to grip the nation on Sunday evenings ▪ People enjoy a little tipple at Christmas ▪ *Baileys Irish-Cream* is a wonderful new alcoholic drink ▪ Motorcar design moves on apace ▪ The all new *MKII* Ford *Escort* is now in showrooms. The range of cars (which will be available in the new year) comprises of: *Popular*, *L*, *GL*, *Ghia* and *RS*. The 1100cc models have a top speed of 81 mph. The 1300cc models have a top speed of 87 mph ▪ Hallmark Records release *The Best of Top of the Pops 1974* - a budget priced, cover-version pop compilation LP with a sensual blonde girl pictured on the sleeve ▪ 22-year-old Helen Morgan from Barry wins the Miss World contest but is forced to resign when it's revealed she's a single mum ▪ "You keep buying and they'll keep the prices down! Alright!?" - Radio One disc jockey Alan 'Fluff' Freeman is on TV, advertising sheets and blankets for *Brentford Nylons* ▪ The 1974/75 football season is at the half way mark ▪ Tony Waddington's Stoke City team (with Shilton, Pejic, Greenhoff, Hurst and Hudson) moves to the top of Division One after winning four of its last five league games, recording victories over Luton Town (4-2), Queens Park Rangers (1-0), Leicester City (1-0) and Birmingham City (3-0) ▪ Alan

Ashman's Carlisle Utd (with Ross, Gorman, Train, O'Neil and Laidlaw) are in the relegation zone after losing five of their last six games, suffering defeats against West Ham Utd (0-1), Queens Park Rangers (1-2), Leeds Utd (1-2), Ipswich Town (1-3) and Chelsea (1-2) ▪ Birmingham City move up to fourteenth with a 3-1 victory over Liverpool in front of 23,608 at St. Andrew's - Gordon Taylor, Howard Kendall and 27-year-old Bob Hatton score the goals for 'The Blues' ▪ 28-year-old Leicester City striker Keith Weller is placed on the transfer list after refusing to play in the second half of a match against Ipswich Town ▪ "There's a new dance that is going around, called the bump. Do..." *The Bump* by Kenny is number three in the pop chart ▪ "Come on baby, do the..." *Juke Box Jive* by The Rubettes is number five ▪ 49-year-old former Labour MP John Stonehouse is caught and arrested in Australia - after faking his own death last month ▪ 28-year-old cricketer Tony Greig scores a century for England in the opening Test of the Ashes series in Brisbane, but Australia go on to win the match. 31-year-old Dennis Amiss and 27-year-old David Lloyd stride out together to open the batting for England in the Boxing Day Test at Melbourne. Amiss scores 4 runs. Lloyd makes 14. The match ends in a draw ▪ Back in Britain - Millions enjoy an evening at the cinema ▪ 'The Who's Who in the Who Dunit!' - An all star cast (including 50-year-old Lauren Bacall, 59-year-old Ingrid Bergman, 44-year-old Sean Connery and 38-year-old Albert Finney) appears in Agatha Christie's *Murder on the Orient Express* ▪ "Goodnight! Goodnight! / Good night, sir" - 47-year-old Roger Moore stars as James Bond (aka 007) in *The Man With The Golden Gun*. 32-year-old Britt Ekland is Bond's beautiful assistant, Mary Goodnight. 66-year-old Bernard Lee is M. 52-year-old Christopher Lee is Bond's arch enemy, Scaramanga ▪ 30-year-old Richard O'Sullivan, 25-year-old Paula Wilcox and 24-year-old Sally Thomsett star in a feature length film version of popular television sit-com *Man About the House* ▪ "So how can you tell me you're lonely and say for you that the sun don't shine. Let me take you by the hand and lead you through the..." *Streets Of London* ("... I'll show you something, to make you change your mind") by Ralph McTell climbs to number two in the pop chart ▪ 31-year-old DJ Tony Blackburn presents the weekday mid-morning show on Radio One ▪ 47-year-old DJ Alan 'Fluff' Freeman presents the afternoon show on Saturdays ▪ Football hoo-

ligans invade the pitch and fighting breaks out at Hillsborough as Sheffield Wednesday draw 4-4 with Manchester Utd in Division Two ▪ 22-year-old aberrant centre-forward Robin Friday scores his tenth league goal of the season (a second half penalty) as Reading lose 1-3 to Stockport County in Division Four ▪ 25-year-old striker Joe Royle transfers from Billy Bingham's Everton to Tony Book's Manchester City for £200,000 ▪ Industrial unrest prevails ▪ The coal mining industry is at an all time low. The National Coal Board has produced just 110 million tonnes this year (down 46 million tonnes from five years ago) ▪ Inflation has risen again - it now stands at 17.2% and Harold Wilson's Labour government is under severe pressure ▪ A bottle of *Johnnie Walker* whisky costs £2.59 ▪ A bottle of *Gordon's* gin is £2.66 ▪ A bottle of *Smirnoff* vodka is £2.95 ▪ A bottle of *Warninks* advocaat is £2.02 ▪ A bottle of *Harveys Bristol Cream* is £1.81 ▪ A four-pack of *Babycham* (small) bottles is 42p ▪ 34-year-old Esther Rantzen presents an edition of *That's Life* on BBC One ▪ Youngsters enjoy a night out on the town, drinking and dancing ▪ *Get Dancing* by Disco Tex and the Sex-O-Lettes (featuring Sir Monti Rock III) is number eight in the pop chart ▪ *Tell Him* ("... that you're always gonna love him") by Hello is number ten ▪ Housewives do the shopping - keeping a watchful eye on those ever rising prices ▪ A packet of McVities *Jaffa Cakes* is 11½p ▪ A jar of *Nescafe* coffee is 34p ▪ At home, millions of TV viewers watch as David Vine and Ron Pickering present *Superstars* on BBC One. 30-year-old David Hemery (athlete), 26-year-old Mick Channon (footballer), 23-year-old John Conteh (boxer), 28-year-old Colin Bell (footballer), 24-year-old John H. Stracey (boxer), 34-year-old Chay Blyth (yachtsman) and 28-year-old Tony Greig (cricketer) take part. John Conteh is the eventual winner ▪ 5.5 million colour TV licenses have been issued this year, increasing from 3.3 million in 1973 ▪ 11.8 million black and white licenses have been issued, falling from 13.8 million in 1973 ▪ On the thirty-first of December, smartly attired, middle-aged men attend New Year's Eve parties ▪ A two-piece *Terylene* suit costs £28.95 ▪ A pair of *Hush Puppies* is £4.99 ▪ All the best 'get togethers' have nibbles and drinks ▪ Small pieces of cubed cheese, with pineapple, on sticks are popular ▪ Golden Wonder *Kung Fuey* crisps are new ▪ Adverts say, 'Try a taste of Martini, the most beautiful drink in the world. It's the bright one, the right one, it's Martini.'

New Year 1975

'Shut it!' - The Sweeney is on telly

Monarch:	Queen Elizabeth II (aged 48)
Prime-minister:	Harold Wilson (aged 58)
Chancellor:	Denis Healey (aged 57)
Home Secretary:	Roy Jenkins (aged 54)
Foreign Secretary:	James Callaghan (aged 62)
Football Manager:	Don Revie (aged 47)
Radio 1 Breakfast DJ:	Noel Edmonds (aged 26)
New car reg. suffix:	'N'

▪ Long-haired rockers in pale-blue denim jackets, and with studded leather bands on their wrists, enjoy their music - loud! ▪ *Down Down* ("… deeper and down") by Status Quo spends a week at number one in the pop chart ▪ "B-b-b-baby, you just ain't seen n-n-nothin' yet. Here's something that you're never gonna forget" - *You Ain't Seen Nothing Yet* by Bachman Turner Overdrive reaches number two ▪ 13-year-old Harry Enfield from Horsham sits at home listening to Radio One ▪ 16-year-old Paul Whitehouse from Enfield watches BBC One television ▪ "Meet the gang 'cause the boys are here, the boys to entertain you" - A new series of *It Ain't Half Hot Mum* begins, with 44-year-old Windsor Davies as Sergeant Major, 41-year-old Don Estelle as Lofty and 39-year-old Melvyn Hayes as Gloria ▪ 49-year-old Richard Baker reads the news ▪ Harold Wilson's Labour government is poised to nationalise the troubled car manufacturer British Leyland. Workers are told to stop going on strike, or risk the bail-out deal being cancelled ▪ "There was a girl / There was a boy" - *Morning Side Of The Mountain* by 17-year-old Donny Osmond and 15-year-old Marie Osmond climbs to number five in the pop chart ▪ "Hey, I…" *Never Can Say Goodbye* ("… boy. Ooh, baby. I never can say goodbye, no, no, no, hey") by 31-year-old Gloria Gaynor is number four ▪ 13-year-old Simon Weston from Caerphilly plays out with his friends ▪ 49-year-old Margaret Thatcher becomes leader of the Conservative Party ▪ 'Who will survive and what will be left of them?' - *The Texas Chain Saw Massacre* is at cinemas ▪ Hollywood disaster movie *Earthquake*, starring 51-year-old Charlton Heston, 59-year-old Lorne Greene, 52-year-old Ava Gardner and 25-year-

old Victoria Principle, is also now showing ▪ Mrs. Thatcher appoints 48-year-old Sir Geoffrey Howe as Shadow Chancellor of the Exchequer ▪ 'He can change his shape like magic' - *Barbapapa* is a popular new TV cartoon show for children on BBC One ▪ *Hong Kong Phooey* - ('Number One Super Guy') is also popular ▪ 29-year-old DJ Tom Browne presents the Top 20 chart rundown (in VHF stereo) on Radio One on Sunday evenings ▪ "Oooh-ooh-ooh…" *Ms Grace* by The Tymes is number one for a week ▪ *January* ("… sick and tired of you picking on me") by Pilot is number one for three weeks ▪ "All alone, once more..." *Angie Baby* by 33-year-old Helen Reddy reaches number five ▪ "Let me help. If your child needs a daddy…" *I Can Help* by 32-year-old Billy Swan peaks at number six ▪ A new seven part drama for children called *The Secret Garden* airs on Wednesday evenings at 5.15 (after *John Craven's Newsround*) ▪ The recent *Blue Peter* Appeal has been a resounding success - almost six million envelopes full of buttons, buckles and badges have been donated and eleven Labrador puppies will now be trained to become guide dogs for blind people ▪ Bread is in short supply after a recent strike by bakers - long queues form outside shops ▪ 18-year-old Ava Cadell (34D) from Budapest is a popular new page three girl in *The Sun* ▪ "Is this the end for our two heroes? Find out next week in another exciting episode" - 45-year-old Ronnie Barker and 44-year-old Ronnie Corbett star as private detectives, Piggy Malone and Charley Farley, in a new series of *The Two Ronnies* on BBC One ▪ "Shut it!" - 32-year-old John Thaw and 26-year-old Dennis Waterman star as Reagan and Carter in *The Sweeney* on ITV ▪ The latest three-litre Ford *Granada GXL* motorcar costs £3,245, has a top speed of 113 mph and accelerates from 0-60 mph in 9 seconds ▪ 42-year-old Reginald Bosanquet reads the *News at Ten* for ITN ▪ 17-year-old Lesley Whittle is kidnapped from her home near Bridgnorth and a ransom demand of £50,000 is made to her parents ▪ Thousands of workers from Birmingham, Manchester and Liverpool converge on London and march from Euston Station to Westminster to demonstrate against the imprisonment of flying-pickets Des Warren and Ricky Tomlinson (aka 'The Shrewsbury Two') ▪ 58-year-old prime-minister Harold Wilson and Foreign Secretary 62-year-old James Callaghan travel to Moscow to meet

with leaders of the Soviet Union ▪ An agreement is signed with 68-year-old General Secretary Leonid Brezhnev on the non-proliferation of nuclear weapons ▪ An agreement is signed with 70-year-old Premier Alexsei Kosygin for Britain and the USSR to collaborate more closely on economic, scientific and technological matters ▪ Back in London - Forty-three people are killed and seventy-four are injured in a morning rush-hour tube-train crash at Moorgate Station. It takes up to thirteen hours for emergency services and rescue workers to cut some of the passengers free from the wreckage ▪ 'There's always another twist to…' *The Spiral Staircase* is at cinemas - 30-year-old Jacqueline Bisset and 45-year-old Christopher Plummer are the stars ▪ *Sugar Candy Kisses* ("... Sugar honey love") by Mac and Katie Kissoon is number three in the pop chart ▪ *Your Kiss Is Sweet* ("... as sweet as candy, but honey beats your kisses by a million miles") by 28-year-old Syreeta is number twelve ▪ 29-year-old reporter Christopher Martin-Jenkins provides regular cricket updates on BBC Radio Two ▪ England captain, Mike Denness, scores 188 runs and Keith Fletcher scores 146 in the final Test of the Ashes series at Sydney. England win the match, but Ian Chappell's Australia (with fast-bowlers Jeff Thompson and Dennis Lillee and wicket-keeper Rodney Marsh) win back the Ashes with a 4-1 series win. D L Amiss, B W Luckhurst, D Lloyd, J H Edrich, M C Cowdrey, M H Denness (cpt), K W R Fletcher, A W Greig, A P E Knott (wk), P Lever, D L Underwood, F J Titmus, R G D Willis, M Hendrick, C M Old and G G Arnold are all downcast by such a resounding Ashes defeat ▪ Back in England - energetic young dancers twist, spin, flip and drop at the *Wigan Casino* nightclub ▪ *Footsee* by Wigan's Chosen Few climbs to number nine in the national pop chart ▪ "Woah, yeah! Wait a minute Mr. Postman" - *Please Mr. Postman* by The Carpenters is number two ▪ "Take the ribbon from your hair, shake it loose and let it fall" - *Help Me Make It Through The Night* by 27-year-old John Holt is number six ▪ People stay up late to watch *Parkinson* on BBC One on Saturday nights ▪ 33-year-old world heavy-weight boxing champion Muhammad Ali is interviewed by 39-year-old Michael Parkinson ▪ "Sing, Muhammad, Muhammad Ali. He floats like a butterfly and stings like a bee" - *Black Superman (Muhammad Ali)* by Johnny Wakelin and the Kinshasa Band is a top

ten hit ▪ Footballers, 30-year-old Franny Lee and 30-year-old Henry Newton score the goals as Dave Mackay's Derby County beat Bob Paisley's Liverpool 2-0 at the Baseball Ground ▪ "Ahhh-a-ah!! Ahhh-ahhh!!" - 36-year-old Ron Ely stars as *Tarzan* on Saturday morning television ▪ 'From Studio Three, ATVland' - 28-year-old Chris Tarrant and 29-year-old John Asher present the brash, outrageous and funny *Tiswas* on ITV in the Midlands region ▪ 66-year-old Magnus Pyke presents ITV's science program *Don't Ask Me* ▪ 29-year-old DJ Johnnie Walker announces the latest Top 20 chart hits on Radio One on Tuesday afternoons ▪ "Oh, baby! I'm losing sleep over..." *The Secrets That You Keep* by Mud is new at number twenty-six ▪ "Just a new man. Yes, you made me live again" - *Now I'm Here* by Queen is number eleven ▪ "I say good-bye my love..." *Goodbye My Love* ("... till we meet once again") by The Glitter Band is number two ▪ Billy Bingham's Everton football team moves back to the top of Division One with a 0-3 victory over Birmingham City - 24-year-old Bob Latchford scores two of Everton's goals against his former club ▪ Dave Mackay's Derby County move up to fifth with a 0-1 victory over Wolverhampton Wanderers at the Molineux ▪ 39-year-old Brian Clough is appointed manager of Second Division Nottingham Forest - Clough signs midfielder John McGovern and striker John O'Hare from Leeds Utd ▪ 19-year-old winger Steve Coppell transfers from Tranmere Rovers to Manchester Utd. Coppell makes his Utd debut in a 4-0 victory over Cardiff City, coming on as a substitute to replace Willie Morgan ▪ "(Oooh-oooh, la-la-la). Blue eyes, blue eyes. (Oooh-oooh, la-la-la). How can you tell so many lies?" - *Make Me Smile (Come Up And See Me)* by Steve Harley and Cockney Rebel climbs to number one ▪ "I said..." *Shame Shame Shame* ("... Shame on you, if you can't dance too") by Shirley and Company is number six ▪ The *J. Lyons & Co* teashop on South Street in Worthing closes down ▪ A new coal-fired power station is now operational at Long Drax in Yorkshire ▪ Middle-class families replace old-fashioned blankets and eiderdowns on their beds with modern Continental Quilts ▪ "Charley says that if you ever see a box of matches lying around, tell mummy because they can hurt you" - a cartoon cat called Charley tells the public not to play with matches ▪ 'One tiny spark becomes a night of blaz-

ing suspense' - 49-year-old Paul Newman and 44-year-old Steve McQueen star at cinemas in Hollywood disaster movie *The Towering Inferno* ▪ Old age pensioners sit together in smoke-filled rooms at the local Working Mens' Club and chat about the good old days ▪ Adverts say, 'Woodbine Taste Great. Always have, always will' ▪ Teenage boys lie about their age in order to gain access to the local *Odeon*, hoping to catch a glimpse of 28-year-old Katy Manning, 27-year-old Diane Langton and 29-year-old Mary Millington (as a stripping traffic warden), all appearing without clothes in *Eskimo Nell* ▪ *Girls* ("... Love the things they know. Love the things they show. Have to be where they go") by Moments & Whatnauts enters the pop chart at number thirty-five ▪ *Only You Can* ("… oh-oh, oh-oh. Only you") by Fox is number three ▪ 27-year-old popstar Elton John features on the front cover of the latest *New Musical Express* ▪ Author P.G. Wodehouse dies aged 93 in New York ▪ 24-year-old boxer Joe Bugner beats Dante Cane by a technical knock-out in round five in Bologna, to retain his European heavy-weight title ▪ Back in England - Police continue their search for missing teenager Lesley Whittle and attempt to track down her kidnapper ▪ In other news, Labour's 50-year-old Secretary of State for Industry, Anthony Wedgwood Benn, asks 58-year-old Sir Don Ryder to report on the future of troubled car manufacturer British Leyland ▪ Grown-ups stay up late, watching television ▪ 57-year-old Googie Withers plays the role of Faye Boswell (a governor at a women's prison) in *Within These Walls* on ITV on Friday nights ▪ On Saturday mornings, children watch *Trumpton*, *Josie and the Pussycats* and *The Flashing Blade* on BBC, or the madcap *Tiswas* on ITV ▪ "Hi, hello, how are you" - *Please Tell Him That I Said Hello* by 23-year-old Dana is number eight on the weekly hit parade ▪ *Good Love Can Never Die* by 32-year-old Alvin Stardust is number eleven ▪ Inflation remains high ▪ Men sit in pubs, complaining about the high price of beer ▪ A pint of bitter costs 17p ▪ A pint of lager is 20p ▪ Housewives go shopping at *Mace*, *Presto* or *Liptons* supermarkets - and keep a watchful eye on those constantly rising prices ▪ A loaf of bread is 15p ▪ A large tub of *Stork SB* margarine is 20½p ▪ A jar of lemon curd is 10p ▪ A quarter pound pack of *Typhoo* tea is 8 ½ p ▪ A pint of milk is 6p ▪ Adverts warn, 'Watch out, watch out! There's a Humphrey about!'

Spring 1975

Bay City Rollers are the best!

Monarch:	Queen Elizabeth II (aged 49)
Prime-minister:	Harold Wilson (aged 59)
Chancellor:	Denis Healey (aged 57)
Home Secretary:	Roy Jenkins (aged 54)
Foreign Secretary:	James Callaghan (aged 63)
Football Manager:	Don Revie (aged 47)
Radio 1 Breakfast DJ:	Noel Edmonds (aged 26)
New car reg. suffix:	'N'

▪ Times are hard ▪ Unemployment is rising ▪ Retail prices are rising ▪ Four-hundred members of the National Front march through London demonstrating against Britain being part of the European Common Market ▪ 11-year-old schoolboy Nigel Farage from Farnborough plays out, alone ▪ "If a picture paints a thousand words, then why can't I paint you?" - *If* by 53-year-old Telly Savalas is number one in the pop chart ▪ *There's A Whole Lot Of Loving* ("... going on, in my heart. It's a feeling I'm feeling through and through") by Guys 'n' Dolls is number two ▪ "Young American, young American. She wants the Young American" - *Young Americans* by 28-year-old David Bowie is number eighteen ▪ Labour prime-minister Harold Wilson is under pressure ▪ Two thousand workers go on strike at British Leyland's Cowley plant ▪ The Transport and General Workers Union calls for a 'One Out, All Out' policy and a further two-thousand indirect workers linked to the plant also go on strike ▪ Workers at Chrysler come out on strike, demanding a weekly pay increase of £15 ▪ 'Your senses will never be the same' - the weird and sinister rock-opera *Tommy* (with 31-year-old Roger Daltrey, 37-year-old Oliver Reed, 33-year-old Ann-Margret and 30-year-old Paul Nicholas) goes on general release at cinemas ▪ 'Big Jim Brannigan takes on London - Chicago Style!' - 57-year-old John Wayne stars in *Brannigan* ▪ 85-year-old actor Charlie Chaplin is knighted by 48-year-old Queen Elizabeth II at Buckingham Palace ▪ *My Eyes Adored You* by 40-year-old Frankie Valli is number five in the pop chart ▪ "Shine a light. Shine the light" - *Philadelphia Freedom* by 27-year-old Elton John is number twelve ▪ *Dreamer* ("... you ain't

nothing but a dreamer") by Supertramp is number thirteen ▪ Heavy snow disrupts the Easter holidays ▪ Children enjoy snowball fights ▪ 11-year-old Michael Edwards (aka Eddie the Eagle) from Cheltenham slides down a steep snow covered hill on his mother's metal baking tray ▪ With high unemployment (it's currently estimated that one million people are out of work), rising prices, industrial action, 'all-out' strikes and disagreement between Labour Ministers (mostly over Britain's membership of the European Common Market), a number of vital issues need to be resolved in Harold Wilson's Cabinet ▪ Troublesome left-winger 53-year-old Eric Heffer is sacked from his position as Minister of State for Industry ▪ 44-year-old Gerald Kaufman is appointed in his place ▪ Inflation continues to rise ▪ 57-year-old Chancellor of the Exchequer Denis Healey presents the Budget ▪ Taxes are raised for the second year running ▪ The price of an annual colour TV license goes up from £12 to £18 ▪ A black and white license rises from £7 to £8 ▪ A vote takes place in Westminster and MPs move in favour of holding a referendum on Britain's membership of the Common Market. The referendum will take place in June ▪ The Labour Cabinet is split on the question of Europe ▪ 50-year-old Tony Benn (Secretary of State for Industry) claims that being part of the European community has cost the country approximately 500,000 jobs ▪ Members in the Conservative opposition campaign for Britain to remain in the Common Market ▪ Opposition leader 49-year-old Margaret Thatcher pays a visit to Scotland ▪ "You're the one girl in town I'd marry" - *Bye Bye Baby* ("… baby, goodbye") by The Bay City Rollers climbs to number one in the pop chart - and stays there for six weeks! ▪ Tartan scarves, flared trousers and high platform shoes are worn with pride. Teenage girls chant, "B-A-Y, B-A-Y, B-A-Y-C-I-T-Y, with an R-O double-L, E-R-S, Bay City Rollers are the best!" ▪ 24-year-old Barry Sheene suffers horrendous injuries when he crashes his Suzuki motorcycle at 170 mph at Daytona in the United States ▪ Back in England - the evil Cambridge Rapist strikes twice more, brutally attacking women in their homes ▪ "One day while I was not at home, while she was there and all alone, the angels came" - A re-issue of *Honey* by Bobby Goldsboro reaches number two in the pop chart ▪ *Fancy Pants* by Kenny is number four ▪ *The Tears I Cried* by The Glitter Band is number eight ▪ Meg Richardson (played by 55-year-old Noele Gordon)

marries Hugh Mortimer (played by 58-year-old John Bentley) in ITV's popular tea-time soap-opera *Crossroads.* 51-year-old comedian Larry Grayson makes a guest appearance, as chauffeur of the couple's wedding car ▪ "Oooh-wap. Ooh-dee, do-ah, doo-wap..." *Swing Your Daddy* ("... Sexy Mama") by Jim Gilstrap is a top five smash hit ▪ 27-year-old footballer Ray Graydon scores the only goal of the match (smashing in the rebound from a saved penalty) as Ron Saunders' Second Division Aston Villa defeat John Bond's Second Division Norwich City 1-0 in the League Cup final at Wembley ▪ 21-year-old Paul Mariner scores twice as Plymouth Argyle beat Preston North End 2-1 in front of 22,063 spectators in a Third Division tie at Home Park ▪ Families sit together watching TV in the evenings ▪ The fourth series of popular sit-com *Man About the House* is on ITV - starring 25-year-old Paula Wilcox, 24-year-old Sally Thomsett and 30-year-old Richard O'Sullivan ▪ "And I mean that most sincerely, folks" - 55-year-old Hughie Green hosts *Opportunity Knocks* and 31-year-old Tammy Jones (a singer from Bangor, North Wales) achieves the highest score on the 'clapometer' ▪ Trendy young people boogie the night away at discos ▪ Dance floors are packed as DJs play *Express*, the funky new single from BT Express ▪ *Pick Up The Pieces* by The Average White Band (with 28-year-old Alan Gorrie and 29-year-old Molly Duncan) is also popular ▪ Richard Hittleman presents *Yoga For Health* on Sunday mornings on ITV ▪ Kenneth Kendall and Richard Whitmore present the *Nine O'Clock News* on weekday evenings on BBC One ▪ The body of missing teenager Lesley Whittle is discovered in a deep drainage shaft at Bathpool Park in Staffordshire. Her evil kidnapper remains at large ▪ 33-year-old George Davis is sentenced to twenty years imprisonment for an armed payroll robbery in Ilford ▪ Sir Don Ryder reports back to Harold Wilson's Labour government and recommends that state intervention is the only way to save ailing car manufacturer British Leyland ▪ "Baby, sweet baby, my babe..." *What Am I Gonna Do With You* by 30-year-old Barry White is number five in the pop chart ▪ *Only Yesterday* ("... when I was sad and lonely, you showed me the way to leave the past behind me") by The Carpenters is number seven ▪ 43-year-old Jack Smethurst and 35-year-old Rudolph Walker star as 'Chalky' and 'Honky' in a new series of *Love Thy Neighbour* on ITV ▪ 'You'll like what's happening at Vaux-

hall' - The brand new *Chevette* 'hatchback' motorcar from Vauxhall is launched - it has a heated rear window, reclining front seats and costs £1,593 ▪ *Red Rum* finishes second in the Grand National behind *L'Escargot* ▪ Cambridge win the Boat Race ▪ 24-year-old footballer Roger Davies scores all five goals as Dave Mackay's Derby County thrash Luton Town 5-0 at the Baseball Ground in Division One ▪ Hooligans invade the pitch and fighting breaks out at White Hart Lane as Tottenham Hotspur beat Chelsea 2-0 in a crucial relegation game ▪ Hooligans invade the pitch and fighting breaks out at the City Ground as Nottingham Forest lose 0-1 to Manchester Utd in Division Two ▪ 22-year-old aberrant centre-forward Robin Friday scores a late winner (in a 2-1 victory) for Reading against Rochdale in Division Four and celebrates his goal by kissing a policeman ▪ 25-year-old Tony Currie of Sheffield Utd and 29-year-old Alan Birchenhall of Leicester City kiss during a First Division match - and the image is captured for posterity by the *Match of the Day* TV cameras ▪ *Oh Boy* ("... when you're with me, oh boy. The world will see that you, were meant for me") by Mud is new at number one in the weekly pop chart - replacing the Bay City Rollers ▪ "And it hurts so good, don't let me know" - *Hurt So Good* by 23-year-old Susan Cadogan is number four ▪ Families sit in front of Ferguson *3713* 19-inch colour television sets and argue about who's going to 'turn over.' (Switching channels involves getting up from the settee!) ▪ 28-year-old Robin Nedwell stars in *Doctor on the Go* on ITV ▪ 28-year-old Felicity Kendal and 35-year-old Penelope Keith star in *The Good Life* on BBC ▪ "So..." *Love Me Love My Dog* ("... We've lived the road too long to break up") by Peter Shelley is number three in the pop chart ▪ *Take Good Care Of Yourself* ("... I worry 'bout you") by The Three Degrees (27-year-old Fayette Pinkney, 27-year-old Valerie Holiday and 27-year-old Sheila Ferguson) is number nine ▪ 33-year-old Fred West and his wife, 21-year-old Rosemary, murder 18-year-old Juanita Mott and bury her body beneath their house at 25 Cromwell Street in Gloucester ▪ 'X' certificate horror films are popular at the cinema ▪ Crowds flock to see *The Ghoul* - starring 61-year-old Peter Cushing, 35-year-old John Hurt, 30-year-old Veronica Carlson and 29-year-old Alexandra Bastedo ▪ *Legend of the Werewolf* is also now showing ▪ 100,000 football supporters gather at Wembley on the third of May for the FA Cup final. 21-year-old

Alan Taylor scores twice, and 19-year-old goalkeeper Mervyn Day makes crucial saves, as John Lyall's West Ham Utd gain a 2-0 victory over Alec Stock's Fulham. 28-year-old captain Billy Bonds lifts the silver trophy for the triumphant Hammers. 33-year-old Fulham captain Alan Mullery and his 34-year-old team-mate Bobby Moore are magnanimous in defeat. A ticket for the standing enclosure at the Empire Stadium costs £1.50 ▪ 25-year-old centre-forward Malcolm 'Supermac' MacDonald scores all five goals (including four headers), as England thrash Cyprus 5-0 at Wembley. England's full line-up for the match is: Shilton, Madeley, Watson, Todd, Beattie, Bell, Ball, Hudson, Channon, MacDonald, Keegan and substitute, Thomas ▪ Dave Mackay's Derby County are the new Division One league champions after a nine match unbeaten run ▪ Colin Boulton, Peter Daniel, David Nish, Colin Todd, Ron Webster, Henry Newton, Archie Gemmill, Bruce Rioch, Franny Lee, Roger Davies and 30-year-old top scorer Kevin Hector have all been outstanding for 'The Rams' ▪ Billy Bingham's Everton finish three points behind Derby, in fourth position, after leading the way for much of the season ▪ Eddie McCreadie's Chelsea are relegated to Division Two along with Luton Town and Carlisle Utd ▪ Tommy 'The Doc' Docherty's Manchester Utd are promoted back to Division One ▪ "There once was an ugly duckling, with feathers all stubby and brown" - *The Ugly Duckling* by 35-year-old Mike Reid peaks at number ten in the pop chart ▪ *Fox On The Run* ("… you scream and everybody comes, a running. Take a run and hide, yourself away. Foxy on the run!") by Sweet is number two ▪ "Rory, Rory, tell us a story" - children watch *Animal Kwackers* (Boots, Bongo, Rory and Twang) on ITV ▪ Miss Diane (played by 32-year-old Susan Hanson) teaches Benny (played by 27-year-old Paul Henry) how to read and write in the popular soap-opera *Crossroads* ▪ Leeds Utd fans invade the pitch at the Parc des Princes in Paris when Peter Lorimer's goal is disallowed against Bayern Munich in the European Cup final. Leeds lose 2-0 to the German team which includes Sepp Maier, Gerd Muller and 29-year-old Franz Beckenbauer ▪ 65-year-old David Niven stars at cinemas in *Paper Tiger* ▪ 33-year-old David Hemmings stars in *Deep Red* ▪ 42-year-old Michael Caine, 31-year-old Helmut Berger and 39-year-old Glenda Jackson star in *The Romantic English-Woman* - the story of a bored housewife who meets a young man on

holiday in Germany ▪ *Loving You* ("… is easy 'cause you're beautiful") by 27-year-old Minnie Riperton is number two in the pop chart ▪ "Oh…" *Mandy* ("… well you came and you gave without taking") by 31-year-old Barry Manilow is number eleven ▪ Veteran centre-forward 37-year-old Derek Dougan of Wolverhampton Wanderers announces his retirement from top-class football ▪ 56-year-old Joe Harvey resigns as manager of Newcastle Utd ▪ Schoolboys buy *Tiger and Scorcher* for 6p from the newsagent and keep up to date with the adventures of 'Johnny Cougar', 'Billy's Boots', 'Martin's Marvellous Mini', 'Nipper Lawrence', 'Skid Solo' and 'Roy of the Rovers' ▪ Groups of teenage girls watch groups of teenage boys at the weekly disco in the local village hall ▪ *I Wanna Dance Wit Choo* by Disco Tex and the Sex-O-Lettes featuring Sir Monti Rock III moves up the pop chart to number six ▪ Ted and Sandra Beckham of Leytonstone are proud parents of a newborn son, David ▪ The England football team (Clemence, Whitworth, Beattie, Bell, Watson, Todd, Ball, Channon, Johnson, G Francis, Keegan and substitute, Thomas) thrashes Scotland 5-1 at Wembley, with goals from Kevin Beattie, Colin Bell, David Johnson and 23-year-old Gerry Francis (2) ▪ Production at British Leyland is brought to a halt yet again and thousands of workers are laid-off due to a strike by staff at tyre manufacturer Dunlop ▪ Prime-minister Harold Wilson visits Bedworth, campaigning for Britain to remain in the Common Market ▪ Employment Secretary Michael Foot speaks at a press conference in London, campaigning for Britain to leave the Common Market ▪ "Do, do, do the funky gibbon. (The funky gibbon). We are here to show you how. Oooh, oooh, oooh, the funky gibbon" - The Goodies (32-year-old Graeme Garden, 33-year-old Bill Oddie and 34-year-old Tim Brooke-Taylor) perform *Funky Gibbon* on *Top of the Pops* ▪ Tight fitting tanktops (with three large star shapes on the front) are in fashion ▪ School children attend birthday parties - where they partake in pass-the-parcel and eat jelly and ice-cream ▪ Housewives water their Spider plants ▪ Husbands decorate the living room - pasting wood-chip paper to the wall ▪ The average price of a house in the UK continues to rise - it's currently at £10,700 ▪ A loaf of bread from the supermarket now costs 16p ▪ Adverts claim, '*Hovis* still has many times more wheatgerm than ordinary bread. It's as good for you today as it's always been.'

Summer 1975

Cresta Pop 'It's frothy, man'

Monarch:	Queen Elizabeth II (aged 49)
Prime-minister:	Harold Wilson (aged 59)
Chancellor:	Denis Healey (aged 58)
Home Secretary:	Roy Jenkins (aged 54)
Foreign Secretary:	James Callaghan (aged 63)
Football Manager:	Don Revie (aged 48)
Radio 1 Breakfast DJ:	Noel Edmonds (aged 26)
New car reg. suffix:	'P'

▪ 'Yes! Britain is where she belongs… in Europe' - Prime-minister Harold Wilson and most of his Labour Party colleagues campaign to remain in the European Common Market ▪ People go to the polls on Thursday the fifth of June and vote (by 17 million to 8 million) to stay in the European community ▪ Rebel Labour MPs Tony Benn, Michael Foot, Eric Heffer and Barbara Castle are disappointed by the outcome ▪ 11-year-old public schoolboy Alexander Boris de Pfeffel Johnson sits at home making models of buses ▪ 3-year-old Dominic Cummings enjoys a day out with his family at Barnard Castle in County Durham ▪ A nearby optician's shop offers a good deal on the price of eye tests ▪ *Stand By Your Man* ("… and show the world you love him. Keep giving all the love you can") by 33-year-old Tammy Wynette (from Mississippi) is number one in the pop chart ▪ "Memories, like the corners of my mind. Memories, misty water colour memories of..." *The Way We Were* by 31-year-old Gladys Knight & The Pips is number four ▪ "I'm not..." *The Proud One* ("... I need you, I'm beggin' to you, baby, please. You're the proud one, believe me, this poor man is down on his knees") by The Osmonds (with 17-year-old 'heart-throb' Donny) is number five ▪ Inflation is rising ▪ 57-year-old Chancellor of the Exchequer Denis Healey plans to put a strict limit on any wage rises - a move which could provoke anger with the trade unions ▪ It's a hot summer ▪ Families travel to the seaside for their annual holiday ▪ Dunlop *Swing Ball* is a fab new game - giving hours and hours of fun ▪ Dads and boys build sandcastles on the beach and paddle together in the sea ▪ Kids enjoy *Haunted House* and *Space 1999* ice-lollies from Lyons Maid ▪ 11-year-old Lena Zavaroni (an *Opportunity Knocks* winner from Gree-

nock in Scotland) appears on stage at the Congress Theatre in Eastbourne. Tickets for the show are priced between £1.00 and £1.50 ▪ "I know I said that I was leaving, but I just couldn't say goodbye" - *Let Me Try Again* by 31-year-old Tammy Jones (an *Opportunity Knocks* winner from Bangor in North Wales) is a Top Five chart hit ▪ *Casey Jones*, *Vision On* and *Robinson Crusoe* are on TV during the school holiday ▪ *Seaside Special* is transmitted by BBC One on Saturday evenings; 36-year-old 'Diddy' David Hamilton introduces the show from Blackpool and, a week later, 26-year-old Noel Edmonds introduces the show from Great Yarmouth ▪ 45-year-old Stuart Hall presents *It's A Knockout* on Friday evenings. A team from Darlington wins a closely fought contest with Berwick-upon-Tweed and Consett. (Darlington will now compete in the Jeux Sans Frontieres competition later in the year) ▪ Teenagers hit the dancefloor at the local youth club ▪ *Disco Stomp* by 33-year-old Hamilton Bohannon climbs to number five in the pop chart ▪ *Disco Queen* by Hot Chocolate is number eleven ▪ 43-year-old Peter Woods reads the news on TV ▪ Trouble is brewing between Harold Wilson's Labour government and some factions of the National Union of Mineworkers ▪ 37-year-old Arthur Scargill (leader of the Yorkshire miners) calls for a wage of £100 a week for men working at the coal face ▪ 58-year-old Joe Gormley (president of the NUM) says some miners have become "a little drunk with power" ▪ Prime-minister Harold Wilson addresses a miners' conference at Scarborough and informs the audience that excessive pay demands will wreck the government's plan to limit pay rises to ten percent. Mr. Wilson says, "democracy is at risk" ▪ In other news - The Cambridge Rapist is caught and arrested after fleeing from the home of an intended victim ▪ A coach crashes at Dibbles Bridge near Hebden, killing the driver and thirty-one elderly female passengers ▪ The dilapidated West Pier at Brighton is closed to the public on safety grounds ▪ Leeds Utd are banned from European football for a year as punishment for the aggressive behaviour of their fans at the recent European Cup Final ▪ "Where are the clowns? There ought to be clowns" - *Send In the Clowns* by Judy Collins moves down the pop chart to number eleven ▪ "Do it! Do..." *The Hustle* by Van McCoy climbs to number four ▪ "Get up in the morning, slaving for bread, sir" - a new version of *The Israelites* by 33-year-old Desmond Dekker is number ten ▪ People enjoy a night out at

the cinema ▪ 'In a town where anything goes, everything does in this funny bedroom farce' - 38-year-old Warren Beatty, 35-year-old Julie Christie and 29-year-old Goldie Hawn star in *Shampoo* - a smash hit at the box-office ▪ 'The dirty window cleaner finds out pop is just a racket!' - 24-year-old Robin Askwith stars as Timmy Lea in *Confessions of a Pop Performer* ▪ "Sing Lofty / Why do you whisper green grass? Why tell the trees what ain't so?" - *Whispering Grass* by Windsor Davis and Don Estelle is new at number one in the pop chart ▪ *Sing Baby Sing* ("... the world is getting better") by The Stylistics is number three ▪ 23-year-old jockey Pat Eddery rides *Grundy* to victory in the Epsom Derby ▪ 61-year-old John Arlott and 63-year-old Brian 'Johnners' Johnston commentate on cricket for BBC radio's *Test Match Special* ▪ England lose the first Test Match of the summer against the touring Australian team. 28-year-old Tony Greig takes over from Mike Denness as England cricket captain. A male streaker runs onto the pitch and hurdles the stumps during the second Test at Lord's. 'Free George Davis' - the third Test at Headingley is abandoned, after the pitch is vandalised by protestors seeking to overturn the conviction of armed robber George Davis. England's debutant batsman, 33-year-old David Steele, performs bravely and scores runs against Australia's pace attack - but it's not enough; Ian Chappell's Aussies win the series, 1-0, and retain the Ashes. England players, J H Edrich, D L Amiss, B Wood, D S Steele, K W R Fletcher, M H Denness, G A Gooch, J H Hampshire, A W Greig (cpt), R A Woolmer, G R J Roope, A P E Knott (wkt), D L Underwood, P H Edmonds, C M Old, J A Snow, G G Arnold and P Lever are all downcast by an Ashes defeat ▪ The England cricket team also takes part in the brand new (one-day, sixty-over) Prudential Cup tournament, but loses to Australia in the semi-finals at Headingley ▪ Union leaders agree to back the government's wage rise policy. A maximum £6 a week rise will be put in place for twelve months ▪ Miners' leader Joe Gormley says, "I feel a lot better now that we have got a sensible approach" ▪ "Roll over lay down and let me in..." *Roll Over Lay Down* by Status Quo is number nine in the pop chart ▪ "Our little boy is four years old and quite a little man. So we spell out the words we don't want him to understand" - *D.I.V.O.R.C.E* by 33-year-old Tammy Wynette is number twelve ▪ 24-year-old Susan George and 37-year-old Vanessa Redgrave star at cinemas in *Out of Season* - a

dark and tense drama set in a rundown hotel at an English seaside resort ▪ The summer is mostly hot with plenty of days of warm sunshine ▪ Kids chase *Corona* lorries down the road as the pop-man delivers bottles of Cherryade and Dandelion and Burdock to local houses ▪ 31-year-old tennis star Arthur Ashe defeats 22-year-old Jimmy Conners (last year's champion) in the men's singles final at Wimbledon ▪ 31-year-old Billie Jean King wins the ladies' singles ▪ A heavy hailstorm towards the end of the British motor racing Grand Prix at Silverstone causes James Hunt and Jody Scheckter to crash. The race is won by 28-year-old Brazilian Emerson Fittipaldi ▪ 40-year-old Gordon Lee is the new football manager of Newcastle Utd. Lee signs striker Alan Gowling from Huddersfield Town for £70,000 and sells midfielder Terry Hibbitt to Birmingham City for £100,000 ▪ 28-year-old centre-half Dave Watson transfers from Sunderland to Manchester City for £175,000 ▪ 24-year-old striker Charlie George transfers from Arsenal to Derby County for £100,000 ▪ 34-year-old Johnny Giles leaves Leeds Utd and joins West Bromwich Albion as player-manager ▪ 30-year-old Angela Rippon presents *News Extra* on BBC Two ▪ The trial begins of six men accused of murdering twenty-one people in last year's Birmingham pub bombings ▪ "Hold on there, Bald Eagle. You wouldn't fire a man till he's finished his *Texan* bar would you?" - Rowntree bring out the *Texan* milk chocolate covered chew bar ▪ 29-year-old Pan's People dancer Barbara 'Babs' Lord marries 31-year-old actor Robert Powell ▪ 19-year-old Deirdre Hunt (played by 21-year-old Anne Kirkbride) marries 28-year-old Ray Langton (played by 32-year-old Neville Buswell) in ITV's *Coronation Street* ▪ *I'm Not In Love* ("… so don't forget it. It's just a silly phase I'm going through") by 10cc is number one in the pop chart ▪ "Now there, are three, steps to heaven. (Wop-wop)" - *Three Steps To Heaven* by Showaddywaddy is number two ▪ The grand final of popular TV show *New Faces* is broadcast live from the London Palladium. 30-year-old all-round entertainer Marti Caine from Sheffield is the eventual winner. 16-year-old comedian and impressionist Lenny Henry from Dudley finishes in fourth place ▪ 'The antidote to panel games' - 54-year-old Humphrey Lyttelton is chairman for a new series of *I'm Sorry I Haven't A Clue* on Radio Four. 32-year-old Graeme Garden, 40-year-old Barry Cryer, 37-year-old Willie Rushton and 35-year-old Tim Brooke-Tay-

lor are panelists on the popular comedy show ▪ 'Prices Soar to All Time High' - Harold Wilson's Labour government presides over record high inflation of 26.9% and unemployment of 1.2 million ▪ Shadow Chancellor Sir Geoffrey Howe describes the latest economic figures as "catastrophic" and says "the action that must be taken [to fix this] will be severe" ▪ Motorbike stuntman Evel Knievel is rushed to hospital after being critically injured in a crash in front of a large crowd at Wembley Stadium. (The 36-year-old was attempting to leap over thirteen parked buses on his Harley-Davidson) ▪ "Now then, now then" - 48-year-old Jimmy Savile OBE makes children's dreams come true in his new TV show, *Jim'll Fix It* ▪ 'Phew! It's a Scorcher!' - The sun continues to shine ▪ Temperatures remain high ▪ Dehydrated families sit in traffic jams on the M5 motorway in Vauxhall *Vivas*, Ford *Cortinas* and Morris *Marinas* - sweaty children are in the back, with bare legs sticking to hot vinyl seats ▪ People rush out to buy the latest 7-inch singles at *Woolworths* for 66p ▪ "Look at me. I'm as helpless as a kitten up a tree" - *Misty* by 36-year-old Ray Stevens is number two in the weekly pop chart ▪ "So..." *If You Think You Know How To Love Me* ("... and you think you know what I need") by Smokie is number three ▪ "It's just your..." *Jive Talkin'* ("... you're tellin' me lies") by The Bee Gees is number five ▪ 25-year-old boxer Joe Bugner is accused of taking a negative approach as he goes fifteen rounds with 33-year-old Muhammad Ali in Kuala Lumpur - but loses on points in a WBA/WBC heavy-weight title fight ▪ Wrestlers Big Daddy (44-year-old Shirley Crabtree) and Giant Haystacks (28-year-old Martin Ruane) form a formidable tag-team on ITV's *World of Sport* on Saturday afternoons ▪ 27-year-old racing driver James Hunt wins the Dutch Grand Prix at Zandvoort in a Hesketh-Ford. 26-year-old Niki Lauda is second in a Ferrari ▪ Back in England - 'P' reg cars go on sale ▪ A new Ford *Cortina 1300L* costs £1,649 and has a top speed of 85 mph ▪ A new Austin *Allegro* costs £1,159 and has a top speed of 78 mph ▪ The board of directors at British Leyland recommends to its shareholders that the government should be allowed to take control of the company - in return for the multi-million pound investment that's needed to keep the car manufacturer solvent ▪ Workers at British Leyland's Triumph factory threaten to go on strike - just as the exciting new *TR7* sports car (with state-of-the-art pop-up headlights) is about to be

launched on the US market ▪ *Tears On My Pillow* ("... Pain in my heart. You on my mind") by Johnny Nash spends a week at the top of the pop chart ▪ More and more foreign cars are being sold in the UK ▪ BMW introduces the all new *3 Series* motorcar - the *316* model comes with two single-set circular headlights. The *320* comes with two dual-set circular headlights ▪ Volkswagen launches the *Golf GTI* with a top speed of 113 mph and capable of 0-60 mph in 8.9 seconds ▪ "Wir fahr'n, fahr'n, fahr'n, auf der..." *Autobahn* by futuristic German pop group Kraftwerk is number eleven on the hit parade ▪ *Listen To What The Man Said* by Wings is number six ▪ 46-year-old Leonard Parkin reads the news for ITN ▪ Three women are injured in separate hammer attacks in Yorkshire ▪ The Birmingham Six are found guilty of last year's pub bombings and each man is given twenty-one life sentences - representing the number of people murdered ▪ Thirty-three people are injured when an IRA bomb explodes at Caterham in Surrey ▪ 'Rollermania' continues - *Give A Little Love* ("... take a little love, be prepared to forsake a little love") by The Bay City Rollers moves to the top of the weekly pop chart ▪ The new football season gets underway ▪ Football kit design moves on apace ▪ Coventry City players wear a striking new outfit (manufactured by *Admiral*) - with two (dark blue and white) downward stripes on the sky-blue jersey, matching up neatly with two similar stripes on the sky-blue shorts ▪ 24-year-old striker David Cross bags a hat-trick as Coventry win their opening game 1-4 away at Everton ▪ 25-year-old Malcolm 'Supermac' MacDonald scores eight goals in the first six games for Newcastle Utd ▪ Manchester Utd's 32-year-old goalkeeper Alex Stepney dislocates his jaw shouting at his own defenders in a match against Birmingham City - Utd win 2-0 with both goals scored by 21-year-old Sammy McIlroy ▪ 21-year-old Jimmy Case scores his first goal for Liverpool in a 3-2 win over Tottenham Hotspur at Anfield ▪ 17-year-old David O'Leary makes his debut for Arsenal in a 0-0 draw against Burnley ▪ 17-year-old Chris Kamara makes his debut for Second Division Portsmouth in a 0-2 defeat against Luton Town ▪ "Ladies and gentlemen this is Captain Tobias Willcock welcoming you aboard Coconut Airways flight 372 to Bridgetown..." *Barbados* by Typically Tropical is the new number one song ▪ "For you are beautiful and I have loved you dearly, more dearly than the spoken word can tell" - *The*

Last Farewell by 39-year-old Roger Whittaker is number two ▪ 9-year-old Denise Jane Lovell is rushed to hospital with a serious head injury, after falling from a swing in a park at Armitage in Staffordshire ▪ Violence has become a major problem on football terraces and in the streets outside grounds ▪ Seventy hooligans are arrested at a First Division match between Wolverhampton Wanderers and Manchester Utd. There's also crowd trouble at Leicester City versus Birmingham City and Nottingham Forest versus Plymouth Argyle ▪ *The Death of Reginald Perrin* - the fourth novel from 40-year-old writer David Nobbs is published ▪ 30-year-old DJ Johnnie Walker announces the new Top 30 chart hits on Tuesdays at 12.45 p.m. ▪ "I..." *Can't Give You Anything (But My Love)* by The Stylistics climbs to number one - and stays there for three weeks ▪ *That's The Way (I Like It)* by KC and the Sunshine Band is number four ▪ *Sealed With A Kiss* by 31-year-old Brian Hyland is number seven ▪ *Sherry* ("... Sherry, baby") by 24-year-old Adrian Baker is number ten ▪ *Fame* ("... Fame, makes a man take things over") by 28-year-old David Bowie is number nineteen ▪ Adolescent boys find discarded pornographic magazines in bushes near the municipal playing fields ▪ 31-year-old actress and glamour model Eve Astor features in a recent volume of *Knave* ▪ The stunning new black and gold *JPS* (special edition) Ford *Capri Mark II* motorcar turns heads on the streets of Britain ▪ Retail prices remain high ▪ There's no let-up in the rate of inflation ▪ Unemployment also continues to rise ▪ Labour prime-minister Harold Wilson and his Chancellor of the Exchequer, Denis Healey, are criticed in the newspapers ▪ *The Lucky Touch* is on general release at cinemas - 47-year-old Roger Moore, 36-year-old Susannah York and 55-year-old Shelley Winters are the stars ▪ *Blanket On The Ground* by 37-year-old Billie Jo Spears is number six in the pop chart ▪ "I saw the light on the night that I passed by her window" - *Delilah* by The Sensational Alex Harvey Band is number seven ▪ 24-year-old footballer Alan Hudson scores the only goal of the game as Tony Waddington's Stoke City beat Arenal 0-1 in Division One at Highbury ▪ 26-year-old Stuart Pearson scores twice as Tommy 'The Doc' Docherty's Manchester Utd thrash Sheffield Utd 5-1 at Old Trafford ▪ Working-class families enjoy a chippy tea and a can of pop on Friday evenings ▪ Fish and chips wrapped in newspaper costs 40p ▪ Adverts say, '*Cresta* pop - "it's frothy man!"'

Autumn 1975

The new TR7 sports car

Monarch:	Queen Elizabeth II (aged 49)
Prime-minister:	Harold Wilson (aged 59)
Chancellor:	Denis Healey (aged 58)
Home Secretary:	Roy Jenkins (aged 55)
Foreign Secretary:	James Callaghan (aged 63)
Football Manager:	Don Revie (aged 48)
Radio 1 Breakfast DJ:	Noel Edmonds (aged 26)
New car reg. suffix:	'P'

▪ "Ooh, you are awful… but I like you." - 60-year-old Dick Emery makes millions laugh on Saturday evenings on BBC One ▪ The fifth series of *Upstairs Downstairs* begins on ITV, with 41-year-old Jean Marsh as Rose, 71-year-old Angela Baddeley as Mrs. Bridges, 51-year-old Gordon Jackson as Hudson and 21-year-old Lesley-Anne Down as Georgina Worsley ▪ "Baby, get down. Come on down to the…" *Summertime City* by 26-year-old Mike Batt with the New Edition is number four in the pop chart ▪ *Scotch On The Rocks* by The Band of the Black Watch is number eight ▪ *The Rochdale Cowboy* by 30-year-old Mike Harding is number twenty-two ▪ Families return home from their summer holidays ▪ 68-year-old Sir Fred Pontin visits his team of Blue Coats at Broadreeds holiday camp in Selsey - and thanks them for their hard work during the main season ▪ 8-year-old Andrew Lovell and his brother, 6-year-old Peter, enjoy a pedalo ride on the pool in Beacon Park, Lichfield ▪ "I am sailing, I am sailing, home again, across the sea" - *Sailing* by 30-year-old Rod Stewart climbs to number one in the pop chart - and stays there for four weeks ▪ *It's Been So Long* by 31-year-old George McCrae is number four ▪ Mororists are excited ▪ The wonderful new *TR7* sportscar which has been developed for the US market, may soon be available in Britain ▪ 47-year-old Sandy Gall reads the evening news for ITN ▪ Three armed robbers hold hostages at gunpoint at the Spaghetti House restaurant in Knightsbridge. A six-day siege ensues before all hostages are released and the robbers hand themselves in to the police. 24-year-old Wesley Dick, 22-year-old Bonsu Munroe and 28-year-old Franklin Davies are taken into custody ▪ Andrew Newton shoots dead a dog called Rinka, in a botched murder attempt. The

intended victim, 34-year-old Norman Scott, a secret former lover of Liberal leader Jeremy Thorpe MP, is unharmed ▪ 31-year-old Michael Fish presents the weather forecast on BBC One ▪ Brisk winds move in from the north ▪ 26-year-old footballer Alan Gowling bags a hat-trick as Gordon Lee's Newcastle Utd thrash Bill McGarry's Wolverhampton Wanderers 5-1 in Division One ▪ Three days later, Willie Bell's Birmingham City beat Newcastle 3-2 with 24-year-old Peter Withe (2) and 21-year-old Trevor Francis scoring the goals ▪ "Need. Need. Got. Need. Got." - schoolboys swap *Soccer Stars '75-'76* football stickers on the playground ▪ Schoolgirls flick through the pages of *Look-In* magazine - searching for pictures of The Bay City Rollers ▪ The fifth series of popular sit-com *Man About the House* is on ITV - starring 25-year-old Paula Wilcox as Chrissie, 25-year-old Sally Thomsett as Jo and with 31-year-old Richard O'Sullivan as Robin Tripp ▪ A new series of *The Liver Birds* is on BBC One, starring 26-year-old Elizabeth Estensen as Carol and 33-year-old Nerys Hughes as Sandra ▪ *Moonlighting* ("… they're leaving everything. Moonlighting, they're losing all their friends") by 27-year-old Leo Sayer is number two in the pop chart ▪ *Heartbeat* ("… why do you miss when my baby kisses me?") by Showaddywaddy is number seven ▪ 58-year-old Chancellor of the Exchequer Denis Healey is under pressure - with record high unemployment and soaring inflation rates, the economy has now moved into recession ▪ Industrial disputes continue - with unions making big demands on the Labour government ▪ Production of British Leyland's new Austin *18/22 (Princess)* motorcar is affected by on-going strike action. Production of Morris *Marinas* and Austin *Allegros* also slows down ▪ "When I get me moped out on the road, I'm gonna ride, ride, ride" - 30-year-old Brummy comedian Jasper Carrott is number five in the pop chart with *Funky Moped* ▪ "Run around now!" - 35-year-old Cockney comedian Mike Reid hosts *Runaround* - a TV game show for children ▪ 45-year-old Brian Redhead is a new presenter on BBC Radio Four's *Today* program on weekday mornings ▪ Iceland extends its territorial fishing waters around its shoreline to two-hundred nautical miles. Previously, it was fifty. British trawlers continue to operate in the disputed zone and political tensions rise between Harold Wilson and Kristjan Eldjarn the president of Iceland ▪ "If you want a sweet, sweet love tonight, call me and

I'll make you feel alright" - *I'm On Fire* by 5000 Volts is number four in the pop chart ▪ *Una Paloma Blanca* ("... I'm just a bird in the sky") by 30-year-old Jonathan King is number ten (and will climb to number five) ▪ 50-year-old Richard Baker and 41-year-old Richard Whitmore present the *9 O'Clock News* on BBC One ▪ 59-year-old prime-minister Harold Wilson and 49-year-old Queen Elizabeth II attend the opening of the new North Sea oil pipeline ▪ Evil 47-year-old Peter Cook (aka The Cambridge Rapist) is sentenced to life in prison and Judge Melford Stevenson concludes, "In your case, I am recommending that life in prison means exactly that." ▪ The IRA steps up its bombing campaign ▪ An explosion at the Hilton Hotel in London kills two and injures sixty-three people ▪ An explosion at Green Park tube station kills one person ▪ An explosion at a London restaurant kills two and injures twenty-three people ▪ Elsewhere in the country - life continues as normal ▪ Children return home at the end of a school day to watch *Play School*, *Deputy Dawg*, *Jackanory*, *Animal Magic*, *John Craven's Newsround*, *The Record Breakers* and *The Magic Roundabout* - before the news begins on BBC One ▪ Over on ITV, children can see *Clapperboard* (with Chris Kelly) on Monday evenings and *Magpie* (with Mick Robertson, Douglas Rae and Jenny Hanley) on Tuesdays and Fridays ▪ Film stars, 43-year-old Elizabeth Taylor and 49-year-old Richard Burton re-marry, after divorcing just sixteen months ago ▪ *There Goes My First Love* ("... with the guy I used to call my friend") by The Drifters is number three in the pop chart ▪ *Motor Bikin'* ("... movin on the Queen's highway lookin' like a streak of lightnin')" by Chris Spedding is number fourteen ▪ The latest Honda *PC50* moped has a top speed of 31 mph ▪ 'Thrilla in Manila' - 33-year-old boxer Muhammad Ali retains his world heavy-weight title - beating 31-year-old Smokin' Joe Frazier by a Technical Knock Out in the fifteenth round in the Philippines ▪ Back in England - football hooligans invade the pitch in an attempt to get the match abandoned as Chelsea lose 0-3 to Luton Town in Division Two ▪ British Rail cancels its 'football specials' due to rowdy behaviour and widespread vandalism on trains ▪ England manager Don Revie calls for birching to be re-introduced as a punishment for football thuggery ▪ "It ain't no big thing, to wait for the bell to ring. It ain't no big thing, the toll of the bell" - *Love Is The Drug* by Roxy Music (with, lead singer, 30-year-

old Bryan Ferry) climbs to number two in the pop chart ▪ "Hey!.." *Fattie Bum Bum* ("… You sweet sugar dumpling") by 29-year-old Carl Malcolm is number eight ▪ Hundreds of thousands of people enjoy a day out at the Earls Court Motor Show - and this year, the annual show is marking its diamond jubilee ▪ 'One size only. Washable. Easy to fit' - *Karobes* sheepskin seat covers are advertised in the motor show's official catalogue ▪ 'The car everyone dreams of. But very, very few can ever own' - Jaguar launches the wonderful *XJ-S* luxury grand tourer as a replacement for the ageing *E-Type*. The new V12 model has a top speed of 150 mph and accelerates from 0-60 mph in 6.8 seconds ▪ 'For a Fortunate Few' - Lotus launches the futuristic, wedge shaped *Esprit* sports car. Top speed is 138 mph and 0-60 mph comes in 6.7 seconds ▪ 'Cavalier is here. Where family and sporty motoring come together' - Vauxhall launches the *Cavalier* (a four door saloon) as a replacement for the ageing *Victor* ▪ 'The new Chrysler Alpine is here' - Chrysler launches the *Alpine* (a 5-door hatchback) as a replacement for the ageing Hillman *Hunter* ▪ Adolescent boys peruse the shelves at newsagents ▪ Diane, Brigit, Shelagh, Mavis and Mandy Moore 'reveal all' in *Knave* magazine - on sale now for 50p ▪ *It's Time For Love* by The Chi-Lites is number five in the pop chart ▪ *Who Loves You* ("… pretty baby. Who's gonna help you through the night?") by The Four Seasons is number six ▪ *Don't Play Your Rock And Roll To Me* by Smokie is number eight ▪ A pale-blue, three-wheeled AC*70 Invacar* is parked at the side of the football pitch at Turf Moor as Burnley draw 4-4 with Norwich City ▪ Tommy 'The Doc' Docherty's newly promoted Manchester Utd are top of Division One, with: Alex Stepney, Stewart Houston, Brian Greenhoff, Martin Buchan, Steve Coppell, Lou Macari, Stuart Pearson, Gerry Daly and 21-year-old Sammy McIlroy all in tremendous form ▪ Working-class lads wear donkey jackets and Dr. Marten boots ▪ 16-year-old Lenny Henry from Dudley is the latest winner on TV talent show *New Faces* ▪ "You're nicked!" - 33-year-old John Thaw and 27-year-old Dennis Waterman star as Reagan and Carter in a new series of *The Sweeney* on Thursday nights at 9 p.m. ▪ "Ahh, Grasshopper" - 38-year-old David Carradine stars in *Kung Fu* on Saturdays nights at 11.30 p.m. ▪ 25-year-old footballer Malcolm 'Supermac' MacDonald (of Newcastle Utd and England) sprints 100m in under eleven seconds on BBC One's *Superstars* ▪

"Don't mention the war!" - 36-year-old John Cleese stars in *Fawlty Towers* on BBC Two ▪ 29-year-old Diane Keen appears in *The Cuckoo Waltz* on ITV ▪ 38-year-old Willie Bell is the new football manager of Birmingham City ▪ 30-year-old Dave Lee Travis is the new presenter of Radio One's tea-time show ▪ *Hold Me Close* ("… don't let me go, oh no") by 28-year-old David Essex is new at number one in the pop chart ▪ "I believe in miracles. Where you from?..." *You Sexy Thing* by Hot Chocolate (with, lead singer, 31-year-old Errol Brown) reaches number two ▪ 34-year-old Bob Dylan and 26-year-old Bruce Springsteen feature on the front cover of the latest *New Musical Express* ▪ Discontented youngsters gather together in groups, frustrated with the banality of (pretty much) everything ▪ Punk rockers - Steve Jones, Paul Cook, Glen Matlock and Johnny Rotten form a group called The Sex Pistols. 29-year-old Malcolm McLaren is the band's promoter and manager ▪ 38-year-old Michael Nicholson reads the lunchtime news for ITN ▪ A woman is found murdered in Yorkshire ▪ 50-year-old Ross McWhirter is shot dead on his doorstep in London by the Provisional IRA ▪ 42-year-old Barry Norman presents the late night movie review program *Film 75* on BBC One ▪ 'The Adventure You Will Never Forget!' - *The Land That Time Forgot* (featuring 26-year-old Susan Penhaligon) is now showing at cinemas across the country ▪ 54-year-old Dirk Bogarde, 52-year-old Ava Gardner and 29-year-old Timothy Dalton star in *Permission to Kill* - a spy thriller from director Cyril Frankel ▪ Popular fictional detective Hercule Poirot takes a final bow in *Curtain* - the latest 'whodunit' novel from 85-year-old crime-writer Agatha Christie ▪ "Are the stars out tonight? I don't know if it's cloudy or bright..." *I Only Have Eyes For You* by 34-year-old Art Garfunkel spends two weeks at number one ▪ *Feelings* ("... Nothing more than feelings") by 24-year-old Morris Albert peaks at number four ▪ Don Revie's England football team draws 1-1 with Portugal in Lisbon and fails to qualify for next year's European Championships. Goalkeeper - Ray Clemence; defenders - Steve Whitworth, Dave Watson, Paul Madeley and Kevin Beattie; midfielders - Colin Todd, Trevor Brooking and Gerry Francis; forwards - Mike Channon, Kevin Keegan and Malcolm 'Supermac' MacDonald; and substitutes - Allan 'sniffer' Clarke and Dave Thomas, all return home disappointed ▪ Back in England - 42-year-old Dickie Davies introduces *World Of Sport*

on ITV on Saturday afternoons ▪ 43-year-old Brian Moore presents *On The Ball* ▪ 31-year-old Franny Lee of Derby County and 32-year-old Norman Hunter of Leeds Utd have a punch-up during a First Division match at the Baseball Ground. Both players are sent off - and continue fighting as they leave the pitch. The game ends in a 3-2 victory for 'The Rams' ▪ 23-year-old Gerry Francis scores twice as Dave Sexton's Queens Park Rangers thrash Everton 5-0 at Loftus Road ▪ 22-year-old Paul Mariner scores twice as Plymouth Argyle beat Oxford Utd 2-1 in Division Two ▪ 19-year-old Laurie Cunningham scores a goal for Orient in a 1-1 draw against Fulham ▪ *Are You Being Served Sir?* ("... I'm Humphries and I'm free!") by 40-year-old John Inman enters the pop chart at number forty-four ▪ "I'm gonna buy a paper doll that I can call my own" - *Paper Doll* by 45-year-old Windsor Davies and 42-year-old Don Estelle is new at number forty-seven ▪ Actot Graham Haberfield (Jerry Booth in ITV's *Coronation Street*) dies of a heart attack, aged 33 ▪ 23-year-old footballer Willie Young (a central defender) transfers from Aberdeen to Tottenham Hotspur for £176,000 and makes his debut in a 1-1 draw against Leeds Utd in front of 27,372 spectators at Elland Road ▪ 23-year-old goalkeeper John 'Budgie' Burridge transfers from Blackpool to Aston Villa for £100,000 and makes his League debut in a 2-1 victory over Birmingham City in front of 53,782 spectators at Villa Park ▪ 19-year-old Andy Gray transfers from Dundee United to Aston Villa for £110,000 - and scores his first League goal in a 1-1 draw against Tottenham Hotspur ▪ "Like a..." *Rhinestone Cowboy* ("... riding out on a horse in a star spangled rodeo") by 39-year-old Glen Campbell is number four in the pop chart ▪ "So when you're near me, darling can't you hear me..." *S.O.S.* by Abba is number six ▪ "Ground control to Major Tom. Take your protein pills and put your helmet on" - *Space Oddity* by 28-year-old David Bowie climbs to number one ▪ Television viewers tune-in to see wrestlers (and former tag-team partners) 45-year-old Big Daddy and 29-year-old Giant Haystacks face each other in a televised bout on ITV's *World Of Sport* ▪ Over on BBC One, a new series of *The Wombles* begins with Bungo getting stuck up a tree ▪ A new series of *Dad's Army* begins with Captain Mainwaring's platoon being mistaken for Nazis ▪ A new series of *Porridge* also begins with a tin of pineapple chunks being stolen from Fletch (46-year-old Ronnie

Barker). The culprit turns out to be prison warder Mr. Barrowclough (48-year-old Brian Wilde) ▪ BBC One TV programs on a Saturday night include: *The Basil Brush Show* - with Roy North and Basil Brush; *Dr. Who* - starring 41-year-old Tom Baker as the Doctor and 29-year-old Elisabeth Sladen as his assistant, Sarah Jane; *Bruce Forsyth and The Generation Game* - with 47-year-old Bruce and his assistant, Anthea Redfern; *Kojak* - with Telly Savalas; and *Match of the Day* - introduced by 47-year-old Jimmy Hill ▪ Footballers, 27-year-old Steve Heighway, 26-year-old John Toshack and 24-year-old Kevin Keegan score the goals as Bob Paisley's Liverpool beat Tommy 'The Doc' Docherty's newly promoted Manchester Utd 3-1 in front of 49,136 spectators at Anfield. (20-year-old Steve Coppell scores Utd's consolation goal) ▪ *What A Diff'rence A Day Make*s ("… There's a rainbow before me") by 39-year-old Esther Phillips climbs to number six in the pop chart ▪ "And I'm going down to the town tonight to get a new B.I.R.D" - *D.I.V.O.R.C.E* (a comedy song) by 33-year-old Billy Connolly from Glasgow spends a week at number one ▪ Motoring technology moves on apace ▪ 'From inside out, a better car' - British Leyland launches the *Austin Allegro 2*, with more leg room in the rear, colour-matched fascias and a new Hydragas suspension system. The *1750HL* model has a top speed of 94 mph and accelerates from 0-60 mph in 11.1 seconds ▪ The futuristic, wedge shaped *Austin Princess* has two-speed wipers, hazard and seat belt warning lights, state-of-the-art quartz halogen headlamps and a hatchback boot. The *2200HL* has a top speed of 104 mph and accelerates from 0-60 mph in 13.5 seconds ▪ *Imagine* ("… all the people, living for today") by 35-year-old John Lennon climbs to number six in the pop chart ▪ "You've blown it all…" *Sky High* ("… by telling me a lie") by Jigsaw is number nine ▪ Retail prices continue to rise ▪ Families save-up for Christmas ▪ A bottle of *Bells* whisky costs £3.45 ▪ A bottle of *Gordon's* gin is £3.35 ▪ A bottle of *Martell* brandy is £4.99 ▪ A bottle of *Smirnoff* vodka is £3.35 ▪ A bottle of *Harveys Bristol Cream* is £1.70 ▪ A bottle of *Croft Original* is £1.69 ▪ A bottle of *Blue Nun* is £1.65 ▪ The weather turns cold ▪ Children (with woollen gloves sewn onto a length of elastic inside the sleeves of their coats) rush home from school ▪ Mum bakes a *Fray Bentos* pie at teatime ▪ Dad makes a warming mug of *Horlicks* before bed.

Christmas 1975

'Oxford Bags' with three-button high waistbands

Monarch:	Queen Elizabeth II (aged 49)
Prime-minister:	Harold Wilson (aged 59)
Chancellor:	Denis Healey (aged 58)
Home Secretary:	Roy Jenkins (aged 55)
Foreign Secretary:	James Callaghan (aged 63)
Football Manager:	Don Revie (aged 48)
Radio 1 Breakfast DJ:	Noel Edmonds (aged 27)
New car reg. suffix:	'P'

▪ Heavy rain and blustery gales give way to mild and dry weather ▪ 'George Davis is Innocent' - the campaign to free convicted armed robber George Davis gathers momentum ▪ In BBC's sit-com *Porridge*, 'Genial' Harry Grout (played by 52-year-old Peter Vaughan) attempts to rig a boxing match between inmates at Slade Prison - and Fletch (played by 46-year-old Ronnie Barker) is coerced into helping fix the result ▪ "I see a little silhouette of a man. Scaramouche. Scaramouche. Will you do the Fandango? Thunderbolt and lightning, very, very frightening me. Gallileo (Gallileo). Gallileo (Gallileo). Gallileo (Gallileo). Figaro. Magnifico" - *Bohemian Rhapsody* by Queen moves up to number one in the pop chart - and stays there for nine weeks! ▪ "Money, money, money, can make you turn your head, now" - *Money Honey* by The Bay City Rollers reaches number three ▪ *This Old Heart Of Mine* ("... been broke a thousand times") by 30-year-old Rod Stewart peaks at number four ▪ The latest 'Cod Wars' continue in the seas off the coast of Iceland ▪ An Icelandic gun boat opens fire on British trawlers after being rammed and Royal Navy frigates are sent to the area ▪ Back in England - 34-year-old cricketer David Steele is voted BBC's 'Sports Personality of the Year' - after his heroic performance in this year's Ashes series ▪ Dave Sexton's Queens Park Rangers lead the way in football's League Division One after an unbeaten run of eight games ▪ Liverpool, Derby County and Manchester Utd are all close behind ▪ 21-year-old Gordon Hill scores his first goal for Manchester Utd - in a 1-4 away win against Sheffield Utd ▪ 23-year-old aberrant centre-forward Robin Friday scores twice (and team-mate 27-year-old John Murray bags a hat-trick) as Charlie Hurley's promotion chasing Reading thrash Stockport County 5-0 in Division Four ▪ Fashion conscious teenagers

wear flared Oxford 'bags' with side pockets and three-button high waist bands ▪ Collars on shirts measure around five-inches ▪ 'Platforms' on shoes and boots measure around six-inches ▪ 19-year-old Richard Madeley reports the local news for BBC Radio Carlisle ▪ 28-year-old disc jockey Simon Bates sits in for 'Diddy' David Hamilton on Radio One's afternoon show ▪ "Sitting in the sun waiting for a senorita to show" - *Happy To Be On An Island In The Sun* by 29-year-old Demis Roussos climbs from number thirteen to number five in the pop chart ▪ *Love Hurts* ("... Love scars, love wounds and mars") by 31-year-old Jim Capaldi falls from number twelve to number sixteen ▪ Hallmark Records release *The Best of Top of the Pops '75* - a budget priced, cover-version pop compilation LP with an energetic blonde girl on the sleeve ▪ "Oggy! Oggy! Oggy! - *We All Had Doctor's Papers* by 32-year-old Max Boyce is number one in the album chart ▪ "The RAF's knocked two years off your life, now isn't that a sin? There's only one way to get out, and that's to get some in. GET SOME IN!" *Get Some In!* - a new sit-com set in the time of National Service (with 37-year-old Tony Selby and 25-year-old Robert Lindsay) is on ITV ▪ 51-year-old Benny Hill stars in a new edition of *The Benny Hill Show*, with 46-year-old Henry McGee, 53-year-old Bob Todd and 30-year-old Diana Darvey in the supporting cast ▪ 31-year-old Angela Rippon presents BBC One's *Nine O'Clock News* ▪ 39-year-old Donald Nielson (aka the Black Panther) is arrested after a fight with two police officers in Mansfield. A few days later, Nielson is charged with the kidnap and murder of Lesley Whittle ▪ 46-year-old champion motor-racing driver Graham Hill and five others die in a plane crash in Hertfordshire ▪ Four members of an IRA unit take two people hostage and occupy a flat on Balcombe Street in Marylebone. The men give themselves up after six days and are taken into custody ▪ The Ulster Defence Association claims responsibility for a bomb which explodes injuring five people at a pub on the Kilburn High Road in London ▪ The weather turns wintery with freezing rain falling across the Midlands and the North ▪ *All Around My Hat* ("... I will wear the green willow, and all around my hat for a twelve month and a day") by Steeleye Span is number five in the pop chart ▪ *Show Me You're A Woman* ("... and I'll show you that I'm a man") by Mud is number eight ▪ "You're gonna need a bigger boat" - *Jaws*, starring 43-year-old Roy Scheider, 28-year-old

Richard Dreyfuss and 48-year-old Robert Shaw, is a huge hit at cinemas ▪ 'The Carry On team: Looking a Site for Sore Thighs!' - *Carry On Behind* (with 49-year-old Kenneth Williams as Professor Crump, 41-year-old Bernard Bresslaw as Arthur Upmore and 57-year-old Kenneth Connor as Major Leap) is also now showing ▪ The number of cars on Britain's roads is increasing ▪ More than 100,000 Ford *Cortinas* have been sold this year. 85,000 *Minis*, 78,000 *Marinas* and 63,000 *Allegros* have also been sold ▪ 129 million tonnes of coal have been mined this year, compared to 110 million in 1974 ▪ TV is the most popular form of entertainment ▪ 7.5 million colour TV licenses have been issued this year, increasing from 5.5 million million in 1974 ▪ Families gather around ITT *CVC9* 26-inch (wood effect) colour television sets ▪ 66-year-old Fanny Cradock shows the nation how to stuff a turkey in *Fanny Cradock Cooks for Christmas* on BBC One ▪ Eleven million people watch the final episode of *Upstairs Downstairs* on ITV on the evening of Sunday the twenty-first of December. Set in the summer of 1930, the Bellamy residence at 165 Eaton Place is put up for sale and Rose (played by 41-year-old Jean Marsh) reminices of times past ▪ "I remember one Christmas morning, a winter's light and a distant choir. And the peal of a bell, and that Christmas tree smell, and their eyes full of tinsel and fire" - *I Believe In Father Christmas* by Greg Lake is number two on the hit parade ▪ The novelty record *Renta Santa* by Chris Hill is number ten ▪ Husbands treat their wives to a bottle of *Tweed* perfume (by Lentheric) for Christmas ▪ Families wrap presents and place them beneath silver/white imitation Christmas trees in the living room ▪ Tinsel and sparkling baubles hang from the branches ▪ Lucky young boys play with their push-along Evel Knievel stunt motorcycles on Christmas morning ▪ A *Kasuga* tape-recorder with microphone is £14.95 from *Argos* ▪ A Mighty *Tonka* Dump Truck is £8.45 ▪ The *Play-Doh 'Fun Factory'* set from Palitoy is 99p ▪ BBC One broadcasts *The Wizard of Oz* (starring Judy Garland) and the TV premiere of *Butch Cassidy and the Sundance Kid* (starring Paul Newman and Robert Redford) ▪ Frank Spencer learns to drive in the Christmas special of *Some Mothers Do 'Ave 'Em* ▪ Captain Mainwaring's drunken brother, Barry, turns up in *Dad's Army* on Boxing Day. 60-year-old Arthur Lowe plays both parts ▪ "In the Blue Ridge Mountains of Virginia, on..." *The Trail Of The Lonesome Pine* by Holly-

wood comedy icons Laurel and Hardy with the Avalon Boys climbs to number two in the pop chart ▪ *Let's Twist Again / The Twist* by 34-year-old Chubby Checker is number five ▪ "Don't let me hear you say life's taking you nowhere, Angel" - *Golden Years* by 28-year-old David Bowie is number eight ▪ 58-year-old Googie Withers makes her final appearance as the prison governor in *Within These Walls* ▪ 'Adventure in all its glory!' - 42-year-old Michael Caine and 45-year-old Sean Connery star at cinemas in *The Man Who Would Be King* ▪ Footballers, John Toshack and Phil Neal score the goals as Bob Paisley's Liverpool move to the top of Division One, by beating Dave Sexton's Queens Park Rangers 2-0 in front of 39,182 at Anfield ▪ Bob Latchford scores for Billy Bingham's Everton and Lou Macari scores for Tommy 'The Doc' Docherty's Manchester Utd in a 1-1 draw in front of 41,732 at Goodison Park ▪ 22-year-old Ronnie Moore scores four goals as Tranmere Rovers thrash Stockport County 5-0 in Division Four ▪ 47-year-old comedian Bob Monkhouse hosts the game show *Celebrity Squares* on TV. Charlie Drake, Des O'Connor, Noele Gordon, John Inman, Pat Coombs, Diana Dors, Alfred Marks, Arthur Mullard, Keith Harris and Cuddles the Monkey are the guest stars ▪ *Bohemian Rhapsody* by Queen (with 24-year-old John Deacon, 26-year-old Roger Taylor, 28-year-old Brian May and 29-year-old Freddie Mercury) remains at number one in the pop chart ▪ *It's Gonna Be A Cold Cold Christmas* ("... without you") by 24-year-old Dana reaches number four ▪ The *Top of the Pops* 'Annual 1976' is available in shops. Radio One DJs: 32-year-old Tony Blackburn, 27-year-old Noel Edmonds and 49-year-old Jimmy Savile OBE are pictured on the front cover ▪ *Can I Take You Home Little Girl* by The Drifters reaches number ten in the pop chart ▪ *Na Na Is The Saddest Word* by The Stylistics is number five ▪ 43-year-old Brian Walden presents *Weekend World* on ITV ▪ The progressive policies of Labour's 55-year-old Home Secretary Roy Jenkins deliver two significant pieces of legislation: The Sex Discrimination Act and the Equal Pay Act become law ▪ Inflation remains high - it's currently standing at 25%! ▪ A pint of milk has gone up from 6p to 8½p ▪ A loaf of bread has risen from 16p to 17p ▪ A bottle of *Warninks* advocaat has risen from £2.02 to £2.27 ▪ A pint of *Carlsberg* in the Red Lion now costs 23p ▪ A pint of Watney's *Special Bitter* is 20p ▪ A packet of twenty cigarettes is 42p.

New Year 1976

Concorde goes supersonic

Monarch:	Queen Elizabeth II (aged 49)
Prime-minister:	Harold Wilson (aged 59)
Chancellor:	Denis Healey (aged 58)
Home Secretary:	Roy Jenkins (aged 55)
Foreign Secretary:	James Callaghan (aged 63)
Football Manager:	Don Revie (aged 48)
Radio 1 Breakfast DJ:	Noel Edmonds (aged 27)
New car reg. suffix:	'P'

▪ The unemployment figure is high and rising - currently standing at 1,430,369 ▪ 62-year-old Michael Foot MP (Employment Minister in Harold Wilson's Labour government) speaks in the House of Commons and warns that "there is likely to be some further rise in the next few months." ▪ This is the worst rate of unemployment since the 1930s ▪ 50-year-old Leader of the Opposition Margaret Thatcher says, "The Labour Party has become the natural party of unemployment" ▪ "Who'll have a fish-ee, on a little dish-ee" - the nation is gripped on Thursday evenings by new TV drama *When The Boat Comes In.* 50-year-old James Garbutt (as Bill Seaton), 34-year-old Susan Jameson (as Jessie Seaton) and 40-year-old James Bolam (as Jack Ford) are the stars ▪ 44-year-old Jimmy Ellis plays Inspector Lynch in a new series of *Z Cars* - shown at 7.20 p.m. on Monday evenings (straight after *Ask The Family*) ▪ Lyn Marshall presents *Wake Up To Yoga* on Sunday mornings on ITV - and people learn how to do the 'bridge' and the 'downward dog' ▪ The comedy song *King Of The Cops* by 25-year-old impressionist Billy Howard is number six in the pop chart ▪ A re-issue of *Itchycoo Park* by The Small Faces is number nine ▪ Children devour *Fizzy Cola* flavoured *Spangles* ▪ 52-year-old Richard 'Dicky' Attenborough becomes a Sir in the New Year's Honours list ▪ Hurricane force winds cause widespread damage to trees and power lines ▪ The economic slump continues ▪ Times are hard for many communities across Britain ▪ A shortage of potatoes sees prices soar in shops. Five pounds of King Edwards now cost four times more than they did twelve months ago ▪ The latest 'Cod Wars' continue in the seas off the coast of Iceland, with British trawlers still operating in the disputed waters. Royal Navy frigate HMS

Andromeda collides with an Icelandic patrol ship - and both captains blame the other. Iceland cuts off diplomatic relations with Britain ▪ Back in England - there's growing speculation that Liberal party leader Jeremy Thorpe MP was involved in a case of attempted murder. Rumours imply Thorpe was acting to silence a former lover who'd threatened to expose their homosexual love affair ▪ After spending nine weeks at number one in the pop chart, *Bohemian Rhapsody* by Queen moves down to number three ▪ "Ooooh..." *Love To Love You Baby* by 27-year-old Donna Summer is number four ▪ *No Regrets* ("... No tears goodbye. I don't want you back, we'd only cry-ie, again. Say goodby, again") by The Walker Brothers (with, lead singer, 32-year-old John Walker) is number seven ▪ "Magic, our Morris!" - *Oh No, It's Selwyn Frogitt* is on ITV, with 47-year-old Bill Maynard in the title role ▪ "Your letter was only the start of it. One letter and now you're a part of it. Now you've done it, Jim has fixed it for you, and you, and you" - a second series of *Jim'll Fix It* (hosted by 49-year-old Jimmy Savile OBE) keeps the kids entertained on BBC One ▪ "I've been cheated by you since I don't know when. So, I made up my mind it must come to an end. Look at me now. Will I ever learn?" - *Mamma Mia* by Abba is number one in the pop chart ▪ "I've got the money, I've got the place. You've got the figure, you've got the face. Let's get together, the two of us over a..." *Glass Of Champagne* by Sailor peaks at number two ▪ *In Dulce Jubilo / On Horseback* by 22-year-old Mike Oldfield is number four ▪ A cold front moves in from the North, bringing sleet and snow ▪ Roads become blocked and many motorists are forced to abandon their cars ▪ A Hillman *Hunter* ('N' reg, in Summer Yellow) is stranded on the A6 near New Mills ▪ A Ford *Consul* ('L' reg, in Daytona Yellow) is stuck on the B6265 at Grassington ▪ Jack Charlton's Middlesbrough football team draws 3-3 against Gordon Lee's Newcastle Utd - playing with an orange ball on a snow covered pitch at Ayresome Park ▪ 26-year-old John Toshack bags a hat-trick (and 24-year-old Kevin Keegan scores once) as Liverpool thrash West Ham Utd 0-4 at Upton Park ▪ "Gimme your love, gimme it all. Gimmie in the kitchen, gimmie in the hall" - *Art For Art's Sake* by 10cc is number five in the weekly pop chart ▪ *Wide Eyed And Legless* ("... I've gone and done it again") by 27-year-old Andy Fairweather-Low is number six ▪ In ITV's popular soap-opera *Coronation Street*,

'The Rovers Return' land-lady Annie Walker (played by 77-year-old Doris Speed) is embarrassed when it comes to light she doesn't possess a TV license ▪ "Come along, Candice Marie / Slow down, Keith" - 28-year-old Alison Steadman is Candice Marie and 29-year-old Roger Sloman is Keith in Mike Leigh's *Nuts In May* - a dark comedy, broadcast as part of BBC's *Play for Today* series ▪ Veteran crime-writer Dame Agatha Christie dies aged 85 in Wallingford ▪ A 42-year-old women is stabbed to death in Leeds ▪ IRA terrorist cells are planning more atrocities in London. Twelve small devices explode in the West End injuring one person ▪ Queen Elizabeth II opens the impressive new National Exhibition Centre near Birmingham ▪ The 49-year-old monarch is greated by cheering crowds ▪ 59-year-old Fred Rought from Solihull begins work as a doorman at the nearby Metropole Hotel, after being made redundant from Rover ▪ 55-year-old Jim Ashford from Acocks Green begins work as a hotel porter, after being made redundant from the BSA ▪ 20-year-old Nottingham Forest footballer Tony Woodcock is loaned out to Graham Taylor's Fourth Division Lincoln City and scores a goal in a 6-0 victory over Southport ▪ 35-year-old Jimmy Greaves plays for non-league Brentwood and fights alcoholism ▪ Non league Wimbledon draw 0-0 against Yeovil Town at Plough Lane ▪ 11-year-old Vinnie Jones from Watford fights boys on the playground at school ▪ 26-year-old ice-skater John Curry wins a gold medal at the Winter Olympics in Innsbruck ▪ "I'm just a…" *Love Machine* ("… and I won't work for nobody but you") by The Miracles is number three on the hit parade ▪ *We Do It* ("… every night, every day, in any possible way, but we do it") by R & J Stone is number five ▪ 18-year-old Denise Perry (36D) from Pinner makes her first appearance on page three of *The Sun* ▪ Supersonic airplane Concorde takes off on its first commercial flight - the *British Airways* jet flies from Heathrow to Bahrain with a cruising speed of 1,350 mph ▪ Wealthy business executives buy 'up-market' sports cars ▪ The new Porsche *911 Turbo* costs £6,930, has a top speed of 153 mph and accelerates from 0-60 mph in just 6.1 seconds ▪ Family men buy sensible cars ▪ The latest Vauxhall *Viva E* 4-door saloon costs £1,646.19 and comes with front disc brakes, reclining front seats, illuminated heater control and 2-speed wipers ▪ Young men hope to impress the girls ▪ A second hand (beige) Ford *Escort 1100 Deluxe*, 1969, taxed and

tested, with recent new clutch and engine overhaul is advertised in the *Nelson Leader* newspaper for £375 ▪ It's the end of an era: The last ever Hillman *Imp* motorcar rolls off the production line at Linwood in Scotland ▪ People enjoy an evening in front of the TV ▪ Light entertainment is thriving ▪ 31-year-old ventriloquist Roger De Courcey and his puppet Nookie the Bear are making names for themselves on ITV's talent show *New Faces* ▪ A crop of young footballers are making names for themselves on the back pages of the daily newspapers ▪ 21-year-old Birmingham City striker Trevor Francis scores his eleventh goal of the season in a 2-1 defeat against high-flying Queens Park Rangers ▪ 19-year-old 'super sub' David Fairclough comes on (for Steve Heighway) and scores twice as Liverpool beat Burnley 2-0. Liverpool are now fourth in Division One - two points behind leaders Queens Park Rangers and one point behind Manchester Utd and Derby County ▪ 18-year-old Glenn Hoddle makes his debut for Tottenham Hotspur and scores the winning goal for Terry Neill's team in a 1-2 away win at Stoke City ▪ 23-year-old Martin O'Neill scores twice as Brian Clough's Nottingham Forest beat Jimmy Frizzell's Oldham Athletic 4-3 in Division Two ▪ 18-year-old Peter Barnes and 26-year-old Dennis Tueart score the goals as Tony Book's Manchester City beat Gordon Lee's Newcastle Utd 2-1 in the League Cup final at Wembley - and the players receive tankards as a memento of the occasion ▪ "I'll dedicate to you, all my love my whole life through. I'll love you..." *Forever And Ever* by Slik (a pop group from Glasgow with, lead singer, 22-year-old Midge Ure) is number one on the hit parade ▪ "Aye 'n' I'll feel safer if we change the subject and call it..." *Dat* by 25-year-old Pluto Shervington is number six ▪ The nation's finances are in a poor state ▪ Labour prime-minister Harold Wilson and Chancellor of the Exchequer Denis Healey stick to their socialist ideals, despite growing criticism over the high levels of unemployment, the faltering economy and the low value of sterling - £1 is now worth just $2.08 ▪ Union leaders and left-wing MPs such as 54-year-old Eric Heffer and 44-year-old Dennis Skinner press for stricter import controls to halt the decline in British industry ▪ 50-year-old Leader of the Opposition Margaret Thatcher makes a speech warning against the threats of communism - and a Russian newspaper describes her as the 'Iron Lady' ▪ "E..." *Evil Woman* by the Electric Light Orchestra is number ten on the

hit parade ▪ "Oh, what a night. Late December back in '63. What a very special time for me, as I remember, what a night" - *December '63 (Oh What A Night)* by The Four Seasons is new at number one ▪ Middle-aged people visit record shops and make discreet purchases ▪ *Rodrigo's Guitar Concerto De Aranjuez (Theme From 2nd Movement)* by Manuel and his Music of the Mountains climbs up the pop chart to number three ▪ Crowds flock to the cinema to see 38-year-old Jack Nicholson (as Randle P. McMurphy) and 41-year-old Louise Fletcher (as Nurse Ratched) in the hit movie *One Flew Over the Cuckoo's Nest* ▪ 26-year-old Susan Penhaligon, 29-year-old Stephanie Beacham and 60-year-old Anthony Sharp star in *House of Mortal Sin* - an 'X' rated horror movie with a religious theme ▪ 65-year-old Arthur Mullard and 52-year-old Queenie Watts star in *Yus My Dear* on ITV ▪ 33-year-old Bob Hoskins and 31-year-old Martin Shaw feature in *On The Move* on BBC One ▪ 26-year-old footballer Malcolm 'Supermac' MacDonald scores the winning goal as Newcastle Utd beat Derby County 4-3 in front of 44,488 spectators at St. James' Park ▪ 26-year-old John Duncan scores for Tottenham Hotspur and 27-year-old Trevor Brooking scores for West Ham Utd in a 1-1 draw in front of 32,832 spectators at White Hart Lane ▪ 25-year-old Asa Hartford, 26-year-old Dennis Tueart and 26-year-old Joe Royle score the goals as Manchester City beat Everton 3-0 in front of 33,148 spectators at Maine Road ▪ Artist (and Manchester City supporter) L. S. Lowry dies aged 88 in Glossop ▪ *It Should Have Been Me* ("... You know that it should have been me!") by 33-year-old Yvonne Fair climbs to number five in the pop chart ▪ "Oh, I love to love, but my baby just loves to dance" - *I Love To Love (But My Baby Loves To Dance)* by 22-year-old Tina Charles moves up to number two ▪ *I Love Music* ("... sweet, sweet music") by The O'Jays peaks at number thirteen ▪ 10cc (31-year-old Eric Stewart, 29-year-old Graham Gouldman, 30-year-old Kevin Godley and 28-year-old Lol Creme) feature on the front cover of the latest *New Musical Express* ▪ Children sit at home, watching TV ▪ 14-year-old Nicholas Lyndhurst stars in BBC One's *The Prince and the Pauper* on Sunday evenings ▪ "Sorry, we cannot return your paintings" - Pat Keysell, Sylveste McCoy and 50-year-old Tony Hart present *Vision On* on Tuesday evenings ▪ *Rise & Shine* - a new cereal from Kellogg's 'Gets you going in the morning'.

Spring 1976

Southampton shock 'The Doc' at Wembley

Monarch:	Queen Elizabeth II (aged 50)
Prime-minister:	James Callaghan (aged 64)
Chancellor:	Denis Healey (aged 58)
Home Secretary:	Roy Jenkins (aged 55)
Foreign Secretary:	Anthony Crossland (aged 57)
Football Manager:	Don Revie (aged 48)
Radio 1 Breakfast DJ:	Noel Edmonds (aged 27)
New car reg. suffix:	'P'

▪ The value of the pound falls below two-dollars for the first time - it's now worth just $1.90 ▪ Out of the blue, 60-year-old Labour prime-minister Harold Wilson resigns and 64-year-old Jim Callaghan takes over at Number 10 ▪ "Stop! I'm spinnin' like a top. We'll dance until we drop, but if I have my way-ah-ayy. Sundown, instead of goin' downtown, we'll stay at home and get down to what I'm tryin' to say-ayy" - *I Love To Love (But My Baby Loves To Dance)* by 22-year-old Tina Charles moves up to number one on the hit parade ▪ "Baby..." *Love Really Hurts Without You* by 26-year-old Billy Ocean climbs to number two ▪ "But these..." *Miss You Nights* ("... are the longest") by 35-year-old Cliff Richard stalls at number fifteen ▪ Jim Callaghan's new Labour Cabinet includes: 62-year-old Michael Foot, (Commons Leader), 57-year-old Anthony Crossland (Foreign Secretary), 51-year-old Peter Shore (Environment Secretary), 47-year-old Albert Booth (Employment Secretary), 54-year-old Edmund Dell (Trade Secretary), 53-year-old David Ennals (Social Services Secretary), 53-year-old Roy Jenkins (Home Secretary), 58-year-old Denis Healey (Chancellor of the Exchequer), 52-year-old Roy Mason (Defence Secretary), 57-year-old Fred Mulley (Education Secretary) and 45-year-old Shirley Williams (as Paymaster General). 64-year-old Barbara Castle moves to the back benches ▪ 47-year-old Jeremy Thorpe is forced to resign as leader of the Liberal party - amidst continuing allegations of his involvement in a plot to commit murder. 62-year-old former leader Jo Grimond takes over from Thorpe on a temporary basis ▪ 24-year-old footballer Gerry Francis is on the score-sheet as Dave Sexton's Queens Park Rangers thrash Coventry

City 4-1 at Loftus Road to keep the pressure on Bob Paisley's Liverpool at the top of Division One ▪ *You Don't Have To Say You Love Me* ("... just be close at hand") by Guys 'n' Dolls is number five in the pop chart ▪ *You See The Trouble With Me* ("... I can't do nothin' without my baby") by 31-year-old Barry White climbs to number two ▪ 38-year-old Jill Gascoine appears in the latest series of *The Onedin Line* on BBC One ▪ 26-year-old Charlotte Cornwell, 29-year-old Julie Covington and 28-year-old Rula Lenska star in *Rock Follies* on ITV ▪ 26-year-old Paula Wilcox, 25-year-old Sally Thomsett and 31-year-old Richard O'Sullivan star in the sixth (and final) series of popular sit-com *Man About the House* on ITV ▪ Eamonn Andrews surprises 80-year-old Arnold Ridley (who plays the role of Private Godfrey in *Dad's Army*) on *This is Your Life* ▪ 30-year-old Radio One DJ Dave Lee Travis takes his turn to introduce *Top of the Pops* on Thursday evenings ▪ *People Like You And People Like Me* ("... need somebody to lean on if we want to stay free") by The Glitter Band is number five in the chart ▪ *I Wanna Stay With You* ("... for the rest of my life") by Gallagher and Lyle is number six ▪ *Funky Weekend* by The Stylistics is number ten ▪ 'Emotion Blazes Across the Big Screen as Bob and Terry Knock Down the Frontiers of Human Knowledge and Newcastle Ale' - 40-year-old James Bolam and 38-year-old Rodney Bewes star at cinemas in *The Likely Lads* - a feature length film spin-off from the popular TV show ▪ 'Love is the Greatest Adventure of All' - 45-year-old Sean Connery (Robin Hood) and 46-year-old Audrey Hepburn (Lady Marian) star in *Robin and Marian*, with 46-year-old Ronnie Barker as Friar Tuck ▪ Brotherhood of Man win the Eurovision song contest in the Netherlands singing *Kisses For Me* ("... bye-bye, baby. Bye-bye") ▪ 45-year-old Princess Margaret and 46-year-old Lord Snowdon split up after fifteen years of marriage ▪ Tensions are growing between celebrity couple 33-year-old Radio One DJ Tony Blackburn and 27-year-old actress Tessa Wyatt, who've been married for four years ▪ "Yes I can't live without the..." *Rain* by Status Quo peaks at number seven in the pop chart ▪ School children return home each day to watch *Play School*, *Crystal Tipps*, *Jackanory*, *Goober and the Ghost Chasers*, *John Craven's Newsround*, *Vision On* and *Ivor the Engine* - before the news begins on BBC One ▪ An IRA bomber explodes a device

at West Ham Railway Station - then shoots and kills a train driver. Twelve days later - a bomb is detonated at the Ideal Home Exhibition at Olympia - killing one person and injuring more than eighty ▪ Elsewhere in the country - life continues as normal ▪ Central London has its warmest Easter for twenty-four years ▪ 20-year-old Stephen Simmons is tried and convicted of robbery after being 'fitted-up' by bent copper DS Derek Ridgewell ▪ 11-year-old catholic schoolboy Piers Stefan O'Meara (later to be known as Piers Morgan) confesses his sins to a priest in the confessional booth - and storms off in a huff when he's instructed to recite ten Hail Marys as penance ▪ Britain's winning song from Eurovision, *Kisses For Me* by Brotherhood of Man, reaches number one in the pop chart - and stays there for six weeks! ▪ "Ah, breaker one-nine. This here's the Rubber Duck. You gotta copy on me?" - *Convoy* by 47-year-old CW McCall from Iowa reaches number two ▪ 27-year-old disc jockey Les Ross joins BRMB radio station in Birmingham ▪ The town centre of Rugeley in Staffordshire is pedestrianised ▪ A six-wheeled Tyrrell racing car driven by Jody Scheckter makes its Formula One debut at the Spanish Grand Prix. The race is won by Britain's James Hunt in a conventional four-wheeled McLaren ▪ 'Tomorrow. Today. The new Rover 3500' - the stunning Rover *SD1* is launched at the Geneva Motor Show. The stylish and luxurious car will go on sale shortly in the UK, with a base level price of £4,750 for a car with a manual gearbox. A Rover *3500* with automatic transmission will cost £4,900 ▪ The new wedge-shaped, wind cheating Triumph *TR7* two-seater sports car will also be available in Britain from the nineteenth of May after a successful launch in the United States. The new model will cost £3,146, comes with pop-up headlights, has a top speed of 109 mph and accelerates from 0-60 mph in 9.8 seconds ▪ The new management team at British Leyland is trying desperately to keep pace with rival European and Japanese car manufacturers ▪ The latest *Dolomite Sprint* now has headrests, radio and a laminated wind-screen as standard ▪ "Just like a rollin' stone, I'm outside lookin' in" - *I'm Mandy Fly Me* by 10cc is number six in the pop chart ▪ "Keep on givin' it to me" - *Don't Stop It Now* by Hot Chocolate is number eleven ▪ *Royal Frolic* (ridden by 23-year-old jockey John Burke) wins the Gold Cup at Cheltenham ▪ 29-year-old footballer Chris Nicholl scores all four goals (including two own goals) as his team, Aston Villa, draws 2-2

with Leicester City in Division One ▪ 26-year-old Stuart Pearson scores twice for Manchester Utd in a 3-4 victory over Gordon Lee's Newcastle Utd ▪ 19-year-old 'super sub' David Fairclough comes on (for John Toshack) and scores a brilliant individual goal in the 87th minute as Liverpool beat Everton 1-0 at Anfield ▪ 23-year-old aberrant centre-forward Robin Friday scores a fantastic thirty-yard volley, after first controlling the ball on his chest, as promotion chasing Reading thrash Tranmere Rovers 5-0 in Division Four ▪ "He's a…" *Pinball Wizard* ("… there has got to be a twist") by 29-year-old Elton John is number seven in the pop chart ▪ *Take It To The Limit* by The Eagles is number twelve ▪ Families sit together and watch TV ▪ Elsie Howard (formerly Elsie Tanner) returns to *Coronation Street* after splitting up with her husband ▪ Fred Gee (played by 46-year-old Fred Feast) is employed as the new 'pot man' at 'The Rovers Return' pub ▪ Minnie Caldwell (played by 79-year-old Margot Bryant) leaves Weatherfield to live in Whaley Bridge ▪ "Goodnight, all" - the final episode of *Dixon of Dock Green* is broadcast on BBC One, with 80-year-old Jack Warner in the title role ▪ Pan's People (Mary Corpe, Cherry Gillespie, Sue Menhenick, Lee Ward and 29-year-old Ruth Pearson) appear on *Top of the Pops* for the last time ▪ "Shy girl, sexy girl. They all like that fancy world" - *Girls Girls Girls* by Sailor is number seven in the pop chart ▪ *S-S-S-Single Bed* ("… S-Single bed, there ain't no room for your sweet head") by Fox (with, lead singer, 31-year-old Susan Traynor - aka Noosha Fox) is number four ▪ The ever popular 62-year-old comedy actor Sid 'Ha-ak-ak' James suffers a heart attack and dies while performing on stage in Sunderland ▪ 43-year-old Ray 'Dracula' Reardon beats 27-year-old Alex 'Hurricane' Higgins in the world snooker final at Middlesbrough ▪ *Rag Trade* (ridden by 23-year-old jockey John Burke) wins the Grand National at Aintree. *Red Rum* (ridden by 30-year-old Tommy Stack) is second ▪ 28-year-old actor Oliver Tobias is on the front cover of the latest *TV Times* magazine ▪ 41-year-old Norman Beaton, 48-year-old Isabelle Lucas and 17-year-old Lenny Henry star in *The Fosters* - a new ITV sitcom set on a council estate in South London ▪ "I was walking through the jungle just the other night. Ah, well I heard a big a rumble and I thought it was a fight" - *Jungle Rock* by 52-year-old Hank Mizell is number three in the pop chart ▪ "Can you hear the drums, Fernando? I remember long ago

another starry night like this" - *Fernando* by Abba (with 26-year-old blonde Agnetha Faltskog and 30-year-old brunette Anni-Frid Lyngstad) is number one ▪ The sun shines ▪ Temperatures rise ▪ 39-year-old Lawrie McMenemy's Second Division Southampton football team causes a major shock in the FA Cup final - by beating Tommy 'The Doc' Docherty's Manchester Utd 1-0. 25-year-old Bobby Stokes scores the winning goal in the eighty-third minute. 32-year-old Peter Rodrigues (captain of 'The Saints') climbs the Wembley steps and lifts the famous silver trophy. A ticket for the standing enclosure at the Empire Stadium costs £2.50 ▪ "Comes up peanuts, slice after slice" - *Marathon* chocolate bars are advertised on ITV ▪ 31-year-old Angela Rippon reads the news on BBC One ▪ 50-year-old Leader of the Opposition Margaret Thatcher visits Coventry to support the local Conservative candidate at a by-election ▪ "She's just a devil woman, with evil on her mind. Beware the devil women, she's gonna get you" - *Devil Woman* by Cliff Richard is number nine in the pop chart ▪ "Thus began the saga on the M1 motorway, of the biggest bloomin' convoy outside the USA" - *Convoy GB* by Laurie Lingo and the Dipsticks is number four ▪ *Shout at the Devil* (with 52-year-old Lee Marvin and 48-year-old Roger Moore) is now showing at cinemas ▪ 35-year-old John Alderton, 45-year-old Colin Blakely and 32-year-old Lisa Harrow star in *It Shouldn't Happen to a Vet* - a film based on the books by 47-year-old James Herriot ▪ The 1975/76 football season is coming to an end ▪ 19-year-old Liverpool 'super sub' David Fairclough comes on (for Jimmy Case) and scores a late goal as 'The Reds' beat Stoke City 5-3. Bob Paisley's team also gains victories over Manchester City (3-0) and Wolverhampton Wanderers (3-1) to become the new champions of Division One. 28-year-old goalkeeper Ray Clemence and 25-year-old full-back Phil Neal have played in every match. 27-year-old John Toshack and 25-year-old Kevin Keegan have scored twenty-eight goals between them. Tommy Smith, Ian Callaghan, Joey Jones, Emlyn Hughes, Phil Thompson, Brian Hall, Peter Cormack, Ray Kennedy, Jimmy Case, Steve Heighway and 'super sub' David Fairclough have also been in fine form ▪ Dave Sexton's Queens Park Rangers (with Phil Parkes, Dave Clement, Ian Gillard, Frank McLintock, Dave Webb, Gerry Francis, John Hollins, Mick Leach, Don Masson, Don Givens, Dave Thomas and 27-year-old Stan Bowles) are runners-up ▪ Tommy

'The Doc' Docherty's Manchester Utd (with Alex Stepney, Alex Forsyth, Stewart Houston, Gerry Daly, Brian Greenhoff, Martin Buchan, Steve Coppell, Sammy McIlroy, Stuart Pearson, Lou Macari and 22-year-old Gordon Hill) are third ▪ Willie Bell's Birmingham City avoid relegation with a 3-1 victory over Tottenham Hotspur ▪ Wolverhampton Wanderers are relegated and sack manager Bill McGarry - 43-year-old Sammy Chung takes over at the Molineux ▪ Bob Stokoe's Sunderland, Alan Dicks' Bristol City and Johnny Giles' West Bromwich Albion all gain promotion from Division Two ▪ 39-year-old John Sillett's Hereford Utd are champions of Division Three ▪ 31-year-old Graham Taylor's Lincoln City are champions of Division Four ▪ 57-year-old Bertie Mee steps down as manager of Arsenal after ten years in charge at Highbury ▪ "For the nine months I carried you, growing inside me..." *No Charge* by JJ Barrie climbs to number one in the pop chart ▪ "Some people want to fill the world with..." *Silly Love Songs* ("... and what's wrong with that, I'd like to know, 'cause here I go, again") by Wings (with, lead singer, 33-year-old Paul McCartney) reaches number two ▪ *Music* ("... was my first love and it will be my last") by 27-year-old John Miles peaks at number three ▪ Liverpool beat Club Bruges 4-3 on aggregate (over two legs) to win the UEFA Cup, with 25-year-old Kevin Keegan (2), 21-year-old Jimmy Case and 24-year-old Ray Kennedy scoring the goals ▪ 50-year-old Richard Baker reads the news on BBC One ▪ A 20-year-old woman is injured in a hammer attack in Leeds ▪ 55-year-old Home Secretary Roy Jenkins authorises the release of George Davis from prison - saying last year's conviction for armed robbery is, "unsafe." ▪ The latest 'Cod Wars' continue in the seas off the coast of Iceland. HMS *Falmouth* rams into an Icelandic patrol ship to prevent it from cutting the fishing lines of a British trawler ▪ Back in England - it's warm and sunny in late May with a long summer heatwave being forecast ▪ 27-year-old England goalkeeper Ray Clemence makes a howler at Hampden Park and allows Kenny Dalglish to score an easy winning goal for Scotland in a 2-1 victory. England's full line-up for the match is: Clemence, Todd, Mills, Thompson, McFarland, Kennedy, Keegan, G Francis, Pearson, Channon, Taylor and substitutes, Doyle and Cherry ▪ 29-year-old Simon Bates is a popular new DJ on BBC Radio One ▪ "Just..." *Let Your Love Flow* ("... like a mountain stream") by The Bel-

lamy Brothers climbs to number seven in the pop chart ▪ *More, More, More* ("… how d'ya like it? How d'ya like it?) by The Andrea True Connection is number five ▪ "Come closer, come closer, my darling, come closer" - *My Resistance Is Low* by 32-year-old Robin Sarstedt is number three ▪ Our Kid, a pop group from Liverpool (comprising of Brian Farrell, Terry McCrieth, Terry Baccino and 12-year-old Kevin Rowan), wins an edition of *New Faces* on ITV ▪ 'The most devastating detective story of this century' - 38-year-old Dustin Hoffman and 39-year-old Robert Redford star at cinemas in *All the President's Men* ▪ 29-year-old David Bowie stars in *The Man Who Fell to Earth* ▪ Family men in well-paid jobs dream of owning a sporty motorcar ▪ A Ford *Escort 1600 Sport* costs £2,099 and has a top speed of 101 mph ▪ A Fiat *131 1600S* costs £2,198 and has a top speed of 99 mph ▪ A Vauxhall *Magnum 1800* costs £2,204 and has a top speed of 96 mph ▪ A Morris *Marina 1.8 S* costs £2,204 and has a top speed of 100 mph ▪ Schoolboys speed down steep hills on Dawes *Galaxy* racing bicycles, and return home to watch *Top of the Pops* ▪ "Oh, how I wish I was lying in the…" *Arms Of Mary* by The Sutherland Brothers and Quiver is number five in the pop chart ▪ "Do you..." *Love Me Like I Love You* (" ... baby") by The Bay City Rollers is number four ▪ Britain's economy continues to struggle ▪ The rate of inflation has fallen slightly but still remains relatively high, at 16% ▪ New prime-minister Jim Callaghan addresses a union rally in Bournemouth and says, "We are still nowhere near where the French or Germans are, or the United States or the Japanese Their inflation rate is 6, 7, 8%. If you can grin and bear it for another twelve months, by the end of 1977 the inflation rate in this country will be where our major competitors' is now" ▪ Mr. Callaghan goes on to say that getting unemployment down is "a more difficult task" ▪ 25-year-old Barry Sheene wins the opening three Grand Prix races in France, Austria and Italy in the 500cc world motorcycle championship ▪ Adolescent boys annoy their neighbours by revving their mopeds, loud ▪ A Honda *Super Sports 50* produces maximum power at 9000 rpm and costs £210 ▪ A Yamaha *FS-1 E* (aka 'Fizzy') produces maximum power at 7000 rpm and costs £220 ▪ A Puch *Grand Prix* produces maximum power at 7400 rpm and costs £249 ▪ A public information film aimed at car drivers says, "Think Once! Think Twice! Think Bike!"

Summer 1976

Long hot sunny days

Monarch:	Queen Elizabeth II (aged 50)
Prime-minister:	James Callaghan (aged 64)
Chancellor:	Denis Healey (aged 59)
Home Secretary:	Roy Jenkins (aged 55)
Foreign Secretary:	Anthony Crossland (aged 58)
Football Manager:	Don Revie (aged 49)
Radio 1 Breakfast DJ:	Noel Edmonds (aged 27)
New car reg. suffix:	'R'

▪ A scorchingly hot summer leads to a nationwide drought ▪ Frozen orange *Jubblys* are in demand ▪ Swarms of ladybirds annoy holiday-makers ▪ Raleigh launches an exciting new range of children's bicycles ▪ The *Grifter* (designed for 8-14 year-olds) has a low-slung frameset, *Sturmey-Archer* 3-speed twist-grip control gears, 20-inch Super-Grip tyres and new style handle-bars with foam plastic fascia. Recommended retail price for this sensational new bike is £67.95 ▪ The smaller *Strika* (designed for 5-8 year olds) has a rrp of £45.95 ▪ The even smaller *Boxer* (designed for 4-7 year olds) has a rrp of £42.95 ▪ "Silver star, there you are…" *Silver Star* by The Four Seasons is number three in the pop chart ▪ "Wise men say, 'only fools rush in', but I…" *Can't Help Falling In Love* ("… with you") by The Stylistics is number four ▪ 'Good, rich and thick. A milk-chocolate brick" - Rowntree's *Yorkie* chocolate bar is new ▪ Children enjoy their six-week holiday from school - playing out all day, only returning home occasionally to gulp down orange squash ▪ The Handsacre Estate Gang throw stones at the Ford Way Gang in the field beside the brook in Old Road, Armitage near Rugeley ▪ Kids chase *Sunblest* vans down the road, as the baker delivers his bread to local houses ▪ *Belle and Sebastian* is on BBC One television on weekday mornings ▪ *It's A Knockout* (presented by 46-year-old Stuart Hall) is on BBC One on Friday evenings. A team from Newbury wins a closely fought contest with Winchcombe and Cirencester and will now compete in the Jeux Sans Frontieres competition later in the year ▪ All across Britain, kids gather in gardens to play *Swing Ball* - a fantastic new game from Dunlop ▪ Retailing at £8.99, *Swing Ball* sets are in high demand. Everybody wants a go ▪ 27-year-old Radio One DJ Noel

Edmonds takes his turn to introduce *Top of the Pops* on Thursday evenings ▪ "Keep on, keep on walking, don't turn around, 'cos if you do..." *You Just Might See Me Cry* by Our Kid shoots up the chart to number two ▪ "Ooh, daddy you're a..." *Fool To Cry* by The Rolling Stones (with, lead singer, 32-year-old Mick Jagger) is number six ▪ A re-issue of *Leader Of The Pack* by The Shangri-Las reaches number seven ▪ *Dr. Kiss Kiss* by 5000 Volts is number eight ▪ 40-year-old jockey Lester Piggott rides *Empery* to victory in the Epsom Derby ▪ The sun continues to shine ▪ Women wear hotpants and bikini tops ▪ Men wear 'cut-off' denim jeans and T shirts ▪ 'They came in search of Paradise' - *Bounty* chocolate bars are advertised on TV ▪ The Smith family from Chigwell enjoys a holiday at *Butlin's* in Bognor Regis - and Mr. Smith is runner-up in the Knobbly Knees competition ▪ 12-year-old Lena Zavaroni appears on stage at the Winter Gardens in Margate ▪ 'The happy sound of Radio One' - 31-year-old DJ Dave Lee Travis presents the afternoon show on Radio One ▪ "I drove my tractor through your haystack last night. Oooh arr! Oooh arr!" - *Combine Harvester (Brand New Key)* by The Wurzels is top of the pop chart ▪ *The Boys Are Back In Town* by Thin Lizzy is number eight ▪ Seedy cinemas are open in the afternoon ▪ 'His Customers are Always Satisfied' - 28-year-old Barry Stokes stars in *The Ups and Downs of a Handyman* ▪ 'What the butler did ... and did ... and did' - 23-year-old Jack Wild, 44-year-old Diana Dors and 34-year-old Aimi MacDonald star in *Keep It Up Downstairs* ▪ 44-year-old Reginald Bosanquet and 48-year-old Sandy Gall present ITN's *News at Ten* program ▪ An agreement is reached between Iceland and the UK over fishing rights and the latest 'Cod Wars' come to an end. A zone of two-hundred nautical miles from the coastline of Iceland is established, with British trawlers being granted limited rights to fish within the newly defined area ▪ 38-year-old David Steel is the new leader of the Liberal party - replacing interim leader Jo Grimond ▪ *British Airways'* Concorde supersonic jet flies on a new commercial route to the USA - from Heathrow to Washington ▪ The value of the pound tumbles further - it's now worth just $1.70 ▪ Pressure grows on 64-year-old prime-minister Jim Callaghan and 59-year-old Chancellor of the Exchequer Denis Healey ▪ Margaret Thatcher's opposition Conservative Party moves ahead of Labour in the opinion polls ▪ *You To Me Are Everything*

("… the sweetest song that I could sing. Oh, baby. Oh baby") by The Real Thing is new at number one in the pop chart ▪ "Oh…" *Young Hearts Run Free* ("… They'll never be hung up, hung up like my man and me. You and me") by 36-year-old Candi Staton is number two ▪ The summer heat-wave continues ▪ Thermometers record temperatures of 100 degrees Fahrenheit - in the shade! ▪ The hot sunshine is relentless ▪ Calamine Lotion soothes the skin of sunburnt children ▪ Weekly discos, held inside the local village hall are popular. Sweaty dancers 'get down' to the sounds of *Disco Connection* by Isaac Hayes (currently number ten on the hit parade) and *Disco Lady* by Johnnie Taylor (currently number twenty-five) ▪ 29-year-old pop star Elton John is the new football chairman at Fourth Division Watford FC. Elton teams up with 36-year-old manager Mike Keen and the two men begin working on an ambitious plan to get 'The Hornets' into Division One ▪ Footballers, 26-year-old Stuart Pearson, 25-year-old Kevin Keegan and 27-year-old Mick Channon score the goals for Don Revie's England team (Clemence, Todd, Mills, Thompson, Madeley, Cherry, Keegan, Channon, Pearson, Brooking, G Francis) in a 1-4 victory over Finland in Helsinki ▪ 29-year-old Tony Greig is England's cricket captain for the summer Test series against Clive Lloyd's West Indians. Lightning fast bowlers Michael Holding and Andy Roberts rip through the English batting line up - and the West Indies win the series, 3-0, with victories at Old Trafford, Headingley and the Oval ▪ "Stay away from my window. Stay away from my back door too" - *Tonight's The Night* by 31-year-old Rod Stewart reaches number five in the pop chart ▪ "I wear my…" *Heart On My Sleeve* by Gallagher and Lyle peaks at number six ▪ Punk rock is becoming popular with some unruly young people ▪ The Sex Pistols play a gig at the Lesser Free Trade Hall in Manchester. 20-year-old Peter Hook, 20-year-old Bernard Sumner and 17-year-old Steven Patrick Morrissey are amongst the audience - each paying 50p to attend ▪ 'You have been warned. The Omen is here' - *The Omen* (starring 60-year-old Gregory Peck and 40-year-old Lee Remick) is now showing at cinemas ▪ 'Girls drive him wild … and he loves it!' - 25-year-old Robin Askwith stars as Timmy Lea in *Confessions of a Driving Instructor* ▪ 44-year-old Elizabeth Taylor and 50-year-old Richard Burton divorce for a second time - just nine months after re-marrying ▪ "Come on, come on…" *Let's Stick To-*

gether by 30-year-old Bryan Ferry reaches number four in the pop chart ▪ "Jolene, Jolene, Jolene…" *Jolene* ("… I'm beggin' of you, please don't take my man") by 30-year-old Dolly Parton reaches number seven ▪ 25-year-old Barry Sheene rides his Suzuki to victory in the Dutch and Swedish 500cc motor cycle Grands Prix and becomes world champion ▪ Formula One driver Jody Scheckter wins the Swedish motor racing Grand Prix at Anderstorp in a six-wheeled Tyrrell car. Britain's James Hunt finishes in fifth position in a conventional four-wheeled McLaren ▪ Back in England - the summer heatwave continues ▪ The hot sunshine beats down ▪ Parched stray dogs roam the streets seeking water and shade ▪ Men go to the pub ▪ 'You're lucky you're thirsty. You've got Harp' - a pint of *Harp* lager costs 26p ▪ "Ever and ever. Forever and ever. You'll be the one, that shines in me, like the morning sun" - *Forever And Ever* by 30-year-old Demis Roussos is number one for a week in July ▪ "Please darlin' don't you cry, let's just…" *Kiss And Say Goodbye* by The Manhattans reaches number four ▪ "Just the thought of you turns my whole world…" *Misty Blue* by 29-year-old Dorothy Moore is number five ▪ 33-year-old tennis player Mark Cox from Leicester loses to Vitas Gerulaitis in the second round of the men's singles at Wimbledon. 20-year-old Bjorn Borg from Sweden becomes the new champion after beating 29-year-old Ilie Nastase (6-4, 6-2, 9-7) in the final ▪ "Don't go breaking my heart. I couldn't if I tried." - *Don't Go Breaking My Heart* by 29-year-old Elton John and 29-year-old Kiki Dee is number one for six weeks in July and August ▪ "Ooh, you make me live" - *You're My Best Friend* by Queen is number seven ▪ 'Save Water. It's Scarce' - the hot weather continues and water is in short supply. Stand-pipes appear on street corners - people queue to fill their pots and pans ▪ 52-year-old Minister for Drought Dennis Howell and his wife share their bath water - Howell goes on television and encourages other people to do the same ▪ At Oxford Crown Court, 39-year-old Donald Nielson (aka the Black Panther) is found guilty of the kidnap and murder of Lesley Whittle and sentenced to life imprisonment ▪ 51-year-old former Labour MP John Stonehouse (who attempted to fake his own death) is found guilty of fraud, theft and deception and sentenced to seven years ▪ Devshi Bhudia is sacked for working too slowly at the Grunwick photographic processing factory in Willesden - a number of fellow workers

walk-out in protest ▪ "When your body's had enough of me and I'm layin' flat out on the floor. When you think I've loved you all I can, I'm gonna love you…" *A Little Bit More* by Dr. Hook is number two in the pop chart ▪ *Heaven Must Be Missing An Angel* ("... Missing an angel, child, 'cause you're here with me right now") by Tavares climbs to number four ▪ The chimes of Big Ben - inside the Great Clock of Westminster - fall silent when metal fatigue damages the mechanism ▪ 'The following information is classified: TOP SECRET' - *The Bionic Woman* is new on TV - with 27-year-old Lindsay Wagner in the title role ▪ Hilda and Stan Ogden (played by 49-year-old Jean Alexander and 61-year-old Bernard Youens) are proud owners of a new mural (depicting three flying ducks) in the living-room at number 13 *Coronation Street* ▪ Trendy young men with moustaches, tight white trousers and Ford *Capri* motorcars take their girlfriends for a night out at the disco ▪ *You Should Be Dancing* ("… Yeah!") by The Bee Gees (a group comprising of the three brothers Gibb: 29-year-old Barry and 26-year-old twins, Robin and Maurice) is new at number five in the pop chart ▪ "When I wake up in the morning light, I pull on my jeans and I feel alright. I pull my blue…" *Jeans On* ("… I pull my old, blue jeans on") by 31-year-old David Dundas is number three ▪ Keith Best presents the weather forecast on BBC One ▪ The heatwave continues ▪ Parks, lawns and grass verges are bleached white in the hot sun ▪ 28-year-old racing driver James Hunt wins the British Grand Prix in his McLaren - but is later disqualified ▪ 27-year-old Niki Lauda crashes and is badly burned in his Ferrari at the German Grand Prix ▪ 'R' reg cars go on sale ▪ 'Ford's new baby. Never has so much advanced engineering gone into a small car' - Ford launches the *Fiesta* - a small hatch-back motorcar designed to give 86% all-round vision. The *1.0 Popular* base model costs £1,856 ▪ Four star leaded petrol rises in price to 77p a gallon ▪ 32-year-old Tony Gubba presents *Grandstand* on BBC One television ▪ 22-year-old swimmer David Wilkie wins gold for Britain in the 200 metre breaststroke at the Montreal Olympics ▪ 28-year-old Brendan Foster wins bronze on the track in the 10,000 metres ▪ 25-year-old Princess Anne is part of the British equestrian team ▪ "Sky rockets in flight…" *Afternoon Delight* by The Starland Vocal Band peaks at number eighteen in the pop chart ▪ "The last time I saw George alive, was in the summer of seventy-five, he said he

was in love, I said 'I'm pleased'" - *The Killing Of Georgie (Parts One And Two)* by 31-year-old Rod Stewart reaches number two ▪ The second series of sit-com *Get Some In!* is on ITV - starring 38-year-old Tony Selby as Corporal Marsh and 26-year-old Robert Lindsay as Jakey Smith ("with three 'f's") ▪ *Don't Go Breaking My Heart* by Elton John and 29-year-old Kiki Dee remains at number one in the pop chart ▪ "Oh, to tell the truth…" *What I've Got In Mind* ("… is making love to you") by 38-year-old Billie Jo Spears is number four ▪ Terry Neill succeeds Bertie Mee as manager of Arsenal and signs 26-year-old striker Malcolm 'Supermac' MacDonald from Newcastle Utd for £333,333 ▪ 24-year-old David Johnson transfers from Ipswich Town to Liverpool for £200,000 ▪ 18-year-old Cyrille Regis from Harlesden joins non-league team Hayes FC ▪ The new football season gets underway ▪ Bob Paisley's Liverpool beat Lawrie McMenemy's Southampton 1-0 in the Charity Shield at Wembley - 27-year-old John Toshack scores the winning goal ▪ A week later hundreds of hooligans fight each other at matches up and down the country ▪ Fans invade the pitch at Derby County versus Manchester Utd - where dozens of supporters are injured and three policeman are taken to hospital ▪ Violence also breaks out at Nottingham Forest versus Wolverhampton Wanderers ▪ Segregation of rival supporters becomes a key issue. The FA considers erecting fences to separate terraced areas ▪ "All those people gathered there (in zire - in Zaire), to see the rumble in the jungle - there, there, there…" *In Zaire* by Johnnie Wakelin is number four in the pop chart ▪ "Someone's knockin' at the door, somebody's ringin' the bell. Do me a favour, open the door and…" *Let 'Em In* by Wings (with, lead singer, 34-year-old Paul McCartney) is number two ▪ Police take a heavy handed approach at the annual Notting Hill street festival - and get a taste of their own medicine when people from the local community fight back ▪ Sex equality takes a small step forward ▪ 25-year-old Mary Langdon joins the fire brigade at Battle, East Sussex - and becomes Britain's first female fire-fighter ▪ The average price of a house in the UK has risen by over £1,000 in the past twelve months - it now stands at £11,700 ▪ A pint of lager in the Red Lion has risen to 28p ▪ Adverts claim, '*Heineken* - refreshes the parts other beers cannot reach'.

Autumn 1976

Four candles. No, fork handles.

Monarch:	Queen Elizabeth II (aged 50)
Prime-minister:	James Callaghan (aged 64)
Chancellor:	Denis Healey (aged 59)
Home Secretary:	Merlyn Rees (aged 55)
Foreign Secretary:	Anthony Crossland (aged 58)
Football Manager:	Don Revie (aged 49)
Radio 1 Breakfast DJ:	Noel Edmonds (aged 27)
New car reg. suffix:	'R'

▪ 38-year-old Barbara Edwards presents the weather forecast on BBC One ▪ Thunderstorms arrive and the great summer heatwave comes to an end ▪ Bosses at the Grunwick photographic processing factory in Willesden sack 137 workers for going on strike in support of a colleague who was dismissed in August ▪ 32-year-old DJ Paul Burnett announces the latest Top 30 chart hits on Radio One on Tuesday afternoons ▪ *You Don't Have To Go* ("... You just wanna see me do some begging") by The Chi-Lites is number three ▪ "I wrote a love song in..." *16 Bars* by The Stylistics is number seven ▪ *I Am A Cider Drinker* ("... I drinks it all of the day") by The Wurzels is new at number twenty-three ▪ Bored youngsters embrace the growing punk rock scene ▪ The Sex Pistols play a gig at the Nag's Head in High Wycombe ▪ 11-year-old schoolboy Robert Brydon from Port Talbot in South Wales sits at home watching TV ▪ A new series of *The Two Ronnies* begins on BBC One on Saturday evenings, with 46-year-old Ronnie Barker and 45-year-old Ronnie Corbett; and featuring a short comedy drama called 'The Phantom Rasberry Blower of Old London Town' (written by Spike Milligan) ▪ 10-year-old schoolboy Stephen Coogan from Middleton in Manchester sits at home watching TV ▪ 'Mah-na, mah-na. Doo-doo, doo-doo-doo' - *The Muppet Show* begins on ITV on Sunday evenings, with puppets - Fozzie, Kermit and Miss Piggy providing a wide variety of entertainment. Statler and Waldorf look on from the balcony of a theatre box - unimpressed ▪ "What's got four legs, walks peculiar, talks with all the choicest words? What's got four arms, loves to grab you? Answer is, two Liver Birds" - A new series of *The Liver Birds* is on BBC One on Sunday evenings, starring 27-year-old Elizabeth Estensen as Carol and

34-year-old Nerys Hughes as Sandra ▪ The haunting sound of pan pipe music draws middle-aged people to record shops ▪ *(Light Of Experience) Doina De Jale* by George Zamfir is number four in the pop chart ▪ Families enjoy an evening at the cinema ▪ 14-year-old John Cassisi is Fat Sam, 13-year-old Jodie Foster is Tallulah and 15-year-old Scott Baio plays the title role in *Bugsy Malone* - a brilliant new musical from 32-year-old director Alan Parker ▪ Energetic teenagers 'get down' to the funky sounds of soul records at 'cool' nightspots ▪ 17-year-old Deborah Meaden gyrates to *The Bottle* by Gil Scott-Heron and Brian Jackson at The Curtain Club in Brighton ▪ "You can dance, you can jive, having the time of your life. See that girl, watch that scene, digging the…" *Dancing Queen* by Abba (with 31-year-old Bjorn Ulvaeus, 29-year-old Benny Andersson, 30-year-old Anni-Frid Lyngstad and 26-year-old Agnetha Faltskog) moves up to number one in the pop chart - and stays there for six weeks! ▪ "When the moon shines on the cow shed and we're rollin' in the hay. All the cows are out there grazing and the milk is on its way." - *I Am A Cider Drinker (Paloma Blanca)* by The Wurzels climbs to number three ▪ *Aria* by 47-year-old Acker Bilk, his Clarinet and Strings is number five ▪ 20-year-old centre-forward Andy Gray bags a hat-trick as Aston Villa thrash Ipswich Town 5-2 in front of 39,916 spectators at Villa Park ▪ 26-year-old Malcolm 'Supermac' MacDonald scores for Arsenal in a 3-1 win over Everton in front of 34,076 at Highbury ▪ *Striker* - a five-part footballing serial for children begins on BBC One on Wednesday evenings ▪ *The New Avengers* begins on ITV, with 54-year-old Patrick Macnee as Steed, 34-year-old Gareth Hunt as Gambit and 30-year-old Joanna Lumley as Purdey (a hot chick driving a yellow *TR7* sports car) ▪ "And I..." *Can't Get By Without You* ("... no way") by The Real Thing is number two in the pop chart ▪ "It happens to be true..." *I Only Wanna Be With You* by The Bay City Rollers is number four ▪ 16-year-old Eddie Kidd from Highbury, London suffers minor injuries as he sets a new world record - leaping over thirteen double-decker buses on his motorbike ▪ "Sunday, Monday, happy days! Tuesday, Wednesday, happy days! Thursday, Friday, happy days! The weekend comes, my cycle hums, ready to race to you. These days are ours, happy and free!" - 'Cool' and 'Ace-a-mundo' are new catch phrases as 30-year-old Henry Winkler stars as The Fonz in *Happy Days* ▪ 33-year-old John

Major is selected as the Conservative parliamentary candidate for Huntingdonshire ▪ *Roy of the Rovers* is a brand new paper for boys - as the footballing saga of Roy Race and his Melchester Rovers team-mates transfers from *Tiger and Scorcher* to its own publication ▪ 25-year-old footballer Kevin Keegan falls off his bike on *Superstars* and is badly injured ▪ *Dance Little Lady, Dance* ("... You know you've only got one chance") by 22-year-old Tina Charles peaks at number six in the pop chart ▪ *Blinded By The Light* ("… Revved up like a deuce, another runner in the night") by Manfred Mann's Earth Band also reaches number six ▪ "Four candles. No, fork handles! Handles for forks!" - Millions of BBC One viewers are in tears of laughter when The Two Ronnies perform an hilarious new comedy sketch set in an iron mongers ▪ "Eleven minutes late. Staff difficulties at Hampton Wick" - 49-year-old Leonard Rossiter stars in *The Fall and Rise of Reginald Perrin* (a new TV comedy based on a novel written by 41-year-old David Nobbs) ▪ "I must get it all down, quickly. Before they finish me off" - 38-year-old Derek Jacobi stars in *I Claudius* on BBC Two - along with 43-year-old Sian Phillips, 40-year-old Brian Blessed, 36-year-old Patrick Stewart and 36-year-old John Hurt ▪ "Please, could Posh Paws roar down the phone to me?" - 27-year-old Noel Edmonds presents *Multi-Coloured Swap Shop* on Saturday mornings - and Nigel from Stroud would like to exchange *Cluedo* for *Ker-Plunk* ▪ "Mii-iss-issippi, you've been on my mind" - *Mississippi* by Pussycat climbs to number one in the pop chart - and stays there for four weeks ▪ "You made a promise, you broke it" - *Hurt* by The Manhattans is number four ▪ *When Forever Has Gone* by 30-year-old Demis Roussos is number five ▪ 43-year-old Dickie Davies presents *World Of Sport* on ITV on Saturday afternoons ▪ 43-year-old Frank Bough presents *Grandstand* on BBC One ▪ 'Mackay Told to Go', 'Mackay Fired!' and 'Mackay Gets the Boot' are back-page newspaper headlines as 42-year-old football manager Dave Mackay takes his leave of Derby County - and is replaced by Colin Murphy at the Baseball Ground ▪ Jack Charlton's Middlesbrough gain a 1-0 victory over John Bond's Norwich City (with a goal from 23-year-old Graeme Souness) and move to the top of Division One ▪ Fighting breaks out at Elland Road as Jimmy Armfield's Leeds Utd lose 0-2 to Tommy 'The Doc' Docherty's Manchester Utd ▪ Even worse crowd trouble breaks out when supporters

invade the pitch at Villa Park during a 'friendly' between Aston Villa and Rangers ▪ 46-year-old Bob Stokoe leaves Sunderland after serving for four years as manager - 47-year-old Jimmy Adamson takes over at Roker Park ▪ *Play That Funky Music* ("… white boy") by Wild Cherry climbs to number seven in the pop chart ▪ "And I kept on looking for a sign in the middle of the night, but I couldn't see the light, no I couldn't see the light" - *Couldn't Get It Right* by The Climax Blues Band is number ten ▪ 26-year-old boxer Joe Bugner beats Richard Dunn by a first round knock-out at Wembley to retain his European heavy-weight title ▪ 43-year-old Barry Norman presents the late night movie review program *Film 76* on BBC One ▪ 'It's the Biggest Bang since the War!' - 58-year-old Kenneth Connor, 46-year-old Windsor Davies and 46-year-old Joan Sims star at cinemas in *Carry On England* ▪ 33-year-old Robert de Niro stars in *Taxi Driver* - with 13-year-old Jodie Foster and 26-year-old Cybill Shepherd in supporting roles ▪ Dads watch *Top of the Pops* on BBC One on Thursday evenings as Legs and Co. make their debut ▪ *You Make Me Feel Like Dancing* ("… I'm gonna dance the night away") by 28-year-old Leo Sayer is number two in the pop chart ▪ "Haah-aah, howzat! You messed about, I caught you out…" *Howzat* by Sherbet is number three ▪ The punk rock 'scene' spreads across the land ▪ Youngsters do creative things with safety pins ▪ The Sex Pistols sign to EMI records ▪ The new super-sleek *Inter-City 125* train runs between London and Bristol ▪ 50-year-old Jimmy Savile OBE says, "This is the age of the train." ▪ School children drink water from *Duralex* glasses at lunch-time - before playing British-Bulldog on the playground ▪ 29-year-old racing driver James Hunt finishes third in the Japanese Grand-Prix to become the new world motor racing champion - pipping his fierce rival Niki Lauda to the title by just one point ▪ Back in England - 30-year-old footballer 'super' Georgie Best makes his debut for Fulham and scores after just seventy-one seconds in a 1-0 win against Bristol Rovers in Division Two ▪ 23-year-old striker Paul Mariner transfers from Second Division Plymouth Argyle to First Division Ipswich Town ▪ Referees use red and yellow cards for the first time ▪ Dave Wagstaffe of Blackburn Rovers sees red and is sent-off just thirty-six minutes into a match against Orient ▪ "Disco…" *Disco Duck* ("… Alright!") by Rick Dees and his Cast of Idiots reaches number six on the hit parade ▪ *I'll*

Meet You At Midnight ("… under the moonlight") by Smokie is number eleven ▪ The annual Motor Show takes place at Earls Court ▪ 'A Car That's Built to Last' - Ford launches the box shaped *Cortina MkIV* motorcar. A basic *Saloon* or *L* model with 1.6 litre engine has a top speed of 94 mph and accelerates from 0-60 mph in 12.4 seconds ▪ A top-of-the-range *Ghia* model with 2.0 litre engine has a top speed of 106 mph and can reach 60 mph in 9.6 seconds ▪ 'Make someone happy with a phone-call' - a yellow cartoon bird called 'Buzby' advertises three-minute, off-peak telephone calls for just 10p ▪ 'The Workers United Will Never Be Defeated' - 43-year-old Jayaben Desai leads the protests of sacked workers from the Grunwick photographic processing factory. 54-year-old Len Murray (General Secretary of the TUC) urges all trade unions to lend their support ▪ The economy is performing badly under 64-year-old Jim Callaghan's Labour government. The unemployment figure is high - standing at 1.3 million. Inflation is also high - at 17%. The balance of payment deficit is almost £1 billion and interest rates are at 15%. The pound falls in value against the dollar to an all-time record low of $1.54 ▪ Chancellor of the Exchequer Denis Healey requests a loan of $3.9 billion from the IMF. The 59-year-old then cancels a foreign trip and arrives back at Labour's party conference in Blackpool to explain why the loan is necessary ▪ Foggy, Compo and Clegg (played by 49-year-old Brian Wilde, 62-year-old Bill Owen and 55-year-old Peter Sallis) get up to no good in *Last of the Summer Wine* on BBC One ▪ Grumpy Albert Tatlock (played by 80-year-old Jack Howarth) and miserable Ena Sharples (played by 78-year-old Violet Carson) get drunk together in the bar of 'The Rovers Return' in *Coronation Street* on ITV. Womaniser Mike Baldwin (played by 41-year-old Johnny Briggs) spends a romantic evening with barmaid Bet Lynch (played by 34-year-old Julie Goodyear) ▪ *Sleeping Murder: Miss Marple's Last Case* - by recently deceased crime-writer Dame Agatha Christie is on sale now in bookshops for £3.50 ▪ 38-year-old Radio One DJ 'Diddy' David Hamilton takes his turn to introduce *Top of the Pops* on Thursday evenings ▪ 33-year-old DJ Tony Blackburn sits at home drowning his sorrows after his actress wife, 28-year-old Tessa Wyatt, walks out on him ▪ *If You Leave Me Now* ("… you'll take away the biggest part of me") by Chicago is the new number one song ▪ *Don't Take Away The Music* ("… it's the only thing I got")

by Tavares is number four ▪ A re-issue of *Substitute* by The Who climbs to number seven ▪ 26-year-old footballer Trevor Whymark scores four goals as Bobby Robson's Ipswich Town move up to second position in Division One with a 7-0 thrashing of West Bromwich Albion. (John Wark, Kevin Beattie and Paul Mariner are also on the score-sheet for the 'Tractor Boys') ▪ Kevin Keegan and Joey Jones score the goals as league leaders Liverpool beat Bristol City 2-1 at Anfield ▪ Bottom-of-the-table West Ham Utd gain a surprise 0-2 away victory over Manchester Utd, with goals from Billy Jennings and Trevor Brooking ▪ Television technology moves on apace - sets with cordless remote controls are now available from *Radio Rentals* ▪ 66-year-old Arthur Mullard and 53-year-old Queenie Watts star in *Yus My Dear* on ITV ▪ 46-year-old Windsor Davies, 43-year-old Don Estelle and 41-year-old Melvyn Hayes star in *It Ain't Half Hot Mum* on BBC One ▪ 33-year-old fascist Martin Webster addresses a group of National Front supporters in Walsall ▪ "Nuts, whole hazel nuts. Urgh! Cadbury's take 'em and they cover them in chocolate" - Cadbury's *Wholenut* bars are advertised on television ▪ The *Bargain Madness* discount store opens in Blackpool - it will eventually become *B&M Bargains* ▪ "Who..." *If Not You* ("... Tell me, who, if not you?") by Dr. Hook is number five in the pop chart ▪ "I am not in love, but I'm open to persuasion" - *Love And Affection* by 25-year-old Joan Armatrading is number ten ▪ "What a..." *Beautiful Noise* ("... coming up from the street") by 35-year-old Neil Diamond is number thirteen ▪ 37-year-old Roger Clark wins the RAC Rally driving a Ford *Escort* (registration POO 505R) ▪ Young children dream of getting a new bike for Christmas ▪ A Raleigh *Budgie* is £31.99 ▪ A Raleigh *Chipper* is £32.99 ▪ 54-year-old Max Bygraves is host for the first ever 'live' TV broadcast of the Royal Variety Performance from the London Palladium. 31-year-old ventriloquist Roger De Courcey and his puppet Nookie the Bear steal the show, appearing in front of 76-year-old Queen Elizabeth the Queen Mother ▪ 41-year-old entertainer Rod Hull and his uncontrollable puppet Emu attack chat-show host Michael Parkinson on late night BBC One television ▪ "I am an anti-Christ! I am an anarchist!" - *Anarchy In The UK* by The Sex Pistols enters the pop chart at number forty-three ▪ The Electric Circus, a club for punk rockers, opens in Manchester.

Christmas 1976

Brut aftershave - 'Splash it all over!'

Monarch:	Queen Elizabeth II (aged 50)
Prime-minister:	James Callaghan (aged 64)
Chancellor:	Denis Healey (aged 59)
Home Secretary:	Merlyn Rees (aged 56)
Foreign Secretary:	Anthony Crossland (aged 58)
Football Manager:	Don Revie (aged 49)
Radio 1 Breakfast DJ:	Noel Edmonds (aged 28)
New car reg. suffix:	'R'

▪ "You derty bar-stud!" - The Sex Pistols (20-year-old Johnny Rotten, 21-year-old Steve Jones, 20-year-old Glen Matlock and 20-year-old Paul Cook) shock millions by swearing on TV ▪ Punk rock divides the nation ▪ Mohair jumpers and PVC trousers are in demand ▪ 12-year-old schoolboy Steve Lamacq from Colne Engaine in Essex plays records in his bedroom ▪ Colchester Utd beat Darlington 4-0 in Division Four, with goals from Bobby Gough, Steve Dowman (2) and Lindsay Smith ▪ 23-year-old centre-forward Paul Mariner scores the only goal of the match as Bobby Robson's Ipswich Town defeat Bob Paisley's Liverpool 1-0 in a top-of-the-table clash in Division One ▪ 24-year-old aberrant centre-forward Robin Friday scores both goals as Reading defeat Wycombe Wanderers 1-2 in the second round of the FA Cup ▪ *A Star is Born* (starring 34-year-old Barbra Streisand and 40-year-old Kris Kristofferson) goes on general release at cinemas ▪ *Marathon Man* (starring 39-year-old Dustin Hoffman, 69-year-old Sir Laurence Olivier and 44-year-old Roy Scheider) is also now showing ▪ 51-year-old Margaret Thatcher MP (leader of the Conservative opposition) travels to Amsterdam for meetings with Dutch officials in the Hague ▪ "I was lost in France, in the fields the birds were singing. I was lost in France and the day was just beginning" - *Lost In France* by 25-year-old Bonnie Tyler is number nine in the pop chart ▪ *Love Me* ("... just a little bit longer") by 24-year-old Yvonne Elliman is number six ▪ Punk band The Sex Pistols cause more controversy in a pre-recorded interview broadcast on Radio Luxembourg. The 30-minute interview has 24 offensive words 'bleeped out' ▪ James Bellini presents *The Money Programme* on BBC Two television on Friday evenings ▪ The UK economy

remains in dire straits ▪ Chancellor of the Exchequer Denis Healey is forced to make cuts in public spending under the terms of the $3.9 billion loan from the IMF ▪ Times are hard for families living in 'run-down' industrial areas of the country ▪ Just 124 million tonnes of coal have been mined in Britain this year ▪ Inflation has fallen slightly to 16.5%, but property prices continue to rise - the average cost of a house is now over £12,000 ▪ Jim Callaghan's Labour government has slipped behind Margaret Thatcher's opposition Tory party in the polls ▪ *Money Money Money* ("... must be funny, in the rich man's world") by Abba is number three in the pop chart ▪ "Let's go for a little walk. Under the moon of love. Let's sit right down and talk..." *Under The Moon Of Love* by Showaddywaddy (with, lead singer, 24-year-old Dave Bartram) is new at number one ▪ 42-year-old John Noakes, 37-year-old Peter Purves and 29-year-old Lesley Judd present *Blue Peter* on BBC One. The Christmas Appeal is underway, with thousands of children sending in old postage stamps and postcards to help raise money for those affected by civil war in Lebanon ▪ *Portsmouth* by 23-year-old Mike Oldfield is number three in the pop chart ▪ Christmas is approaching ▪ Middle-class families enjoy an evening at the Pantomime ▪ 51-year-old comedian Charlie Drake appears in *Jack and the Beanstalk* at the Birmingham Hippodrome ▪ TV adverts declare, 'That's the Wonder of *Woolworths*' ▪ Schoolboys make their lists for Santa Claus ▪ *Up Periscope* costs £5.49 ▪ *Super Flight Deck* is £4.50 ▪ *Buck-a-Roo* is £2.75 ▪ The latest *All Star Super Striker* table-top football game (from *Palitoy*) now comes with a 'super texture pitch' ▪ *Matey* bubble bath is a popular stocking filler ▪ Dads know what to expect ▪ The *Ronco* Record Vacuum is £5.99 ▪ A gift set of *Old Spice* aftershave and talc for men is £1.69 ▪ "And it went, la-la-la-la-la-la-la-la-la-lah, la-la-la-la-la-la-lah. Peace and goodwill to all men, and love for the child" - *A Spaceman Came Travelling* by 28-year-old Chris de Burgh plays on a transistor ▪ 29-year-old entrepreneur Alan Sugar sells imported car radios and music cassette players to independent electrical retailers in London ▪ 41-year-old actor Johnny Briggs plays hard-headed businessman Mike Baldwin in ITV's popular soap-opera *Coronation Street* - and refuses to employ Elsie Howard (played by 53-year-old Pat Phoenix) as she's too old ▪ "Leave it out, guv'nor!" - the third series of hard-hitting cop drama *The Sweeney* (star-

ring 34-year-old John Thaw as Jack Reagan and 28-year-old Dennis Waterman as George Carter) comes to an end ▪ 'Bargain of the Week' - a 1973 Ford *Granada GXL*, (automatic) is advertised for just £1,750 at Brook Bridge Garage, Prescot ▪ "Can anybody find me…" *Somebody To Love* by Queen (with, lead singer, 30-year-old Freddie Mercury) is number two in the singles chart ▪ *Sorry Seems To Be The Hardest Word* by 29-year-old Elton John is number eleven ▪ Hallmark Records release *The Best of Top of the Pops '76* - a budget priced, cover-version pop compilation LP with blonde Jilly Johnson in a sultry pose on the sleeve ▪ "What do you hear on the street these days, Huggy?" - *Starsky & Hutch* (starring Paul Michael Glaser, David Soul and with 30-year-old Antonio Fargas as Huggy Bear) is a popular new TV program for Saturday nights ▪ 'Mah-na, mah-na. Doo-doo, doo-doo-doo' - Millions tune in to ITV's *Muppet Show* on Sunday evenings - where the outrageous Miss Piggy attempts to make Kermit jealous by flirting with the male guest stars ▪ The second series of *When the Boat Comes In* (starring 41-year-old James Bolam and 35-year-old Susan Jameson) is on BBC One on Friday nights ▪ Housewives keep jars of spices on a wooden rack, mounted on the wall of the kitchen ▪ Food is served on a push-a-long, three-tiered dinner trolley ▪ 'Splash it all over' - 42-year-old Henry Cooper, 26-year-old Barry Sheene and 25-year-old Kevin Keegan are on TV, promoting *Brut* aftershave ▪ *Brut 33* is on offer at Rackhams for just £1.95 ▪ 27-year-old Olympic ice-skating champion John Curry is BBC's 'Sports Personality of the Year' ▪ 30-year-old footballer Fabio Capello plays in the Italian team which beats Don Revie's England 2-0. England's line-up for the match is: Clemence, Clement, Mills, B Greenhoff, McFarland, Hughes, Keegan, Channon, Bowles, Cherry, Brooking and substitute, Beattie ▪ Last season's Division One champions and current league leaders, Liverpool, are thrashed 5-1 by Ron Saunders' Aston Villa, with 21-year-old Andy Gray and 19-year-old John Deehan both scoring twice for the Midlands' club ▪ "It's a…" *Living Thing* ("… it's a terrible thing to lose") by Electric Light Orchestra (with, lead singer, 28-year-old Jeff Lynne) climbs to number four on the hit parade ▪ *Lean On Me* by Mud (with, lead singer, 30-year-old Les Gray) is number seven ▪ 26-year-old footballer Malcolm 'Supermac' MacDonald bags a hat-trick as Terry Neill's Arsenal beat Gordon Lee's Newcastle Utd 5-3 at

Highbury ▪ 30-year-old 'super' Georgie Best makes a rude gesture and swears at the referee in a match between Fulham and Chelsea ▪ There's a flurry of activity on football's transfer market ▪ 28-year-old Larry Lloyd leaves Coventry City and joins Brian Clough's Nottingham Forest ▪ 28-year-old Bruce Rioch leaves Derby County and joins Billy Bingham's Everton ▪ 31-year-old Alan Ball leaves Arsenal and signs for Southampton for £60,000 ▪ BBC One's TV sit-com *Porridge* draws millions of viewers. 47-year-old Ronnie Barker (Fletch), 29-year-old Richard Beckinsale (Godber) and 49-year-old Brian Wilde (Mr. Barrowclough) are held hostage, at gunpoint, in the governor's office at Slade Prison ▪ 44-year-old movie star Elizabeth Taylor marries her sixth husband - 49-year-old US politician John Warner at Richmond in Virginia, USA ▪ Back in Britain - the economy continues to struggle and retail prices are rising ▪ Prime-minister Jim Callaghan and his Labour government are criticised for their poor handling of the country's finances ▪ In the House of Commons, Conservative MPs call for the resignation of Chancellor of the Exchequer Dennis Healey ▪ "I'm backing Dennis" says prime-minister Callaghan. "He has my full support in what he is doing" ▪ People escape the grim pressures of life with a night out at the pictures ▪ "Do you have a rheum? / I do not know what a rheum is" - 51-year-old Peter Sellers stars in *The Pink Panther Strikes Again* ▪ 'Welcome to the 23rd Century. The perfect world for total pleasure' - 34-year-old Michael York, 29-year-old Farrah Fawcett and 23-year-old Jenny Agutter star in *Logan's Run* ▪ 20-year-old Koo Stark stars in the 'X' rated movie *Emily* ▪ 18-year-old Linda Lusardi (36C) from Wood Green is a popular new page three girl in *The Sun* ▪ The Christmas rush begins ▪ Shops are crowded with eager shoppers ▪ A bottle of *Bells* whisky costs £3.79 ▪ A bottle of *Courvoisier* is £5.35 ▪ A bottle of *Smirnoff* vodka is £3.69 ▪ A bottle of *Harveys Bristol Cream* is £1.79 ▪ A bottle of *Croft Original* is £1.79 ▪ A four-pack of *Babycham* (small) bottles is 57p ▪ 37-year-old Bill Giles presents the weather forecast on BBC One ▪ There's widespread heavy snow in the week before Christmas ▪ "A ray of hope flickers in the sky. A tiny star lights up way up high. All across the land, dawns a brand new morn. This comes to pass..." *When A Child Is Born* by 41-year-old Johnny Mathis is number one in the pop chart ▪ Digital watches are all the rage ▪ A gold *Seiko* with red digital display

(which illuminates at the press of a button) is £78.95 ▪ A silver *Imado* with red digital display costs £53.50 ▪ A five-function digital watch from *Metac* is £39.95 ▪ A *Trafalgar 61036* is £21.95 ▪ On Christmas morning, excitable kids play out on their new bikes ▪ A Silver Jubilee special edition of the Raleigh *Chopper* bicycle has a silver coloured frame and 10-spoke alloy wheels ▪ A Bantel *Hugh Porter* racer has dropped handlebars, 5-speed Derailleur gears and sports mudguards ▪ "Don't forget the cuddly toy" - 48-year-old TV presenter Bruce Forsyth hosts the ever popular *Generation Game* on BBC One ▪ 32-year-old newsreader Angela Rippon shows her legs on *Morecambe and Wise* in front of 28 million viewers ▪ The musical *Oliver!* (starring Mark Lester, Ron Moody and Oliver Reed) is broadcast in the afternoon on Christmas Day. The film *Airport* (starring Burt Lancaster, Dean Martin and Jacqueline Bisset) is broadcast in the evening. *The Wizard of Oz* (starring Judy Garland) is shown on Boxing Day ▪ "Oh, I don't know why she's leaving, or where she's gonna go. I guess she's got her reasons but I just don't want to know, 'cause for twenty-four years I've been..." *Living Next Door To Alice* by Smokie is number five in the pop chart ▪ "The stars are shining bright, and I'm feelin' just right for..." *Grandma's Party* ("... tonight") by 31-year-old Paul Nicholas is number nine ▪ 8.6 million colour TV licenses have been issued this year, compared to 9.1 million black and white licenses ▪ A new eight part drama for children called *The Phoenix and the Carpet* airs on BBC One on Wednesday evenings at ten past five (after *Goober and the Ghost Chasers*) ▪ Southampton footballer Mick Channon scores twice in a 2-1 victory over Bristol Rovers and celebrates his goals by making a windmill action with one arm ▪ 24-year-old aberrant centre-forward Robin Friday transfers from Third Division Reading to Second Division Cardiff City for £28,000 ▪ On Sunday mornings, mums and dads enjoy a well earned lie-in ▪ A Goblin *Teasmade* costs £32.59 and provides an automatic early morning cuppa ▪ A Pifco *1846* electric toaster costs £12.95 ▪ 'Gaz + Julie' - Trendy young courting couples in Vauxhall *Viva* motorcars, with personalised green-coloured sun visor strips bearing their names across the top of the windscreen, enjoy a night out at *Berni Inn* ▪ Steak (well-done) and chips is a popular choice from the menu, followed by Black Forest gateau ▪ Adverts say, 'Martini Rosso - Anytime, any place, anywhere'.

New Year 1977

Footballer Trevor Francis makes his debut for England

Monarch:	Queen Elizabeth II (aged 50)
Prime-minister:	James Callaghan (aged 64)
Chancellor:	Denis Healey (aged 59)
Home Secretary:	Merlyn Rees (aged 56)
Foreign Secretary:	David Owen (aged 38)
Football Manager:	Don Revie (aged 49)
Radio 1 Breakfast DJ:	Noel Edmonds (aged 28)
New car reg. suffix:	'R'

▪ 32-year-old Michael Fish presents the weather forecast on BBC One ▪ A cold, north-easterly wind brings snow ▪ Men attempt to keep warm - turning the collars up on their fleece lined sheerling lumberjack jackets ▪ Punk rock continues to thrill and shock in equal measure ▪ Gangs of spiky haired teenagers pogo, spit, and push and shove one another, at raucous gigs all around the country ▪ 22-year-old Stuart Goddard from London changes his name to Adam Ant ▪ The Clash begin recording their first album at CBS Studios ▪ Troublesome band The Sex Pistols are sacked by record company EMI. 'The Pistols' sign with A&M - have another fall out - and eventually sign for 26-year-old Richard Branson's Virgin label ▪ 31-year-old Malcolm McLaren sits at home, counting his money ▪ The football season continues ▪ 24-year-old aberrant centre-forward Robin Friday scores two goals on his debut for Cardiff City in a 3-0 victory over Fulham in front of 20,268 spectators at Ninian Park ▪ 19-year-old Alan Biley scores for Cambridge Utd in a 4-0 win against Darlington in Division Four ▪ More heavy snow in mid January causes chaos on the roads, with many motorists forced to abandon their cars ▪ A Vauxhall *Viva* ('K' reg, in Flamenco Red) is stranded on the A6 near New Mills ▪ A BMW *1602* ('M' reg, in Colorado Orange) is stuck on the B676 at Bourne ▪ Schoolboys make 'slides' on the pavement - and take turns to see who can glide the furthest over the compacted snow ▪ "So let the..." *Sideshow* ("... begin. Hurry, hurry. Step right on in") by 30-year-old Barry Biggs is number three in the pop chart ▪ "You gave up the only one that ever loved you, and went back to that..." *Wild Side Of Life* by Status Quo (with, lead singer,

27-year-old Francis Rossi and guitarist 28-year-old Rick Parfitt) is number nine ▪ 30-year-old David Bowie releases the *Low* album. The tracks *Breaking Glass* and *Sound And Vision* are on side one. *Subterraneans* is the closing track on side two ▪ 48-year-old Bruce Forsyth is the guest star (appearing alongside Fozzie, Kermit, Animal and Miss Piggy) on ITV's hugely popular Sunday evening program *The Muppet Show* ▪ 38-year-old Christopher Robbie presents the weather forecast ▪ Heavy rain and thawing snow lead to widespread flooding ▪ 44-year-old Andrew Gardner and 44-year-old Reginald Bosanquet present the *News at Ten* for ITN ▪ 50-year-old Queen Elizabeth II travels to Tonga to begin her Silver Jubilee tour, before moving onto Fiji and New Zealand ▪ 64-year-old Labour prime-minister Jim Callaghan is under pressure ▪ Inflation has risen to 17% and unemployment now stands at 1.4 million ▪ Sacked workers continue to picket the Grunwick photographic processing factory in Willesden ▪ A homeless woman is murdered in Leeds ▪ Police confirm that the recent murders of women in Yorkshire could be linked ▪ The IRA sets off seven bombs around London's West End - thankfully there are no fatalities ▪ 'The roughest, toughest men from London's greatest crime squad smash their way onto the BIG SCREEN!' - John Thaw and Dennis Waterman star in an 'X' rated film version of *Sweeney!* ▪ "Don't give up on us, baby. Don't make the wrong seem right. The future isn't just one night. It's written in the moonlight, and painted on the stars; we can't change ours" - *Don't Give Up On Us* by 33-year-old David Soul climbs to number one in the pop chart - and stays there for four weeks ▪ *The Things We Do For Love* by 10cc is number six ▪ 'Ding-dong. Avon calling' - Housewives order perfumes and cosmetics from their local Avon rep ▪ Young girls wear *Pretty Peach* talc and lotions ▪ 40-year-old Gordon Honeycombe reads the daytime news for ITN ▪ 38-year-old David Owen is the new Foreign Secretary in Jim Callaghan's Labour government ▪ 36-year-old convicted murderer Gary Gilmore says, "Let's do it!" - and is executed by firing squad in Utah ▪ 52-year-old Jimmy Carter is inaugurated as US president in Washington ▪ Back in England - around 18 million TV viewers watch *Coronation Street* twice a week (on Mondays and Wednesdays at 7.30 p.m.). Ray and Deirdre Langton (played by 34-year-old Neville

Buswell and 22-year-old Anne Kirkbride) are proud parents of a newborn baby girl called Tracy. 25-year-old Cheryl Murray makes her first appearance as Suzie Birchall ▪ "She's crazy like a fool. What about..." *Daddy Cool* by Boney M climbs to number six in the pop chart ▪ "Working at the..." *Car Wash* by Rose Royce reaches number nine ▪ "Beep-beep, beep-beep, yeah! Traffic news on Radio One" - the latest traffic updates are transmitted on Radio One ▪ A new twelve-mile stretch of M11 motorway opens between Redbridge and Harlow ▪ More and more foreign cars are being sold in the UK ▪ The new Alfa Romeo *Alfasud Sprint* (with disc-brakes and a top speed of 103 mph) is now in showrooms ▪ The new Fiat *127 Sport* (with cloth upholstered seats and a top speed of 100 mph) is also available ▪ 2.5 litre tins of *Finnigan's* (rust-proofing) underbody seal with *Waxoyl* fly off the shelves at *Halfords* ▪ 55-year-old Trevor Baker presents the weather forecast on ITV ▪ There's more heavy rain in mid February ▪ Footballers play 'the beautiful game' on muddy pitches ▪ 27-year-old Brian Kidd scores four goals as Tony Book's Manchester City thrash Leicester City 5-0 at Maine Road ▪ Kevin Keegan, John Toshack and Joey Jones score the goals as Bob Paisley's Liverpool beat Derby County 3-1 at Anfield ▪ Brian Talbot, John Wark, Keith Bertschin and Paul Mariner score the goals as Bobby Robson's Ipswich Town beat Arsenal 1-4 at Highbury ▪ Aston Villa's 21-year-old centre-forward Andy Gray is fined £75 for making a 'V' sign at Manchester Utd fans ▪ 34-year-old Radio One DJ Tony Blackburn tells listeners of his sorrow and regret after the breakdown in his marriage to 28-year-old actress Tessa Wyatt ▪ *Dr. Love* ("... please come running can't you see I'm in pain") by 22-year-old Tina Charles climbs to number four in the pop chart ▪ *Isn't She Lovely* ("... isn't she wonderful") by 28-year-old David Parton reaches the same position ▪ 18-year-old Linda Lusardi (36C) appears nude in the latest edition of *Mayfair* magazine ▪ 19-year-old Sid Vicious replaces Glen Matlock as bass player in troublesome punk band The Sex Pistols ▪ 29-year-old Jim Rosenthal presents *Sport on 2* on BBC Radio Two on Saturday afternoons ▪ Sammy Chung's Wolverhampton Wanderers are top of Division Two ▪ Peter Morris' Mansfield Town are top of Division Three ▪ Big Ron Atkinson's Cambridge Utd are top of Division Four ▪ Everton sack manager Billy Bingham and appoint 42-year-old Gordon Lee ▪ 22-year-old Trevor

Francis (of Birmingham City) makes his debut for England in a 0-2 defeat against Holland at Wembley. England's full line-up for the match is: Clemence, Clement, Beattie, Doyle, Watson, Madeley, Keegan, Greenhoff, T Francis, Bowles, Brooking and substitutes, Pearson and Todd ▪ 30-year-old 'super' Georgie Best spends a few days in hospital after crashing his car in the early hours in Knightsbridge ▪ *You're More Than A Number In My Little Red Book* ("… you're more than a one night date") by The Drifters is number five in the pop chart ▪ "Just got back from the downtown Palais where the music was so sweet it knocked me right back in the alley. I'm ready. Yeah, yeah, yeah I'm ready" - *Rockaria!* by Electric Light Orchestra is number nine ▪ Hi-fi audio technology moves on apace ▪ 29-year-old entrepreneur Alan Sugar promotes his new *Amstrad 8000* stereo amplifier to independent electrical retailers in London ▪ Television technology moves on apace ▪ 36-year-old inventor Clive Sinclair markets a new two-inch TV set for £175.95 ▪ *Robin's Nest* (with 32-year-old Richard O'Sullivan, 28-year-old Tessa Wyatt and 52-year-old Tony Britton) is new on TV ▪ "Once upon a time there were three little girls who went to the police academy" - Men watch spellbound as *Charlie's Angels* (with 28-year-old Kate Jackson as Sabrina, 31-year-old Jaclyn Smith as Kelly and 29-year-old Farrah Fawcett-Majors as Jill) is shown on British television for the first time ▪ 'If you've got a taste for terror … take Carrie to the prom' - 22-year-old John Travolta, 44-year-old Piper Laurie and 27-year-old Sissy Spacek star at cinemas in *Carrie* - a film based on the novel by 29-year-old Stephen King ▪ 46-year-old Clint Eastwood stars in *The Enforcer* ▪ Motoring technology moves on apace ▪ The wonderful new 'up-market' Chrysler *Alpine GLS* comes with front head restraints, headlamp wash/wipe system and electronically operated front windows. This luxurious five-door hatchback is available now in showrooms for £3,040 ▪ Footballers, Alan Gowling and Micky Burns score the goals for Newcastle Utd in a 2-0 victory over Tottenham Hotspur. Spurs are now bottom of Division One and in real danger of being relegated to Division Two ▪ *Don't Cry For Me Argentina* ("… the truth is, I never left you") by 30-year-old Julie Covington spends a week at number one in the pop chart ▪ *Boogie Nights* ("… ain't no doubt, we are here to party") by Heatwave climbs to number two ▪ Boys play out - racing against each other on bicycles ▪

10-year-old Andrew Lovell, 9-year-old Neil Roper and 9-year-old Anthony Sutton speed around 'the block' on their bikes at Ford Way in Armitage ▪ A red Raleigh BSA *Tour-de-France* with dropped handle bars, 10-speed Derailleur gears, water bottle and toe-clips costs £96.95 (or £2.56 for 38 weeks from mum's catalogue) ▪ Girls attend gymnastics class ▪ 10-year-old Julie Walkeden from Rugeley achieves the B.A.G.A Level 2 award and sews a small oval badge onto her leotard to prove it ▪ The weather brightens ▪ Middle aged men spend Sunday afternoons in the garden ▪ A push-along *Qualcast Q7* side lawn mower (with five cutting blades) costs £11.45 at *Argos* ▪ A *Black & Decker* mains electric hedge trimmer is £15.95 ▪ *When I Need You* ("… I just close my eyes and I'm with you") by 28-year-old Leo Sayer spends three weeks at number one in the pop chart ▪ "Step back in time, me Ro-me-oh. My Juliet and take me home" - *Romeo* by Mr. Big is number four ▪ The *J. Lyons & Co* Corner House on The Strand in London closes down ▪ 47-year-old Ronnie Barker, 29-year-old Richard Beckinsale, 49-year-old Brian Wilde and 54-year-old Fulton Mackay star in a new series of BBC One sit-com *Porridge* ▪ "Now is the time to send us a line, for your Hoseason's boating brochure. We've got all kinds of craft that'll suit you just for fine for messing about on the water" - Middle-class families peruse glossy holiday pamphlets, before booking a two week summer break on the Norfolk Broads ▪ Travelling sales representatives (driving white Ford *Cortina* estate cars) hog the outside lane on motorways ▪ Music blares from 8-track cartridge tapes inserted into dashboard players ▪ "Oh, Jack comes out of the box. The bears came home and caught Goldilocks" - *Jack In The Box* by The Moments is number seven in the pop chart ▪ "I am the melody…" *Sing Me* by The Brothers is number eight ▪ Inflation has risen again - retail prices are now 17.5% higher than they were last year ▪ 64-year-old Labour prime-minister Jim Callaghan and his Chancellor of the Exchequer, 59-year-old Denis Healey, are under pressure to fix the failing economy ▪ Housewives go shopping at *Fine Fare* or *Gateway* supermarkets ▪ A loaf of bread costs 20p ▪ A jar of lemon curd is 14p ▪ A pint of milk is 11½p ▪ A pack of twenty cigarettes is 55p ▪ 'The double filling bar for the double filling feeling' - The new *Double Decker* chocolate bar from Cadbury's tastes good ▪ "Tell 'em about the honey, mummy!" - the Honey Monster advertises *Sugar Puffs* on TV.

Spring 1977

Lucious Linda Lusardi on page three

Monarch:	Queen Elizabeth II (aged 51)
Prime-minister:	James Callaghan (aged 65)
Chancellor:	Denis Healey (aged 59)
Home Secretary:	Merlyn Rees (aged 56)
Foreign Secretary:	David Owen (aged 38)
Football Manager:	Don Revie (aged 49)
Radio 1 Breakfast DJ:	Noel Edmonds (aged 28)
New car reg. suffix:	'R'

▪ Fathers take their sons to the cinema ▪ 'By train, by plane, by the edge of your seat - It's the Most Hilarious Suspense Ride of Your Life!' - *Silver Streak* (with 43-year-old Gene Wilder, 36-year-old Richard Pryor and 33-year-old Jill Clayburgh) is now showing ▪ Prime-minister Jim Callaghan zooms across the Atlantic Ocean on Concorde to meet president Carter in the US ▪ Queen Elizabeth II's Silver Jubilee tour moves onto Australia - the 50-year-old monarch visits Canberra for the State Opening of Parliament and then travels to Newcastle, Sydney, Nuriootpa and Perth ▪ 51-year-old Mrs. Thatcher (Leader of the Conservative Opposition) travels to her home town of Grantham and pays a visit to Kesteven and Grantham Girls' School - where she was head girl in 1942 ▪ "I can't stop running to ya, feel love coming through ya. Girl with you beside me, hold on, heaven guide me..." *Red Light Spells Danger* by 27-year-old Billy Ocean enters the pop chart at number forty-eight ▪ "When, when you smile, when you smile at me. Well, well I know our love will always be" - *When* by Showaddywaddy (with, lead singer, 25-year-old Dave Bartram) is number four ▪ "Only this time I'm..." *Going In With My Eyes Open* ("... I won't make the same mistake again") by 33-year-old David Soul is number two ▪ *Red Rum* wins the Grand National for a third time - 31-year-old Tommy Stack is the jockey and 46-year-old Ginger McCain is the trainer ▪ The rate of inflation remains high ▪ Unemployment remains high ▪ The economy is in a mess ▪ Jim Callaghan returns from his trip to America just as his Labour government looks set to fall ▪ A vote of confidence at the House of Commons is expected to go against Mr. Callaghan and a general election seems to be inevitable ▪ 'By Jimmy, he's done it!' - then suddenly in an amazing turn of events, prime Callaghan negotiates a last minute

deal with David Steel's Liberals and the vote of confidence is defeated by a majority of twenty-four ▪ Labour clings to power, but has been forced into making a number of concessions to the Liberal Party ▪ *Torn Between Two Lovers* ("... feeling like a fool. Loving both of you is breaking all the rules") by 28-year-old Mary MacGregor is number four in the pop chart ▪ "Don't you wonder sometimes, about..." *Sound And Vision* by 30-year-old David Bowie climbs to number three ▪ The under-fire Labour Party loses a crucial by-election at Ashfield (usually a safe seat) to the Conservatives ▪ The Lib-Lab Pact is now in place, with thirteen Liberal MPs voting with the government on crucial issues ▪ 59-year-old Chancellor of the Exchequer Denis Healey delivers his fifth Budget and announces a cut in the basic rate of income tax ▪ "Silly Billy!" - 35-year-old Mike Yarwood impersonates the Chancellor on Saturday night television and eighteen million viewers tune in to BBC One ▪ 57-year-old Hughie Green hosts *Opportunity Knocks* on ITV on Monday evenings (before *Coronation Street*) and 24-year-old Berni Flint (a singer from Southport) achieves the highest score on the 'clapometer' ▪ 'The antidote to panel games' - 55-year-old Humphrey Lyttelton is chairman for a new series of *I'm Sorry I Haven't A Clue* on BBC Radio Four. 34-year-old Graeme Garden, 41-year-old Barry Cryer, 39-year-old Willie Rushton and 36-year-old Tim Brooke-Taylor are panelists on the popular comedy show ▪ People buy the latest 7-inch pop singles at *Our Price* for 75p ▪ "Chanson d'amour. (Ra-da-da-da-da). Je t'adore" - *Chanson D'Amour* by Manhattan Transfer spends three weeks at number one on the hit parade ▪ "Oh, Moody Blue, tell me am I getting' through" - *Moody Blue* by 42-year-old Elvis Presley reaches number six ▪ Footballers, Kevin Keegan and Steve Heighway score the goals for Liverpool as Bob Paisley's team beats Tony Book's Manchester City 2-1 in a top-of-the-table clash in Division One. (Brian Kidd scores City's goal) ▪ 25-year-old Steve Perryman makes his three-hundredth appearance for Tottenham Hotspur in a 3-0 victory over Queens Park Rangers - the win gives Spurs two vital points in their fight against relegation ▪ The Easter holidays arrive ▪ Families gather around Ferguson *Colourstar TX* television sets ▪ BBC One broadcasts a six-part mini-series called *Roots* - with Kunta Kinte, Kizzy and Chicken George ▪ "Behold, the lamb of God who takes unto himself the sins of the world" - 32-year-old Robert Powell

stars in the title role in ITV's new blockbuster mini-series, *Jesus of Nazareth* ▪ "Magic, our Morris!" - 48-year-old Bill Maynard stars as Selwyn Frogitt in series two of *Oh No, It's Selwyn Frogitt* ▪ Approximately 20 million viewers tune-in to see Len Fairclough (played by 47-year-old Peter Adamson) marry Rita Littlewood (played by 43-year-old Barbara Knox) in the popular soap-opera *Coronation Street.* Womaniser Mike Baldwin (played by 41-year-old Johnny Briggs) is in a complicated love triangle with his London mistress Anne Woodley and his Weatherfield girlfriend Bet Lynch ▪ *Sunny* ("… yesterday my life was filled with rain") by Boney M (24-year-old Liz Mitchell, 28-year-old Marcia Barrett, 26-year-old Maizie Williams and 27-year-old Bobby Farrell) is number three in the pop chart ▪ *Red Light Spells Danger* ("… Can't hold out much longer") by Billy Ocean climbs to number two ▪ 32-year-old Angela Rippon reads the news on BBC television ▪ Two Boeing *747* jumbo jets collide on the ground in Tenerife killing 583 people - it's the world's worst aviation disaster ▪ Queen Elizabeth II's Silver Jubilee tour moves onto Papua New Guinea, Bombay and Oman ▪ Back in England - sacked workers continue to picket the Grunwick photographic processing factory in Willesden. Flying pickets also target any chemist shops that use the services of Grunwick ▪ Car production at British Leyland grinds to a halt when three-thousand tool-makers walk out on strike ▪ 49-year-old Derek Robinson (aka Red Robbo) is union convener at the Longbridge factory ▪ 52-year-old US president Jimmy Carter pays a flying visit to Newcastle-upon-Tyne and is given a warm welcome by the Geordie crowds ▪ The economy continues to falter under Jim Callaghan's Labour government ▪ Mrs. Thatcher's opposition Conservative Party takes a significant lead in the opinion polls ▪ Political leaders from the richest seven countries in the world travel to London for the G7 summit. Helmut Schmidt represents West Germany, Valery Giscard d'Estaing represents France and Jimmy Carter represents the USA. The leaders discuss the global economy and also attend a state dinner with Queen Elizabeth II and the Duke of Edinburgh ▪ Life continues as normal for families around the country ▪ *Hawaii Five-O* is on ITV on Tuesday evenings - with 56-year-old Jack Lord as Steve McGarrett ▪ *It's A Knockout* is on BBC One on Friday evenings. A team from Beverley wins a closely fought contest against Wakefield and

Calderdale and will now compete in the Jeux Sans Frontieres competition later in the year ▪ The final episode of *Porridge* is shown on Friday the twenty-fifth of March. Young Lenny Godber leaves Slade Prison at the end of his sentence and goes off on a romantic holiday with Fletch's daughter ▪ Queens Park Rangers star footballer 27-year-old Stan Bowles is currently out of the team injured after breaking his ankle in a match against Bristol City ▪ 11-year-old schoolboy Stephen Coogan from Middleton in Manchester sits in his bedroom listening to records ▪ *Knowing Me Knowing You* ("… Ah-haa") by Abba is number one in the pop chart for five weeks! ▪ "If you want to leave me, well that's all right" - *I Don't Want To Put A Hold On You* by 24-year-old Berni Flint (an *Opportunity Knocks* winner from Southport) climbs to number three ▪ *Pearl's A Singer* ("… she stands up when she plays the piano") by 31-year-old Elkie Brooks peaks at number eight ▪ "Where are we..." *Rock Bottom* (Britain's entry for the Eurovision Song Contest) by 28-year-old Lynsey De Paul and 29-year-old Mike Moran stalls at number nineteen ▪ The rebellious 'punk' movement gathers momentum ▪ Siouxsie and the Banshees play a gig in London ▪ The Clash release their first album and thousands of young punk rockers listen to the tracks: *Remote Control*, *White Riot* and *London's Burning* on their record players - with the volume turned up loud ▪ The Damned release *Damned, Damned, Damned* ▪ The Stranglers release *Rattus Norvegicus* ▪ At lunch times, working men sit in canteens, browsing through *The Sun* newspaper ▪ 18-year-old Luscious Linda Lusardi (36C) is on page three ▪ 26-year-old cricketer Derek Randall scores 174 runs in England's second innings total of 417, but England lose the Centenary Test Match against Australia in Melbourne, after being bowled out for just 95 in the first innings ▪ 26-year-old Barry Sheene wins the 500cc motorcycle Grand Prix in Venezuela ▪ 22-year-old footballer Trevor Francis scores a goal for England (Clemence, Gidman, Cherry, Kennedy, Watson, Hughes, Keegan, Channon, Royle, T Francis, Hill and substitute, Mariner) in a 5-0 victory over Luxembourg. Keegan, Kennedy and Channon (2) are also on the score-sheet. John Gidman and Paul Mariner make their international debuts. The victory gives England a faint hope of reaching next year's world cup finals ▪ 24-year-old Brian Little scores the winning goal as Ron Saunders' Aston Villa achieve a 3-2 victory (after extra-time) over

Gordon Lee's Everton in the second replay of the League Cup final ▪ 20-year-old Alan Biley scores twice as Big Ron Atkinson's Cambridge Utd beat Aldershot 4-1 in Division Four ▪ 24-year-old Robin Friday scores twice as Cardiff City beat Luton Town 4-2 in Division Two - and the aberrant centre-forward celebrates by flicking a 'V' sign at Luton goalkeeper, Milija Aleksic ▪ "And I just got to be me-ee, free-ee, free-ee" - *Free* by Deniece Williams is the new number one pop single ▪ *Whodunit* ("… who killed my baby?") by Tavares is number five ▪ *White Riot* ("… I wanna riot. White riot, a riot of my own") by The Clash is number thirty-eight ▪ 41-year-old John Spencer collects £6,000 after winning the *Embassy* World Snooker Championship at the Crucible in Sheffield - by beating Cliff Thorburn from Canada in the final ▪ The domestic football season ends ▪ Bob Paisley's Liverpool are champions of Division One for the second year running. Ray Clemence, Phil Neal, Emlyn Hughes, Tommy Smith, Joey Jones, Phil Thompson, Ian Callaghan, Jimmy Case, Steve Heighway, Ray Kennedy, David Johnson, John Toshack, Terry McDermott and 26-year-old Kevin Keegan have all been outstanding ▪ Tony Book's Manchester City (with Joe Corrigan, Willie Donachie, Dave Watson, Mike Doyle, Asa Hartford, Peter Barnes, Gary Owen, Joe Royle, Brian Kidd and 27-year-old Dennis Tueart) are runners-up ▪ Keith Burkinshaw's Tottenham Hotspur are relegated along with Sunderland and Stoke City ▪ Andy Gray (of Aston Villa) and Malcolm 'Supermac' MacDonald (of Arsenal) share the accolade of top goal scorer - both men having scored twenty-five league goals for the season ▪ 42-year-old Brian Clough's Nottingham Forest gain promotion from Division Two ▪ "I would have given you all of my heart, but there's someone who's torn it apart" - Rod Stewart's double A-sided single, *I Don't Want To Talk About It / First Cut Is The Deepest* climbs to number one ▪ "Well good morning Judge, how are you today?" - *Good Morning Judge* by 10cc is number five ▪ *You Don't Have To Be A Star (To Be In My Show)* by Marilyn McCoo and Billy Davis Jr. is number seven ▪ 51-year-old Queen Elizabeth II visits Dundee, Aberdeen and Edinburgh as part of her Silver Jubilee tour ▪ 'In 1943, sixteen German paratroopers landed in England. In three days, they almost won the war' - 44-year-old Michael Caine, 46-year-old Robert Duvall and 41-year-old Donald Sutherland star at cinemas in *The Eagle Has Landed* ▪ 'It's not

what we do - it's the way we do it' - 31-year-old Mary Millington features in *Come Play With Me* at 'special' cinemas ▪ "Only the crumbliest flakiest chocolate, tastes like chocolate never tasted before" - Cadbury's *Flake* adverts are on TV ▪ 43-year-old *Blue Peter* presenter John Noakes is filmed at the top of Nelson's Column, helping workman clean the 169 foot high monument in Trafalgar Square ▪ "Oh, what a..." *Lonely Boy* by Andrew Gold reaches number eleven in the pop chart ▪ *Mah-Na, Mah-Ma* ("... Doo-doo, doo-doo-doo") by Piero Umiliani reaches number eight ▪ Repairs are completed on Big Ben and the historic Great Clock of Westminster is working again for the first time in nine months ▪ 30-year-old footballer Jimmy Greenhoff scores the winning goal in the FA Cup final as Tommy 'The Doc' Docherty's Manchester Utd defeat champions Liverpool 2-1. A ticket for the standing enclosure at the Empire Stadium in Wembley costs £2.50 ▪ Four days after the cup final - Terry McDermott, Tommy Smith and Phil Neal score the goals as Liverpool win the European Cup for the first time by beating Borussia Monchengladbach 3-1 in Rome ▪ "Welcome to the..." *Hotel California* ("... Such a lovely place. Such a lovely place. Such a lovely face") by The Eagles is number eight in the pop chart ▪ *Solsbury Hill* by 27-year-old Peter Gabriel is number thirteen ▪ The *Spot the Pigeon E.P.* (with tracks: *Match Of The Day*, *Pigeons* and *Inside and Out*) by Genesis is number fourteen ▪ 19-year-old footballer Cyrille Regis transfers from non-league Hayes FC to First Division West Bromwich Albion for a fee of £10,000 ▪ "You can feel it all over. You can feel it all over, people" - *Sir Duke* by 26-year-old Stevie Wonder is number two on the weekly hit parade ▪ *Love Theme From 'A Star Is Born' (Evergreen)* by 35-year-old Barbara Streisand peaks at number three and stays in the chart for nineteen weeks ▪ *Smoke On The Water* by Deep Purple is number twenty-one ▪ 38-year-old Terry Wogan presents the breakfast show on BBC Radio Two ▪ 51-year-old Pete Murray, 55-year-old Jimmy Young and 38-year-old 'Diddy' David Hamilton host programs during the day ▪ 43-year-old John Dunn presents the teatime show ▪ Housewives peg out the washing on 'new-fangled' galvanised tubular steel framed rotary clothes lines, before sitting down to read *Weekend* magazine ▪ A 4oz pack of *Co-op 99* tea costs 11½p ▪ An 8oz pack of *Co-op 99* coffee is 79p ▪ Adverts say, '*Twix* - the longer lasting snack'.

Summer 1977

Young Ian Botham makes his Test Match debut

Monarch:	Queen Elizabeth II (aged 51)
Prime-minister:	James Callaghan (aged 65)
Chancellor:	Denis Healey (aged 60)
Home Secretary:	Merlyn Rees (aged 56)
Foreign Secretary:	David Owen (aged 39)
Football Manager:	Ron Greenwood (aged 55)
Radio 1 Breakfast DJ:	Noel Edmonds (aged 28)
New car reg. suffix:	'S'

▪ Street parties are held to celebrate Queen Elizabeth II's Silver Jubilee ▪ It rains ▪ Children devour cup cakes and jelly with ice-cream ▪ 'How's that for taste?" - Cans of *Top Deck* are available in 'Lemonade Shandy' and 'Limeade & Lager' flavours ▪ Discarded ring-pulls litter the country's parks and communal spaces ▪ 'DESTROY' - "God save the queen. She ain't no human being. There is no future, in England's dreaming" - *God Save The Queen* by The Sex Pistols reaches number two in the pop chart. The controversial group takes a Jubilee boat trip along the River Thames ▪ The Ramones perform a gig at the Roundhouse in Camden and hundreds of youngsters push and shove in the mosh-pit to the sounds of *Sheena Is A Punk Rocker* and *Blitzkrieg Bop* ▪ Joe Strummer of The Clash appears in court to answer charges of stealing a pillowcase from a hotel in Newcastle ▪ Johnny Rotten of The Sex Pistols is attacked by a gang of thugs outside a pub in north London ▪ Punk bands play at dingy music venues; performing in front of crowds of pogo-ing youths ▪ 13-year-old schoolboy Nigel Blackwell from Birkenhead plays *Subbuteo* 'round his friend's house - and gets palmed off with a headless centre-forward ▪ Millions of people stay indoors and enjoy watching television ▪ *Celebrity Squares* (hosted by 'the big square himself' 49-year-old Bob Monkhouse) is on ITV on Saturday evenings ▪ The fifth series of *The Onedin Line* (with 45-year-old Peter Gilmore as James Onedin) is on BBC One on Sunday evenings ▪ The annual cost of a colour TV license increases from £18 to £21 ▪ A black and white license goes up from £8 to £9 ▪ Inflation remains high ▪ The economic policies of Jim Callaghan's Labour government appear to be failing ▪ 51-year-old Margaret Thatcher's opposition Conservative Party is ahead

in the polls ▪ 39-year-old Australian businessman Kerry Packer causes a huge furore by signing thirty-five leading international cricketers to appear in an unofficial world series. 30-year-old England captain Tony Greig is one of the players choosing to join the 'Packer Circus' and, as a consequence, is sacked by the MCC ▪ 41-year-old jockey Lester Piggott rides *The Minstrel* to victory in the Epsom Derby ▪ The school holidays begin ▪ *Jackanory*, *Inch High Private Eye* and *Flash Gordon's Trip to Mars* are broadcast on BBC One during the day ▪ Children play-out, despite the inclement weather ▪ The Ford Way Gang throw stones at the Handsacre Estate Gang in the field beside the brook in Old Road, Armitage near Rugeley ▪ Kids chase *Corona* lorries down the road as the pop-man delivers bottles of Cream Soda and Orangeade to local houses ▪ "You've picked a fine time to leave me..." *Lucille* ("... with four hungry children and a crop in the field") by 38-year-old Kenny Rogers is number one in the pop chart ▪ "Oh, that's why I'm..." *Easy* ("... I'm easy like Sunday morning, yeah") by The Commodores is number nine ▪ *Too Hot To Handle* by Heatwave is number fifteen ▪ Grown-ups buy tickets for the cinema ▪ 'Out of the sky comes the screen's most incredible spectacle of men and war!' - *A Bridge Too Far* is now showing, with a multi-star cast which includes: 46-year-old Sean Connery, 44-year-old Michael Caine, 40-year-old Edward Fox, 39-year-old Anthony Hopkins and 56-year-old Dirk Bogarde ▪ 'England expects that every man will do his duty!' - *Stand Up Virgin Soldiers* (with 26-year-old Robin Askwith, 29-year-old Lynda Bellingham and 27-year-old Pamela Stephenson) is also on general release ▪ *Show You The Way To Go* by The Jacksons spends a week at number one in the pop chart ▪ *Halfway Down The Stairs* by The Muppets is number seven ▪ 51-year-old Queen Elizabeth II visits Lancaster, Preston, Manchester, Liverpool, Llandudno, Bangor, Hollyhead, Harlech, Milford Haven, Carmarthen, Llanelli, Swansea, Barry and Cardiff as part of her Silver Jubilee tour ▪ 32-year-old DJ Dave Lee Travis hosts the travelling Radio One Roadshow for five days in July. DLT's Roadshow week begins on the Marine Parade in Clacton-on-Sea and ends at Steyne Gardens in Worthing ▪ *So You Win Again* ("... You win again. Here I stand again, the loser") by Hot Chocolate (with, lead singer, 33-year-old Errol Brown) is new at number one ▪ *Fanfare For The Common Man* by Emerson, Lake & Palmer is number two ▪

"Hey-eehh!" - 31-year-old Henry Winkler stars as The Fonz in *Happy Days* on ITV ▪ 47-year-old Brian Redhead and 33-year-old Nigel Rees present Radio Four's *Today* news program ▪ A young woman is murdered in Leeds and it's feared that she's the fifth victim of the Yorkshire Ripper ▪ A mass-picket takes place outside the Grunwick photo processing plant in Willesden. Hundreds of representatives from various unions attend, including 39-year-old Arthur Scargill of the Yorkshire NUM ▪ *The Return of Reginald Perrin* - the fifth novel from 42-year-old writer David Nobbs is published ▪ 46-year-old Windsor Davies and 44-year-old Don Estelle (from BBC One's *It Ain't Half Hot Mum*) appear in summer season at the White Rock Pavilion in Hastings ▪ 29-year-old ventriloquist Keith Harris is a guest star on *The Black and White Minstrel Show* ▪ Police use Perspex riot-shields for the first time, during a violent demonstration against members of the National Front in Lewisham. More than two-hunderd people are arrested and fifty-six police officers injured ▪ "So pack your toys away, your pretty boys away. Your 45s away, your alibis away. Your Spanish flies away, your one more tries away. Your old tye-dyes away…" *You're Moving Out Today* by 30-year-old Carole Bayer Sager reaches number six in the pop chart at the end of June ▪ "Oh, Sam, Sam, you know where I am" - *Sam* by 28-year-old Olivia Newton-John reaches number six in early July ▪ 30-year-old pop star/football chairman Elton John appoints 32-year-old Graham Taylor as manager of Fourth Division Watford FC ▪ 29-year-old defender Trevor Cherry (of Leeds Utd) is sent off for England in a friendly against Argentina ▪ 21-year-old striker Andy Gray (of Aston Villa) is voted PFA 'Player of the Year' and PFA 'Young Player of the Year' ▪ Scottish fans invade the pitch and break a crossbar, after Scotland have beaten England by two goals to one at Wembley - Gordon McQueen and Kenny Dalglish score for the Scots. Mick Channon scores a late penalty for England ▪ Families book their holidays ▪ *Lunn Poly* travel agents do a roaring trade on the high street ▪ People enjoy a week at *Butlin's* or in a static caravan at the seaside ▪ 'Holiday campers exposed! The funniest take off of the season!' - 26-year-old Robin Askwith stars at cinemas - playing the character Timmy Lea in *Confessions from a Holiday Camp* ▪ Young men with hairy chests, gold medallions and shirts unbuttoned to the waist 'strut their stuff' on Saturday nights - hoping to impress the ladies ▪

Ain't Gonna Bump No More ("... with no big fat woman") by Joe Tex is number two in the pop chart ▪ *The Crunch* (a catchy instrumental tune) by The Rah Band is number six ▪ "Burn baby, burn" - *Disco Inferno* by The Trammps is number sixteen ▪ There's a flurry of activity on football's transfer market ▪ Kevin Keegan leaves Liverpool and joins SV Hamburg for £500,000 ▪ 26-year-old Kenny Dalglish leaves Celtic and joins Liverpool as Keegan's replacement ▪ 28-year-old striker Mick Channon transfers from Southampton to Manchester City ▪ 23-year-old defender Kenny Burns transfers from Birmingham City to Brian Clough's newly promoted Nottingham Forest ▪ 29-year-old goalkeeper Jimmy Rimmer leaves Arsenal and joins Aston Villa ▪ 32-year-old Pat Jennings leaves relegated Tottenham Hotspur to become Arsenal's new number one ▪ 49-year-old Tommy 'The Doc' Docherty is sensationally sacked by Manchester Utd after conducting an affair with the wife of the team's physiotherapist ▪ "Oooh, love. Oooh, lover boy. What're you doin' tonight, hey boy?" - *Good Old Fashioned Lover Boy* by Queen reaches number seventeen in the pop chart ▪ 47-year-old Dave Sexton succeeds 'The Doc' and is appointed manager of Manchester Utd ▪ 35-year-old Mike Brearley succeeds Tony Greig as England's cricket captain ▪ The first Test Match of the Ashes series against Australia at Lord's is drawn - with fast bowler Bob Willis taking 7 for 78. England then go on to win the next three matches (at Old Trafford, Trent Bridge and Headingley) and regain the Ashes. 21-year-old Ian Botham makes his Test debut at Trent Bridge and takes 5 wickets and scores 25 runs. Yorkshireman Geoffrey Boycott scores a magnificent (and hard fought) 191 at his home ground, Headingley. It's the 36-year-old batsman's one-hundredth first-class century. D L Amiss, J M Brearley (cpt), G Boycott, R A Woolmer, D W Randall, A W Greig, G D Barlow, G R J Roope, A P E Knott (wk), I T Botham, G Miller, C M Old, J K Lever, D L Underwood, M Hendrick and R G D Willis have all played a part in this fantastic Ashes victory ▪ Queen Elizabeth II's Silver Jubilee tour moves onto Ipswich, Norwich, Grimsby, Doncaster, Sheffield, Leeds, Wakefield, Harrogate, York, Hull, Middlesbrough, Sunderland and Newcastle-upon-Tyne ▪ Discotheques are all the rage ▪ Youngsters in flared trousers groove and gyrate on the dance floor at the local village hall, be-

neath flashing lights and a glittery disco ball ▪ "Oooh, I feel love, I feel love, I feel love, I feel love…" *I Feel Love* by 28-year-old Donna Summer climbs to number one in the pop chart - and stays there for four weeks ▪ "Baby, my love is on the line…" *Baby Don't Change Your Mind* ("… Don't change it") by Gladys Knight and the Pips reaches number four ▪ 'Suzuki, 7' - 26-year-old Barry Sheene is crowned 500cc motorcycle racing world champion for the second year running. Sheene wins a race at Spa in Belgium at an average speed of 135 mph - it's the fastest motorcycle Grand Prix, ever! ▪ "Adrian! Adrian!" - *Rocky*, with 30-year-old Sylvester Stalone, is a huge hit at cinemas ▪ 49-year-old Roger Moore stars as James Bond (aka 007) in *The Spy Who Loved Me* - 29-year-old Barbara Bach is Anya Amasova and 37-year-old Richard Kiel is Jaws. Schoolboys watch, amazed, as Bond's white Lotus *Esprit S1* sports car (registration PPW 306R) transforms into a submarine ▪ *Nobody Does It Better* ("... Makes me feel sad for the rest") by 32-year-old Carly Simon climbs to number seven in the pop chart ▪ 45-year-old Brian Moore presents *On The Ball* on Saturday lunchtimes on ITV ▪ 50-year-old Don Revie resigns as England football manager to take up a coaching role in the United Arab Emirates on a salary of £60,000 a year - tax free! Revie is vilified by the press as he still had two years of his contract to run ▪ 55-year-old Ron Greenwood from West Ham Utd succeeds Revie as England manager ▪ 21-year-old tennis star Bjorn Borg defeats 24-year-old Jimmy Conners in the men's singles final at Wimbledon ▪ 32-year-old Virginia Wade from Bournemouth wins the ladies' singles, beating Bette Stove from the Netherlands (4-6, 6-3, 6-1) in the final. (21-year-old Sue Barker loses in the semi-finals) ▪ "Hello, how are you? Have you been alright, through all these lonely, lonely, lonely, lonely, lonely nights? - *Telephone Line* by Electric Light Orchestra is number eight in the pop chart ▪ *Give A Little Bit* ("… Give a little bit of your love to me") by Supertramp is number twenty-nine ▪ Queen Elizabeth II's Silver Jubilee tour moves onto Wolverhampton, West Bromwich, Walsall, Birmingham, Coventry, Leicester, Chesterfield, Derby and Nottingham ▪ "Long ago, high on a mountain in Mexico, lived a young shepherd boy…" *Angelo* ("…Who met a young girl and he loved her so") by Brotherhood of Man is top of the pop chart ▪

Ma Baker ("… she taught her four sons. Ma-ma-ma-ma. Ma Baker, to handle their guns") by Boney M peaks at number two ▪ *Oh Lori* by Alessi reaches number eight ▪ 'S' reg cars go on sale ▪ More and more foreign cars are being purchased in the UK ▪ The new Skoda *105 Estelle* from Czechoslovakia has a top speed of 81 mph and accelerates from 0-60 mph in 22 seconds ▪ The latest Renault *12TL* from France has a top speed of 87 mph and accelerates from 0-60 mph in 16.1 seconds ▪ The latest Volvo *244DL* from Sweden has a top speed of 95 mph and accelerates from 0-60 mph in 15 seconds ▪ Four star leaded petrol is 78p a gallon ▪ "It's your life, ahh-ahh…" *It's Your Life* ("… Ooh-ooh") by Smokie is number five in the pop chart ▪ "Blamin' it all on the…" *Nights On Broadway* by 37-year-old Candi Staton is number six ▪ Queen Elizabeth II's Silver Jubilee tour moves onto Southampton, Torbay, Exeter, Plymouth, Falmouth, Truro, Bodmin, St. Austell, Bristol, Bath and Weston-super-Mare ▪ Families enjoy the late summer Bank Holiday - walking along the sea-front, eating ice-creams ▪ Frozen ice-lollies now come with jokes and riddles printed on the sticks ▪ 12-year-old schoolboy Matthew Hall (aka Harry Hill) from Staplehurst in Kent enjoys a *Count Dracula.* His sister has a *Lemonade Fizz* ▪ 'Just one Cornetto, give it to me' - *Cornettos* are new ▪ "Aquarius, and my name is Ralph" - *Float On* by The Floaters reaches number one on the weekly hit parade ▪ "But baby (yeah, yeah)…" *You Got What It Takes* by Showaddywaddy is number two ▪ "Outside, the rain begins and it may never end, so cry no more, on the shore, a dream will take us out to sea, forever more, forever more" - *We're All Alone* by 32-year-old Rita Coolidge is number six ▪ Noisy schoolboys sit together in the local cinema ▪ A ticket for a seat in the stalls costs 40p ▪ 'New!! Sinbad's boldest and most daring adventure!' - 38-year-old Patrick Wayne and 26-year-old Jane Seymour star in *Sinbad and the Eye of the Tiger* ▪ 'A fantastic, incredible world of savage mystery!' - 38-year-old Patrick Wayne and 24-year-old Sarah Douglas star in *The People that Time Forgot* ▪ The new football season gets underway ▪ 28-year-old Lou Macari bags a hat-trick as Dave Sexton's Manchester Utd beat Willie Bell's Birmingham City 1-4 in front of 28,005 spectators at St. Andrews ▪ Kenny Dalglish scores on his league debut for Liverpool in a 1-1 draw against Middlesbrough ▪ Brian Clough's

newly promoted Nottingham Forest win their opening three matches in Division One; 25-year-old centre-forward Peter Withe scores four goals in victories over Everton, Bristol City and Derby County. 24-year-old winger John Robertson and 25-year-old midfielder Martin O'Neill also get their names on the score-sheet for Forest ▪ 38-year-old 'Diddy' David Hamilton presents the afternoon show on Radio One ▪ "There's no point in asking, you'll get no reply. Oh just remember, I don't decide. I got no reason, it's all too much. You'll always find us, out to lunch" - *Pretty Vacant* by The Sex Pistols (with, lead singer, 21-year-old Johnny Rotten and, bassist, 20-year-old Sid Vicioius) is number six in the pop chart ▪ "Walking on the beaches, looking at the…" *Peaches* by The Stranglers (with, lead singer, 27-year-old Hugh Cornwell and, bassist, 25-year-old Jean-Jacques Burnel) is number eight ▪ "I'd go the…" *Whole Wide World* by 23-year-old Wreckless Eric fails to make the *Top 50* ▪ Spiky haired adolescent kids sit in bus shelters, drinking *Olde English* cider and smoking *Benson & Hedges* cigarettes ▪ Graffiti on walls says, 'Oi! Punks Punks Punks rule OK' ▪ The availability of 'fast-food' has increased ▪ *McDonalds* now has ten restaurants in the UK ▪ Elvis Presley dies on the toilet in Memphis, aged 42.

Autumn 1977

Never mind the bollocks, here's the Sex Pistols

Monarch:	Queen Elizabeth II (aged 51)
Prime-minister:	James Callaghan (aged 65)
Chancellor:	Denis Healey (aged 60)
Home Secretary:	Merlyn Rees (aged 56)
Foreign Secretary:	David Owen (aged 39)
Football Manager:	Ron Greenwood (aged 56)
Radio 1 Breakfast DJ:	Noel Edmonds (aged 28)
New car reg. suffix:	'S'

▪ The Silver Jubilee tour continues ▪ 51-year-old Queen Elizabeth II visits Northern Ireland before jetting off to Canada with her 56-year-old husband Prince Philip, Duke of Edinburgh ▪ The nation watches on television as 21-year-old athlete Steve Ovett wins a gold medal in the IAAF World Cup in Dusseldorf by showing an incredible burst of pace on the final bend

of the 1500 metres ▪ 'Spearmint Flavoured Chewy Sweets' - *Pacers* go on sale ▪ Children return to school after the summer holiday ▪ Boys play conkers in the corner of the playground and exchange skateboarding stories ▪ A packet of Smiths *Football Crazy* smokey bacon crisps from the school tuck-shop costs 4½p ▪ 28-year-old DJ Noel Edmonds presents the breakfast show on BBC Radio One ▪ "Way Down, where the music plays. Way down, like a tidal wave" - *Way Down* by the late Elvis Presley climbs to the top of the pop chart - and stays there for five weeks! ▪ "Whoa, whoa, you've got the..." *Best Of My Love* by The Emotions enters at number twenty-seven ▪ "Gimme dat, gimme dat ..." *Gimme Dat Banana* by Black Gorilla is number twenty-nine ▪ 'Raising More Than a Temperature!' - the 'X' rated comedy film *What's Up, Nurse!* (starring 26-year-old Felicity Devonshire, 27-year-old Angela Grant and 65-year-old John Le Mesurier) is at cinemas ▪ 'They're free!! Ready to serve you on the big screen!' - A feature length version of *Are You Being Served?* (starring 42-year-old John Inman, 55-year-old Mollie Sugden, 42-year-old Trevor Bannister, 56-year-old Frank Thornton, 78-year-old Harold Bennett and 34-year-old Wendy Richard) is also now showing ▪ 33-year-old comedy actor Richard O'Sullivan enjoys a romantic night out with his girlfriend (and co-star in popular sit-com *Robin's Nest*) 29-year-old actress Tessa Wyatt - the estranged wife of DJ Tony Blackburn ▪ The Labour Party Conference takes place in Brighton ▪ 65-year-old prime-minister Jim Callaghan and 60-year-old Chancellor of the Exchequer Denis Healey continue to battle rising inflation rates. Retail prices are currently 18% higher than they were twelve months ago ▪ 16-year-old William Hague makes a witty speech about old people at the Conservative Party conference in Blackpool ▪ 13-year-old Alexander Boris de Pfeffel Johnson is a new border at Eton College ▪ "Whatever happened to dear old Lenin?" - *No More Heroes* ("... anymore") by The Stranglers enters the pop chart at number forty-nine ▪ "We like the music. We like that disco sound" - *Black Is Black* ("... I want my baby back) by La Belle Epoque climbs to number two ▪ 28-year-old goalkeeper Peter Shilton leaves George Eastham's Stoke City and joins Brian Clough's newly promoted Nottingham Forest for £250,000 ▪ Football hooligans travel abroad to fight opposing fans on the terraces ▪ French police arrest dozens of rampaging Manchester Utd fans at a European Cup

Winners' Cup tie between United and St. Etienne in Paris ▪ In the UEFA Cup, Newcastle Utd fans fight on the pitch with Bohemians' supporters in Dublin ▪ "Why don't you ask them what they expect from you?" - *Do Anything You Wanna Do* by The Rods reaches number nine in the pop chart ▪ "Looking through..." *Gary Gilmore's Eyes* by The Adverts stalls at number nineteen ▪ 35-year-old Gordon Burns presents *The Krypton Factor* on television - a tough new 'game show' where contestants are put through their paces in rounds of mental and physical agility ▪ "Remember to tell a grown-up where you're going" - 20-year-old Keith Chegwin encourages children to turn up at his Saturday morning 'Swaparama' on BBC's *Multi-Coloured Swap Shop* ▪ Dads cut the grass on Sunday mornings ▪ The standard colour of *Flymo* 'hover' lawn-mowers has changed from blue and white to bright orange ▪ "It's time to play the music, it's time to light the lights. It's time to meet the Muppets on the Muppet Show tonight" - Fozzie, Kermit, Animal, Miss Piggy and the Swedish Chef star in a new series of ITV's hugely popular *Muppet Show* ▪ "Meet the gang 'cause the boys are here, the boys to entertain you" - 47-year-old Windsor Davies, 44-year-old Don Estelle and 42-year-old Melvyn Hayes star in a new series of BBC One's hugely popular situation comedy *It Ain't Half Hot Mum* ▪ 28-year-old Elizabeth Estensen, 35-year-old Nerys Hughes and 55-year-old Mollie Sugden star in a new series of *The Liver Birds* ▪ "What's that lipstick taste of? / Woman, Stanley. Woman" - Stanley Ogden (62-year-old Bernard Youens) kisses his wife Hilda (51-year-old Jean Alexander) on ITV's popular soap-opera *Coronation Street* ▪ 13-year-old schoolgirl Sally Wainwright from Sowerby Bridge stays up late to watch *Rock Follies of '77*, and dreams of one day writing dramas for TV ▪ 32-year-old Angela Rippon and 47-year-old Tom Coyne present *Top Gear* on BBC One in the Midlands' region ▪ A Bill to make the wearing of seat-belts in cars compulsory fails to get through parliament ▪ Ford launches the all new *Granada* motorcar, with prices from £5,913. There's a choice of 2.0 litre, 2.3 litre and 2.8 litre petrol engines, and (for the first time) there's also a 2.1 litre diesel engine. The top-of-the-range *Ghia* model comes complete with headlamp washers as standard ▪ 'From Georgia to Texas ... and back, in 28 hours, with a truck-load of bootleg beer' - fathers and sons rush to the cinema to see *Smokey and the Bandit*, starring 41-year-

old Burt Reynolds, 40-year-old Jerry Reed, 30-year-old Sally Field and a black Pontiac *Trans-Am* car ▪ The songs: *It's Now Or Never*, *Jailhouse Rock*, *Crying In The Chapel*, *Return To Sender* and *All Shook Up* by the late Elvis Presley all enter the Top 50 hit parade ▪ "I remember Elvis Presley, Lord how I love to hear him sing. So, I'll adore him just forever, for he's the one and only king" - Danny Mirror sings *I Remember Elvis Presley (The King Is Dead)* ▪ The dark nights draw in and families spend their evenings watching TV together ▪ The *Dutchess of Duke Street* (with 34-year-old Gemma Jones) is on BBC One on Saturday nights ▪ *Poldark* (with 35-year-old Robin Ellis) is broadcast on Sunday nights ▪ "I rented my apartment on a Monday at one, a-singin' doo-lolly-lolly, shicky-bum, shicky-bum" - *Telephone Man* by 28-year-old Meri Wilson climbs to number six on the weekly hit parade ▪ "From L.A. to New York..." *From New York To L.A.* by 29-year-old Patsy Gallant also reaches number six ▪ 30-year-old footballer Archie Gemmill transfers from Derby County to Brian Clough's newly promoted Nottingham Forest for £25,000 ▪ Liverpool sign 21-year-old defender Alan Hansen for £110,000 from Partick Thistle ▪ 19-year-old Cyrille Regis makes his debut for Ronnie Allen's West Bromwich Albion - and scores the winning goal in a 2-1 victory over Middlesbrough. (20-year-old Bryan Robson is also on the score-sheet for 'The Baggies') ▪ 49-year-old Tommy 'The Doc' Docherty is installed as the new manager of Derby County ▪ 57-year-old Sir Alf Ramsey takes over from Willie Bell as manager of Birmingham City ▪ 27-year-old DJ David 'Kid' Jensen presents an edition of *Top of the Pops* ▪ Futuristic electronic music is becoming popular ▪ *Magic Fly* by Space is number two in the pop chart ▪ "De, de-de, de-der" - *Oxygene Part IX* by Jean-Michel Jarre is number four ▪ Pop star Marc Bolan dies in a car crash at Barnes in London - just two weeks before his 30th birthday ▪ 44-year-old Frank Bough presents *Grandstand* on BBC One on Saturday afternoons ▪ 54-year-old Murray Walker commentates on motor racing events ▪ The six-wheeled Tyrrell Formula One racing car is used for the final time - Frenchman Patrick Depailler drives the experimental machine to a third placed finish in the Japanese Grand Prix. The race is won by Britain's James Hunt in a conventional four-wheeled McLaren ▪ Back in England

- 10-year-old Andrew Lovell undergoes an operation at Stafford Hospital to remove a burst appendix. Nurse Hart, on the Thomas Ward, looks after young Andrew as he convalesces ▪ 6-year-old Helena Lovell from Armitage receives a *Fisher Price* Kermit the Frog hand-puppet for her birthday ▪ *No More Heroes* ("…anymore") by The Stranglers climbs to number eight in the pop chart ▪ 23-year-old footballer Trevor Francis scores twice as Sir Alf Ramsey's Birmingham City beat John Neal's Middlesbrough 1-2 at Ayresome Park ▪ 23-year-old Mick Ferguson bags a hat-trick as Gordon Milne's Coventry City beat Tony Book's Manchester City 4-2 at Highfield Road ▪ 27-year-old Malcolm 'Supermac' MacDonald and 21-year-old Frank Stapleton score the goals as Terry Neill's Arsenal beat Dave Sexton's Manchester Utd 1-2 at Old Trafford ▪ 21-year-old Andy Gray scores twice as Ron Saunders' Aston Villa beat Bob Paisley's Liverpool 1-2 at Anfield ▪ "I-I-I don't wanna be like you" - *Looking After Number One* by The Boomtown Rats climbs to number eleven in the pop chart - 25-year-old Bob Geldof (the band's charismatic lead singer) has become one of the best known and most popular punk rockers in Britain ▪ The Sex Pistols' LP *Never Mind The Bollocks Here's The Sex Pistols* is number one in the album chart - 21-year-old Johnny Rotten and 20-year-old Sid Vicious are the two most infamous punk rockers in Britain ▪ 23-year-old Lucinda Prior-Palmer wins the three-day horse trial event at Burghley House on *George* ▪ "Woah-oh" *Black Betty* ("Bam-ba-lam!") by Ram Jam climbs to number seven in the pop chart ▪ "Ah, here we are, and here we are, and here we go. All aboard and we're hitting the road. Here we go-oh…" *Rockin' All Over The World* by Status Quo reaches number three ▪ The second series of *The New Avengers* begins on ITV, with Patrick Macnee as Steed, Gareth Hunt as Gambit and 31-year-old Joanna Lumley as Purdey ▪ The final series of *Dad's Army* begins on BBC - and sees Private Pike (played by 31-year-old Ian Lavender) running out of petrol, as he drives his girlfriend home from the pictures ▪ "Don't you find shopping boring though, Ange? Oh, I do. I hate it" - 31-year-old Alison Steadman stars in BBC One's Play For The Day, *Abigail's Party* ▪ 44-year-old Barry Norman presents the late night movie review program *Film 77* on Sundays ▪ 'A moment of love becomes a crime of passion' - 24-year-old Jenny

Agutter gets naked with 23-year-old Peter Firth in *Equus* - now showing at cinemas ■ 19-year-old Luscious Linda Lusardi (36C) appears nude in the latest edition of *Fiesta* magazine ■ Dads suddenly become interested in Saturday morning television when 27-year-old Sally James joins *Tiswas* ■ *You're In My Heart* ("... you're in my soul. You'll be my breath should I grow old. You are my lover, you're my best friend. You're in my soul") by 32-year-old Rod Stewart is number three in the pop chart ■ "Come on Silver Lady take my word, I won't run out on you again, believe me. Oh, I've seen the light, it's just one more night without you" - *Silver Lady* by 34-year-old David Soul climbs to number one ■ Pam Ayres, Little and Large and the Muppets appear in front of 51-year-old Queen Elizabeth II at the Silver Jubilee Royal Variety Performance ■ 45-year-old Reginald Bosanquet and 50-year-old Sandy Gall present ITN's *News at Ten* program ■ Fire brigades across the country go on strike for higher pay. Army operated 'Green Goddess' vehicles are used in place of fire-engines for the first time in nine years ■ 47-year-old Michael Edwardes is the new chairman of car manufacturer British Leyland ■ 50-year-old Derek Robinson (aka Red Robbo) addresses a mass meeting of workers at Longbridge ■ An official enquiry into the strike at the Grunwick photographic processing factory in Willesden concludes that the sacked workers should now be re-instated. The bosses at Grunwick decide not to do so - and picketing continues ■ "Yes sir, I can boogie, but I need a certain song. I can boogie. Boogie, boogie all night long" - *Yes Sir I Can Boogie* by Baccara is top of the hit parade ■ "But still they'd begin - ah..." *Needles and Pins* ("... ah") by Smokie is number ten ■ 11-year-old David Cameron from Marylebone watches television ■ 'Power to the people!' - *Citizen Smith*, with 27-year-old Robert Lindsay as Wolfie Smith (leader of the Tooting Popular Front) is broadcast on BBC One on Thursday evenings ■ Eamonn Andrews hosts *This is Your Life* on ITV on Wednesday evenings - 30-year-old Richard Beckinsale is one of the celebrities to be presented with the big red book ■ Children rush home from school to watch *Secret Squirrel* and *Ivor the Engine* ■ After peaking at number seven in the pop chart, *Star Wars Theme* by Meco moves down to number ten ■ "I had to leave to hear your ..." *Wonderous Stories* by Yes is number eighteen ■ Home entertainment technology moves on apace ■ Families have hours of fun playing Football,

Tennis, Squash and Squash (Practice) on the Binatone *TV Master Mk IV* games console ▪ The new *Atari 2600* game system is launched - with the exciting *Combat* cartridge as part of the bundle ▪ Home communication technology moves on apace ▪ The iconic GPO trimphone now comes with state-of-the-art push-buttons and is available in green, ivory or two-tone blue ▪ *British Airways'* Concorde supersonic jet begins a new commercial route - flying direct to New York's John F. Kennedy Airport for the first time ▪ 55-year-old entrepreneur Freddie Laker launches his 'low price' *Skytrain* service - flying from Gatwick to New York for just £59 one-way ▪ Mrs. Thatcher's opposition Conservative Party is ahead in the opinion polls. The 52-year-old leader continues to challenge the Labour government on its poor economic record - and in particular, the high rate of inflation ▪ "She is…" *Watching The Detectives* by 22-year-old Elvis Costello reaches number fifteen in the pop chart ▪ "Sitting in the front row..." *Mary Of The 4th Form* ("... turning all the boys on") by The Boomtown Rats (with 26-year-old punk rocker Bob Geldof) also peaks at number fifteen ▪ Siouxsie and the Banshees perform a night-time session for 38-year-old Radio One disc jockey John Peel ▪ 27-year-old Princess Anne gives birth to baby Peter - and Queen Elizabeth II becomes a grandmother in her Silver Jubilee year ▪ 24-year-old footballer Graeme Souness scores twice as Middlesbrough beat Leeds Utd 2-1 at Ayresome Park ▪ Brian Clough's newly promoted Nottingham Forest are top of Division One after thrashing Bobby Robson's Ipswich Town 4-0 at the City Ground, with all four goals scored by 26-year-old centre-forward Peter Withe ▪ Keith Burkinshaw's Tottenham Hotspur are second (behind Bolton Wanderers) in Division Two after thrashing Bristol Rovers 9-0 at White Hart Lane, with 21-year-old Colin Lee (a recent signing from Torquay Utd) scoring four goals and 23-year-old Ian Moores bagging a hat-trick ▪ Cardiff City's 25-year-old centre-forward Robin Friday is sent off for kicking opponent Mark Lawrenson (of Brighton and Hove Albion) in the face. The anomalous Friday then walks into the Brighton changing room and defecates in Lawrenson's kit bag ▪ "We are your friends"- *Calling Occupants Of Interplanetary Craft (The Recognised Anthem Of World Contact Day)* by The Carpenters climbs to number nine in the pop chart ▪ "2-4-6-8 ain't never too late. Me and my radio truckin' on through the night. 3-5-7-9 on a dou-

ble white line. Motorway sun coming up on the morning light" - *2-4-6-8 Motorway* by The Tom Robinson Band reaches number five ▪ 32-year-old Russell Brookes from Redditch finishes third in the RAC Rally, driving a Ford *Escort* (registration ODA 622R) ▪ "Twenty-two minutes late. Badger ate a junction box at New Malden" - 51-year-old Leonard Rossiter stars in the second series of *The Fall and Rise of Reginald Perrin* (a TV comedy based on a novel by 42-year-old David Nobbs) ▪ 'Stop! You're Killing Me' - 48-year-old Ronnie Barker and 46-year-old Ronnie Corbett return as private detectives, Piggy Malone and Charley Farley, in a new series of *The Two Ronnies* ▪ In ITV's *Coronation Street*, Suzi Birchall (played by 25-year-old Cheryl Murray) dumps businessman Mike Baldwin (played by 42-year-old Johnny Briggs) for being too old ▪ "I was an impossible case, no-one ever could reach me. But I think I can see in your face, there's a lot you can teach me. So I wanna know, what's..." *The Name Of The Game* by Abba (with 32-year-old Bjorn Ulvaeus, 30-year-old Benny Andersson, 31-year-old Anni-Frid Lyngstad and 27-year-old Agnetha Faltskog) is number one in the pop chart ▪ "I would love you till forever and..." *I Will* by 35-year-old Ruby Winters is number four ▪ There's been a slight improvement in the economy ▪ Unemployment has dipped to 1.3 million under Jim Callaghan's Labour government ▪ The annual rate of inflation is also down - to 12% (after reaching a record high of 26.9% two years ago) ▪ Sensible people queue at building societies, to pay small deposits into their savings account ▪ 'Security, it's good to know it's there when you need it. Get the Abbey habit with Abbey National' - *Abbey National* advertises its services on TV ▪ *We Are The Champions* ("... my friend. And we'll keep on fightin', till the end") by Queen climbs to number two in the pop chart ▪ *She's Not There* by Santana is number eleven ▪ 34-year-old Radio One DJ Tony Blackburn is granted a divorce from his wife, 29-year-old actress Tessa Wyatt, on grounds of her adultery with comedy actor Richard O'Sullivan ▪ Young men with long hair and leather-jackets tear through housing estates on Yamaha *FS-1 E* (aka 'Fizzy') motorbikes ▪ Middle-aged men with side-partings and polyester jackets drive along 'B' roads in metallic green Austin *Allegro Special L.E.* motorcars ▪ Schoolboys are excited - Christmas is coming ▪ The annual *Beezer Book* (with characters 'Pop, Dick and Harry' on the front cover) is now on sale.

Christmas 1977

Flight Deck for Christmas

Monarch:	Queen Elizabeth II (aged 51)
Prime-minister:	James Callaghan (aged 65)
Chancellor:	Denis Healey (aged 60)
Home Secretary:	Merlyn Rees (aged 57)
Foreign Secretary:	David Owen (aged 39)
Football Manager:	Ron Greenwood (aged 56)
Radio 1 Breakfast DJ:	Noel Edmonds (aged 29)
New car reg. suffix:	'S'

▪ The weather is cold and frosty in the North. It's mostly mild in the South ▪ "Long ago, outside a chip-shop in Walthamstow was a young rocker called Greasy Joe, he put on his helmet and said, 'Let's go.' He was keen, off up the high street like Barry Sheene" - *Live In Trouble* a comedy song by The Barron Knights climbs to number seven in the pop chart ▪ Parents take their children to matinee screenings at the local cinema during the school holiday ▪ 'The love bug turns the great race into a HERBIE-DERBY!' - Walt Disney's *Herbie Goes to Monte Carlo*, featuring a very special, racing liveried Volkswagen *Beetle* motorcar (number 53), is on general release ▪ 'Is anything worth the terror of…' *The Deep* - a 'PG' rated movie starring 50-year-old Robert Shaw, 36-year-old Nick Nolte and 33-year-old Jacqueline Bisset is also now showing ▪ Groups of skateboarding teenagers meet up in carparks and shopping centres ▪ A new 'Play Safe' campaign promotes the use of safety equipment such as helmets and joint padding ▪ 65-year-old Labour prime-minister Jim Callaghan makes a surprise visit to Ulster. Speaking at Stormont Castle, Mr. Callaghan says, "I would like to see Northern Ireland taking over more responsibility for its own affairs." ▪ 32-year-old DJ Tom Browne presents the Top 20 chart rundown (in VHF stereo) on Radio One on Sunday evenings ▪ *Egyptian Reggae* by Jonathan Richman and the Modern Lovers is number five in the pop chart ▪ "I turn to stone when you are gone, I..." *Turn To Stone* by the Electric Light Orchestra is number eighteen ▪ The Jam, a little known new-wave band, play a gig at the Greyhound in Croydon ▪ England's footballers play a crucial match against Italy at Wembley.

26-year-old Kevin Keegan and 29-year-old Trevor Brooking score the goals as Ron Greenwood's team achieves a 2-0 victory, but still fails to qualify for next year's world cup finals. Keegan and Brooking, along with Ray Clemence, Phil Neal, Trevor Cherry, Emlyn Hughes (captain), Dave Watson, Ray 'Butch' Wilkins, Steve Coppell, Bob Latchford and Peter Barnes, will all miss out on the finals in Argentina ▪ Life continues ▪ Families prepare for Christmas ▪ Housewives serve food on heated *Hostess* trollies ▪ 'Get busy with the fizzy - Sodastream' - *Sodastreams* make refreshing fizzy drinks ▪ *Superglue* is now available in shops ▪ Firemen continue their industrial action ▪ Army operated 'Green Goddess' vehicles attend emergency 999 call-outs ▪ The Yorkshire Ripper strikes again - attacking a 25-year-old woman in Leeds ▪ Chrysler launches the *Horizon* motorcar. Showroom price for the entry level *LS* model is £3,320 and top speed is 95 mph. Fuel consumption is 50 mpg - when driven sensibly ▪ Supermarkets are busy ▪ Shopping trollies are full ▪ A bottle of *John Haig* whisky costs £4.19 ▪ A bottle of *Courvoisier* is £5.99 ▪ A bottle of *Cossack* vodka is £3.99 ▪ A bottle of *Warninks* advocaat is £2.99 ▪ A bottle of *Harveys Bristol Cream* is £1.99 ▪ A four-pack of *Carling Black Label* cans is 89p ▪ Husbands treat their wives to a bottle of new *Opium* perfume (by Yves Saint Laurent) for Christmas ▪ "Let's have a ball at the hall tonight. Boogie girl till the early bright. Make a scene with the record machine…" *Dancin' Party* ("… tonight") by Showaddywaddy is number four in the pop chart ▪ "And you come to me on a summer breeze, keep me warm in your love, then you softly leave, and it's me you need to show..." *How Deep Is Your Love* by The Bee Gees is number three ▪ 'We are not alone' - Steven Spielberg's *Close Encounters of a Third Kind* (with 30-year-old Richard Dreyfuss and 38-year-old Melinda Dillon) is on general release at picture houses ▪ "Magic, our Morris!" - series three of *Oh No, It's Selwyn Frogitt* (with 49-year-old Bill Maynard in the title role) is on TV ▪ 26-year-old footballer Alex Cropley breaks his leg playing for Aston Villa in a local derby match against West Bromwich Albion ▪ Non league part-timers Blyth Spartans defeat Third Division Chesterfield 1-0 in the second round of the FA Cup. 21-year-old Steve Jones scores the winning goal for Spartans ▪ 32-year-old Wimbledon tennis champion Virginia Wade is voted BBC's 'Sports Personality of the Year' ▪ 30-year-old DJ Simon Bates is

the new presenter of Radio One's mid morning show ▪ "Far have I travelled and much have I seen. Dark distant mountains with valleys of green" - *Mull Of Kintyre* by 36-year-old Paul McCartney and his band, Wings, is number one ▪ The *Floral Dance* by The Brighouse and Rastrick Brass Band is number two ▪ Hallmark Records release *The Best of Top of the Pops '77* - a budget priced, cover-version pop compilation LP with blonde Jilly Johnson pictured on a sheep-skin rug on the sleeve ▪ Hi-fi technology moves on apace ▪ A Ferguson *Music Centre* (comprising of LW/MW/VHF decoder, multi-speed record deck and cassette player/recorder) costs £129.95 at *Argos* ▪ A pair of Alba stereo headphones are £5.95 ▪ 'Is it live, or is it Memorex?' - *Memorex* recordable tapes offer high quality music reproduction ▪ 22-year-old footballer Tony Woodcock scores twice as Brian Clough's newly promoted Nottingham Forest beat Dave Sexton's Manchester Utd 0-4 at Old Trafford. Forest follow-up this win with a 1-1 draw against Liverpool and then a 0-2 victory over Newcastle Utd - to stay top of Division One ▪ Trevor Brooking is on the score-sheet for struggling West Ham Utd in a rare victory (2-1 over Manchester Utd) at Upton Park ▪ Four children die at a house fire in Wednesbury. Troops in 'Green Goddess' vehicles attend the tragedy, as the fireman's strike continues ▪ 30-year-old convicted murderer Leslie Grantham is out of prison (after serving ten years) and is now forging a career as an actor ▪ "I'm dreaming of a..." *White Christmas* ("... just like the ones I used to know") by the late Bing Crosby reaches number five in the pop chart ▪ *Mull Of Kintyre* (... Oh, mist rollin' in from the sea, my desire, is always to be here") by Wings stays at number one for the festive period ▪ Boyfriends impress their girlfriends with romantic Christmas gifts ▪ A box of Cadbury's *Milk Tray* chocolates costs £1.40 ▪ A box of *Black Magic* is £1.48 ▪ A box of Terry's *All Gold* is £1.50 ▪ Excited schoolboys make a Christmas wish - hoping to receive a skateboard or *Tin Can Alley* or *Flight-Deck* ▪ The new *Sportel* TV games console (with simulated tennis, squash and football) is also popular ▪ A *Hornby* model train set (with a high-speed 125 British Rail engine) costs £19.50 ▪ A *Kodak EK4* instant camera is £29.95 ▪ *Ker-Plunk* is £2.45 ▪ Families settle down in front on the telly ▪ "Follow the yellow brick road" - *The Wizard of Oz* is on BBC One on Christmas Day ▪ 30-year-old Elton John and 37-year-old Penelope Keith are special guests on the

Morecambe and Wise Christmas Show in the evening ▪ On Boxing Day - millions enjoy *It's a Christmas Knockout* (presented by 67-year-old Eddie Waring and 48-year-old Stuart Hall) and *The Two Ronnies* (with 48-year-old Ronnie Barker and 47-year-old Ronnie Corbett) ▪ Over on ITV, Eamonn Andrews presents his big red book to 77-year-old Earl Mountbatten of Burma (a cousin of Queen Elizabeth II and great grandson to Queen Victoria) on *This Is Your Life* ▪ "You're gonna get your fucking head kicked in!" - Groups of young men attend football matches, standing together on packed terraces and taunting supporters of the opposing team ▪ Sammy Chung's Wolverhampton Wanderers gain a 3-1 victory over Jimmy Armfield's Leeds Utd at the Molineux and fans clash in the subway behind the South Bank ▪ Tony Book's Manchester City beat Bill McGarry's Newcastle Utd 4-0 at Maine Road with 28-year-old Dennis Tueart bagging a hat-trick ▪ "You can try. (You can try). You can try. (You can try). You can try, to tell the world the reason why…" *Belfast* by Boney M climbs to number eight on the hit parade ▪ *It's A Heartache* ("… nothing but a heartache. Hits you when it's too late. Hits you when you're down") by Bonnie Tyler is number four ▪ Television remains the nation's favourite form of entertainment ▪ Fot the first time ever, more colour TV licences (9.9 million) have been issued than black and white licenses (8.1 million) ▪ "Didn't he do well?" - 49-year-old Bruce Forsyth bows out of BBC One's *Generation Game* ▪ 30-year-old Farrah Fawcett-Majors leaves ITV's *Charlie's Angels* and is replaced by 26-year-old Cheryl Ladd ▪ "Ah-So!" - 64-year-old Robert Ya Fu Lee, 34-year-old Barry Evans and 28-year-old Francoise Pascal feature in *Mind Your Language* - a popular new comedy ▪ 51-year-old Jimmy Savile OBE presents *Jimmy Savile's Old Record Club* on Sunday afternoons on Radio One ▪ 63-year-old 'Cheerful' Charlie Chester presents *Your Sunday Soapbox* on Radio Two ▪ The Phantom Flan Flinger appears on children's TV show *Tiswas* ▪ 28-year-old Patrick Duffy is *The Man from Atlantis* - a person with super-human strength and the ability to breath underwater ▪ "Oh yeah? Shoo-ey, magoo-ey!" is a common phrase used by disbelieving kids - as they rub their chins in an exaggerated style ▪ Movie star Charlie Chaplin dies aged 88 in Switzerland ▪ Back in England - men enjoy an evening at the pub ▪ A pint of lager in the Red Lion is 32p ▪ A pint of bitter is 27p.

New Year 1978

Flippin' 'eck, Tucker!

Monarch:	Queen Elizabeth II (aged 51)
Prime-minister:	James Callaghan (aged 65)
Chancellor:	Denis Healey (aged 60)
Home Secretary:	Merlyn Rees (aged 57)
Foreign Secretary:	David Owen (aged 39)
Football Manager:	Ron Greenwood (aged 56)
Radio 1 Breakfast DJ:	Noel Edmonds (aged 29)
New car reg. suffix:	'S'

▪ Richard Baker reads the news on BBC One ▪ An 18-year-old woman is murdered in Huddersfield ▪ A 21-year-old woman goes missing in Leeds ▪ The firemen's strike comes to an end - with a negotiated pay increase of ten percent ▪ Red fire-engines are operational once again and the army's 'Green Goddess' emergency vehicles are moved back into storage ▪ "I was dancin' to the beat, feel the heat, I'm movin' my feet" - *Dance Dance Dance (Yowsah Yowsah Yowsah)* by Chic is number six in the pop chart ▪ "You're a..." *Native New Yorker* ("... You should know the score by now") by Odyssey is number five ▪ There's some rare good news on the economy ▪ Inflation has fallen slightly ▪ The opinion polls show that 65-year-old prime-minister Jim Callaghan and his Labour government are closing the gap on Margaret Thatcher's Conservative opposition ▪ 24-year-old footballer Paul Mariner scores twice as Ipswich Town beat Cardiff City 0-2 in the third round of the FA Cup ▪ Part-timers Blyth Spartans beat Enfield 1-0 with a goal from 24-year-old Alan Shoulder ▪ 26-year-old centre-forward Joe Jordan transfers from Leeds Utd to Manchester Utd for £350,000 ▪ "As they carry me back to the..." *Mull Of Kintyre* by Paul McCartney and Wings remains at number one in the pop chart until late January ▪ "Don't know when I've been so blue. Don't know what's come over you" - *Don't It Make My Brown Eyes Blue* by 27-year-old Crystal Gayle is number five ▪ Elton John is the special guest on ITV's hugely popular program *The Muppet Show*, where the 30-year-old pop star performs *Don't Go Breaking My Heart* as a duet with Miss Piggy ▪ 58-year-old movie star Richard Todd is a special guest on *Celebrity Squares* ▪

Children devour *Old English Flavours* of *Spangles* ▪ Bill Giles presents the weather forecast on BBC One ▪ Heavy snowstorms hit the UK and some schools and factories are forced to close. The East of the country is worst hit - and the seaside piers at Herne Bay, Margate and Skegness are battered by a raging North Sea ▪ "Well Daddy who? Daddy Cool. Daddy who..?" *Daddy Cool* ("... Daddy Cool, Daddy Cool. Cool, Daddy Cool") by Darts climbs to number six in the pop chart ▪ *Love's Unkind* ("... 'cause he's not mine") by 29-year-old Donna Summer is number three ▪ *The Professionals* is new on ITV, with 53-year-old Gordon Jackson as Cowley, 32-year-old Martin Shaw as Doyle and 31-year-old Lewis Collins as Bodie - all three men, part of a national security agency called CI5 ▪ *All Creatures Great and Small* is new on BBC, with 52-year-old Robert Hardy as Siegfried Farnon, 37-year-old Christopher Timothy as James Herriot and 26-year-old Peter Davison as Tristan Farnon - all three men, part of a 1930s veterinary practice in the Yorkshire Dales ▪ "May the force be with you" - Queues form outside cinemas as *Star Wars* arrives in Britain. 25-year-old Mark Hamill is Luke Skywalker, 34-year-old Harrison Ford is Han Solo and 20-year-old Carrie Fisher is Princess Leia ▪ *Blake's 7* is on TV, with 32-year-old Gareth Thomas as Roj Blake and with 27-year-old Sally Knyvette as Jenna Stannis ▪ "I thought I could hear the curious tone of the cornet, clarinet and big trombone" - 39-year-old Terry Wogan performs his own version of the *Floral Dance* on *Top of the Pops* and the song climbs to number twenty-one in the pop chart ▪ "We're..." *Jamming* ("... jamming, and I hope you like jamming, too") by 32-year-old Bob Marley & The Wailers reaches number nine ▪ There's a major shock in the world of boxing: 24-year-old underdog Leon Spinks defeats favourite Muhammad Ali by a split-decision (after fifteen rounds in Las Vegas) and becomes the new undisputed heavy-weight champion ▪ Back in England - Brian Clough's recently promoted Nottingham Forest are six points clear at the top of Football League Division One. 35,743 people are at the City Ground to see Archie Gemmill score in Forest's 2-0 victory over Terry Neill's Arsenal ▪ In the fourth round of the FA Cup, non league Blyth Spartans cause a major upset by beating Second Division Stoke City 2-3 at the Victoria Ground, with late goals from 20-year-old Steve Carney and 28-year-old Terry Johnson ▪ First Division West Bromwich Albion ap-

point 38-year-old Big Ron Atkinson as manager ▪ 38-year-old Leighton Rees (from Wales) is the first ever World Darts Champion, defeating 32-year-old John Lowe (from England) 11-7 in the final at the Heart of the Midlands Club in Nottingham. Rees receives a prize payout of £3,000 ▪ A new, smaller one-pound note is issued, with an image of Isaac Newton on the front ▪ "Nah pop no style. A strictly roots" - *Uptown Top Ranking* by Althia and Donna (two teenage girls from Jamaica) is new at number one in the pop chart ▪ *If I Had Words* ("... to make a day for you, I'd sing you a morning golden and new") by Scott Fitzgerald and Yvonne Keeley is number three ▪ Millions of people enjoy an evening in front of the telly ▪ Ernest Bishop (played by 52-year-old Stephen Hancock) is shot and killed at Mike Baldwin's factory in *Coronation Street* on ITV ▪ "Flippin' 'eck, Tucker!" - school kids rush home to watch *Grange Hill* on BBC One. 14-year-old Todd Carty (as Tucker Jenkins), 13-year-old Terry Sue-Patt (as Benny Green), 15-year-old George Armstrong (as Alan Hargreaves) and 12-year-old Michelle Herbert (as Trisha Yates) are the stars ▪ Fletch and Godber are out of Slade Prison as a new TV sit-com called *Going Straight* begins on Friday evenings at 8.30 p.m. ▪ "He's out to make a killing girl, he's out to make a score. And maybe if you're willing girl, he's gonna ask for more. Oh-oh Figaro, he's got magic, oh-oh!" - *Figaro* by The Brotherhood of Man (33-year-old Nicky Stevens, 31-year-old Martin Lee, 28-year-old Lee Sheridan and 33-year-old Sandra Stevens) spends a week at number one in the pop chart ▪ "Ooooh, here comes that man again. Something in the way he moves makes me..." *Sorry I'm A Lady* by Baccara (27-year-old Mayte Mateos and 25-year-old Maria Mendiola) is number eight ▪ "Could I stay, could I please stay. Could-a, could-a, could-a please stay..." *Just One More Night* by Yellow Dog is number eight ▪ BBC One programs on a Saturday night include: *Jim'll Fix It* - with 51-year-old Jimmy Savile OBE; *Dr. Who* - with 44-year-old Tom Baker as the Doctor, 26-year-old Louise Jameson as his assistant, Leela, and K9 as the dog shaped robot, K9; *Saturday Night at the Movies*; *Mike Yarwood in Persons* - with 36-year-old impersonator Mike Yarwood; *Starsky and Hutch* - starring 34-year-old Paul Michael Glaser as Starsky and 34-year-old David Soul as Hutch; *News* - read by 53-year-old Kenneth Kendall; and *Match of the Day* - introduced by 49-year-old Jimmy Hill ▪ "Well you can tell by the

way I use my walk I'm a woman's man, no time to talk" - *Stayin' Alive* by The Bee Gees (a group comprising of the three brothers Gibb: 31-year-old Barry and 28-year-old twins, Robin and Maurice) climbs to number four in the pop chart ▪ *Five Minutes* ("… and you're almost there. Five minutes and you're almost dead") by The Stranglers (with, lead singer, 28-year-old Hugh Cornwell, and, drummer, 39-year-old Jet Black) is number eleven ▪ 26-year-old goalkeeper John 'Budgie' Burridge moves (on loan) from First Division Aston Villa to Fourth Division Southend Utd and keeps a clean sheet on his debut for 'The Shrimpers' in a 0-1 away win against Crewe Alexandra ▪ "If you change your mind, I'm the first in line. Honey I'm still free…" *Take A Chance On Me* by Abba is number one for three weeks ▪ *Hotlegs* ("… I love ya honey!") by 33-year-old Rod Stewart is number five ▪ 34-year-old Anna Ford is ITN's first female news reader ▪ 56-year-old Jimmy Young from Cinderford presents the mid morning show on Radio Two, before *Waggoners' Walk* comes on at 12.15 ▪ Prosperous people keep a cactus in a pot on the kitchen windowsill ▪ Primary school children are forced to learn 'country dancing' in time for the school Spring Fayre ▪ 29-year-old Noel Edmonds presents *Multi-Coloured Swap Shop* on BBC One on Saturday mornings - assisted by 37-year-old John Craven and 21-year-old Keith Chegwin ▪ 45-year-old Frank Bough introduces *Grandstand* straight afterwards ▪ 36-year-old Bob Wilson presents *Football Focus* ▪ 25-year-old defender Gordon McQueen transfers from Jimmy Armfield's Leeds Utd to Dave Sexton's Manchester Utd for £500,000 ▪ 24-year-old midfielder Graeme Souness transfers from John Neal's Middlesbrough to Bob Paisley's Liverpool for £350,000 ▪ 'The Chilling Story of a Psycho!' - 34-year-old Donald Sumpter is Donald Nielson in real-life terror film *The Black Panther* - now showing at cinemas ▪ 17-year-old striker Craig Johnston makes his debut for Middlesbrough in a 1-2 away win against Sir Alf Ramsey's Birmingham City ▪ Ken Shellito's Chelsea beat Bobby Robson's Ipswich Town 5-3 at Stamford Bridge and move up to thirteenth in Division One ▪ Tottenham Hotspur remain top of Division Two after a 1-1 draw against Orient in front of 32,869 spectators at White Hart Lane. 21-year-old striker Colin Lee is on the score-sheet for Spurs ▪ "I'm..." *Wishing On A Star* ("... to follow where you are") by Rose Royce (with, lead singer, 24-year-old

Gwen Dickey) is number three in the pop chart ▪ *Mr. Blue Sky* ("… please tell us why you had to hide away for so long (so long)? Where did we go wrong?" by Electric Light Orchestra (with, lead singer, 30-year-old Jeff Lynne) is number six ▪ 24-year-old music journalist Mark Ellen meets 27-year-old record plugger David Hepworth at an Earthquake gig at Salford University ▪ Motoring technology moves on apace ▪ A 'push-button' radio/cassette player, power assisted steering, central locking, electrically operated front windows and tinted glass are all fitted 'as standard' in the top-of-the-range Ford *Granada Ghia* - the luxurious 2.8 litre (V6) motor-car has a top speed of 112 mph and is available now for £7,315 ▪ Working class men set their sights slightly lower ▪ A brand new Morris *Marina 1.3L* has a top speed of 86 mph and costs less than £3,000 ▪ People enjoy a night out on the town ▪ Courting couples make the most of dimly lit back row seats at their local cinema ▪ 'Where do you go when the record is over' - 24-year-old John Travolta stars in *Saturday Night Fever* ▪ 'Cool' young men blow-dry their hair and 'style-in' a centre parting ▪ 'Cool' young women have bubble perms ▪ Tear-away teenagers sniff glue near the garages behind the shopping precinct ▪ *Monster Munch* crisps go on sale ▪ "Denis, Denis, oh with your eyes so blue. Denis, Denis, I got a crush on you. Denis, Denis, I'm so in love with you, oh-ohh" - *Denis* by Blondie (featuring 32-year-old Debbie Harry) climbs from number eleven to number five in the pop chart ▪ *Come Back My Love* ("... don't stay away. I need your loving every day. I love you so, well I want you to know, I need your love so badly") by Darts moves down from number two to number three ▪ A new series of *Robin's Nest* begins on television, with 33-year-old Richard O'Sullivan, 29-year-old Tessa Wyatt and 53-year-old Tony Britton ▪ The impressive FA Cup run of non league football team Blyth Spartans comes to an end as Wrexham (current leaders of Division Three) win a fifth round replay, 1-2. The match is played in front of 42,157 spectators at Newcastle Utd's St. James' Park ▪ Modern couples with young children visit car showrooms ▪ A new Ford *Fiesta 950* costs £2,100 and has a top speed of 86 mph ▪ Schoolboys begin saving up for a skateboard ▪ A plywood *Flyer De Lux* (with double ball-bearing rubber wheels) costs £7.40 at toy-shops ▪ A tub of *Slime* by Matel is £1.25 ▪ Adverts say, 'Wrigley's Spearmint Gum - carry the big fresh flavour!'

Spring 1978

Cloughie's Forest are champions

Monarch:	Queen Elizabeth II (aged 52)
Prime-minister:	James Callaghan (aged 66)
Chancellor:	Denis Healey (aged 60)
Home Secretary:	Merlyn Rees (aged 57)
Foreign Secretary:	David Owen (aged 39)
Football Manager:	Ron Greenwood (aged 56)
Radio 1 Breakfast DJ:	Dave Lee Travis (aged 33)
New car reg. suffix:	'S'

▪ "Ten-four good buddy" - the cult of CB radio sweeps the country, despite it being illegal to own and use transceiver sets ▪ Ford introduces a new version of the *Transit* van - this latest model has a redesigned radiator grill and stylish new indicator lights at the front ▪ Chrysler introduces the *Rancho* - a rugged and capacious 'off-road' estate car, with auxiliary lamps positioned close to the windscreen, a roof-rack and towing hitch. Priced at £5,645, supply of the 'quirky' new vehicle will be limited to two-hundred per month ▪ "Out on the wiley, windy moors we'd roll and fall in green. You had a temper like my jealousy, too hot, too greedy" - *Wuthering Heights* by 19-year-old Kate Bush moves to the top of the hit parade - and stays there for four weeks ▪ "Oh, no, it does not move me, even though I've seen the movie" - *(I Don't Wanna Go To) Chelsea* by 23-year-old Elvis Costello and the Attractions is number sixteen ▪ 14-year-old David Thewlis is beaten up by a gang of thugs (and has his Harrington jacket stolen) after attending a Blondie gig at Salford University ▪ 48-year-old Julian Haviland is Political Editor for ITV ▪ 39-year-old Vivian Bendall is elected as a new Tory MP after winning a by-election at Ilford North ▪ After a short period of relative stability in retail prices, inflation is now rising again ▪ A loaf of bread costs 24p ▪ A pint of milk is 12p ▪ The opinion polls put Margaret Thatcher's opposition Conservative Party slightly ahead of Jim Callaghan's governing Labour Party ▪ 60-year-old Chancellor of Exchequer Denis Healey cuts income tax rates for the lowest paid workers ▪ "Silly Billy!" - 36-year-old Mike Yarwood impersonates the Chancellor on Saturday night television and approximately fifteen million viewers tune in ▪ 36-year-old Fred West and his wife, 24-year-old Rose-

mary, murder 18-year-old Shirley Robinson and bury her body beneath their house at 25 Cromwell Street in Gloucester ▪ Brian Clough's recently promoted Nottingham Forest football team remains top of Division One with three consecutive home victories: 2-0 versus West Ham Utd, 1-0 versus Leicester City and 2-0 versus Newcastle Utd. Forest's left-winger, 25-year-old John Robertson, scores a penalty in each of the matches ▪ 33-year-old Angela Rippon reads the news on BBC television ▪ Charlie Chaplin's coffin is stolen from a cemetery in Switzerland ▪ The *Amoco Cadiz* oil tanker sinks and spills its cargo into the sea ▪ 33-year-old bent copper DS Derek Ridgewell is arrested and charged with conspiring to steal mailbags from the Royal Mail ▪ 'They're back - Tougher than ever!' - John Thaw and Dennis Waterman star in *Sweeney 2* at cinemas ▪ Ford launches the sporty *MkIII Capri* motorcar with four circular headlights replacing the two rectangular ones on the old *MKII*. The new *1.3L* model costs £2,998.51, has a top speed of 91 mph and accelerates from 0-60 mph in 17.4 seconds. The new *3.0S* costs £4,421.52, has a top speed of 124 mph and accelerates from 0-60 mph in 8 seconds ▪ A pint of lager in the Red Lion costs 36p ▪ A pint of bitter is 29p ▪ TV information films say, 'Think before you drink before you drive' ▪ *I Love The Sound Of Breaking Glass* ("... especially when I'm lonely") by 29-year-old Nick Lowe is number seven in the pop chart ▪ "Winding your way down on…" *Baker Street* by 30-year-old Gerry Rafferty (with a catchy and distinctive saxophone break) is number three ▪ 49-year-old Bob Holness presents the breakfast show on LBC Radio ▪ ITV axes *Opportunity Knocks* (presented by 58-year-old Hughie Green) and replaces it with *The Kenny Everett Video Show* ▪ Alf Roberts (played by 46-year-old Bryan Mosley) marries Renee Bradshaw (played by 40-year-old Madge Hindle) in *Coronation Street* ▪ A new comedy series called *Mixed Blessings*, starring Christopher Blake and Muriel Odunton (as a newly wed mixed race couple), begins on ITV ▪ 27-year-old Simon Groom replaces 39-year-old Peter Purves as a presenter on BBC One's children show *Blue Peter* ▪ Oxford win the Boat Race, after the Cambridge boat sinks in the River Thames ▪ 18-year-old dare-devil stunt rider Eddie Kidd sets a new world record - leaping over fourteen double-decker buses on his motorbike in front of a crowd of 30,000 people at a disused airport in Hertfordshire ▪ "And he painted…"

Matchstalk Men And Matchstalk Cats And Dogs by Brian and Michael is number one in the pop chart ▪ *I Can't Stand The Rain* ("… 'gainst my window, bringing back sweet memories") by Eruption is number five ▪ 58-year-old football manager Sir Alf Ramsey is sacked by Birmingham City after his team is beaten 4-0 by Coventry City ▪ 37-year-old Jim Smith is installed as the new boss at St. Andrews ▪ 18-year-old goalkeeper Chris Woods is man-of-the-match for Nottingham Forest in a 0-0 draw against Liverpool in the League Cup final at Wembley. In the replay at Old Trafford, referee Pat Partridge awards a penalty to Forest, which left-winger John Robertson scores to give Brian Clough's men a 1-0 victory over Bob Paisley's team ▪ In Division One, 29-year-old Trevor Brooking scores a consolation goal as John Lyall's relegation threatened West Ham Utd lose 4-1 against Ron Saunders' Aston Villa in front of 28,275 spectators at Villa Park ▪ 28-year-old striker Malcolm 'Supermac' MacDonald scores twice as Arsenal beat Manchester Utd 3-1 in front of 40,739 spectators at Highbury ▪ "I wanna love you, and treat you right" - *Is This Love* by 33-year-old Bob Marley and the Wailers is number nine in the pop chart ▪ "I will follow you. Will you follow me?" - *Follow You Follow Me* by Genesis (with, drummer / lead singer, 27-year-old Phil Collins) is number seven ▪ Robin Tripp (played by Richard O'Sullivan) marries Vicky Nicholls (played by Tessa Wyatt) in the series finale of sit-com *Robin's Nest* ▪ Football hooligans invade the pitch and fighting breaks out at an FA Cup quarter-final match between Millwall and Ipswich Town ▪ 29-year-old striker Alan Gowling transfers from First Division Newcastle Utd to Second Division Bolton Wanderers for £120,000 ▪ 20-year-old Sian Adey-Jones (36C) from Denbighshire is a popular new page three girl in *The Sun* ▪ 'Is she or isn't she?' - adverts for *Harmony Hairspray* are on TV ▪ "Cause she's good for me, and it would really make me happy to…" *Never Let Her Slip Away* by 26-year-old Andrew Gold is number five on the hit parade ▪ *I Wonder Why* ("… you love me like you do") by Showaddywaddy is number two ▪ The eastern side of the UK lies under thick snow ▪ Roads become impassable and traffic is disrupted ▪ An Austin *Princess* ('R' reg, in Reynard Metallic) is stranded on the A142 near Chatteris ▪ A Datsun *120Y* four-door saloon ('P' reg, in Cameo Beige) is stuck on the B1053, just north of Braintree ▪ 'Forty-two!' - *The Hitch-Hiker's Guide to the*

Galaxy, a fantastic new sci-fi comedy written by 26-year-old Douglas Adams, is on Radio Four ▪ *The Little and Large Show*, featuring 36-year-old Eddie Large and 35-year-old 'Supersonic' Syd Little, airs for the first time on BBC One ▪ 19-year-old footballer Gordon Cowans scores a goal for Aston Villa in a 2-0 victory over Newcastle Utd. 22-year-old Andy Gray is also on the score-sheet for Villa, after returning from a knee injury ▪ After his recent loan move to Southend Utd, 26-year-old goalkeeper John 'Budgie' Burridge transfers from Villa to Crystal Palace for £50,000 ▪ 19-year-old centre-back Terry Butcher makes his debut for Bobby Robson's Ipswich Town in a match against Gordon Lee's Everton at Goodison Park ▪ "So..." *If You Can't Give Me Love* ("... honey, that ain't enough") by 27-year-old Suzi Quatro is number four in the pop chart ▪ *Too Much Too Little Too Late* ("... to lie again with you") by 42-year-old Johnny Mathis & 26-year-old Deniece Williams climbs to number three ▪ 43-year-old Brian Clough leads Nottingham Forest to the Division One football title - just twelve months after gaining promotion from Division Two. Peter Shilton, Viv Anderson, Colin Barrett, Kenny Burns, Larry Lloyd, Ian Bowyer, Archie Gemmill, John McGovern, Martin O'Neill, John Robertson, Peter Withe and 22-year-old Tony Woodcock have all been outstanding ▪ Bob Paisley's Liverpool are runners-up ▪ John Lyall's West Ham Utd, Bill McGarry's Newcastle Utd and Ian MacFarlane's Leicester City are relegated to Division Two ▪ Youngsters queue outside *Tiffany's* night-club in Exeter on Thursday and Saturday evenings - hoping to gain access past the thick-set bouncers ▪ "Then I get…" *Night Fever* ("… night fever. We know how to do it") by The Bee Gees is number one in the pop chart ▪ *Everybody Dance* ("... der-der-doo-doo, clap your hands, clap your hands") by Chic is number twelve ▪ 33-year-old Graham Taylor leads Watford to the Division Four title - just twelve months after becoming manager at Elton John's football club ▪ The St. Joseph's Junior School (under-11) football team from Rugeley defeats local rivals Pear Tree 7-3 in a top-of-the-table clash - Gary Till, Peter Deeley, Nick Bates and twins Robert and Donald Harvey, all get their names on the score-sheet ▪ 45-year-old Ray 'Dracula' Reardon wins the *Embassy* World Snooker Championship at the Crucible in Sheffield - beating Perrie Mans from South Africa in the final ▪ *With A Little Luck* ("… we can help it out") by

Wings (with, lead singer, 35-year-old Paul McCartney) is number five in the pop chart ▪ "Ooha, ooha..." *Let's All Chant* by The Michael Zager Band is number eight ▪ Approximately 100,000 people march from Trafalgar Square to Victoria Park to watch an Anti Nazi League / Rock Against Racism concert, featuring X-Ray Spex, Steel Pulse, The Clash and the Tom Robinson Band ▪ 24-year-old Altab Ali is stabbed to death on Alder Street in Whitechapel ▪ Men flock to the cinema to see 44-year-old Joan Collins (36-24-37) in a raunchy new film called *The Stud* ▪ *Leopard in the Snow*, starring 28-year-old Susan Penhaligon, is also now showing ▪ "She's so, twentieth century. She's so, nineteen-seventies. She's a modern girl. (Oh yeah!)" - *She's So Modern* by the Boomtown Rats is number twelve in the pop chart ▪ *News Of The World* by The Jam is number twenty-seven ▪ 31-year-old Dave Lee Travis (aka The Hairy Cornflake) takes over from Noel Edmonds as host of Radio One's breakfast show ▪ "By the rivers of Babylon, there we sat down. Ye-eah we wept, when we remembered Zion" / "Brown girl in the ring, tra-la-la-la-la" - the double A sided pop single *Rivers Of Babylon* and *Brown Girl In The Ring* by Boney M is number one for five weeks! ▪ "Now, why do you think, Jack snuck down the hill?" - *Jack And Jill* by Raydio is number eleven ▪ 28-year-old footballer Roger Osborne scores the only goal of the game as Bobby Robson's Ipswich Town beat Terry Neill's Arsenal 1-0 in the FA Cup final. 47-year-old Derek Nippard is referee. A ticket for the standing enclosure at the Empire Stadium in Wembley costs £2.50 ▪ 27-year-old Kenny Dalglish scores the only goal of the game as Liverpool win the European Cup for the second year running by beating Club Brugge 1-0 at Wembley. 30-year-old left-back (and captain) Emlyn Hughes lifts the gleaming silver trophy ▪ 11-year-old Andrew Lovell performs a dos-a-dos with his class-mate Teresa Hurley in a country dancing display at the St. Joseph's Junior School Spring Fayre in Rugeley ▪ 30-year-old Steve Heathcote runs the weekly Youth Club in Armitage on Wednesday evenings ▪ "Ooh-wah, ooh-wah, cool, cool kitty, tell us about..." *The Boy From New York City* by Darts is number two on the weekly hit parade ▪ *What A Waste* ("... what a waste, but I don't mind") by 36-year-old Ian Dury climbs to number nine ▪ The Yorkshire Ripper strikes twice - murdering women in Leeds and Manchester ▪ Footballers, Bob Latchford, Tony Currie and 20-year-old

Peter Barnes score the goals as Ron Greenwood's England team (Shilton, Mills, Cherry, B Greenhoff, Watson, Wilkins, Coppell, T Francis, Latchford, Brooking, Barnes and substitutes, Currie and Mariner) beats Wales 1-3 at Ninian Park ▪ "Miss Jones! Miss Jones!" - the final episode of *Rising Damp* airs on ITV, with Frances de la Tour, Richard Beckinsale, Don Warrington and starring 52-year-old Leonard Rossiter as Rigsby ▪ *Because The Night* ("… belongs to lovers. Because the night belongs to lust") by the Patti Smith Group is number five in the pop chart ▪ *Do It, Do It Again* ("... Do it, do it again with love") by 35-year-old Raffaella Carra is number nine ▪ Middle-aged men mow the lawn on Sunday mornings ▪ Adverts say, 'Qualcast Concorde - It's a lot less bother than a hover!' ▪ Keep fit fanatics, wearing iridescent lycra tracksuits and headbands, go jogging in the park ▪ Trendy kids, in Brutus stretch jeans, Adidas *Mamba* trainers and with (red, white and blue) sweatbands on their wrists hang about in bus-shelters ▪ "We're the people you don't wanna know, we come from places you don't wanna go" - *Angels With Dirty Faces* by Sham 69 is number nineteen in the pop chart ▪ *Nice 'n' Sleazy* by The Stranglers is number twenty-one ▪ The sex comedy films - *Let's Get Laid* (with 33-year-old Fiona Richmond and 27-year-old Robin Askwith) and *What's Up Superdoc!* (with 28-year-old Angela Grant and 53-year-old Harry H. Corbett) attract crowds of men to the cinema ▪ 'A story of today' - *Tomorrow Never Comes*, an 'X' rated movie (with 27-year-old Susan George and 40-year-old Oliver Reed) is also now showing ▪ "I am your…" *Automatic Lover* by 23-year-old Dee D Jackson from Oxford climbs to number four in the pop chart ▪ *(I'm Always Touched By Your) Presence Dear* by Blondie is number ten ▪ 34-year-old Anna Ford reads the news for ITN ▪ Retail prices continue to rise ▪ Inflation is now at 8.3% ▪ 66-year-old prime-minister Jim Callaghan and his Labour government are coming under more and more pressure ▪ Charlie Chaplin's coffin turns up in Switzerland - just a few short miles from where it was stolen six weeks ago ▪ Back in Britain - music lovers stay up late, watching TV or listening to the radio ▪ "The sirens are screaming and the fires are howling way down in the valley tonight" - 30-year-old Meat Loaf performs *Bat Out Of Hell* on BBC Two's *Old Grey Whistle Test* ▪ "Bingo Master's Breakout!" - The Fall perform a night-time session for Radio One disc jockey John Peel.

Summer 1978

Grease is the word

Monarch:	Queen Elizabeth II (aged 52)
Prime-minister:	James Callaghan (aged 66)
Chancellor:	Denis Healey (aged 61)
Home Secretary:	Merlyn Rees (aged 57)
Foreign Secretary:	David Owen (aged 40)
Football Manager:	Ron Greenwood (aged 56)
Radio 1 Breakfast DJ:	Dave Lee Travis (aged 33)
New car reg. suffix:	'T'

▪ The sun shines ▪ *Grease* mania sweeps the nation ▪ "I got chills, they're multiplying, and I'm losing control, 'cause the power you're supplying, it's electrifying!" - *You're The One That I Want* by 29-year-old Olivia Newton-John and 24-year-old John Travolta is number one in the pop chart ▪ *Love Is In The Air* ("... everywhere I look around") by 27-year-old John Paul Young is number five ▪ *More Than A Woman* ("... More than a woman to me") by Tavares is number seven ▪ 33-year-old Angela Rippon reads the news for BBC Two ▪ Jim Callaghan's Labour government takes a new course of action to get the high rate of inflation under control ▪ 60-year-old Chancellor of the Exchequer Denis Healey imposes a 5% pay rise restriction and threatens sanctions against any companies or organisations failing to comply ▪ 51-year-old Derek Robinson (aka Red Robbo) leads a mass walk-out of workers at British Leyland ▪ 65-year-old Jack Jones retires from his position as leader of the Transport and General Workers Union ▪ 45-year-old Ishaque Ali dies of heart failure after being attacked by a gang of racists in Hackney ▪ 52-year-old Warren Mitchell stars in *The Saga of Alf Garnett* on ITV ▪ Matt (played by Frederick Pyne) marries Dolly (played by Katherine Barker) in popular soap-opera *Emmerdale Farm* ▪ 24-year-old Karl Howman, 24-year-old Philip Davis and 29-year-old John Duttine star in the final episode of ITV's Friday night drama *People Like Us* - based on 'The Avenue' novels from R. F. Delderfield ▪ The weather turns cool and rain clouds gather ▪ The summer holidays begin ▪ School children enjoy a six week break from the classroom ▪ 15-year-old Georgios Kyriacos Panayiotou from Hertfordshire and his

best friend, Andrew Ridgeley, write pop songs together in Georgios' bedroom ▪ *If I Can't Have You* ("… I don't want nobody, baby") by 26-year-old Yvonne Elliman moves down the weekly pop chart after peaking at number four ▪ "Oh Carol, you've opened the door..." *Oh Carol* ("... you can do it some more") by Smokie is number five ▪ "I've been holdin' out so long. I've been sleepin' all alone. Lord, I…" *Miss You* by The Rolling Stones is number three ▪ Kids rush to the sweet-shop for a Sherbet *Dip Dab* ▪ 11-year-old Paul 'Gazza' Gascoigne from Gateshead pulls a daft face and makes his friends laugh ▪ BBC One broadcasts *Jackanory*, *Help! It's the Hair Bear Bunch* and *Belle and Sebastian* during the school summer holiday ▪ 44-year-old John Noakes leaves children's TV show *Blue Peter* - after serving as a presenter for twelve and a half years ▪ "Where are you all coming from? / From Smurfland where we belong / Are you talking just like us? / No, we Smurf, it's much less fuss" - *The Smurf Song* by Father Abraham and the Smurfs shoots up the pop chart to number two ▪ *Annie's Song* by 38-year-old flautist James Galway is number three ▪ 38-year-old jockey Greville Starkey rides *Shirley Heights* to victory in the Epsom Derby ▪ 42-year-old Jock Wallace is appointed football manager of Second Division Leicester City ▪ *Dancing In The City* ("… alleys that we run through, now we've just begun to, have fun tonight") by Marshall Hain is number three in the pop chart ▪ *Rock 'n Roll Damnation* ("… take a chance while you still got the choice") by AC/DC is number twenty-four ▪ Industrial unrest continues ▪ Thousands of union members attend mass meetings ▪ The TUC votes to reject the government's 5% pay rise guideline ▪ Workers at Ford in Dagenham are expected to make a large pay demand; one that reflects the huge profits the company is making ▪ The *Cortina* and *Escort* motorcars are the two best selling models in Britain ▪ The number of foreign cars sold in the UK continues to increase ▪ A Datsun *Cherry* costs £2,335 ▪ A Datsun *Bluebird* is £3,097 ▪ A sporty Datsun *260Z* (two--seater) is £5,850 ▪ The last remaining pickets at the Grunwick photographic processing factory in Willesden call off their dispute - the workers have lost ▪ Mike Baldwin sacks Hilda Ogden from his factory on ITV's *Coronation Street* - Hilda's co-workers show their support by going on strike ▪ 48-year-old Stuart Hall presents *It's A Knockout* on BBC One. A team from Cleethorpes comes out on top after a closely fought contest

with Gainsborough and Lincoln. Cleethorpes will now compete in the Jeux Sans Frontieres competition later in the year ▪ The Lib-Lab pact (a political arrangement between David Steel's Liberals and the Labour government) comes to an end ▪ With high inflation and unions demanding pay increases greater than 5%, the economic outlook for the country is grim ▪ Labour prime-minister Jim Callaghan is determined to turn things around ▪ 52-year-old leader of the Conservative opposition Margaret Thatcher pushes for a general election but Mr. Callaghan resists ▪ 52-year-old Queen Elizabeth II welcomes 60-year-old Romanian President Nicolae Ceausescu and his wife, First Lady Elena, on an official state visit to Britain ▪ "Oooh, he's here again. The..." *Man With The Child In His Eyes* by 19-year-old Kate Bush is number six in the pop chart ▪ "Come on, baby..." *(Don't Fear) The Reaper* by Blue Oyster Cult is number sixteen ▪ The sixth series of BBC One's popular historical drama *The Onedin Line* (with 46-year-old Peter Gilmore and 41-year-old Jill Gascoine) begins on Sunday evenings ▪ The twelfth series of *Z Cars* (with 32-year-old Douglas Fielding as PC Alec Quilley and 47-year-old Jimmy Ellis as Inspector Bert Lynch) is transmitted on Wednesday evenings, after *The Big Time* (presented by 38-year-old Esther Rantzen) ▪ "Don't make me angry. You wouldn't like me when I'm angry" - *The Incredible Hulk* begins on ITV, with 44-year-old Bill Bixby as David Bruce Banner and with 26-year-old Lou Ferrigno as Banner's alter-ego - a giant, powerful, green coloured creature ▪ Teenagers attend discos at (council-run) youth centres ▪ A carton of orange squash (with a straw) costs 3½p ▪ A packet of KP *Outer-Spacer*s is 5p ▪ *Ca Plane Pour Moi* ("... moi, moi, moi, moi. Ca plane pour moi") by Plastic Bertrand climbs to number five on the hit parade ▪ *Pump It Up* ("... when you don't really need it") by 23-year-old Elvis Costello and the Attractions is number twenty-four ▪ *Shame* by 17-year-old Evelyn 'Champagne' King from New York is number thirty-nine ▪ 18-year-old Joanne Latham (36DD) from Wolverhampton is a popular new page three girl in *The Sun* ▪ Trendy young girls wear long 'gypsy' style skirts with bold floral prints and a decorative white frill showing at the hem ▪ Trendy young boys wear 'capped sleeve' T-shirts and dark blue jeans ▪ Assorted *Toffos* are now available - with regular, chocolate, strawberry and banana flavours all in one packet ▪ Like, old hippies wear denim

jeans and sandals, and smoke spliffs round their mate's flat, man ▪ *Davy's On The Road Again* ("... wearin' different clothes again") by Manfred Mann's Earth Band is number six in the pop chart ▪ *Run For Home* ("… Run as fast, as I can. Oh, oh, running man, running for home") by Lindisfarne reaches number ten ▪ 22-year-old tennis star Bjorn Borg wins the Wimbledon men's championship for the third consecutive year, beating 25-year-old Jimmy Conners (6-2, 6-2, 6-3) in the final ▪ 21-year-old Martina Navratilova wins the women's title for the first time, defeating 23-year-old Chris Evert (2-6, 6-4, 7-5) in the final ▪ There's a spell of hot weather in July ▪ The Savin family from Kings Norton spends two weeks in a static caravan at Barmouth Bay Holiday Village ▪ 36-year-old racing driver Carlos Reutemann from Argentina wins the British Grand Prix at Brands Hatch, driving a Ferrari ▪ 29-year-old Niki Lauda from Austria (in a Brabham) is second ▪ 32-year-old John Watson from Belfast (also in a Brabham) is third ▪ 31-year-old DJ Simon Bates presents the *Top 20* chart show on Radio One on Sunday evenings ▪ Teenagers wait for their favourite songs, then press 'play' and 'record' on their radio/cassettes ▪ *You're The One That I Want* by Olivia Newton-John and John Travolta is still number one in the pop chart ▪ "Don't you know I'll be your…" *Substitute* ("… whenever you want me, ooh, a-ooh") by Clout moves up to number two ▪ *Rivers Of Babylon / Brown Girl In The Ring* by Boney M moves back up to number ten after being in the chart for fifteen weeks ▪ *Identity* ("... is the crisis, can't you see?") by X-Ray Spex (with, lead singer, 21-year-old Poly Styrene) is number twenty-four ▪ Schoolboy John 'Fuzz' Townshend celebrates his fourteenth birthday with a hamburger and a side order of French fried potatoes at the *Wimpy* bar in Wolverhampton ▪ Teenage boys sneak into their local picture house to see *The Playbirds* - a raunchy new film starring 32-year-old Mary Millington ▪ Many elderly TV viewers are disappointed when *The Black and White Minstrel Show* is broadcast for a final time before being taken off-air. (The program has been running for twenty years) ▪ England's footballers take no part in the Argentinian world cup ▪ Ally MacLeod's Scotland team beats the Netherlands 3-2 with goals from Archie Gemmill and Kenny Dalglish ▪ *Ole Ola (Mulher Brasileira)* by 33-year-old Rod Stewart featuring the Scottish World Cup Squad is a Top Five chart hit ▪ A pair of black and white Adidas

World Cup 78 football boots (with six red screw-in studs) cost £19.75 ▪ A pack of World Cup '78 *Top Trumps* costs 50p ▪ "Ride the range all the day, till the first fading light. Be with my western girl, around the fire, oh so bright" - *Wild West Hero* by Electric Light Orchestra is number six on the hit parade ▪ *A Little Bit Of Soap* ("... will wash away your lipstick on my face") by Showaddywaddy reaches number five ▪ 'T' reg cars go on sale ▪ 'Princess. Not the car for Mr. Average' - British Leyland launches its range of *Princess Series 2* motorcars priced from £4,232. All models come with *Triplex 10/20* laminated windscreens. The 4-cylinder *1700 L* also has a clock and a heated rear window - and a top speed of 99 mph. The top-of-the-range 6-cylinder *2200 HLS* (priced at £5,030) has front headrests, centre folding armrests and a push-button radio - and a top speed of 104 mph ▪ 43-year-old Barrie Gill and 33-year-old Angela Rippon present *Top Gear* on BBC Two ▪ 13-year-old schoolgirl Genette Tate goes missing as she's delivering newspapers near her home in Devon ▪ 28-year-old DJ Kid Jensen hosts the travelling Radio One Roadshow for five days in August. The Kid's Roadshow week begins at the Glebe in Bowness and ends at Eirias Park in Colwyn Bay ▪ *Airport* ("... you've got a smiling face") by The Motors is number four in the pop chart ▪ "Tick-tock, tick-tock, tick-tock" - *Like Clockwork* by The Boomtown Rats is number six ▪ 35-year-old Mike Brearley is England's cricket captain for the summer series against Pakistan and New Zealand. 21-year-old batsman David Gower makes his Test debut at Edgbaston and hits a boundary off his first ball. 22-year-old 'all-rounder' Ian Botham scores a century and takes eight wickets in one innings at Lord's ▪ 27-year-old Barry Sheene finishes third in a rain affected 500cc motorcycle Grand Prix at Silverstone. Kenny Roberts wins to become the new world champion ▪ Pope Paul VI dies in Rome at the age of 80 and is succeeded by 65-year-old Pope John Paul ▪ Back in England - people enjoy a night out at the cinema ▪ *Revenge of the Pink Panther* (with 52-year-old Peter Sellers as Inspector Clouseau and with 60-year-old Herbert Lom as Chief Inspector Dreyfus) goes on general release ▪ 'The First Time was Only a Warning' - *Damien: Omen II* is also now showing ▪ *Evita* by Andrew Lloyd Webber opens in the West End ▪ Children go round to their (well-off) mate's house and have hours of fun playing on the electronic *Atari 2600* games console ▪ Teenagers 'hang-out' in

amusement arcades ▪ The *Pong* video game is hugely popular ▪ "She is cruel and heartless to pack me for Gordon. Just 'cause he's better looking than me, just 'cause he's cool and trendy. But I know he's a moron. GORDON IS A MORON!' - *Jilted John* by Jilted John (19-year-old Graham Fellows) is number four on the hit parade ▪ *If The Kids Are United* ("... they will never be divided") by Sham 69 (with, lead singer, 23-year-old Jimmy Pursey) is number nine ▪ *You're The One That I Want* ("... You are the one for. Ooh, ooh, ooh, honey") by Olivia Newton-John and John Travolta is still number one - and remains at the top of the chart for nine weeks! ▪ *Grease* mania continues to grip the nation ▪ Tim Sparks (an ex-port shipping controller) has a new side-line - as a John Travolta 'look-a-like' ▪ The 21-year-old from Hillingdon dresses in a black leather jacket, black drainpipe trousers, combs his hair in a 50's style - and stops traffic in the West End of London ▪ BBC One TV programs on a Saturday night include: *Emu's Broadcasting Company* - with 43-year-old Rod Hull and his uncontrollable puppet, Emu; *News* - read by 44-year-old Richard Whitmore; *Wonder Woman* - starring 27-year-old Lynda Carter (37-25-35) as Diana Prince; *Saturday Night at the Movies*; *Seaside Special* - with various star acts including Jim 'Nick Nick' Davidson, Roger de Courcey with Nookie Bear, Bernie Clifton (riding an ostrich), The Black Abbotts, Stu Francis and The Krankies; *Kojak* - with 56-year-old Telly Savalas; and *Sailor* - a documentary on life in the Royal Navy ▪ "Loose fallen leaves lie undisturbed now, 'cause you're not here" - *Forever Autumn* by 31-year-old Justin Hayward is number five in the pop chart ▪ *5.7.0.5.* ("... but there's no reply") by City Boy moves down from number eight to number thirteen ▪ "Everybody's on..." *Top Of The Pops* by The Rezillos is number twenty-six ▪ ITV programs on a Saturday night include: *Celebrity Squares* - hosted by 50-year-old Bob Monkhouse; *Happy Days* - featuring 32-year-old Henry Winkler as the Fonz and 24-year-old Ron Howard as Richie Cunningham; *Gambit* - with Fred Dinenage and Michelle Lambourne; *The Life and Times of Grizzly Adams*; a feature film at 8 p.m; *ITN News* at 10 p.m; and *The South Bank Show* - introduced by 38-year-old Melvyn Bragg ▪ 57-year-old Humphrey Lyttelton is chairman for a new series of *I'm Sorry I Haven't A Clue* on BBC Radio Four. Panelists Graeme Garden, Barry Cryer, Willie Rushton and Tim Brooke-Taylor partake in a new

game called 'Mornington Crescent' ▪ Middle aged, long haired men, clad in denim (and in possession of a 'twin-deck' record turntable unit, a dry ice 'fog' machine and a battered old Ford *Transit* van) advertise their services in local newspapers as mobile disco operators ▪ "If you're thinkin' you're too cool to boogie; boy, oh boy, have I got news for you" - *Boogie Oogie Oogie* by A Taste of Honey is number three in the pop chart ▪ *It's Raining* ("... raining down on me, yeah") by Darts is number two ▪ After the wettest summer for ten years, the sun breaks through the clouds and there's a mini heatwave in late August ▪ Temperatures rise into the seventies on the beaches of Blackpool, Bournemouth, Clacton, Eastbourne and Scarborough ▪ The going rate for B&B accomodation in a sea-side guest house is £18 per person, per night ▪ Toolmakers at British Leyland in Birmingham come out on strike ▪ Argentinian World Cup footballers Ossie Ardiles (aged 25) and Ricardo Villa (aged 26) sign for newly promoted Tottenham Hotspur ▪ 23-year-old left-back Alan Kennedy transfers from Newcastle Utd to Liverpool for £330,000 ▪ 29-year-old midfielder Colin Suggett moves from Norwich City to Newcastle Utd on a free transfer ▪ 26-year-old centre-forward Peter Withe transfers from Nottingham Forest to Newcastle Utd for £225,000 ▪ "By the..." *Rivers Of Babylon / Brown Girl In The Ring* ("... tra-la-la-la-lah") by Boney M moves back up to number two in the pop chart after being in the chart for twenty weeks ▪ "The..." *Northern Lights* ("... are in my mind, they guide me back to you") by Renaissance is number ten ▪ *Don't Be Cruel* ("... to a heart that's true") by the late Elvis Presley is number twenty-four ▪ Siouxsie and the Banshees (with, lead singer, 21-year-old Siouxsie Sioux) feature on the front cover of the latest *New Musical Express* ▪ The European Athletics Championships get underway in Prague. 22-year-old Steve Ovett and 21-year-old Sebastian Coe compete against each other for the first time - both taking part in the final of the 800 metres. Ovett wins a silver medal, Coe gets a bronze ▪ Back in England - Trendy boys (in suede 'brothel creeper' shoes) pluck up the courage to ask girls (in knee-high 'crazy boots') for the last dance at the mobile disco in the village hall ▪ "And now that we've come to the end of our rainbow, there's something I must say out loud. You're once, twice..." *Three Times A Lady* ("... and I love you") by The Commodores is new at number one in the pop chart.

Autumn 1978

Ossie Ardilles and Ricky Villa join Spurs

Monarch:	Queen Elizabeth II (aged 52)
Prime-minister:	James Callaghan (aged 66)
Chancellor:	Denis Healey (aged 61)
Home Secretary:	Merlyn Rees (aged 57)
Foreign Secretary:	David Owen (aged 40)
Football Manager:	Ron Greenwood (aged 57)
Radio 1 Breakfast DJ:	Dave Lee Travis (aged 33)
New car reg. suffix:	'T'

▪ The weather is inclement ▪ Children return to school after the summer holidays ▪ Boys play *Top Trumps* in the corner of the playground ▪ 19-year-old student Simon Le Bon moves from Bushey to Birmingham to study drama - and holds ambitions of one day becoming a famous pop star ▪ "I say, I don't like cricket. Oh no. I love it" - *Dreadlock Holiday* by 10cc spends a week at number one ▪ "Space travel's in my blood. There ain't nothin' I can do about it" - *Another Girl, Another Planet* by The Only Ones is a minor hit - the record fails to make the Top 75 ▪ British Leyland toolmakers are still on strike and Michael Edwardes (Leyland's chairman) warns that continued industrial action could result in 70,000 workers being laid-off ▪ Inflation remains high, but the rate of increase has slowed slightly ▪ "I shall not be calling for a general election at this time. Instead, I ask every one of you to carry on with the task of consolidating the improvement now taking place in our country's position. Let's see it through together" - 66-year-old Labour prime-minister Jim Callaghan decides not to call a general election just yet ▪ 52-year-old Leader of the Opposition Margaret Thatcher accuses Mr. Callaghan of running scared ▪ 22-year-old athlete Steve Ovett wins a gold medal in the final of the 1500 metres at the European Athletics Championships. 25-year-old David Moorcroft finishes in third place and gets a bronze ▪ *British Hustle* by Hi Tension is number eight in the pop chart ▪ "You've been…" *Talking In Your Sleep* ("… Sleeping in your dreams") by 27-year-old Crystal Gayle is number eleven ▪ "I woke up in a Soho doorway, a policeman knew my name" - *Who Are You* by The Who slides down the chart to number twenty-two. The group's

drummer, 32-year-old Keith Moon, dies at Flat 12, Number 9 Curzon Place, Mayfair in London ▪ Pope John Paul dies just thirty-three days after becoming leader of the Catholic church. 58-year-old Karol Wojtyla from Poland succeeds the late pontiff - and takes the name John Paul II ▪ "Seems like a nice boy" - 55-year-old Larry Grayson is the new host of *The Generation Game* on BBC One. 26-year-old Isla St. Clair is Grayson's assistant ▪ 51-year-old Terry Scott goes searching up the loft, hoping to find an old '78' recording of *The Hut-Sut Song* by The Melba Trio in BBC sit-com *Happy Ever After* ▪ The film *Grease* is now on general release at cinemas throughout the UK - and hundreds of thousands of people make multiple visits, queuing up to see the popular movie again and again ▪ 45-year-old Barry Norman interviews John Travolta on the late night movie review program *Film 78* on BBC One ▪ Teenage boys chalk 'T-birds' on the back of their black PVC ('leather-look') zip-up jackets ▪ "Well-a-well-a-well-a-huh. Tell me more, tell me more. Did you get very far? Tell me more, tell me more. Like, does he have a car?" - *Summer Nights* by John Travolta and Olivia Newton-John reaches number one in the pop chart - and stays there for seven weeks! ▪ *Grease* ("... is the word") by 44-year-old Frankie Valli is number three ▪ 62-year-old singing superstar Frank Sinatra appears at the Royal Festival Hall in London - performing in front of a packed house for eight nights ▪ The new football season is underway ▪ Bob Paisley's Liverpool thrash Keith Burkinshaw's Tottenham Hotspur (with Argentinian World Cup stars Ossie Ardiles and Ricardo Villa in the Spurs' team) by seven goals to nil at Anfield. 26-year-old Liverpool midfielder Terry McDermott heads home the seventh goal, after running the length of the pitch to get on the end of a Steve Heighway cross ▪ A pale-blue, three-wheeled AC*70 Invacar* is parked at the side of the football pitch at St. Andrews as Birmingham City lose 0-1 to rivals Aston Villa, with a goal from 22-year-old Andy Gray ▪ 36-year-old Muhammad Ali regains the WBA heavy-weight world boxing title by beating 25-year-old Leon Spinks in New Orleans ▪ Back in England - 13-year-old paper boy Carl Bridgewater is murdered at a farmhouse near Stourbridge and a nation-wide search begins to find the brutal killer. Police officers interview tens of thousands of owners of light blue Ford *Cortina* and *Escort* estate cars. (A vehicle of similar description was seen near the scene of the

crime) ▪ In a separate incident - a crazed gunman kills three people in West Bromwich before driving off in his Ford *Capri* and murdering a fourth person at a petrol station in Nuneaton. Police chase the killer to Buxton where he's eventually caught and arrested ▪ *Oh What A Circus* ("... Oh, what a show. Argentina has gone to town over the death of an actress called Eva Peron") by 31-year-old David Essex is number three in the pop chart ▪ "You abandoned me..." *Love Don't Live Here Anymore* by Rose Royce is number two ▪ Workers at Ford go on strike, demanding a 30% pay increase - way above the government's 5% guideline ▪ Labour prime-minister Jim Callaghan and Chancellor of the Exchequer Denis Healey negotiate with union leaders, but fail to reach a satisfactory agreement ▪ In other news - Fifty Vietnamese boat people are given sanctuary in England after being rescued by a British ship in the South China Sea ▪ Bulgarian defector Georgi Markov is murdered at a bus stop in London - by poison injected through the point of an umbrella ▪ "Do me a favour, Guv!" - 36-year-old John Thaw and 30-year-old Dennis Waterman star as Reagan and Carter in a new series of ITV's popular, hard-hitting cop drama *The Sweeney* ▪ The last ever episode of BBC's *Z Cars* is broadcast on Wednesday the twentieth of September. 32-year-old Douglas Fielding (as Sgt. Alec Quilley, 44-year-old David Jackson (as DC Jim Braithwaite), 41-year-old Brian Grellis (as DS Bernard Bowker) and 50-year-old Frank Windsor (as DS John Watt) make their final appearances in the popular drama, which first aired in January, 1962 ▪ 'Just when you thought it was safe to go back in the water…' *Jaws 2* (with 45-year-old Roy Scheider) is now showing at cinemas ▪ "Ra-ra…" *Rasputin* ("… Russia's greatest love machine") by Boney M climbs to number three in the pop chart ▪ "Waiting for the sunrise, soul dancin' in the dark…" *Summer Night City* by Abba reaches number five ▪ The Slits (with 23-year-old Viv Albertine, 19-year-old Tessa Pollitt and 16-year-old Ari Up) feature on the front cover of the latest *New Musical Express* ▪ *The Better World of Reginald Perrin* - the sixth novel from 43-year-old writer David Nobbs is published ▪ "S'alright. Por favor" - 55-year-old Ricardo Montez, 35-year-old Barry Evans and 28-year-old Francoise Pascal feature in a new series of *Mind Your Language* on ITV ▪ 22-year-old Argentinian footballer Alberto Tarantini signs for Birmingham City ▪ 19-year-old Kevin Mabbutt scores a hat-trick as

Alan Dicks' Bristol City beat Manchester Utd 1-3 at Old Trafford ▪ Brian Clough's Nottingham Forest win 0-1 against Ian Greaves' Bolton Wanderers - and Forest remain unbeaten after sixteen league games ▪ 28-year-old striker Malcolm 'Supermac' MacDonald of Arsenal is out, injured - awaiting an operation on his knee ▪ Brendan Batson plays alongside Cyril Regis and Laurie Cunningham in Big Ron Atkinson's West Bromwich Albion team ▪ The Three Degrees perform their new song *Givin' Up Givin' In* on *Top of the Pops* ▪ Queen release the single *Bicycle Race* - a 'limited edition' disc comes with a free poster showing a group of naked women on bikes ▪ *Picture This* ("… a sky full of thunder. Picture this, my telephone number") by Blondie (featuring 33-year-old Debbie Harry) is number twelve in the pop chart ▪ "Where did you go? I was searchin' (searchin') on a one-way street. I was hopin' (hopin') for a chance to meet. I was waitin' for the operator on the line" - *Sweet Talkin' Woman* by Electric Light Orchestra is number six ▪ Bakers go on strike, demanding a 26% pay increase - way above the government's 5% guideline ▪ Labour prime-minister Jim Callaghan and Chancellor of the Exchequer Denis Healey negotiate with union leaders, but fail to reach a satisfactory agreement ▪ 'We Regret No Bread Owing to Bakers Strike!' - Bread is now in short supply. Queues form outside shops as panic buying breaks out ▪ *Summer Nights* by John Travolta and Olivia Newton-John remains at number one in the pop chart ▪ "Harmful elements in the air, symbols clashing everywhere" - *Hong Kong Garden* by Siouxsie and the Banshees is number seven ▪ *Supernature* by Cerrone is number eight ▪ Sid Vicious' girlfriend, Nancy Spungen, is found stabbed to death in a hotel room in New York ▪ Back in England - 'We Ain't Going Back Till We Get Our Fair Wack' - Pickets brandish placards outside Ford factories, holding firm with their strike for higher pay ▪ Trendy kids spend evenings at roller-discos ▪ *You Make Me Feel (Mighty Real)* by Sylvester is number eight in the pop chart ▪ "I wanna…" *Kiss You All Over* ("… and over again") by Exile is number six ▪ Poorly children stay home and miss out on the disco fun ▪ 'Sore throat need soothing?' - Gargling with *TCP Antiseptic* relieves irritation' ▪ Tony Adamson presents *Sport on 2* on BBC Radio Two ▪ Footballers, Garry Birtles and Colin Barrett score the goals as Brian Clough's Nottingham Forest knock Bob Paisley's Liverpool out of the European Cup in the first

round. Forest will now face AEK Athens in round two ▪ 20-year-old David O'Leary is on the score-sheet for Terry Neill's Arsenal in a 2-3 victory over John Neal's Middlesbrough at Ayresome Park in Division One ▪ "Aaah, it's-an-up-and-unda!" - 68-year-old Eddie Waring commentates on Rugby League for BBC's *Grandstand* on Saturday afternoons ▪ Widnes beat Workington 15-13 in the Lancashire Cup Final ▪ "Well how am I supposed to feel with all the things you don't reveal, and you can thank your lucky stars that we're not as smart as we'd like to think we are" - *Lucky Stars* by 23-year-old Dean Friedman reaches number three in the pop chart ▪ "Let's all smurf together. It's smurfing kind of weather and it's very easy if you try" - *Dippety Day* by 43-year-old Father Abraham and The Smurfs reaches number two ▪ Miss Piggy performs a duet with 38-year-old Raquel Welch on *The Muppet Show*. Fozzie the bear tries to be more assertive. Animal the drummer is wild and crazy. Kermit the frog attempts to hold things together ▪ The annual cost of a colour TV license increases from £21 to £25 ▪ A black and white license goes up from £9 to £10 ▪ Affluent families purchase the latest electronic goods from *Rumbelows* ▪ VHS and Betamax video recorders are now available ▪ "Confused? You Will Be" - the American sit-com *Soap* is on late night ITV ▪ "Magic, our Morris!" - series four of *Oh No, It's Selwyn Frogitt* (starring 49-year-old Bill Maynard) is on evening-time ITV ▪ Twenty-million people watch *Coronation Street* as the dastardly Ray Langton (played by 35-year-old Neville Buswell) walks out on his wife Deirdre and baby Tracy and goes off to build a new life in Holland ▪ 35-year-old Ian Ogilvy drives a white Jaguar *XJ-S* and stars as Simon Templar in *The Return of the Saint* ▪ A sport hatch version of the Vauxhall *Cavalier* motorcar goes on sale ▪ Car theft is increasing ▪ Ford make 'central-locking' a standard feature on the *Granada GL* model ▪ 33-year-old DJ Dave Lee Travis (aka 'The Hairy Cornflake') takes his turn to introduce *Top of the Pops* on BBC One on Thursday evenings ▪ "Come on, come on …" *Hurry Up Harry* ("… come on. We're goin' down the pub") by Sham 69 reaches number ten in the pop chart ▪ *Winker's Song (Misprint)* by Ivor Biggun and the Red Nosed Burglars stalls at number twenty-two ▪ After nine weeks of industrial action, union leaders at Ford negotiate a 17% pay increase for workers ▪ Jim Callaghan's Labour government has allowed a dangerous precedent to be

set and strikes in other sectors are now more likely ▪ *The Sun* newspaper predicts that the country is facing a winter of discontent ▪ "Someone left the cake out in the rain. I don't think that I can make it, 'cause it took so long to bake it" - *MacArthur Park* by 29-year-old Donna Summer is number five in the pop chart ▪ *Darlin'* ("… I'm feeling pretty lonesome. I'd call you on the phone-some, but I don't have a dime") by 28-year-old Frankie Miller is number six ▪ Suburban housewives take turns to host tea and coffee mornings ▪ 'A drink's too wet without one' - *Rich Tea* biscuits are advertised on telly ▪ 29-year-old David Sullivan opens a new sex shop at Tunbridge Wells ▪ 21-year-old Marie Forsa stars in a video cassette recording of *Sex in Sweden* ▪ 24-year-old Lina Romay stars in *Barbed Wire Dolls* ▪ 'When it comes to foreign affairs' - 21-year-old Suzanne Danielle, 60-year-old Kenneth Connor and 52-year-old Kenneth Williams star on the big screen at cinemas in *Carry On Emmanuelle* ▪ "Bright eyes, burning like fire" - *Watership Down* is also now showing ▪ "Oooh, Betty" - 36-year-old Michael Crawford plays Frank Spencer in a new series of *Some Mothers Do 'Ave 'Em* on BBC One ▪ 28-year-old pop star Suzi Quatro plays the role of Leather Tuscadero in *Happy Days* on ITV ▪ *I Lost My Heart To A Starship Trooper* ("… Crashin' light in hyper-space") by 18-year-old Sarah Brightman and Hot Gossip is number six in the pop chart ▪ Van drivers buy a copy of *The Sun* newspaper on their way to work ▪ 20-year-old Luscious Linda Lusardi (36C) is on page three ▪ 'Reach for the Star, it's Britain's Best Buy' - the brand new *Daily Star* newspaper costs 6p ▪ 'Free. The Boomtown Rats Pull-Out Poster' - the brand new *Smash Hits* magazine (aimed at teenagers) costs 25p ▪ "The pulse of the corner boys just sprang into action, and young Billy watched it under the yellow street light, and said, tonight, of all nights, there's gonna be a fight" - *Rat Trap* by The Boomtown Rats reaches number one in the pop chart, replacing *Summer Nights* which had held top spot for seven weeks. To mark the occasion, 27-year-old Bob Geldof rips up a photograph of John Travolta and Olivia Newton-John on *Top of the Pops* ▪ Here she comes again, when she's dancin' 'neath the starry sky" - *My Best Friend's Girl* by The Cars is number three ▪ "10-9-8-7-6-5-4-3-2-1. Aahhh, ahh-ahh-ahh, ah-ah" - *Instant Replay* ("… You got to have it") by 27-year-old Dan Hartman is number eight ▪ Firemen are called out to tackle a fire in the kitchen

of a flat at 58A Mount Ephraim, Tunbridge Wells. The flat is severely damaged but Miss A. Marshall (the resident) is unharmed. The fire was started by a short circuit in an extractor fan ▪ Kitchen appliance technology moves on apace ▪ A Toshiba *ER556* microwave oven costs £199 ▪ A Toshiba *ER638* microwave oven (with a new-fangled turntable) costs £275 ▪ Trendy families enjoy chilli con carne for dinner with a glass of Liebfraumilch wine ▪ Grease mania continues ▪ "Stranded at the drive-in, branded a fool. What will they say Monday at school?" - *Sandy* by 24-year-old John Travolta is number two in the pop chart in early November ▪ "But now there's nowhere to hide since you pushed my love aside. I'm out of my head..." *Hopelessly Devoted To You* by 30-year-old Olivia Newton John is number two in mid November ▪ Bread remains in short supply as 26,000 bakers continue their industrial action ▪ A *Sunblest* van (a Leyland *FG*) is attacked by pickets outside Cookson's bakery in Lytham St. Annes ▪ Elsewhere, husbands and wives enjoy an evening out at the cinema ▪ 'A murderer strikes on board the luxury Nile steamer Karnak' - 56-year-old Peter Ustinov stars as Hercule Poirot in Agatha Christie's *Death on the Nile*. 70-year-old Bette Davis, 31-year-old Jane Birkin, 26-year-old Simon MacCorkindale, 27-year-old Olivia Hussey, 43-year-old Maggie Smith and 68-year-old David Niven are also in the cast ▪ 'One step beyond horror' - 40-year-old John Nolan and 31-year-old Carolyn Courage star in *Terror* ▪ 33-year-old Dennis Nilsen strangles 14-year-old Stephen Holmes at Melrose Avenue in Cricklewood and hides his body beneath the floorboards ▪ 12-year-old Mark Gatiss from Sedgefield scares his friends by telling chilling ghost stories ▪ 11-year-old Steve Pemberton from Blackburn visits the local shop (for local people) with his mum and the two of them join the long queue for bread ▪ A loaf costs 27p ▪ A pint of milk is 13p ▪ The bakers' strike continues ▪ Supermarkets experience shortages and shelves are bare ▪ Tesco and Asda turn to smaller bakeries for an alternative means of supply ▪ Fed up with the situation, many people are now baking their own bread at home ▪ Despite strikes, high inflation and food shortages, Labour prime-minister Jim Callaghan still believes he can turn the country's fortunes around ▪ "Everyone's a fruit and nut case" - Frank Muir advertises Cadbury's *Fruit & Nut* on TV.

Christmas 1978

Labour isn't working

Monarch:	Queen Elizabeth II (aged 52)
Prime-minister:	James Callaghan (aged 66)
Chancellor:	Denis Healey (aged 61)
Home Secretary:	Merlyn Rees (aged 58)
Foreign Secretary:	David Owen (aged 40)
Football Manager:	Ron Greenwood (aged 57)
Radio 1 Breakfast DJ:	Dave Lee Travis (aged 33)
New car reg. suffix:	'T'

▪ "Solid Gold. Ray-dee-oh One" - Radio One's frequency moves from 247m to 275m and 285m on medium wave transmission ▪ "But what was the year?" - 32-year-old disc jockey Simon Bates presents the *Golden Hour* during his mid morning show ▪ "Ahhh, freak out! Le Freak c'est Chic" - *Le Freak* by Chic climbs to number seven in the pop chart ▪ "Well, this car could be systematic, hydromatic, ultramatic. Why, it could be..." *Greased Lightnin'* by 24-year-old John Travolta is number eleven ▪ Hallmark Records release *The Best of Top of the Pops '78* - a budget priced, cover-version pop compilation LP with a hot disco babe pictured on the sleeve ▪ KP *Discos* - a new type of crisps are now on sale in shops ▪ Families enjoy an evening in, playing *Connect Four*, *Frustration* and *Hungry Hippos* ▪ The IRA resumes its bombing campaign on mainland Britain. Devices are activated in Manchester, Liverpool, Coventry, Bristol and Southampton - thankfully there are no fatalities ▪ "There's nothin' for us in Belfast, the Pound's old and that's a pity" - Stiff Little Fingers perform *Alternative Ulster* ▪ "He's a germ free adolescent. Cleanliness is her obsession. Cleans her teeth ten times a day. Scrub away, scrub away, scrub away, the SR way" - *Germ Free Adolescents* by X-Ray Spex (with 21-year-old Poly Styrene) reaches number nineteen in the weekly pop chart ▪ *You Don't Bring Me Flowers* ("... anymore") by 36-year-old Barbra Steisand and 37-year-old Neil Diamond is number five ▪ 66-year-old Labour prime-minister Jim Callaghan refuses to join a new currency plan being put in place by the European Common Market ▪ 53-year-old Leader of the Opposition Mrs. Thatcher criticises Mr. Callaghan, saying, "This is a sad day for Europe." ▪ Concrete cows stand proudly in a field near the ul-

tra-modern town of Milton Keynes ▪ The final episode of series two of *The Professionals* (with Doyle driving a 'Diamond White' Ford *Escort RS2000* and Bodie driving a 'Strato Silver' Ford *Capri 3.0S*) grips late night TV viewers on Saturday the ninth of December ▪ 35-year-old Radio One DJ Tony Blackburn takes his turn to introduce *Top of The Pops*, on Thursday the fourteenth of December ▪ 23-year-old Sue Menhenick dances with Legs & Co ▪ *Pretty Little Angel Eyes* by Showaddywaddy moves up to number five in the chart ▪ *Always And Forever / Mind Blowing Decisions (re-mix)* by Heatwave peaks at number nine ▪ *New York New York* ("… so good they named it twice. New York, New York, all the scandal and the vice. I love it") by 31-year-old Gerard Kenny stalls at number forty-three ▪ 27-year-old Bob Geldof of the Boomtown Rats is pictured on the front cover of the latest *New Musical Express* ▪ Labour prime-minister Jim Callaghan loses a vote in the House of Commons to restrict pay increases to 5% ▪ Leader of the Opposition Mrs. Thatcher senses that a Conservative victory could well be on the cards at the next general election ▪ "It's behind you!" - Middle-class families enjoy an evening at the Pantomime ▪ 63-year-old Peter Butterworth appears as Widow Twankey in *Aladdin* at the Coventry Theatre ▪ 'The image of an adult world through a child's eyes' - 13-year-old Brooke Shields plays a child prostitute in the film *Pretty Baby* ▪ "If you want my body and you think I'm sexy, come on sugar tell me so" - *Da Ya Think I'm Sexy?* by Rod Stewart climbs to number one in the pop chart ▪ "Where are you all coming from? / We're from Dartmoor on the run / How did you work out your route? / We followed the arrows on our suit" - the comedy song *A Taste Of Aggro* by The Barron Knights reaches number three ▪ The final section of M180 motorway opens near Scunthorpe and motorists can now speed between Doncaster and Grimsby in less than one hour ▪ 124 million tonnes of coal have been mined in the UK this year - roughly the same amount as last year - but the number of miners has decreased to just 240,000 ▪ The total number of unemployed people has risen to 1.5 million ▪ Pressure is intensifying on prime-minister Jim Callaghan ▪ More than one-million council workers are planning to go on strike in January unless their demand for a 20 per cent pay increase is met ▪ Almost half a million haulage workers are demanding an extra £20 a week and the men (mainly lorry drivers) are prepared to strike to get it ▪

Coal miners want a 40 per cent pay rise - which would take the basic rate for men at the coalface to £110 a week ▪ Power station workers are demanding a 20 per cent increase ▪ Bill-board posters say, 'Labour Isn't Working' ▪ Jim Callaghan's Labour government survives a vote of confidence in the House of Commons - but there's a growing consensus that the 66-year-old premier's time at Number 10 is now coming to an end ▪ On-going industrial action by print workers forces *The Times* newspaper to close down ▪ 'We are unable to show the published programmes at the moment because of an Industrial Dispute' - workers at BBC are on an overtime ban ▪ Away from workplace strife and unrest, Ron Greenwood's England football team beats Czechoslovakia 1-0 at Wembley with a goal from 23-year-old Steve Coppell of Manchester Utd. 22-year-old Nottingham Forest full-back Viv Anderson makes his international debut and becomes England's first black player. The full line-up for the match is: Shilton, Anderson, Cherry, Thompson, Watson, Wilkins, Keegan, Coppell, Woodcock, Currie, P Barnes and substitute, Latchford ▪ *Tommy Gun* ("... you ain't happy 'less you got one") by The Clash reaches number nineteen in the pop chart ▪ "Oh, how can you ever let me down? (Down)" - *Promises* by The Buzzcocks peaks at number twenty ▪ Nottingham Forest's long unbeaten run comes to an end when Liverpool win a top-of-the-table clash by two goals to nil at Anfield - with both goals scored by 27-year-old Terry McDermott ▪ Big Ron Atkinson's West Bromwich Albion achieve a 3-5 victory over Dave Sexton's Manchester Utd at Old Trafford - with goals from Tony 'bomber' Brown (2), Len Cantello, Laurie Cunningham and 20-year-old Cyril Regis ▪ Terry Neill's Arsenal thrash Tottenham Hotspur 0-5 at White Hart Lane - with 22-year-old Liam Brady scoring a sublime chip shot and 25-year-old Alan Sunderland bagging a hat-trick ▪ In Division Two, Terry Venables' Crystal Palace stay top-of-the-table with a 0-0 draw away at Cambridge Utd. (Palace goalkeeper John 'Budgie' Burridge keeps a clean sheet) ▪ In Division Three, Graham Turner's Shrewsbury Town move up to second place (behind leaders Watford) with a 3-0 victory over promotion rivals Swansea City. (Ian Atkins, Steve Biggins and Paul Maguire score the goals for 'Town') ▪ In Division Four, Jimmy Dickinson's Portsmouth move up to second place (behind leaders Wimbledon) with a 4-0 victory over promotion rivals Reading. (Pete De-

nyer, Leigh Barnard, Jeff Hemmerman and Steve Davey score the goals for 'Pompey') ▪ Four days before Christmas, workers at the BBC go on strike and television programs are suspended ▪ With no transmissions from the BBC, a record number of nineteen million people tune in to watch a repeat of *The Sweeney* on ITV ▪ Mums and dads carry out the last minute Christmas shopping ▪ A bottle of *White Horse* whisky costs £4.19 ▪ A bottle of *Gordon's* gin is £4.19 ▪ A bottle of *Martell* brandy is £6.35 ▪ A bottle of *Smirnoff* vodka is £4.19 ▪ A bottle of *Harveys Bristol Cream* is £1.99 ▪ A bottle of *Baileys Irish Cream* is £3.69 ▪ A tin of *Family Circle* biscuits is £1.41 ▪ "Hark now hear the angels sing, a King was born today. And man will live for evermore, because of Christmas Day" - *Mary's Boy Child - Oh My Lord* by Boney M is number one in the pop chart ▪ *Christmas In Smurfland* by Father Abraham and the Smurfs is number nineteen ▪ Parents take their young children to department stores to visit Father Christmas' grotto. Reluctant girls and boys sit on the knee of an elderly stranger (who's dressed in a red coat and wearing a false white beard) and claim to have "been good" - in the hope of getting the Christmas present they most desire ▪ A 'figure-of-eight' *Scalextric* race set costs £23.95 from *Argos* ▪ A *Hornby* British Rail High Speed Passenger (oval shaped) train set is £19.75 ▪ A *Palitoy* Family Tree House is £7.95 ▪ A *Palitoy* 'Girl's World' head with growing hair is £8.45 ▪ An *Action Man* soldier with 'Eagle-Eyes' is £3.60 ▪ *Lego* sets now contain realistic mini figures of people ▪ 14-year-old public schoolboy Alexander Boris de Pfeffel Johnson opens his Christmas presents and is pleased to receive a bottle of aftershave ▪ 'Denim - for men who don't have to try too hard' - *Denim* is advertised on television ▪ 43-year-old Ted Rogers stars with Dusty Bin in the Christmas special of ITV's popular game show *3-2-1* ▪ At the final hour in negotiations, a pay settlement is reached with unions and management at the BBC and programs are back up and running in time for the festive period ▪ 30-year-old Noel Edmonds introduces a special edition of *Top of the Pops* ▪ 52-year-old Queen Elizabeth II addresses the nation at three o'clock on Christmas Day ▪ Frank Spencer (played by 36-year-old Michael Crawford) learns to fly in the Christmas special of *Some Mothers Do 'Ave 'Em* ▪ BBC One broadcasts the television network premiere of *The Sound of Music* ▪ ITV transmits the James Bond film *Diamonds Are Forever* ▪

Mary's Boy Child - Oh My Lord by Boney M remains at the top of the hit parade for the Yuletide holiday ▪ "Nobody gets…" *Too Much Heaven* ("… no more, it's much harder to come by, I'm waiting in line") by The Bee Gees is number four ▪ *Dr. Who* by Mankind is number twenty-five ▪ 36-year-old Mike Brearley leads England's cricketers on an Ashes tour of Australia. England win the opening Test in Brisbane by seven wickets. In the second Test (at Perth), England win again, with 21-year-old batsman David Gower scoring a century and 29-year-old fast bowler Bob Willis taking 5 wickets for 44 runs. Graham Yallop's Aussies gain a victory in the third Test at Melbourne and England take a 2-1 lead into the new year ▪ Back in Britain - the weather turns cold and snow begins to fall ▪ Families stay indoors and turn up the central heating ▪ 'Make someone happy with a phone-call' - cartoon bird 'Buzby' advertises the services of the Post Office's telecommunications department on TV ▪ The new fangled *Key-phone* telephone set (with state-of-the-art push-buttons and a distinctive 'warble' ring tone) is in high demand ▪ "I'm in the phone booth, it's the one across the hall. If you don't answer, I'll just ring it off the wall" - *Hanging On The Telephone* by Blondie (featuring 33-year-old Debbie Harry) climbs to number five in the pop chart ▪ "Hello, this is Joanie, I'm sorry but I'm not home" - *Hello This Is Joanie (The Telephone Answering Machine Song)* by 40-year-old Paul Evans is number six ▪ "There is nothing in the world that we can't do to stop the light of love come shining through" - *Mirrors* by 31-year-old Sally Oldfield stalls at number nineteen ▪ "Leave it alone!'" - the fourth (and final) series of ITV's popular, hard-hitting cop drama *The Sweeney* (starring 36-year-old John Thaw as Jack Reagan and 30-year-old Dennis Waterman as George Carter) comes to an end ▪ Crossroads Motors at Challock near Ashford in Kent advertise a 1973 Ford *Granada GXL*, in red with automatic gearbox, for £1,495 ▪ Clarks Car Sales at Ilkeston, Derbyshire have a 1973 Ford *Granada GXL*, in bronze with brown interior, for £1,475 ▪ Young men pop into the newsagent on their way to work ▪ 'Meet her on Page Seven' - a photograph of a topless 'Starbird' is a popular feature in the new *Daily Star* newspaper ▪ A copy of the latest *Mayfair* magazine is 60p ▪ Miniature models of *Coca-Cola* cans on silver chain necklaces are popular Christmas gifts for girls ▪ *Stretch Armstrong* is popular for boys.

New Year 1979

Winter of discontent

Monarch:	Queen Elizabeth II (aged 52)
Prime-minister:	James Callaghan (aged 66)
Chancellor:	Denis Healey (aged 61)
Home Secretary:	Merlyn Rees (aged 58)
Foreign Secretary:	David Owen (aged 40)
Football Manager:	Ron Greenwood (aged 57)
Radio 1 Breakfast DJ:	Dave Lee Travis (aged 33)
New car reg. suffix:	'T'

▪ Freezing weather with drifting snow ▪ Public sector workers go on strike ▪ Lorry drivers go on strike ▪ Disgruntled workers stand on picket lines outside factory gates - warming themselves beside fires in rusty oil drums ▪ Rubbish piles up on the streets ▪ There's a shortage of food in shops ▪ Across the country, power cuts occur on a daily basis ▪ 66-year-old prime-minister Jim Callaghan leaves the UK to attend an international conference in Guadalupa followed by a holiday in Barbados ▪ *The Sun* newspaper uses the headline, 'Crisis? What Crisis?' ▪ "Young man, there's no need to feel down. I said, young man, pick yourself off the ground" - *YMCA* by The Village People is new at number one in the pop chart ▪ "Night, is draggin' her feet. I wait, alone in the heat" - *A Little More Love* by 30-year-old Olivia Newton-John is number four ▪ "They got me on…" *Milk And Alcohol* by Dr. Feelgood is number nine ▪ *Every Which Way But Loose* is now showing at cinemas. 48-year-old Clint Eastwood, 34-year-old Sondra Locke and an orangutan called Clyde are the stars of the film ▪ England's cricketers are successful down-under. 27-year-old Derek Randall scores 150 runs in Sydney. 23-year-old 'all-rounder' Ian Botham scores 74 runs and takes 4 wickets for 42 at Adelaide - and Brearley's team wins the Ashes by five Test Matches to one. G Boycott, G A Gooch, D W Randall, J M Brearley (cpt), D I Gower, I T Botham, G Miller, R W Taylor (wk), P H Edmonds, J E Emburey, C M Old, R G D Willis, J K Lever and M Hendrick have all played a part in England's resounding victory ▪ Back in England - power cuts continue and shops and businesses are forced to close early ▪ The winter is cold and grim ▪ Labour prime-minister Jim Callaghan blames the media for 'talking down' the prospects of the coun-

try ▪ The freezing weather continues ▪ There's no heating in schools ▪ 'Low Paid Workers Need a Minimum Wage' - members of NALGO and NUPE brandish placards and huddle for warmth on picket lines ▪ Grave diggers in Liverpool go on strike ▪ For most people, this is truly a winter of discontent ▪ "Life, isn't everything. Isn't everything" - *Song For Guy* by 31-year-old Elton John climbs to number four in the pop chart ▪ "Ooh, baby..." *Lay Your Love On Me* by Racey is number three ▪ Football matches go ahead in icy conditions ▪ Bob Paisley's Liverpool (top of Division One) play against Dave Smith's Southend Utd (eighth in Division Three) in an FA Cup tie on a snow covered pitch with an orange ball - the game ends in a 0-0 draw, with Liverpool going on to win the replay ▪ 31-year-old Keith Weller wears white tights, and scores a brilliant goal for Leicester City in a 3-0 victory over Norwich City ▪ "I don't care what you say anymore..." *This Is My Life* ("... Go ahead with your own life, leave me alone") by 29-year-old Billy Joel is number twelve in the pop chart ▪ "And baby I want you now, now, now and hold on fast, could this be the magic at last? And..." *Could It Be Magic* by 35-year-old Barry Manilow is number twenty-five ▪ 40-year-old Terry Wogan hosts the first edition of *Blankety Blank* on BBC One ▪ 63-year-old actor Peter Butterworth dies of heart failure in Coventry ▪ 52-year-old Jimmy Savile OBE takes part in a charity pancake flipping contest at a *Little Chef* restaurant in Old Windsor ▪ 'The Night *He* Came Home!' - Horror movie *Halloween* (with 20-year-old Jamie Lee Curtis) is now showing at cinemas ▪ "A finger of Fudge is just enough to give your kids a treat. A finger of Fudge is just enough until it's time to eat" - Cadbury's *Fudge* bars are advertised on telly ▪ Another cold weather front moves in, bringing sub-zero temperatures ▪ 'Trains are being delayed because of bad weather' - notices at railway stations inform of hold-ups and cancellations ▪ Power cuts persist and industrial unrest continues across the whole country ▪ Sixteen-hundred car workers are laid-off at British Leyland's Cowley factory because of a shortage of components ▪ 51-year-old Derek Robinson (aka Red Robbo) leads a mass walk-out of thousands of workers at Longbridge ▪ "Control this is six-seven here, I can hear you loud and I can hear you clear" - *Car 67* by Driver 67 is on *Top of the Pops* ▪ "In the deserts of Sudan and the gardens of Japan. From Milan to Yucatan, every woman, every man" - *Hit Me With*

Your Rhythm Stick by Ian and the Blockheads is number one ▪ *Don't Cry For Me Argentina* by The Shadows is number nine ▪ Radio One's weekday schedule of disc jockeys is: 33-year-old Dave Lee Travis - aka 'The Hairy Cornflake' (7 a.m. to 9 a.m.), 32-year-old Simon Bates (9 a.m. to 11.30 a.m.), 35-year-old Paul Burnett (11.30 p.m. to 2 p.m.), 36-year-old Tony Blackburn (2 p.m. to 4 p.m.) and 30-year-old Andy Peebles (4 p.m. to 5.30 p.m.) ▪ "Walk, in silence" - Joy Division perform a night-time session for 39-year-old DJ John Peel ▪ "Do you remember, twenty-first night of..." *September* by Earth Wind and Fire is number three in the pop chart ▪ In between the power cuts, mobile discos are held at village halls ▪ Hit tunes such as *Contact* by Edwin Starr and *I Was Made For Dancin'* by Leif Garrett are played, loud ▪ Teenagers dance, snog and choke on smokey dry-ice ▪ 21-year-old punk-rocker Sid Vicious suffocates on his own vomit and dies in his sleep after a party in New York ▪ Back in England - kids rush home from school to watch the second series of *Grange Hill* on BBC One. Mr. Llewellyn is new headmaster at the fictional North London comprehensive school. Mr. 'Bullet' Baxter is the new PE teacher. Cathy Hargreaves is a new friend for Trisha Yates. Tucker Jenkins leads a fight against the boys from neighbouring Brookdale School ▪ 35-year-old Richard O'Sullivan stars as *Dick Turpin* on ITV. 22-year-old Michael Deeks is Swift Nick, Turpin's trusty sidekick ▪ People love soap operas ▪ Bert and Ivy Tilsley (played by 43-year-old Peter Dudley and 46-year-old Lynne Perrie) purchase the terraced house at number five *Coronation Street* from Deirdre Langton for £7,000 ▪ *Chiquitita* ("... tell me what's wrong. You're enchained by your own sorrow") by Abba is number two in the pop chart ▪ "I am a..." *Woman In Love* by The Three Degrees is number three ▪ 33-year-old John Lowe is the World Darts Champion after beating Leighton Rees in the final at *Jollees* nightclub in Stoke-on-Trent ▪ 'Zip goes a million! Cloughie gets his man' - 24-year-old footballer Trevor Francis leaves Birmingham City and joins Brian Clough's high-flying Nottingham Forest for a new record transfer fee of £1,180,000 ▪ 23-year-old Steve Coppell scores twice as Dave Sexton's Manchester Utd beat Tony Book's Manchester City 0-3 at Maine Road - Utd move up to ninth in Division One ▪ 30-year-old Neil Warnock scores the winning goal for Crewe Alexandra in a 1-0 victory over Halifax Town - a bottom-of-the-table clash in

Division Four ▪ Schoolboys hang posters of 33-year-old Debbie Harry on their bedroom walls ▪ *Parallel Lines* by Blondie is number one in the LP chart ▪ "Once I had a love and it was a gas, soon turned out, had a..." *Heart Of Glass* by Blondie is number one in the singles chart ▪ *King Rocker* by Generation X climbs to number eleven ▪ All across the nation, people enjoy an evening in front of the television set ▪ 7 million black and white TV licenses were issued last year ▪ 11 million colour TV licenses were issued ▪ "A cup o' tea an' a slice o' cake" - *Worzel Gummidge* (starring 59-year-old Jon Pertwee and with 41-year-old Una Stubbs as Aunt Sally) is on ITV ▪ BBC One programs on a Saturday night include: *The Pink Panther Show*; *News* - read by Peter Woods; *Jim'll Fix It* - presented by Jimmy Savile OBE; *Dr. Who* - starring Tom Baker; *Saturday Night at the Movies*; *The Two Ronnies* - with 49-year-old Ronnie Barker and 48-year-old Ronnie Corbett; *Starsky and Hutch* - starring Paul Michael Glaser and David Soul; and *Match of the Day* - introduced by 50-year-old Jimmy Hill ▪ 'From Deep Space...' *Invasion of the Body Snatchers* (starring 43-year-old Donald Sutherland, 47-year-old Leonard Nimoy, 26-year-old Jeff Goldblum and 29-year-old Brooke Adams) draws fans of horror movies to the cinema. A ticket for a seat in the circle costs £1.20 ▪ *Oliver's Army* ("... is here to stay. Oliver's Army are on their way, and I would rather be anywhere else but here today") by 24-year-old Elvis Costello and the Attractions is number two in the pop chart ▪ "This is..." *The Sound Of The Suburbs* by The Members (with 23-year-old Nicky Tesco and 23-year-old JC Carroll) is number twelve ▪ Punk poet, 30-year-old John Cooper Clarke performs to crowds of 'new-wave' kids at rock venues around the country ▪ Striking workers at British Leyland's Longbridge factory vote to return to work - just as a new strike begins at Leyland's Rover plant in Solihull ▪ Fashions are shifting ▪ A London based pop group called Gentry changes its name to Spandau Ballet - at the suggestion of 19-year-old journalist Robert Elms ▪ Trendy young things in garish costumes gather once a week at *Billy's* nightclub in Soho ▪ *Boots* sell out of Max Factor make-up ▪ Moulinex curling tongs cost £3.29 at *Argos* ▪ A Braun *SDE850* hairstyling set with a two-speed hair-dryer is £18.99 ▪ A set of hair-crimpers is £16.99 ▪ A can of *Silvikrin* hair laquer is 70p from any good chemist on the High Street.

Spring 1979

Mrs. Thatcher at Number 10

Monarch:	Queen Elizabeth II (aged 53)
Prime-minister:	Margaret Thatcher (aged 53)
Chancellor:	Geoffrey Howe (aged 52)
Home Secretary:	William Whitelaw (aged 60)
Foreign Secretary:	Peter Carrington (aged 59)
Football Manager:	Ron Greenwood (aged 57)
Radio 1 Breakfast DJ:	Dave Lee Travis (aged 34)
New car reg. suffix:	'T'

▪ There's more heavy snow ▪ 63-year-old MP Airey Neave is killed by a car bomb at Westminster - the Irish National Liberation Army claims responsibility ▪ The country remains in crisis ▪ Public sector services are delayed or even cancelled because of striking workers ▪ 66-year-old Labour prime-minister Jim Callaghan and his 61-year-old Chancellor of the Exchequer Denis Healey are under severe pressure ▪ 53-year-old Leader of the Opposition Margaret Thatcher is waiting in the wings, ready to take power ▪ "At first I was afraid, I was petrified. Kept thinking I could never live without you by my side" - *I Will Survive* by 29-year-old Gloria Gaynor spends four weeks at number one in the pop chart ▪ "I'm having so much fun. My lucky number's one. Ah! Ooh! Ah! Ooh!" - *Lucky Number* by 29-year-old Lene Lovich reaches number three ▪ "Ahoy! Ahoy! Land, sea and sky" - *Into The Valley* by The Skids peaks at number ten ▪ "Another car strike. Marvellous, isn't it? Taxpayers pay 'em millions each year, they get the money, go on strike. It's called Socialism" - 39-year-old John Cleese stars as Basil in a new series of *Fawlty Towers* on BBC Two ▪ 38-year-old Esther Rantzen presents *That's Life* on BBC One - aided by reporters Paul Heiney, Chris Serle and 65-year-old Cyril Fletcher - who delivers funny little odes at the end of the show ▪ "Sausages!" - Prince the talking dog (a Yorkshire Terrier) is an unlikely TV star ▪ 61-year-old Peter O'Sullevan reports on horse racing for BBC One ▪ *Rubstick* (ridden by 28-year-old Maurice Barnes) wins the Grand National, at odds of twenty-five to one ▪ 11-year-old schoolboy Paul Merson from Harlesden plays football with his friends in the park ▪ 21-year-old midfielder Graham Rix and 22-year-old striker Frank Stapleton score the goals as Arsenal beat

Bristol City 2-0 in League Division One at Highbury ▪ "Wow! Wow! Wow! Wow! Unbelievable" - *Wow* by 20-year-old Kate Bush is number fourteen on the weekly hit parade ▪ "It's just around the corner in the..." *English Civil War* by The Clash (with, lead singer, 26-year-old Joe Strummer) is number twenty-five ▪ *Strange Town* by The Jam (with, lead singer, 20-year-old Paul Weller) climbs to number fifteen ▪ TV viewers are gripped by exciting storylines in soap-operas: In *Coronation Street* - Deirdre Langton fears her young daughter is trapped beneath rubble after a lorry crashes into 'The Rovers Return' pub. Thankfully, 2-year-old Tracy is unhurt ▪ In *Crossroads* - Jill Harvey has a scatterbrained idea and Adam Chance tries to talk her out of it ▪ In *Emmerdale Farm* - Joe Sugden deals with the death of a ewe ▪ A new series of ITV's popular sit-com *Robin's Nest* is broadcast on Thursday evenings. 34-year-old Richard O'Sullivan, 30-year-old Tessa Wyatt and 49-year-old David Kelly (as a one-armed waiter called Albert Riddle) are the stars of the show ▪ *In The Navy* ("... yes you can sail the seven seas") by The Village People is number two in the pop chart ▪ *I Want Your Love* ("... I want. Your love") by Chic is number four ▪ *Can You Feel The Force?* by The Real Thing is number five ▪ Million pound footballer Trevor Francis scores a goal for Nottingham Forest in a 1-3 victory over Chelsea at Stamford Bridge ▪ 26-year-old Ossie Ardiles scores twice as Keith Burkinshaw's Tottenham Hotspur defeat Tommy Docherty's Derby County 2-0 at White Hart Lane ▪ 23-year-old Aston Villa striker Andy Gray returns after a four month injury lay-off and scores in a 3-0 victory over Ian Greaves' Bolton Wanderers at Villa Park ▪ 17 million people stay in to watch *Top of the Pops* on Thursday evenings ▪ 7-inch pop singles have risen in price - they now cost 85p ▪ "The Sweeney's doin' ninety 'cause they've got the word to go. They get a gang of villains in a shed up at Heathrow" - *Cool For Cats* by Squeeze is number two in the pop chart ▪ *Something Else / Friggin' In The Riggin'* by The Sex Pistols moves down to number eleven after peaking at number three ▪ *Painter Man* by Boney M is number ten ▪ *Pop Muzik* by M is a new entry at number twenty-eight ▪ Public sector workers continue to strike ▪ Skilled workers at British Leyland factories threaten to 'down-tools' unless a pay demand of £90 a week is met ▪ The economy remains in crisis ▪ Power

cuts and food shortages prevail ▪ Leader of the Opposition Mrs. Thatcher calls for a vote of confidence in the failing Labour government ▪ 'Never have so few taken so much from so many' - 48-year-old Sean Connery, 43-year-old Donald Sutherland and 24-year-old Lesley-Anne Down star at cinemas in *The First Great Train Robbery* ▪ 31-year-old actor Richard Beckinsale dies of a heart attack at his home in Sunningdale ▪ 'A Tennis Love Match' - 24-year-old tennis player John Lloyd marries 24-year-old tennis player Chris Evert in Florida ▪ Back in England - Jim Callaghan's Labour government loses the motion of confidence (by a single vote) in the House of Commons and a general election is called ▪ Campaigning gets underway ▪ Mr. Callaghan promises to improve industrial relations and return the country to full employment ▪ Bill board posters in support of Labour say, 'Labour. The Better Way' ▪ Bill board posters in support of the Tories say, 'Labour Still Isn't Working' ▪ The country goes to the polls in early May ▪ The Conservatives are triumphant ▪ 53-year-old Margaret Thatcher becomes prime-minister. (Conservatives: 339 seats, Labour: 269 seats, Liberals: 11 seats). Britain's first ever female prime-minister enters 10 Downing Street saying, "Where there is doubt, may we bring faith. And where there is despair, may we bring hope" ▪ *Tragedy* ("… When the feeling's gone and you can't go on, it's tragedy") by The Bee Gees slides down the pop chart after peaking at number one ▪ "Try some, buy some, fe-fi-fo-fum. Talk about…" *Pop Muzik* by M moves up to number two ▪ 52-year-old Sir Geoffrey Howe is the new Chancellor of the Exchequer ▪ 60-year-old Willie Whitelaw is Home Secretary and 59-year-old Lord (Peter) Carrington is Foreign Secretary ▪ 32-year-old Edwina Curry is a Conservative councillor for Northfield in Birmingham ▪ 36-year-old John Major is the new MP for Huntingdonshire ▪ "Oh, what, wow…" *He's The Greatest Dancer* by Sister Sledge is number six in the pop chart ▪ "Let's dance. Let's shout..." *Shake Your Body (Down To The Ground)* by The Jacksons is number four ▪ Families queue outside cinemas, eager to get a ticket for the latest Hollywood blockbuster movie ▪ 'You'll Believe A Man Can Fly' - 26-year-old Christopher Reeve is *Superman*. 30-year-old Margot Kidder is Lois Lane ▪ 'She was born into a world where they called it seduction not rape. What she did would shatter that world for ever' -

17-year-old Nastassja Kinski stars in *Tess* - the latest film from Roman Polanski ▪ 44-year-old (over-worked) writer David Nobbs collapses in Manchester and spends a few days in hospital ▪ "How can the light that burned so brightly, suddenly burn so pale..." *Bright Eyes* by 37-year-old Art Garfunkle climbs to number one in the pop chart - and stays there for six weeks! ▪ *Some Girls* ("... will. Some girls won't. Some girls need a lot of lovin', and-a, some girls don't") by Racey reaches number two ▪ "Money talks, but it don't sing and dance, and it don't walk"- *Forever In Blue Jeans* by 38-year-old Neil Diamond stalls at number sixteen ▪ 28-year-old Barry Sheene rides his Suzuki to victory in the opening Grand Prix of the 500cc motorcycle racing season ▪ 22-year-old footballer Garry Birtles scores twice, and 23-year-old Tony Woodcock scores once, as Brian Clough's high-flying Nottingham Forest achieve a 3-2 victory over Lawrie McMenemy's Southampton in the League Cup final at Wembley ▪ "Choo-choo train, truckin' down the track" - *One Way Ticket* by Eruption reaches number five in the pop chart ▪ "There's a place I know where we should go. Hi-de-hi-de-ho" - *Hooray Hooray It's A Holi-Holiday* by Boney M is number three ▪ "Were you truly wafted here from paradise? / No, Luton Airport" - 27-year-old Lorraine Chase advertises *Campari* on TV ▪ Fifteen million TV viewers watch teams compete in a new series of BBC One's ever popular outdoor games show *It's a Knockout*. 49-year-old Stuart Hall is presenter of the program. 64-year-old Arthur Ellis is referee - ensuring fair use of 'the joker' ▪ 31-year-old Bob Carolgees and his puppet 'Spit the Dog' are new on ITV's children's show *Tiswas* ▪ The word 'bagsy' is new in the dictionary ▪ 'Soft, Juicy, Delicious. Big Bubbles, No Troubles' - *Hubba Bubba* bubble gum goes on sale ▪ 49-year-old Leonard Parkin reads the *News at 5.45* for ITN ▪ The evil Yorkshire Ripper strikes again - a 19-year-old female is murdered in Halifax ▪ A fire in a crowded *Woolworths* store in the centre of Manchester claims the lives of ten people ▪ 46-year-old Frank Bough presents *Grandstand* on BBC One on Saturday afternoons ▪ 46-year-old Dickie Davies presents *World Of Sport* on ITV ▪ 18-year-old footballer Gary Lineker scores the winning goal for Second Division Leicester City in a match against Notts County ▪ 17-year-old Ian Rush makes his debut for Third Division Chester City in a match against Sheffield Wednesday ▪ 18-year-old Mark Falco scores on his debut

for First Division Tottenham Hotspur in a 1-3 win against Bolton Wanderers ▪ 29-year-old Malcolm 'Supermac' MacDonald returns from a long term injury and scores for Arsenal in a 1-1 draw against Chelsea at Stamford Bridge. (37-year-old goalkeeper Peter 'the cat' Bonetti makes his 600th and final appearance for Chelsea in the same match) ▪ 30-year-old striker Frank Worthington scores a sublime individual goal, turning 180 degrees while keeping the ball in the air with four touches before volleying into the back of the net in a match against Ipswich Town ▪ "I close my eyes and dance 'til dawn..." *Dance Away* ("... the heartache") by Roxy Music (with, lead singer, 33-year-old Bryan Ferry) is new at number two in the pop chart ▪ "Dance! ..." *Boogie Wonderland* by Earth Wind and Fire is number eight ▪ Footballers, 28-year-old Kenny Dalglish, 24-year-old Alan Kennedy and 27-year-old Terry McDermott score the goals as Bob Paisley's Liverpool beat Aston Villa 3-0 (in front of 50,570 spectators at Anfield) to become the new champions of Division One - with two games of the season still remaining. Liverpool players, Ray Clemence, Phil Neal, Phil Thompson, Alan Hansen, Emlyn Hughes, Alan Kennedy, Ray Kennedy, Terry McDermott, Steve Heighway, David Johnson, Kenny Dalglish, Jimmy Case and 25-year-old Graeme Souness have all been in fine form ▪ Cloughie's Forest are runners-up ▪ Big Ron Atkinson's West Bromwich Albion (with Tony Godden, Brendan Batson, Derek Statham, John Wile, Ally Robertson, Len Cantello, Ally Brown, Tony 'bomber' Brown, Cyrille Regis, Laurie Cunningham and 22-year-old Bryan Robson) are third ▪ Steve Burtenshaw's Queens Park Rangers, Jim Smith's Birmingham City and Danny Blanchflower's Chelsea are relegated to the Second Division ▪ *Boys Keep Swinging* by 32-year-old David Bowie climbs to number seven in the pop chart ▪ "Breaking rocks in the hot sun. I fought the law, and the law won" - *The Cost Of Living E.P* (with tracks: *I Fought The Law*, *Groovy Times*, *Gates Of The West* and *Capital Radio*) by The Clash is number twenty-two ▪ 51,482 spectators turn out at Selhurst Park to see 36-year-old Terry Venables' Crystal Palace team record a 2-0 victory over 58-year-old Harry Potts' Burnley and 'The Eagles' are champions of Division Two ▪ 34-year-old Graham Taylor leads Watford to runners-up position in Division Three - and Elton John's football club gains promotion to Division Two ▪ "There are times when all the world's asleep, the questions run too

deep, for such a simple man" - *The Logical Song* by Supertramp (with, lead singer, 29-year-old Roger Hodgson) is number seven in the pop chart ■ "Re-mem-mem, remember-member" - *Remember Then* by Showaddywaddy (with, lead singer, 27-year-old Dave Bartram) is number seventeen ■ Great excitement builds for the FA Cup final between Terry Neill's Arsenal and Dave Sexton's Manchester Utd on Saturday the twelfth of May. With just five minutes of the game remaining, Arsenal are 2-0 in front, with goals from Brian Talbot and Frank Stapleton. Gordon McQueen and Sammy McIlroy then grab two quick goals to bring Utd level, before the match turns on its head again when 25-year-old Alan Sunderland scores a dramatic (last minute) winner for Arsenal. The thrilling cup final ends in a 3-2 victory for 'The Gunners'. A ticket for the standing enclosure at the Empire Stadium in Wembley costs £2.50 ■ "It's like thunder, lightning. The way you love me is frightening. You better knock, knock…" *Knock On Wood* ("... baby") by 23-year-old Amii Stewart is number six in the pop chart ■ "It's number one all over heaven" - *The Number One Song In Heaven* by Sparks is number fourteen ■ *Danger UXB* is a popular new drama on ITV ■ 50-year-old politician Jeremy Thorpe stands trial at the Old Bailey - accused of conspiring to commit murder ■ 20-year-old Crystal Palace footballer Kenny Sansom (a left-back) makes his debut for Ron Greenwood's England team (Corrigan, Cherry, Sansom, Wilkins, Watson, Hughes, Keegan, Currie, Latchford, McDermott, Cunningham and substitutes, Brooking and Coppell) in a 0-0 draw against Wales at Wembley ■ *Ain't No Stoppin'Us Now* ("… we're on the move") by McFadden and Whitehead is number five in the pop chart ■ *Parisienne Walkways* by 27-year-old Gary Moore is number eight ■ 25-year-old million pound striker Trevor Francis scores a diving header as Brian Clough's high-flying Nottingham Forest defeat Malmo 1-0 to win the European Cup. 29-year-old captain John McGovern lifts the silver trophy in front of Forest's jubilant fans at the Olympic Stadium in Munich - Forest are champions of Europe! ■ "Fan-dabi-dozi!" - TV comedy duo The Krankies (32-year-old Ian Tough and his wife, 31-year-old Janette) make millions of people laugh ■ 32-year-old DJ Simon Bates presents the *Top 40* chart rundown on Radio One on Sunday evenings ■ "I know a girl from a lonely

street. Cold as ice cream but still as sweet. Dry your eyes…" *Sunday Girl* by Blondie (featuring 33-year-old Debbie Harry) is number one ▪ *Reunited* ("… and it feels so good") by Peaches and Herb is number four ▪ "Don't say it. Don't say it" - *Good Night Tonight* by Wings (with 36-year-old Paul McCartney) is number five ▪ 31-year-old snooker player Terry Griffiths wins the *Embassy* World Championship - beating 29-year-old Dennis Taylor in the final at the Crucible in Sheffield ▪ 32-year-old Elton John performs a pop concert in the USSR - becoming the first Western pop star to play behind the Iron Curtain ▪ Back in England - property prices continue to rise at a rapid rate. The average cost of a house now stands at £19,000 ▪ Mrs. Thatcher's Conservative government is working on five key objectives, as set out in the recent election manifesto: 1. To restore economic health (and impose greater control on the unions). 2. To make hard work pay by cutting income taxes and rewarding success. 3. To uphold the law of the land. 4. To support families and create a property owning democracy. 5. To strengthen Britain's defences ▪ Chancellor of the Exchequer Sir Geoffrey Howe slashes the top rate of income tax from 83% to 60% and increases VAT from 8% to 15% ▪ 3-year-old Mary Elizabeth Truss from Oxford practices her sums at home - and gets them all wrong ▪ 'Forward with the People' - *The Sun* embraces the bright new world promised by the Tory government ▪ 17-year-old Joanne Latham (36-23-36) from Wolverhampton appears topless on page three of the nation's most popular newspaper ▪ "You're so hot, teasing me, so you're blue but I can't take a chance on a chick like you, that's something I couldn't do" - *Does Your Mother Know* by Abba is number four in the pop chart ▪ "When I saw her there, she was a real disgrace. I thought..." *Nice Legs Shame About Her Face* by The Monks is number nineteen ▪ 'Beep! Beep!' - *Space Invaders* arcade game is exciting and new ▪ Progressive middle-class families enjoy the convenience of small, hatch-back motorcars ▪ 'Ah, bravo Figaro. Bravo, bravissimo. Sono il factotum. Della citt-ah. Della citt-ah. Della citt-ah. DELLA CITT-AH! La la la la la la la la la! - The ultra-modern Fiat *Strada* is 'Handbuilt by Robots' ▪ British Leyland introduces a new *Maxi 1750 HLS* with twin carburettor and walnut dash.

Summer 1979

Are friends electric?

Monarch:	Queen Elizabeth II (aged 53)
Prime-minister:	Margaret Thatcher (aged 53)
Chancellor:	Geoffrey Howe (aged 52)
Home Secretary:	William Whitelaw (aged 61)
Foreign Secretary:	Peter Carrington (aged 60)
Football Manager:	Ron Greenwood (aged 57)
Radio 1 Breakfast DJ:	Dave Lee Travis (aged 34)
New car reg. suffix:	'V'

▪ The summer is mostly dull with thundery showers ▪ "You…" *Shine A Little Love* ("… on my life, and let me see") by Electric Light Orchestra (with, lead singer, 31-year-old Jeff Lynne) is number six in the pop chart ▪ "Yes, I get lonely when the sun gets low. And I end up looking for somewhere to go" - *Night Owl* by 32-year-old Gerry Rafferty is number five ▪ *Theme From The 'Deer Hunter'* by The Shadows, led by 37-year-old Hank Marvin, is number nine ▪ The new prime-minister, 53-year-old Mrs. Thatcher, addresses the European Youth Rally at the National Exhibition Centre in Birmingham ▪ 11-year-old Chris Boardman from Hoylake on Merseyside plays out with his friends ▪ Schoolboys do 'no-handed' on racer bicycles ▪ A Raleigh *Europa* 5-speed racer (in 'Team Raleigh' racing colours - red, yellow and black) costs £89.95 ▪ A Raleigh *Hustler* 3-speed racer (in silver) costs £79.95 ▪ 10-year-old Peter Lovell and 9-year-old Darren Rock race around 'the block' on their bikes at Ford Way in Armitage ▪ 36-year-old jockey Willie Carson rides *Troy* to victory in the Epsom Derby ▪ "Hi ho Silver, away. Ride into tomorrow today, but who was that masked man you say. That was…" *The Lone Ranger* by Quantum Jump enters the pop chart at number forty-one and climbs to number five ▪ "And it looks like I'm falling all over again…" *Head Over Heels In Love* ("… with you") by 28-year-old football superstar Kevin Keegan peaks at number thirty-one ▪ 37-year-old Gordon Burns presents a new series of *The Krypton Factor* on ITV ▪ *Seaside Special* is on BBC One on Saturday evenings - Ken Dodd, Cilla Black and Rod Hull (with his uncontrollable puppet, Emu) take turns presenting the show ▪ 30-year-old punk poet John

Cooper Clarke features on the front cover of the latest *New Musical Express* ▪ Skinny kids in 'drainpipe' jeans listen to portable radio/cassette machines in bus-shelters, while smoking Player's *No. 6* cigarettes ▪ "Roxanne, you don't have to put on the red light. Those days are over. You don't have to sell your body to the night" - *Roxanne* by The Police (with, lead singer, 27-year-old Sting) is number twelve in the pop chart ▪ "Little mummy's boy, he wasn't very old. Though he was very small, he did what he was told" - *Jimmy Jimmy* by The Undertones (with, lead singer, 20-year-old Feargal Sharkey) is number sixteen ▪ 48-year-old Michael Edwardes is knighted in the Queen's Birthday Honours list ▪ 52-year-old union leader Derek Robinson (aka Red Robbo) addresses a mass meeting of workers at Longbridge ▪ *The Comedy Store* opens in Soho - a new venue for 'alternative' comedians, with 27-year-old anarchist Alexei Sayle introducing the acts and challenging the audience to a fight ▪ The new prime-minister Mrs. Thatcher travels to Tokyo, along with Foreign Secretary Peter Carrington and Chancellor of the Exchequer Sir Geoffrey Howe, for a leaders' conference of the G7 nations. Japan's prime-minister 69-year-old Masayoshi Ohira is chairman for the meeting. 54-year-old Jimmy Carter represents the USA, 60-year-old Helmut Schmidt represents West Germany, 60-year-old Giulio Andreotti represents Italy, 53-year-old Valery Giscard d'Estaing represents France and 40-year-old Joe Clark represents Canada ▪ Back in Britain - 23-year-old tennis star Bjorn Borg defeats 27-year-old Roscoe Tanner (6-7, 6-1, 3-6, 6-3, 6-4) at Wimbledon in the men's singles final - to make it three consecutive championship victories in last three years ▪ 22-year-old Martina Navratilova beats 24-year-old Chris Evert-Lloyd (6-4, 6-4) in the women's final. It's Navratilova's second Wimbledon singles' title ▪ Cricketers, Mike Brearley and Geoffrey Boycott stride out together to open the batting for England against India at Edgbaston. 37-year-old Brearley makes 24 runs. 38-year-old Boycott hits 155. 22-year-old David Gower (batting at number five) scores 200 not out and England win by 83 runs ▪ 23-year-old 'all-rounder' Ian Botham takes 5 wickets for 35 runs in the second Test at Lord's ▪ England's cricketers progress to the final of the (one-day, sixty-over) Prudential Cup tournament, but lose to the West Indies after a dramatic batting collapse ▪

33-year-old racing driver John Watson from Belfast finishes fourth in the British Grand Prix at Silverstone, driving a McLaren. 39-year-old Clay Regazzoni from Switzerland is the winner, driving a Williams - it's the Williams' team first ever Grand Prix victory! ▪ 'It's everything about being seventeen' - Teenage boys sneak into their local picture house to see *Lemon Popsicle* (an 'X' rated film with some nudity) ▪ "You can..." *Ring My Bell* by 22-year-old Anita Ward moves to the top of the pop chart ▪ *C'mon Everybody* by The Sex Pistols is number three ▪ "Something happened along the way, and yesterday was all we had" - *After The Love Has Gone* by Earth Wind and Fire reaches number four ▪ "Come on, baby..." *Light My Fire* ("... Try to set the night on fire") by 23-year-old Amii Stewart peaks at number five ▪ 38-year-old DJ Ed 'stewpot' Stewart hosts the travelling Radio One Roadshow for five days in August. Stewpot's Roadshow week begins at Torre Abbey Meadows in Torquay and ends on The Island in St. Ives, Cornwall ▪ Retail prices have risen after the recent hike in VAT ▪ Prime-minister Mrs. Thatcher announces that gas and electricity prices will also be increased next year ▪ 33-year-old Dennis Nilsen spends a night at home at Melrose Avenue in Cricklewood, with the dead body of a young boy buried beneath the floor-boards ▪ 37-year-old Fred West and his wife, 25-year-old Rosemary, spend a night at home at 25 Cromwell Street in Gloucester, with the dead bodies of multiple young women buried beneath the floorboards ▪ MPs vote against the reintroduction of capital punishment ▪ "A bit of grin and bear it, a bit of come and share it. You're welcome, we can spare it. Yellow socks" - *Reasons To Be Cheerful (Pt 3)* by 37-year-old Ian Dury and the Blockheads is number three in the pop chart ▪ "'Cause you left me..." *Just When I Needed You Most* by 24-year-old Randy VanWarmer climbs to number eight ▪ 'The antidote to panel games' - 58-year-old Humphrey Lyttelton is chairman for a new series of *I'm Sorry I Haven't A Clue* on BBC Radio Four. 36-year-old Graeme Garden, 44-year-old Barry Cryer, 41-year-old Willie Rushton and 39-year-old Tim Brooke-Taylor are panelists on the popular comedy show ▪ "I never thought it would happen, with me and the girl from Clapham" - *Up The Junction* by Squeeze (with 21-year-old Glenn Tilbrook, 24-year-old Chris Difford and 21-year-old Jools Holland) is number two in the pop chart ▪ "When the kids are swinging on the gate..." *Gertcha* by Chas &

Dave (35-year-old Chas Hodges and 34-year-old Dave Peacock) is number twenty ▪ *CHiPs* is on ITV on Saturday evenings with 30-year-old Erik Estrada as Ponch - a Californian motorcycle highway patrol cop ▪ *Police Woman* is on ITV on Saturday nights with 47-year-old Angie Dickinson (38-23-36) as Pepper - an under-cover police officer in L.A ▪ 28-year-old DJ Peter Powell presents the lunchtime show on weekdays on Radio One ▪ 29-year-old Kid Jensen presents the teatime show ▪ *We Are Family* ("... I got all my sisters with me") by Sister Sledge is number eight in the pop chart ▪ "Looking for some..." *Hot Stuff* ("... baby, this evening") by 30-year-old Donna Summer is number twelve ▪ 'Nude at Last' - 18-year-old Joanne Latham (36-23-36) from Wolverhampton bares all in *Penthouse* magazine ▪ "Rock on Tommy!" - 41-year-old Tommy Cannon and 35-year-old Bobby Ball are on TV ▪ 51-year-old Roger Moore stars as James Bond (aka 007) at cinemas in *Moonraker*. 71-year-old Bernard Lee is M. 64-year-old Desmond Llewelyn is Q. 52-year-old Lois Maxwell is Miss Moneypenny ▪ 33-year-old Sylvester Stallone stars as Rocky Balboa in *Rocky II* ▪ A seventh series of *The Onedin Line* (with 47-year-old Peter Gilmore and 42-year-old Jill Gascoine) begins on BBC One on Sunday evenings ▪ *Ask The Family* (with 51-year-old Robert Robinson) is broadcast at teatime on Mondays ▪ *Petrocelli* (with 40-year-old Barry Newman) is broadcast on Friday nights ▪ "It's cold outside, and the paint's peeling off of my walls. There's a man outside, in a long coat, grey hat, smoking a cigarette" - *Are 'Friends' Electric?* by Tubeway Army (with, lead singer, 21-year-old Gary Numan) climbs to number one in the pop chart - and stays there for four weeks ▪ "No, I've got no time to play your silly games..." *Silly Games* by Janet Kay is number two ▪ Movie star John Wayne dies aged 72 in California ▪ Back in England - prominent politician Jeremy Thorpe is cleared of attempted murder. As Thorpe leaves court, he tells reporters the verdict was, "totally fair, just and a complete vindication." ▪ The nation watches on television as 22-year-old athlete Sebastian Coe sets a new world record by running 800 metres in just 42.33 seconds at a meeting in Oslo. Twelve days later, Coe sets another world record - running a mile in just 3 minutes 48.95 seconds ▪ "I can't, I can't, I can't stand losin'. I..." *Can't Stand Losing You* by The Police peaks at number two in the pop chart ▪ "Look into his angel eyes, one look and you're hyp-

notized" - The double A sided single *Angel Eyes / Voulez-Vous* ("… a-ha! Take it now or leave it") by Abba (with 34-year-old Bjorn Ulvaeus, 32-year-old Benny Andersson, 33-year-old Anni-Frid Lyngstad and 29-year-old Agnetha Faltskog) reaches number three ▪ Adolescent schoolboys congregate in the corner of the playground and pass around a copy of *The Sun* newspaper ▪ 20-year-old Luscious Linda Lusardi (36C) is on page three ▪ "M-m-m…" *My Sharona* by The Knack is number six in the pop chart ▪ "Take a look at my girlfriend, she's the only one I got" - *Breakfast In America* by Supertramp is number nine ▪ 31-year-old Camille Keaton stars at 'special' cinemas in *I Spit On Your Grave* ▪ 68-year-old Thora Hird stars on ITV in the sit-com *In Loving Memory* ▪ 28-year-old Richard Thomas is John Boy and 21-year-old Judy Norton is Mary Ellen in *The Waltons* on BBC Two ▪ 'V' reg cars go on sale ▪ The Ford *Cortina MkIV* now has wrap-around bumpers, redesigned indicator lights and a new front grill. The top-of-the-range 2.3 litre *Cortina Ghia* has a top speed of 108 mph and accelerates from 0-60 mph in 10.5 seconds ▪ Volkswagen introduces a right-hand drive version of the *Golf GTI* for the British market. Top speed of this German 'pocket-rocket' is 113 mph and acceleration time from 0-60 mph is 8.9 seconds ▪ Chrysler cars are rebranded as Talbots ▪ Four star leaded petrol has risen to an all time high price of 98p a gallon ▪ "Wanted, boy you're everything I ever..." *Wanted* by The Dooleys is number three in the pop chart ▪ "Horace Wimp, this is your life, go out and find yourself a wife" - *The Diary Of Horace Wimp* by Electric Light Orchestra is number eight ▪ People enjoy a day out at the seaside ▪ 'Sooper-dooperlooper!' - 'The Revolution' is a new and thrilling ride (looping the loop at 38 feet per second) at Blackpool Pleasure Beach ▪ ' Skin is in!' - a nudist beach is set to open in Brighton ▪ Rock band Led Zeppelin (Jimmy Page, John Bonham, John Paul Jones and 30-year-old Robert Plant) play in front of 200,000 people at Knebworth ▪ Crowds flock to watch summer motorcycling events ▪ At White City, 26-year-old Dave Jessup takes part in the finals of the International Speedway championship ▪ At Silverstone, 27-year-old Kenny Roberts (on a Yamaha) pips 28-year-old Barry Sheene (on a Suzuki) by the narrowest of margins to win the 500cc Grand Prix ▪ 'Fletcher's inside story - Even funnier as a film' - 49-year-old Ronnie Barker, 57-year-old Fulton Mackay and the late Richard Beckinsale star at

cinemas in *Porridge* - a feature length movie spin-off from the popular TV show ▪ "Good times, these are the…" *Good Times* by Chic is number five in the pop chart ▪ "There are some things you can't cover up with lipstick and powder" - *Girls Talk* by 35-year-old Dave Edmunds is number four ▪ There's a flurry of activity on football's transfer market ▪ 23-year-old Laurie Cunningham leaves West Bromwich Albion and joins Real Madrid for £995,000 ▪ 23-year-old Tony Woodcock leaves Nottingham Forest and joins Cologne for £600,000 ▪ 31-year-old Emlyn Hughes leaves Liverpool (after twelve years) and joins Wolverhampton Wanderers for £90,000 ▪ 29-year-old Malcolm 'Supermac' MacDonald of Arsenal is forced into early retirement after failing to recover from a knee injury ▪ The new season begins ▪ Terry McDermott scores twice as Bob Paisley's Liverpool beat Terry Neill's Arsenal 3-1 in the FA Charity Shield at Wembley ▪ After a £700,000 transfer from Chelsea, 22-year-old Ray 'Butch' Wilkins makes his debut for Manchester Utd in a 1-1 draw against Lawrie McMenemy's Southampton in Division One ▪ 51-year-old Tommy 'The Doc' Docherty is the new manager of Queens Park Rangers in Division Two. Rangers defeat Bristol Rovers 2-0 at Loftus Road with goals from Clive Allen and Paul Goddard ▪ 36-year-old George Kerr is the new manager of Grimsby Town in Division Three. 'The Mariners' thrash Exeter City 4-1 at Blundell Park with goals from Bob Cumming, Gary Liddell (2) and Joe Waters ▪ "And daddy doesn't understand it, he always said she was good as gold. And he can see no reason, 'cause there are no reasons. What reason do you need to be shown? Tell me why…" *I Don't Like Mondays* by The Boomtown Rats (with, lead singer, 27-year-old Bob Geldof) spends four weeks at number one in the pop chart ▪ *Hersham Boys* ("… Hersham boys! Laced up boots and corduroys!") by Sham 69 (with, lead singer, 24-year-old Jimmy Pursey) enters the chart at number twenty-three and climbs to number six two weeks later ▪ 'For God's Sake, Get Out!' - 39-year-old James Brolin, 30-year-old Margot Kidder and 54-year-old Rod Steiger star at cinemas in *The Amityville Horror* ▪ 37-year-old Fred West and his wife, 25-year-old Rosemary, murder 16-year-old Alison Chambers and bury her body beneath their house at 25 Cromwell Street in Gloucester ▪ *Is She Really Going Out With Him?* ("… 'Cause if my eyes don't deceive me, there's something going wrong around here") by 25-year-old Joe Jackson

is number thirteen in the pop chart ▪ "We were born, born, born..." *Born To Be Alive* by 30-year-old Patrick Hernandez is number ten ▪ 'We did it, say Provos' - the headline in *The Sun* newspaper tells the bloody story from Ireland: 79-year-old Earl Mountbatten of Burma (a cousin of Queen Elizabeth II and great grandson to Queen Victoria) and three other people are killed by an IRA bomb at County Sligo. A few hours later - eighteen British soldiers are killed when booby-trap bombs explode at Warrenpoint in Northern Ireland ▪ Back in England - inflation continues to rise under the new Conservative government. Prime-minister Mrs. Thatcher and her Chancellor of the Exchequer, Sir Geoffrey Howe, hold meetings late into the night, fine-tuning economic policy ▪ Elsewhere, people settle down for a night in front of the telly ▪ 'We are sorry that programmes have been interrupted. There is an industrial dispute. Transmissions will start again as soon as possible' - ITV technicians go on strike for eleven weeks - and soap-opera fans are deprived of *Crossroads*, *Emmerdale Farm* and *Coronation Street* ▪ 22-year-old athlete Sebastian Coe sets a third world record of the summer - running 1500 metres in 3 minutes 32.1 seconds ▪ 33-year-old glamour model Mary Millington commits suicide at her home in Surrey ▪ "It's so funny, how..." *We Don't Talk Anymore* by 38-year-old Cliff Richard climbs to number one in the pop chart - and stays there for four weeks ▪ "Why must you record my phone calls? Are you planning a bootleg LP?" - *Gangsters* by The Special AKA is number six ▪ "Life is timeless, days are long when..." *When You're Young* by The Jam is new at number twenty-five ▪ Trendy kids wear black *Harrington* jackets ▪ Really trendy kids wear red *Harrington* jackets ▪ The art of 'consumer-marketing', with compelling slogans and clever copy, is conveyed by smart young businessmen in open-neck shirts and tight *Farah* trousers ▪ Adverts for Austin Morris compact family cars boast that, '*Allegro's* got Vroom. Miles and miles of vroom' ▪ Adverts for instant coffee claim, '*Mellow Birds* will make you smile' ▪ Adverts for chocolate bars pose the question, 'Would you risk it for a *Swisskit*?' ▪ Adverts for lager beer pose the question, 'Wouldn't you rather be *Hemeling*?' ▪ A four-can pack of *Hemeling Lite* is £1.16.

Autumn 1979

Don't panic

Monarch:	Queen Elizabeth II (aged 53)
Prime-minister:	Margaret Thatcher (aged 54)
Chancellor:	Geoffrey Howe (aged 52)
Home Secretary:	William Whitelaw (aged 61)
Foreign Secretary:	Peter Carrington (aged 60)
Football Manager:	Ron Greenwood (aged 58)
Radio 1 Breakfast DJ:	Dave Lee Travis (aged 34)
New car reg. suffix:	'V'

▪ "Blankety-blank. Blankety-blank. Blankety Blank!" - 41-year-old Terry Wogan hosts a new series of *Blankety Blank* on BBC One ▪ 32-year-old Simon Bates presents Radio One's *Top 40* show for the final time before handing over to 36-year-old Tony Blackburn ▪ *We Don't Talk Anymore* by Cliff Richard remains at number one ▪ *Bang Bang* ("... the mighty fall") by 23-year-old B.A. Robertson is number two ▪ "Oh..." *Angel Eyes* ("... am I deceived, or did you sigh?") by Roxy Music is number four ▪ 53-year-old Conservative prime-minster Margaret Thatcher and 52-year-old Chancellor of the Exchequer Sir Geoffrey Howe are under pressure ▪ Inflation is running high - at over 11% ▪ The Minimum Lending Rate is raised to 17% ▪ Britain's economy has moved into recession ▪ NHS prescription charges are increased from 20p to 45p ▪ The annual cost of a colour TV license increases from £25 to £34 ▪ A black and white license goes up from £10 to £12 ▪ A loaf of bread goes up from 28p to 30p ▪ 'Don't Panic' - *The Hitch-Hiker's Guide to the Galaxy*, a novel by 27-year-old Douglas Adams is published ▪ "I want…" *Money* ("… That's what I want. That's what I want. That's what I want!") by The Flying Lizzards (with, lead singer, 23-year-old Deborah Evans-Stickland) climbs to number five in the pop chart ▪ "Only, love's gotta hold of my mind, taking all of my time with you" - *Love's Gotta Hold On Me* by Dollar (a duo comprising of 22-year-old David Van Day and 24-year-old Thereza Bazar) is number four ▪ 'It'll never take off' - 35-year-old Michael Rodd presents a feature on a new-fangled concept called the 'portable telephone' on BBC's science program *Tomorrow's World* ▪ ITV is back on air after three months of industrial

action by technicians ▪ "I could be so good for you. Love you like you want me to" - a brand new program called *Minder* begins on Monday evenings at 9.00 p.m. - starring 31-year-old Dennis Waterman as Terry and 54-year-old George Cole as Arthur ▪ Series three of *The Professionals* is on Saturday evenings at 9.00 p.m. - with Bodie in a Ford *Capri 3.0S*, Doyle in a Ford *Escort RS2000* and Cowley in a Ford *Granada 2.8 Ghia* ▪ *Streetlife* ("… it's the only way I know") by The Crusaders is a Top Five hit song ▪ Vauxhall replaces the ageing *Viva* motorcar with the all new, front-wheel drive *Astra.* The 1200cc model has a top speed of 88 mph and prices start from just £3,404 ▪ "Here in my car, I feel safest of all. I can lock all my doors, it's the only way to live in…" *Cars* by 21-year-old Gary Numan spends a week at number one in the pop chart ▪ *Don't Bring Me Down* ("… Grooss!!") by Electric Light Orchestra is number three ▪ *Sail On* ("... down the line") by The Commodores (with 30-year-old Lionel Richie) is number eight ▪ "Rolling the ball. Rolling the ball. Rolling the ball to me" - The *On Stage E.P.* (which includes the tracks *Them Heavy People* and *James And The Cold Gun*) by 21-year-old Kate Bush is number ten ▪ 'The summer you'll never forget' - 22-year-old Ray Winstone stars at cinemas in *That Summer!* ▪ 'Love hasn't been like this since 1943' - 37-year-old Harrison Ford and 25-year-old Lesley-Anne Down star in *Hanover Street* ▪ "Oh, Melissa, darling. You're early." [Looks at watch and accidently spills drink over Ms. Collins] "Would you like a Cinzano? / No thanks, I've already had one" - 52-year-old Leonard Rossiter and 46-year-old Joan Collins advertise *Cinzano Bianco* on TV ▪ 53-year-old prime-minister Mrs. Thatcher opens the Central Milton Keynes Shopping Centre - where there are more than 130 shops, including *John Lewis*, *C&A*, *Boots*, *Woolworths*, *Our Price*, *British Home Stores* and *Waitrose* ▪ "Just a castaway, on an island lost at sea-oh. Another lonely day, with no one here but me-oh" - *Message In A Bottle* by The Police climbs to number one - and stays there for three weeks ▪ "When, I met you in the restaurant, you could tell I was no debutante. You asked me what's my pleasure, 'a movie or a measure?' I'll have a cup of tea and tell you of my…" *Dreaming* by Blondie (featuring 34-year-old Debbie Harry) is number two ▪ *If I Said You Had A Beautiful Body Would You Hold It Against Me* by The Bellamy Brothers is number three ▪ 49-year-old business leader Sir Mi-

chael Edwardes proposes a major restructuring of British Leyland - which involves factory closures and thousands of job losses. 52-year-old union leader Derek Robinson (aka Red Robbo) is sacked ▪ 'In space no one can hear you scream' - *Alien* (a terrifying new film) is now showing at the pictures - starring 29-year-old Sigourney Weaver and 39-year-old John Hurt ▪ *Not The Nine O'Clock News* (a new topical comedy program) debuts on television - with 24-year-old Rowan Atkinson, 26-year-old Mel Smith, 29-year-old Pamela Stephenson and 30-year-old Chris Langham ▪ A mod revival is underway, with youngsters wearing fishtail parka coats and loafer shoes ▪ "I got ya number, written on the…" *Back Of My Hand* by The Jags climbs to number seventeen in the pop chart ▪ "This is the time, the…" *Time For Action* by Secret Affair is number thirteen ▪ Adverts for motor scooters say - 'Give your life a little Vespa' ▪ The Vespa *P200E* has a 198cc engine and a top speed of 68 mph ▪ Millions listen in to Radio One's *Top 40* show on Sunday evenings ▪ "Oh-a-ho, you were the first one. Oh-a-ho, you were the last one…" *Video Killed The Radio Star* by Buggles (with 30-year-old Trevor Horn) is new at number one ▪ "We're only…" *Making Plans For Nigel* ("... We only want what's best for him") by XTC is number seventeen ▪ At lunchtimes, schoolboys come rushing out of double Maths to play Humbug on the playground ▪ 12-year-old Michael Bayliss from Burntwood dislocates a finger ▪ 13-year-old Peter Deeley from Rugeley sprains a wrist ▪ 23-year-old Aston Villa footballer Andy Gray has a fall-out with his manager Ron Saunders and transfers to John Barnwell's Wolverhampton Wanderers for a new record fee of £1.47 million. (Gray scores his first goal for Wolves in a 2-3 away win against Everton) ▪ 25-year-old Trevor Francis and 23-year-old Tony Woodcock each score twice as Ron Greenwood's England team (Shilton, Neal, Mills, Thompson, Watson, Wilkins, Keegan, Coppell, T Francis, Brooking, Woodcock and substitute, McDermott) defeats Northern Ireland 1-5 in Belfast ▪ "This thing called love, I just can't handle it. This thing called love, I must get round to it. I ain't ready…" *Crazy Little Thing Called Love* by Queen reaches number two in the pop chart ▪ *Gimme Gimme Gimme (A Man After Midnight)* ("… won't somebody help me chase the shadows away?") by Abba peaks at number three ▪ "Just tell me that you want me..." *Tusk* by Fleetwood Mac is number six ▪ The Police (28-year-

old Sting, 36-year-old Andy Summers and 27-year-old Stewart Copeland) release their new album, *Reggatta de Blanc* - which enters the LP chart at number one ▪ 50-year-old Leonard Parkin presents ITN's *News at 5.45* ▪ A female student is murdered in Bradford and it's feared she's the twelfth victim of the evil Yorkshire Ripper ▪ 15-year-old schoolboy Martin Allen goes missing as he's travelling on the underground in London ▪ *Shoestring* is an exciting new TV drama on BBC One - starring 28-year-old Trevor Eve as private detective Eddie Shoestring ▪ *Cloppa Castle* is popular with children ▪ *One Day At A Time* ("… sweet Jesus, that's all I'm asking from you") by 39-year-old Lena Martell climbs to number one on the hit parade - and stays there for three weeks ▪ "Keep on, with the force, don't stop…" *Don't Stop 'Til You Get Enough* by 21-year-old Michael Jackson is number three ▪ *OK Fred* ("… now you're a Yaga Yaga. OK Fred, bully for you") by 28-year-old Errol Dunkley is number eleven ▪ ITV programmes on a Saturday night include: *Magpie* - presented by 26-year-old Tommy Boyd, 33-year-old Mick Robertson and 32-year-old Jenny Hanley; *Mr. and Mrs.* - hosted by 51-year-old Derek Batey; *The Muppet Show*; *3-2-1* - featuring Ted Rogers and Dusty Bin; *The Comedians* - with Lee Wilson, Mick Miller, Stan Boardman and 39-year-old Roy Walker; *Hawaii Five-O* - starring 58-year-old Jack Lord as Steve McGarrett; and *News at Ten* - read by 51-year-old Alastair Burnet ▪ "Who's the daddy?" - 22-year-old Ray Winstone stars at cinemas in *Scum* ▪ *Pot Noodle* is launched - it's the latest concept in 'quick and easy' hot food ▪ "Hey you! Don't watch that! Watch this! This is the heavy, heavy monster sound…" *One Step Beyond* by Madness (with, lead singer, 18-year-old Suggs) climbs to number seven in the pop chart ▪ "I bought my baby, a red radio. He played it all, a go-go, a go-go" - *On My Radio* by The Selecter (with, lead singer, 26-year-old Pauline Black) is number eight ▪ "Rudy…" *A Message To You Rudy* by The Specials (with, lead singer, 20-year-old Terry Hall, and keyboard player, 24-year-old Jerry Dammers) is number ten ▪ Kids gather together at *Tiffany's* club in Coventry and enjoy a night of Ska and 2-Tone music. Rude Boys wear tight-fitting 'tunic' suits, shirts with cutaway collars and narrow ties. Rude Girls wear black and white chequered dresses ▪ Northern Soul enthusiasts head for the *Wigan Casino* and attend 'all-nighters' - spinning and dropping to the sounds of Jimmy Radcliffe, Edwin Starr and

Dean Parrish. Trendy young men wear black *Solatio* basket-weave shoes with metal segs in the soles ▪ Heavy-metal rockers douse themselves in patchouli oil (aka hippy juice) and head for the *Bandwagon* in North-West London or *The Highwayman* at Threapwood ▪ "It's a bomber, it's a bomber, it's a…" *Bomber* ("… Hey, hey") by Motorhead (with, lead singer, 33-year-old Lemmy) enters the hit-parade at number sixty-seven ▪ *Since You've Been Gone* ("I'm outta my head, can't take it") by Rainbow (with, lead singer, 31-year-old Graham Bonnet) is number six ▪ *Whatever You Want* ("… Whatever you like") by Status Quo (with, lead singer, 30-year-old Francis Rossi) is number four ▪ Flashy London teenagers swirl and flounce on the dancefloor at *The Blitz* nightclub in Covent Garden - 20-year-old Steve Strange decides who will (and who won't) be admitted to hear the 'futuristic' electronic music played inside ▪ "Please, keep them away. Don't let them touch me" - *Complex* by Gary Numan enters the pop chart at number fifteen ▪ The Human League's debut LP, *Reproduction*, is number thirty-four in the album chart ▪ The weather turns cold ▪ Families stay in, watching television ▪ "Oh, blimey. Yes, indeed" - 49-year-old Dino Shafeek, 36-year-old Barry Evans and 30-year-old Francoise Pascal feature in a new series of *Mind Your Language* on ITV on Saturday evenings ▪ "Ha-ha-ha. Bum! Bum!" - *The Basil Brush Show* (presented by 34-year-old Billy Boyle) is on BBC One ▪ Finnish rally driver Hannu Mikkola wins the RAC Rally, driving a Ford *Escort*. 34-year-old Russell Brookes from Redditch is second (also in an *Escort*) ▪ "Every day that I'm without you hurts, just, a little bit more than I've ever been hurt before" - *Every Day Hurts* by Sad Café reaches number three in the pop chart ▪ "I do love you..." *Still* by The Commodores is number four ▪ "Oh, yes it's…" *Ladies Night* ("… and the feeling's right") by Kool and the Gang peaks at number nine ▪ *Luton Airport* ("… Oooh-ee-oooh!") by Cats UK stalls at number twenty-two ▪ A scandal is reported at Buckingham Palace - 72-year-old Anthony Blunt (Queen Elizabeth II's former art advisor) is exposed as a Soviet spy ▪ 26-year-old Jilly Johnson (34A) and 24-year-old Rita Pennington (34D) are popular page three girls in *The Sun* newspaper ▪ *When You're In Love With A Beautiful Woman* ("… it's hard") by Dr. Hook moves to the top of the pop chart.

Christmas 1979

'We are the mods!' - Quadrophenia at cinemas

Monarch:	Queen Elizabeth II (aged 53)
Prime-minister:	Margaret Thatcher (aged 54)
Chancellor:	Geoffrey Howe (aged 53)
Home Secretary:	William Whitelaw (aged 61)
Foreign Secretary:	Peter Carrington (aged 60)
Football Manager:	Ron Greenwood (aged 58)
Radio 1 Breakfast DJ:	Dave Lee Travis (aged 34)
New car reg. suffix:	'V'

▪ Cold and frosty weather ▪ 36-year-old DJ Tony Blackburn presents the *Top 40* show on Radio One on Sunday afternoons ▪ "I hope my leg don't break..." *Walking On The Moon* by The Police is new at number one - glossy posters of band members: 28-year-old Sting, 36-year-old Andy and 27-year-old Stewart, adorn the bedroom walls of trendy teenagers ▪ "Hey you! Don't watch that! Watch this! - *One Step Beyond* by Madness (with, lead singer, 18-year-old Suggs) moves down from number seven to number ten ▪ "Enough is enough, I can't go on, I can't go on no more, no" - *No More Tears (Enough Is Enough)* by 30-year-old Donna Summer and 37-year-old Barbra Streisand peaks at number three ▪ 54-year-old prime-minister Margaret Thatcher and her 60-year-old Foreign Secretary Lord Carrington visit the USA - it's Mrs. Thatcher's first visit across the Atlantic since taking office seven months ago. Meetings are held in the White House with 55-year-old President Jimmy Carter and on Capitol Hill with sixty or so leading senators and congressmen. Mrs. Thatcher hopes to draw Britain and America closer together by discussing a range of topics such as economic policy, energy and military issues, but talks are largely overshadowed by the on-going US/Iranian hostage crisis, which is the main focus of attention for President Carter and his staff ▪ Back in Britain - the weather turns wet and windy ▪ Schoolboys venture outside, wearing rain-proof kagools ▪ 20-year-old dare-devil stunt rider Eddie Kidd jumps 80ft across the River Blackwater in Essex on a 400cc motorbike ▪ 11-year-old Matt Le Tissier from Saint Peter Port in Guernsey plays football with

his friends in the park ▪ First Division footballers, Mick Channon (aged 31) and Phil Boyer (aged 30) score the goals as Lawrie McMenemy's Southampton defeat Alan Durban's Stoke City 3-1 at The Dell ▪ Andy Gray (aged 24) scores twice as John Barnwell's Wolverhampton Wanderers beat Ian Greaves' Bolton Wanderers 3-1 at the Molineux ▪ Gary Lineker (aged 18) scores for Leicester City in a 1-1 draw against Preston North End in Division Two ▪ Peter Beardsley (aged 18) scores for Carlisle Utd in a 1-1 draw against Colchester Utd in Division Three ▪ Ian Robins (aged 27) scores for Huddersfield Town in a 5-1 victory over Rochdale in Division Four ▪ "Sup up your beer and collect your fags. There's a row going on down near Slough" - *Eton Rifles* by The Jam peaks at number three in the pop chart ▪ "But if the rhythm is hot then they never can stop the dance of the teenage idol..." *Let Your Heart Dance* by Secret Affair stalls at number thirty-two ▪ Young mods sew beer towels onto their fish-tail parka coats ▪ 'A Way of Life' - 21-year-old Phil Daniels and 19-year-old Leslie Ash star at cinemas in *Quadrophenia* ▪ 23-year-old Bo Derek (36-24-34) stars in the movie *"10"* - alongside 44-year-old Dudley Moore ▪ 34-year-old Helen Mirren stars in *Caligula* - alongside 24-year-old Teresa Ann Savoy, 47-year-old Peter O'Toole and 36-year-old Malcom McDowell ▪ Husbands treat their wives to a bottle of *Anais Anais* perfume (by Cacherel) for Christmas ▪ "Oh-oh, what are we gonna do?" - *Union City Blue* by Blondie (with 34-year-old Debbie Harry) is number thirteen in the pop chart ▪ "He knocked it off..." *Knocked It Off* by 23-year-old B. A. Robertson is number eight ▪ *Nights In White Satin* ("... never reaching the end") by The Moody Blues is number nine ▪ 55-year-old Kenneth Kendall reads the news on BBC One ▪ Inflation rises to 13.4% ▪ A loaf of bread goes up from 30p to 32p ▪ Road tax is set to rise from £50 a year to £60 ▪ Prime-minister Mrs. Thatcher and her Conservative government demand a multi-million pound rebate from the European Union ▪ The Conservative government introduces a new Housing Bill giving council house tenants the right to buy their homes ▪ A Welsh nationalist group called Meibion Glyndwr sets fire to English-owned cottages in Wales ▪ 24-year-old Tim Martin opens *Martin's Free House* in Muswell Hill - the first *JD Wetherspoon's* pub ▪ "I didn't get where I am today by being nice" -

58-year-old John Barron is C. J. and 53-year-old Leonard Rossiter is Reginald Perrin in the third series of *The Fall and Rise of Reginald Perrin* (a TV comedy based on a novel by 44-year-old David Nobbs) ▪ "It's behind you!" - Middle-class families enjoy an evening at the Pantomime ▪ 36-year-old singer Cilla Black appears in *Aladdin* at the Wimbledon Theatre ▪ 26-year-old comedian Jim 'Nick Nick' Davidson stars alongside The Krankies in *Babes in the Wood* at the Bristol Hippodrome ▪ Millions of people stay indoors watching television ▪ The character Gail Potter (played by 28-year-old Helen Worth) marries Brian Tilsley (played by 22-year-old Christopher Quinten) in ITV's popular soap-opera *Coronation Street* ▪ 46-year-old Barry Norman presents late night film review program *Film 79* on BBC One ▪ *Meteor*, a disaster movie (starring 41-year-old Natalie Wood, 49-year-old Sean Connery and 67-year-old Karl Malden) is now showing at cinemas ▪ Ford launches a limited edition *Escort Harrier* motorcar - with a rear boot spoiler, 1.6 litre engine and twin carburetors ▪ "If you should go, go, go. If you should go, go, go" - *Que Sera Mi Vida* by The Gibson Brothers is number five in the pop chart ▪ "Live your life off the wall. Live it..." *Off The Wall* by 21-year-old Michael Jackson is number seven ▪ The double A sided single *Confusion / Last Train To London* ("... just leaving town") by Electric Light Orchestra is number eight ▪ Hallmark Records release *The Best of Top of the Pops '79* - a budget priced, cover-version pop compilation LP with blonde Carolyn Evans in a see-through body stocking on the sleeve ▪ 23-year-old record breaking athlete Sebastian Coe is BBC's 'Sports Personality of the Year' ▪ "He's a spacer, a star chaser" - *Spacer* by Sheila B Devotion is number eighteen in the singles chart ▪ "Ace, a journey on a train. Always been the same. Lookin' out windows" - *Word Salad* (containing the track *The Worker*) by Fischer Z is number sixty-six in the album chart ▪ *Greatest Hits* by 34-year-old Rod Stewart is number one ▪ 18-year-old Boy George is the new cloakroom attendant at *The Blitz* nightclub in Covent Garden ▪ "He's not the Messiah, he's a very naughty boy!" - *The Life of Brian* (a film from Monty Python) is now showing at cinemas ▪ BBC One TV programs on a Saturday night include: *Dr. Who* - with 45-year-old Tom Baker as the Doctor, 28-year-old Laila Ward as his assistant, Romana, and with K9 as the dog shaped robot, K9; *Larry Grayson's Generation Game* - starring

56-year-old Larry Grayson and 27-year-old Isla St Clair; *Secret Army* - featuring Clifford Road as Kessler and Angela Richards as Monique; *Shirley Bassey* - a music show hosted by the popular 42-year-old singer from Cardiff; *Dallas* - with Larry Hagman as JR and Linda Gray as Sue Ellen; *News* - read by 49-year-old Peter Woods; *Match of the Day* - introduced by 51-year-old Jimmy Hill; and *Parkinson* - a chat-show hosted by 44-year-old Michael Parkinson ▪ *John, I'm Only Dancing (Again)* by 32-year-old David Bowie is number thirteen in the pop chart ▪ *Living On An Island* ("... looking at another line. Waiting for my friend to come and we'll get high") by Status Quo is number sixteen ▪ *The Times* newspaper is back on sale after almost a year away ▪ 22-year-old footballer Glenn Hoddle scores on his debut for Ron Greenwood's England in a 2-0 victory over Bulgaria. (32-year-old defender Dave Watson is also on the score-sheet). England's full line-up for the match is: Shilton, Neal, Mills, Thompson, Watson, Wilkins, Keegan, Coppell, T Francis, Brooking, Woodcock and substitute, McDermott ▪ "We don't need no education. We don't need no thought control. No dark sarcasm in the classroom, teachers leave those kids alone" - *Another Brick In The Wall (Part 2)* by Pink Floyd (with 36-year-old Roger Waters, 33-year-old David Gilmour, 35-year-old Nick Mason, 36-year-old Richard Wright and the children of Islington Green School) is number one at Christmas ▪ "I believe in angels, something good in everything I see" - *I Have A Dream* by Abba (with 34-year-old Bjorn Ulvaeus, 33-year-old Benny Andersson, 34-year-old Anni-Frid Lyngstad and 29-year-old Agnetha Faltskog) is number two ▪ *My Simple Heart* by The Three Degrees is number nine ▪ 37-year-old Mike Brearley leads England's cricketers, on a three-match tour down-under, against Greg Chappell's Australians. 24-year-old all-rounder Ian Botham takes 11 wickets and 39-year-old batsman Geoff Boycott scores 99 not out in the opening Test Match at Perth, but England lose by 138 runs ▪ Back in Britain - The nights are dark and drizzly ▪ 34-year-old Dennis Nilsen strangles 23-year-old Kenneth Ockenden at Melrose Avenue in Cricklewood and hides his body beneath the floorboards ▪ "I'm only a poor little sparrow. No colourful feathers have I" - *The Sparrow* by The Ramblers is number eleven in the pop chart ▪ *Blue Peter* by 26-year-old Mike Oldfield is number nineteen ▪ 29-year-old Simon Groom, 25-year-old Christopher Wen-

ner and 26-year-old Tina Heath light the candles on the tinsel covered Advent Crown on children's TV show *Blue Peter* ▪ 30-year-old Noel Edmonds presents *Multi-Coloured Swap Shop* on Saturday mornings. 53-year-old Jimmy Savile OBE is a special guest on the fifteenth of December - dropping by the studio to tell viewers what he's been up to ▪ Excited children look forward to Christmas ▪ 'The Total Control Slotless Racing System' - schoolboys make a wish at Christmas for a *TCR* racing set - with cars that really overtake ▪ The ultra-modern electronic game *Simon* (from MB Electronics) costs £21.95 ▪ The *Big Trak* remote control vehicle (also from MB Electronics) is £39.95 ▪ An Atari video computer system (with two 'joy-stick' remote controllers) is £155.00 ▪ On Christmas Day, housewives cook turkey, boil sprouts and take a drink in the kitchen ▪ Adverts say, '*Harvey's Bristol Cream* - the best sherry in the world' ▪ An estimated 25 million viewers watch *Larry Grayson's Generation Game* on Christmas night on BBC One. Larry's Christmas conveyor belt contains: a tumbler dryer, a food hamper, an oven/toaster/grill, a 'cuddly' Rudolph the Red Nosed Reindeer, an automatic tea maker, three bottles of Champagne and a bucket, TV game, Christmas cake and a box of chocolates, a slow cooker, silver plated goblets and a tray, food mixer, 'cuddly' type-writer, a hair dryer and a stand, bottle of port/ stilton cheese and biscuits, sherry decanter and six glasses, two baby Orvilles, electric car racing set and a silver plated candelabra ▪ "Oh, I wish I'd looked after me teeth" - 32-year-old Pam Ayres' *Christmas Special* is on ITV ▪ "The moon is right. The spirit's up. We're here tonight and that's enough. Simply having a..." *Wonderful Christmas Time* by 38-year-old Paul McCartney peaks at number six ▪ Bob Paisley's Liverpool and Dave Sexton's Manchester Utd are neck and neck at the top of Division One. The two teams meet on Boxing Day at Anfield, where 24-year-old Alan Hansen and 29-year-old David Johnson score the goals in a 2-0 victory for Liverpool ▪ Terry Neill's Arsenal beat Keith Burkinshaw's Tottenham Hotspur 1-0 on the same day, with a goal from Alan Sunderland ▪ Ron Saunders' Aston Villa beat Alan Dicks' Bristol City 1-3, with 18-year-old Gary Shaw bagging a hat-trick ▪ In Division Two, Bill McGarry's Newcastle Utd defeat Tommy 'The Doc' Docherty's Queens Park Rangers 4-2, with goals from Tommy Cassidy, Alan Shoulder and Peter Withe (2) ▪ 35-year-old

Michael Fish presents the weather forecast on BBC One ▪ Temperatures plummet ▪ Heavy frost and thick fog descend on the country ▪ 34-year-old DJ Dave Lee Travis (aka 'The Hairy Cornflake') presents the breakfast show on Radio One ▪ "Now, what you hear is not a test, I'm rappin' to the beat" - *Rapper's Delight* by The Sugar Hill Gang reaches number three ▪ "We wish you a merry Christmas and a happy New Year" - *A Merry Jingle* by The Greedies is number twenty-eight ▪ The total number of music cassettes being sold each year is increasing - it's currently estimated at around 20 million units ▪ *Smash Hits* magazine costs 30p and is available fortnightly. Blondie (with, lead singer, 34-year-old Debbie Harry) are on the front cover of the latest edition ▪ Prime-minister Mrs. Thatcher and Foreign Secretary Lord Carrington return to Britain after their visit to the US ▪ The weather is cold and bleak - snow and sleet moves in across the north of the country ▪ Football supporters tune-in to *Sport on 2* (with 32-year-old Jim Rosenthal) on BBC Radio Two on Saturday afternoons for the latest results ▪ Manchester Utd bounce back from their recent defeat against Liverpool with a 3-0 victory over Arsenal, playing with an orange ball on a snow covered pitch at Old Trafford. Sammy McIlroy, Joe Jordan and Gordon McQueen are the goal scorers ▪ On television, 39-year-old Michael Brunson reports on diplomatic affairs for ITN ▪ 61-year-old Keith Joseph (Secretary of State for Industry) and 43-year-old David Howell (Secretary of State for Energy) meet with prime-minister Mrs. Thatcher ▪ Efficiencies must be found to help improve the country's finances ▪ 122 million tonnes of coal have been mined in Britain this year - roughly the same amount for each of the past five years ▪ The average price of a house has almost doubled in three years - it now stands at £22,000 ▪ The average weekly wage is £110.70 ▪ Families all across the country enjoy *Vesta* curry with rice for tea. Some indulge in *Arctic Roll* (from Birds Eye) for pudding ▪ People visit their local pub on New Year's Eve to celebrate by raising a glass (or two) to toast in the 1980s ▪ Good wishes are exchanged ▪ There's an air of happiness and hope ▪ A pint of *Carling Black Label* in the Red Lion costs 40p.

--o--

Books by the same author:

- LIFE IN ENGLAND non-stop through the 1940s (ISBN 978-1-840-41035-8)
- LIFE IN ENGLAND non-stop through the 1950s (ISBN 978-1-840-41036-5)
- LIFE IN ENGLAND non-stop through the 1960s (ISBN 978-1-840-41037-2)
- LIFE IN ENGLAND non-stop through the 1980s (ISBN 978-1-840-41039-6)

Coming soon:

- LIFE IN ENGLAND non-stop through the 1990s (ISBN 978-1-840-41040-2)

Printed in Great Britain
by Amazon

58779427R00169

RAISING READERS

Books Build Bright Futures

Dear Reader,

We'd love your attention for one more page to tell you about the crisis in children's reading, and what we can all do.

Studies have shown that reading for fun is the **single biggest predictor of a child's future life chances** – more than family circumstance, parents' educational background or income. It improves academic results, mental health, wealth, communication skills, ambition and happiness.[1]

The number of children reading for fun is in rapid decline. Young people have a lot of competition for their time. In 2024, 1 in 10 children and young people in the UK aged 5 to 18 did not own a single book at home.[2]

Hachette works extensively with schools, libraries and literacy charities, but here are some ways we can all raise more readers:

- Reading to children for just 10 minutes a day makes a difference
- Don't give up if children aren't regular readers – there will be books for them!
- Visit bookshops and libraries to get recommendations
- Encourage them to listen to audiobooks
- Support school libraries
- Give books as gifts

There's a lot more information about how to encourage children to read on our website: **www.RaisingReaders.co.uk**

Thank you for reading.

hachette UK

---

[1] OECD, '21st-Century Readers: Developing Literacy Skills in a Digital World', 2021, https://www.oecd.org/en/publications/21st-century-readers_a83d84cb-en.html

[2] National Literacy Trust, 'Book Ownership in 2024', November 2024, https://literacytrust.org.uk/research-services/research-reports/book-ownership-in-2024

THE UNFORGETTABLE DEBUT
FROM SARAH HORNSLEY

NOW AVAILABLE IN PAPERBACK,
EBOOK AND AUDIO